P9-AFA-888

THE HARDY BOYS®

UNDERCOVER BROTHERS™

PAPERCUTZ™

THE **HARDY BOYS** ®

Graphic Novels
Available from Papercutz

#1 The Ocean of Osyria
#2 Identity Theft
#3 Mad House
#4 Malled
#5 See You, Sea Me (Coming May 2006)

$7.95 each in paperback
$12.95 each in hardcover

THE HARDY BOYS

#4

UNDERCOVER BROTHERS™

Malled

SCOTT LOBDELL • Writer
DANIEL RENDON • Artist
Based on the series by
FRANKLIN W. DIXON

New York

Malled
SCOTT LOBDELL – Writer
DANIEL RENDON — Artist
BRYAN SENKA – Letterer
LAURIE E. SMITH — Colorist
JIM SALICRUP
Editor-in-Chief

ISBN-10: 1-59707-014-9 paperback edition
ISBN-13: 978-1-59707-014-0 paperback edition
ISBN-10: 1-59707-015-7 hardcover edition
ISBN-13: 978-1-59707-015-7 hardcover edition

10 9 8 7 6 5 4 3 2 1

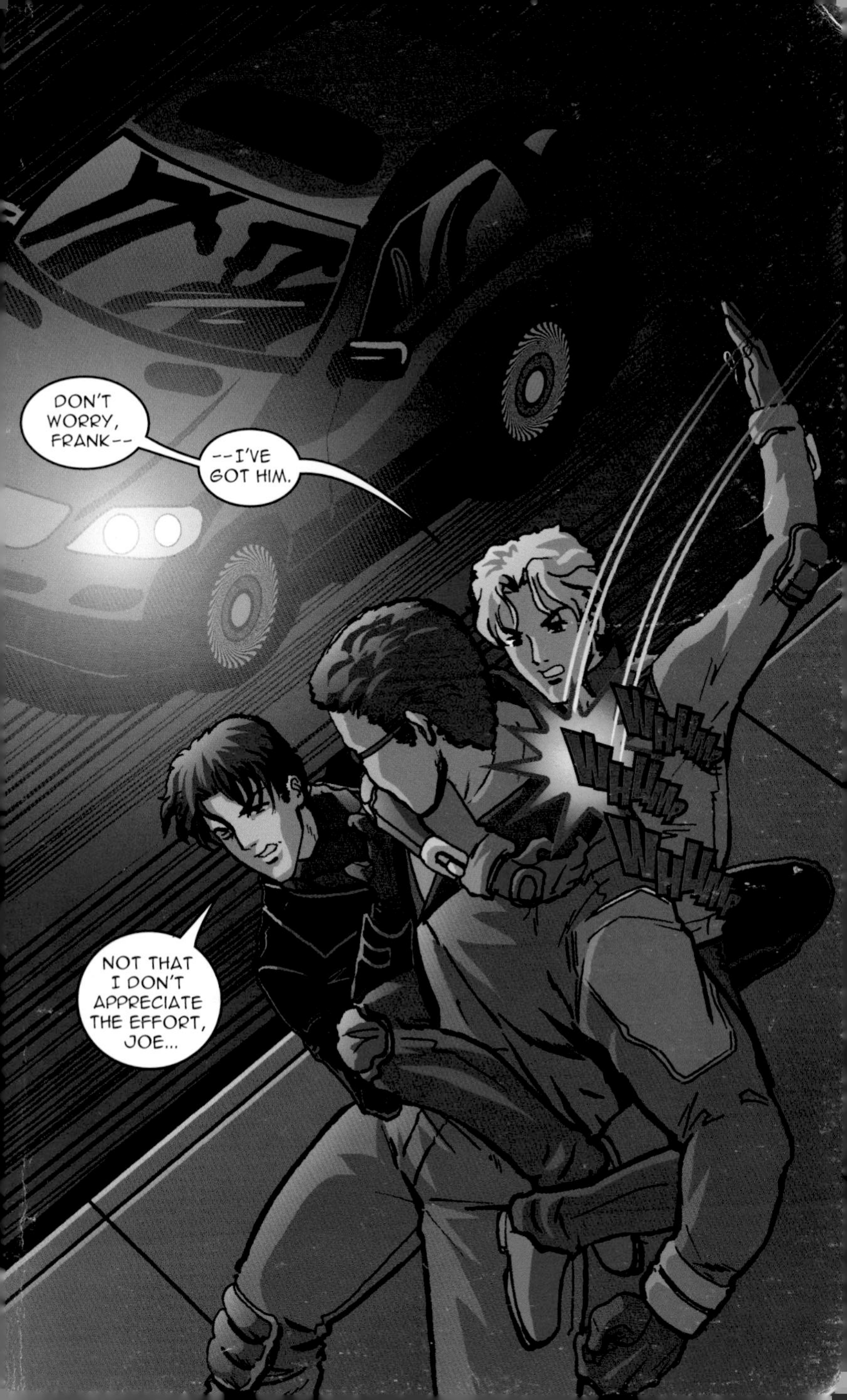
DON'T WORRY, FRANK--
--I'VE GOT HIM.
WHUMP
WHUMP
WHUMP
NOT THAT I DON'T APPRECIATE THE EFFORT, JOE...

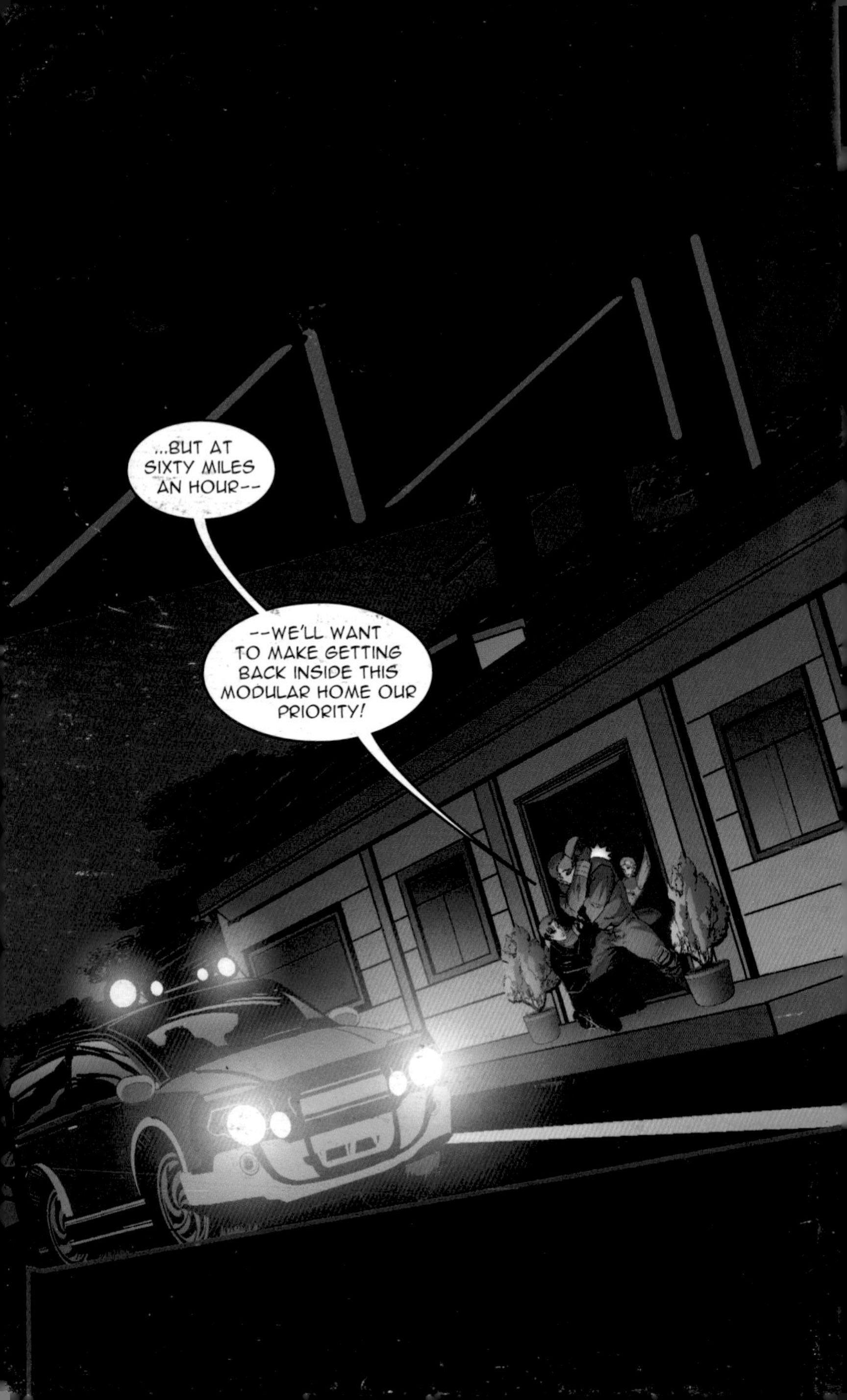
...BUT AT SIXTY MILES AN HOUR--
--WE'LL WANT TO MAKE GETTING BACK INSIDE THIS MODULAR HOME OUR PRIORITY!

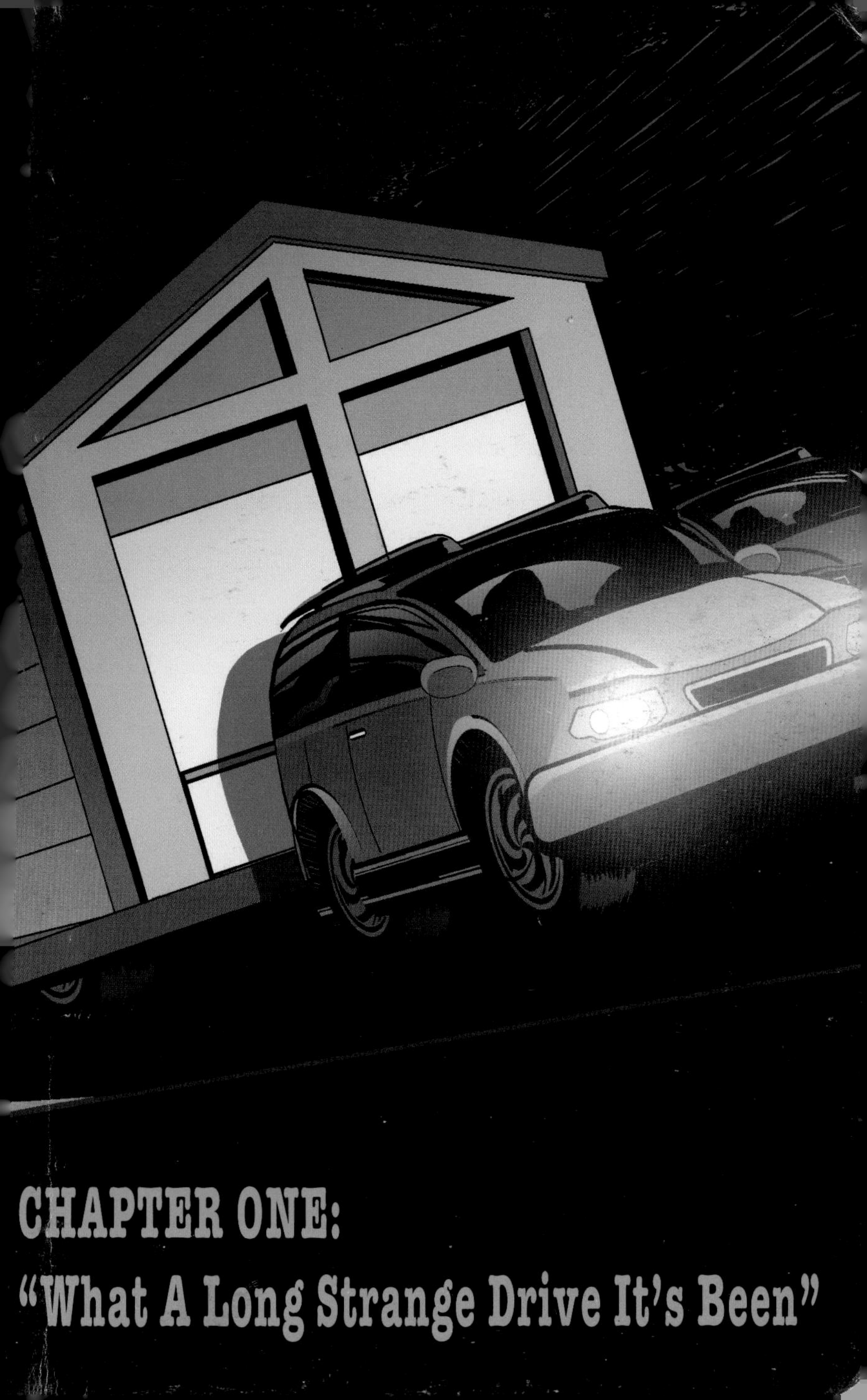

CHAPTER ONE:
"What A Long Strange Drive It's Been"

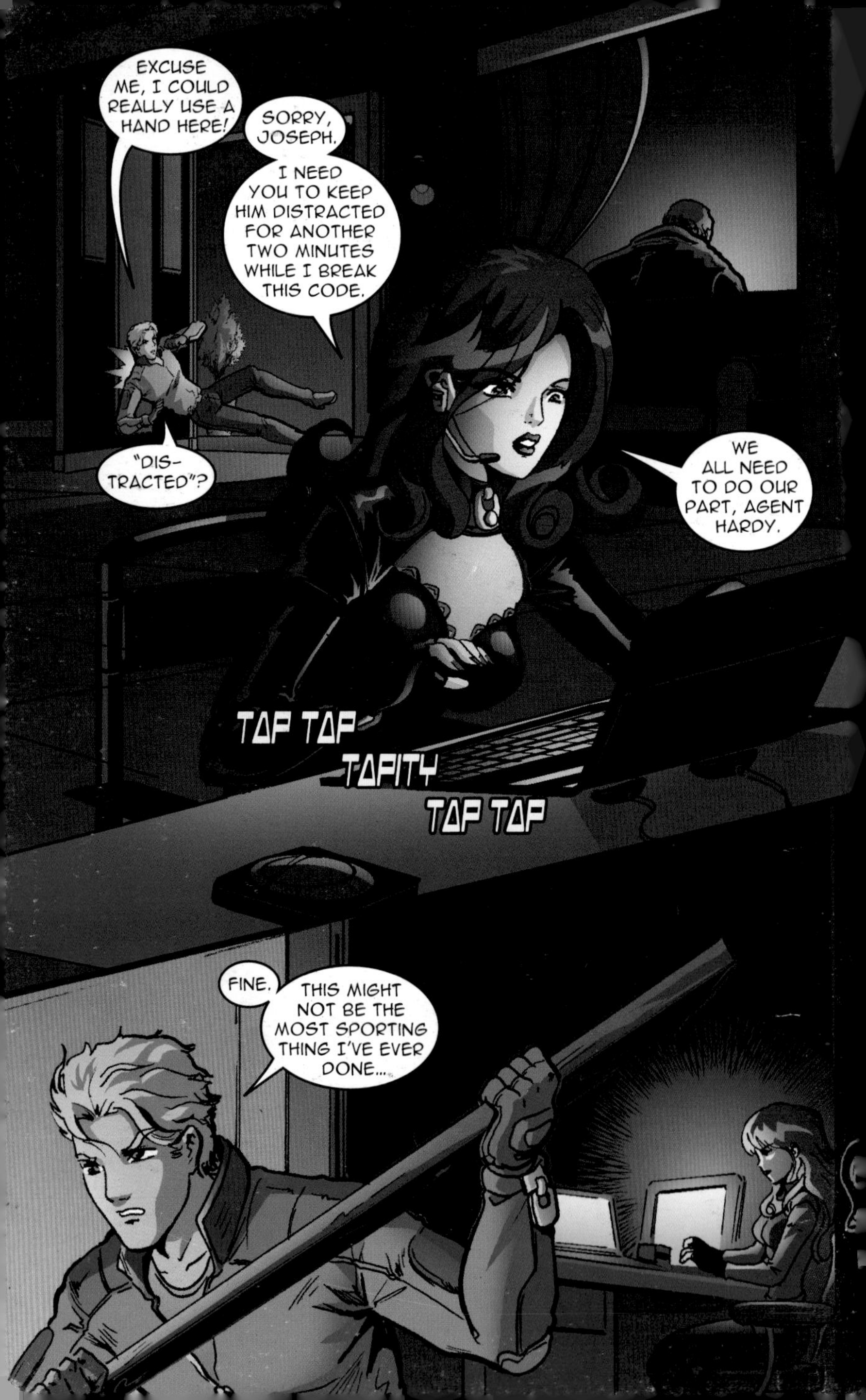
EXCUSE ME, I COULD REALLY USE A HAND HERE!
SORRY, JOSEPH.
I NEED YOU TO KEEP HIM DISTRACTED FOR ANOTHER TWO MINUTES WHILE I BREAK THIS CODE.
"DIS-TRACTED"?
WE ALL NEED TO DO OUR PART, AGENT HARDY.
TAP TAP
TAPITY
TAP TAP
FINE.
THIS MIGHT NOT BE THE MOST SPORTING THING I'VE EVER DONE...

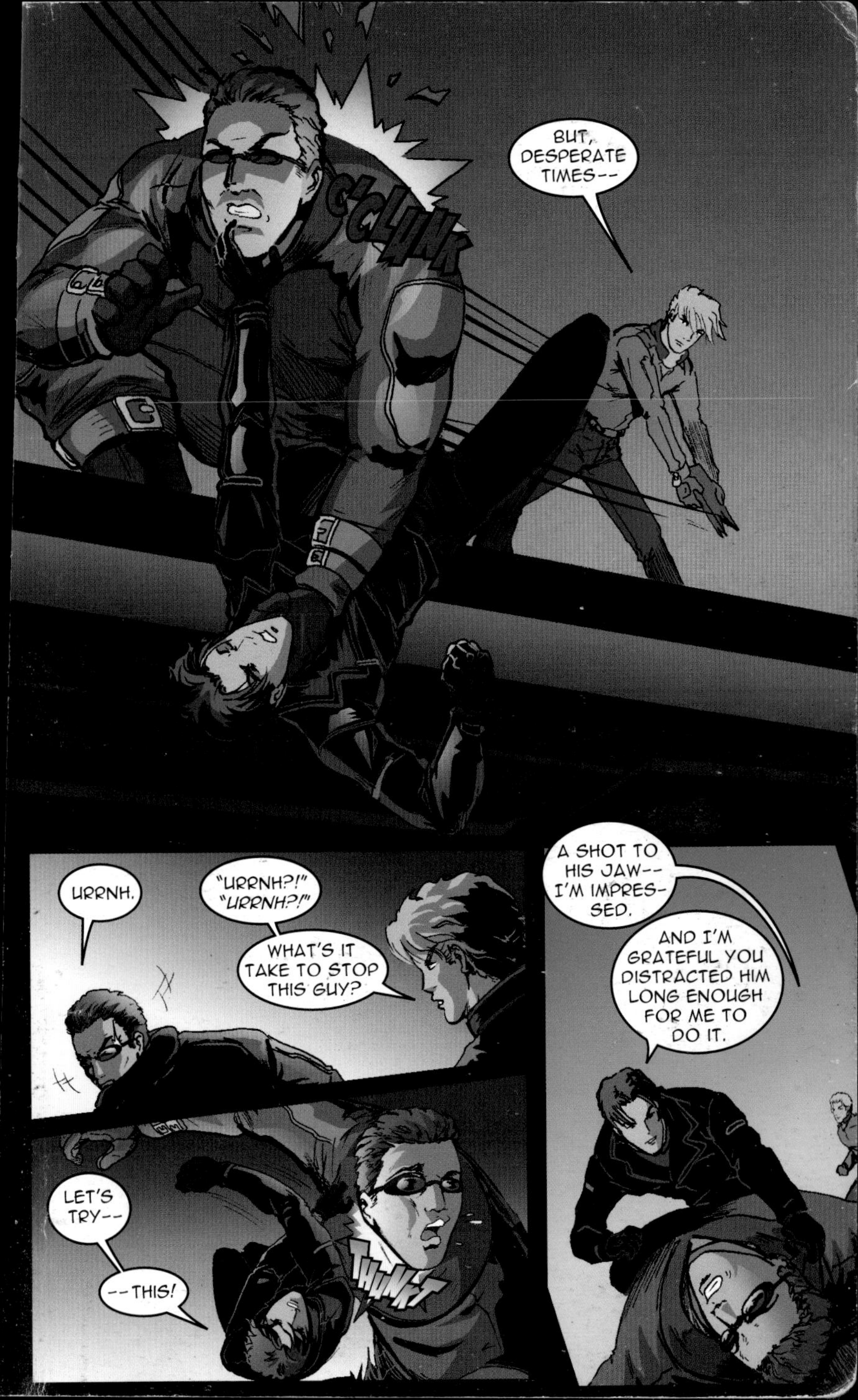
BUT, DESPERATE TIMES--
C'CLUNK
A SHOT TO HIS JAW-- I'M IMPRES-SED.
AND I'M GRATEFUL YOU DISTRACTED HIM LONG ENOUGH FOR ME TO DO IT.
"URRNH?!" "URRNH?!"
WHAT'S IT TAKE TO STOP THIS GUY?
URRNH.
LET'S TRY--
THUNK
--THIS!

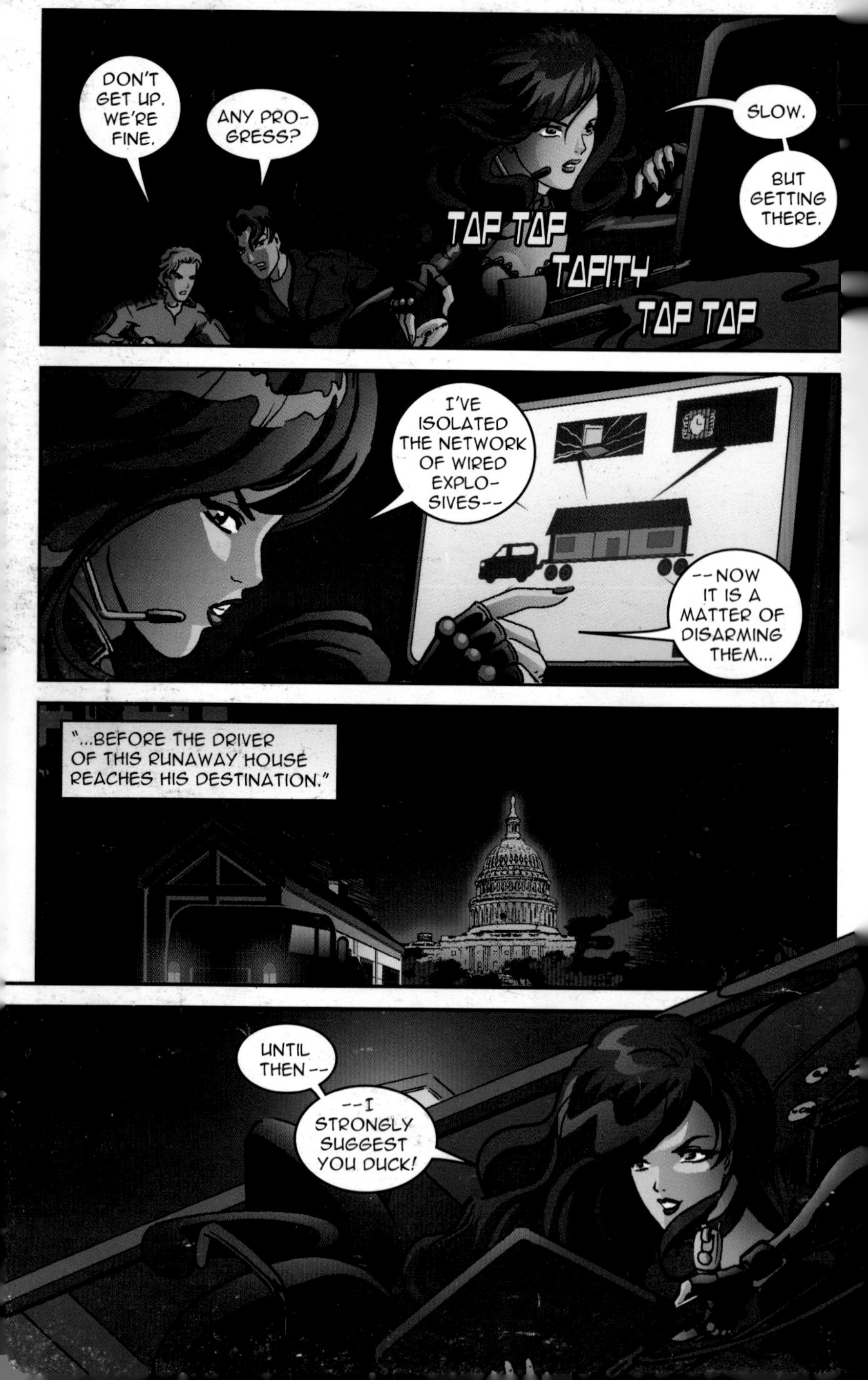
SLOW.
BUT GETTING THERE.
ANY PROGRESS?
DON'T GET UP. WE'RE FINE.
TAP TAP
TAPITY
TAP TAP
I'VE ISOLATED THE NETWORK OF WIRED EXPLOSIVES--
--NOW IT IS A MATTER OF DISARMING THEM...
"...BEFORE THE DRIVER OF THIS RUNAWAY HOUSE REACHES HIS DESTINATION."
UNTIL THEN--
--I STRONGLY SUGGEST YOU DUCK!

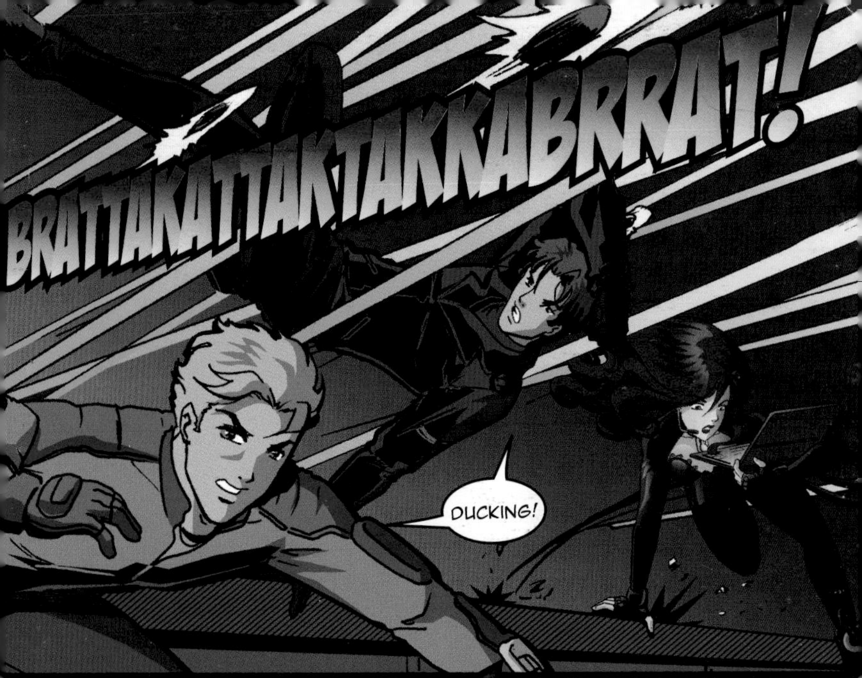
BRATTAKATTAKTAKKABRRAT!
DUCKING!

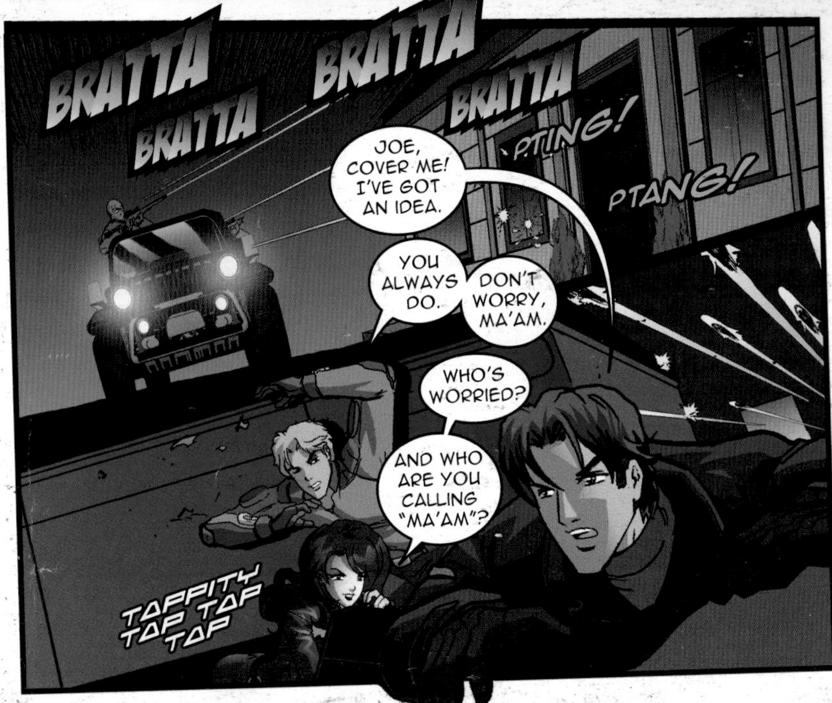
BRATTA
BRATTA
BRATTA
BRATTA
PTING!
JOE, COVER ME! I'VE GOT AN IDEA.
PTANG!
DON'T WORRY, MA'AM.
YOU ALWAYS DO.
WHO'S WORRIED?
AND WHO ARE YOU CALLING "MA'AM"?
TAPPITY TAP TAP TAP

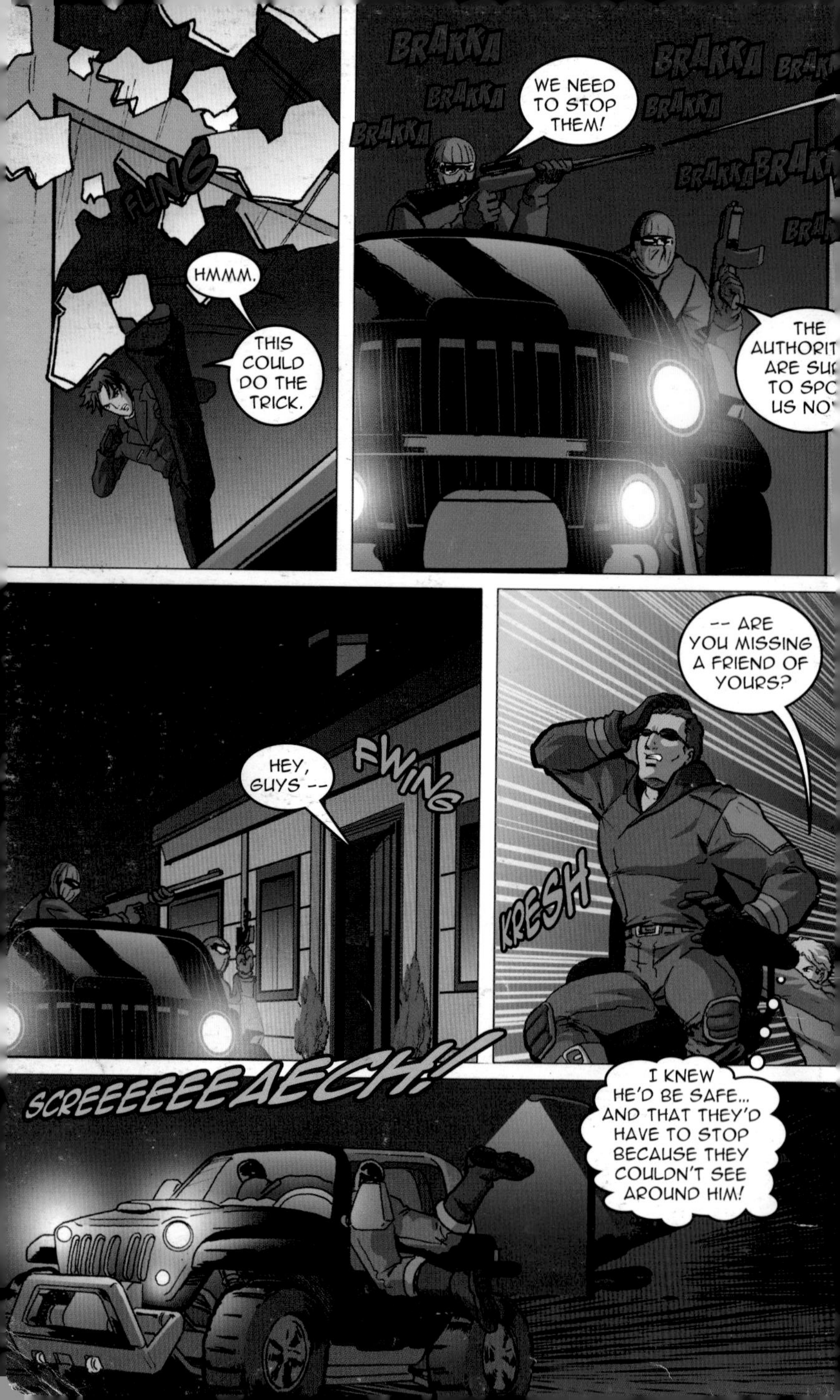

BRAKKA
BRAKKA
BRAKKA
BRAKKA
BRAKKA
BRAKKABRAKK
WE NEED TO STOP THEM!
THE AUTHORIT ARE SU TO SPO US NO
FLING
HMMM.
THIS COULD DO THE TRICK.
-- ARE YOU MISSING A FRIEND OF YOURS?
KRESH
HEY, GUYS --
FWING
SCREEEEEEEAECH!!
I KNEW HE'D BE SAFE... AND THAT THEY'D HAVE TO STOP BECAUSE THEY COULDN'T SEE AROUND HIM!

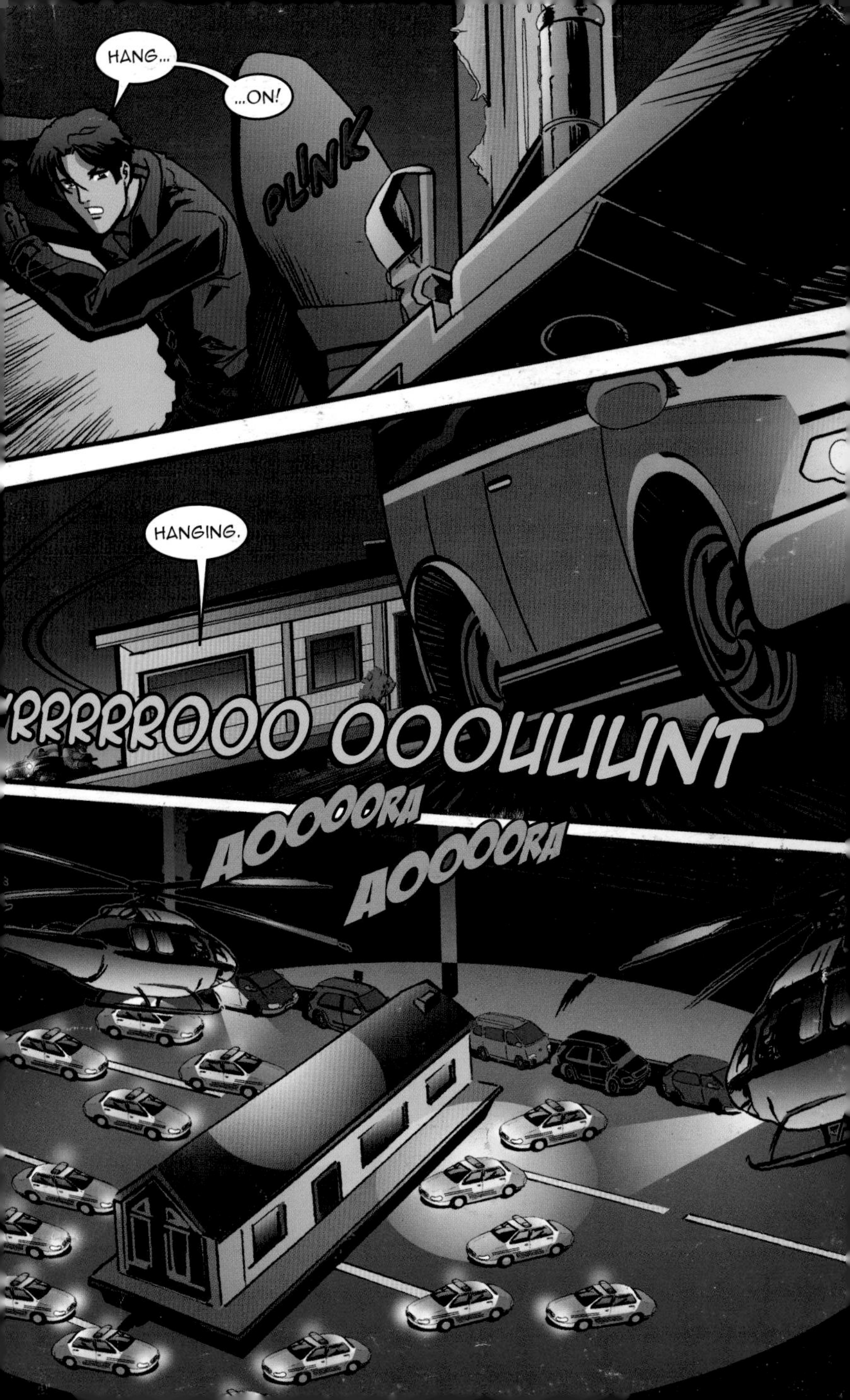
HANG...
...ON!
PLINK
HANGING.
RRRRROOO OOOUUUNT
AOOOORA
AOOOORA

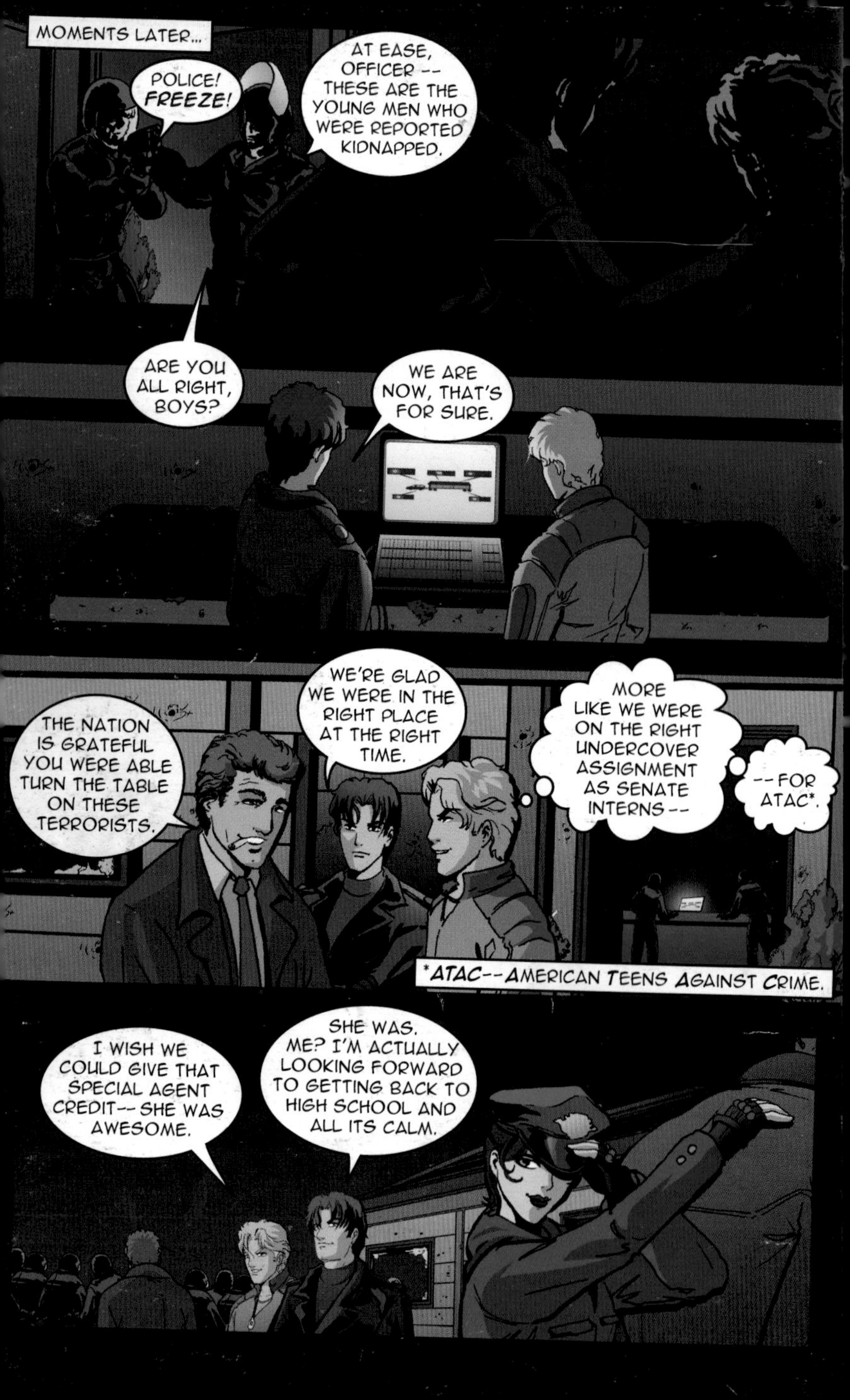
MOMENTS LATER...
POLICE! FREEZE!
AT EASE, OFFICER -- THESE ARE THE YOUNG MEN WHO WERE REPORTED KIDNAPPED.
ARE YOU ALL RIGHT, BOYS?
WE ARE NOW, THAT'S FOR SURE.
THE NATION IS GRATEFUL YOU WERE ABLE TURN THE TABLE ON THESE TERRORISTS.
WE'RE GLAD WE WERE IN THE RIGHT PLACE AT THE RIGHT TIME.
MORE LIKE WE WERE ON THE RIGHT UNDERCOVER ASSIGNMENT AS SENATE INTERNS --
-- FOR ATAC*.
*ATAC--AMERICAN TEENS AGAINST CRIME.
I WISH WE COULD GIVE THAT SPECIAL AGENT CREDIT-- SHE WAS AWESOME.
SHE WAS. ME? I'M ACTUALLY LOOKING FORWARD TO GETTING BACK TO HIGH SCHOOL AND ALL ITS CALM.

CHAPTER TWO: "First and Ten!"

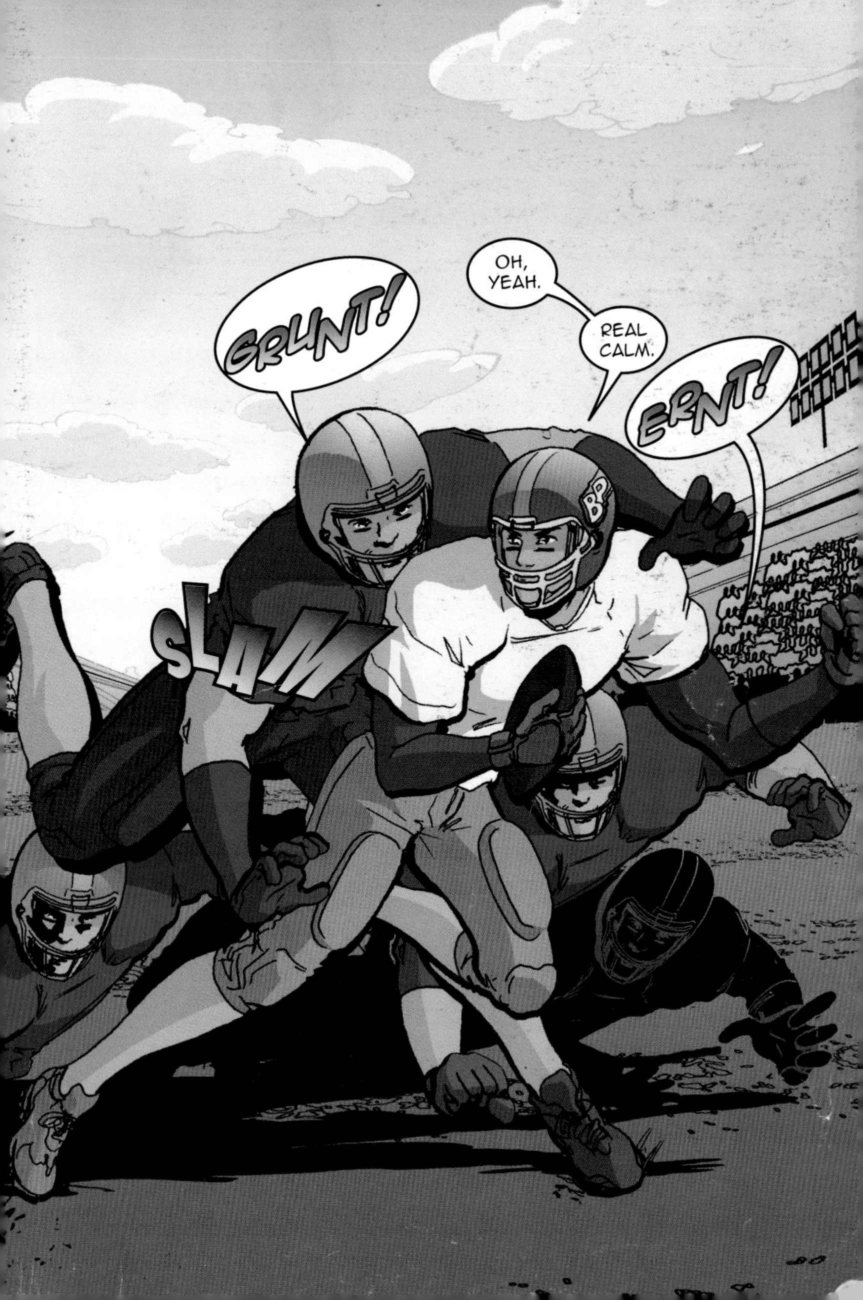
OH, YEAH.
REAL CALM.
ERNT!
GRUNT!
SLAM

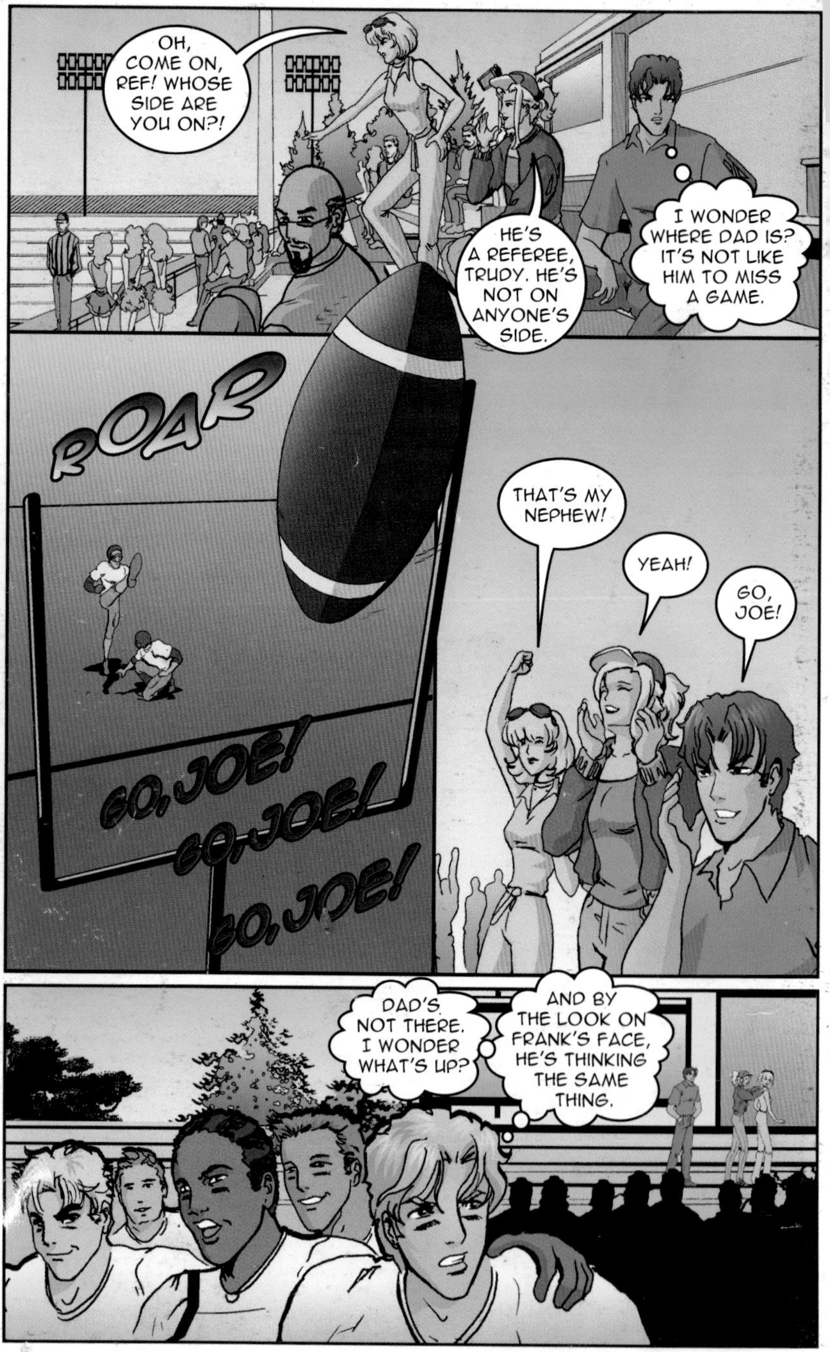
OH, COME ON, REF! WHOSE SIDE ARE YOU ON?!
I WONDER WHERE DAD IS? IT'S NOT LIKE HIM TO MISS A GAME.
HE'S A REFEREE, TRUDY. HE'S NOT ON ANYONE'S SIDE.
THAT'S MY NEPHEW!
YEAH!
GO, JOE!
ROAR
GO, JOE!
GO, JOE!
GO, JOE!
AND BY THE LOOK ON FRANK'S FACE, HE'S THINKING THE SAME THING.
DAD'S NOT THERE. I WONDER WHAT'S UP?

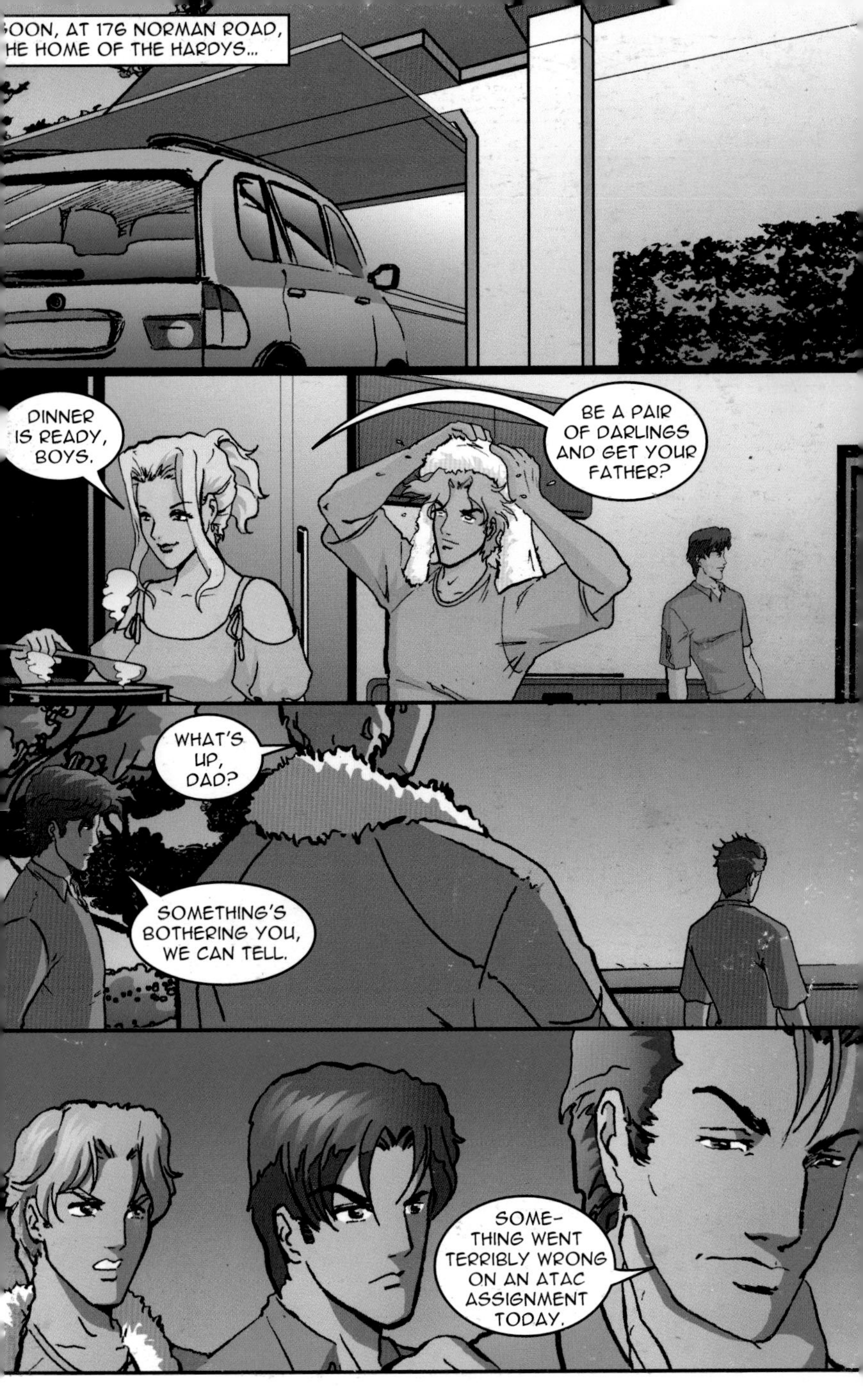
OON, AT 176 NORMAN ROAD, HE HOME OF THE HARDYS...
BE A PAIR OF DARLINGS AND GET YOUR FATHER?
DINNER IS READY, BOYS.
WHAT'S UP, DAD?
SOMETHING'S BOTHERING YOU, WE CAN TELL.
SOME-THING WENT TERRIBLY WRONG ON AN ATAC ASSIGNMENT TODAY.

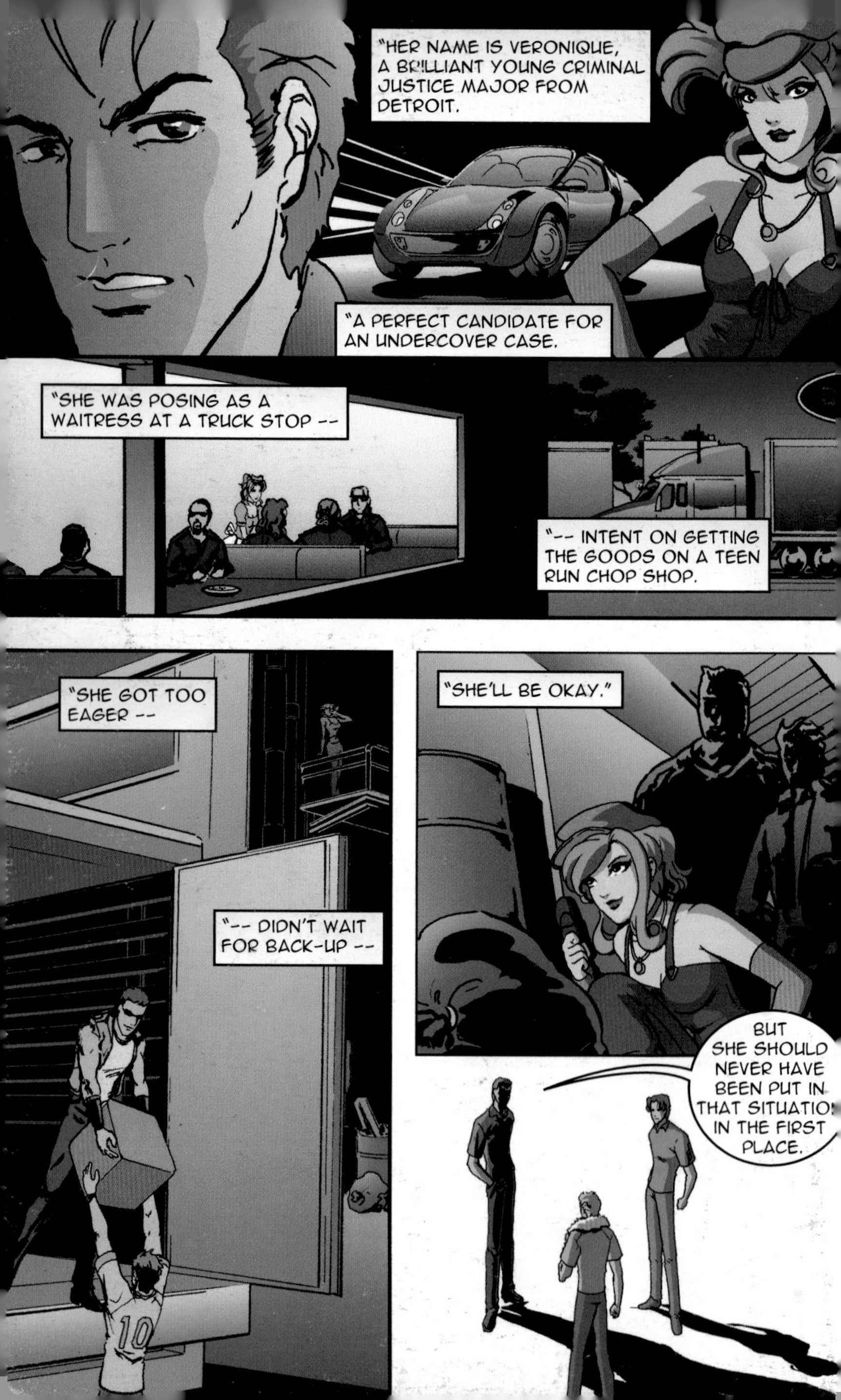
"HER NAME IS VERONIQUE, A BRILLIANT YOUNG CRIMINAL JUSTICE MAJOR FROM DETROIT.
"A PERFECT CANDIDATE FOR AN UNDERCOVER CASE.
"SHE WAS POSING AS A WAITRESS AT A TRUCK STOP --
"-- INTENT ON GETTING THE GOODS ON A TEEN RUN CHOP SHOP.
"SHE GOT TOO EAGER --
"-- DIDN'T WAIT FOR BACK-UP --
"SHE'LL BE OKAY."
BUT SHE SHOULD NEVER HAVE BEEN PUT IN THAT SITUATIO IN THE FIRST PLACE.

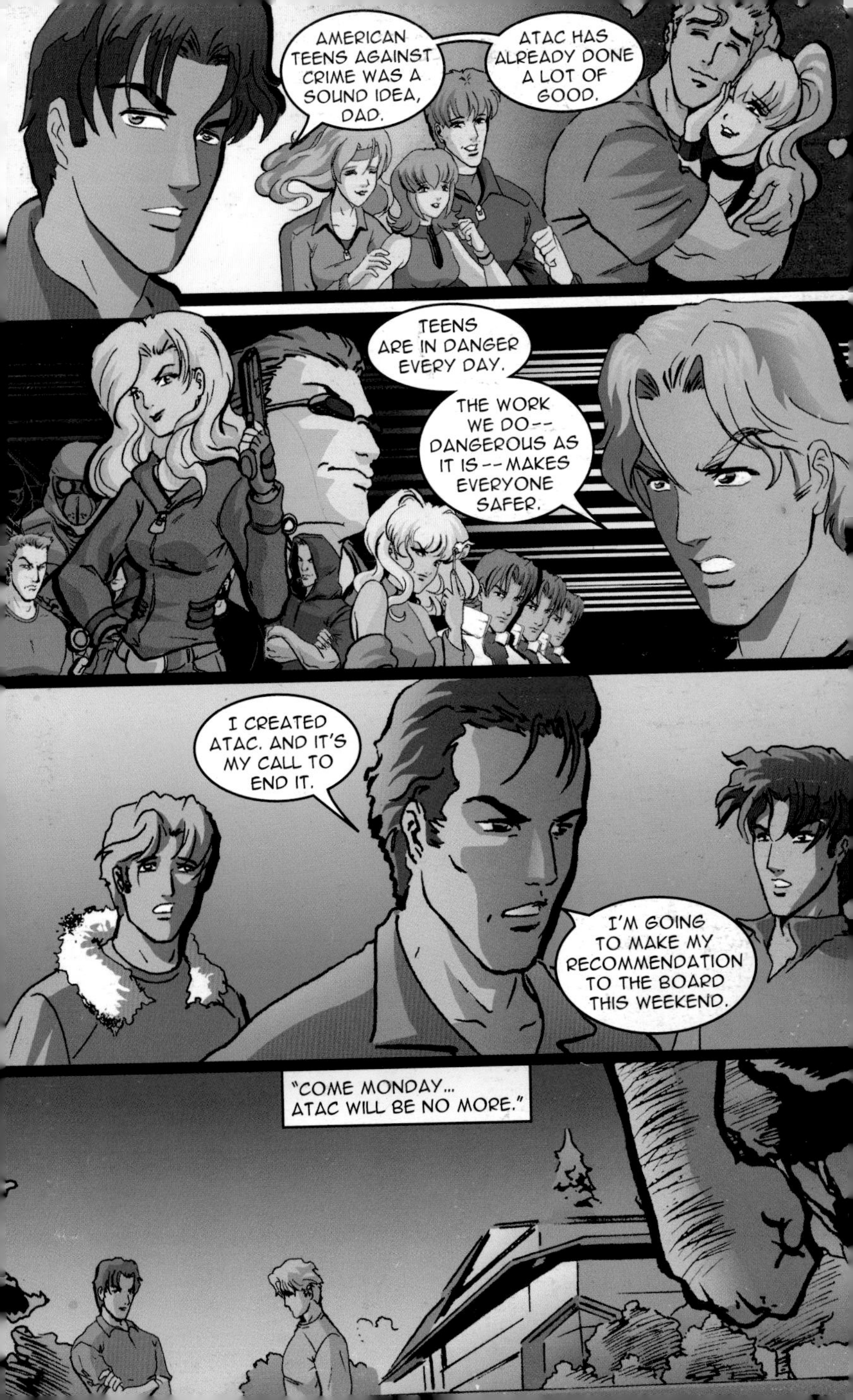
ATAC HAS ALREADY DONE A LOT OF GOOD.
AMERICAN TEENS AGAINST CRIME WAS A SOUND IDEA, DAD.
TEENS ARE IN DANGER EVERY DAY.
THE WORK WE DO-- DANGEROUS AS IT IS--MAKES EVERYONE SAFER.
I CREATED ATAC. AND IT'S MY CALL TO END IT.
I'M GOING TO MAKE MY RECOMMENDATION TO THE BOARD THIS WEEKEND.
"COME MONDAY... ATAC WILL BE NO MORE."

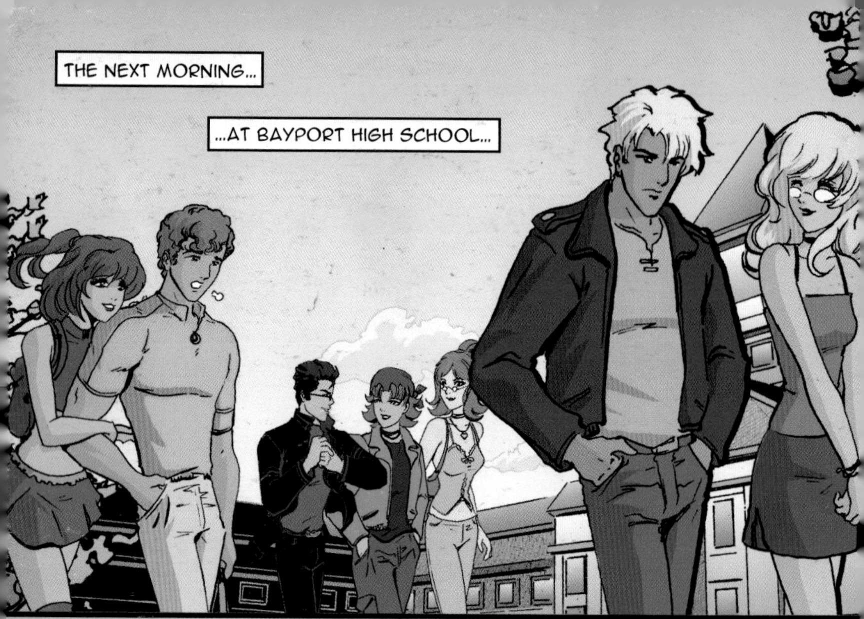
THE NEXT MORNING...
...AT BAYPORT HIGH SCHOOL...

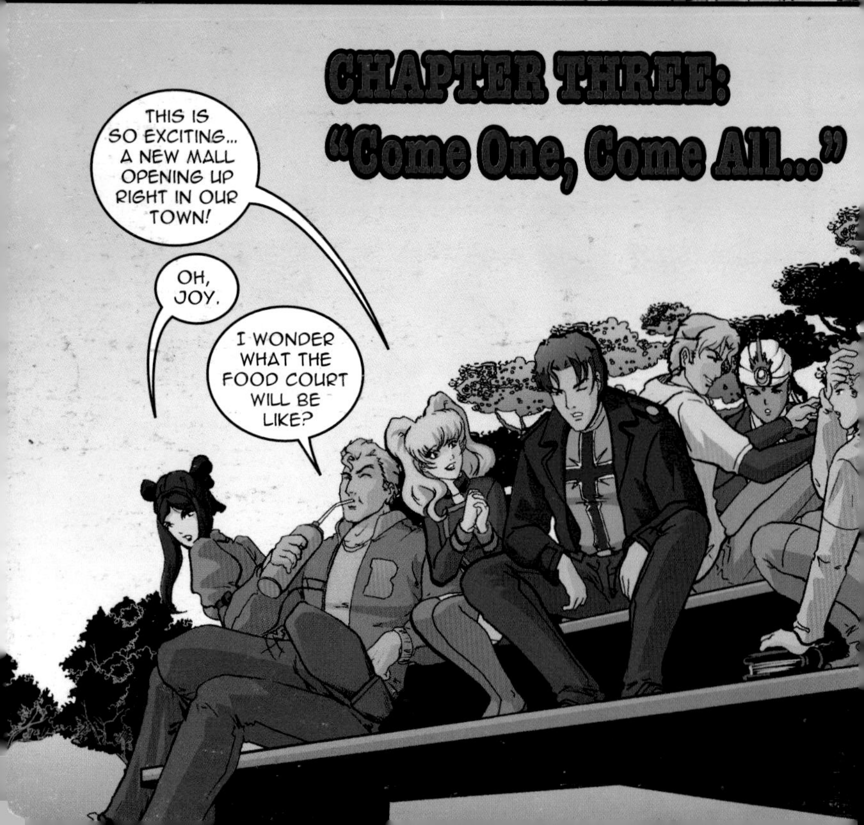
CHAPTER THREE:
"Come One, Come All..."
THIS IS SO EXCITING... A NEW MALL OPENING UP RIGHT IN OUR TOWN!
OH, JOY.
I WONDER WHAT THE FOOD COURT WILL BE LIKE?

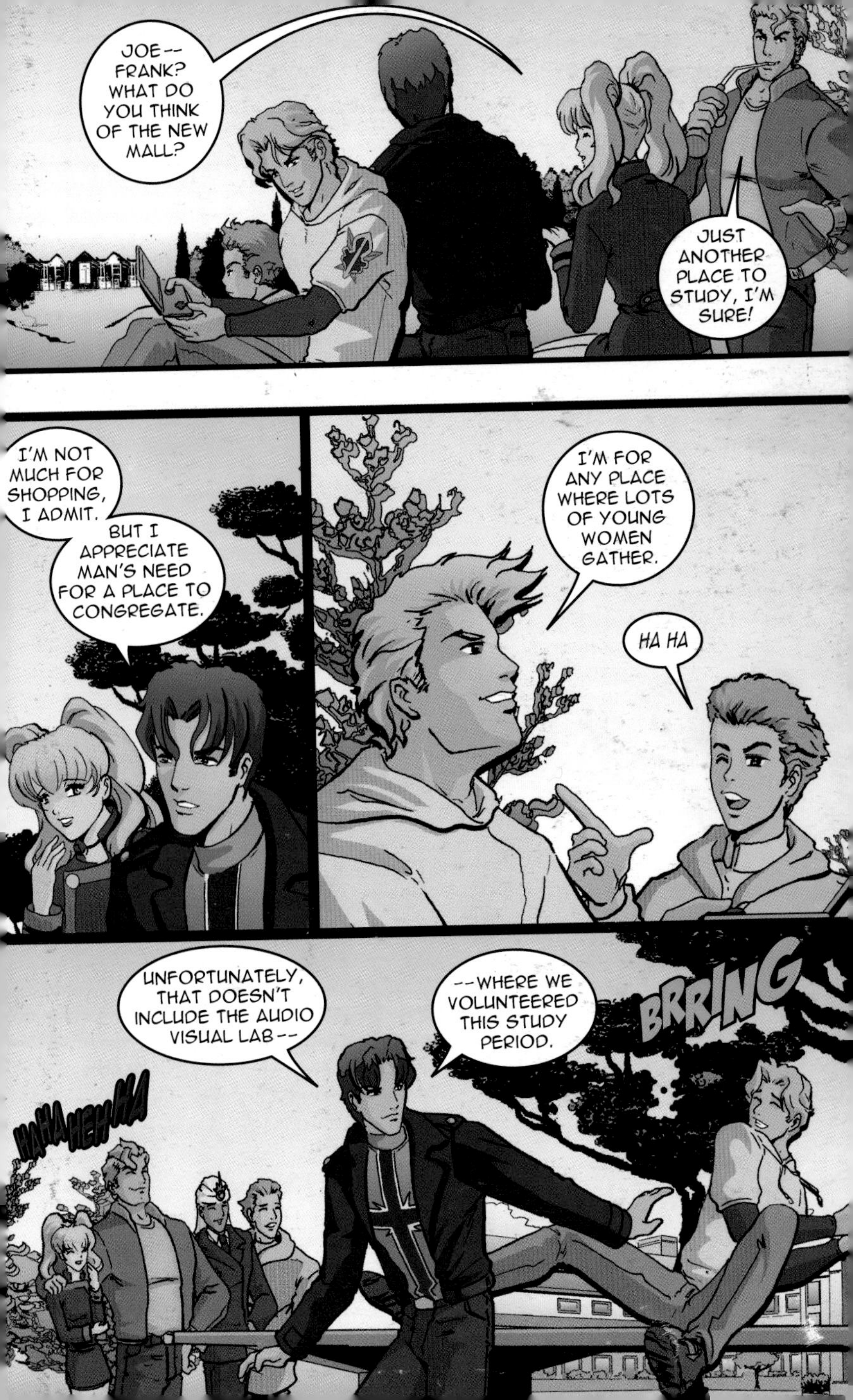
JOE-- FRANK? WHAT DO YOU THINK OF THE NEW MALL?
JUST ANOTHER PLACE TO STUDY, I'M SURE!
I'M NOT MUCH FOR SHOPPING, I ADMIT.
BUT I APPRECIATE MAN'S NEED FOR A PLACE TO CONGREGATE.
I'M FOR ANY PLACE WHERE LOTS OF YOUNG WOMEN GATHER.
HA HA
UNFORTUNATELY, THAT DOESN'T INCLUDE THE AUDIO VISUAL LAB--
--WHERE WE VOLUNTEERED THIS STUDY PERIOD.
BRRING
HAHA HEH HA

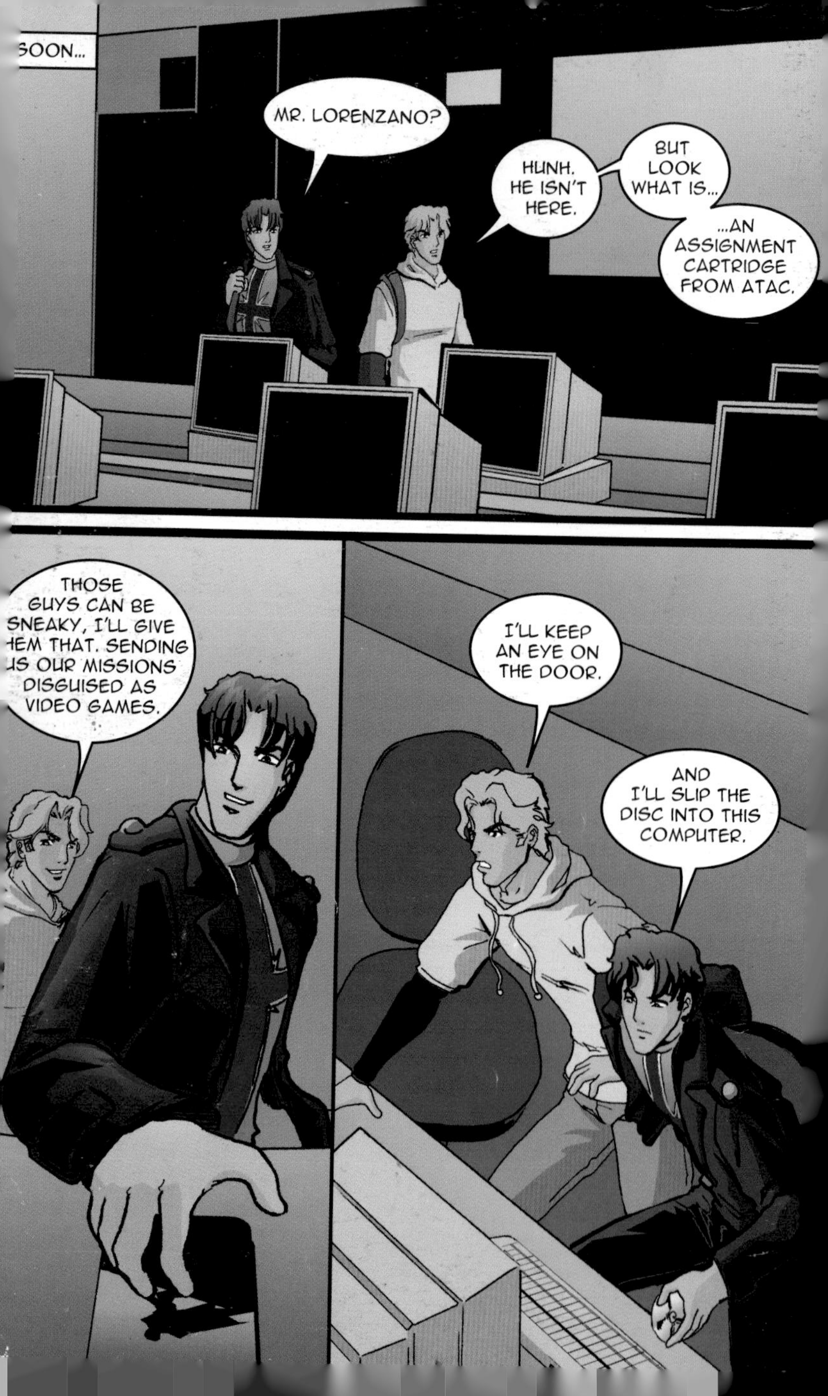
SOON...
MR. LORENZANO?
HUNH. HE ISN'T HERE.
BUT LOOK WHAT IS...
...AN ASSIGNMENT CARTRIDGE FROM ATAC.
I'LL KEEP AN EYE ON THE DOOR.
AND I'LL SLIP THE DISC INTO THIS COMPUTER.
THOSE GUYS CAN BE SNEAKY, I'LL GIVE HEM THAT. SENDING US OUR MISSIONS DISGUISED AS VIDEO GAMES.

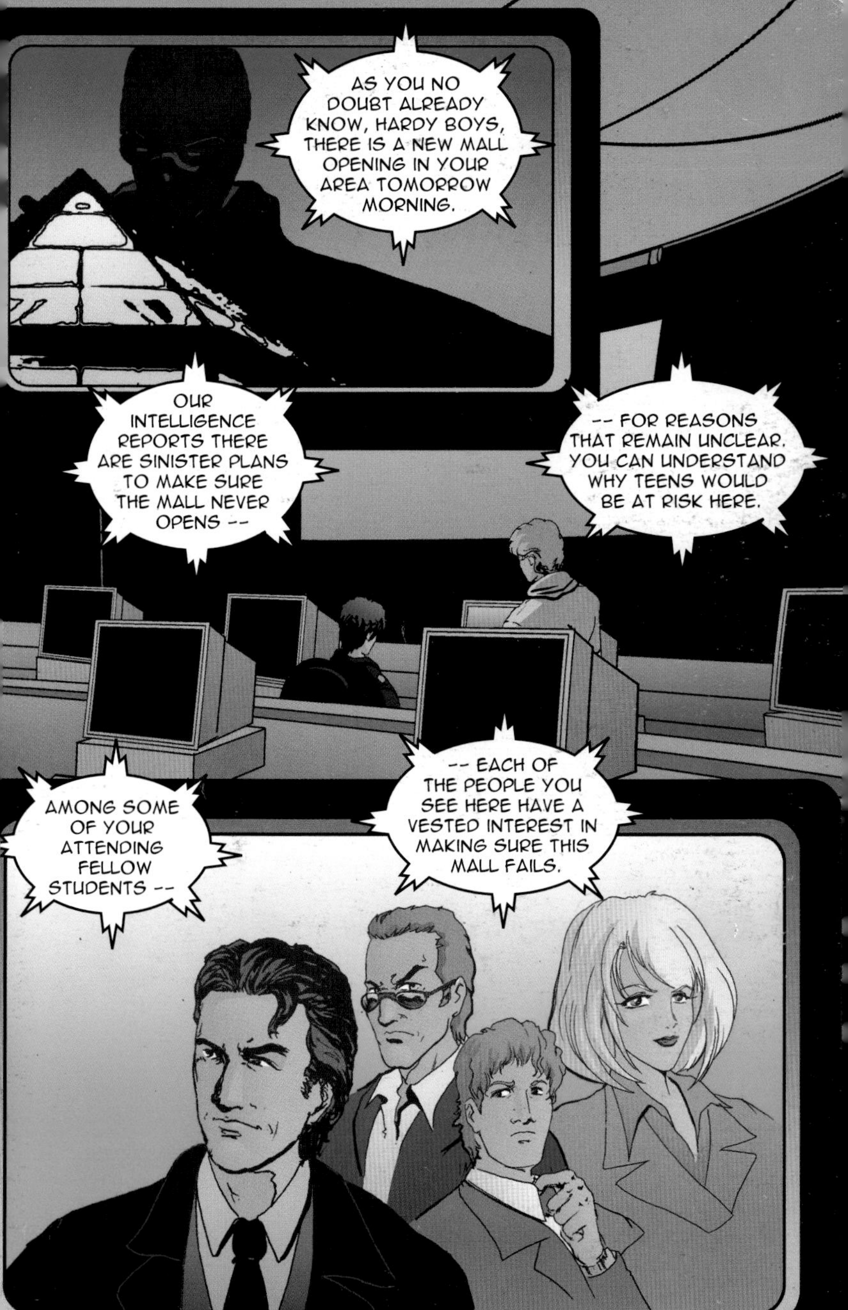
AS YOU NO DOUBT ALREADY KNOW, HARDY BOYS, THERE IS A NEW MALL OPENING IN YOUR AREA TOMORROW MORNING.
OUR INTELLIGENCE REPORTS THERE ARE SINISTER PLANS TO MAKE SURE THE MALL NEVER OPENS --
-- FOR REASONS THAT REMAIN UNCLEAR. YOU CAN UNDERSTAND WHY TEENS WOULD BE AT RISK HERE.
AMONG SOME OF YOUR ATTENDING FELLOW STUDENTS --
-- EACH OF THE PEOPLE YOU SEE HERE HAVE A VESTED INTEREST IN MAKING SURE THIS MALL FAILS.

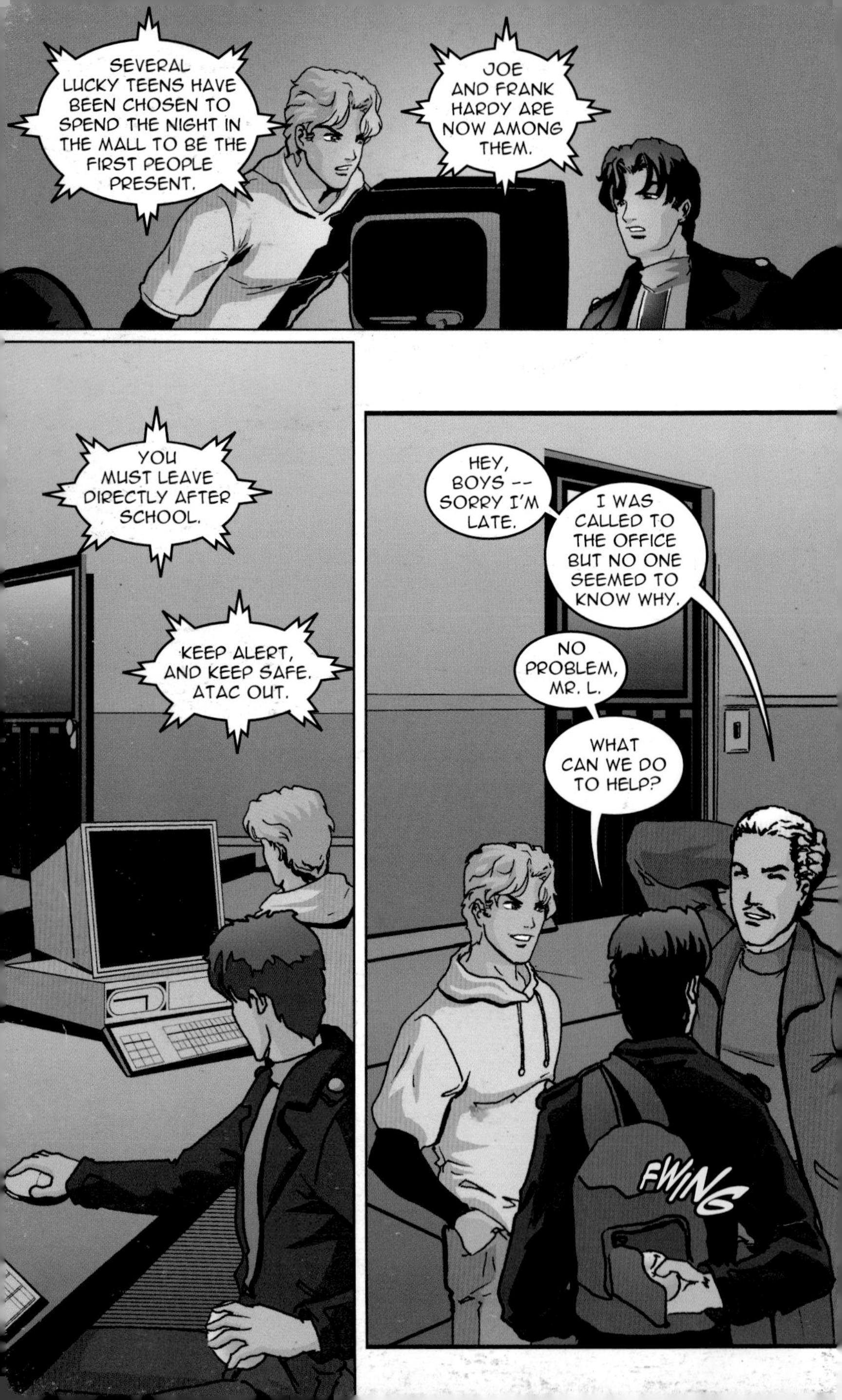
JOE AND FRANK HARDY ARE NOW AMONG THEM.
SEVERAL LUCKY TEENS HAVE BEEN CHOSEN TO SPEND THE NIGHT IN THE MALL TO BE THE FIRST PEOPLE PRESENT.
HEY, BOYS -- SORRY I'M LATE.
I WAS CALLED TO THE OFFICE BUT NO ONE SEEMED TO KNOW WHY.
NO PROBLEM, MR. L.
WHAT CAN WE DO TO HELP?
FWING
YOU MUST LEAVE DIRECTLY AFTER SCHOOL.
KEEP ALERT, AND KEEP SAFE. ATAC OUT.

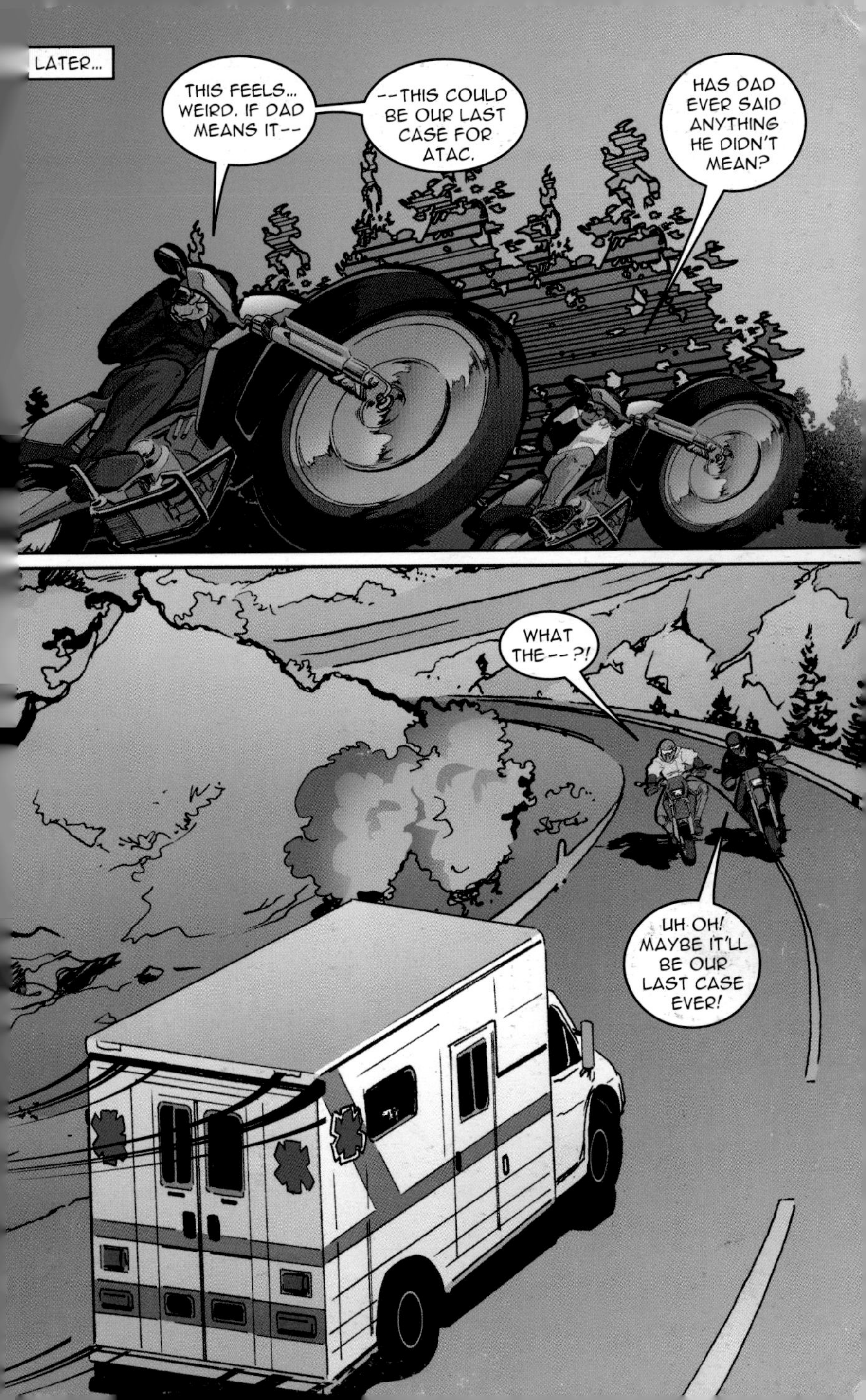
LATER...
THIS FEELS... WEIRD. IF DAD MEANS IT--
--THIS COULD BE OUR LAST CASE FOR ATAC.
HAS DAD EVER SAID ANYTHING HE DIDN'T MEAN?
WHAT THE--?!
UH OH! MAYBE IT'LL BE OUR LAST CASE EVER!

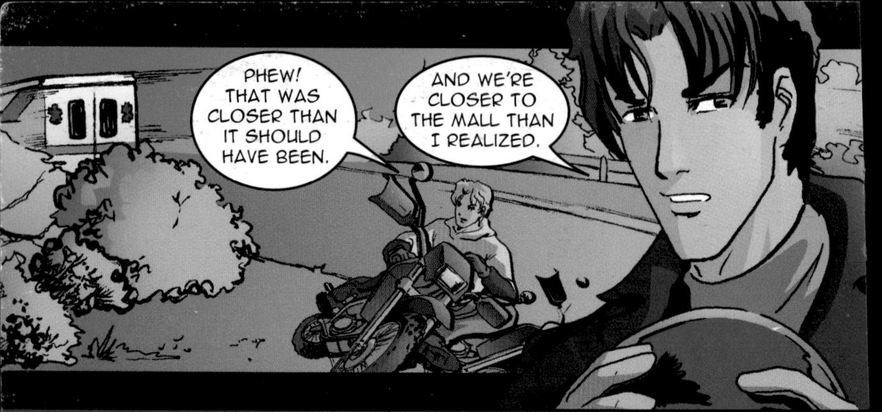
AND WE'RE CLOSER TO THE MALL THAN I REALIZED.
PHEW! THAT WAS CLOSER THAN IT SHOULD HAVE BEEN.

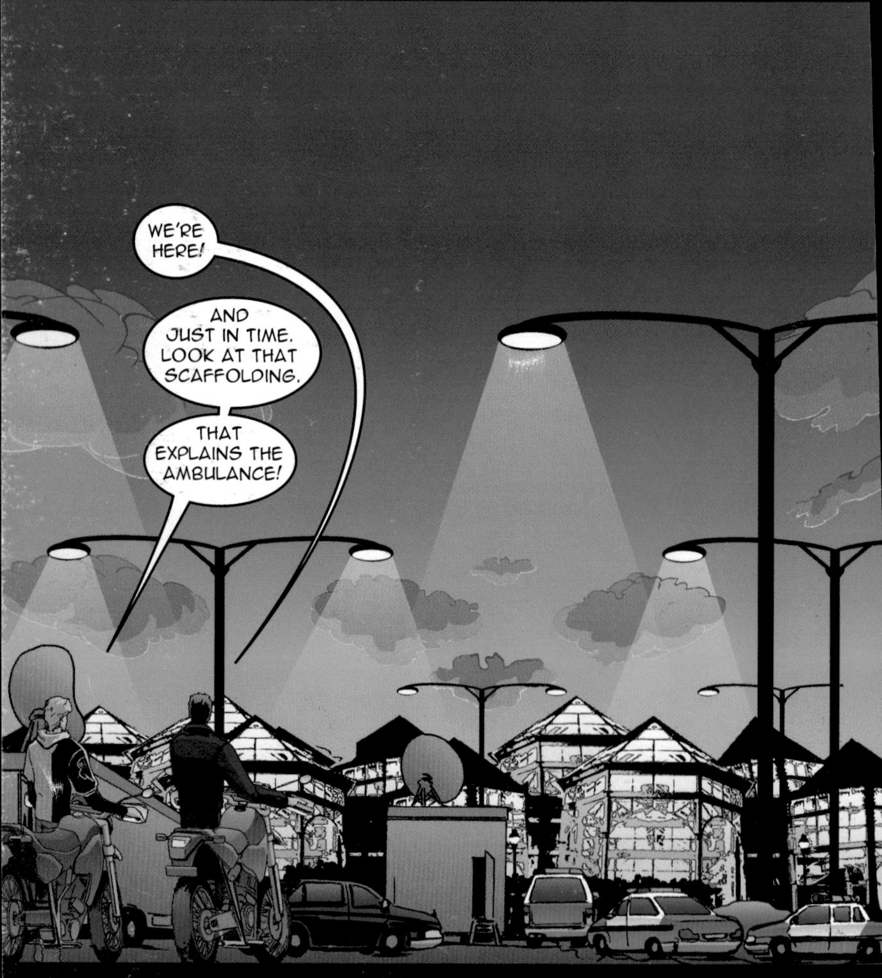
WE'RE HERE!
AND JUST IN TIME. LOOK AT THAT SCAFFOLDING.
THAT EXPLAINS THE AMBULANCE!

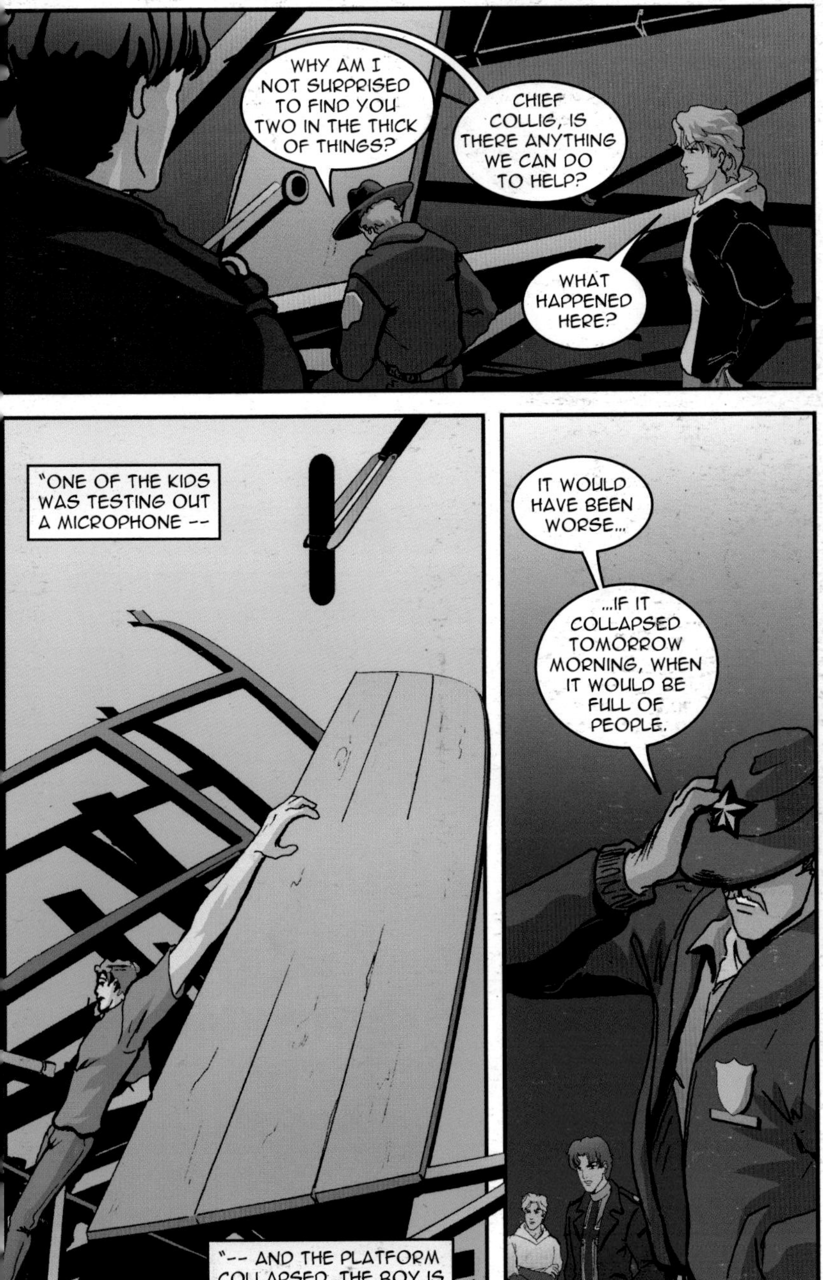
CHIEF COLLIG, IS THERE ANYTHING WE CAN DO TO HELP?
WHY AM I NOT SURPRISED TO FIND YOU TWO IN THE THICK OF THINGS?
WHAT HAPPENED HERE?
IT WOULD HAVE BEEN WORSE...
...IF IT COLLAPSED TOMORROW MORNING, WHEN IT WOULD BE FULL OF PEOPLE.
"ONE OF THE KIDS WAS TESTING OUT A MICROPHONE --
"-- AND THE PLATFORM COLLAPSED. THE BOY IS BRUISED, BUT OKAY."

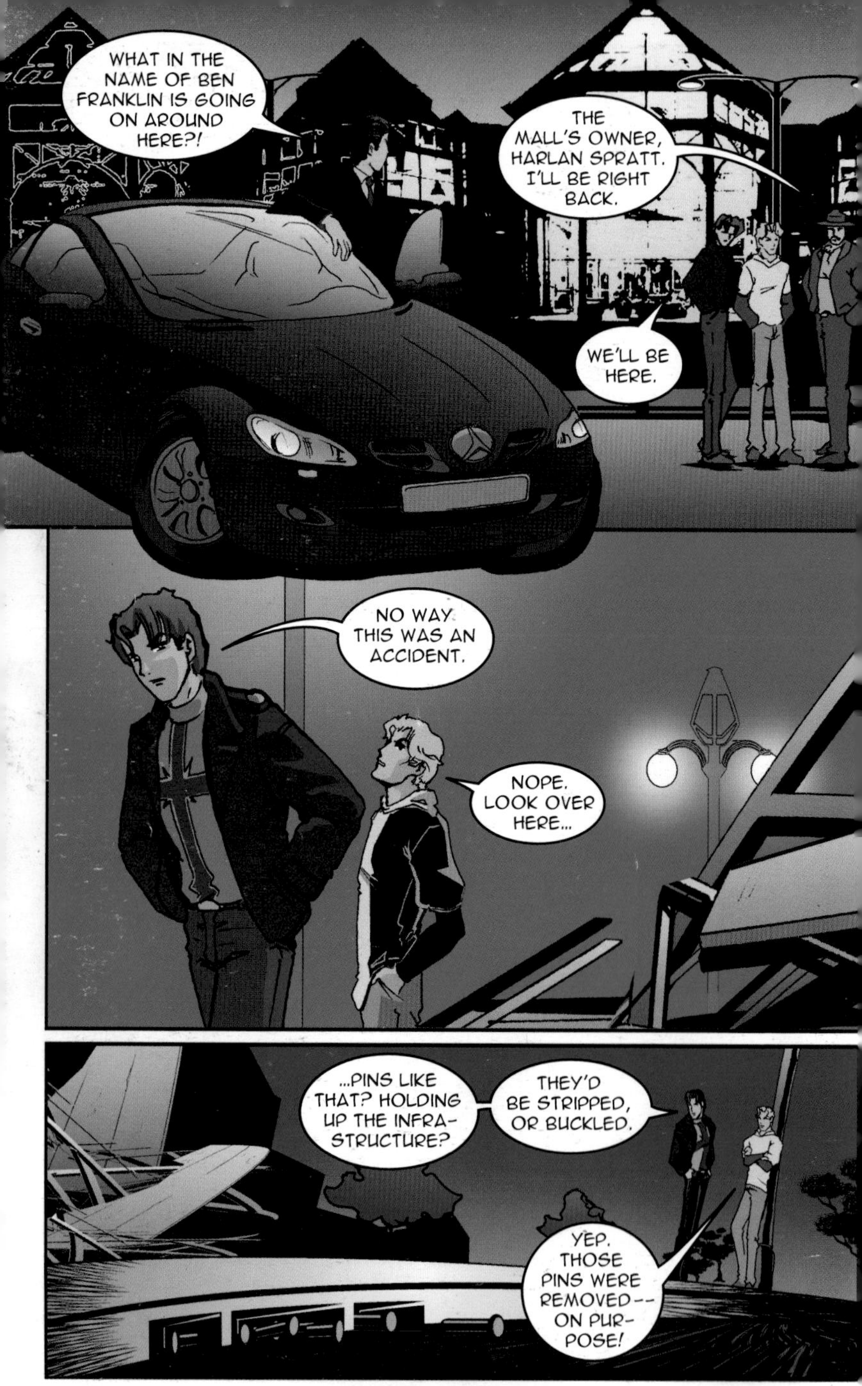
WHAT IN THE NAME OF BEN FRANKLIN IS GOING ON AROUND HERE?!
THE MALL'S OWNER, HARLAN SPRATT. I'LL BE RIGHT BACK.
WE'LL BE HERE.
NO WAY THIS WAS AN ACCIDENT.
NOPE. LOOK OVER HERE...
...PINS LIKE THAT? HOLDING UP THE INFRA-STRUCTURE?
THEY'D BE STRIPPED, OR BUCKLED.
YEP. THOSE PINS WERE REMOVED--ON PUR-POSE!

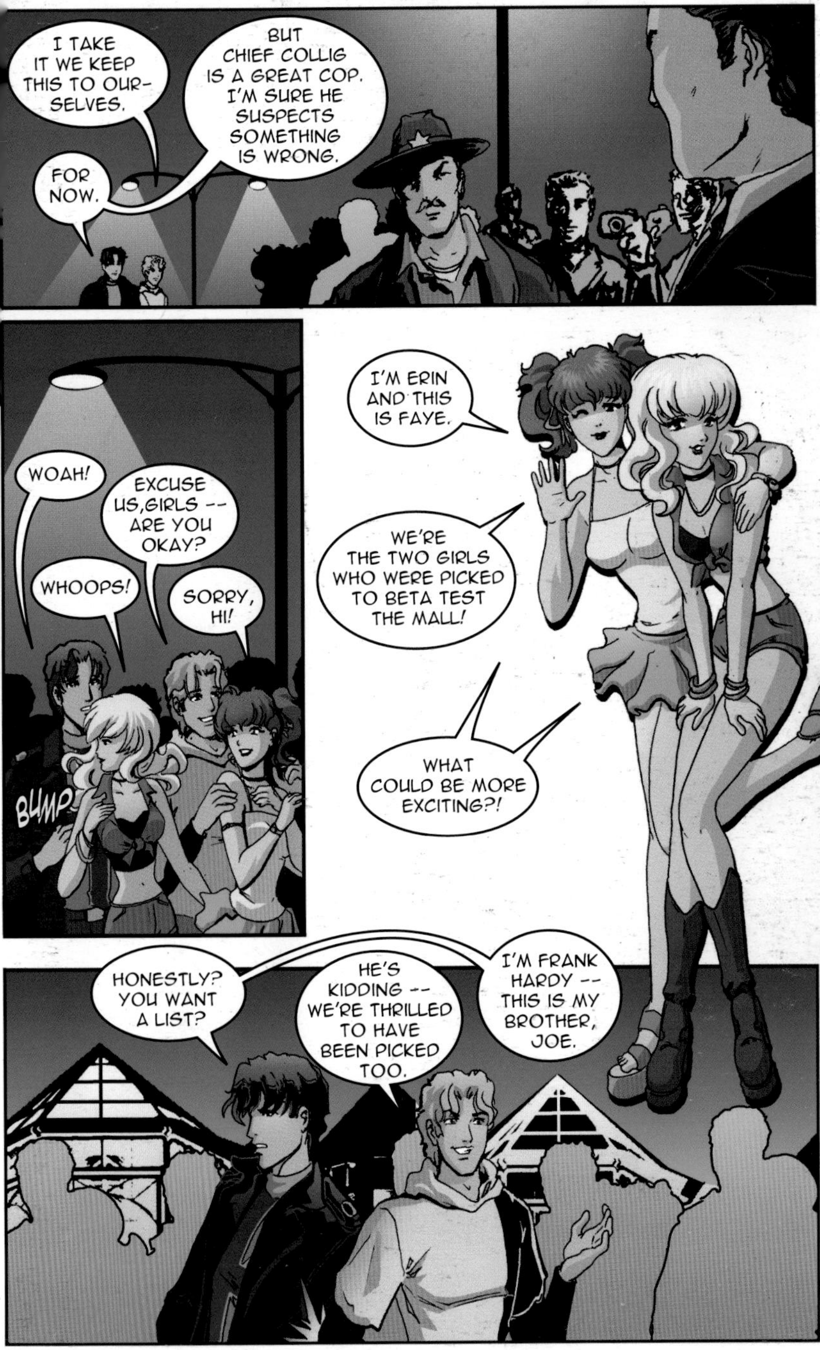
I TAKE IT WE KEEP THIS TO OUR-SELVES.
FOR NOW.
BUT CHIEF COLLIG IS A GREAT COP. I'M SURE HE SUSPECTS SOMETHING IS WRONG.
I'M ERIN AND THIS IS FAYE.
WE'RE THE TWO GIRLS WHO WERE PICKED TO BETA TEST THE MALL!
WHAT COULD BE MORE EXCITING?!
SORRY, HI!
EXCUSE US,GIRLS -- ARE YOU OKAY?
WOAH!
WHOOPS!
BUMP
I'M FRANK HARDY -- THIS IS MY BROTHER, JOE.
HE'S KIDDING -- WE'RE THRILLED TO HAVE BEEN PICKED TOO.
HONESTLY? YOU WANT A LIST?

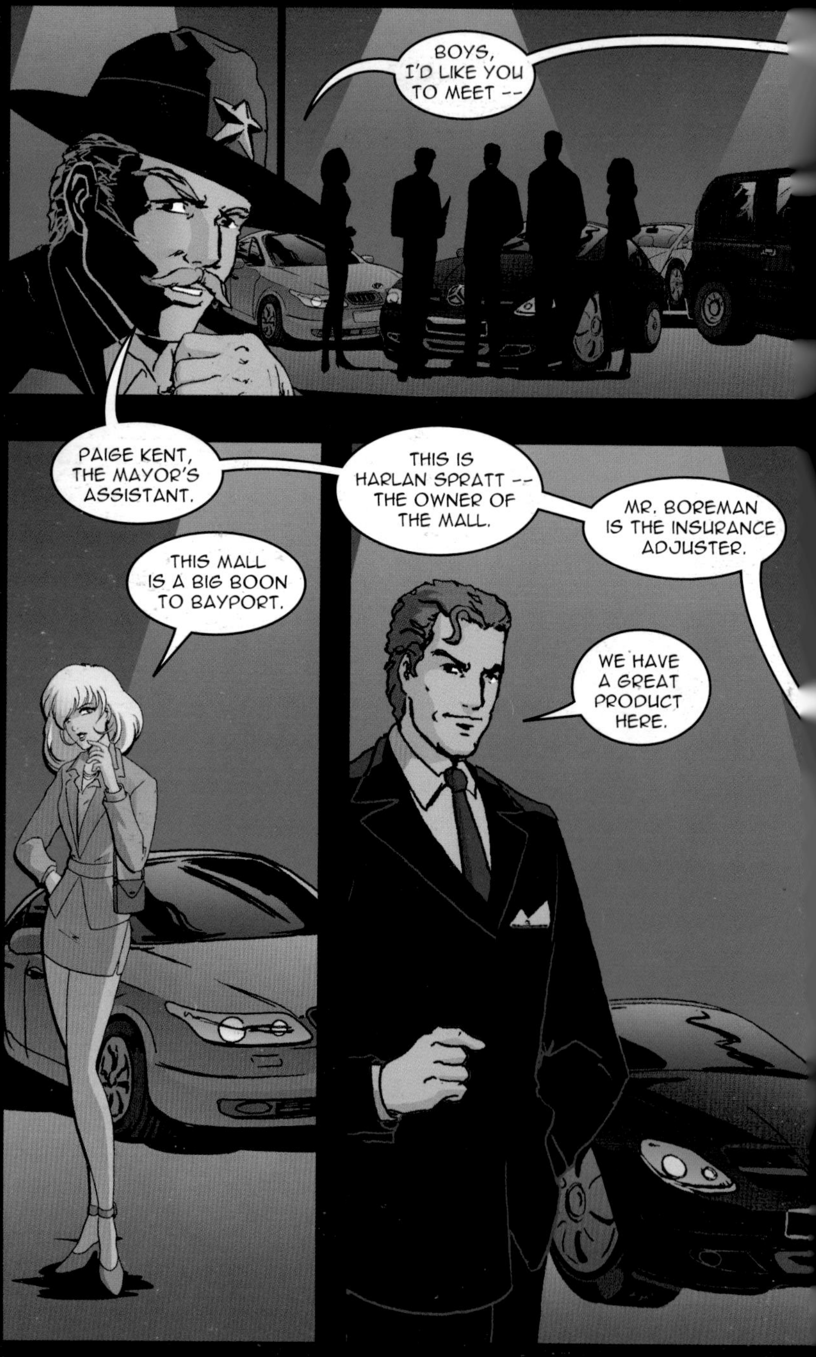
BOYS, I'D LIKE YOU TO MEET --
PAIGE KENT, THE MAYOR'S ASSISTANT.
THIS MALL IS A BIG BOON TO BAYPORT.
THIS IS HARLAN SPRATT -- THE OWNER OF THE MALL.
MR. BOREMAN IS THE INSURANCE ADJUSTER.
WE HAVE A GREAT PRODUCT HERE.

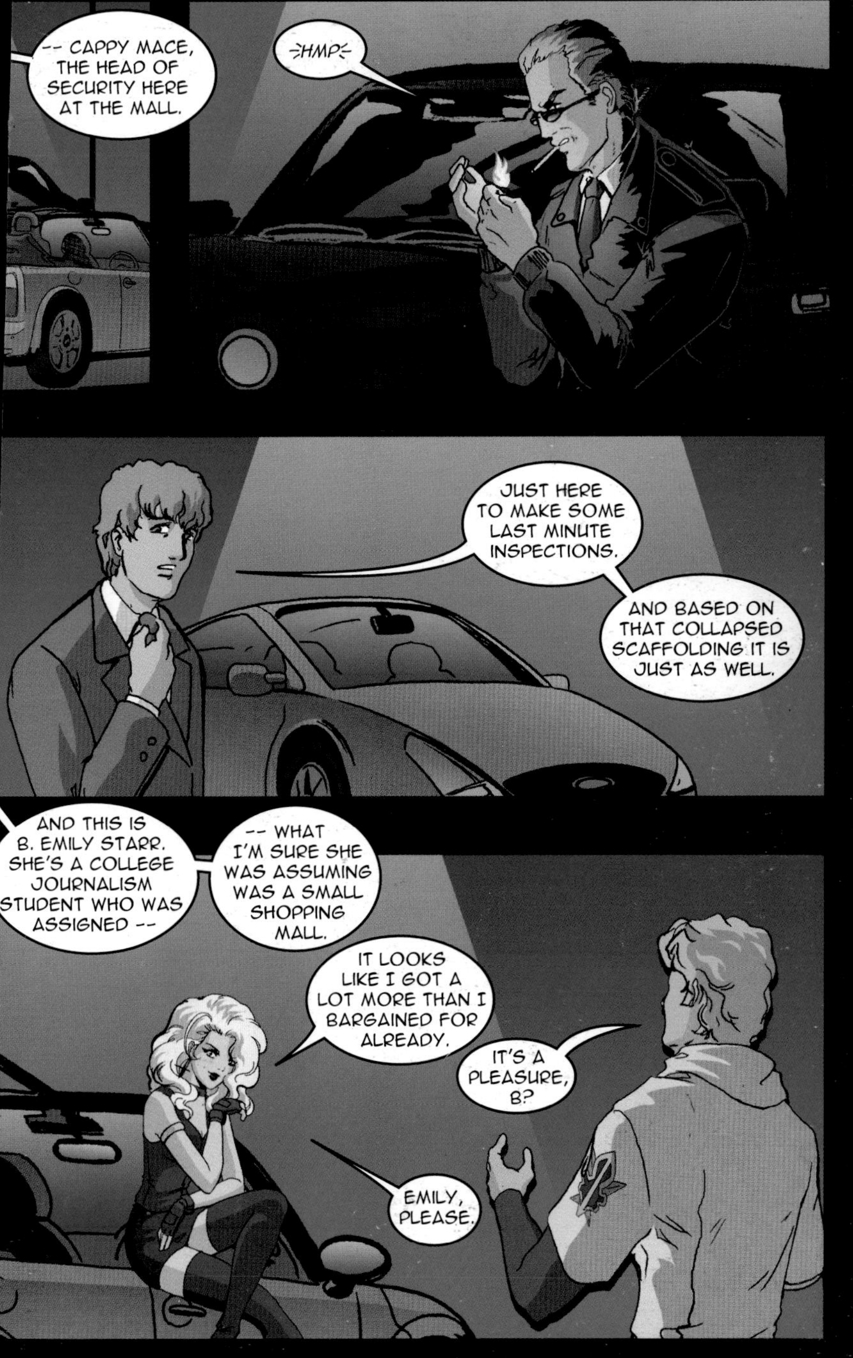
-- CAPPY MACE, THE HEAD OF SECURITY HERE AT THE MALL.
HMP
JUST HERE TO MAKE SOME LAST MINUTE INSPECTIONS.
AND BASED ON THAT COLLAPSED SCAFFOLDING IT IS JUST AS WELL.
AND THIS IS B. EMILY STARR. SHE'S A COLLEGE JOURNALISM STUDENT WHO WAS ASSIGNED --
-- WHAT I'M SURE SHE WAS ASSUMING WAS A SMALL SHOPPING MALL.
IT LOOKS LIKE I GOT A LOT MORE THAN I BARGAINED FOR ALREADY.
IT'S A PLEASURE, B?
EMILY, PLEASE.

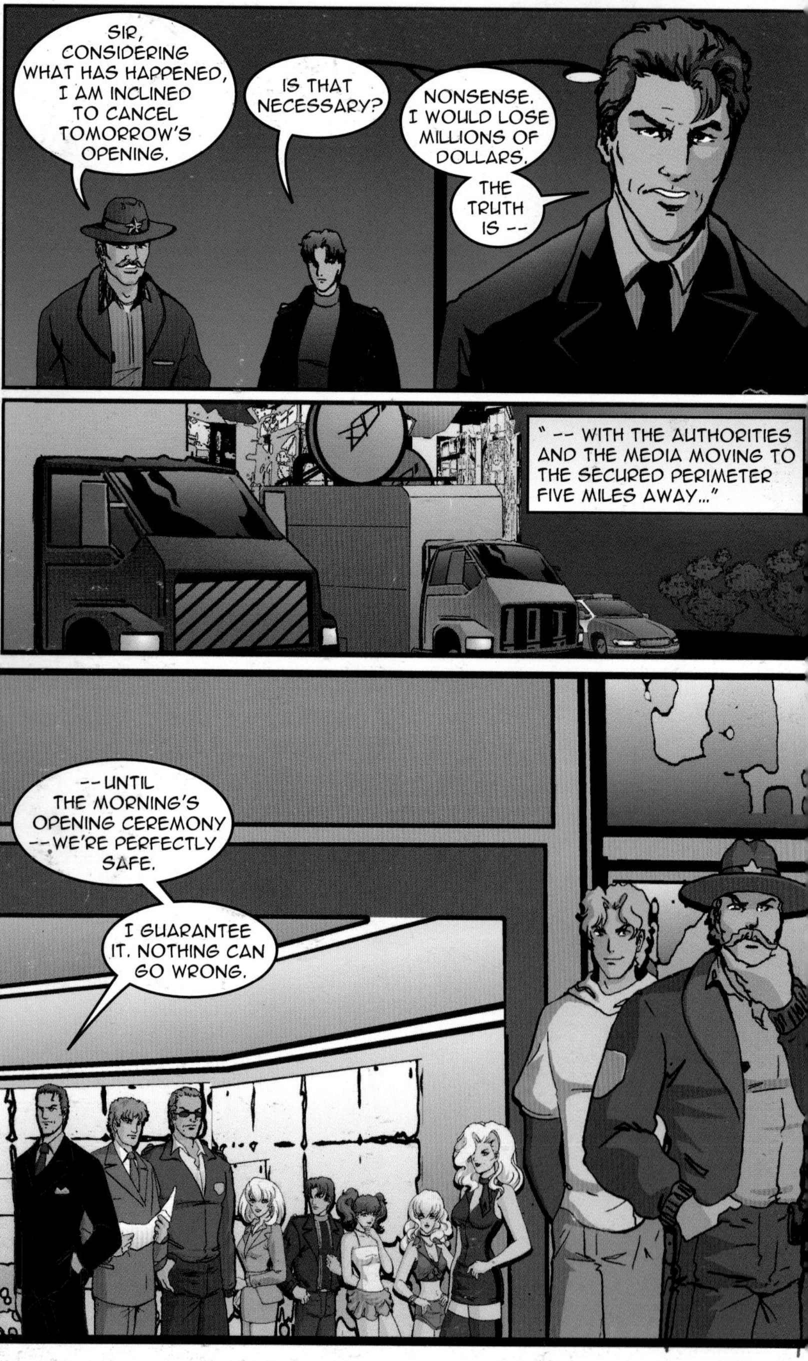
SIR, CONSIDERING WHAT HAS HAPPENED, I AM INCLINED TO CANCEL TOMORROW'S OPENING.
IS THAT NECESSARY?
NONSENSE. I WOULD LOSE MILLIONS OF DOLLARS.
THE TRUTH IS --
" -- WITH THE AUTHORITIES AND THE MEDIA MOVING TO THE SECURED PERIMETER FIVE MILES AWAY..."
-- UNTIL THE MORNING'S OPENING CEREMONY -- WE'RE PERFECTLY SAFE.
I GUARANTEE IT. NOTHING CAN GO WRONG.

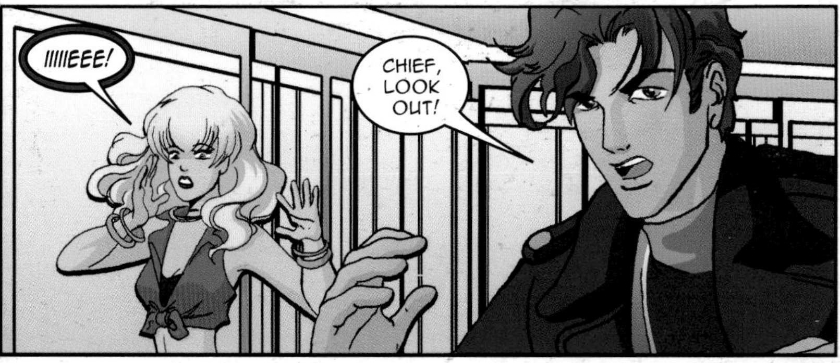
CHIEF, LOOK OUT!
IIIIIEEE!

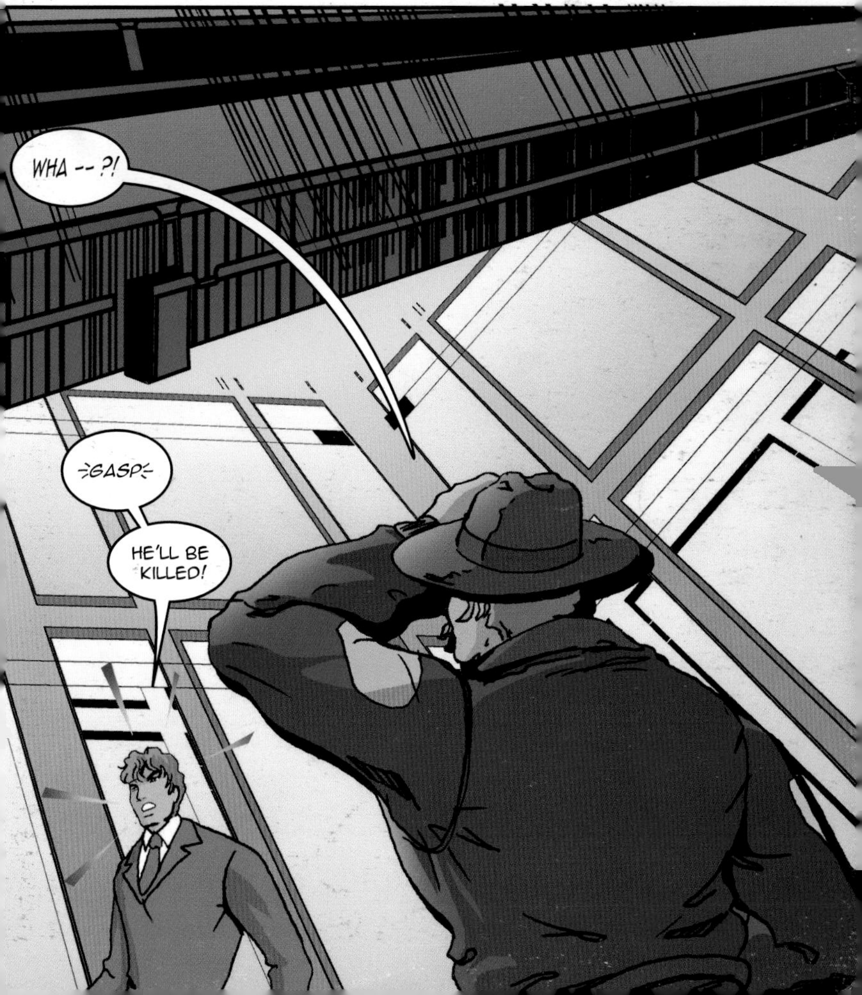
WHA -- ?!
GASP
HE'LL BE KILLED!

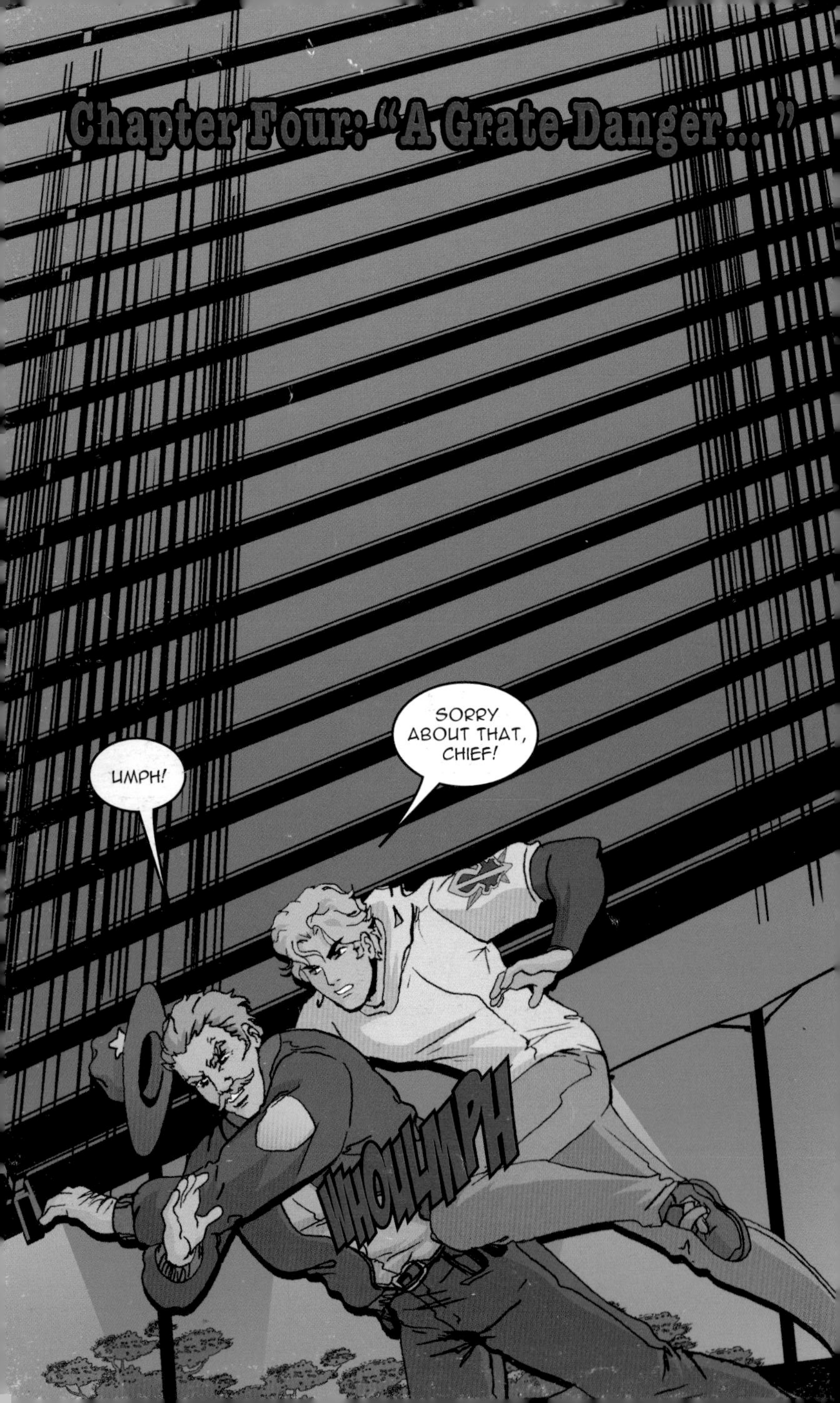
Chapter Four: "A Grate Danger..."
SORRY ABOUT THAT, CHIEF!
UMPH!
WHOOUMPH

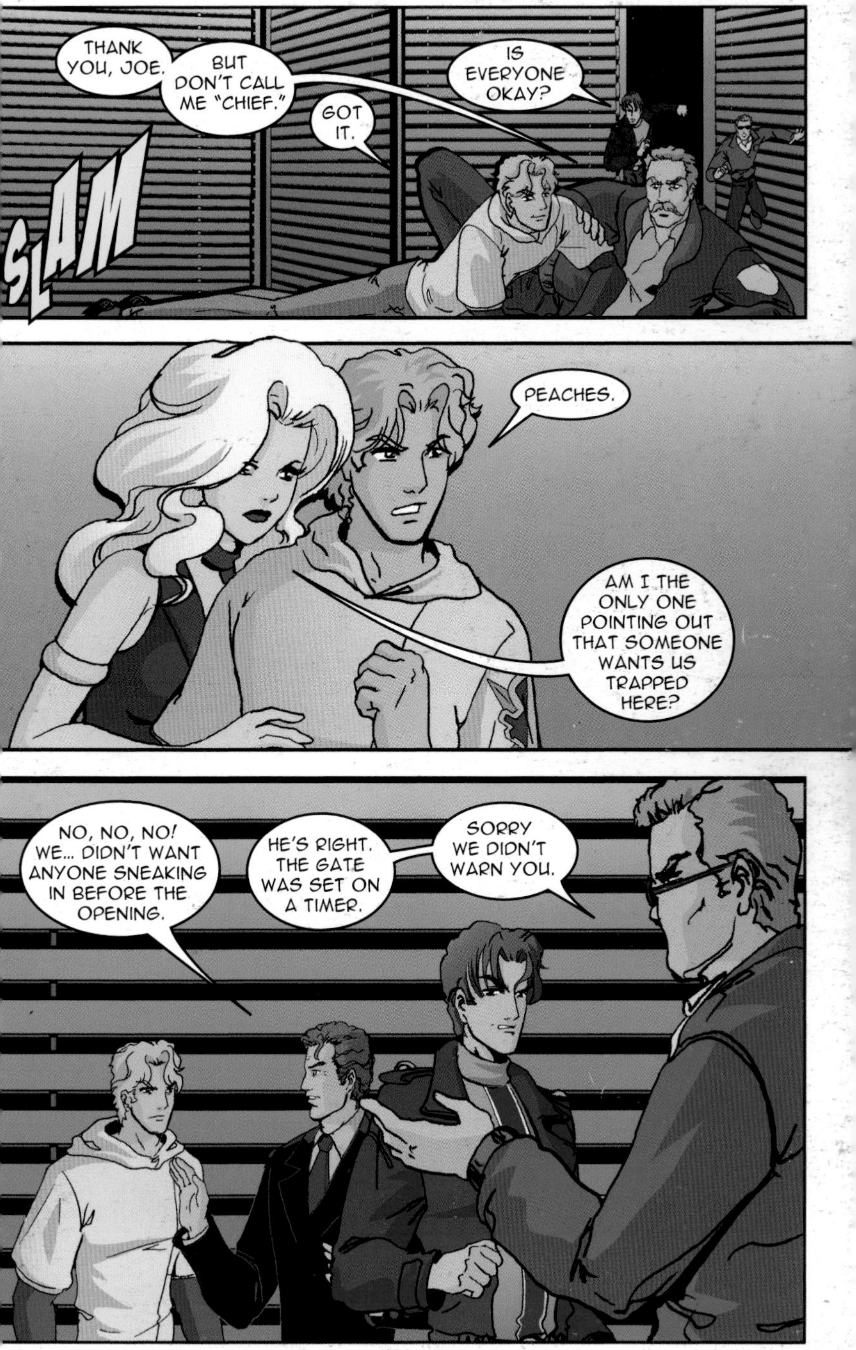
THANK YOU, JOE.
BUT DON'T CALL ME "CHIEF."
GOT IT.
IS EVERYONE OKAY?
SLAM
PEACHES.
AM I THE ONLY ONE POINTING OUT THAT SOMEONE WANTS US TRAPPED HERE?
NO, NO, NO! WE... DIDN'T WANT ANYONE SNEAKING IN BEFORE THE OPENING.
HE'S RIGHT. THE GATE WAS SET ON A TIMER.
SORRY WE DIDN'T WARN YOU.

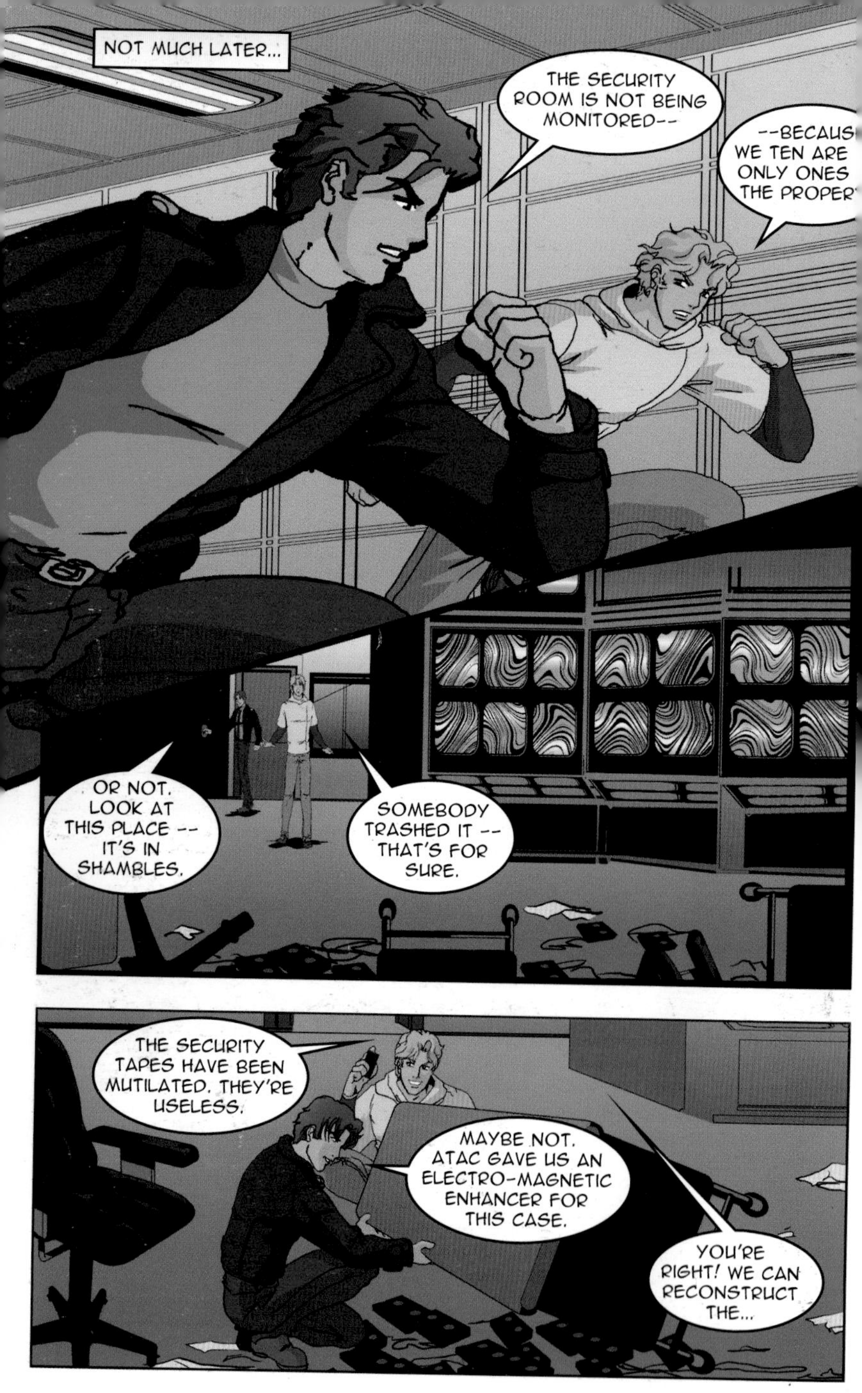
NOT MUCH LATER...
THE SECURITY ROOM IS NOT BEING MONITORED--
--BECAUS WE TEN ARE ONLY ONES THE PROPER
OR NOT. LOOK AT THIS PLACE -- IT'S IN SHAMBLES.
SOMEBODY TRASHED IT -- THAT'S FOR SURE.
THE SECURITY TAPES HAVE BEEN MUTILATED. THEY'RE USELESS.
MAYBE NOT. ATAC GAVE US AN ELECTRO-MAGNETIC ENHANCER FOR THIS CASE.
YOU'RE RIGHT! WE CAN RECONSTRUCT THE...

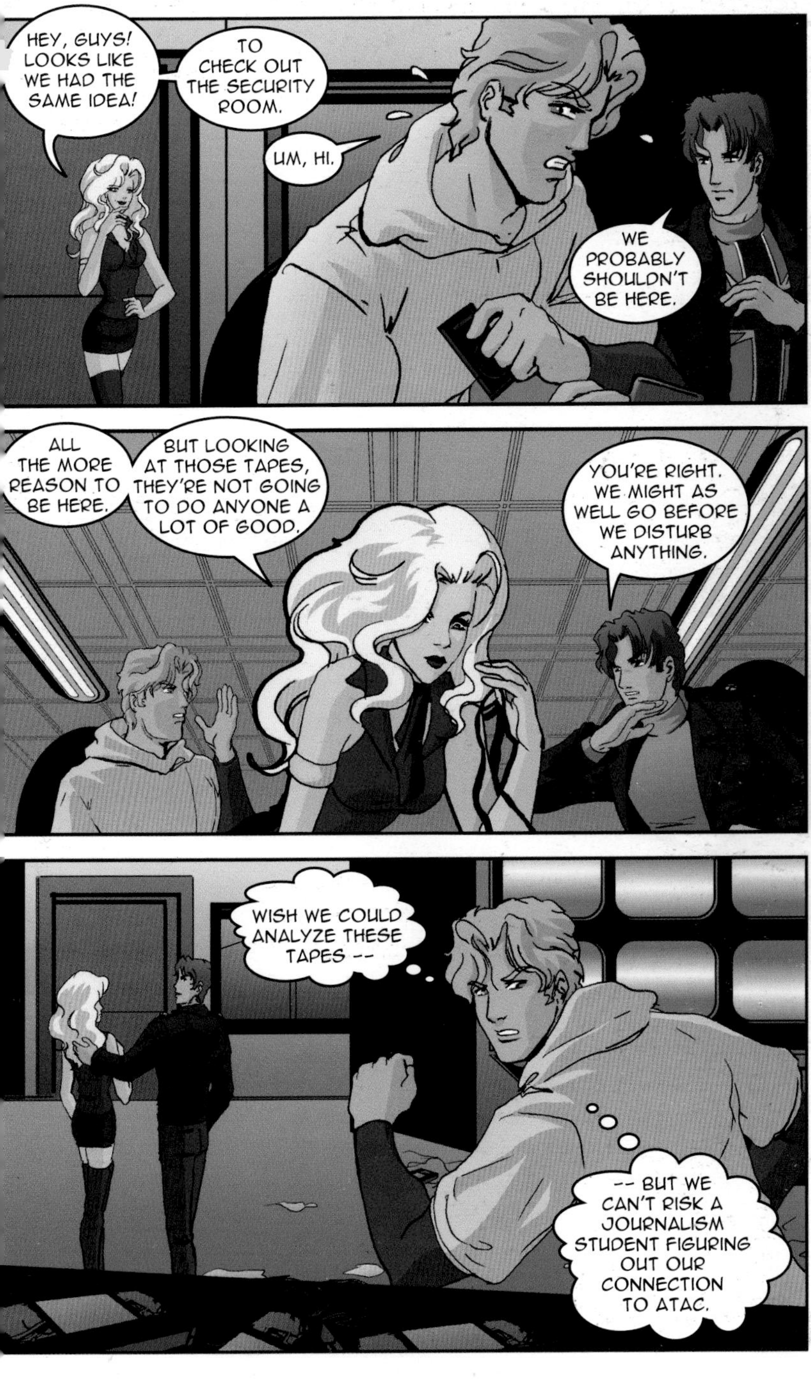
HEY, GUYS! LOOKS LIKE WE HAD THE SAME IDEA!
TO CHECK OUT THE SECURITY ROOM.
UM, HI.
WE PROBABLY SHOULDN'T BE HERE.
YOU'RE RIGHT. WE MIGHT AS WELL GO BEFORE WE DISTURB ANYTHING.
ALL THE MORE REASON TO BE HERE.
BUT LOOKING AT THOSE TAPES, THEY'RE NOT GOING TO DO ANYONE A LOT OF GOOD.
WISH WE COULD ANALYZE THESE TAPES --
-- BUT WE CAN'T RISK A JOURNALISM STUDENT FIGURING OUT OUR CONNECTION TO ATAC.

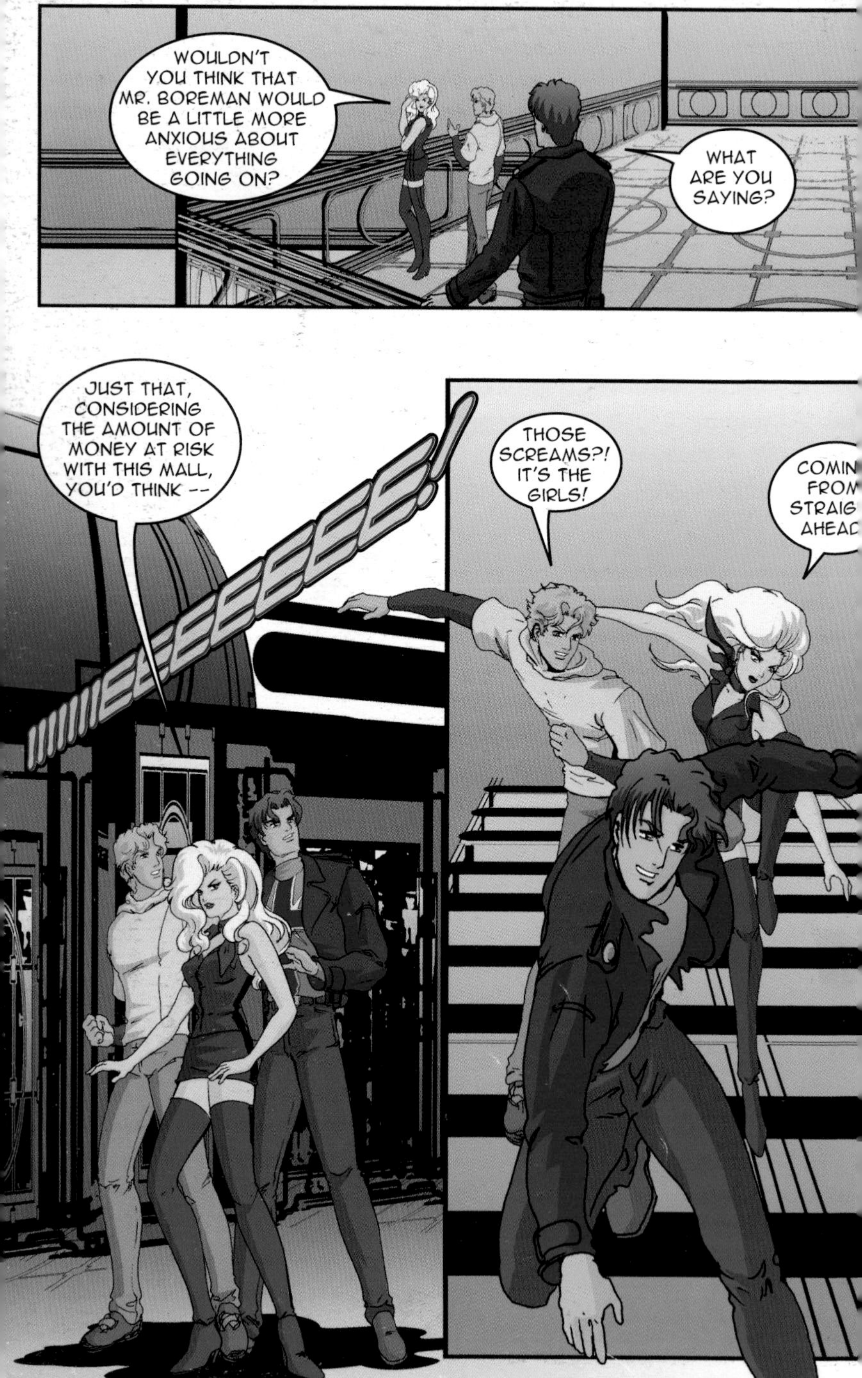

WOULDN'T YOU THINK THAT MR. BOREMAN WOULD BE A LITTLE MORE ANXIOUS ABOUT EVERYTHING GOING ON?
WHAT ARE YOU SAYING?
JUST THAT, CONSIDERING THE AMOUNT OF MONEY AT RISK WITH THIS MALL, YOU'D THINK --
IIIIIIEEEEEEEEE!!
THOSE SCREAMS?! IT'S THE GIRLS!
COMIN FROM STRAIG AHEA

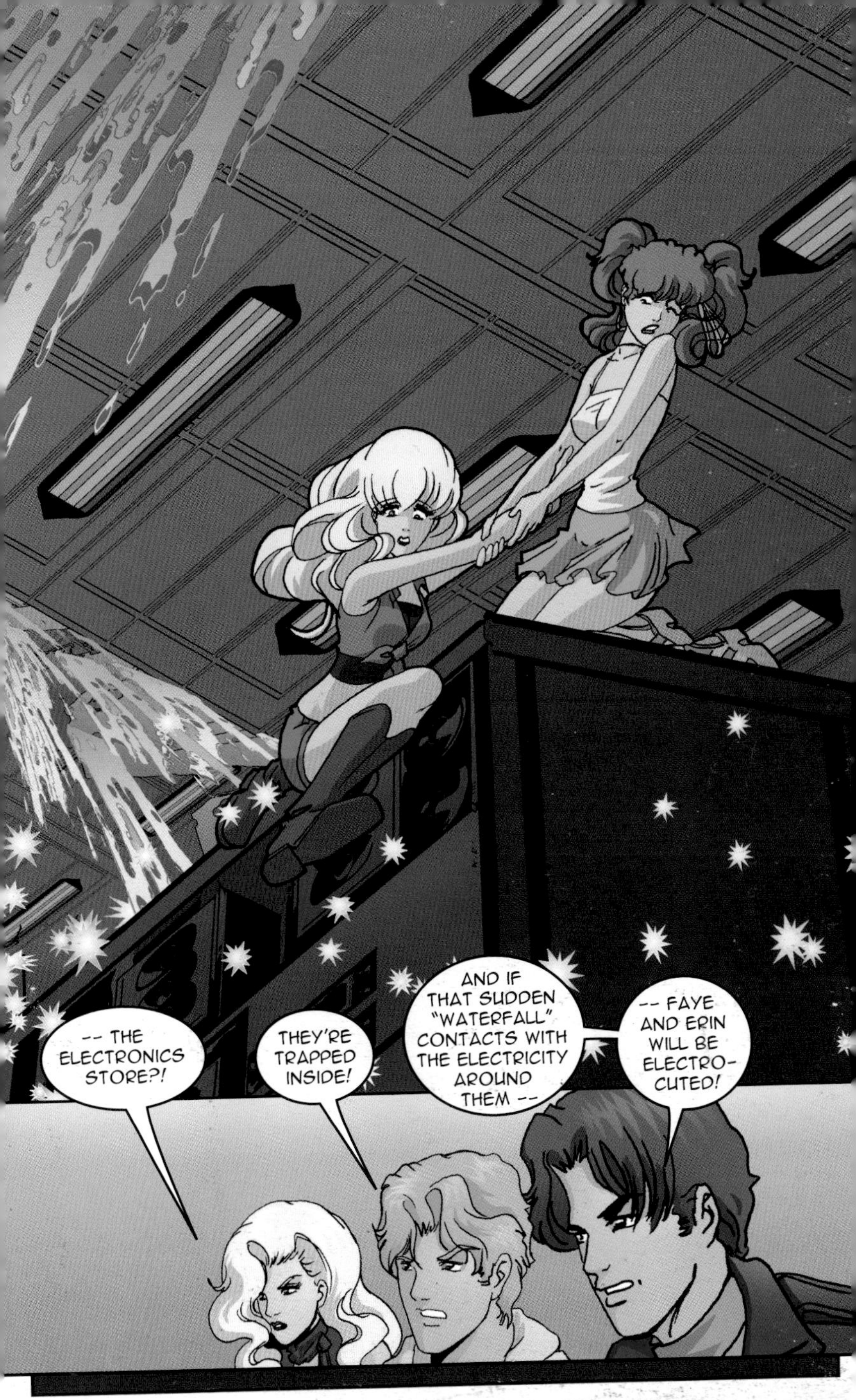
-- THE ELECTRONICS STORE?!
THEY'RE TRAPPED INSIDE!
AND IF THAT SUDDEN "WATERFALL" CONTACTS WITH THE ELECTRICITY AROUND THEM --
-- FAYE AND ERIN WILL BE ELECTRO-CUTED!

CHAPTER FIVE: "Rain of Terror!"

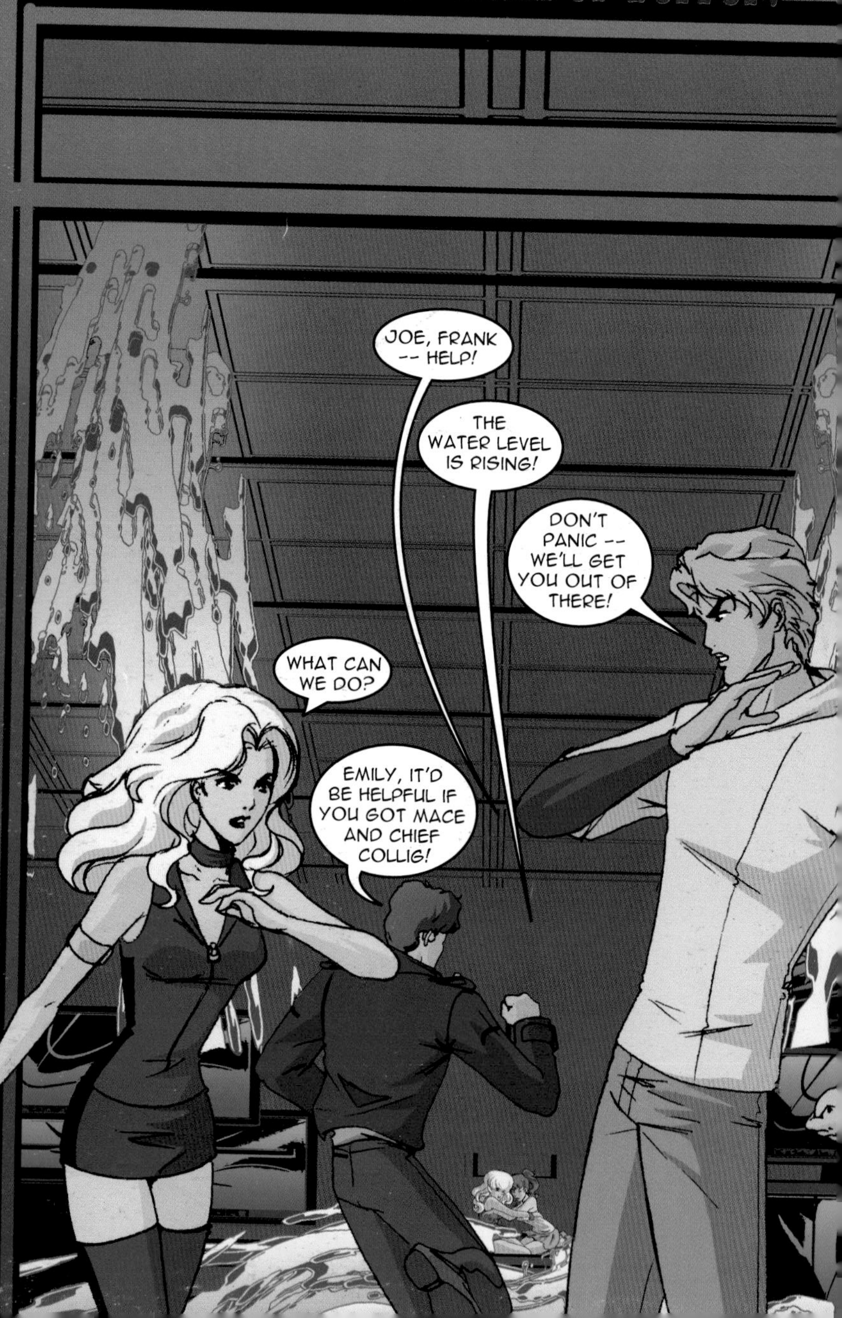
JOE, FRANK -- HELP!
THE WATER LEVEL IS RISING!
DON'T PANIC -- WE'LL GET YOU OUT OF THERE!
WHAT CAN WE DO?
EMILY, IT'D BE HELPFUL IF YOU GOT MACE AND CHIEF COLLIG!

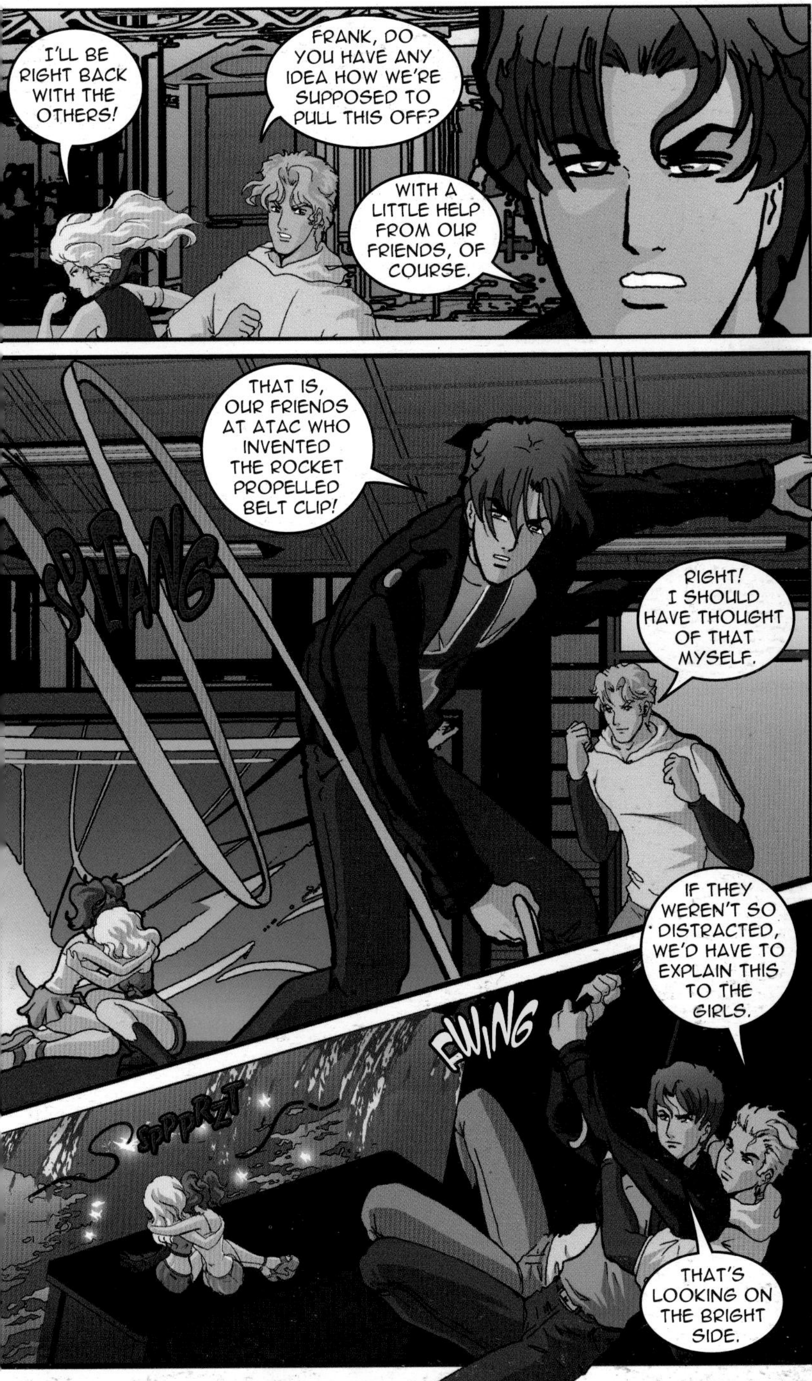
FRANK, DO YOU HAVE ANY IDEA HOW WE'RE SUPPOSED TO PULL THIS OFF?
I'LL BE RIGHT BACK WITH THE OTHERS!
WITH A LITTLE HELP FROM OUR FRIENDS, OF COURSE.
THAT IS, OUR FRIENDS AT ATAC WHO INVENTED THE ROCKET PROPELLED BELT CLIP!
SPLIANG
RIGHT! I SHOULD HAVE THOUGHT OF THAT MYSELF.
IF THEY WEREN'T SO DISTRACTED, WE'D HAVE TO EXPLAIN THIS TO THE GIRLS.
FWING
SPPPRZT
THAT'S LOOKING ON THE BRIGHT SIDE.

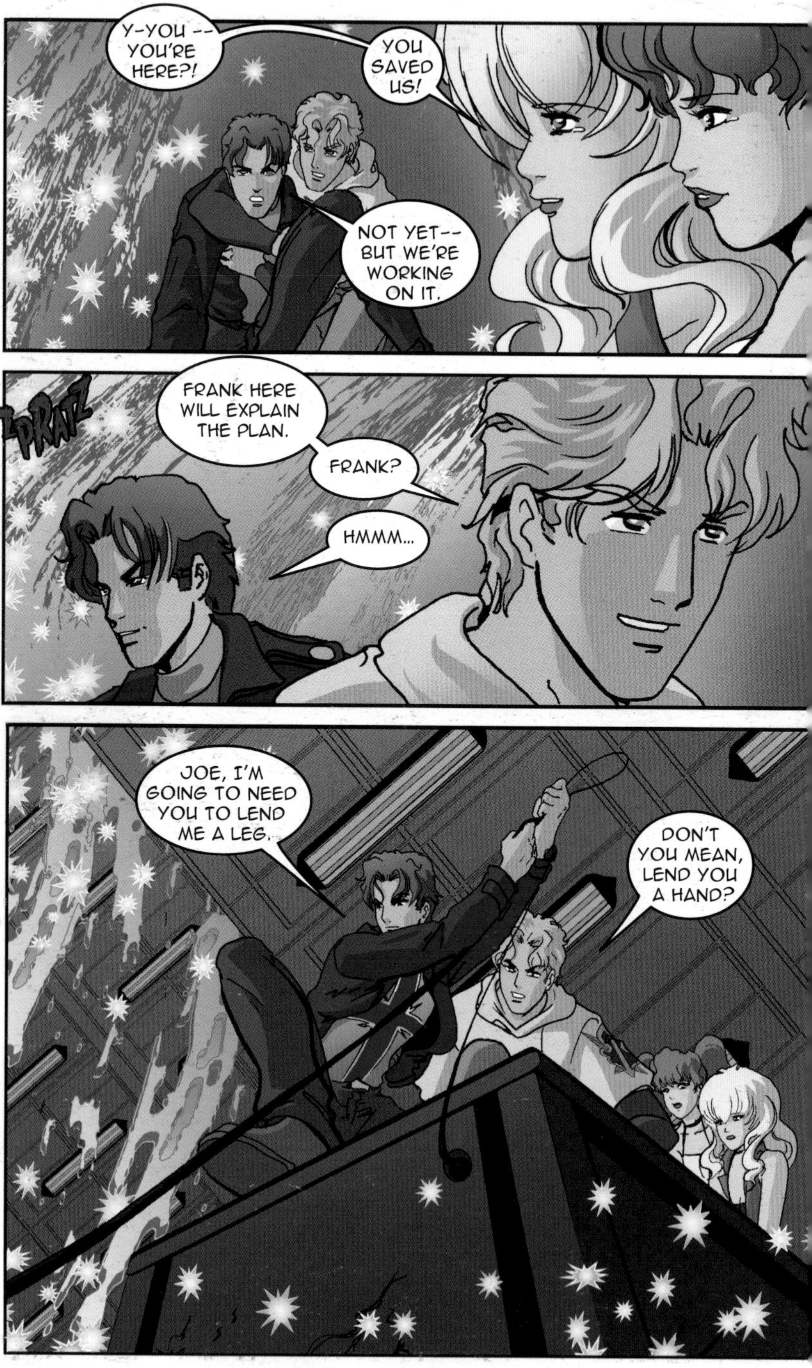
Y-YOU -- YOU'RE HERE?!
YOU SAVED US!
NOT YET-- BUT WE'RE WORKING ON IT.
FRANK HERE WILL EXPLAIN THE PLAN.
FRANK?
HMMM...
ZPRATZ
JOE, I'M GOING TO NEED YOU TO LEND ME A LEG.
DON'T YOU MEAN, LEND YOU A HAND?

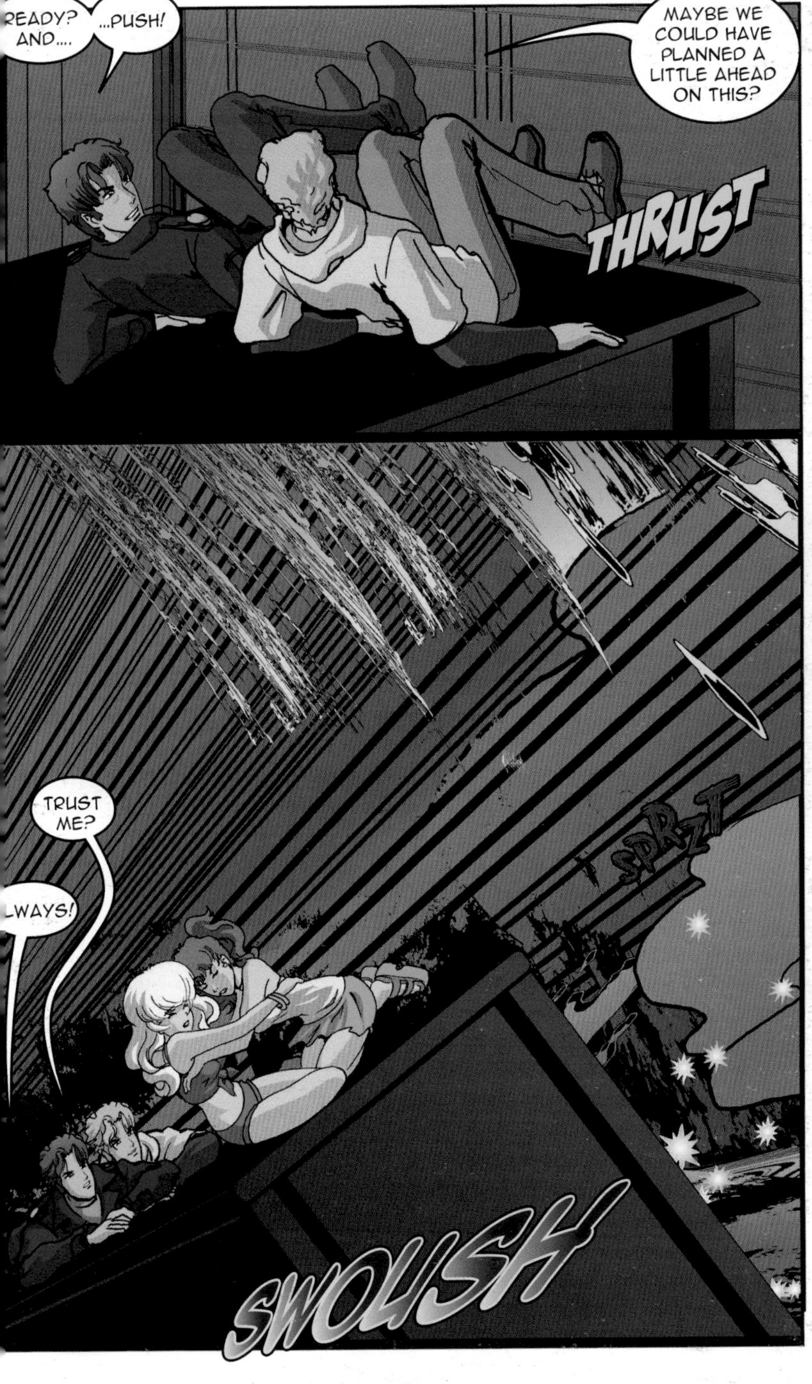
READY? AND....
...PUSH!
MAYBE WE COULD HAVE PLANNED A LITTLE AHEAD ON THIS?
THRUST
TRUST ME?
LWAYS!
SPRZT
SWOUSH

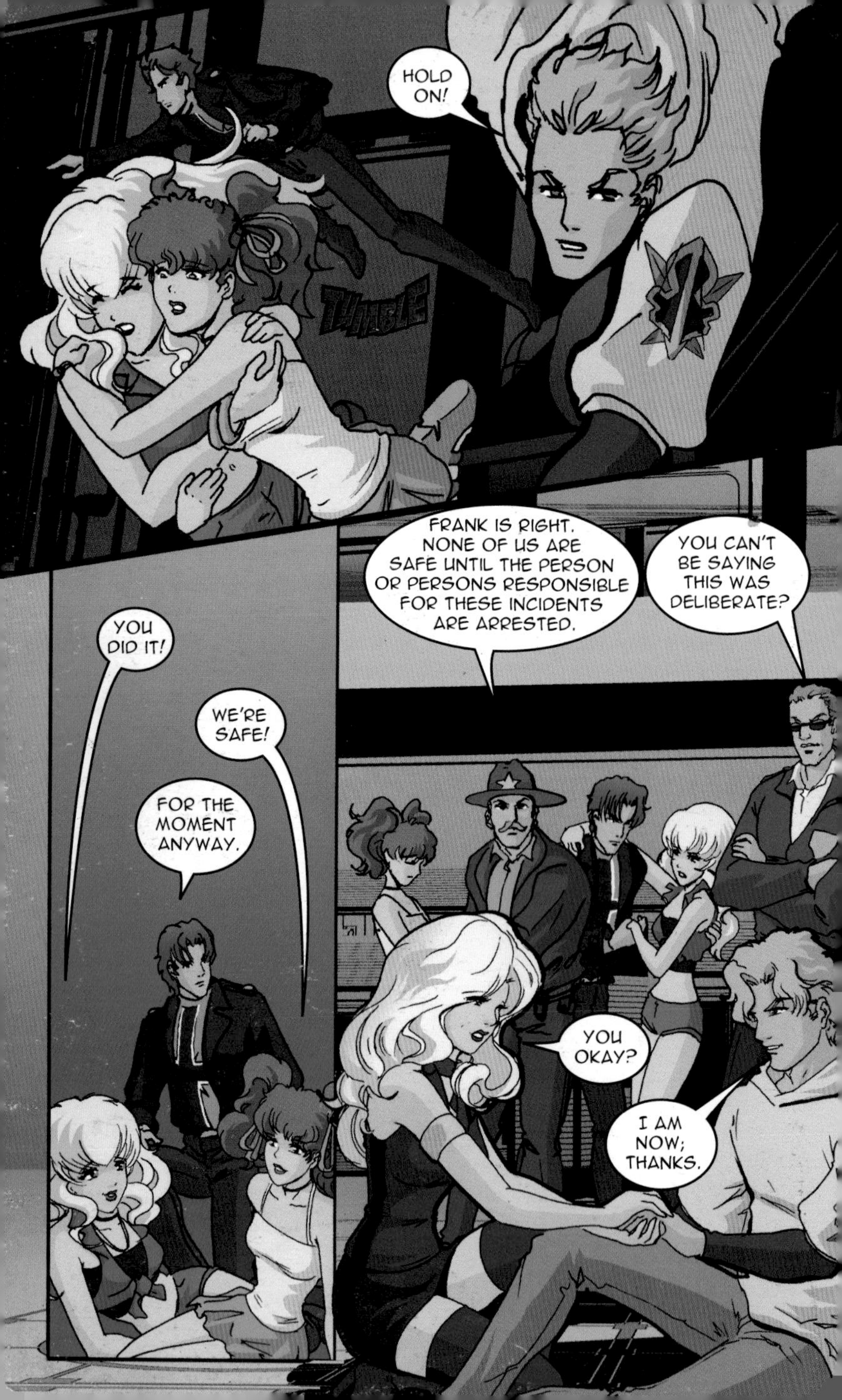
HOLD ON!
YOU CAN'T BE SAYING THIS WAS DELIBERATE?
FRANK IS RIGHT. NONE OF US ARE SAFE UNTIL THE PERSON OR PERSONS RESPONSIBLE FOR THESE INCIDENTS ARE ARRESTED.
YOU OKAY?
I AM NOW; THANKS.
YOU DID IT!
WE'RE SAFE!
FOR THE MOMENT ANYWAY.

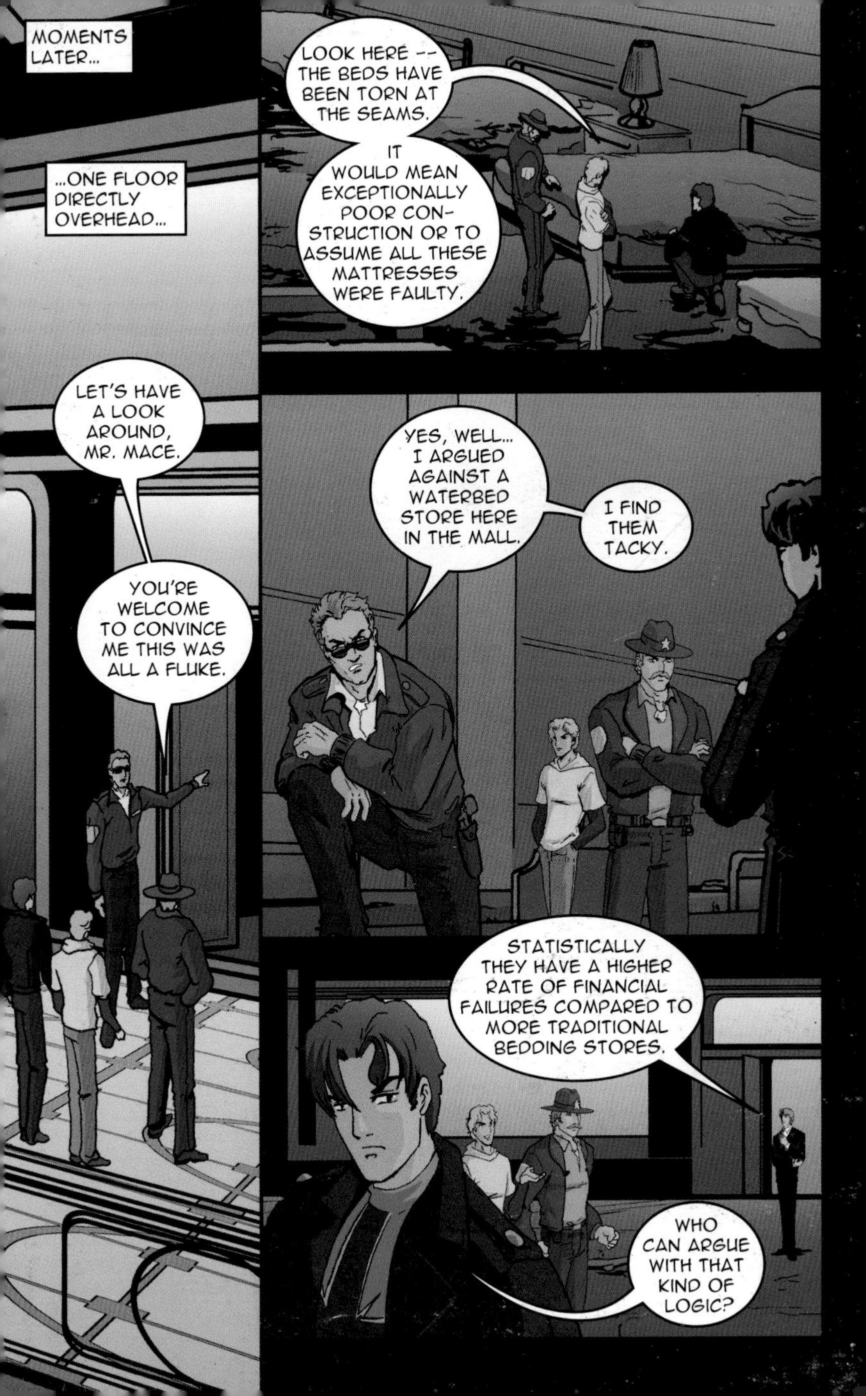
LOOK HERE -- THE BEDS HAVE BEEN TORN AT THE SEAMS.
IT WOULD MEAN EXCEPTIONALLY POOR CON- STRUCTION OR TO ASSUME ALL THESE MATTRESSES WERE FAULTY.
YES, WELL... I ARGUED AGAINST A WATERBED STORE HERE IN THE MALL.
I FIND THEM TACKY.
STATISTICALLY THEY HAVE A HIGHER RATE OF FINANCIAL FAILURES COMPARED TO MORE TRADITIONAL BEDDING STORES.
WHO CAN ARGUE WITH THAT KIND OF LOGIC?
MOMENTS LATER...
...ONE FLOOR DIRECTLY OVERHEAD...
LET'S HAVE A LOOK AROUND, MR. MACE.
YOU'RE WELCOME TO CONVINCE ME THIS WAS ALL A FLUKE.

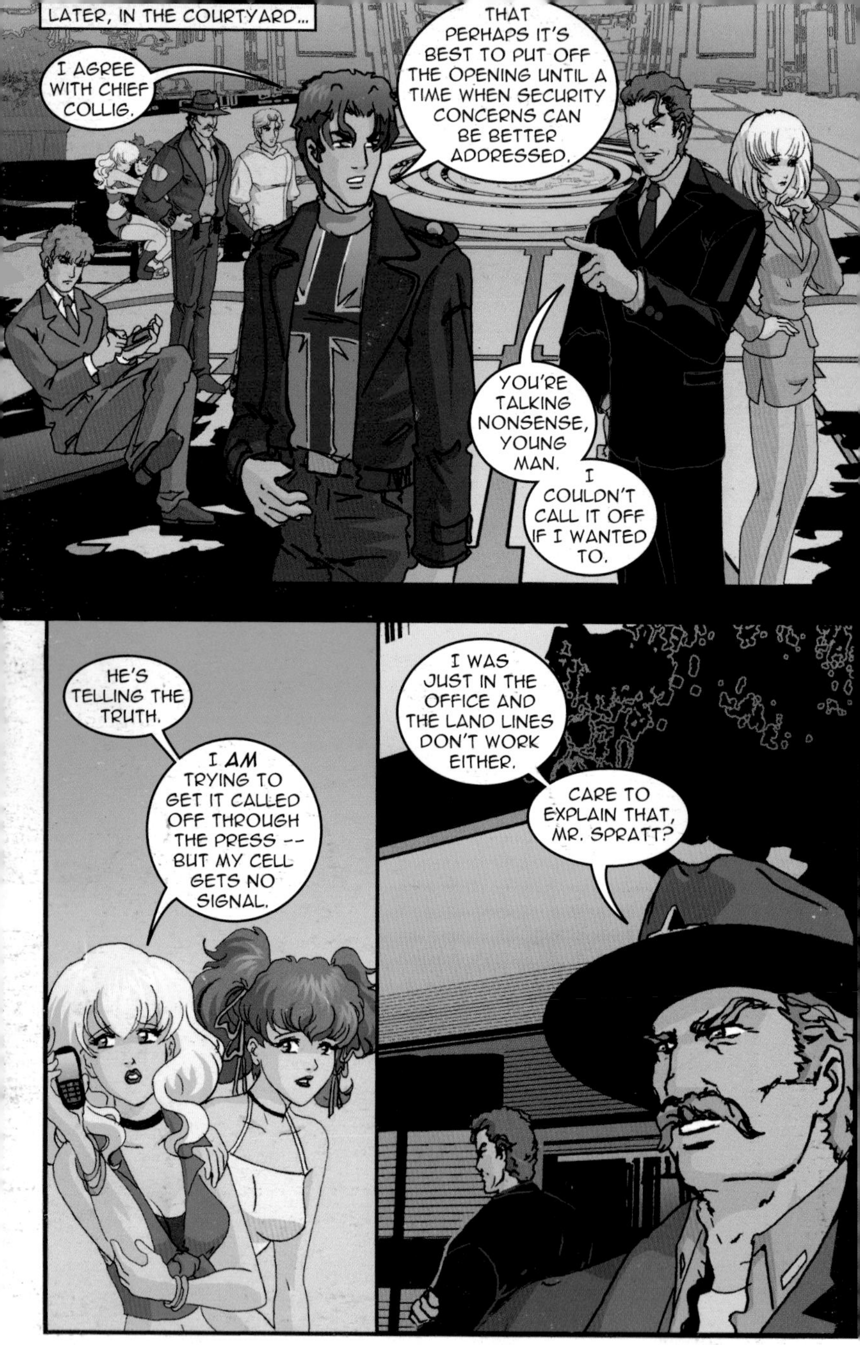
LATER, IN THE COURTYARD...
I AGREE WITH CHIEF COLLIG.
THAT PERHAPS IT'S BEST TO PUT OFF THE OPENING UNTIL A TIME WHEN SECURITY CONCERNS CAN BE BETTER ADDRESSED.
YOU'RE TALKING NONSENSE, YOUNG MAN.
I COULDN'T CALL IT OFF IF I WANTED TO.
HE'S TELLING THE TRUTH.
I AM TRYING TO GET IT CALLED OFF THROUGH THE PRESS -- BUT MY CELL GETS NO SIGNAL.
I WAS JUST IN THE OFFICE AND THE LAND LINES DON'T WORK EITHER.
CARE TO EXPLAIN THAT, MR. SPRATT?

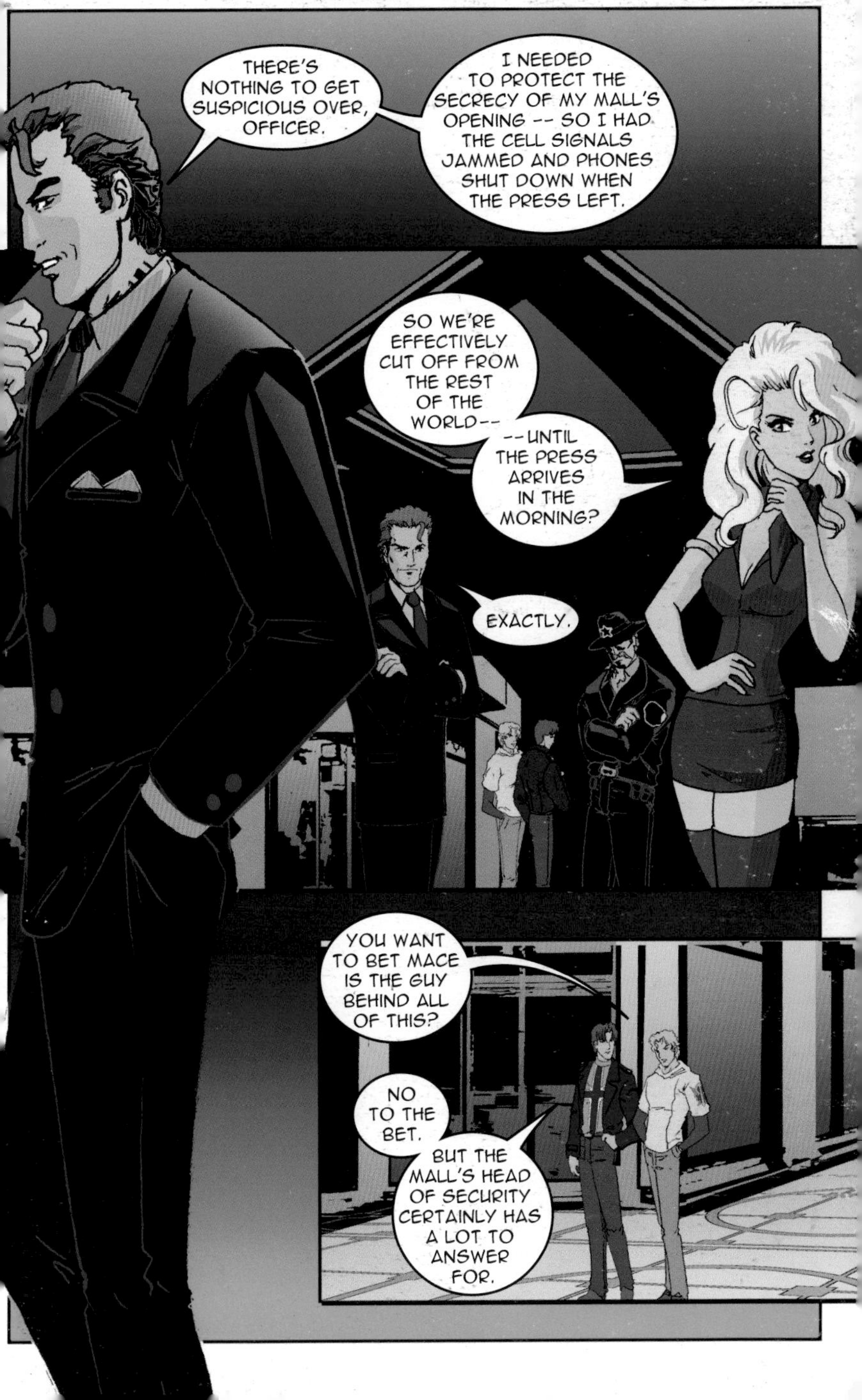

THERE'S NOTHING TO GET SUSPICIOUS OVER, OFFICER.
I NEEDED TO PROTECT THE SECRECY OF MY MALL'S OPENING -- SO I HAD THE CELL SIGNALS JAMMED AND PHONES SHUT DOWN WHEN THE PRESS LEFT.
SO WE'RE EFFECTIVELY CUT OFF FROM THE REST OF THE WORLD--
--UNTIL THE PRESS ARRIVES IN THE MORNING?
EXACTLY.
YOU WANT TO BET MACE IS THE GUY BEHIND ALL OF THIS?
NO TO THE BET.
BUT THE MALL'S HEAD OF SECURITY CERTAINLY HAS A LOT TO ANSWER FOR.

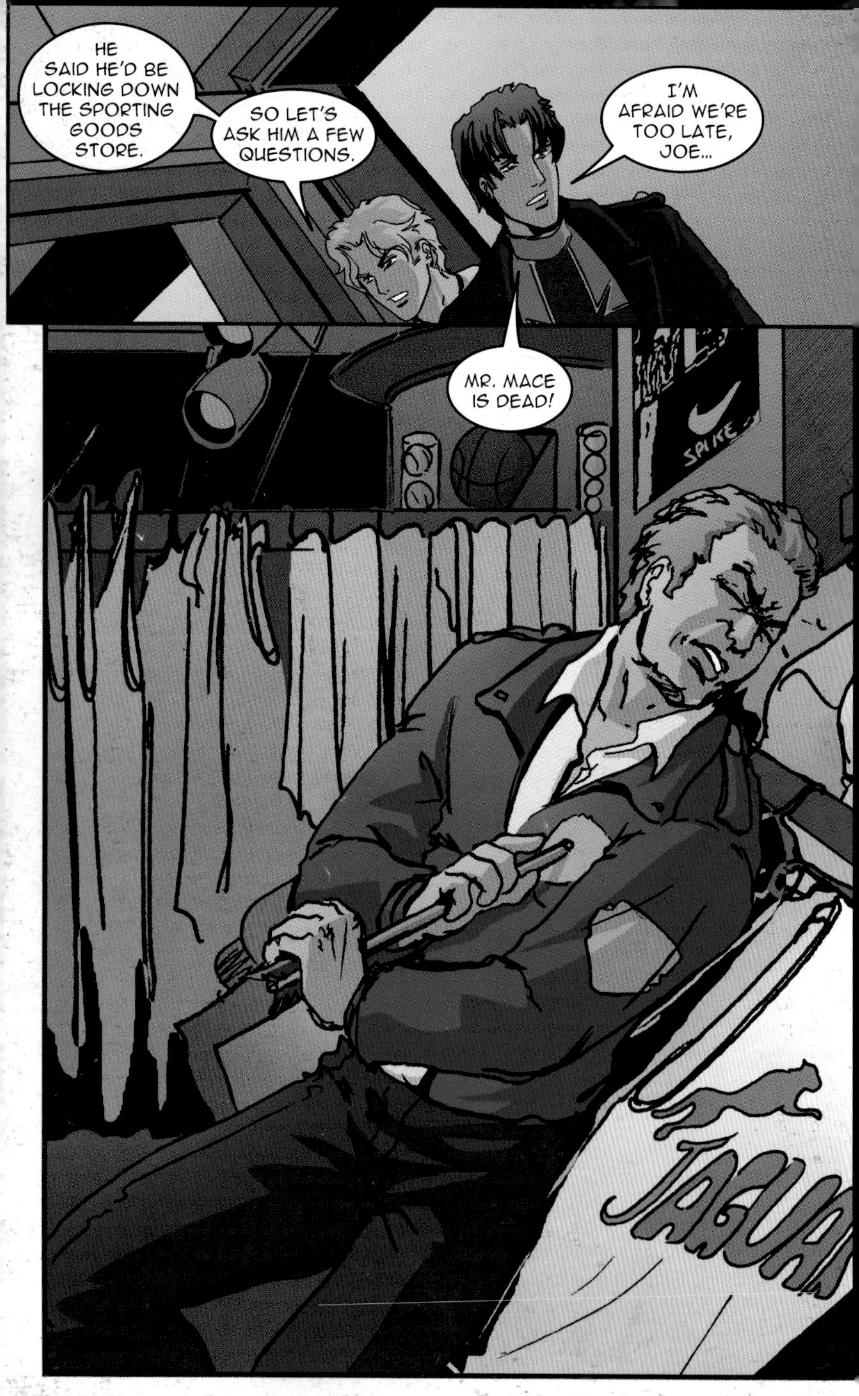
HE SAID HE'D BE LOCKING DOWN THE SPORTING GOODS STORE.
SO LET'S ASK HIM A FEW QUESTIONS.
I'M AFRAID WE'RE TOO LATE, JOE...
MR. MACE IS DEAD!
SPIKE
JAGUA

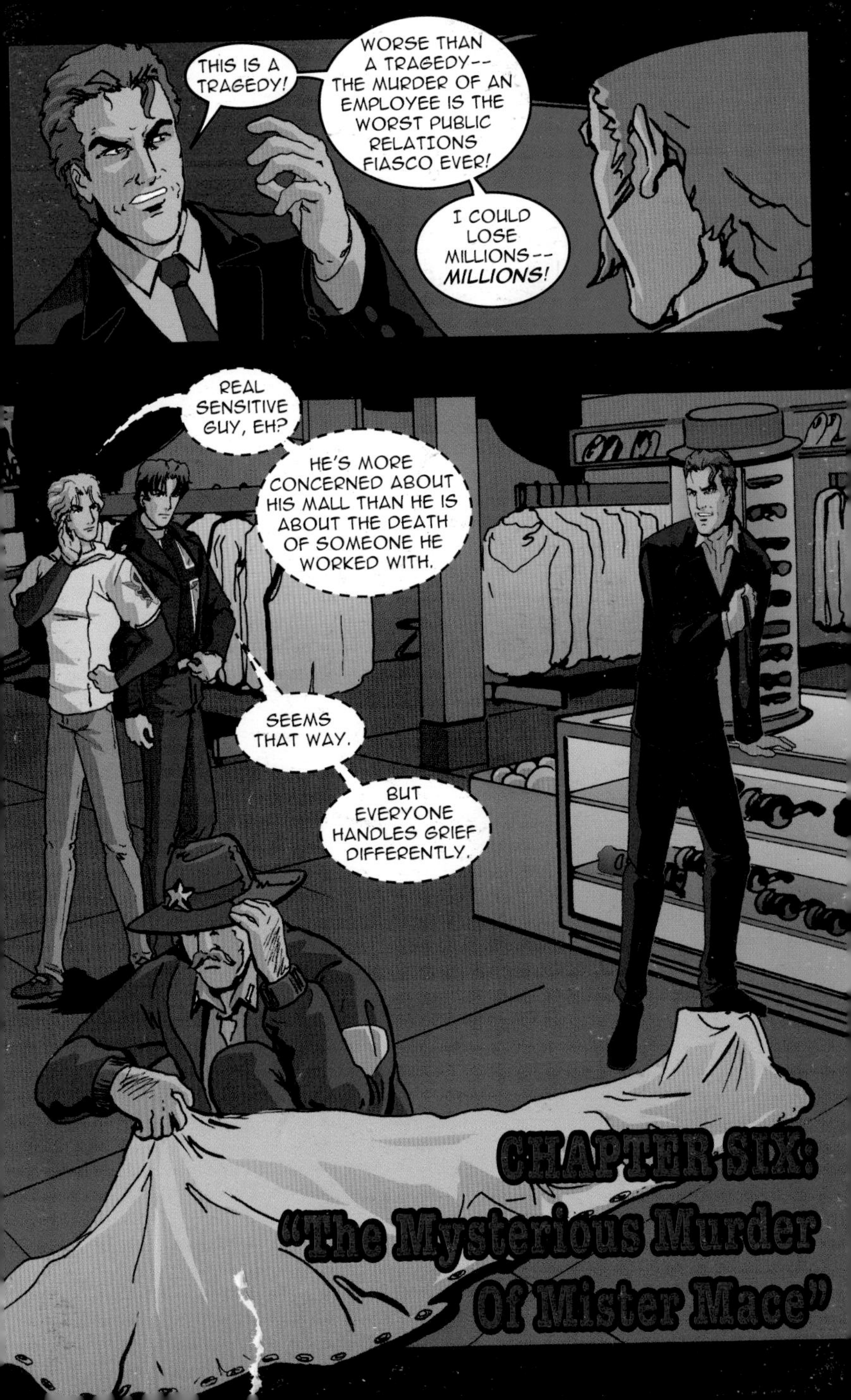

THIS IS A TRAGEDY!
WORSE THAN A TRAGEDY-- THE MURDER OF AN EMPLOYEE IS THE WORST PUBLIC RELATIONS FIASCO EVER!
I COULD LOSE MILLIONS-- *MILLIONS!*
REAL SENSITIVE GUY, EH?
HE'S MORE CONCERNED ABOUT HIS MALL THAN HE IS ABOUT THE DEATH OF SOMEONE HE WORKED WITH.
SEEMS THAT WAY.
BUT EVERYONE HANDLES GRIEF DIFFERENTLY.
CHAPTER SIX:
"The Mysterious Murder Of Mister Mace"

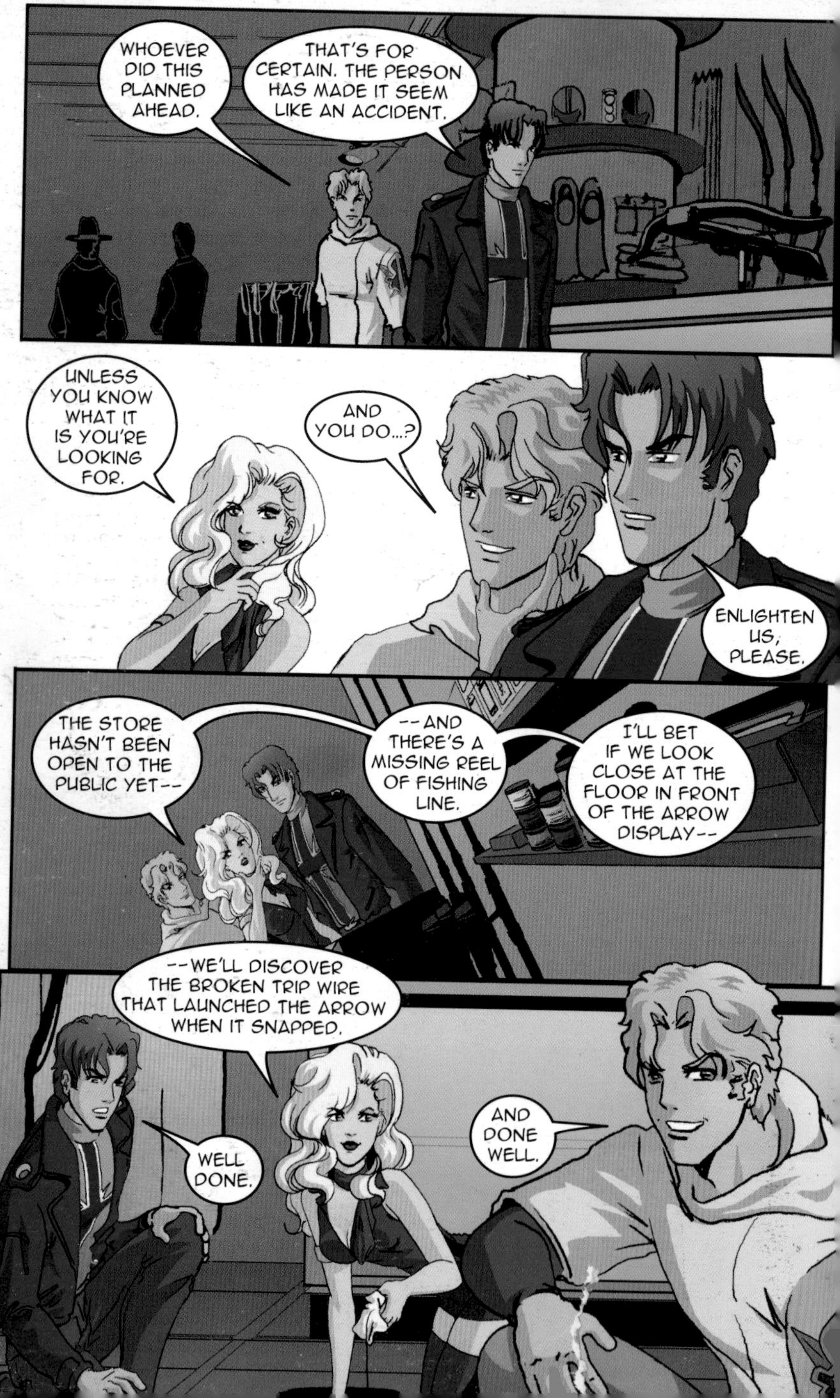
WHOEVER DID THIS PLANNED AHEAD.
THAT'S FOR CERTAIN. THE PERSON HAS MADE IT SEEM LIKE AN ACCIDENT.
UNLESS YOU KNOW WHAT IT IS YOU'RE LOOKING FOR.
AND YOU DO...?
ENLIGHTEN US, PLEASE.
THE STORE HASN'T BEEN OPEN TO THE PUBLIC YET--
--AND THERE'S A MISSING REEL OF FISHING LINE.
I'LL BET IF WE LOOK CLOSE AT THE FLOOR IN FRONT OF THE ARROW DISPLAY--
--WE'LL DISCOVER THE BROKEN TRIP WIRE THAT LAUNCHED THE ARROW WHEN IT SNAPPED.
WELL DONE.
AND DONE WELL.

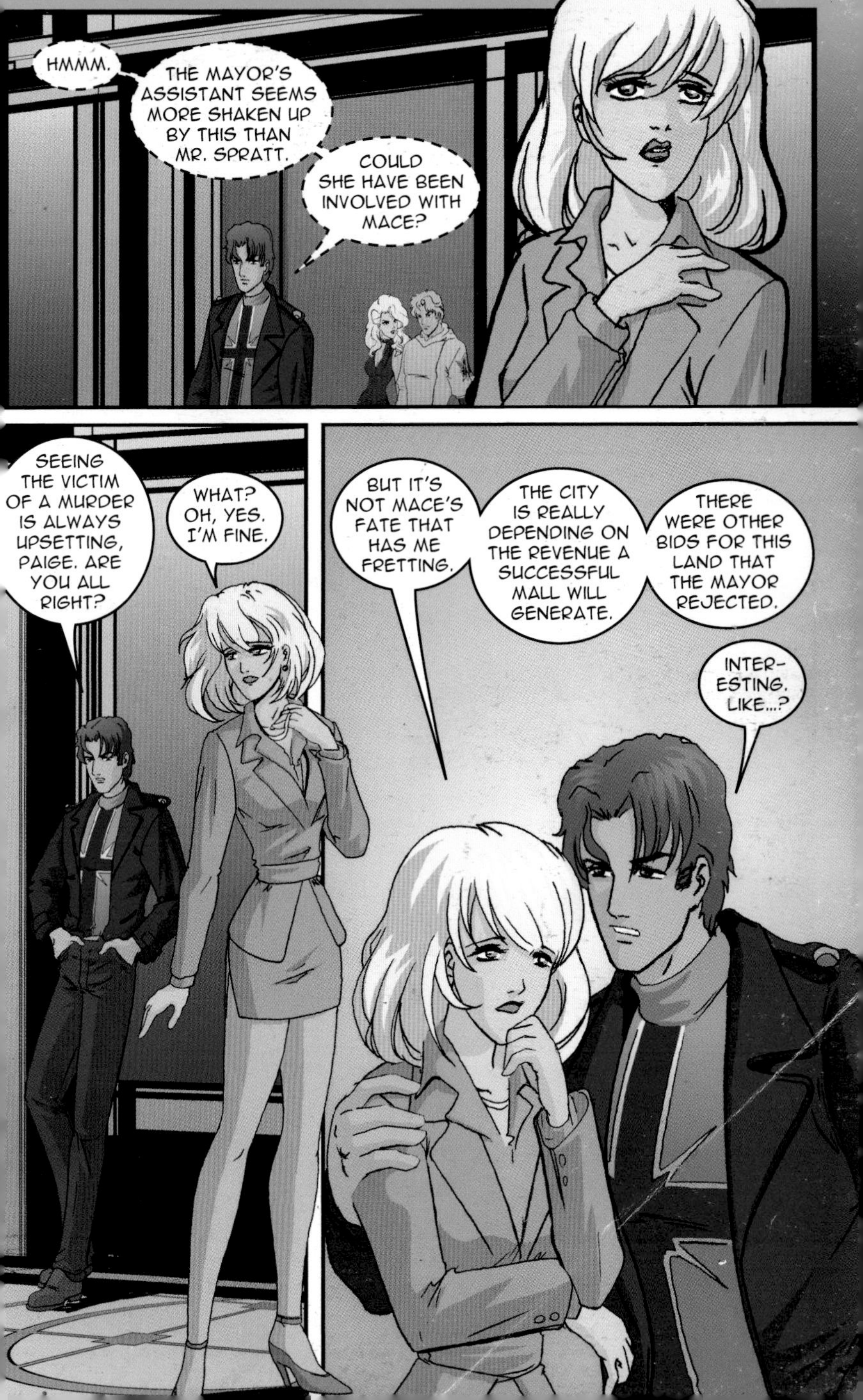
HMMM.
THE MAYOR'S ASSISTANT SEEMS MORE SHAKEN UP BY THIS THAN MR. SPRATT.
COULD SHE HAVE BEEN INVOLVED WITH MACE?
SEEING THE VICTIM OF A MURDER IS ALWAYS UPSETTING, PAIGE. ARE YOU ALL RIGHT?
WHAT? OH, YES. I'M FINE.
BUT IT'S NOT MACE'S FATE THAT HAS ME FRETTING.
THE CITY IS REALLY DEPENDING ON THE REVENUE A SUCCESSFUL MALL WILL GENERATE.
THERE WERE OTHER BIDS FOR THIS LAND THAT THE MAYOR REJECTED.
INTER-ESTING. LIKE...?

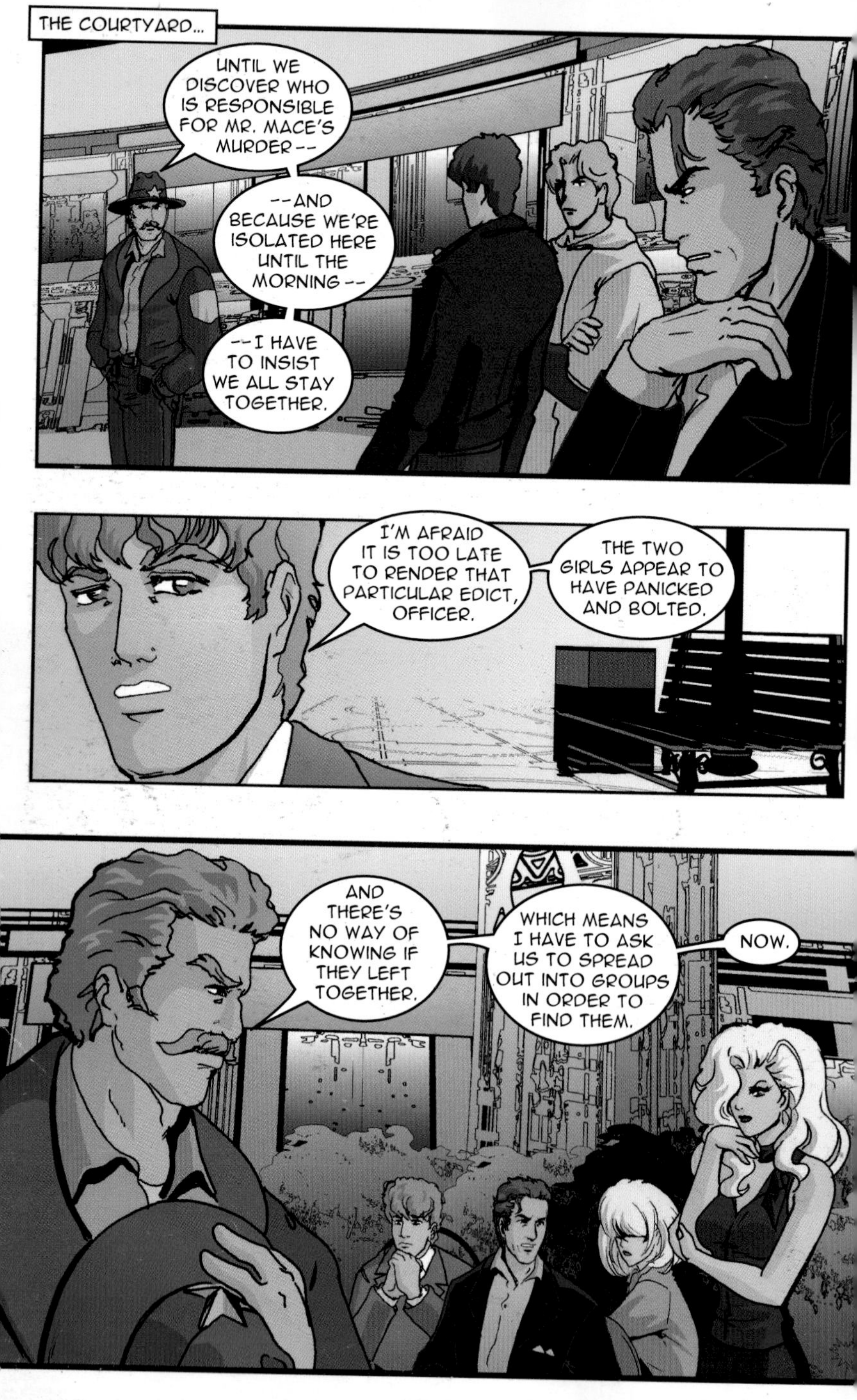
THE COURTYARD...
UNTIL WE DISCOVER WHO IS RESPONSIBLE FOR MR. MACE'S MURDER--
--AND BECAUSE WE'RE ISOLATED HERE UNTIL THE MORNING--
--I HAVE TO INSIST WE ALL STAY TOGETHER.
I'M AFRAID IT IS TOO LATE TO RENDER THAT PARTICULAR EDICT, OFFICER.
THE TWO GIRLS APPEAR TO HAVE PANICKED AND BOLTED.
AND THERE'S NO WAY OF KNOWING IF THEY LEFT TOGETHER.
WHICH MEANS I HAVE TO ASK US TO SPREAD OUT INTO GROUPS IN ORDER TO FIND THEM.
NOW.

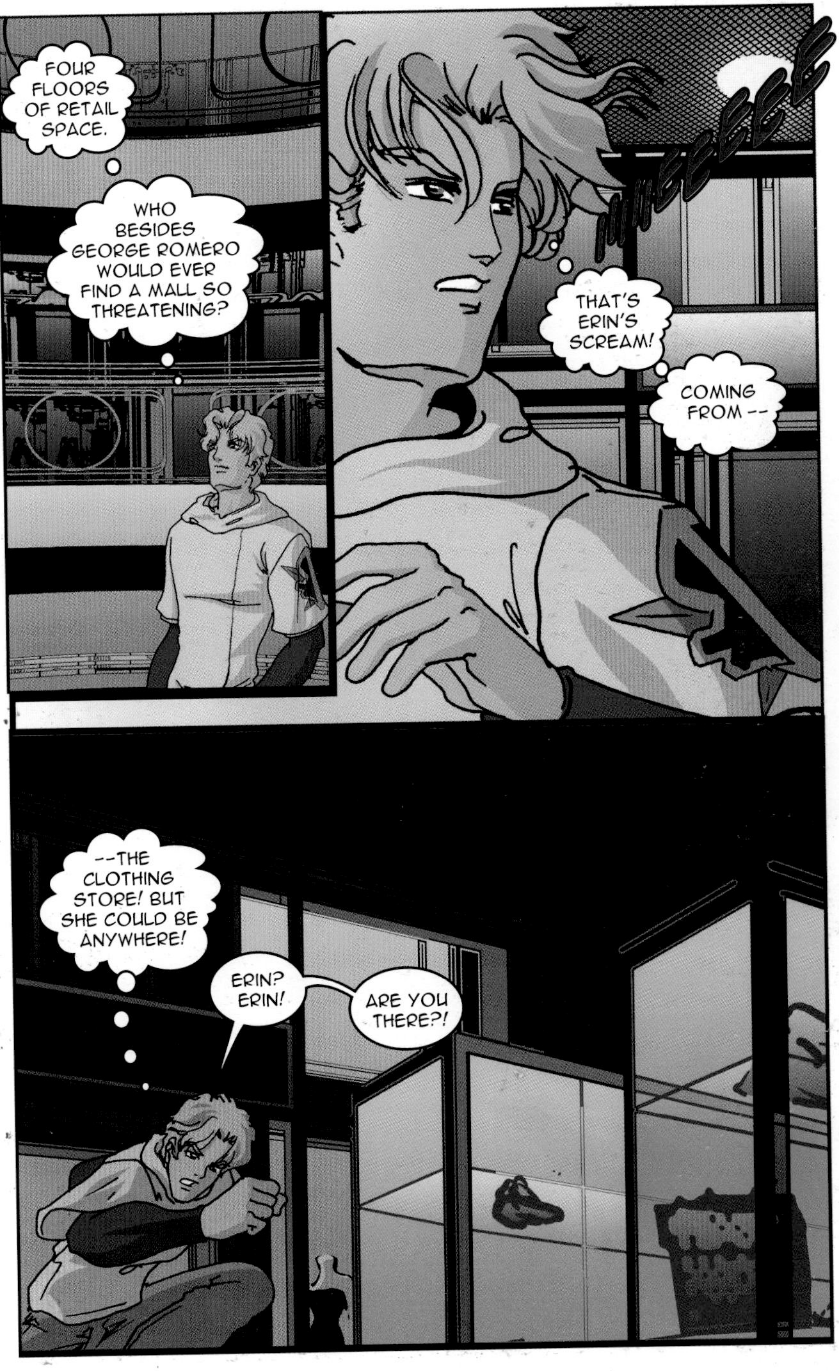
THAT'S ERIN'S SCREAM!
COMING FROM --
FOUR FLOORS OF RETAIL SPACE.
WHO BESIDES GEORGE ROMERO WOULD EVER FIND A MALL SO THREATENING?
--THE CLOTHING STORE! BUT SHE COULD BE ANYWHERE!
ERIN? ERIN!
ARE YOU THERE?!

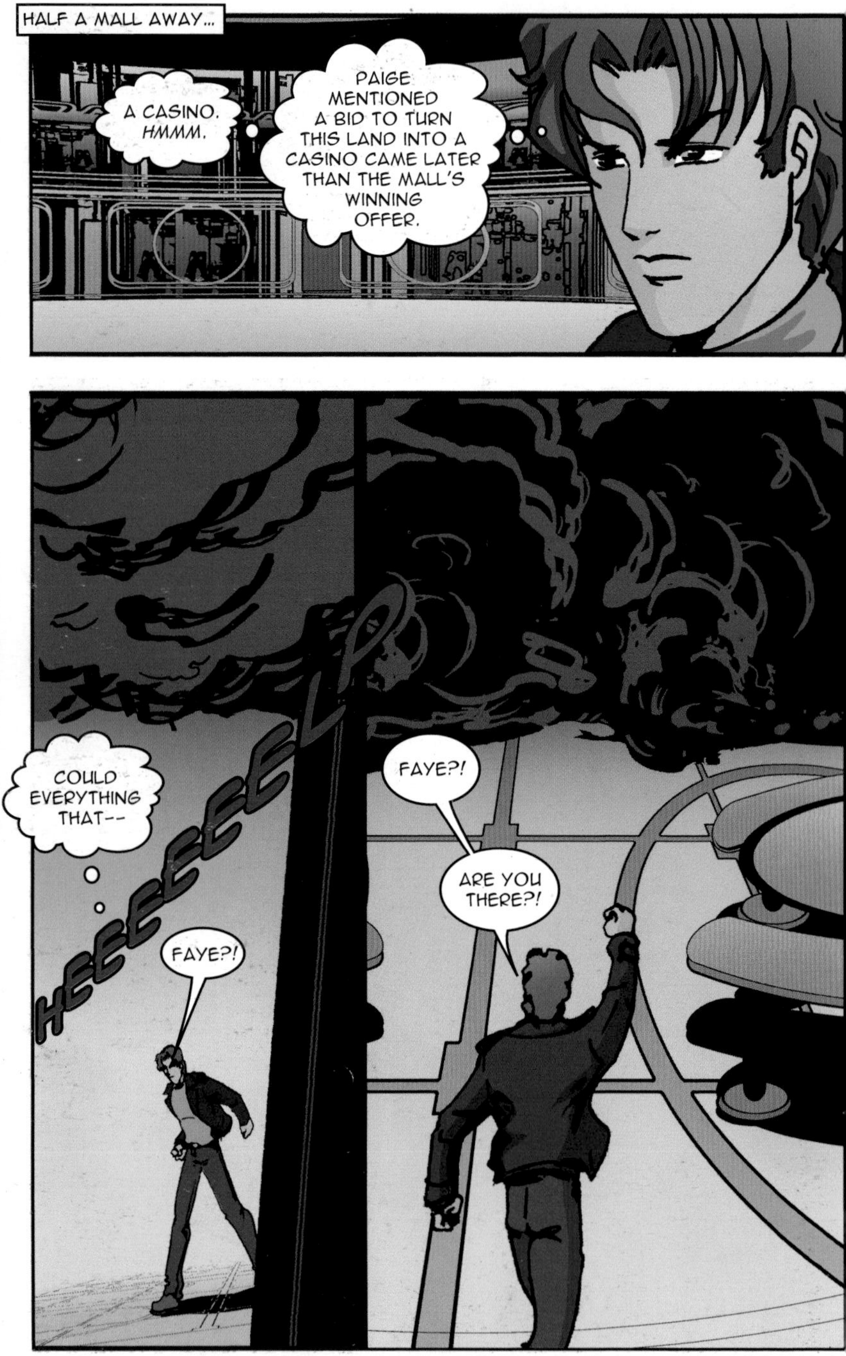
HALF A MALL AWAY...
PAIGE MENTIONED A BID TO TURN THIS LAND INTO A CASINO CAME LATER THAN THE MALL'S WINNING OFFER.
A CASINO. HMMM.
FAYE?!
ARE YOU THERE?!
COULD EVERYTHING THAT--
HEEEEEEELP
FAYE?!

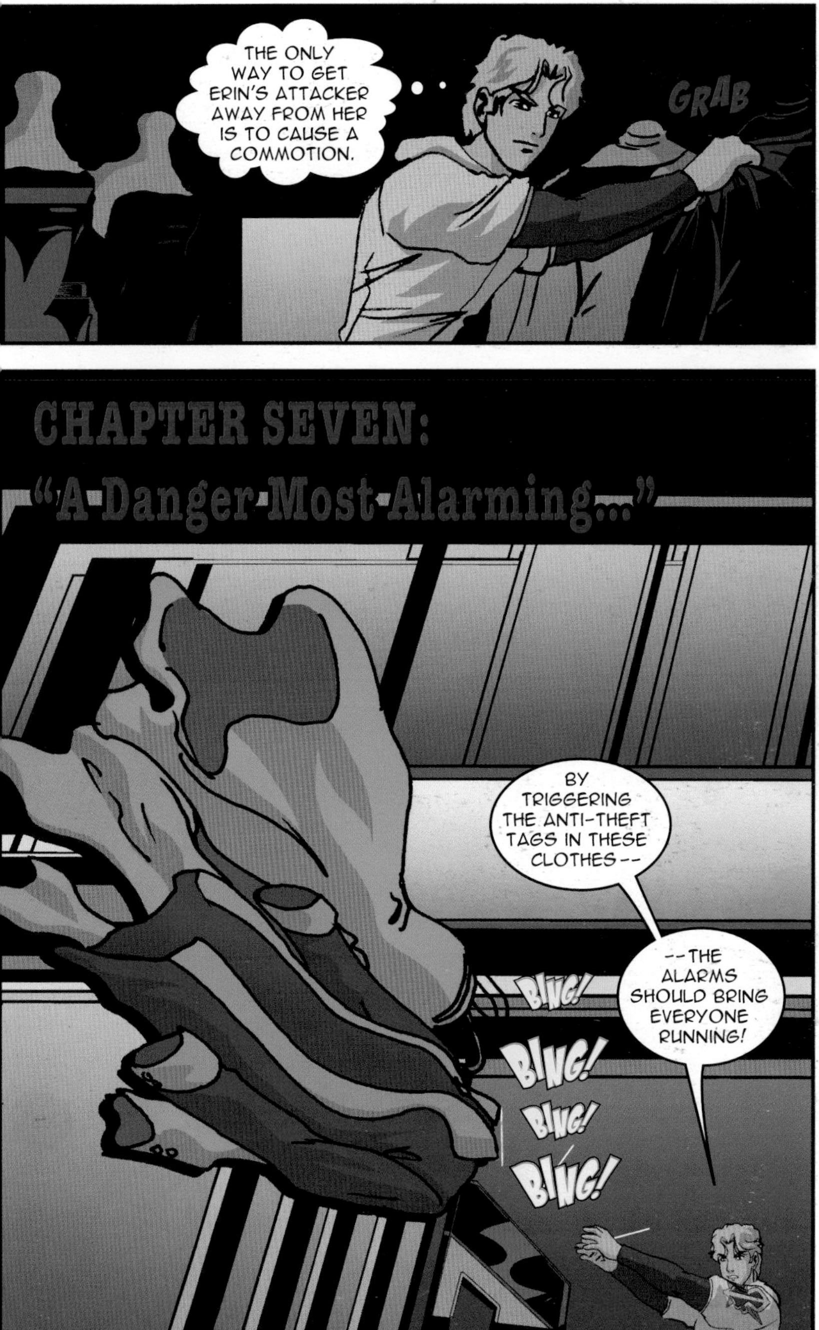
GRAB
THE ONLY WAY TO GET ERIN'S ATTACKER AWAY FROM HER IS TO CAUSE A COMMOTION.
CHAPTER SEVEN:
"A Danger Most Alarming..."
BY TRIGGERING THE ANTI-THEFT TAGS IN THESE CLOTHES --
-- THE ALARMS SHOULD BRING EVERYONE RUNNING!
BING!
BING!
BING!
BING!

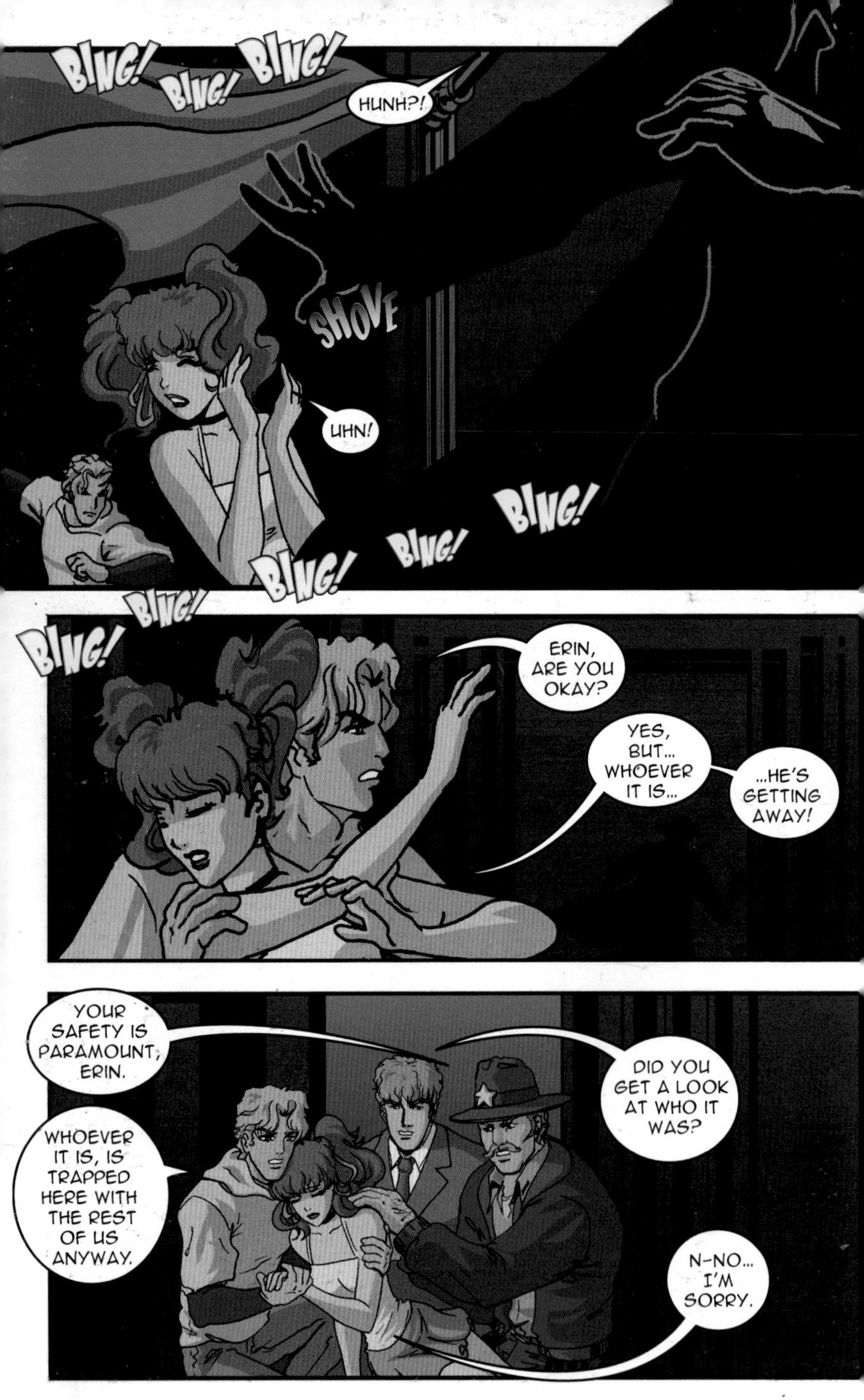
BING! BING! BING!
HUNH?!
SHOVE
UHN!
BING! BING! BING!
BING! BING!
ERIN, ARE YOU OKAY?
YES, BUT... WHOEVER IT IS...
...HE'S GETTING AWAY!
DID YOU GET A LOOK AT WHO IT WAS?
N-NO... I'M SORRY.
YOUR SAFETY IS PARAMOUNT, ERIN.
WHOEVER IT IS, IS TRAPPED HERE WITH THE REST OF US ANYWAY.

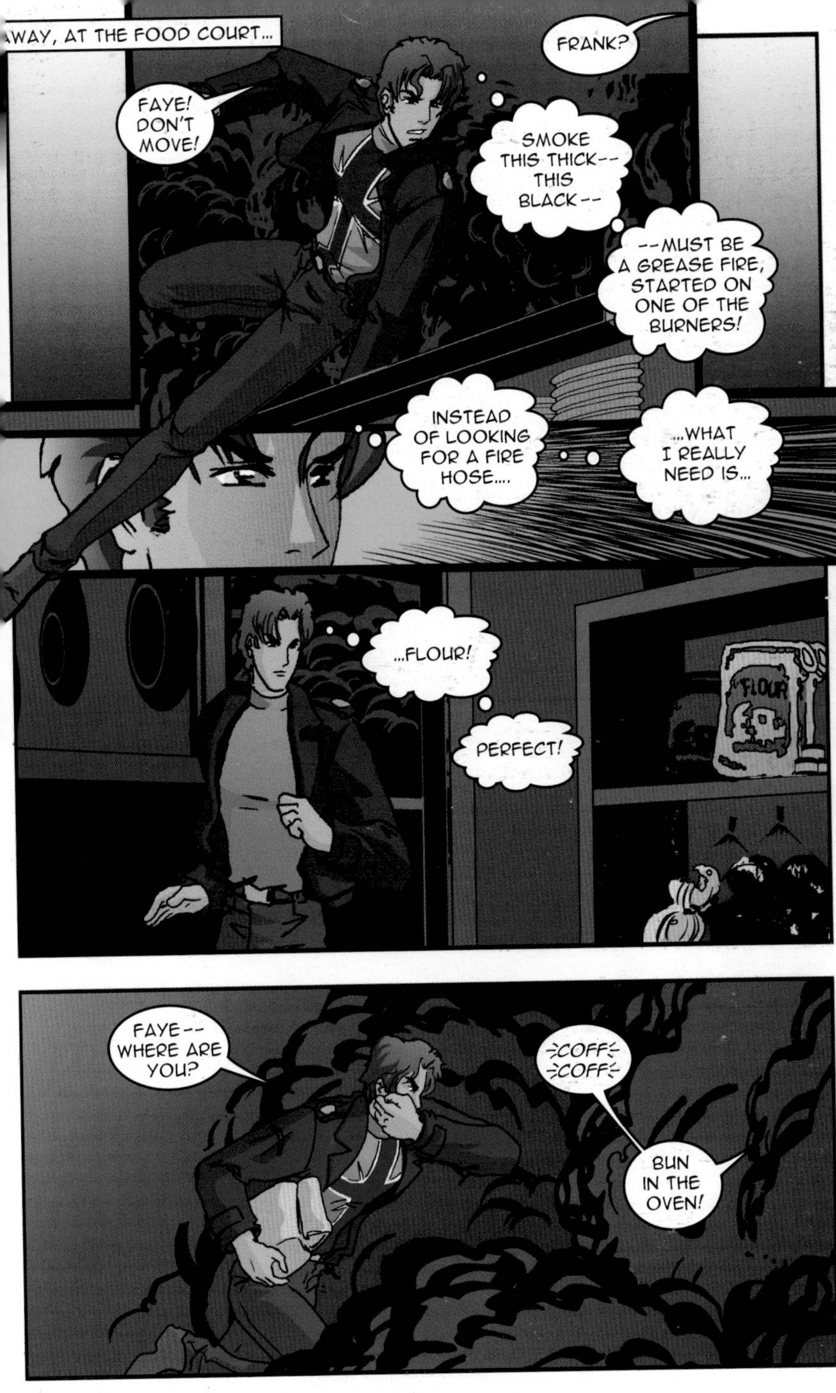
AWAY, AT THE FOOD COURT...
FRANK?
FAYE! DON'T MOVE!
SMOKE THIS THICK-- THIS BLACK--
--MUST BE A GREASE FIRE, STARTED ON ONE OF THE BURNERS!
INSTEAD OF LOOKING FOR A FIRE HOSE....
...WHAT I REALLY NEED IS...
...FLOUR!
PERFECT!
FAYE-- WHERE ARE YOU?
COFF COFF
BUN IN THE OVEN!

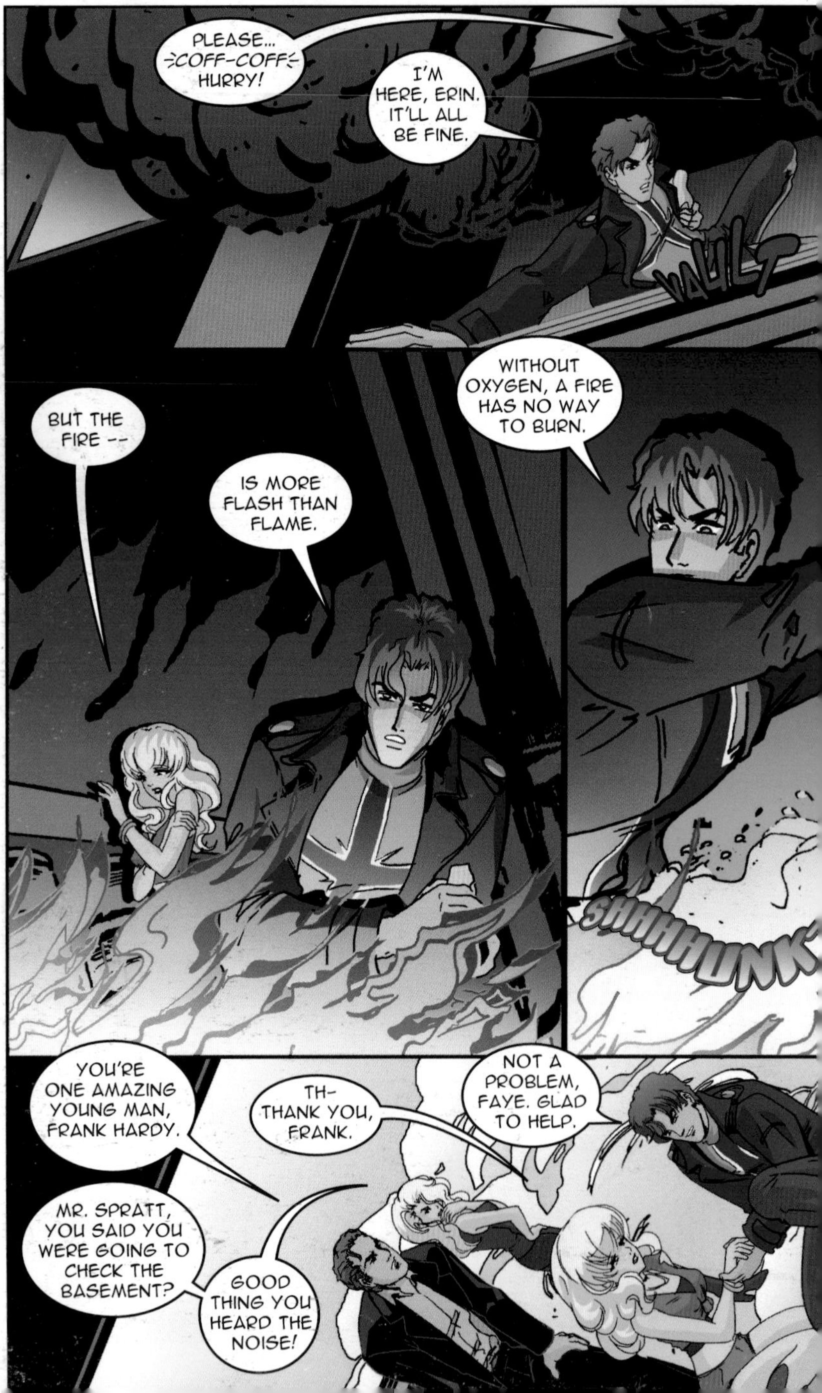
PLEASE... COFF-COFF HURRY!
I'M HERE, ERIN. IT'LL ALL BE FINE.
VAULT
WITHOUT OXYGEN, A FIRE HAS NO WAY TO BURN.
SHHHHUNK
BUT THE FIRE --
IS MORE FLASH THAN FLAME.
NOT A PROBLEM, FAYE. GLAD TO HELP.
TH- THANK YOU, FRANK.
YOU'RE ONE AMAZING YOUNG MAN, FRANK HARDY.
MR. SPRATT, YOU SAID YOU WERE GOING TO CHECK THE BASEMENT?
GOOD THING YOU HEARD THE NOISE!

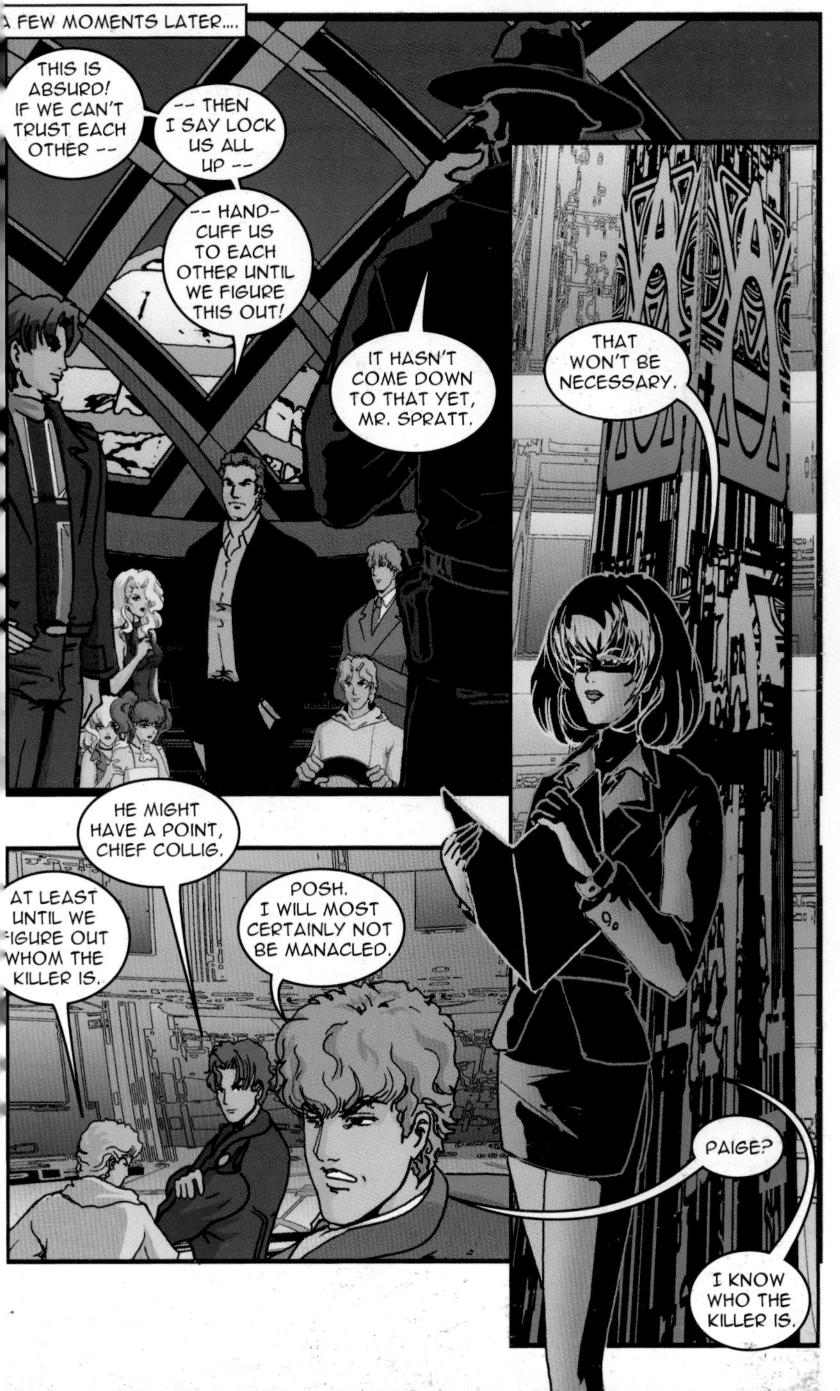
THAT WON'T BE NECESSARY.
PAIGE?
I KNOW WHO THE KILLER IS.
A FEW MOMENTS LATER....
THIS IS ABSURD! IF WE CAN'T TRUST EACH OTHER --
-- THEN I SAY LOCK US ALL UP --
-- HAND-CUFF US TO EACH OTHER UNTIL WE FIGURE THIS OUT!
IT HASN'T COME DOWN TO THAT YET, MR. SPRATT.
HE MIGHT HAVE A POINT, CHIEF COLLIG.
POSH. I WILL MOST CERTAINLY NOT BE MANACLED.
AT LEAST UNTIL WE FIGURE OUT WHOM THE KILLER IS.

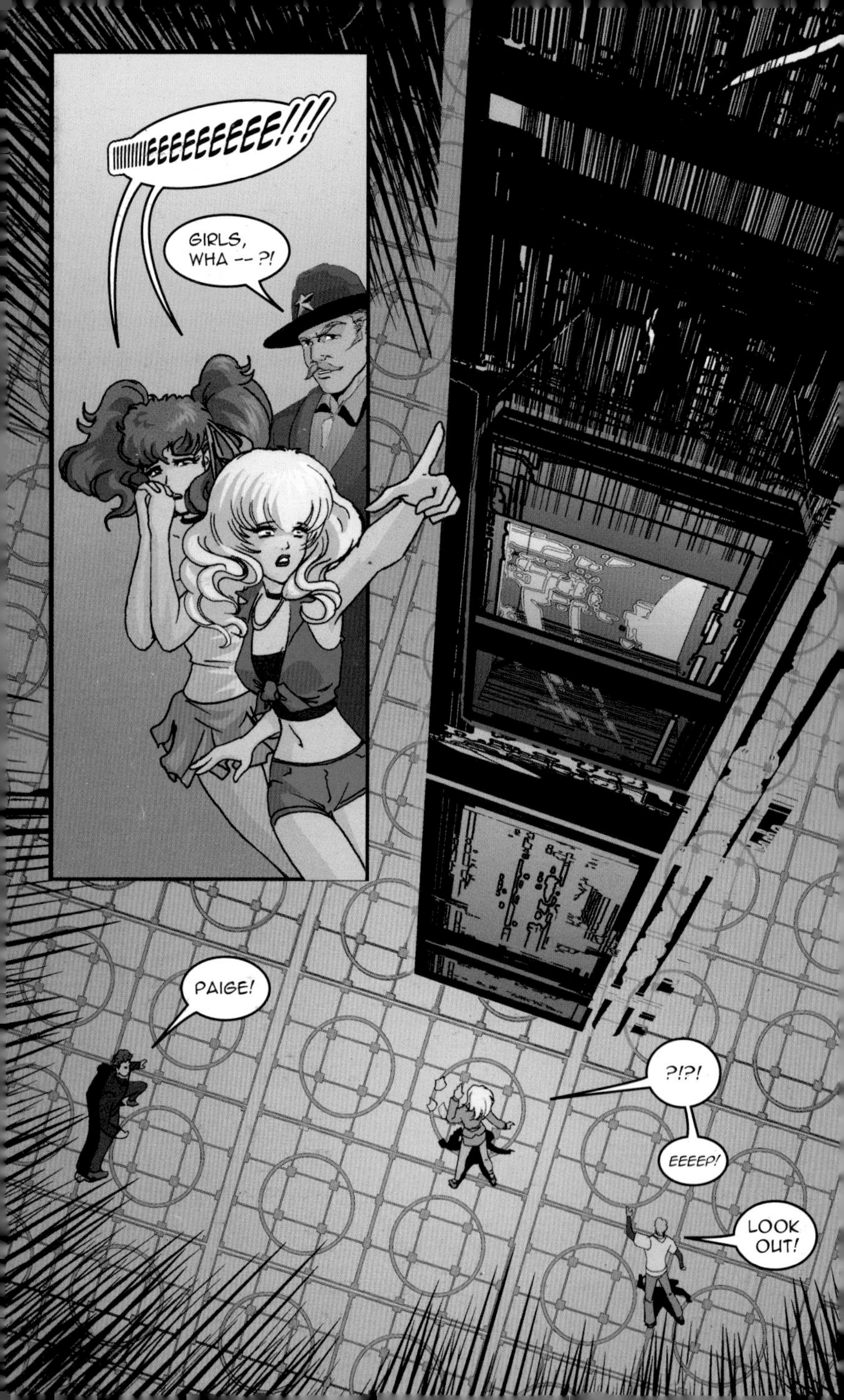
IIIIIIIIIIEEEEEEEEEE!!!
GIRLS, WHA -- ?!
PAIGE!
?!?!
EEEEP!
LOOK OUT!

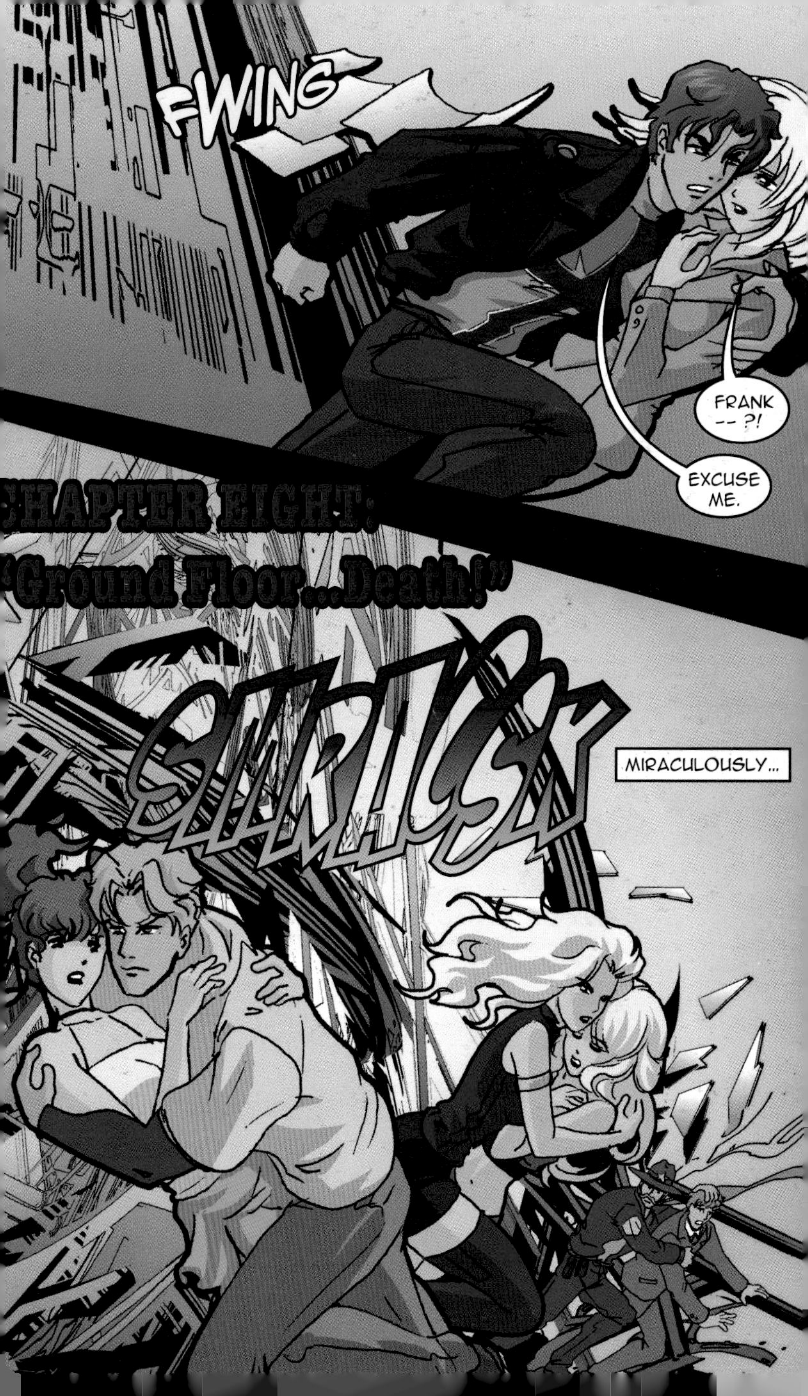
FWING
FRANK -- ?!
EXCUSE ME.
CHAPTER EIGHT:
"Ground Floor...Death!"
MIRACULOUSLY...

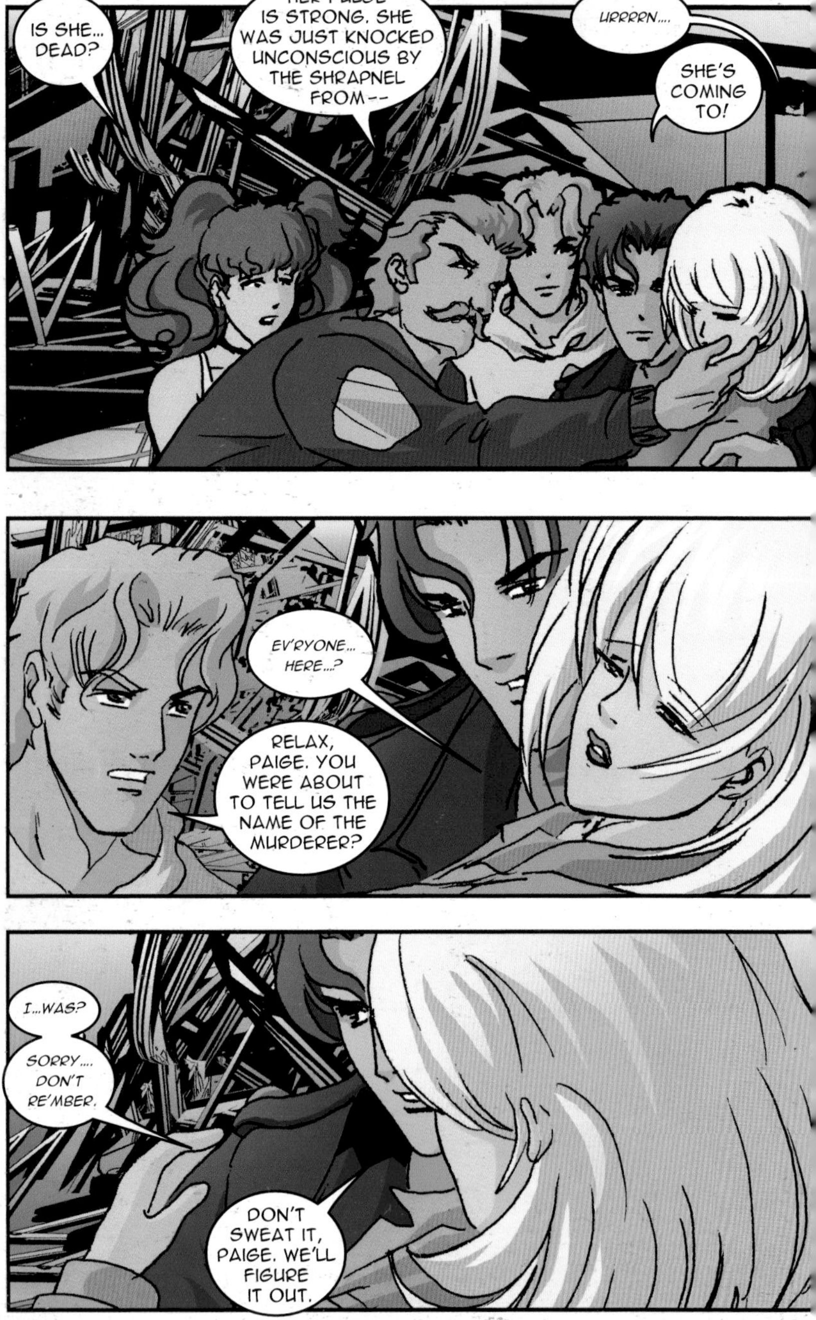
URRRRN....
SHE'S COMING TO!
HER PULSE IS STRONG. SHE WAS JUST KNOCKED UNCONSCIOUS BY THE SHRAPNEL FROM--
IS SHE... DEAD?
EV'RYONE... HERE...?
RELAX, PAIGE. YOU WERE ABOUT TO TELL US THE NAME OF THE MURDERER?
I...WAS?
SORRY.... DON'T RE'MBER.
DON'T SWEAT IT, PAIGE. WE'LL FIGURE IT OUT.

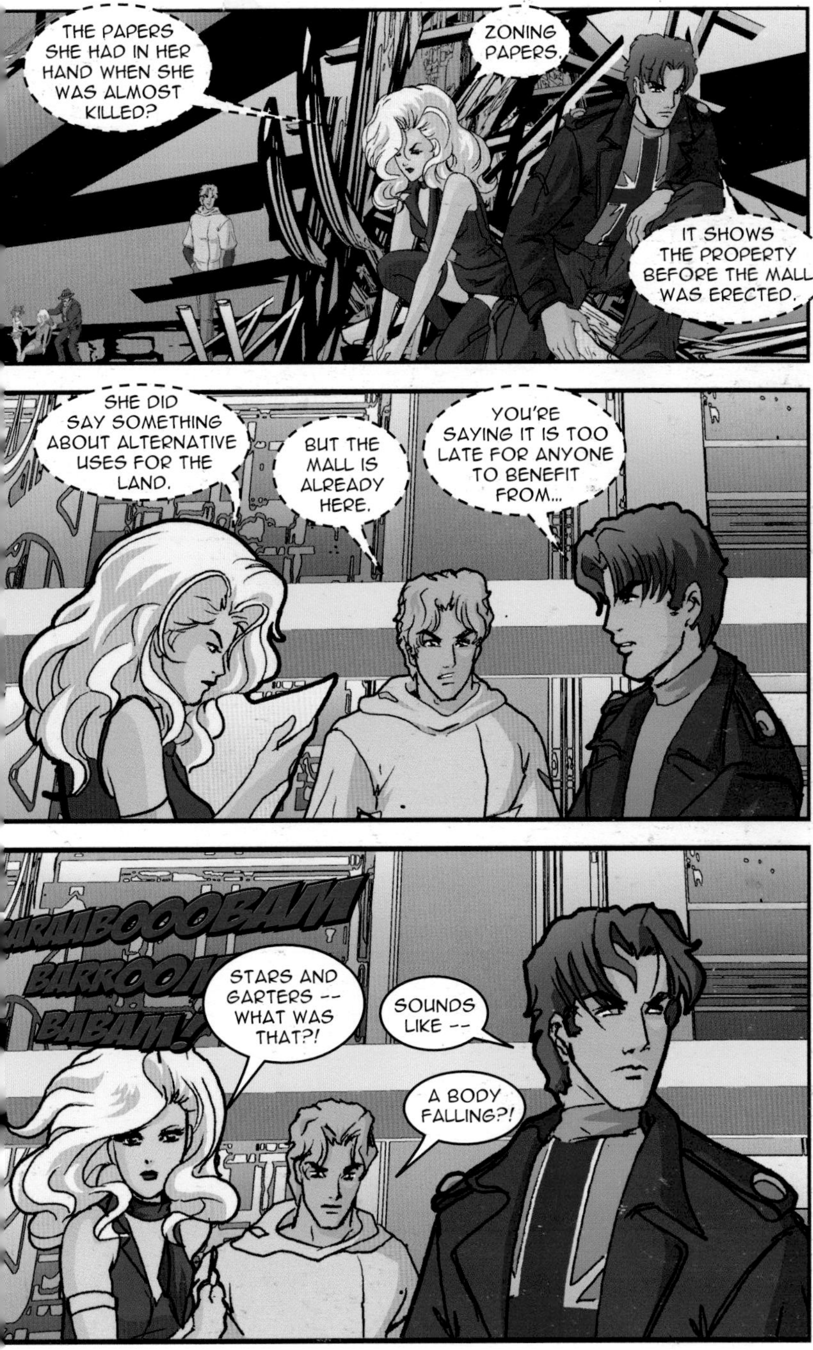
ZONING PAPERS.
THE PAPERS SHE HAD IN HER HAND WHEN SHE WAS ALMOST KILLED?
IT SHOWS THE PROPERTY BEFORE THE MALL WAS ERECTED.
YOU'RE SAYING IT IS TOO LATE FOR ANYONE TO BENEFIT FROM...
BUT THE MALL IS ALREADY HERE.
SHE DID SAY SOMETHING ABOUT ALTERNATIVE USES FOR THE LAND.
SOUNDS LIKE --
A BODY FALLING?!
STARS AND GARTERS -- WHAT WAS THAT?!
BARROOM
BABAM!

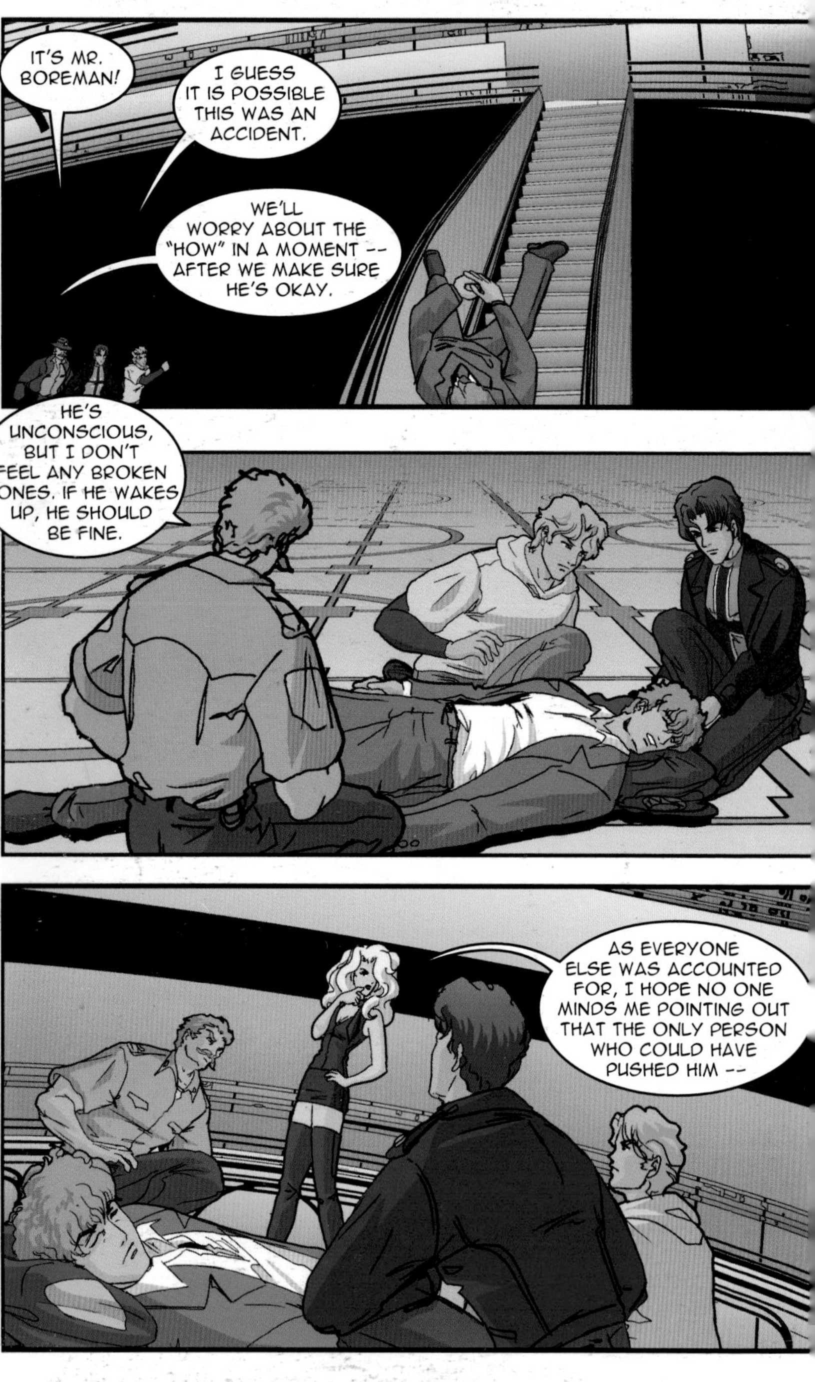
IT'S MR. BOREMAN!
I GUESS IT IS POSSIBLE THIS WAS AN ACCIDENT.
WE'LL WORRY ABOUT THE "HOW" IN A MOMENT -- AFTER WE MAKE SURE HE'S OKAY.
HE'S UNCONSCIOUS, BUT I DON'T FEEL ANY BROKEN BONES. IF HE WAKES UP, HE SHOULD BE FINE.
AS EVERYONE ELSE WAS ACCOUNTED FOR, I HOPE NO ONE MINDS ME POINTING OUT THAT THE ONLY PERSON WHO COULD HAVE PUSHED HIM --

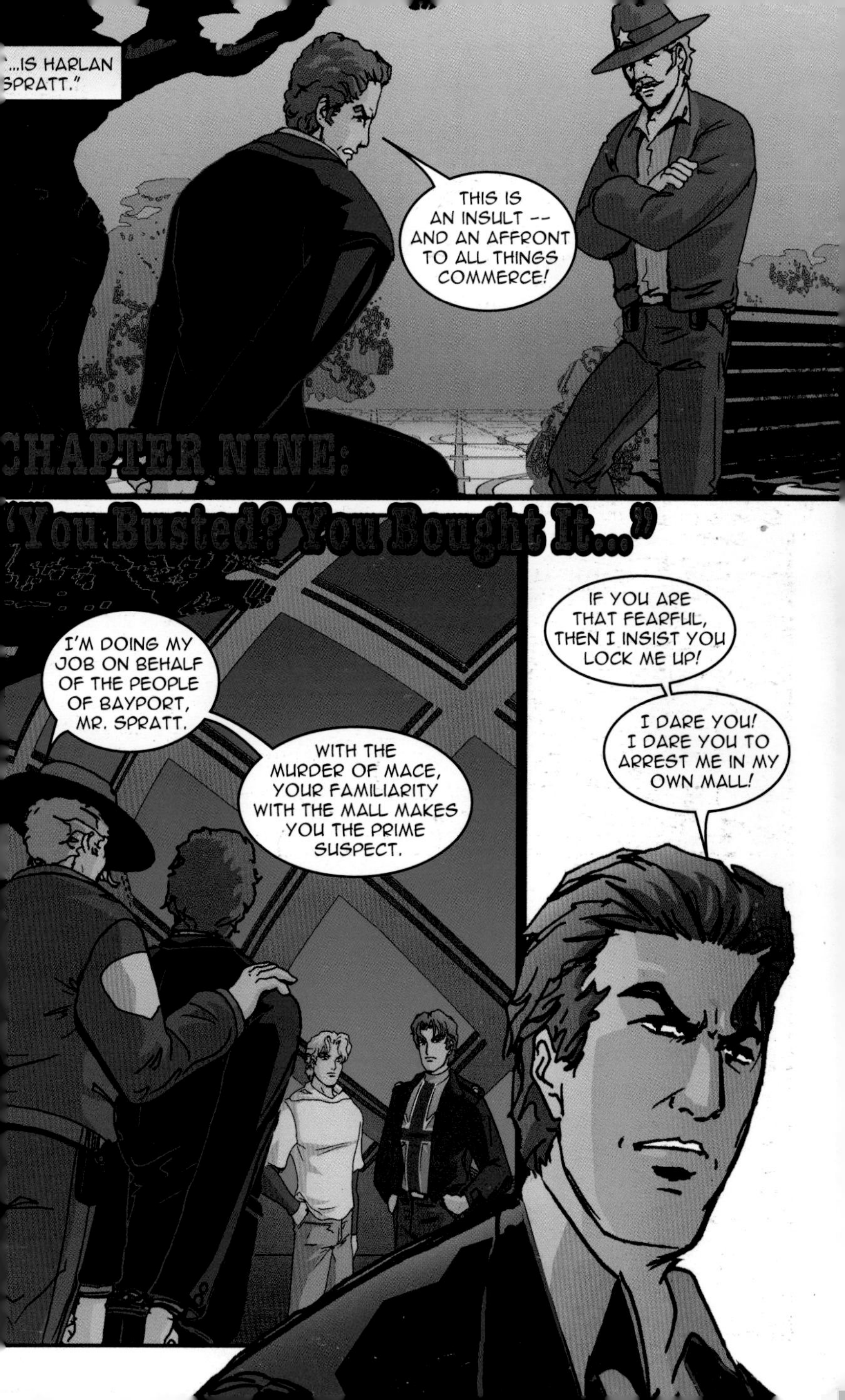
"...IS HARLAN SPRATT."
THIS IS AN INSULT -- AND AN AFFRONT TO ALL THINGS COMMERCE!
CHAPTER NINE:
"You Busted? You Bought It..."
IF YOU ARE THAT FEARFUL, THEN I INSIST YOU LOCK ME UP!
I DARE YOU! I DARE YOU TO ARREST ME IN MY OWN MALL!
I'M DOING MY JOB ON BEHALF OF THE PEOPLE OF BAYPORT, MR. SPRATT.
WITH THE MURDER OF MACE, YOUR FAMILIARITY WITH THE MALL MAKES YOU THE PRIME SUSPECT.

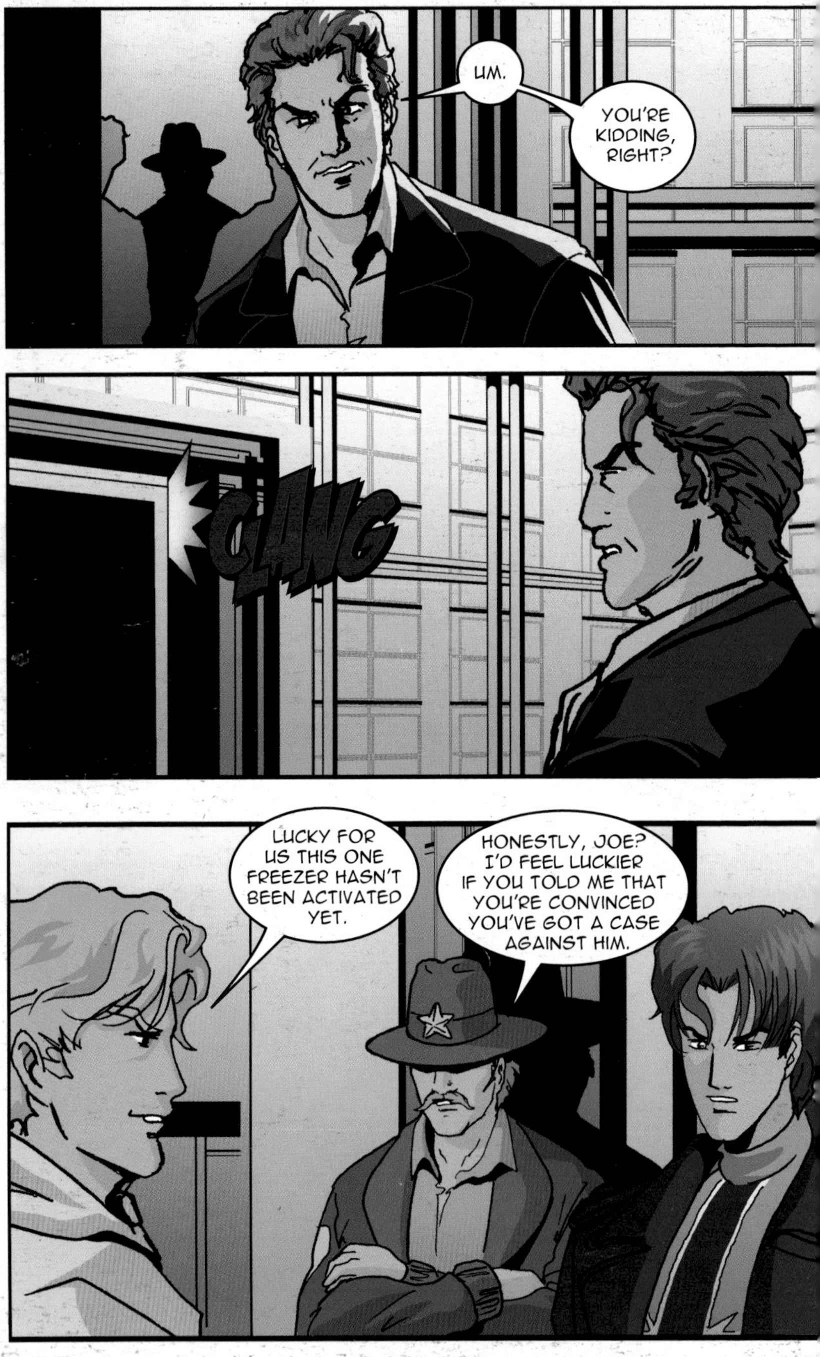
UM.
YOU'RE KIDDING, RIGHT?
CLANG
LUCKY FOR US THIS ONE FREEZER HASN'T BEEN ACTIVATED YET.
HONESTLY, JOE? I'D FEEL LUCKIER IF YOU TOLD ME THAT YOU'RE CONVINCED YOU'VE GOT A CASE AGAINST HIM.

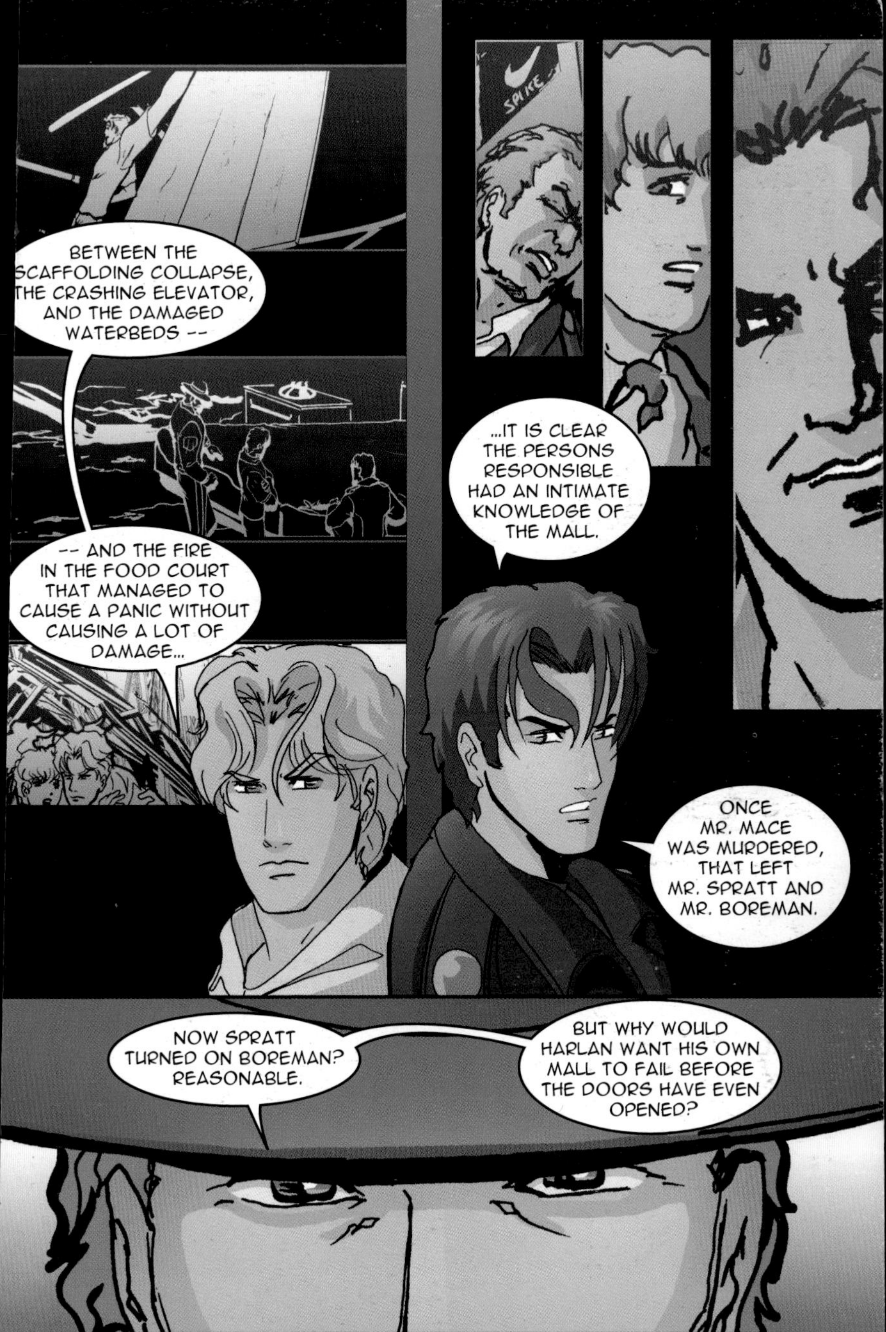
BETWEEN THE SCAFFOLDING COLLAPSE, THE CRASHING ELEVATOR, AND THE DAMAGED WATERBEDS --
-- AND THE FIRE IN THE FOOD COURT THAT MANAGED TO CAUSE A PANIC WITHOUT CAUSING A LOT OF DAMAGE...
...IT IS CLEAR THE PERSONS RESPONSIBLE HAD AN INTIMATE KNOWLEDGE OF THE MALL.
ONCE MR. MACE WAS MURDERED, THAT LEFT MR. SPRATT AND MR. BOREMAN.
NOW SPRATT TURNED ON BOREMAN? REASONABLE.
BUT WHY WOULD HARLAN WANT HIS OWN MALL TO FAIL BEFORE THE DOORS HAVE EVEN OPENED?

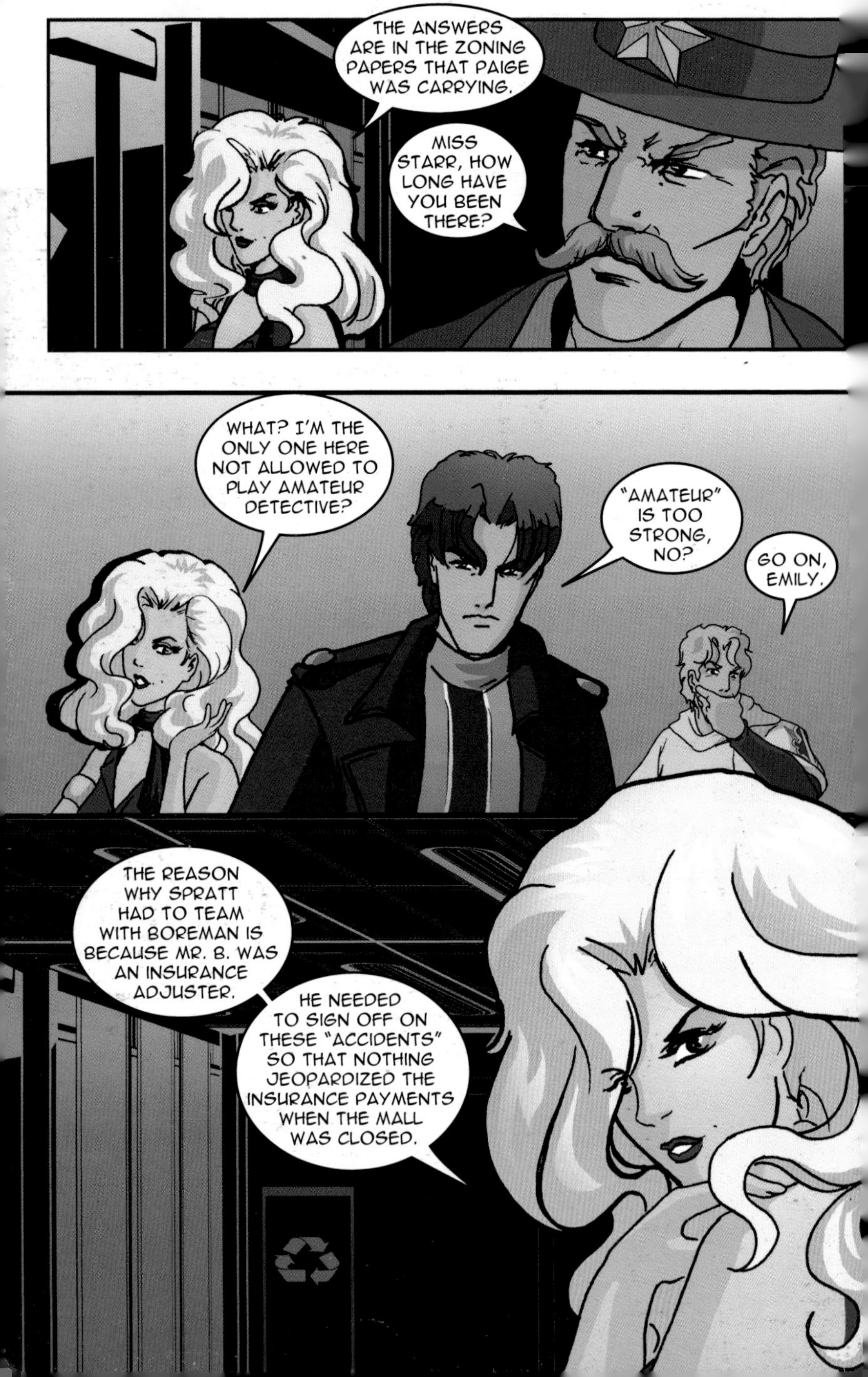
THE ANSWERS ARE IN THE ZONING PAPERS THAT PAIGE WAS CARRYING.
MISS STARR, HOW LONG HAVE YOU BEEN THERE?
WHAT? I'M THE ONLY ONE HERE NOT ALLOWED TO PLAY AMATEUR DETECTIVE?
"AMATEUR" IS TOO STRONG, NO?
GO ON, EMILY.
THE REASON WHY SPRATT HAD TO TEAM WITH BOREMAN IS BECAUSE MR. B. WAS AN INSURANCE ADJUSTER.
HE NEEDED TO SIGN OFF ON THESE "ACCIDENTS" SO THAT NOTHING JEOPARDIZED THE INSURANCE PAYMENTS WHEN THE MALL WAS CLOSED.

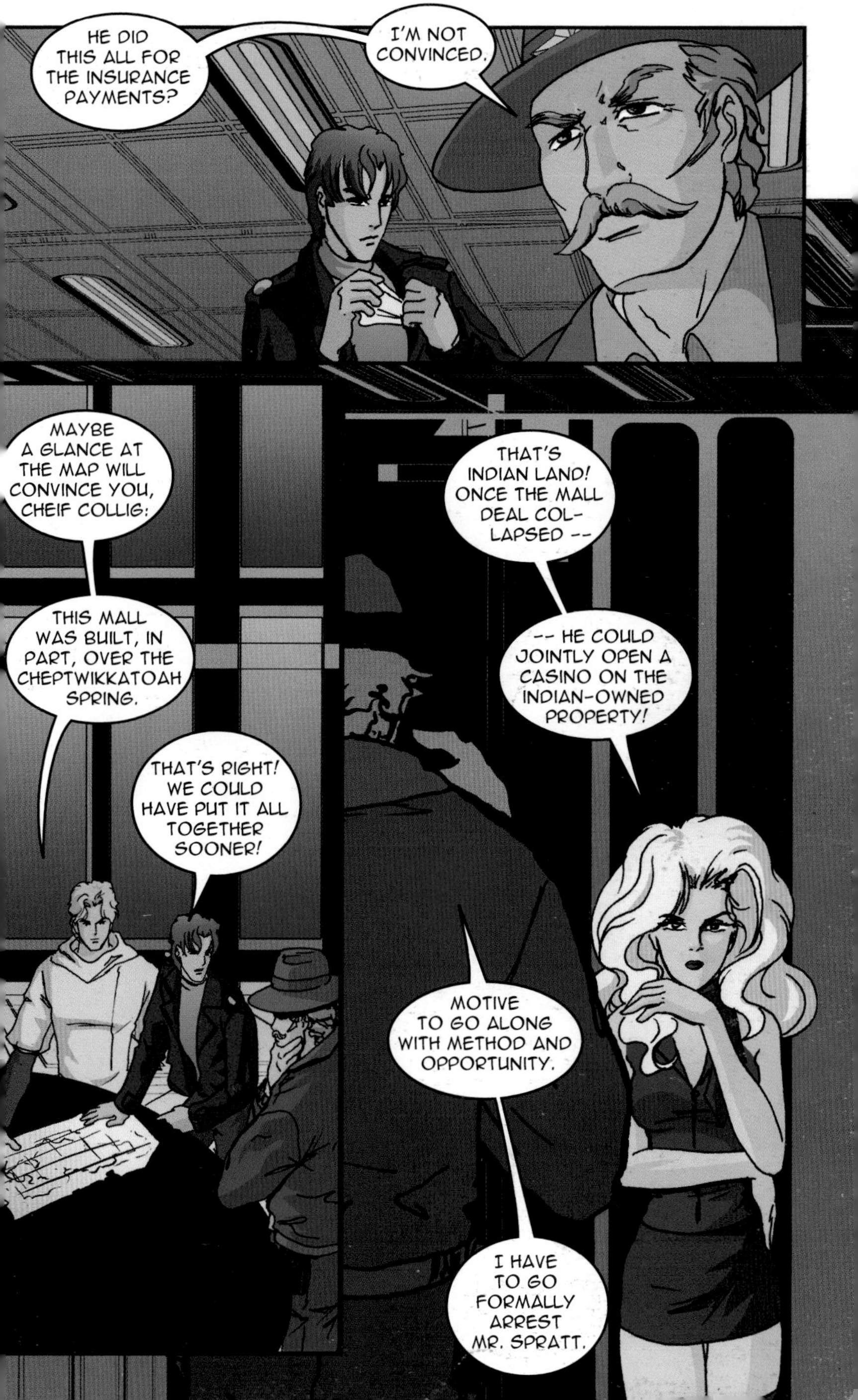
I'M NOT CONVINCED.
HE DID THIS ALL FOR THE INSURANCE PAYMENTS?
THAT'S INDIAN LAND! ONCE THE MALL DEAL COL-LAPSED --
-- HE COULD JOINTLY OPEN A CASINO ON THE INDIAN-OWNED PROPERTY!
MOTIVE TO GO ALONG WITH METHOD AND OPPORTUNITY.
I HAVE TO GO FORMALLY ARREST MR. SPRATT.
MAYBE A GLANCE AT THE MAP WILL CONVINCE YOU, CHEIF COLLIG:
THIS MALL WAS BUILT, IN PART, OVER THE CHEPTWIKKATOAH SPRING.
THAT'S RIGHT! WE COULD HAVE PUT IT ALL TOGETHER SOONER!

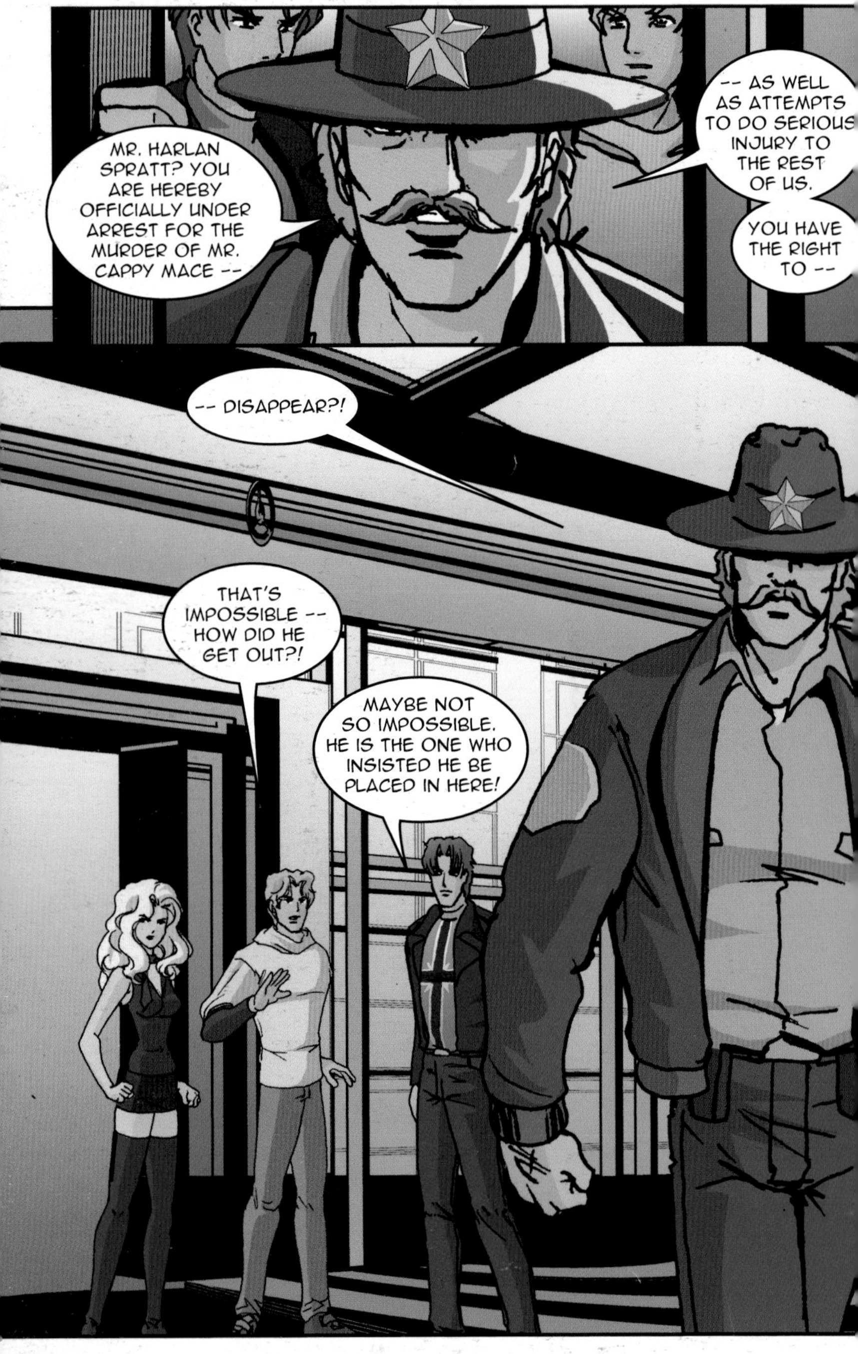
MR. HARLAN SPRATT? YOU ARE HEREBY OFFICIALLY UNDER ARREST FOR THE MURDER OF MR. CAPPY MACE --
-- AS WELL AS ATTEMPTS TO DO SERIOUS INJURY TO THE REST OF US.
YOU HAVE THE RIGHT TO --
-- DISAPPEAR?!
THAT'S IMPOSSIBLE -- HOW DID HE GET OUT?!
MAYBE NOT SO IMPOSSIBLE. HE IS THE ONE WHO INSISTED HE BE PLACED IN HERE!

CHAPTER TEN: "Attention, Shoppers..."

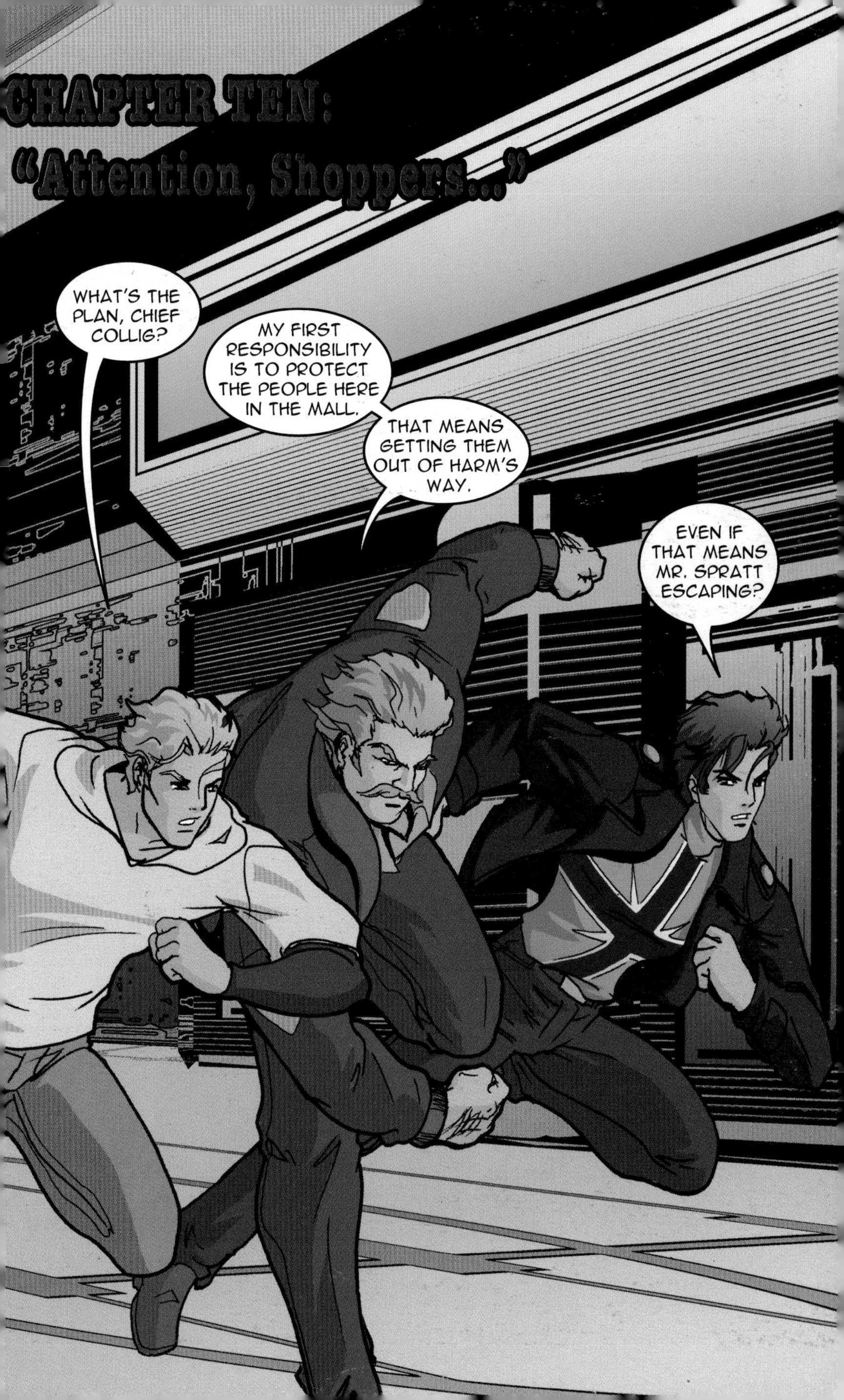
WHAT'S THE PLAN, CHIEF COLLIG?
MY FIRST RESPONSIBILITY IS TO PROTECT THE PEOPLE HERE IN THE MALL.
THAT MEANS GETTING THEM OUT OF HARM'S WAY.
EVEN IF THAT MEANS MR. SPRATT ESCAPING?

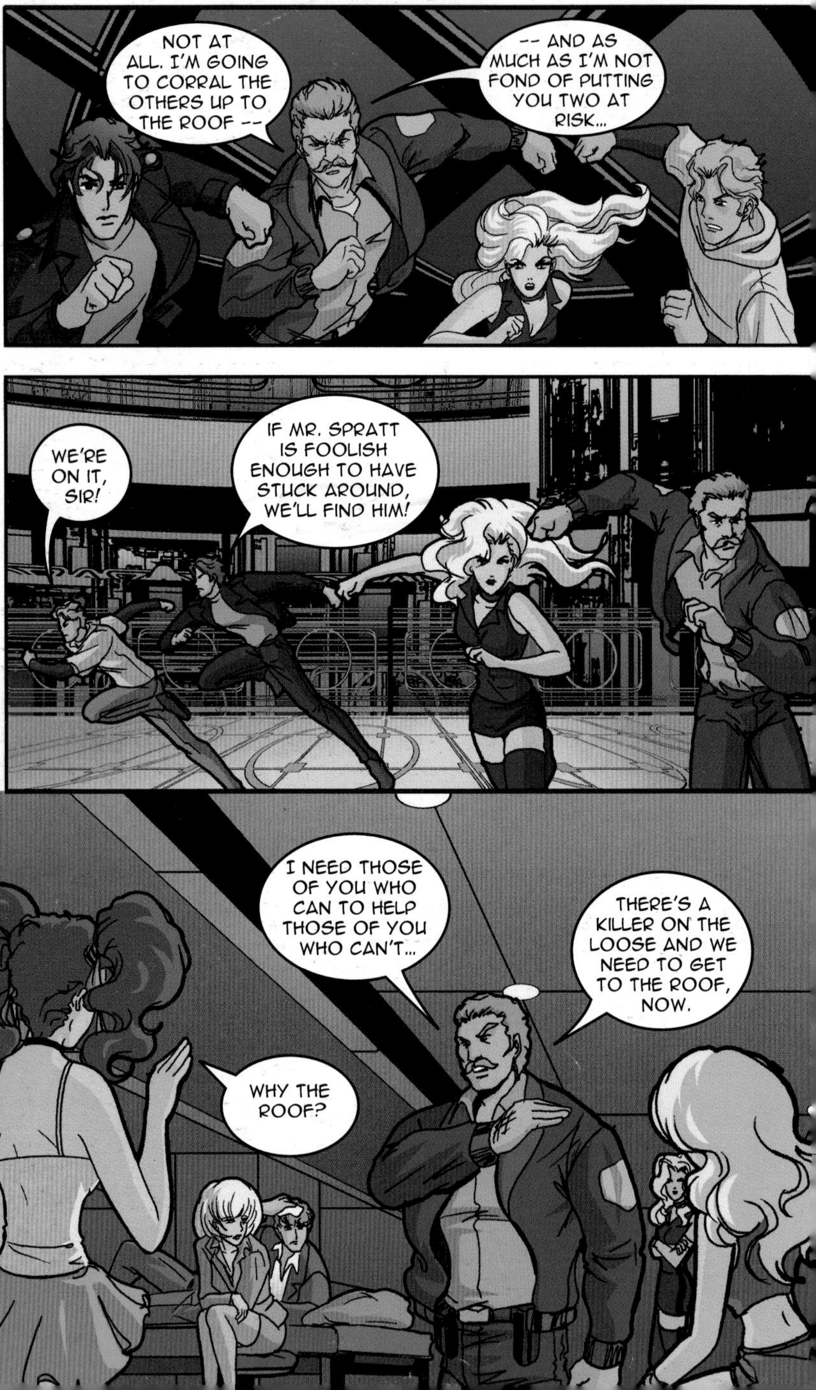
NOT AT ALL. I'M GOING TO CORRAL THE OTHERS UP TO THE ROOF --
-- AND AS MUCH AS I'M NOT FOND OF PUTTING YOU TWO AT RISK...
WE'RE ON IT, SIR!
IF MR. SPRATT IS FOOLISH ENOUGH TO HAVE STUCK AROUND, WE'LL FIND HIM!
I NEED THOSE OF YOU WHO CAN TO HELP THOSE OF YOU WHO CAN'T...
THERE'S A KILLER ON THE LOOSE AND WE NEED TO GET TO THE ROOF, NOW.
WHY THE ROOF?

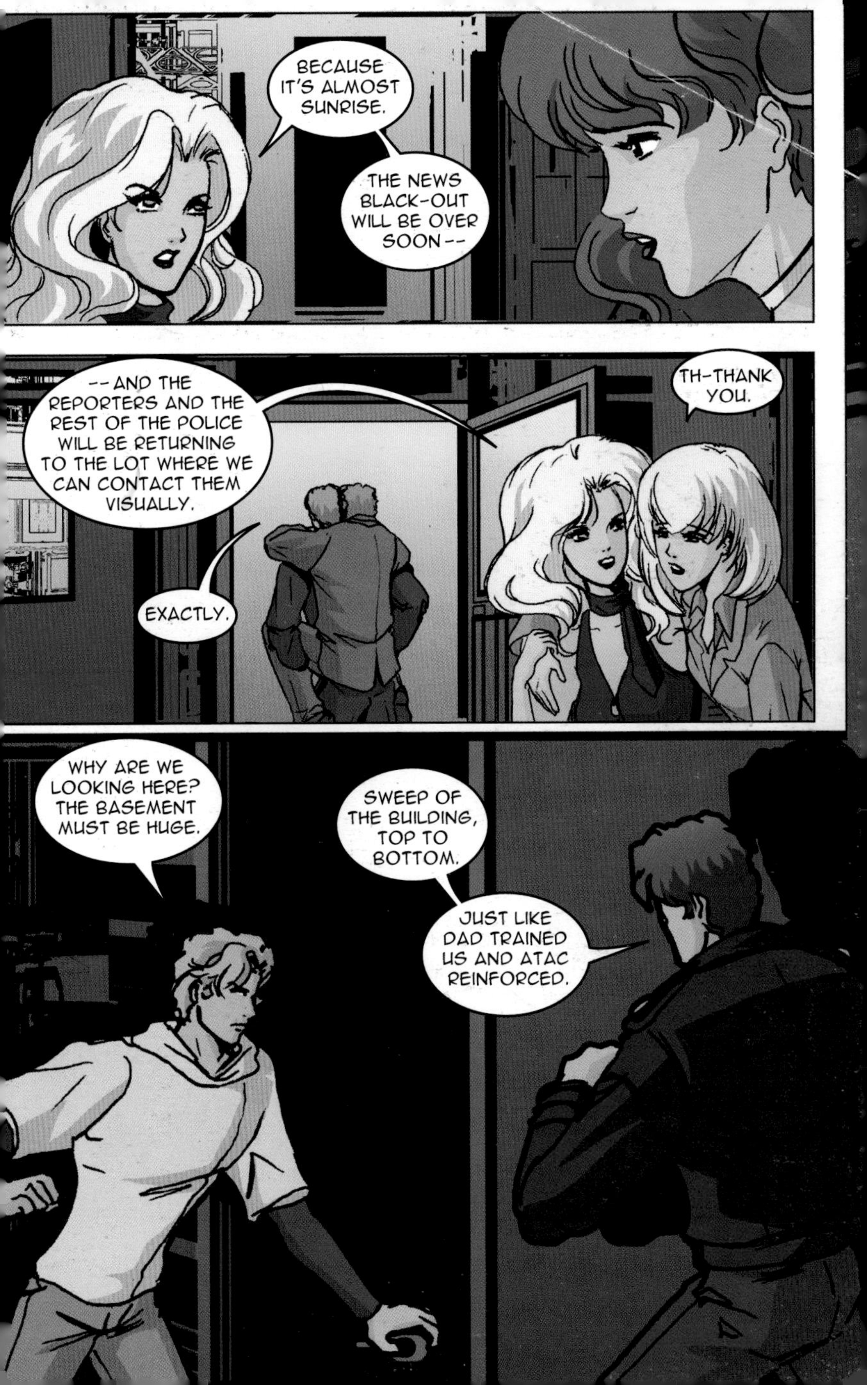
BECAUSE IT'S ALMOST SUNRISE.
THE NEWS BLACK-OUT WILL BE OVER SOON--
--AND THE REPORTERS AND THE REST OF THE POLICE WILL BE RETURNING TO THE LOT WHERE WE CAN CONTACT THEM VISUALLY.
EXACTLY.
TH-THANK YOU.
WHY ARE WE LOOKING HERE? THE BASEMENT MUST BE HUGE.
SWEEP OF THE BUILDING, TOP TO BOTTOM.
JUST LIKE DAD TRAINED US AND ATAC REINFORCED.

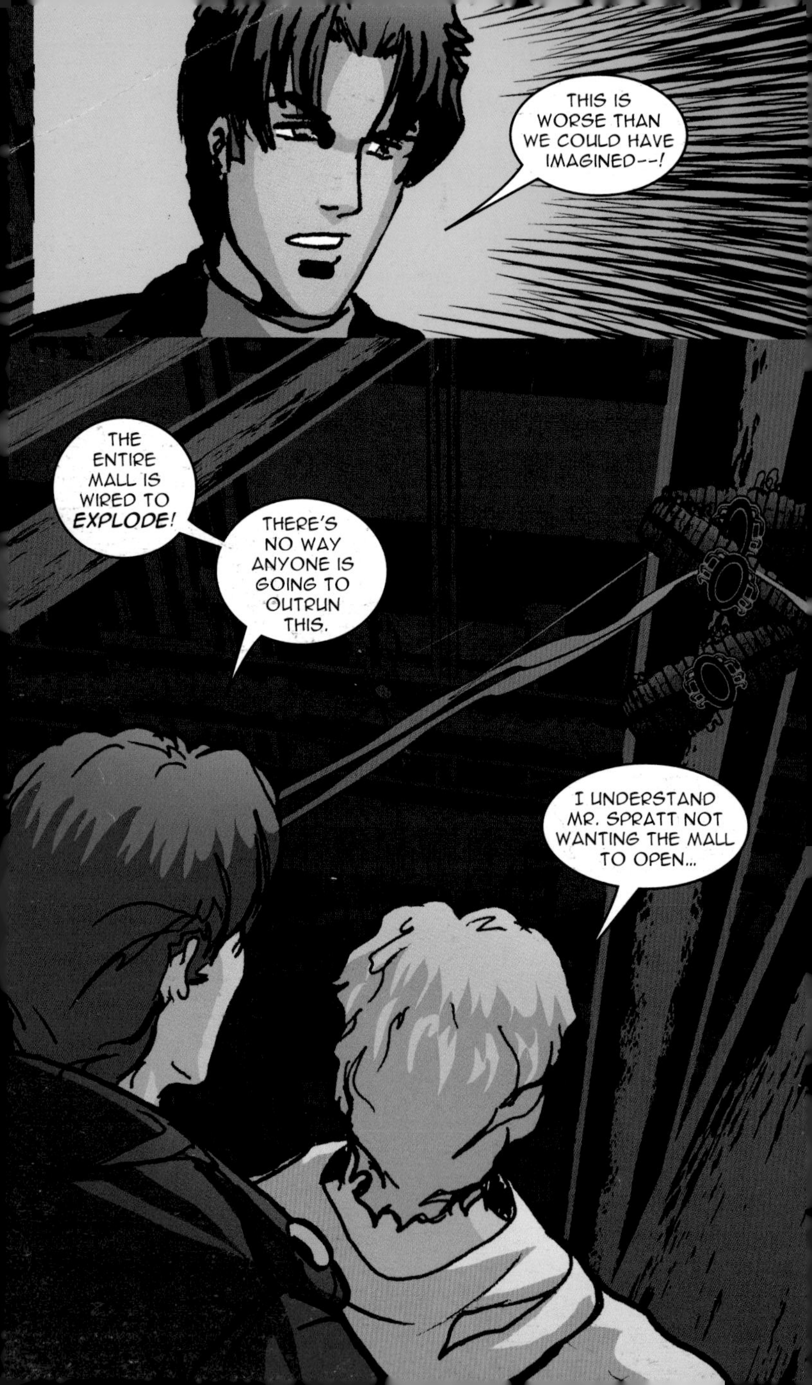
THIS IS WORSE THAN WE COULD HAVE IMAGINED--!
THE ENTIRE MALL IS WIRED TO *EXPLODE*!
THERE'S NO WAY ANYONE IS GOING TO OUTRUN THIS.
I UNDERSTAND MR. SPRATT NOT WANTING THE MALL TO OPEN...

CHAPTER ELEVEN
"...The Mall Will Be Exploding In Five Minutes!"

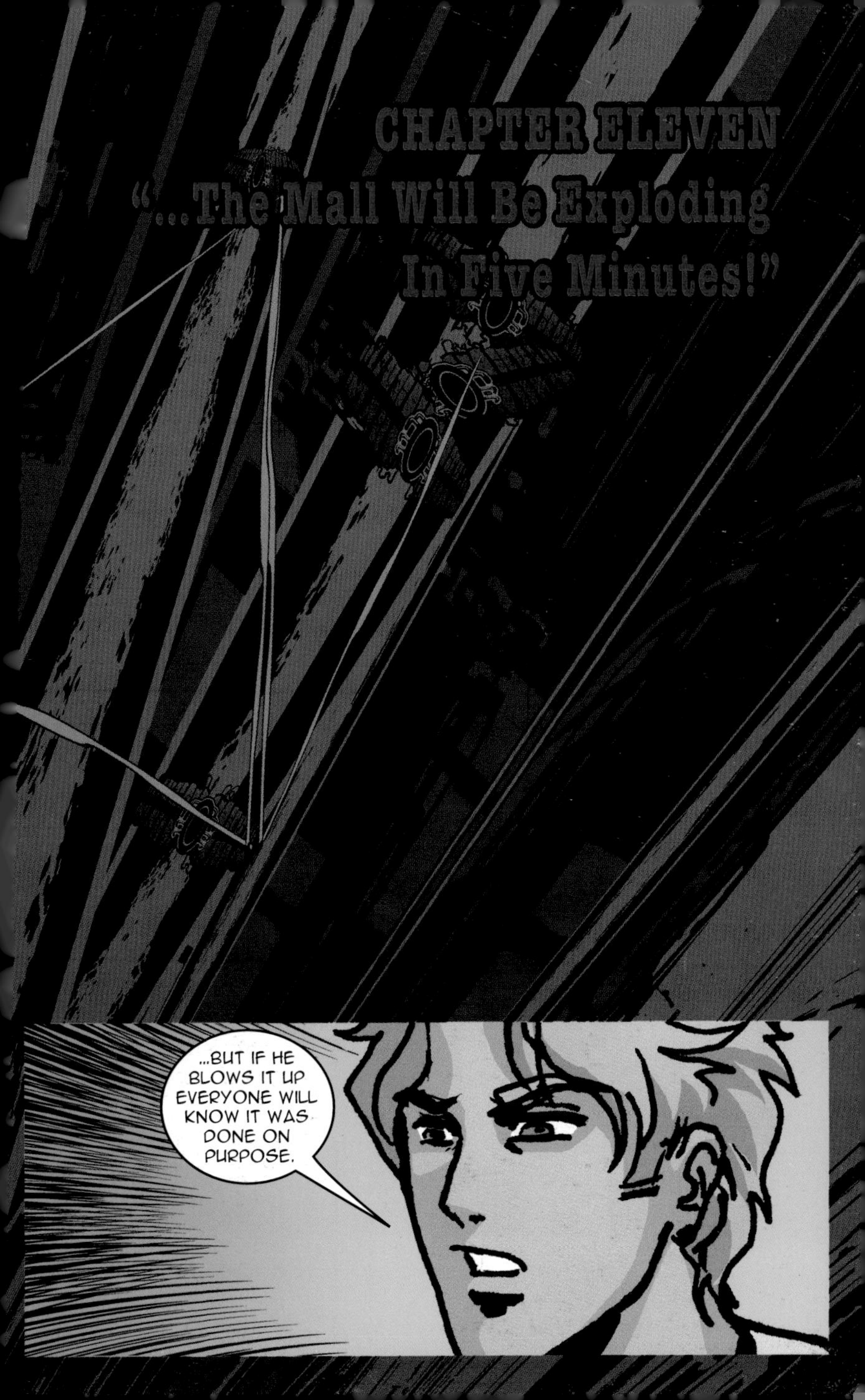
...BUT IF HE BLOWS IT UP EVERYONE WILL KNOW IT WAS DONE ON PURPOSE.

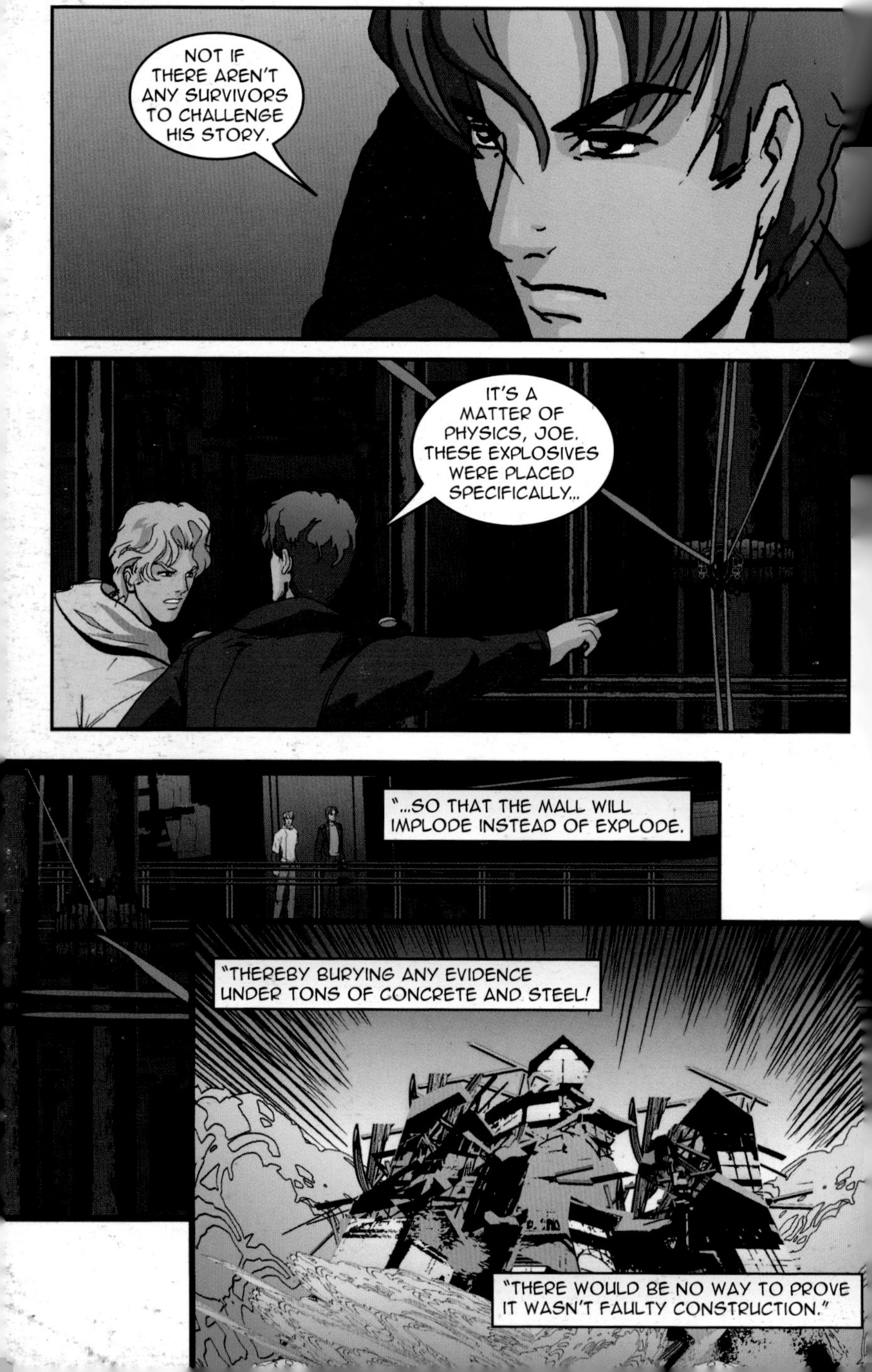
NOT IF THERE AREN'T ANY SURVIVORS TO CHALLENGE HIS STORY.
IT'S A MATTER OF PHYSICS, JOE. THESE EXPLOSIVES WERE PLACED SPECIFICALLY...
"...SO THAT THE MALL WILL IMPLODE INSTEAD OF EXPLODE.
"THEREBY BURYING ANY EVIDENCE UNDER TONS OF CONCRETE AND STEEL!
"THERE WOULD BE NO WAY TO PROVE IT WASN'T FAULTY CONSTRUCTION."

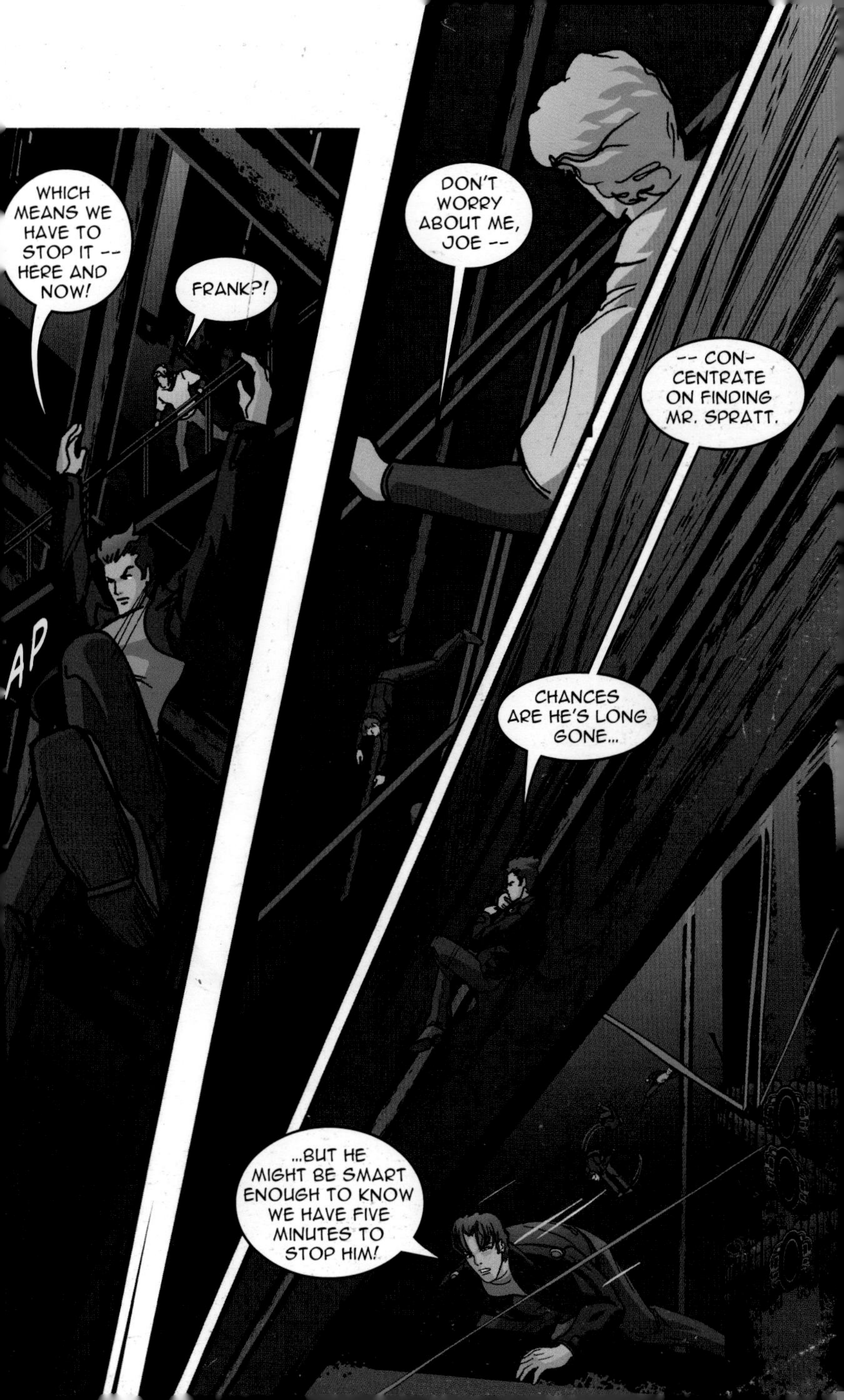
DON'T WORRY ABOUT ME, JOE --
-- CONCENTRATE ON FINDING MR. SPRATT.
CHANCES ARE HE'S LONG GONE...
...BUT HE MIGHT BE SMART ENOUGH TO KNOW WE HAVE FIVE MINUTES TO STOP HIM!
WHICH MEANS WE HAVE TO STOP IT -- HERE AND NOW!
FRANK?!

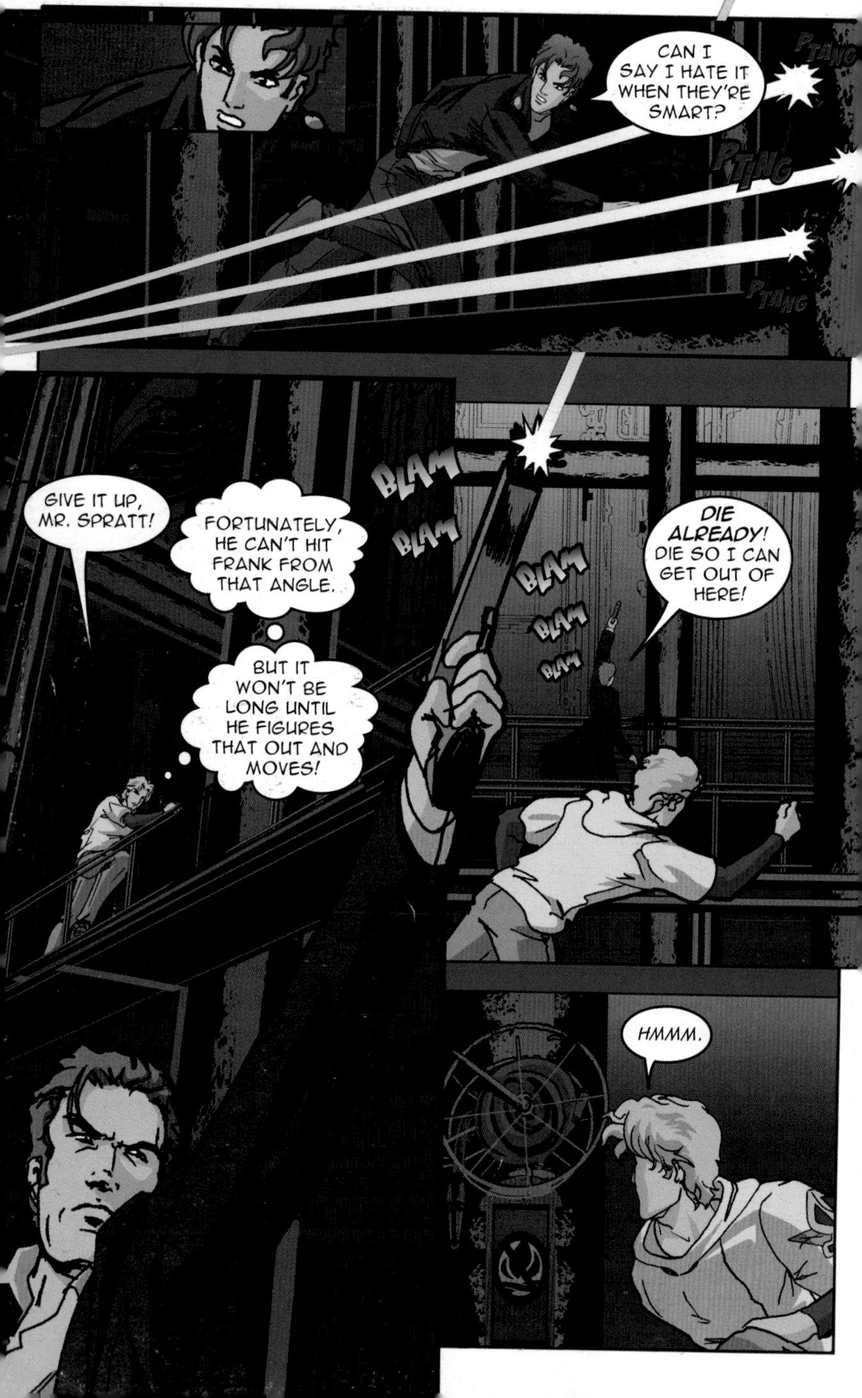
PTANG
CAN I SAY I HATE IT WHEN THEY'RE SMART?
PTING
PTANG
BLAM
BLAM
BLAM
BLAM
BLAM
DIE ALREADY! DIE SO I CAN GET OUT OF HERE!
HMMM.
GIVE IT UP, MR. SPRATT!
FORTUNATELY, HE CAN'T HIT FRANK FROM THAT ANGLE.
BUT IT WON'T BE LONG UNTIL HE FIGURES THAT OUT AND MOVES!

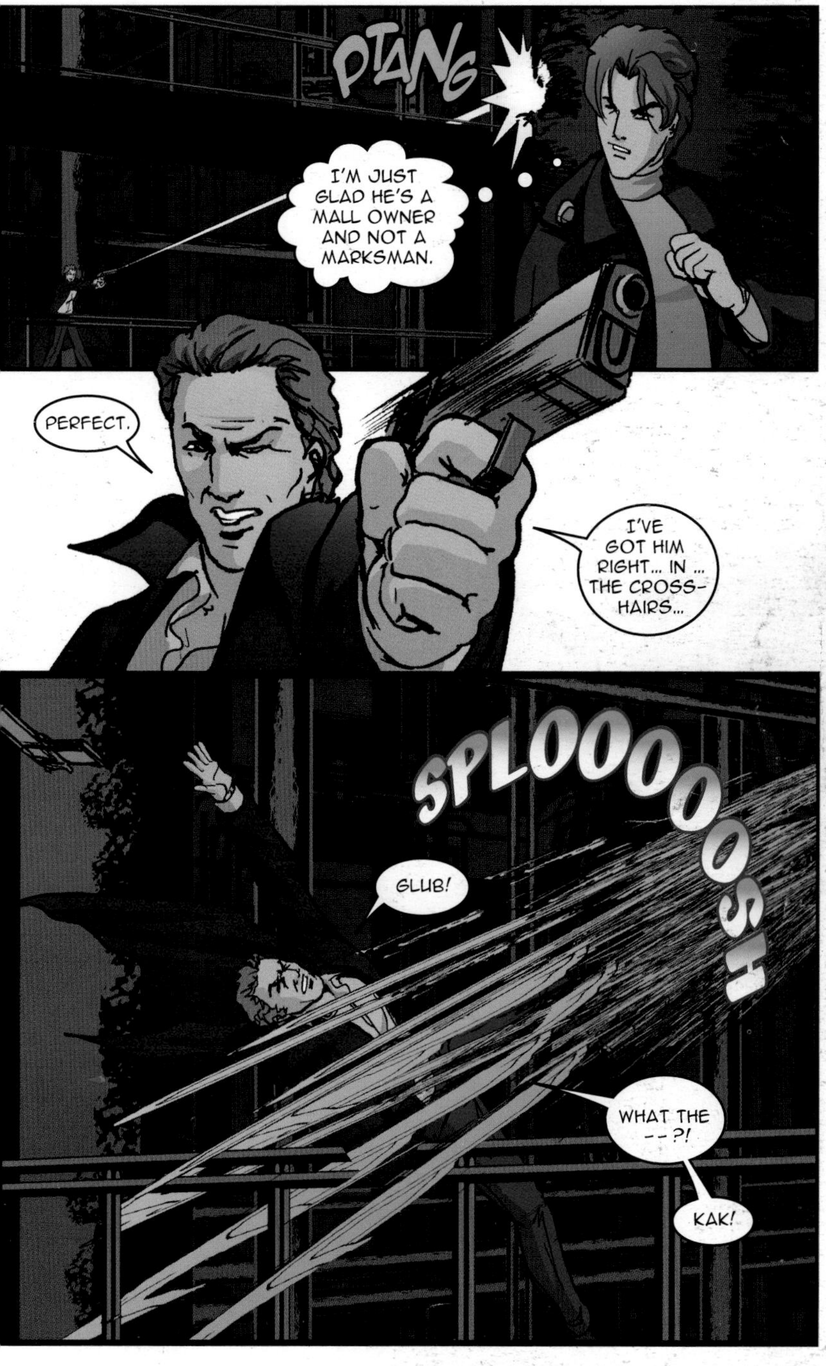
PTANG
I'M JUST GLAD HE'S A MALL OWNER AND NOT A MARKSMAN.
PERFECT.
I'VE GOT HIM RIGHT... IN ... THE CROSS-HAIRS...
SPLOOOOOOSH
GLUB!
WHAT THE --?!
KAK!

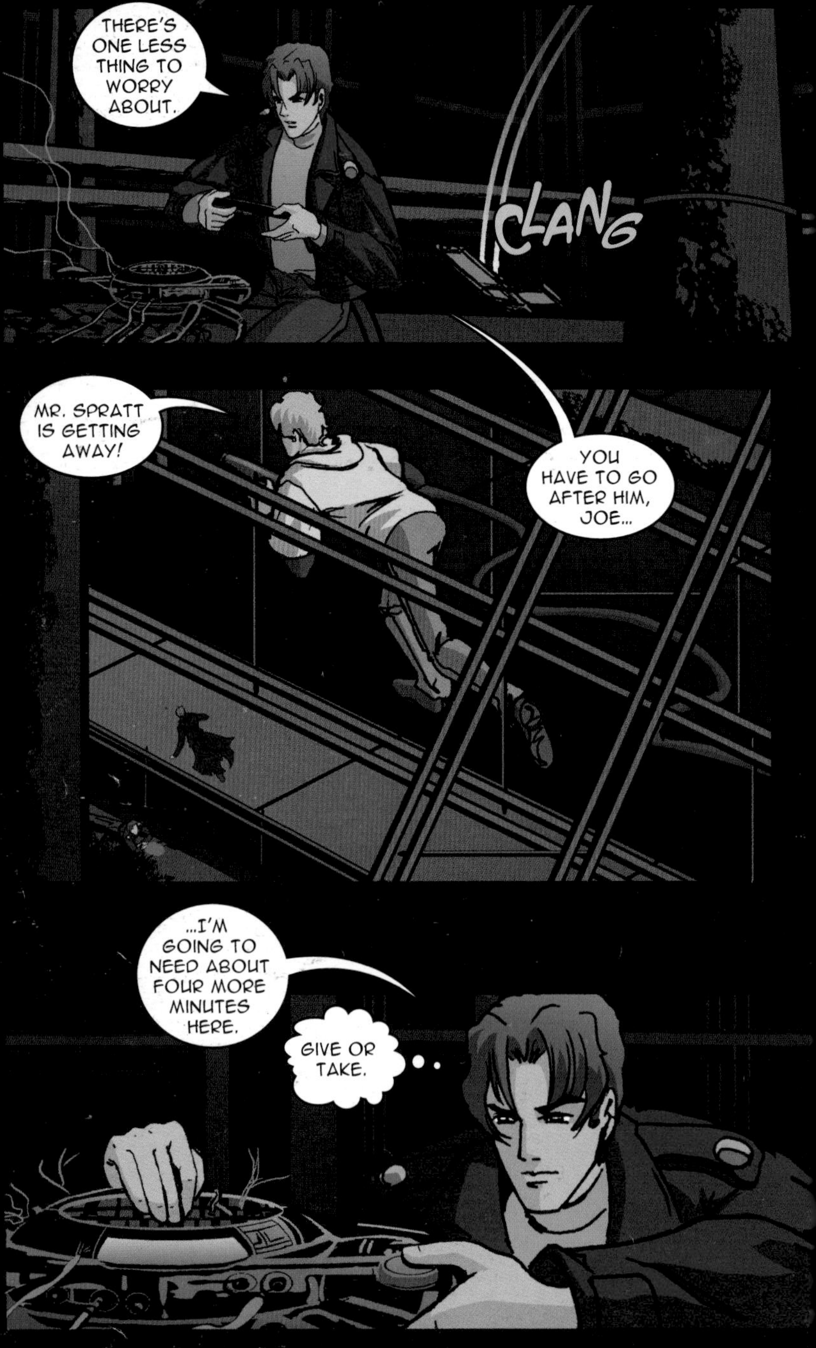
THERE'S ONE LESS THING TO WORRY ABOUT.
CLANG
MR. SPRATT IS GETTING AWAY!
YOU HAVE TO GO AFTER HIM, JOE...
...I'M GOING TO NEED ABOUT FOUR MORE MINUTES HERE.
GIVE OR TAKE.

CHAPTER TWELVE: "Up on the roof..."

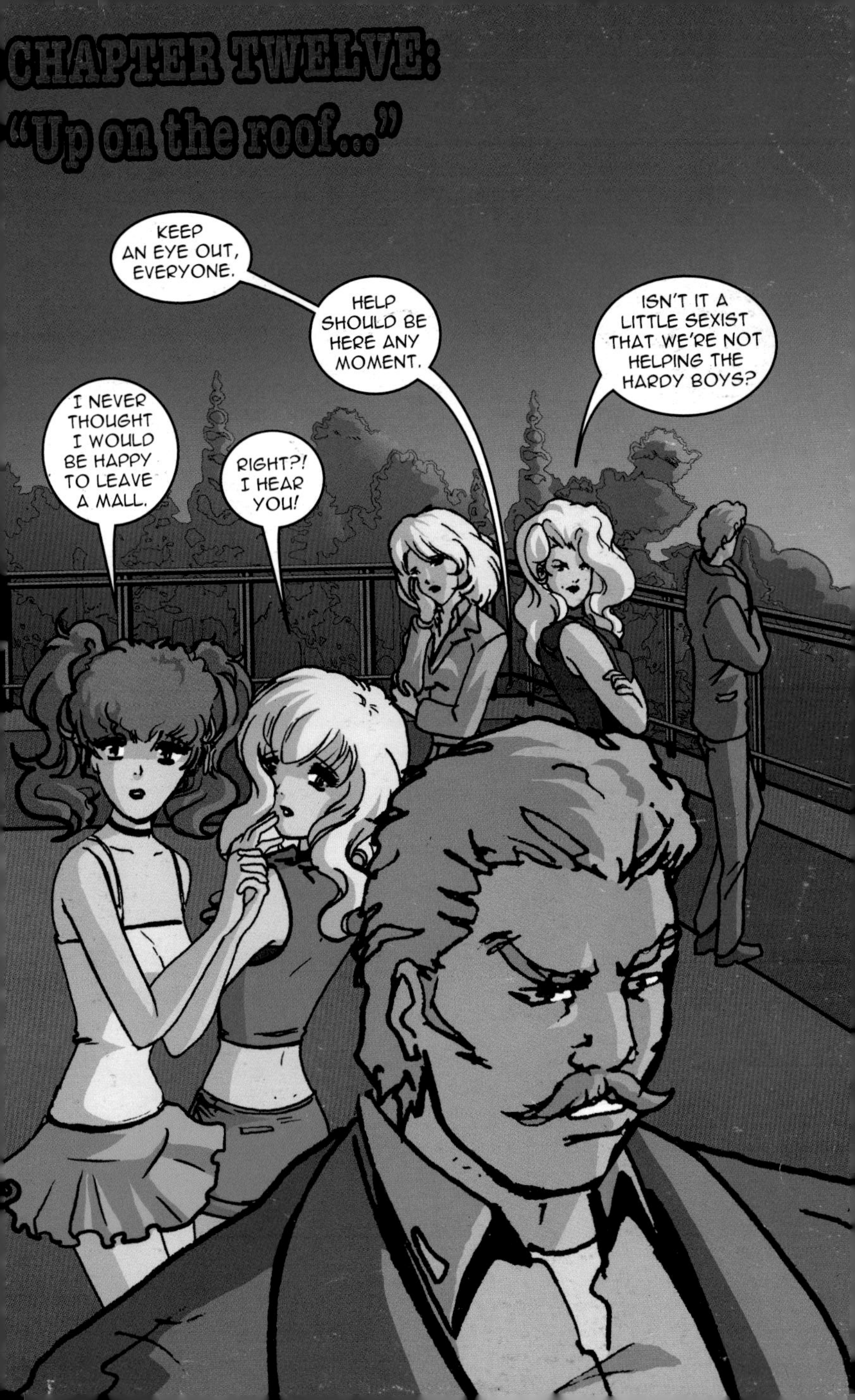
KEEP AN EYE OUT, EVERYONE.
HELP SHOULD BE HERE ANY MOMENT.
ISN'T IT A LITTLE SEXIST THAT WE'RE NOT HELPING THE HARDY BOYS?
I NEVER THOUGHT I WOULD BE HAPPY TO LEAVE A MALL.
RIGHT?! I HEAR YOU!

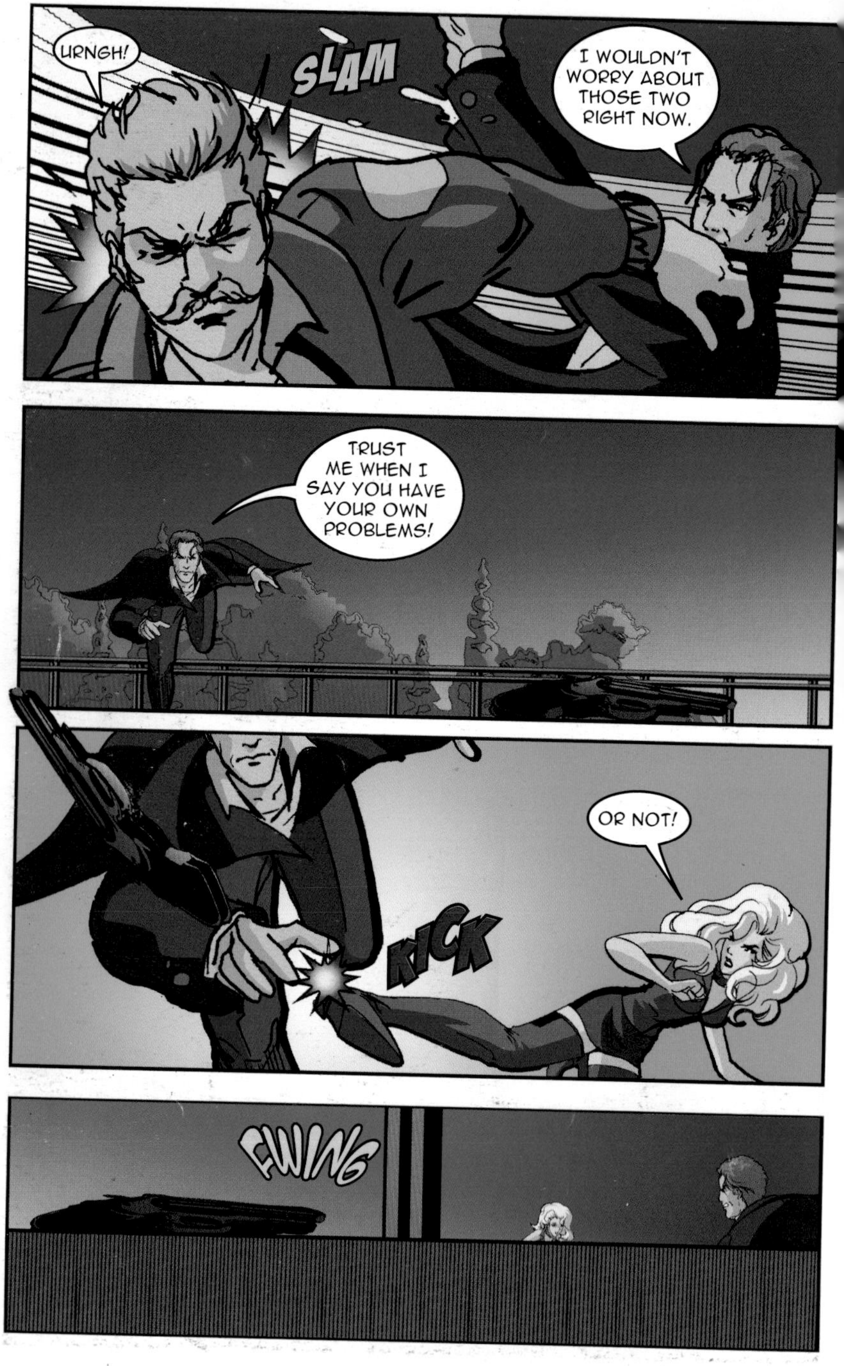
I WOULDN'T WORRY ABOUT THOSE TWO RIGHT NOW.
SLAM
URNGH!
TRUST ME WHEN I SAY YOU HAVE YOUR OWN PROBLEMS!
OR NOT!
KICK
FWING

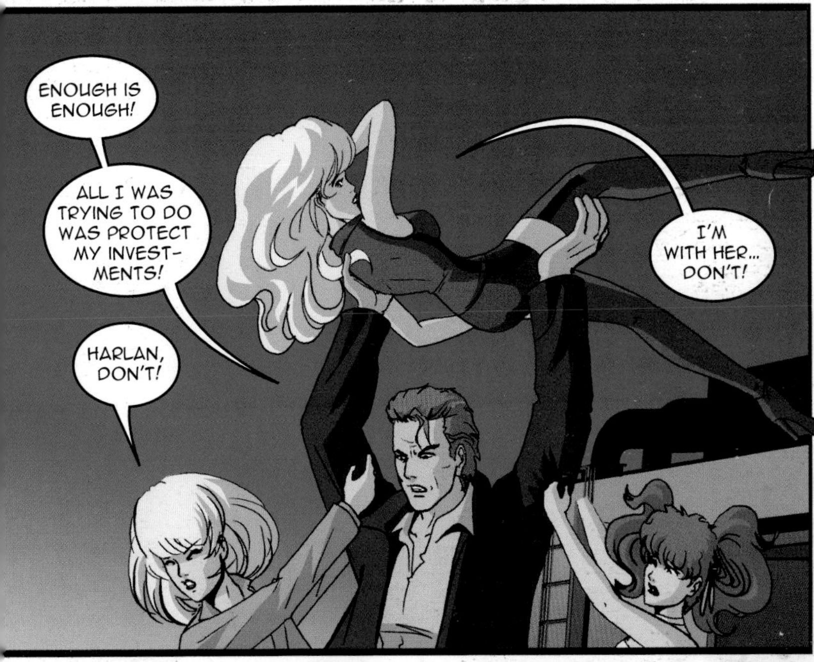
ENOUGH IS ENOUGH!
ALL I WAS TRYING TO DO WAS PROTECT MY INVEST-MENTS!
I'M WITH HER... DON'T!
HARLAN, DON'T!

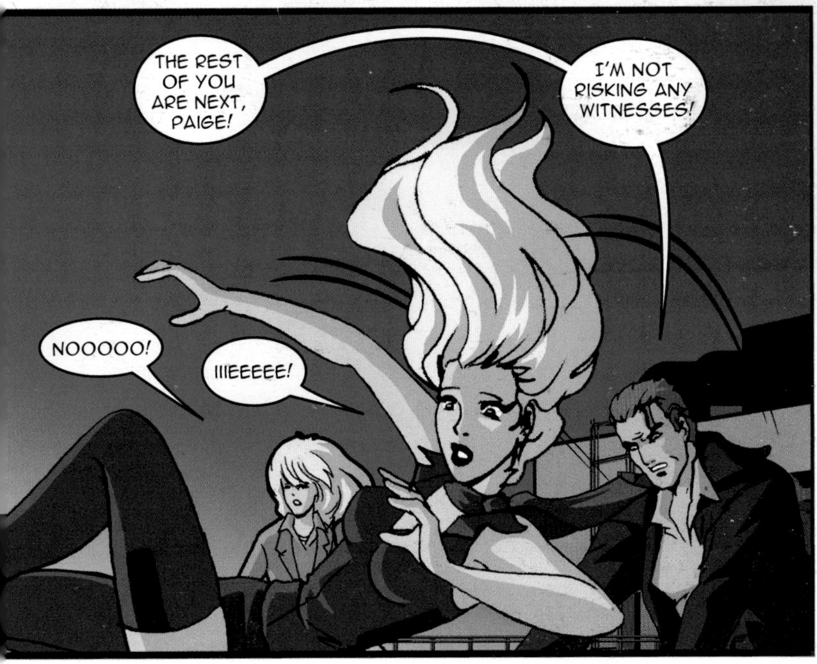
THE REST OF YOU ARE NEXT, PAIGE!
I'M NOT RISKING ANY WITNESSES!
IIIEEEEE!
NOOOOO!

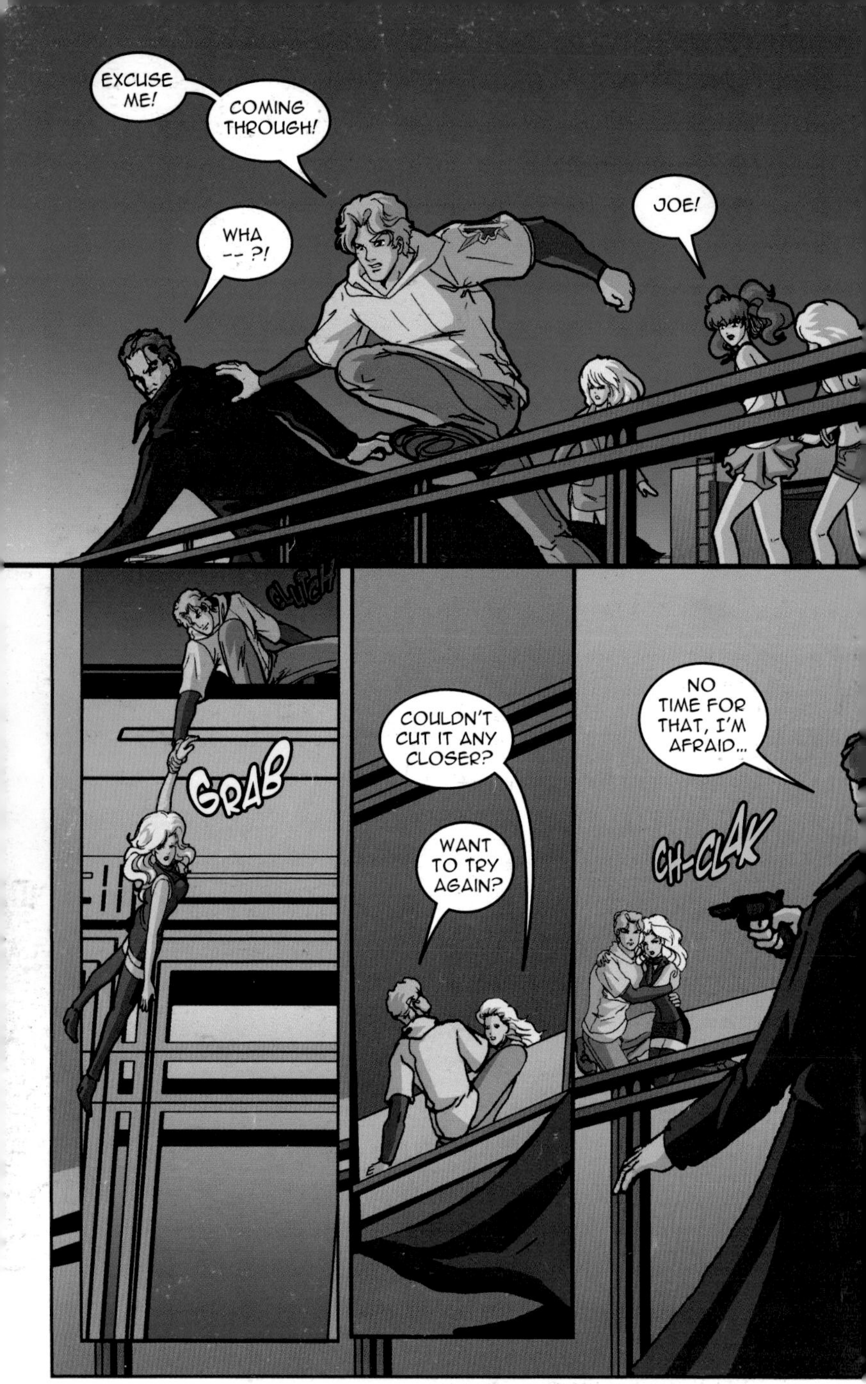
EXCUSE ME!
COMING THROUGH!
JOE!
WHA -- ?!
NO TIME FOR THAT, I'M AFRAID...
CH-CLAK
COULDN'T CUT IT ANY CLOSER?
WANT TO TRY AGAIN?
CLUTCH
GRAB

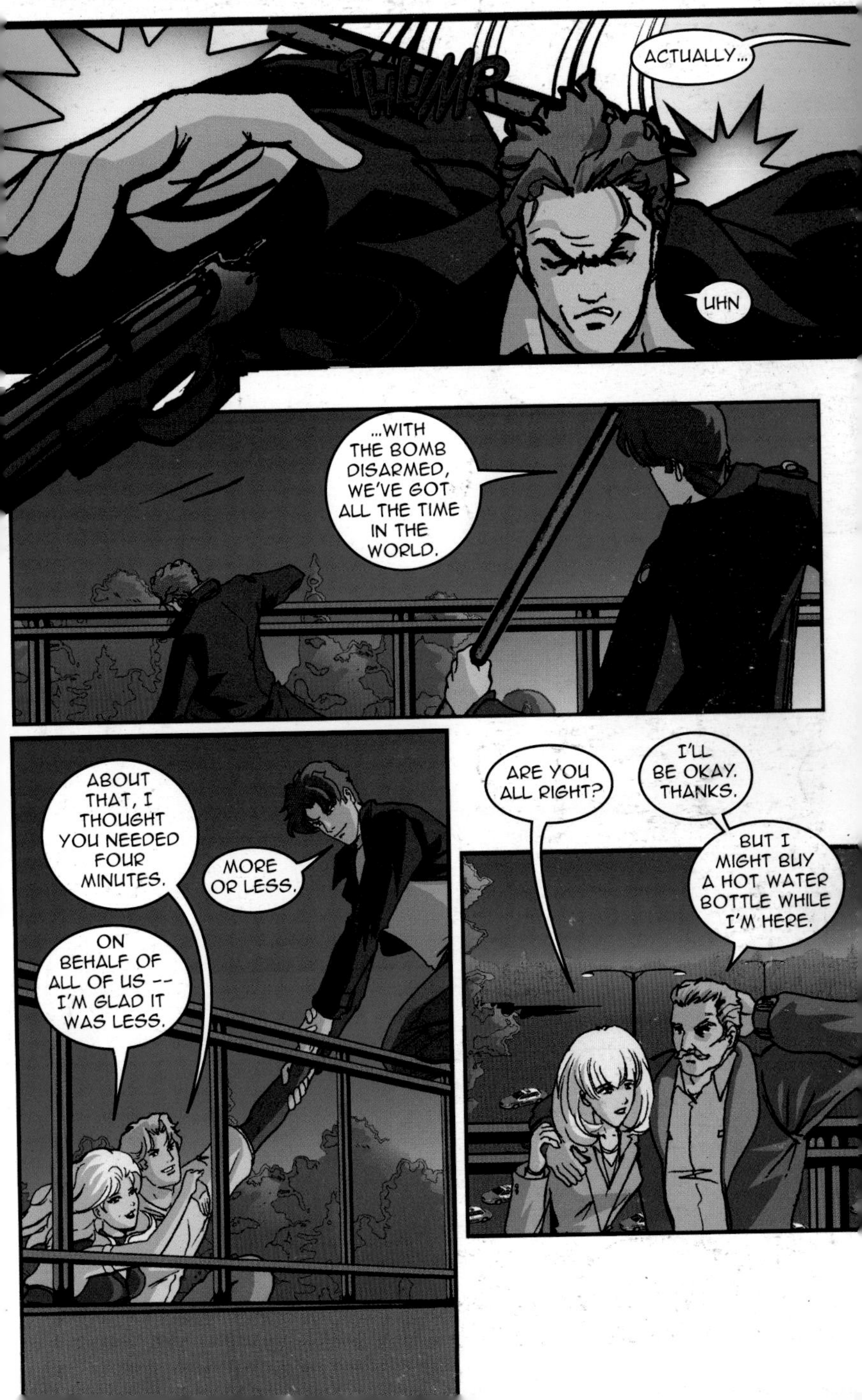
ACTUALLY...
THUMP
UHN
...WITH THE BOMB DISARMED, WE'VE GOT ALL THE TIME IN THE WORLD.
ARE YOU ALL RIGHT?
I'LL BE OKAY. THANKS.
BUT I MIGHT BUY A HOT WATER BOTTLE WHILE I'M HERE.
ABOUT THAT, I THOUGHT YOU NEEDED FOUR MINUTES.
MORE OR LESS.
ON BEHALF OF ALL OF US -- I'M GLAD IT WAS LESS.

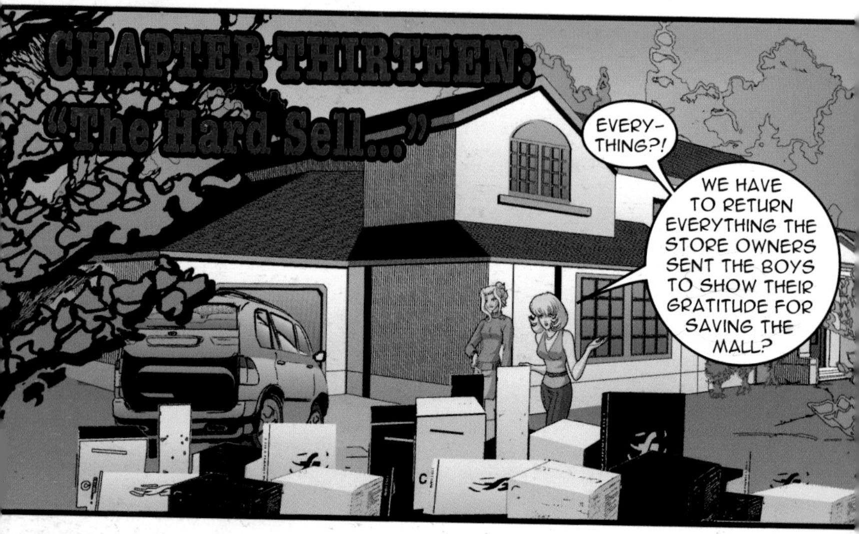
CHAPTER THIRTEEN:
"The Hard Sell..."
EVERY-THING?!
WE HAVE TO RETURN EVERYTHING THE STORE OWNERS SENT THE BOYS TO SHOW THEIR GRATITUDE FOR SAVING THE MALL?

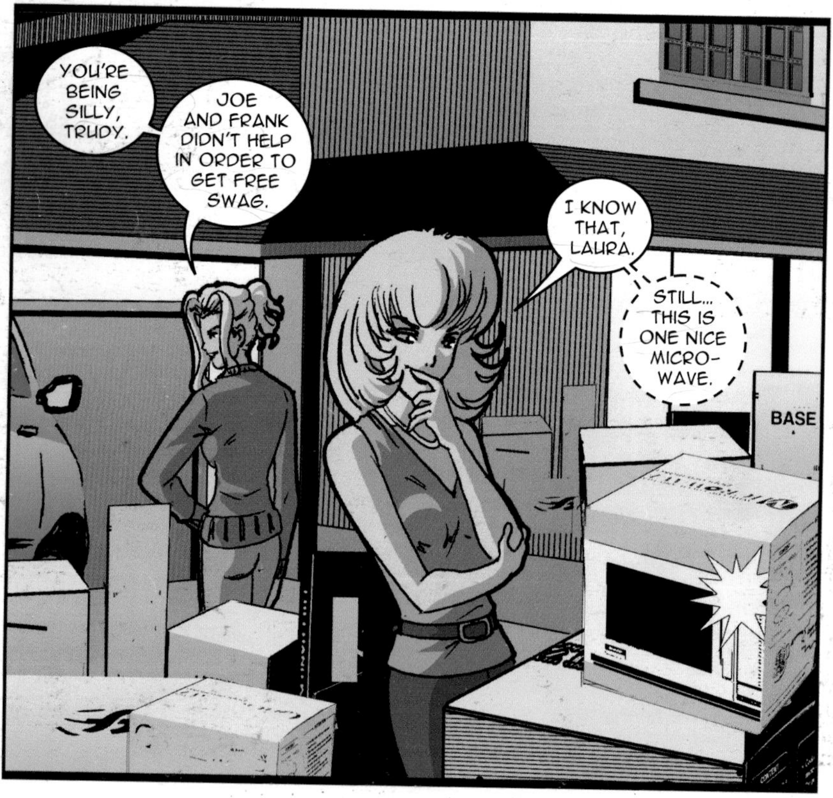
YOU'RE BEING SILLY, TRUDY.
JOE AND FRANK DIDN'T HELP IN ORDER TO GET FREE SWAG.
I KNOW THAT, LAURA.
STILL... THIS IS ONE NICE MICRO-WAVE.
BASE

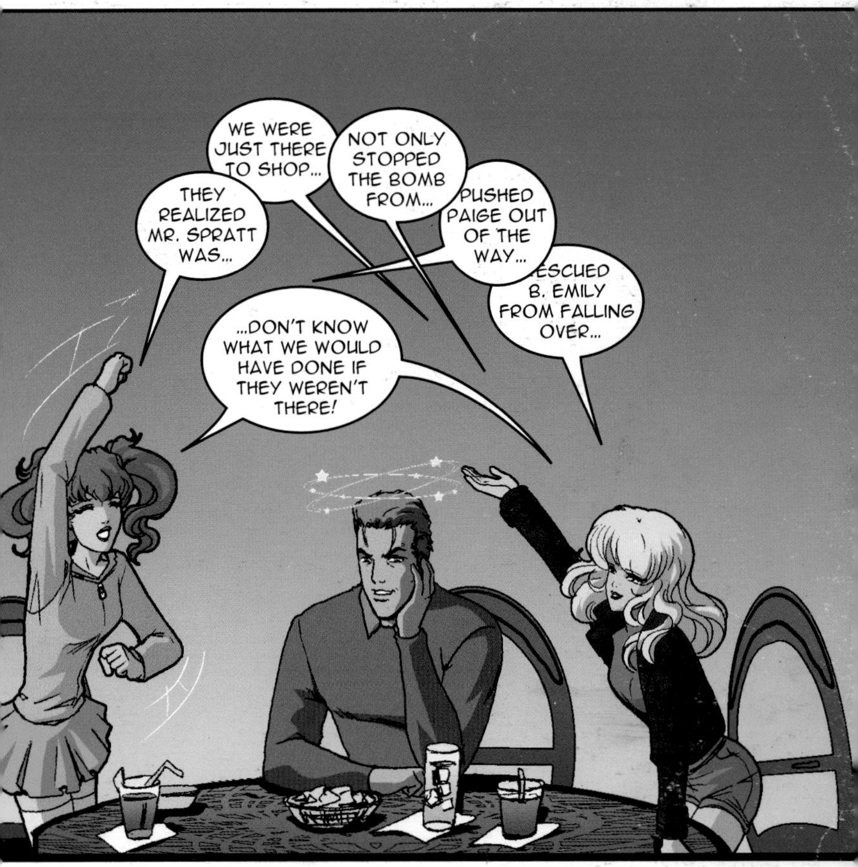
NOT ONLY STOPPED THE BOMB FROM...
PUSHED PAIGE OUT OF THE WAY...
RESCUED B. EMILY FROM FALLING OVER...
WE WERE JUST THERE TO SHOP...
THEY REALIZED MR. SPRATT WAS...
...DON'T KNOW WHAT WE WOULD HAVE DONE IF THEY WEREN'T THERE!

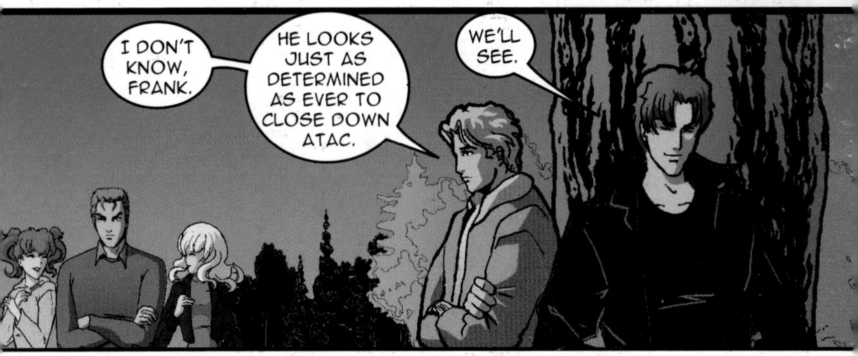
WE'LL SEE.
HE LOOKS JUST AS DETERMINED AS EVER TO CLOSE DOWN ATAC.
I DON'T KNOW, FRANK.

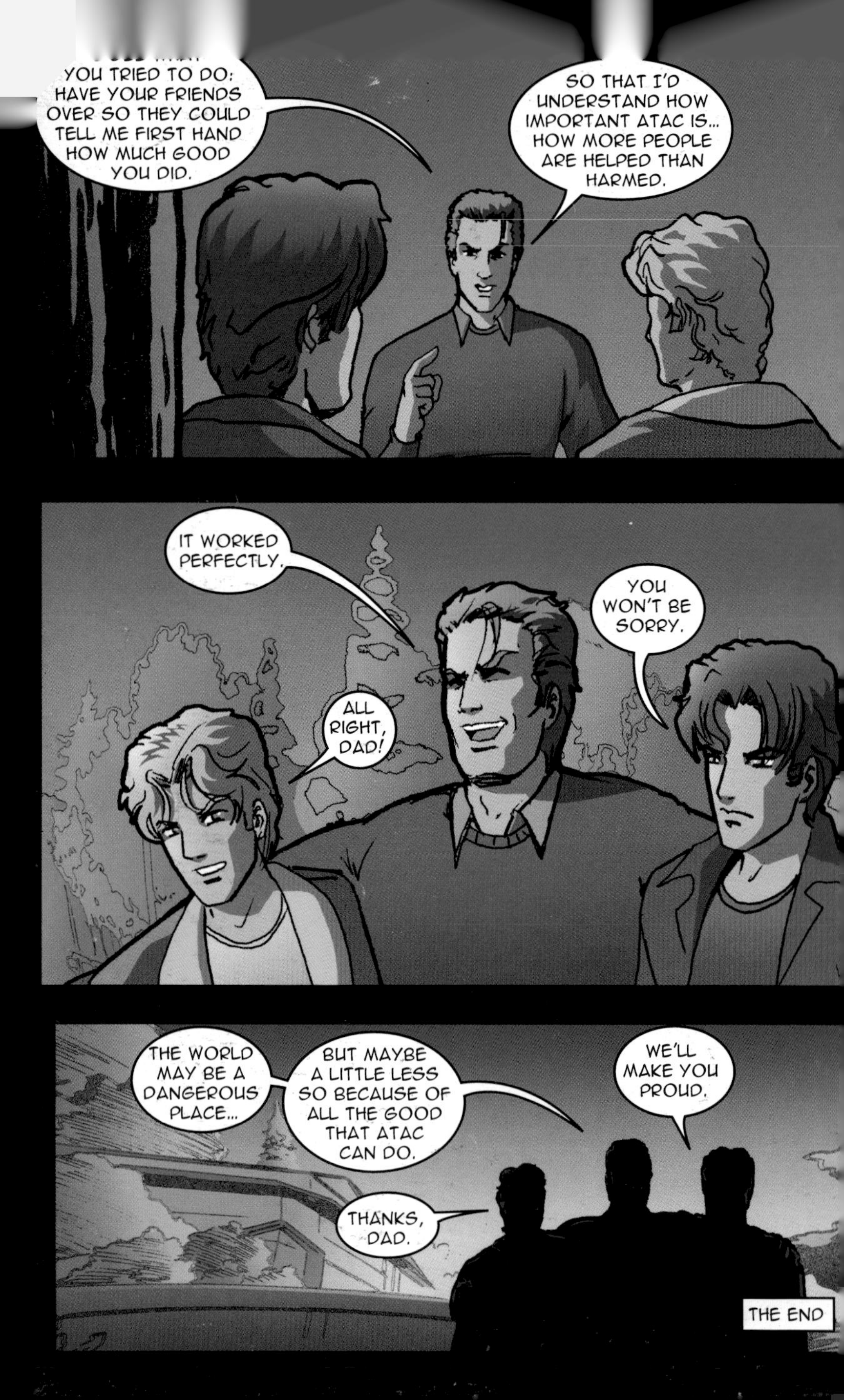
YOU TRIED TO DO: HAVE YOUR FRIENDS OVER SO THEY COULD TELL ME FIRST HAND HOW MUCH GOOD YOU DID.
SO THAT I'D UNDERSTAND HOW IMPORTANT ATAC IS... HOW MORE PEOPLE ARE HELPED THAN HARMED.
IT WORKED PERFECTLY.
YOU WON'T BE SORRY.
ALL RIGHT, DAD!
THE WORLD MAY BE A DANGEROUS PLACE...
BUT MAYBE A LITTLE LESS SO BECAUSE OF ALL THE GOOD THAT ATAC CAN DO.
WE'LL MAKE YOU PROUD.
THANKS, DAD.
THE END

Chapter One: "En Garde!"

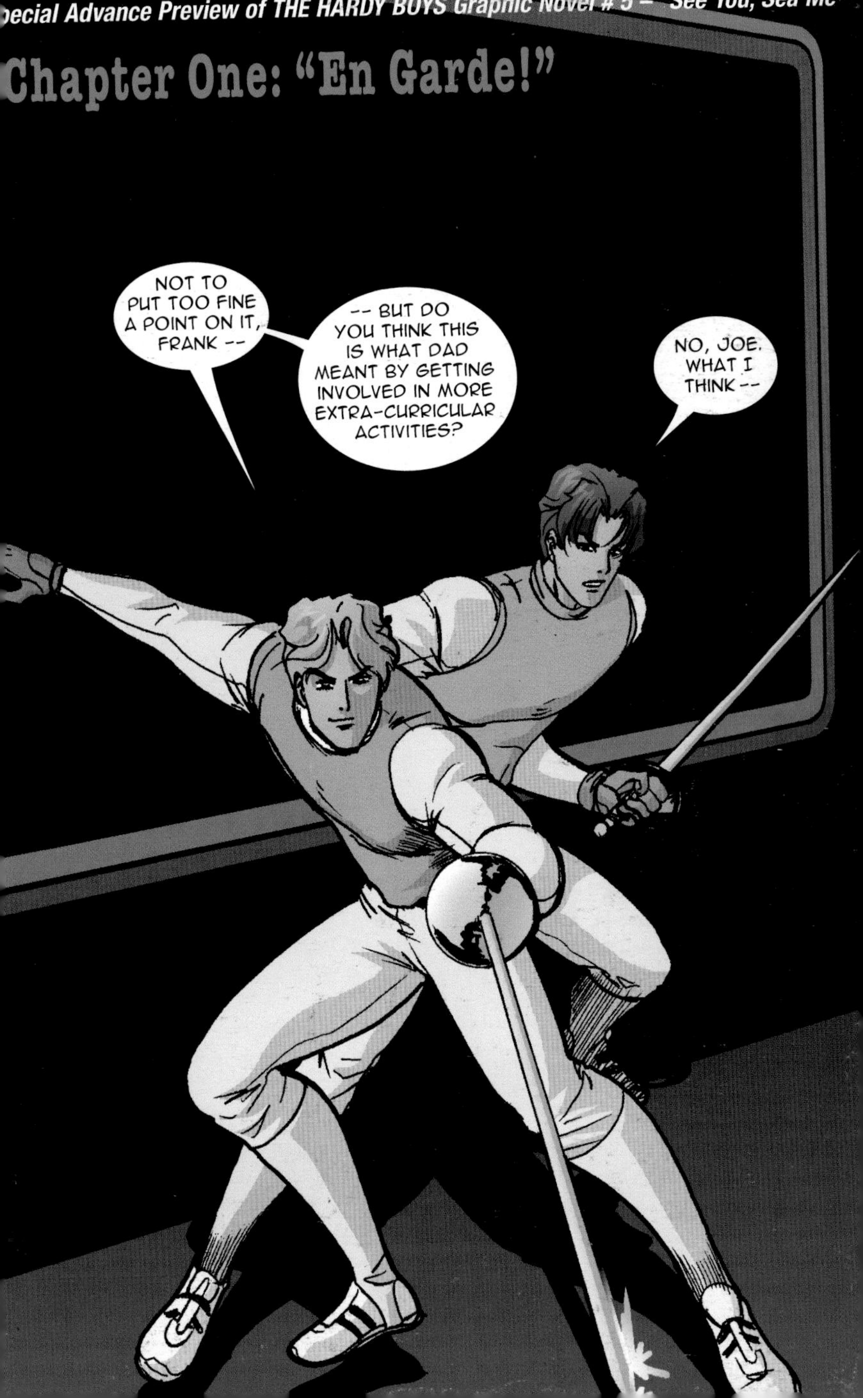
NOT TO PUT TOO FINE A POINT ON IT, FRANK --
-- BUT DO YOU THINK THIS IS WHAT DAD MEANT BY GETTING INVOLVED IN MORE EXTRA-CURRICULAR ACTIVITIES?
NO, JOE. WHAT I THINK --

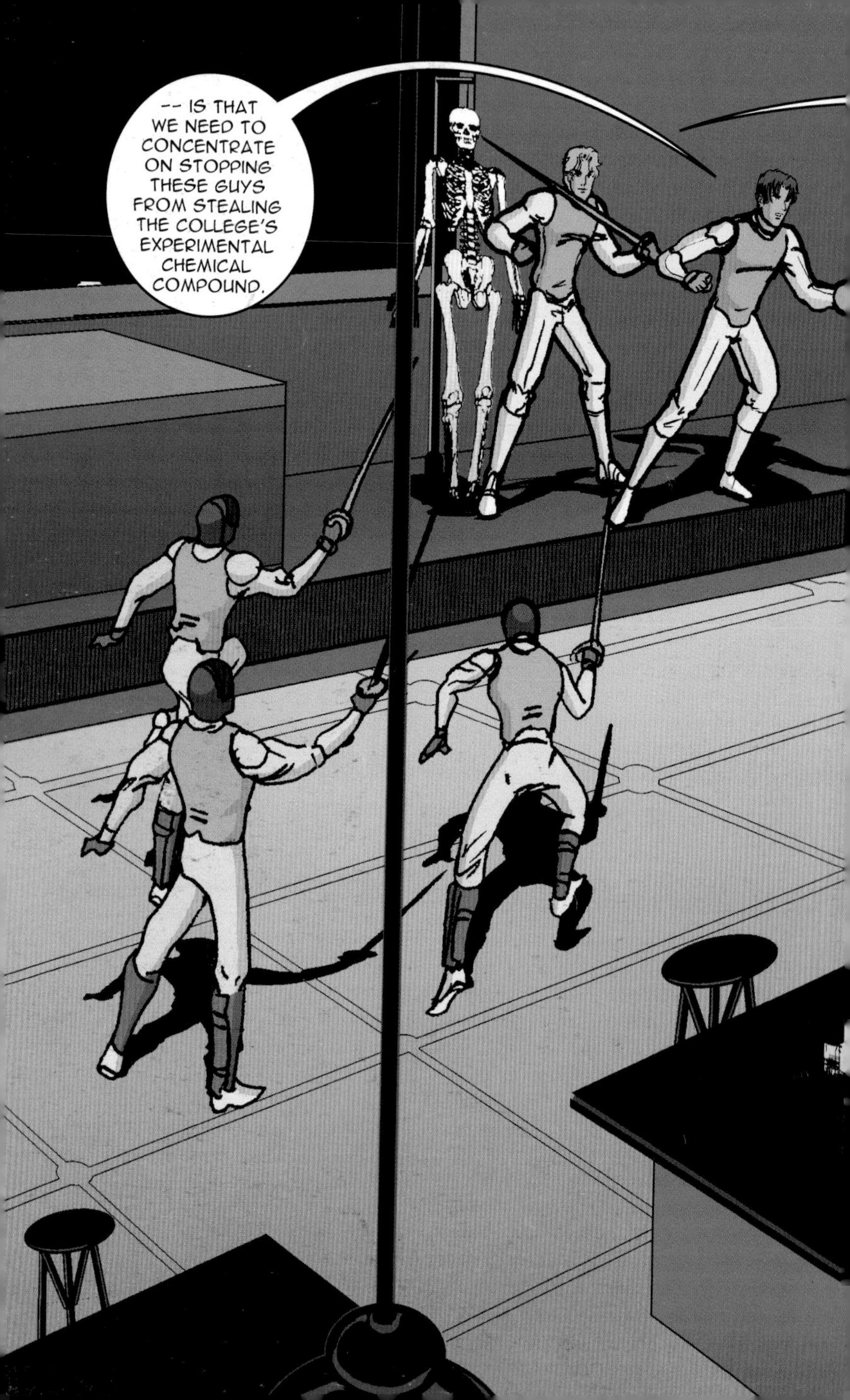
-- IS THAT WE NEED TO CONCENTRATE ON STOPPING THESE GUYS FROM STEALING THE COLLEGE'S EXPERIMENTAL CHEMICAL COMPOUND.

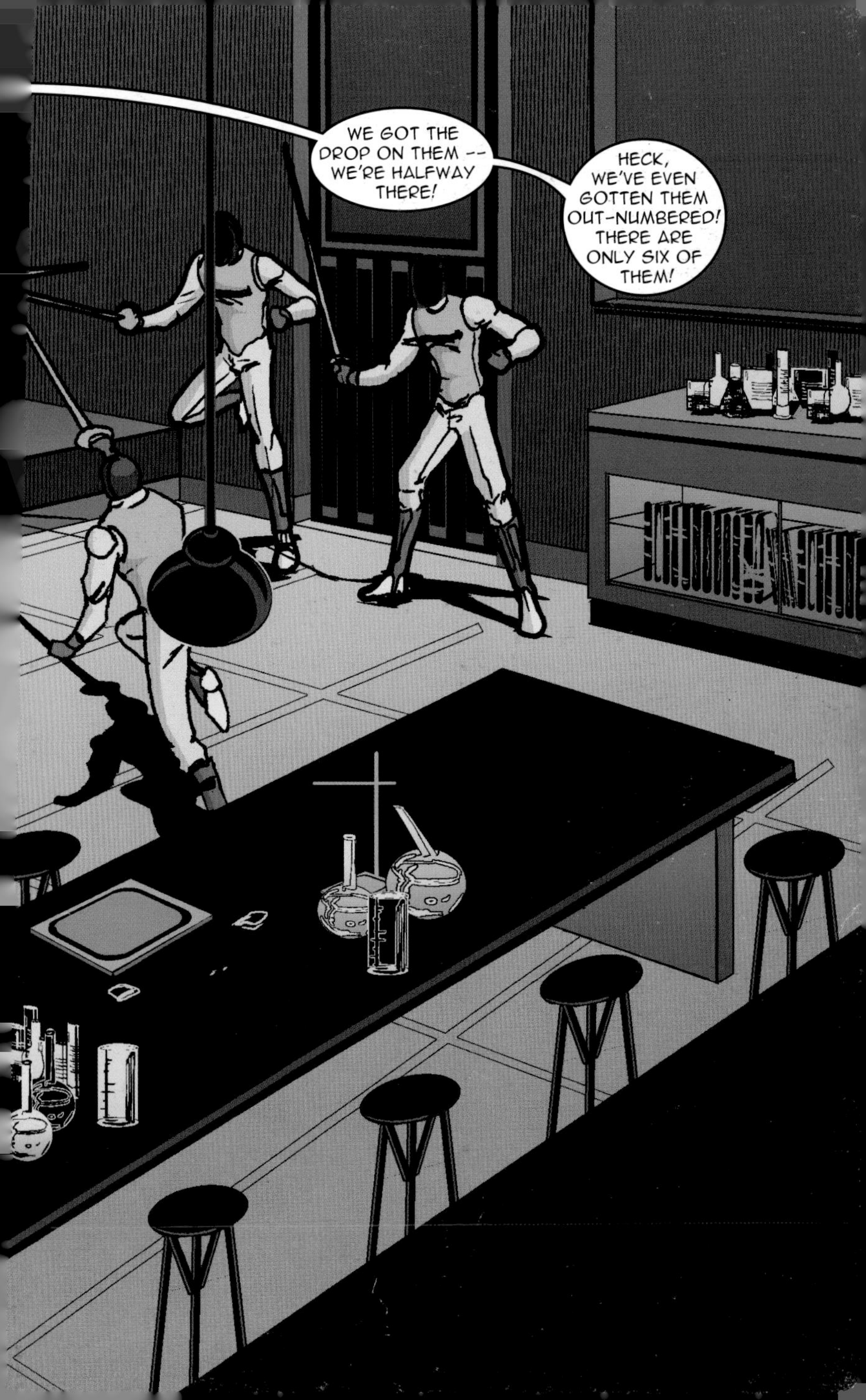
WE GOT THE DROP ON THEM -- WE'RE HALFWAY THERE!
HECK, WE'VE EVEN GOTTEN THEM OUT-NUMBERED! THERE ARE ONLY SIX OF THEM!

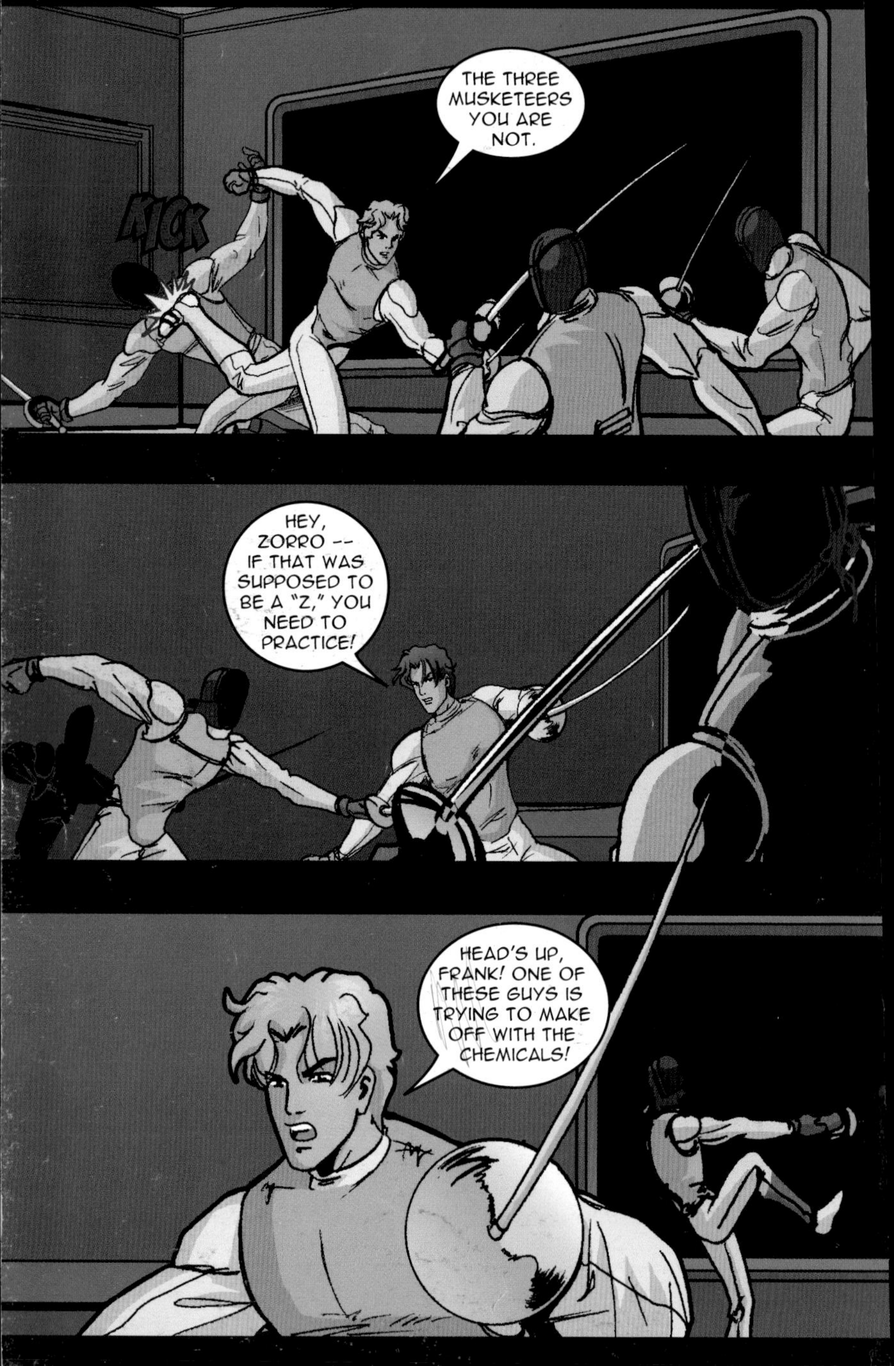
THE THREE MUSKETEERS YOU ARE NOT.
KICK
HEY, ZORRO -- IF THAT WAS SUPPOSED TO BE A "Z," YOU NEED TO PRACTICE!
HEAD'S UP, FRANK! ONE OF THESE GUYS IS TRYING TO MAKE OFF WITH THE CHEMICALS!

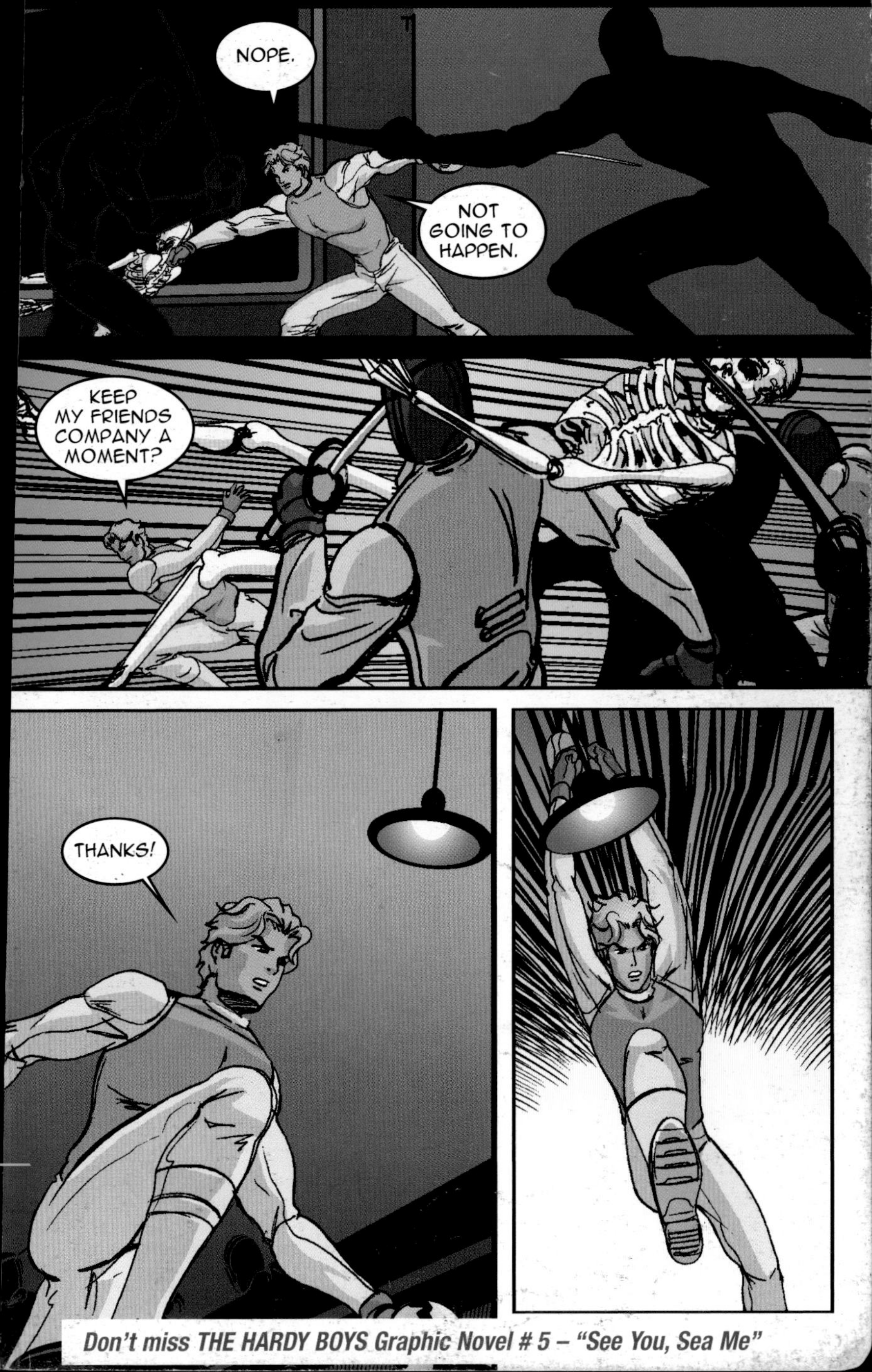
NOPE.
NOT GOING TO HAPPEN.
KEEP MY FRIENDS COMPANY A MOMENT?
THANKS!

CRIMINALS BEWARE!

THE HARDY BOYS

UNDERCOVER BROTHERS

ARE ON YOUR TRAIL.

Read the paperback series that started it al

ALL NEW ALL NEW ALL NEW #8

Top Ten Ways to Die

Available February 2006

Madison Vee is the biggest thing to hit pop music since Britney—and someone is trying to kill her. To protect the young star, Frank and Joe join the tech crew of Madison's latest music video shoot. But a bunch of threatening notes and technical accidents make them realize that the wanna-be-pop-star-killer is right there, waiting in the wings—and ready to make Madison's next hit her last.

Have you read Frank and Joe's latest stories of crime, danger, mystery, and death-defying stunts

BOARDWALK BUST

THRILL RIDE

ROCKY ROAD

BURNED

OPERATION: SURVIVAL

Look for a new book every other month, and collect them all!
Visit www.SimonSaysSleuth.com for more Hardy Boys adventures.

ALADDIN PAPERBACKS • SIMON & SCHUSTER CHILDREN'S PUBLISHING • WWW.SIMONSAYSKIDS.COM

The Hardy Boys © Simon & Schuster, Inc.

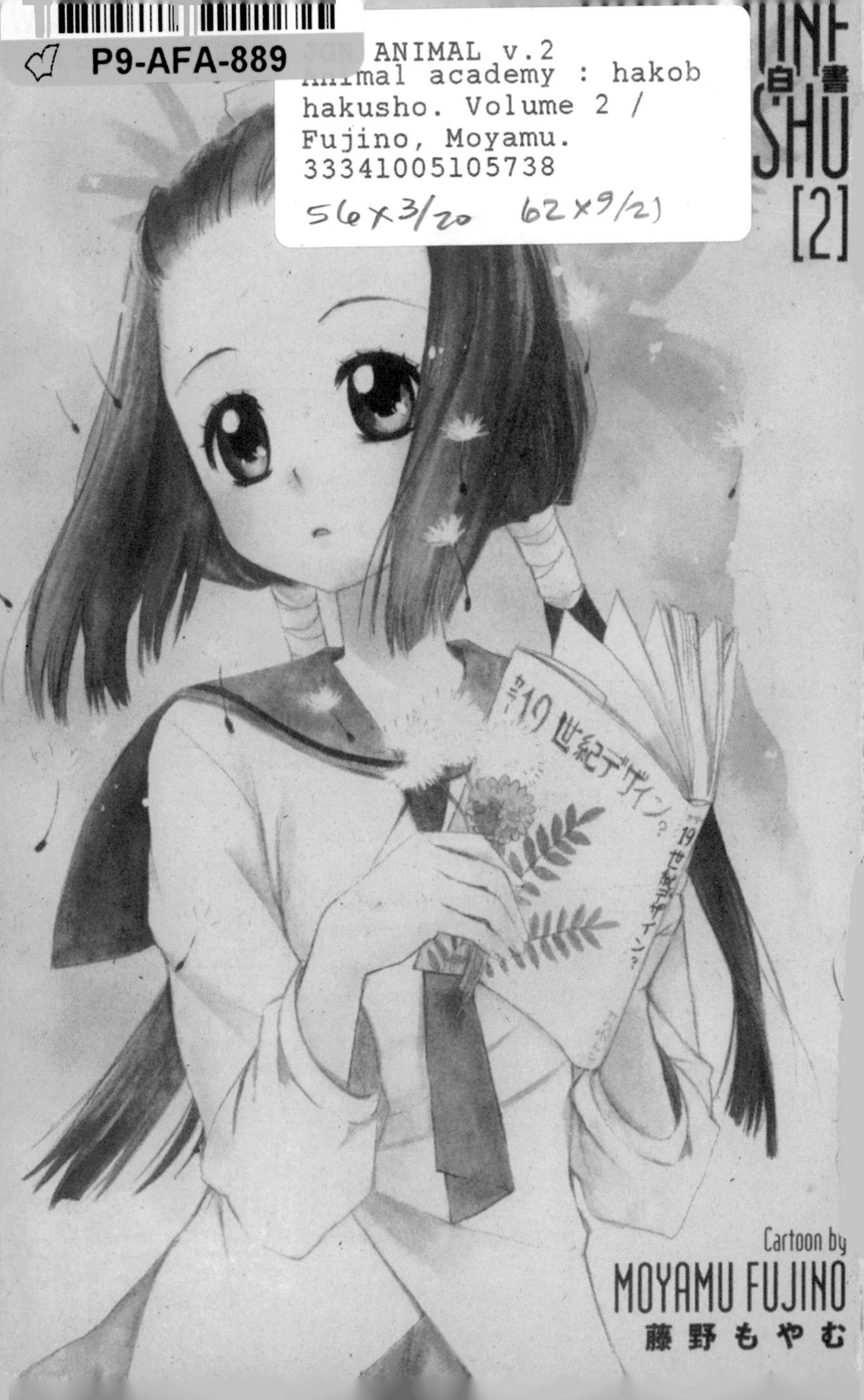

...INE 白書 SHU [2]

Cartoon by MOYAMU FUJINO
藤野もやむ

Animal Academy: Hakobune Hakusho Volume 2
Created by Moyamu Fujino

Translation - Alexis Kirsch
English Adaptation - Ysabet Reinhardt MacFarlane
Retouch and Lettering - Star Print Brokers
Production Artist - Rui Kyo
Graphic Designer - Louis Csontos

Editor - Lillian Diaz-Przybyl
Print Production Manager - Lucas Rivera
Managing Editor - Vy Nguyen
Senior Designer - Louis Csontos
Director of Sales and Manufacturing - Allyson De Simone
Associate Publisher - Marco F. Pavia
President and C.O.O. - John Parker
C.E.O. and Chief Creative Officer - Stu Levy

A **TOKYOPOP** Manga

TOKYOPOP and 🌀 are trademarks or registered trademarks of TOKYOPOP Inc.

TOKYOPOP Inc.
5900 Wilshire Blvd. Suite 2000
Los Angeles, CA 90036

E-mail: info@TOKYOPOP.com
Come visit us online at www.TOKYOPOP.com

ISBN: 978-1-4278-1096-0

First TOKYOPOP printing: September 2009
10 9 8 7 6 5 4 3 2 1
Printed in the USA

Animal ACADEMY

HAKOBUNE HAKUSHO

はこぶね白書

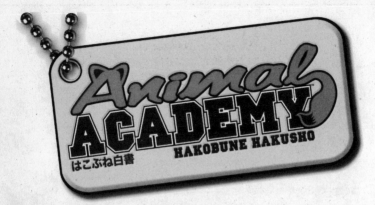

Volume 2

by

MOYAMU FUJINO

TOKYOPOP®

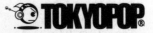

HAMBURG // LONDON // LOS ANGELES // TOKYO

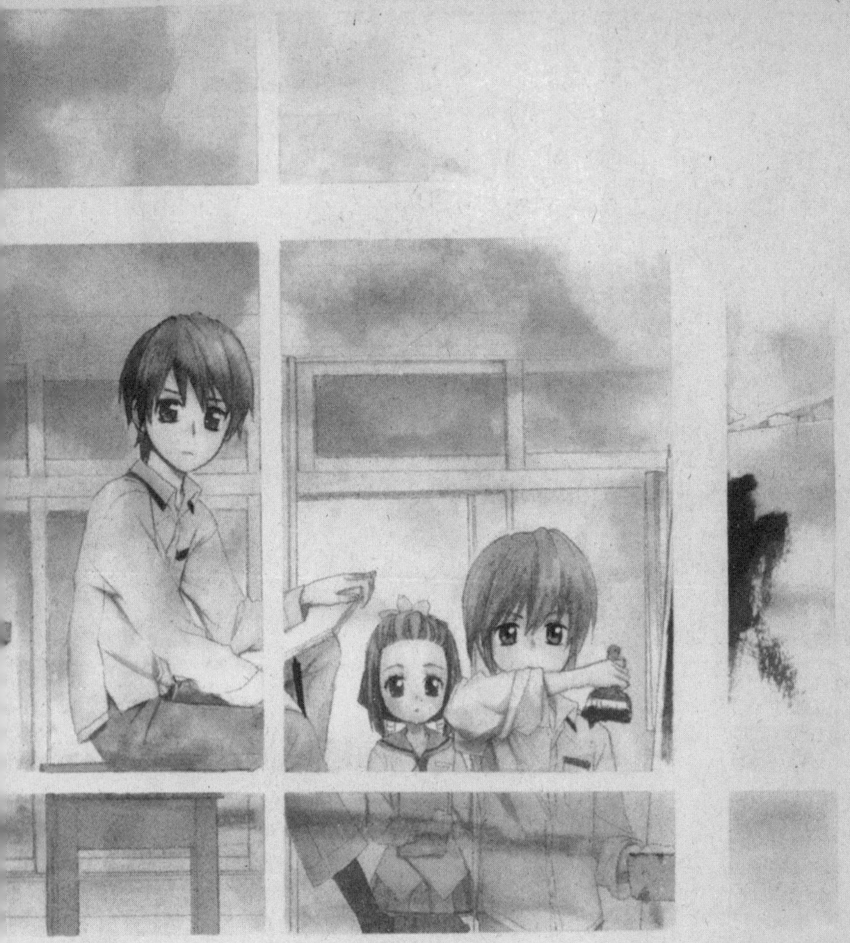

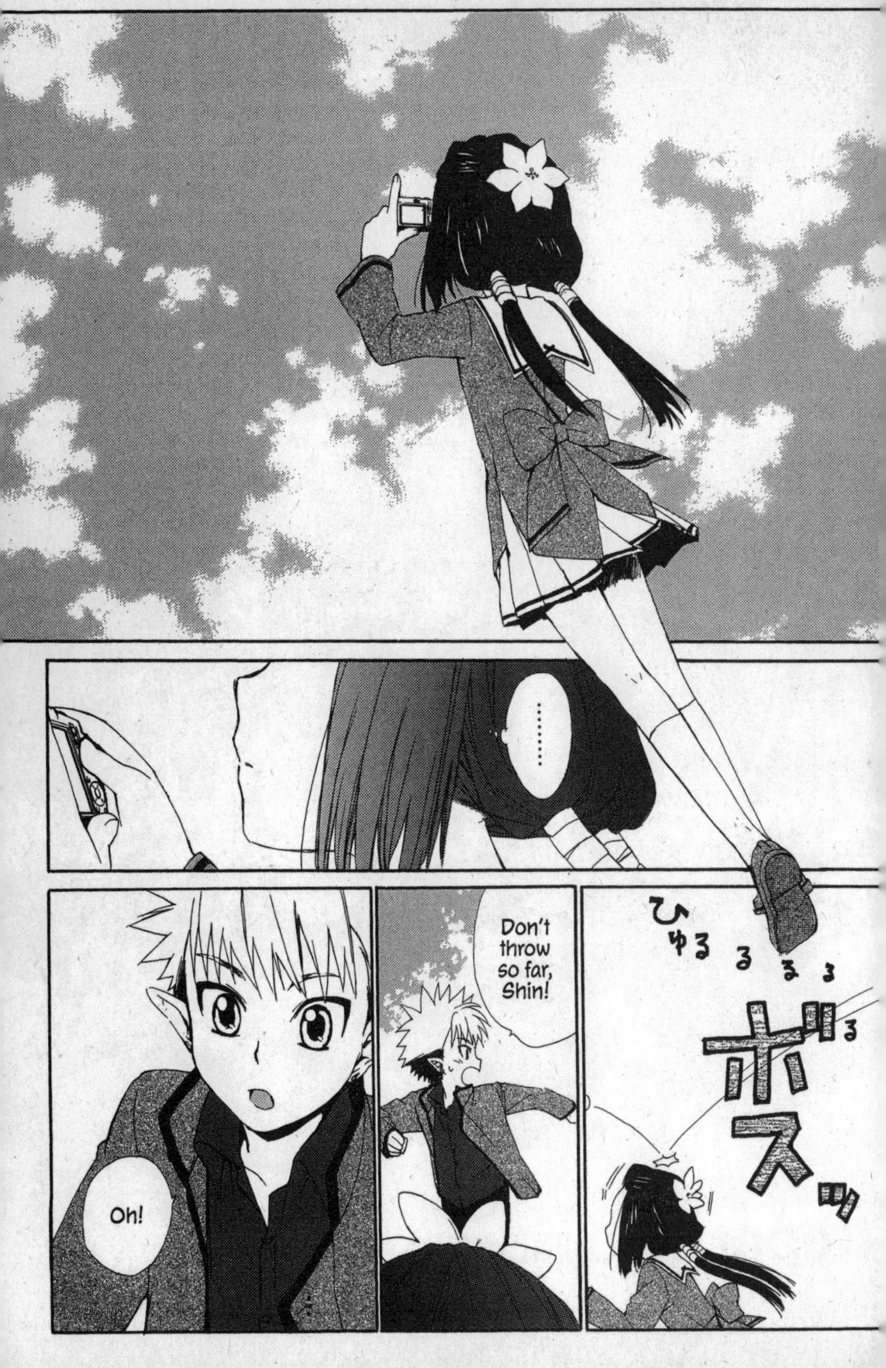
……
ひゅるるるるる
ボスッ
Don't throw so far, Shin!
Oh!

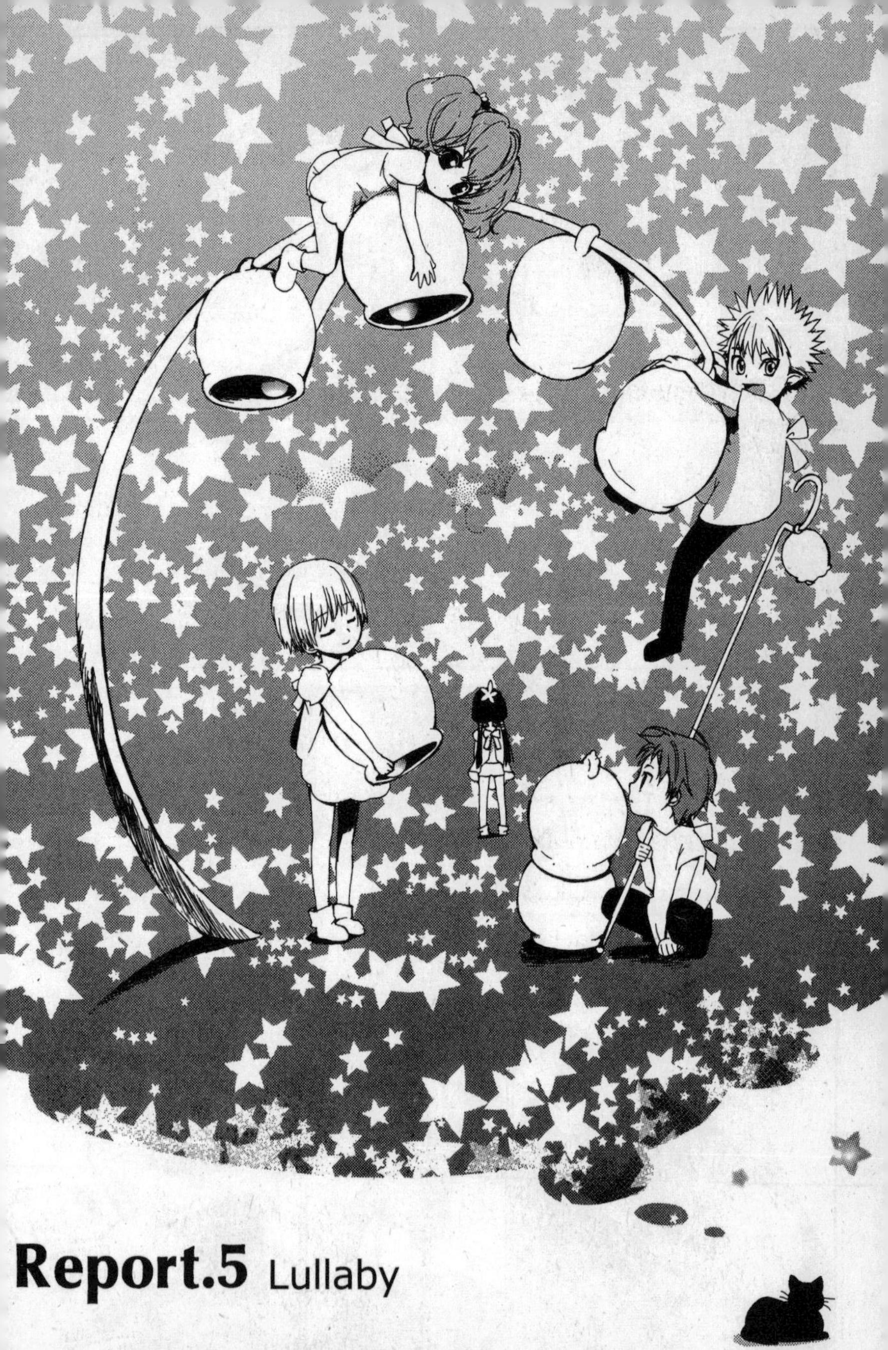

Report.5 Lullaby

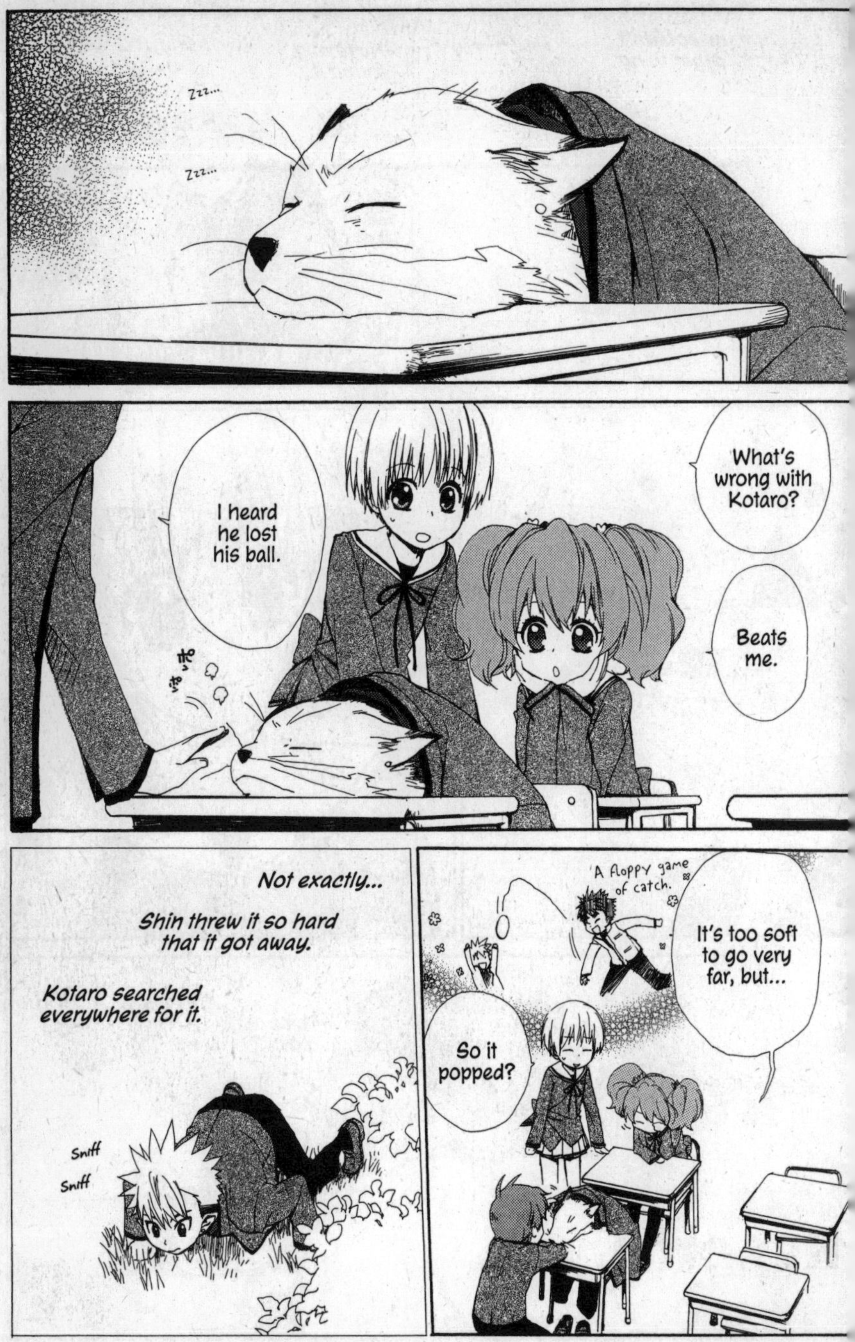
Zzz...
Zzz...
What's wrong with Kotaro?
Beats me.
I heard he lost his ball.
A floppy game of catch.
It's too soft to go very far, but...
So it popped?
Not exactly...
Shin threw it so hard that it got away.
Kotaro searched everywhere for it.
Sniff
Sniff

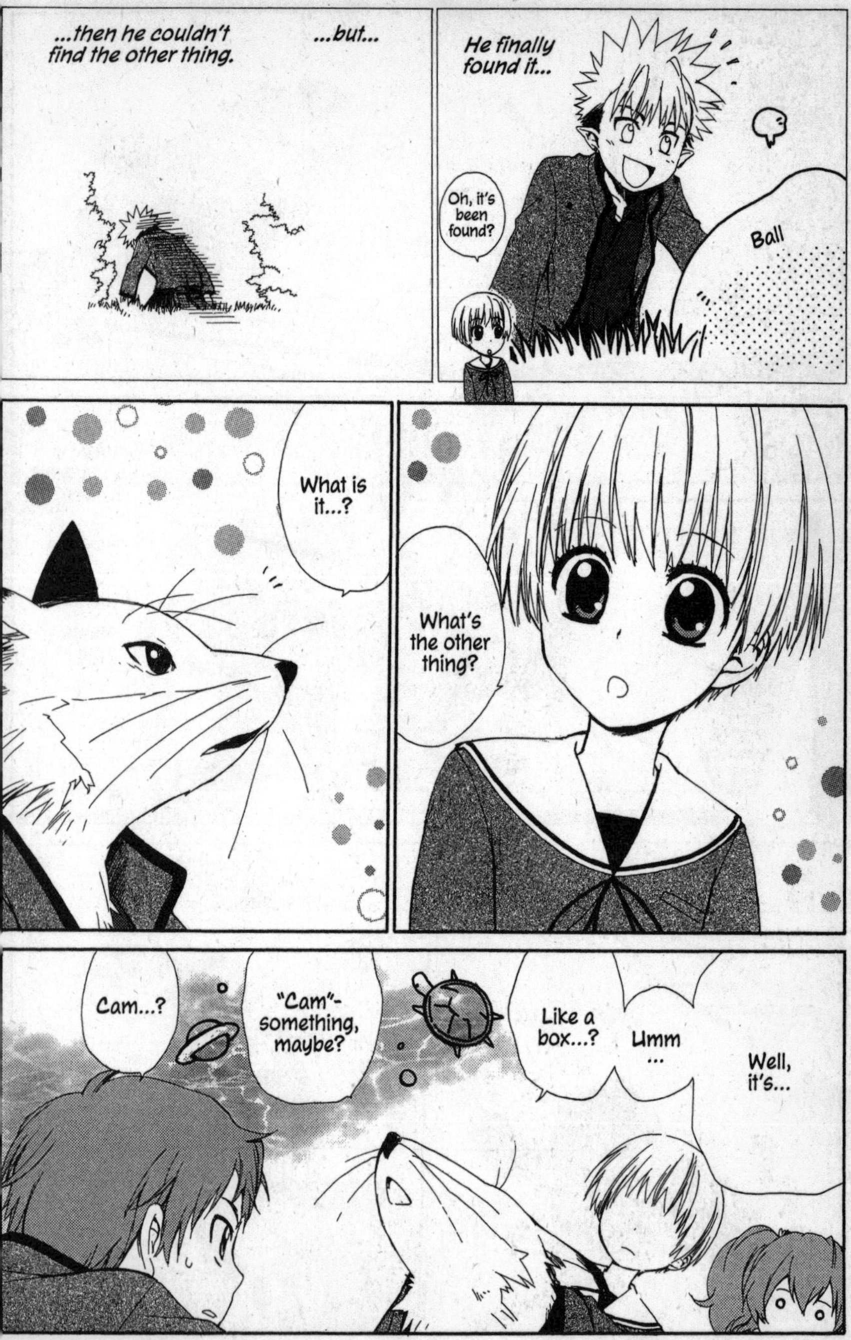
He finally found it...
Ball
Oh, it's been found?
...but...
...then he couldn't find the other thing.
What's the other thing?
What is it...?
Well, it's...
Umm ...
Like a box...?
"Cam"-something, maybe?
Cam...?

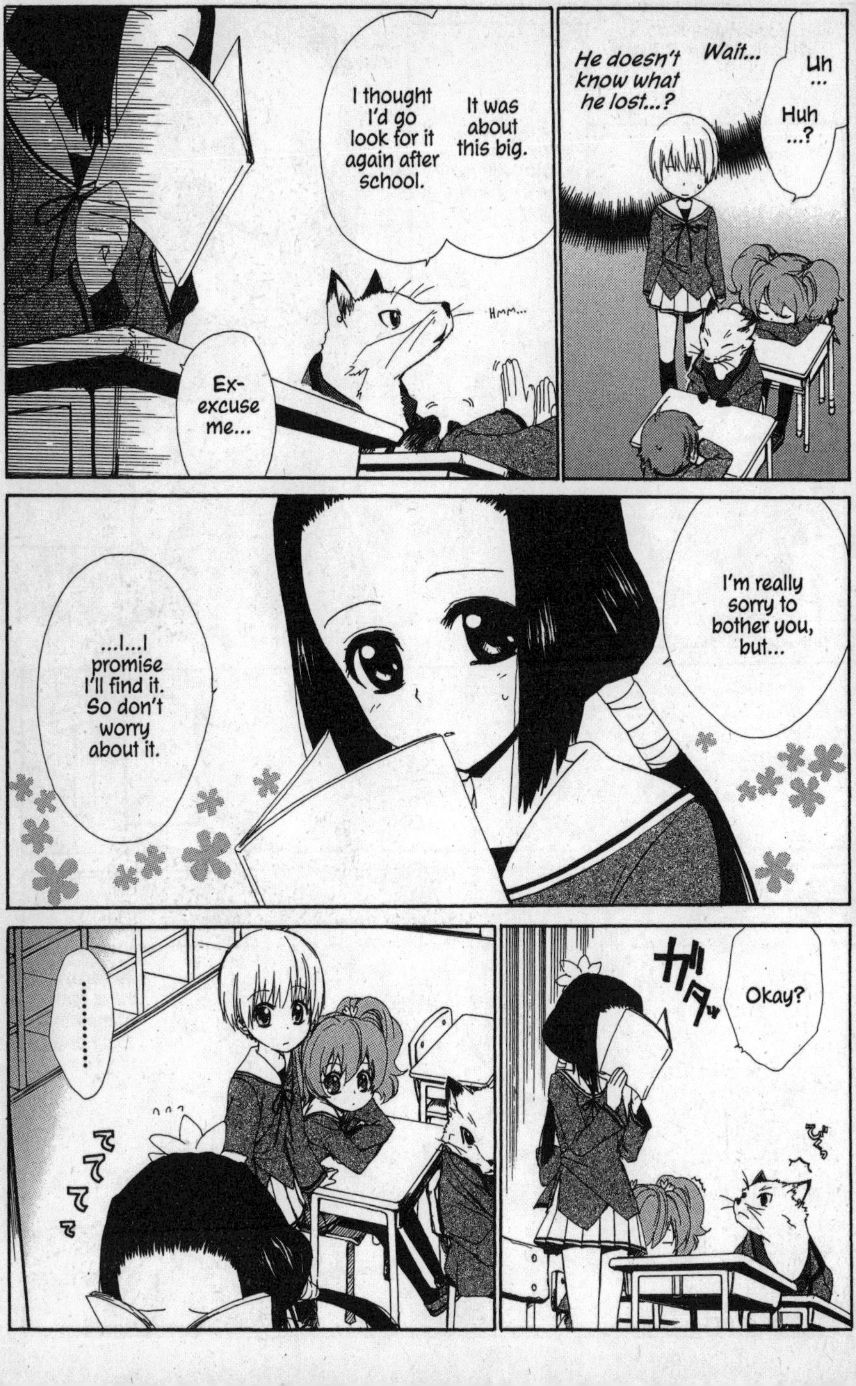
Uh ... Huh ...?
Wait...
He doesn't know what he lost...?
It was about this big.
I thought I'd go look for it again after school.
Hmm...
Ex-excuse me...
I'm really sorry to bother you, but...
...I...I promise I'll find it. So don't worry about it.
Okay?
ガタッ
....

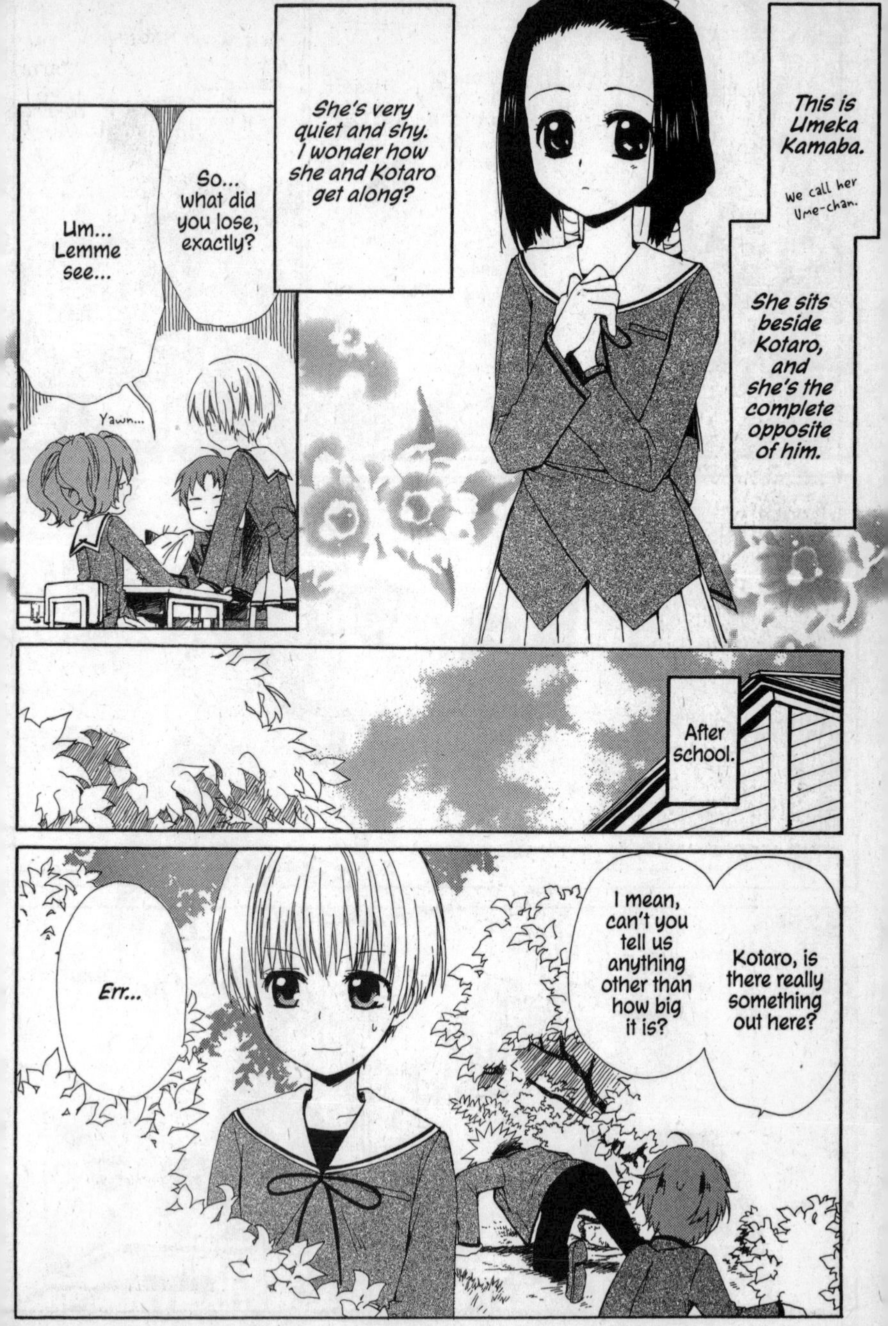

This is Umeka Kamaba.
We call her Ume-chan.
She sits beside Kotaro, and she's the complete opposite of him.
She's very quiet and shy. I wonder how she and Kotaro get along?
So... what did you lose, exactly?
Um... Lemme see...
Yawn...
After school.
Kotaro, is there really something out here?
I mean, can't you tell us anything other than how big it is?
Err...

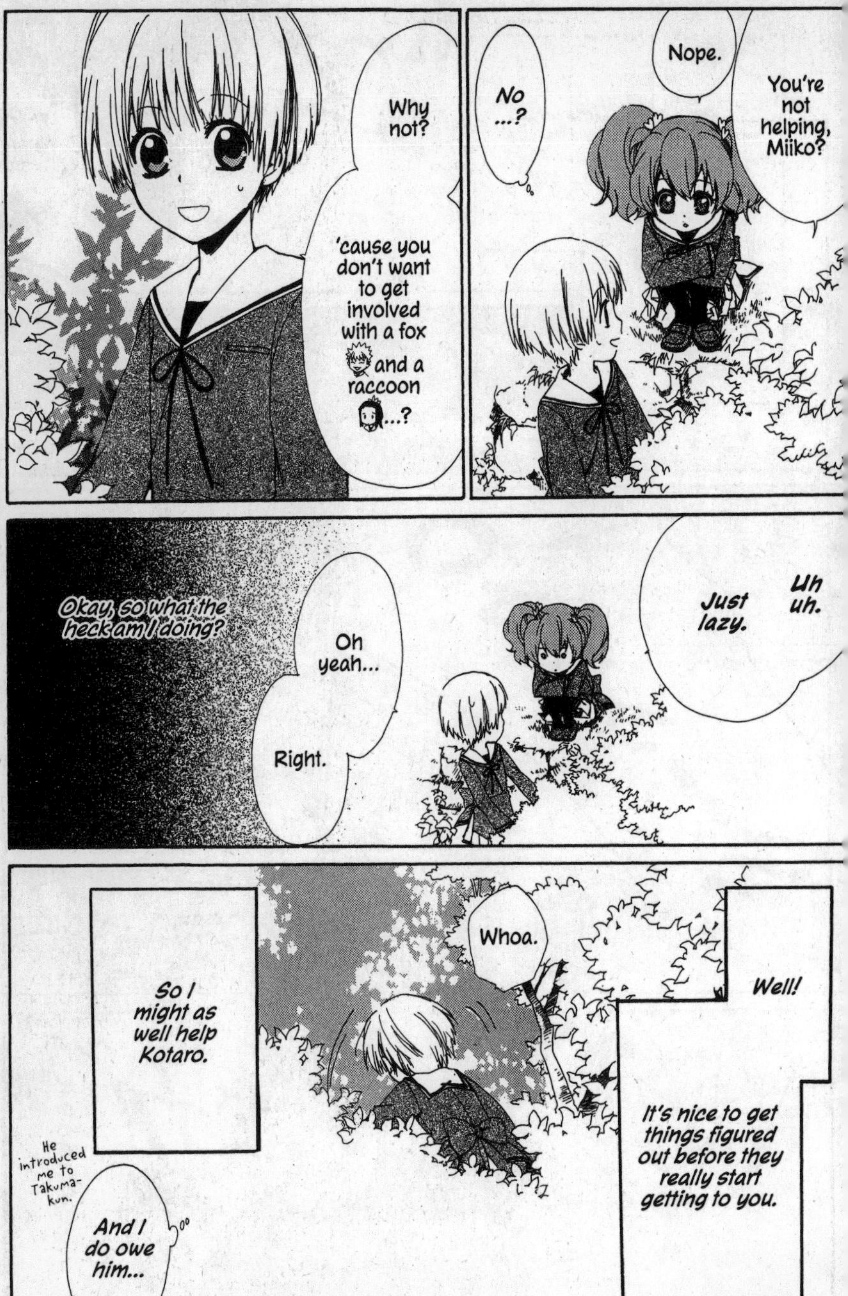
You're not helping, Miiko?
Nope.
No ...?
Why not?
'cause you don't want to get involved with a fox and a raccoon ...?
Uh uh.
Just lazy.
Oh yeah...
Right.
Okay, so what the heck am I doing?
Well!
It's nice to get things figured out before they really start getting to you.
Whoa.
So I might as well help Kotaro.
He introduced me to Takuma-kun.
And I do owe him...

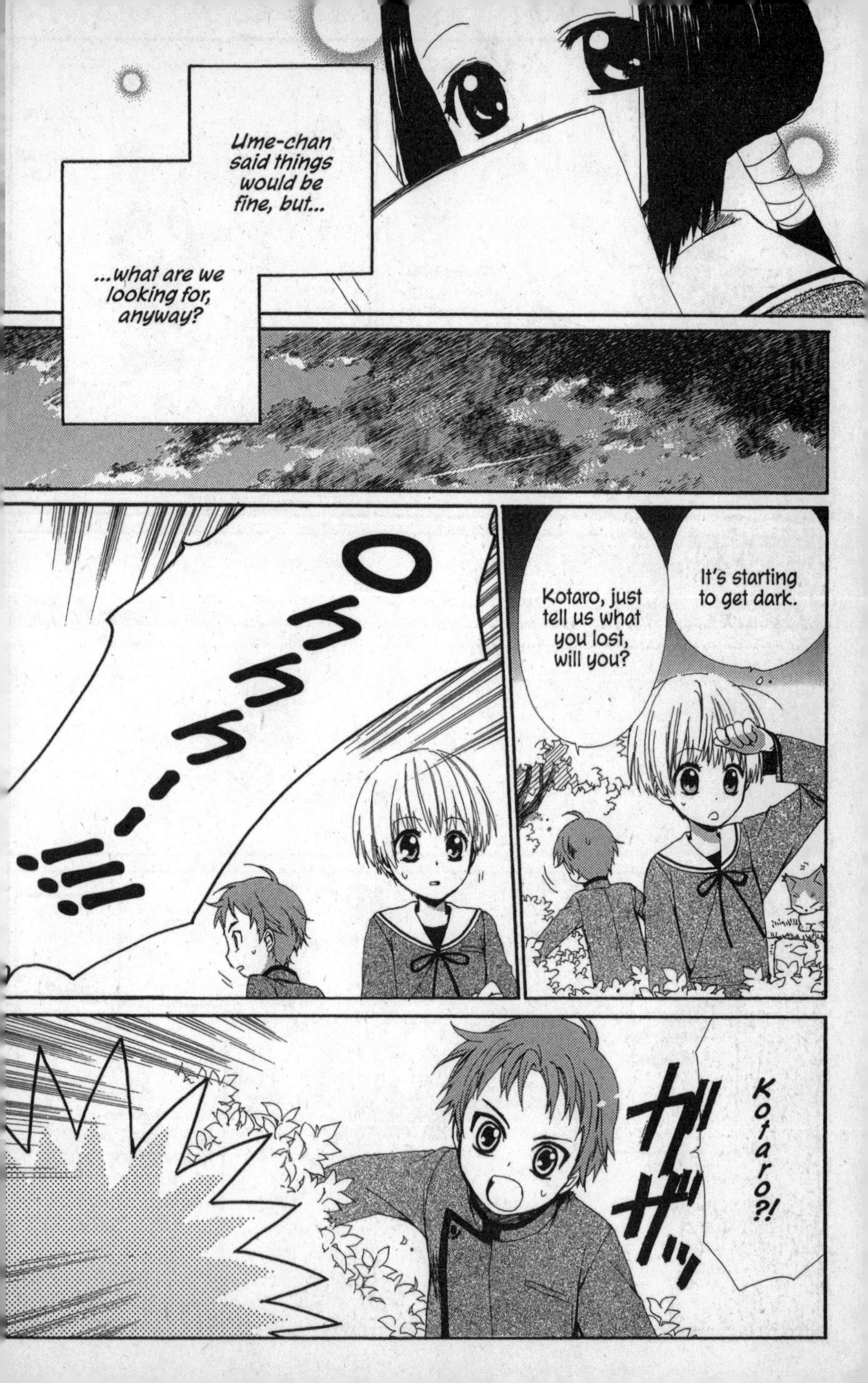
Ume-chan said things would be fine, but...
...what are we looking for, anyway?
It's starting to get dark.
Kotaro, just tell us what you lost, will you?
Kotaro?!
ガザッ

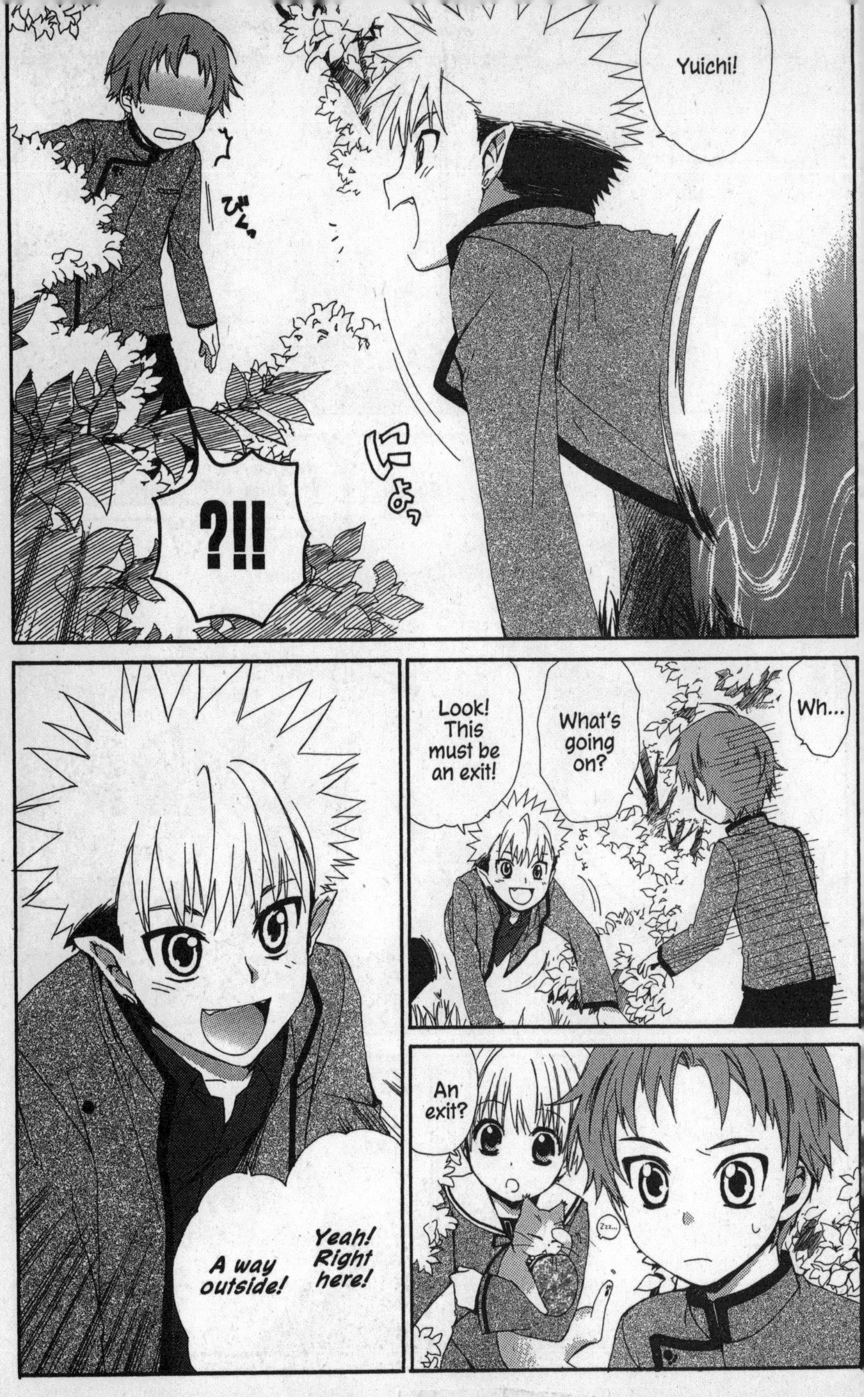
Yuichi!
?!!
Wh...
What's going on?
Look! This must be an exit!
An exit?
Zzz...
Yeah! Right here!
A way outside!

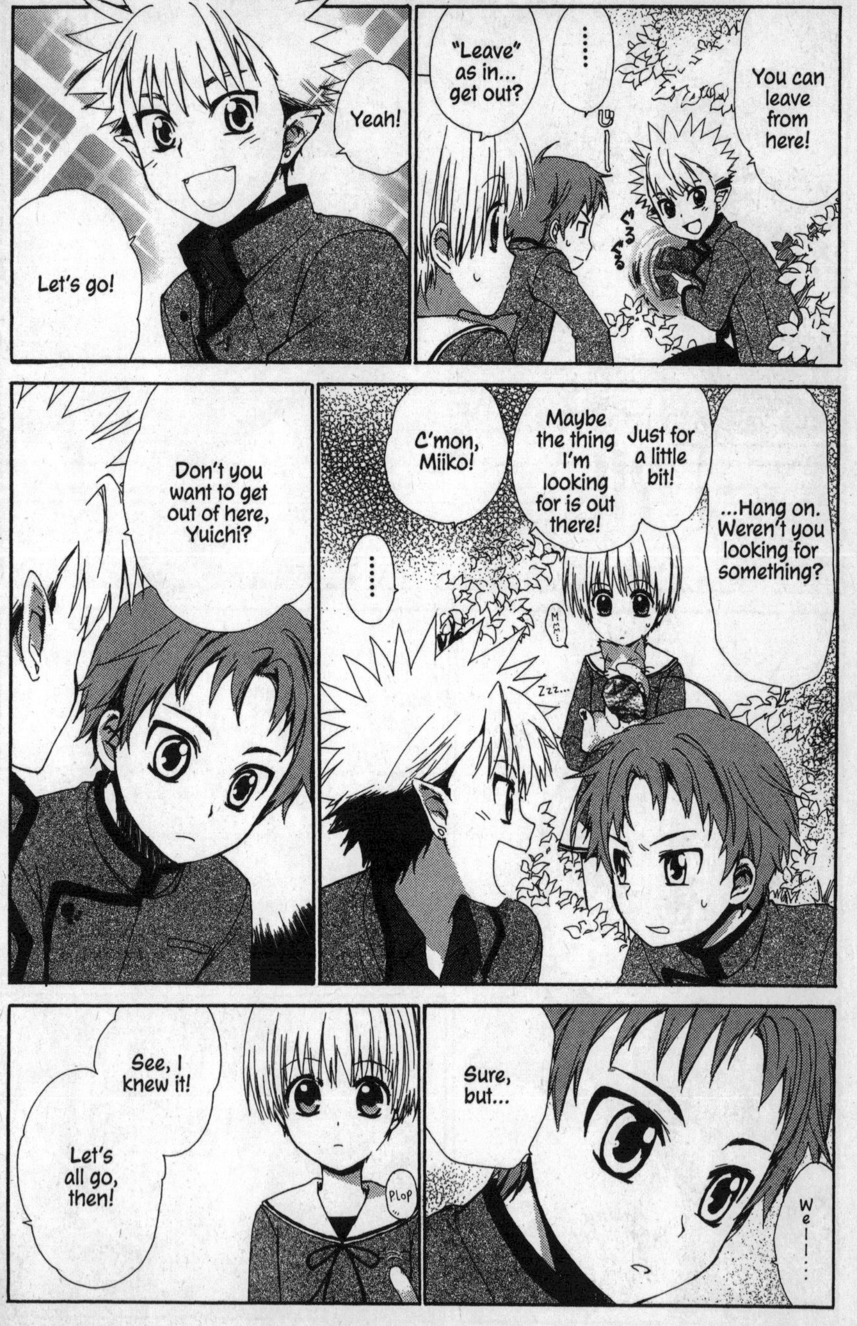
You can leave from here!
......
"Leave" as in... get out?
Yeah!
Let's go!
...Hang on. Weren't you looking for something?
Just for a little bit!
Maybe the thing I'm looking for is out there!
C'mon, Miiko!
......
Mmm...
Zzz...
Don't you want to get out of here, Yuichi?
Well...
Sure, but...
See, I knew it!
Plop
Let's all go, then!

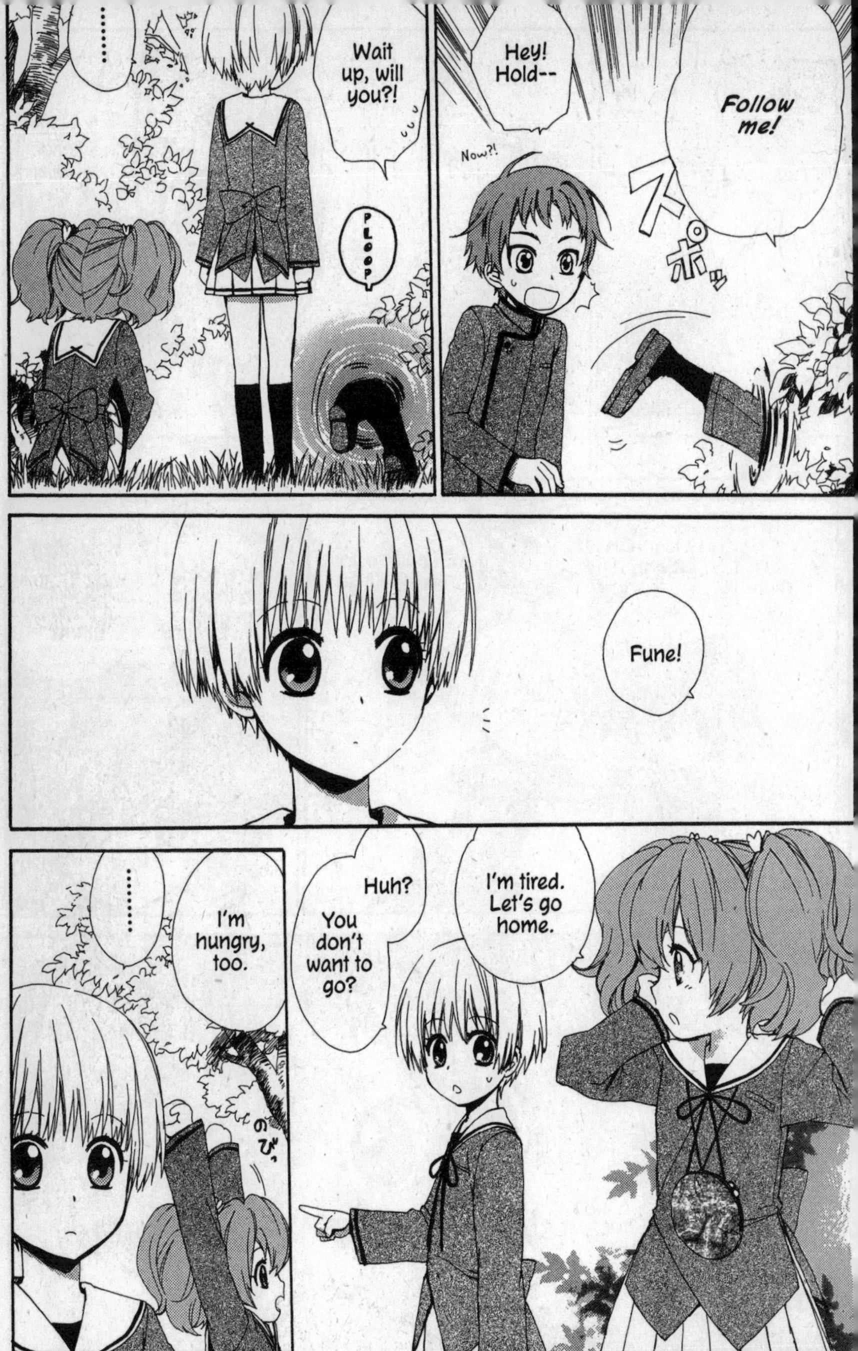
Follow me!
Hey!
Hold--
Now?!
スポッ
Wait up, will you?!
PLOOP
……
Fune!
I'm tired. Let's go home.
Huh?
You don't want to go?
I'm hungry, too.
……
のび

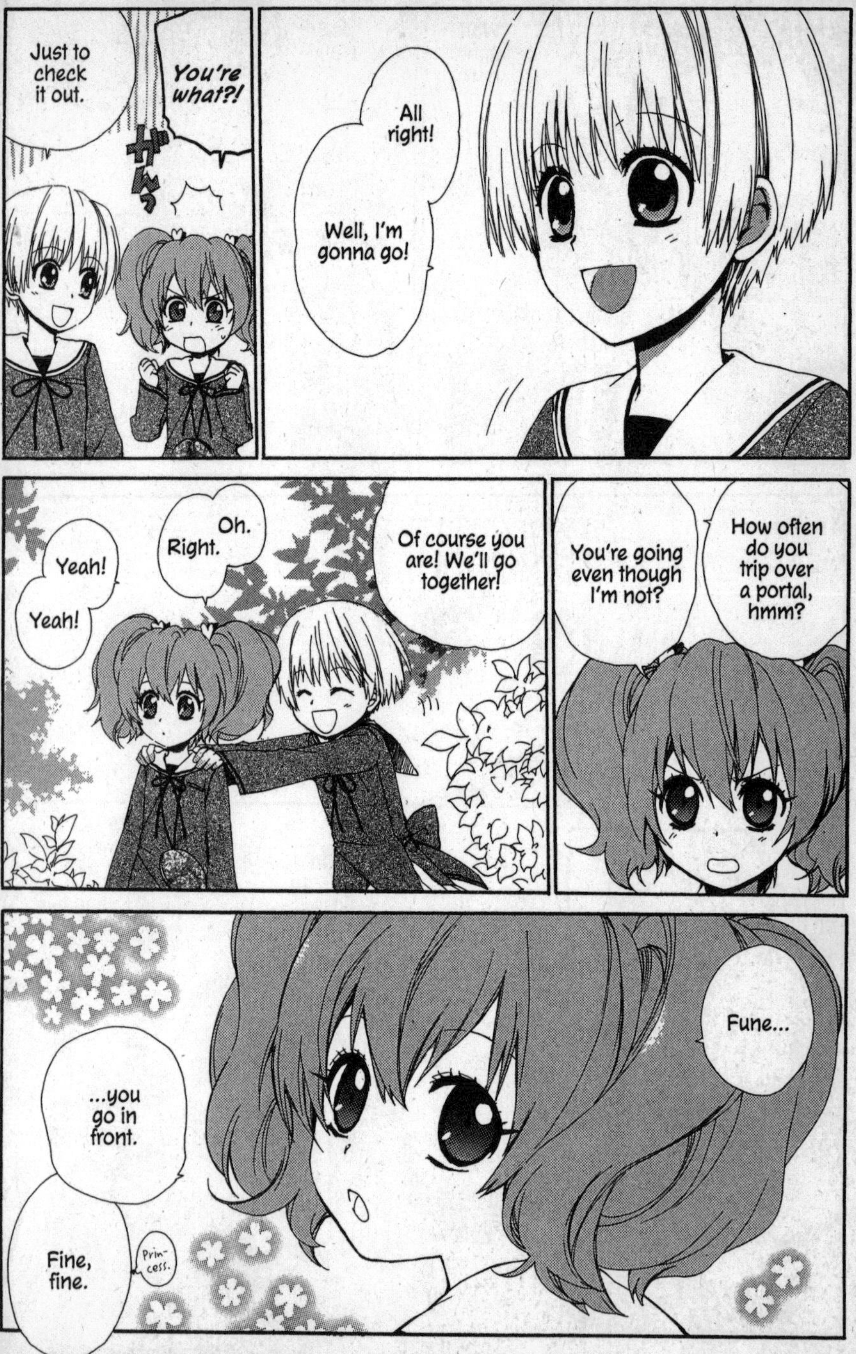
All right!
Well, I'm gonna go!
You're what?!
がんっ
Just to check it out.
How often do you trip over a portal, hmm?
You're going even though I'm not?
Of course you are! We'll go together!
Oh. Right.
Yeah!
Yeah!
Fune...
...you go in front.
Prin-cess.
Fine, fine.

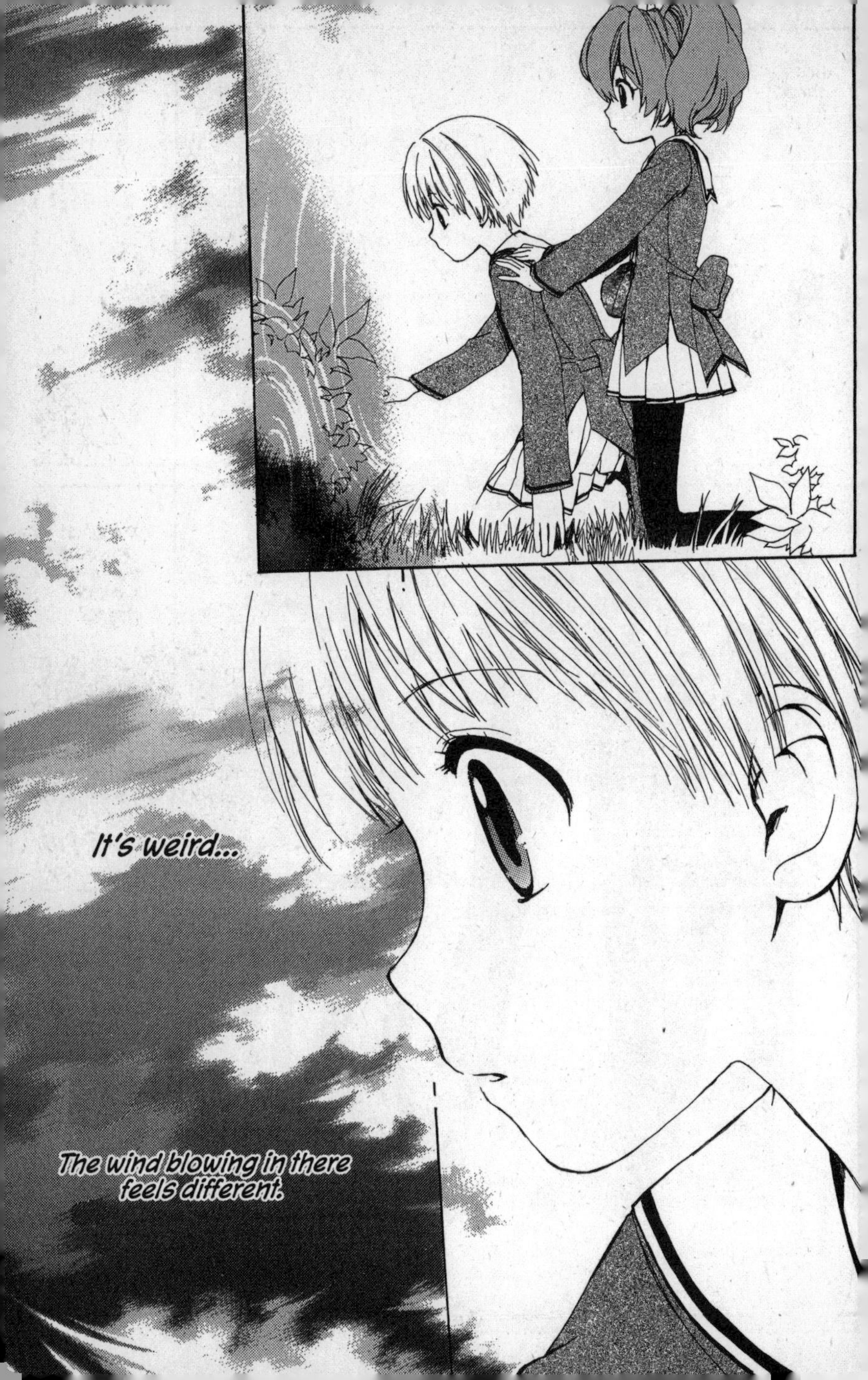
It's weird...
The wind blowing in there feels different.

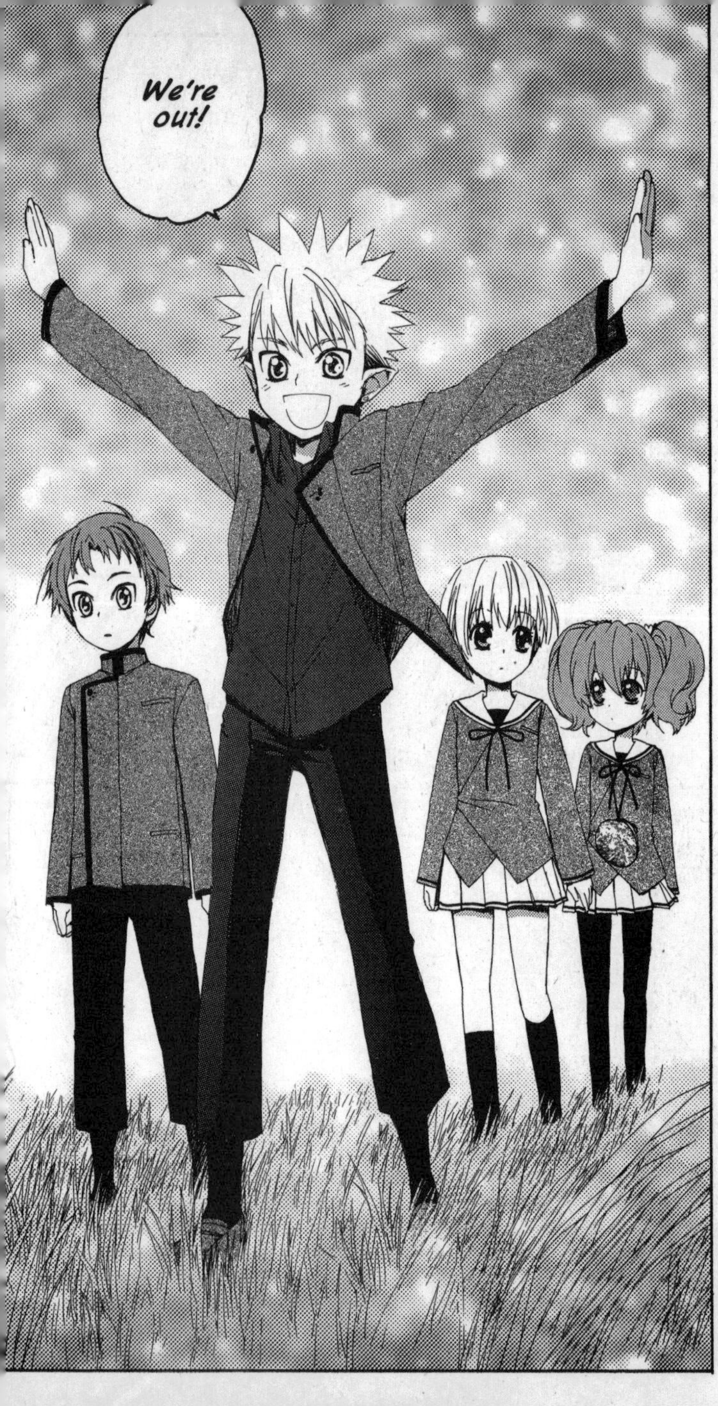
We're out!

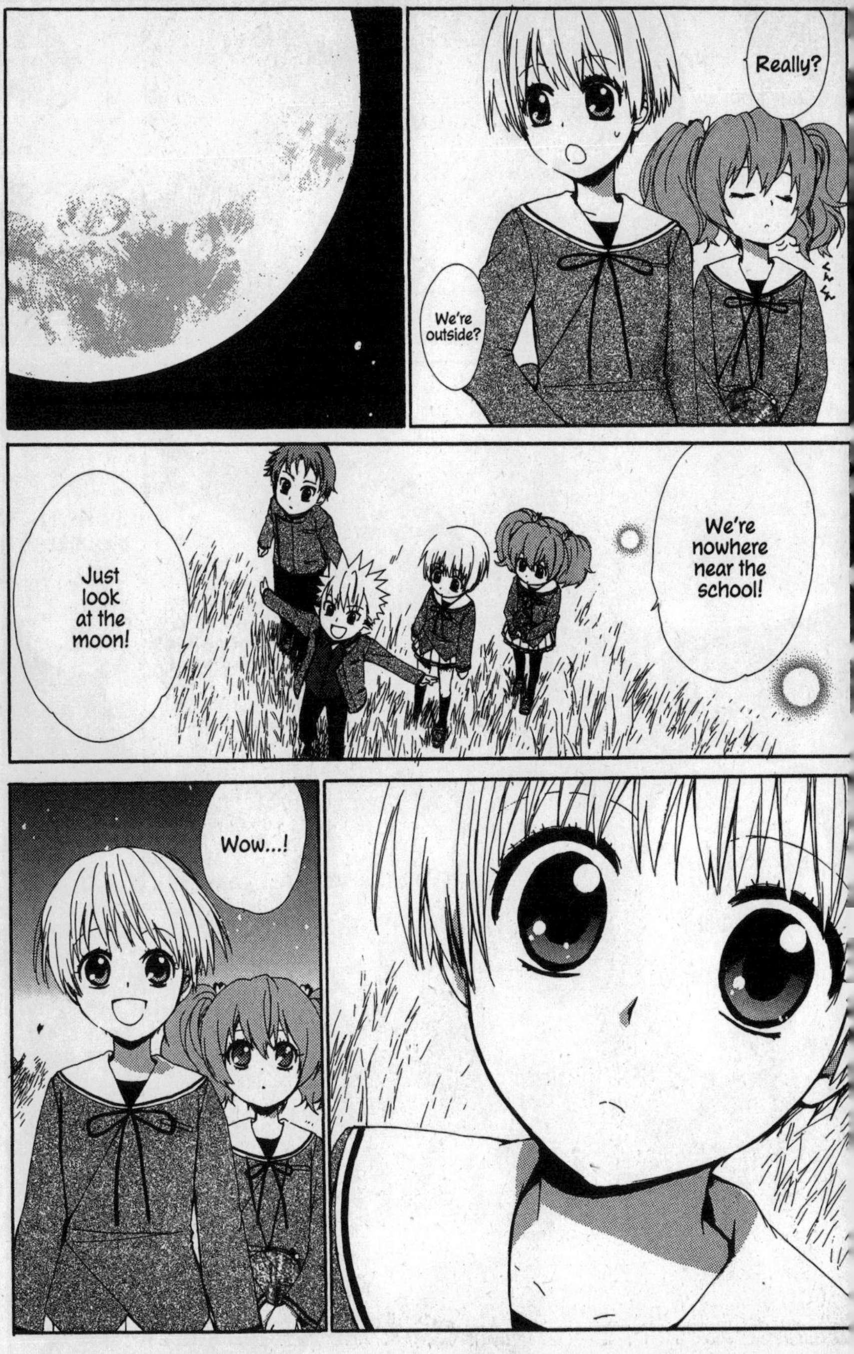
Really?
We're outside?
We're nowhere near the school!
Just look at the moon!
Wow...!

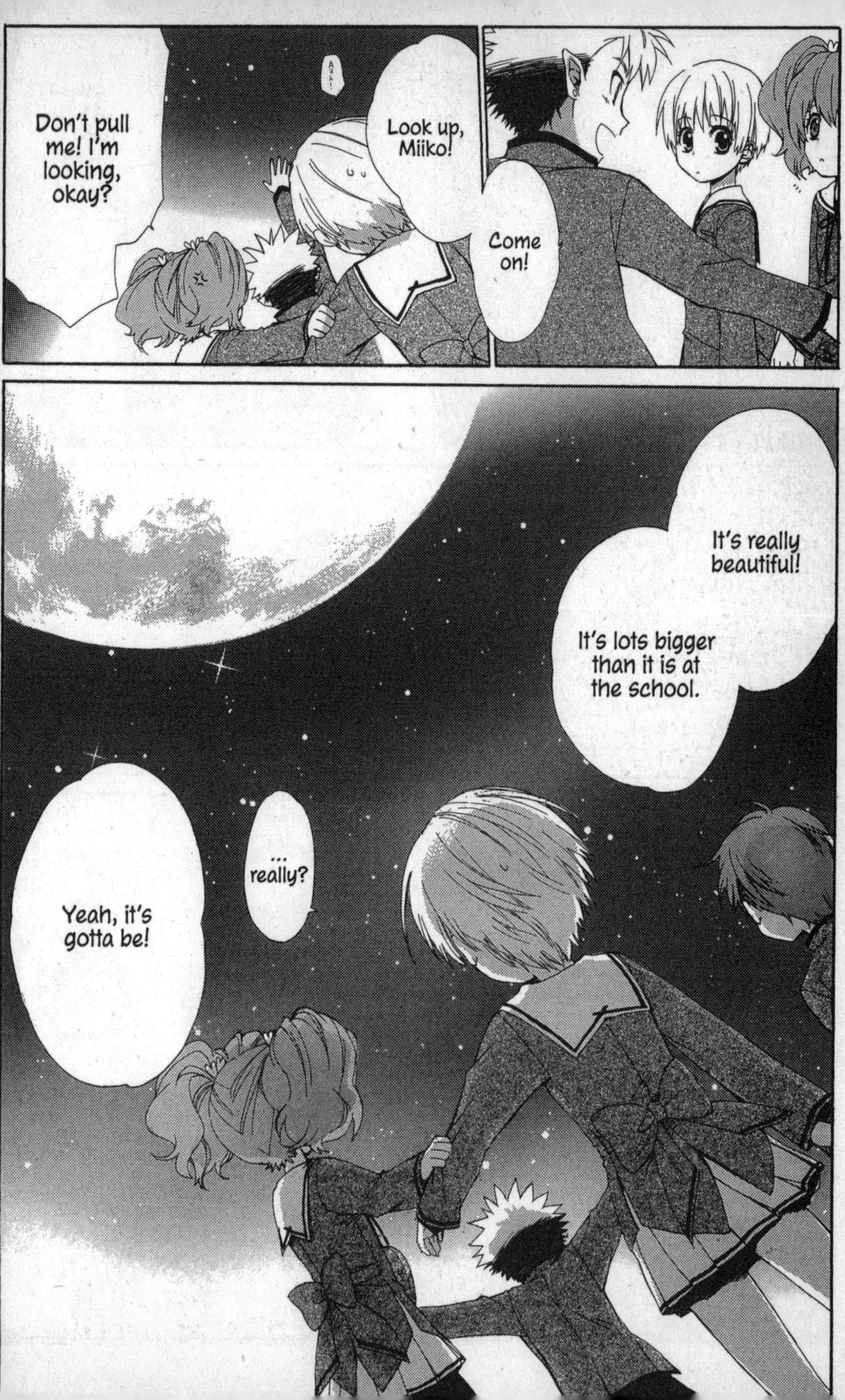
Come on!
Look up, Miiko!
Aah!
Don't pull me! I'm looking, okay?
It's really beautiful!
It's lots bigger than it is at the school.
...really?
Yeah, it's gotta be!

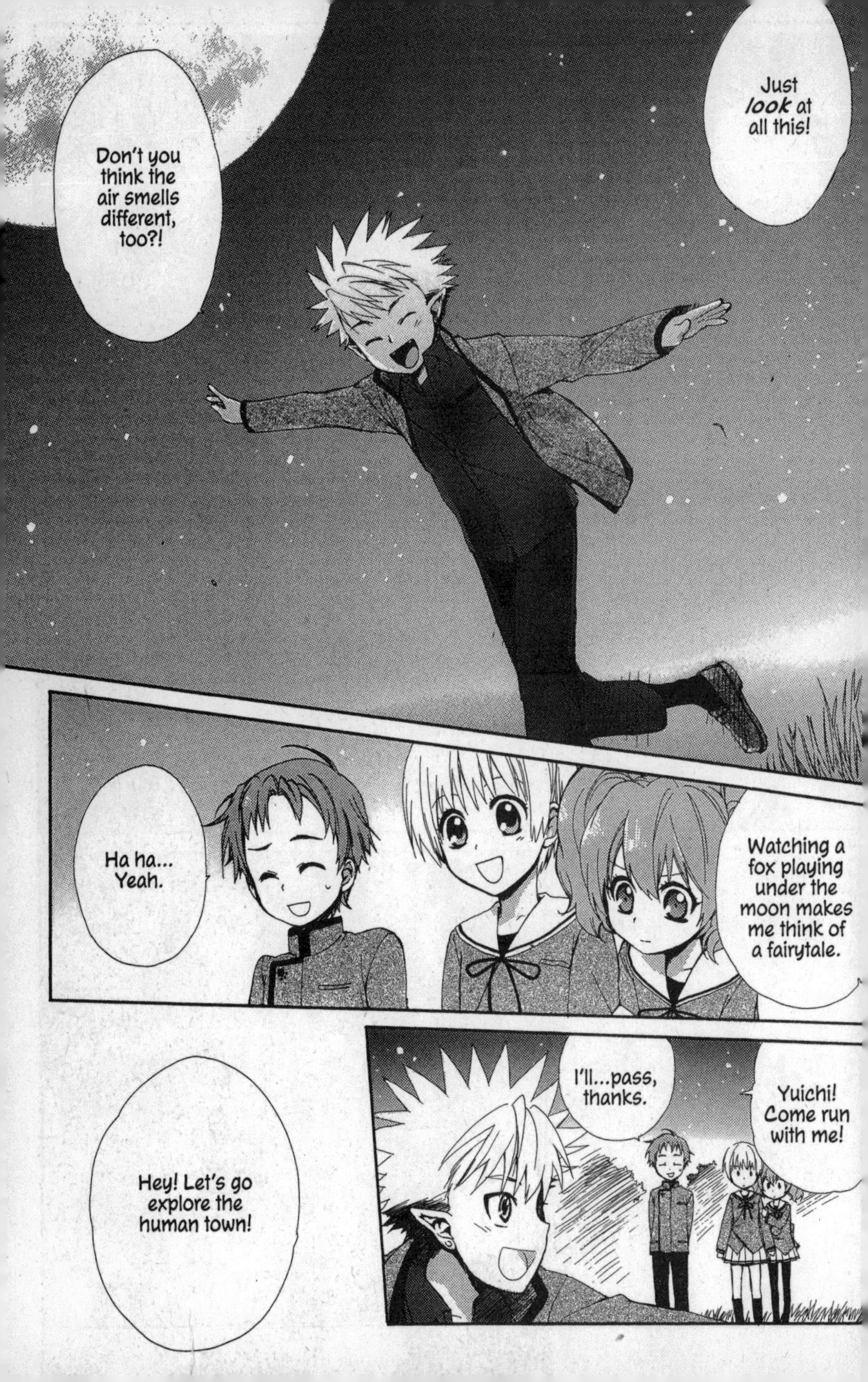
Just *look* at all this!
Don't you think the air smells different, too?!
Watching a fox playing under the moon makes me think of a fairytale.
Ha ha... Yeah.
Yuichi! Come run with me!
I'll...pass, thanks.
Hey! Let's go explore the human town!

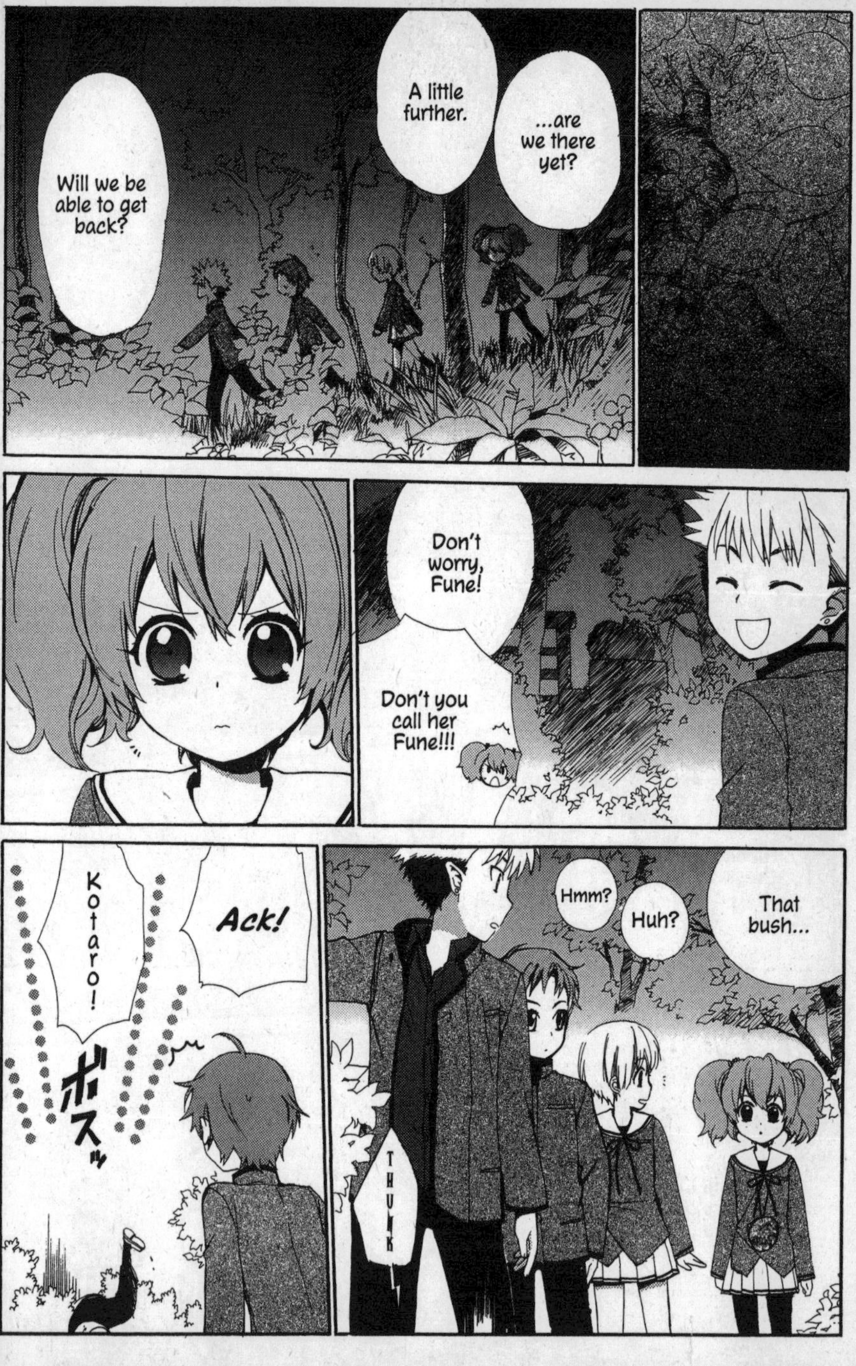
...are we there yet?
A little further.
Will we be able to get back?
Don't worry, Fune!
Don't you call her Fune!!!
That bush...
Huh?
Hmm?
THUNK
Ack!
Kotaro!
ボスッ

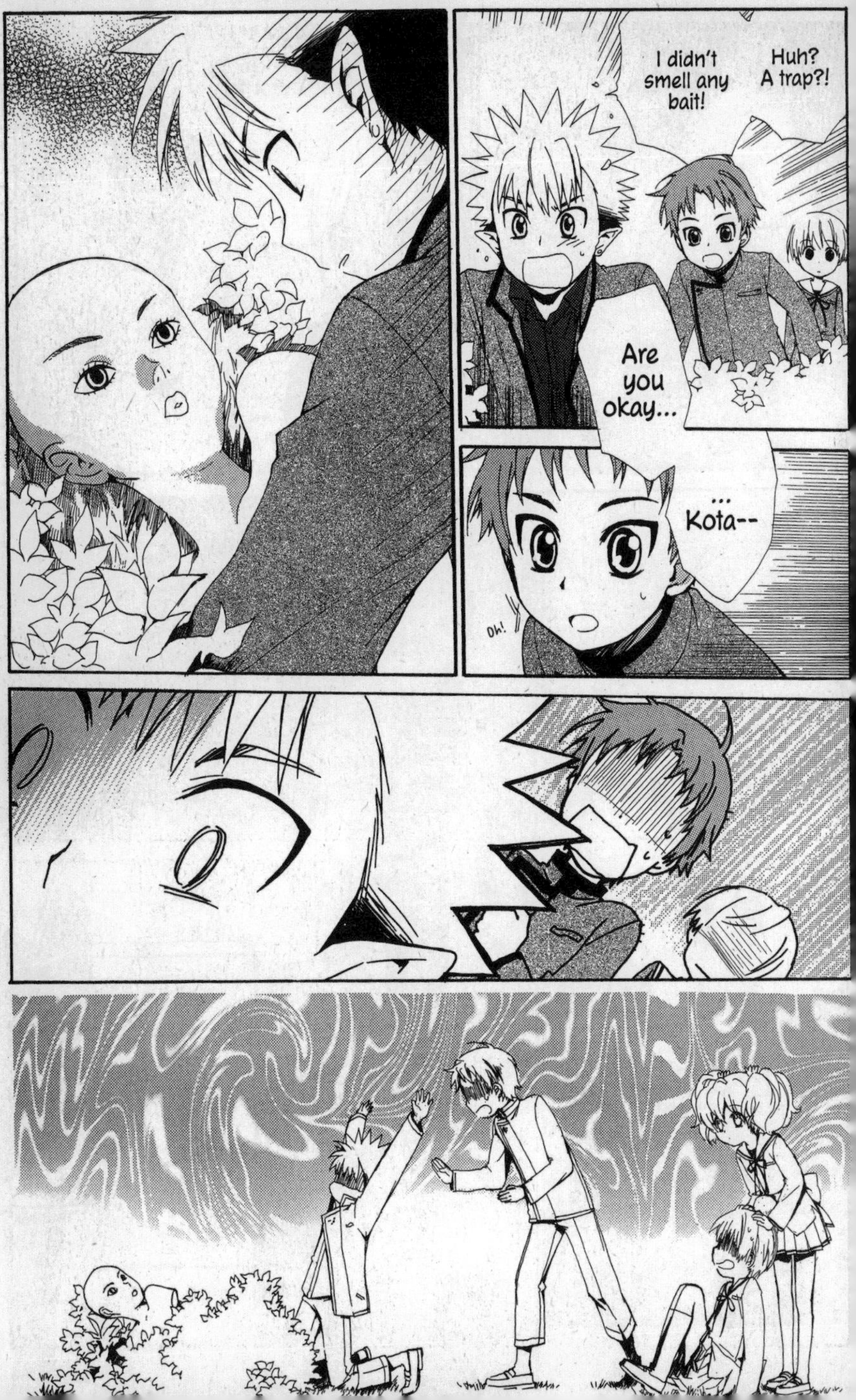
Huh? A trap?!
I didn't smell any bait!
Are you okay...
... Kota--
Oh!

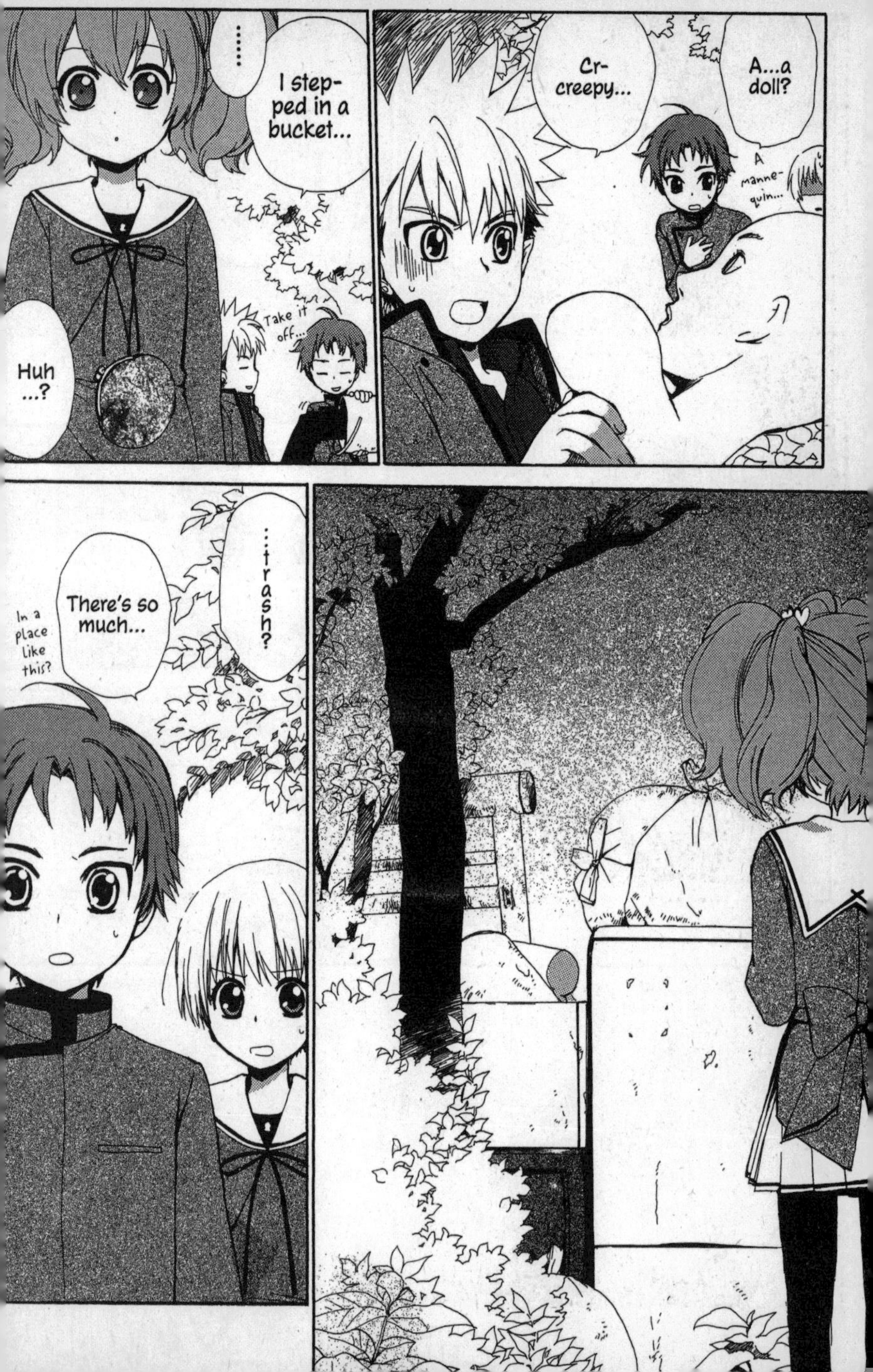
A...a doll?
A manne-quin...
Cr-creepy...
......
I step-ped in a bucket...
Take it off...
Huh ...?
...trash?
There's so much...
In a place like this?

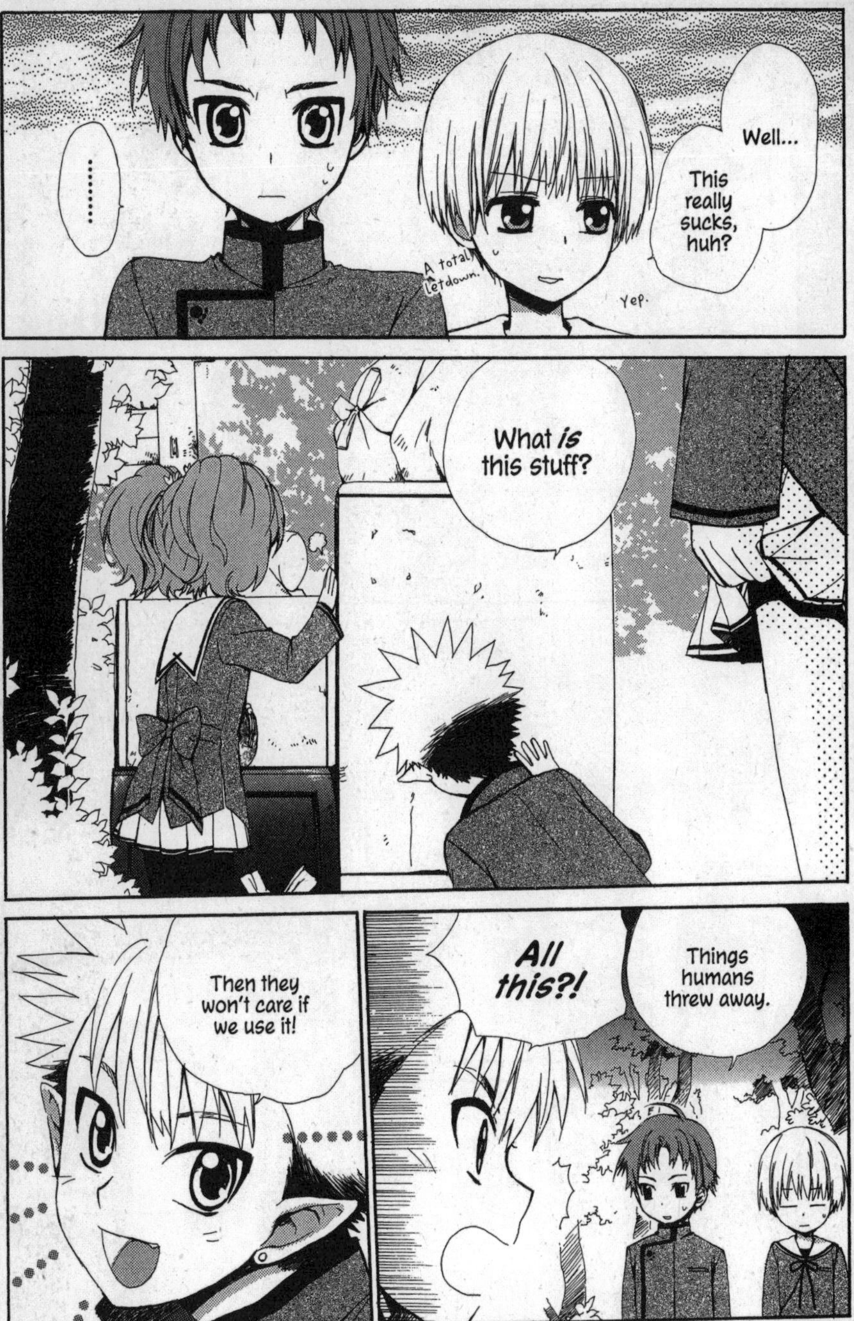
Well...
This really sucks, huh?
A total letdown.
Yep.
......
What *is* this stuff?
Things humans threw away.
All this?!
Then they won't care if we use it!

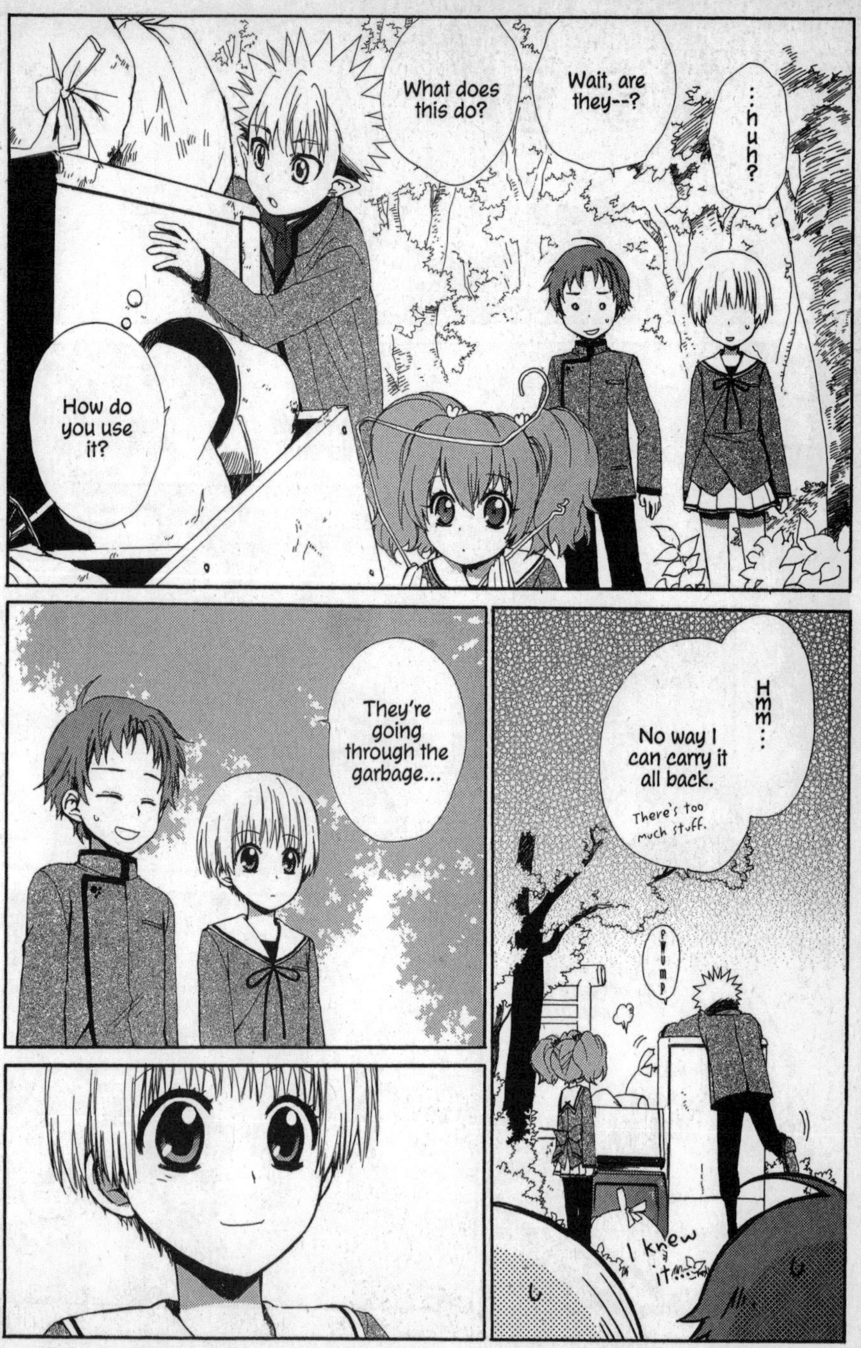
...huh?
Wait, are they--?
What does this do?
How do you use it?
Hmm...
No way I can carry it all back.
There's too much stuff.
FWUMP
I knew it...
They're going through the garbage...

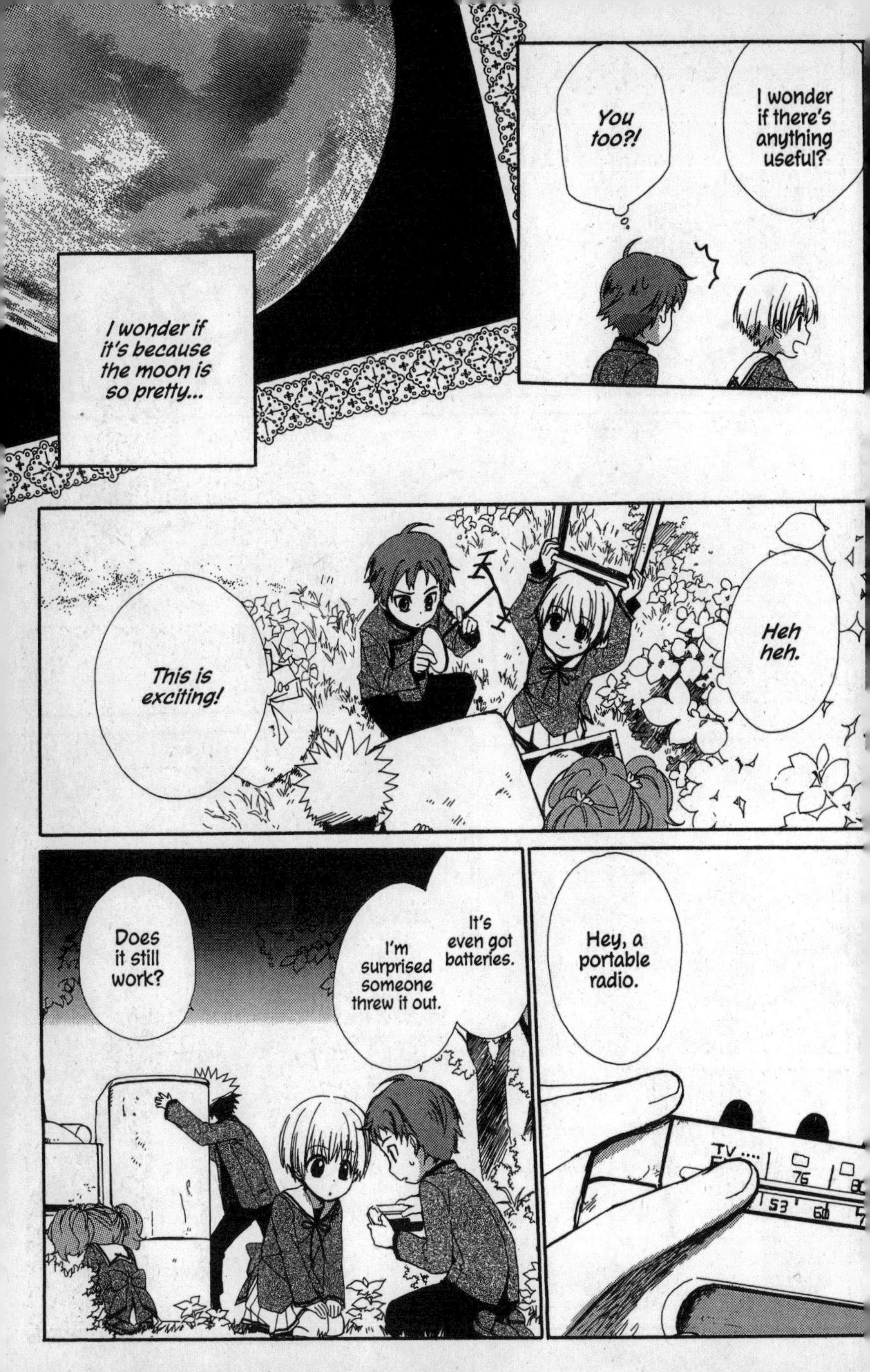
I wonder if there's anything useful?
You too?!
I wonder if it's because the moon is so pretty...
Heh heh.
This is exciting!
Hey, a portable radio.
It's even got batteries.
I'm surprised someone threw it out.
Does it still work?

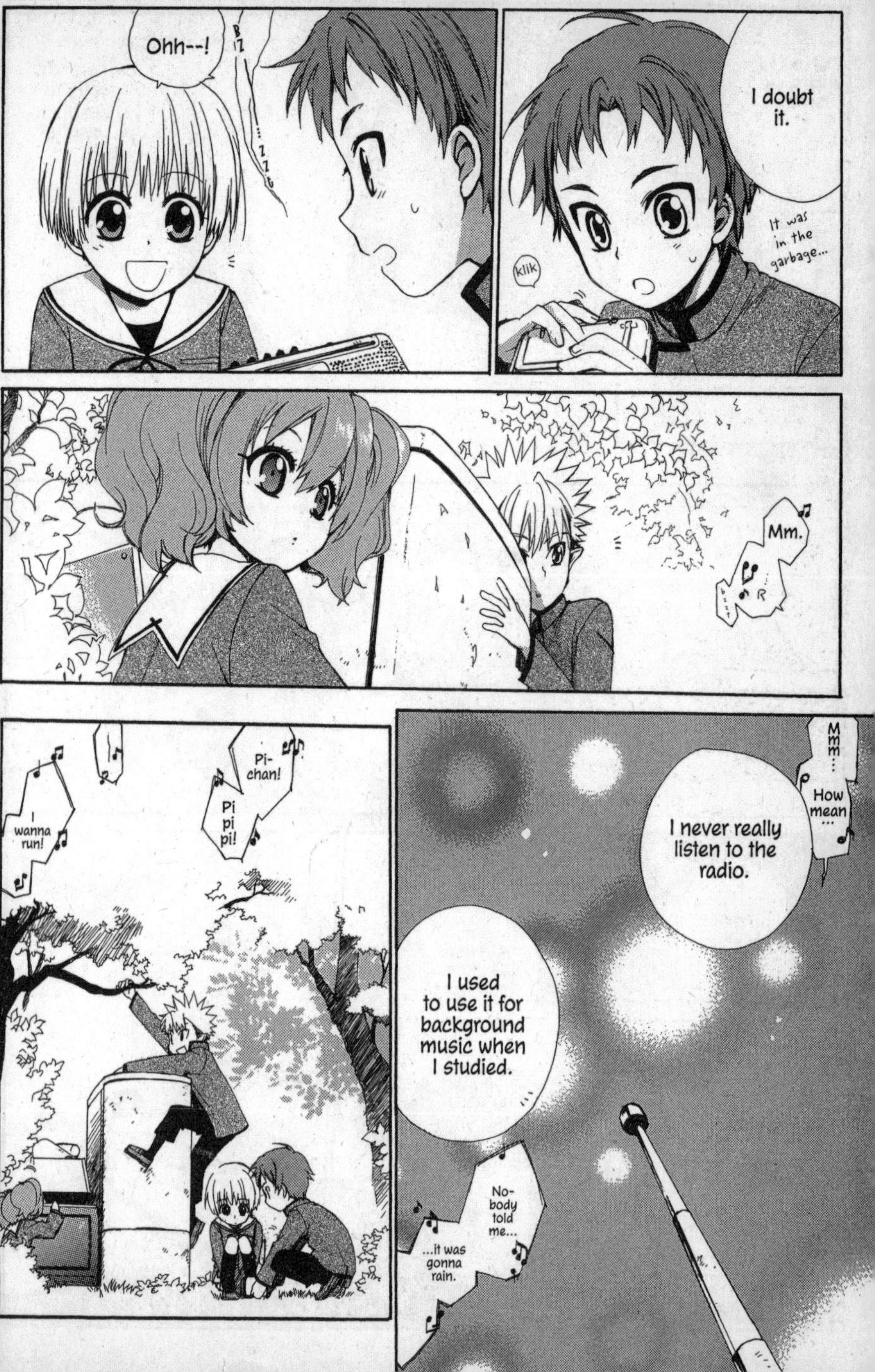
I doubt it.
It was in the garbage...
klik
Ohh--!
Mm.
Mmm... How mean...
I never really listen to the radio.
I used to use it for background music when I studied.
No-body told me...
...it was gonna rain.
Pi-chan!
Pi pi pi!
I wanna run!

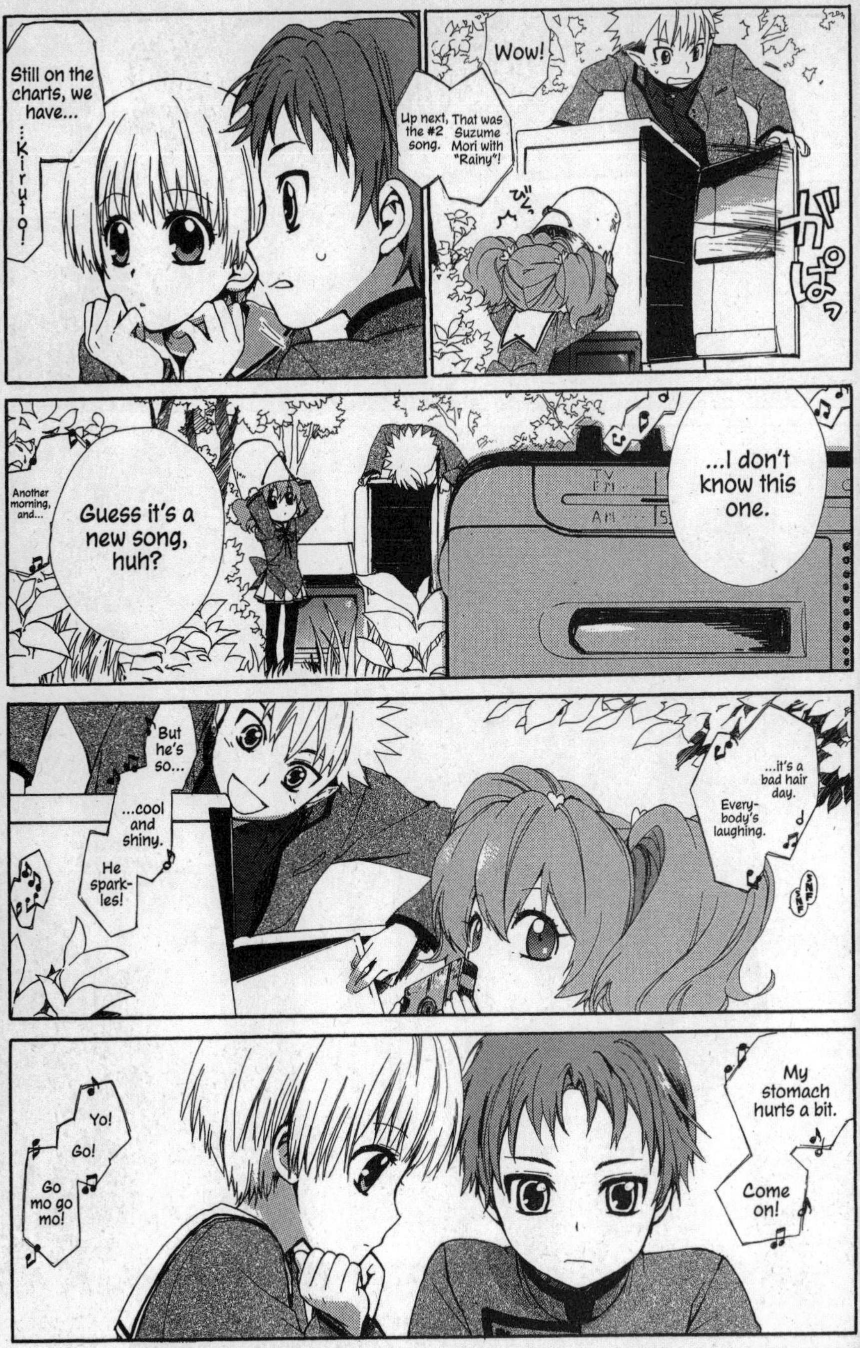

Wow!
That was Suzume Mori with "Rainy"!
Up next, the #2 song.
がぱっ
Still on the charts, we have...
...Kiruto!
...I don't know this one.
Guess it's a new song, huh?
Another morning, and...
...it's a bad hair day.
Everybody's laughing.
SNF SNF
But he's so...
...cool and shiny.
He sparkles!
My stomach hurts a bit.
Come on!
Yo!
Go!
Go mo go mo!

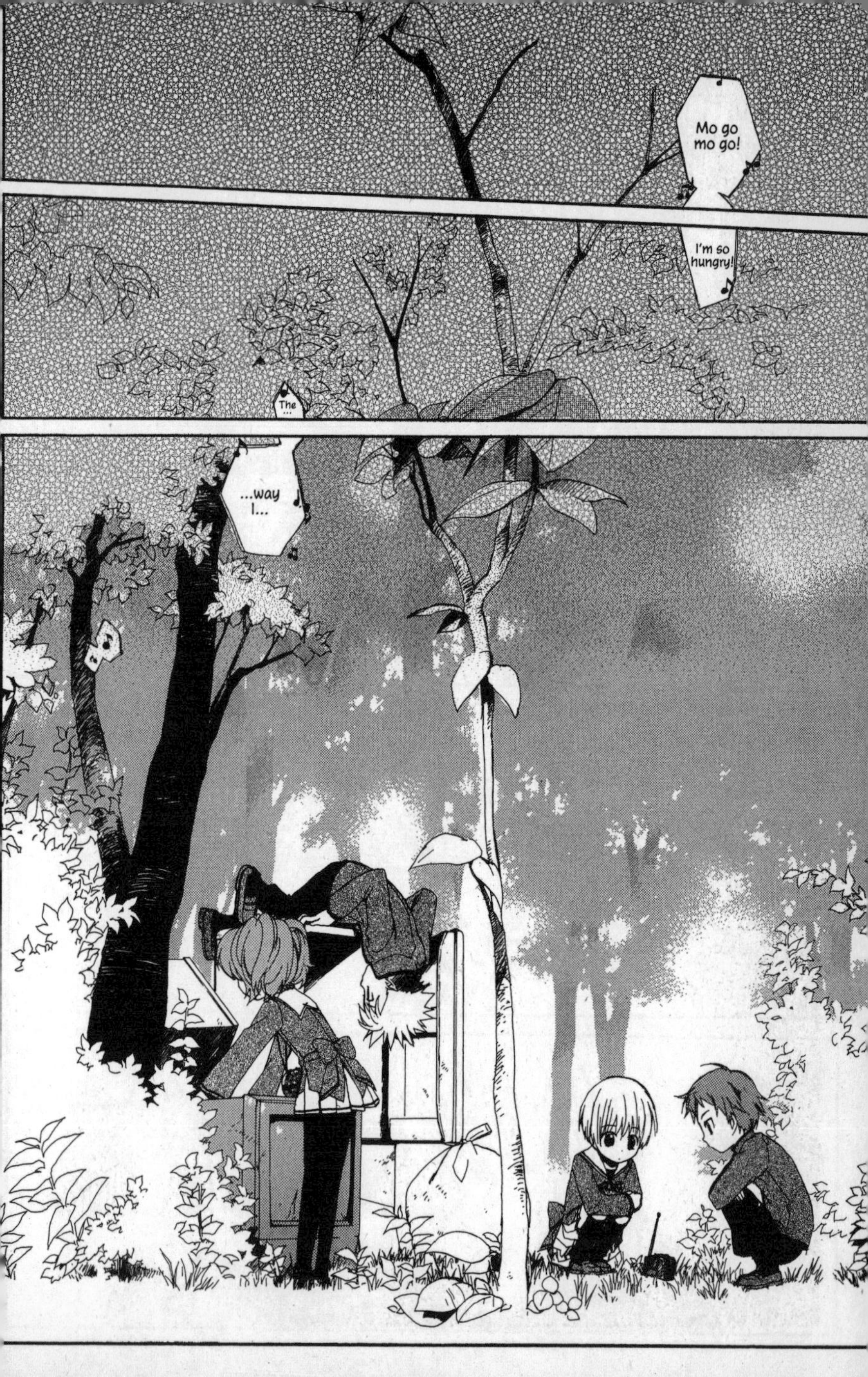
Mo go mo go!
I'm so hungry!
The...
...way I...

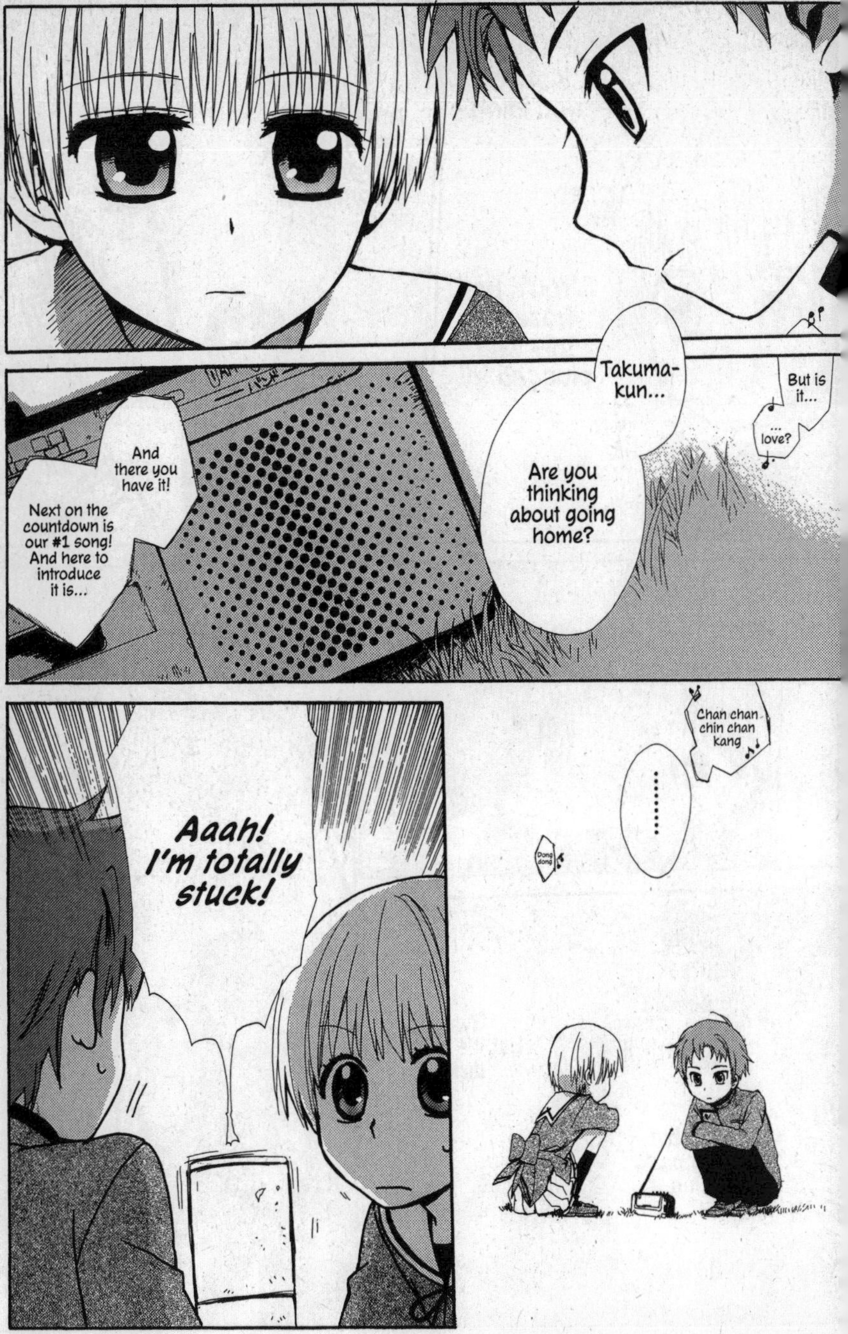
But is it...
... love?
Takuma-kun...
Are you thinking about going home?
And there you have it!
Next on the countdown is our #1 song! And here to introduce it is...
Chan chan chin chan kang
......
Dong dong
Aaah! I'm totally stuck!

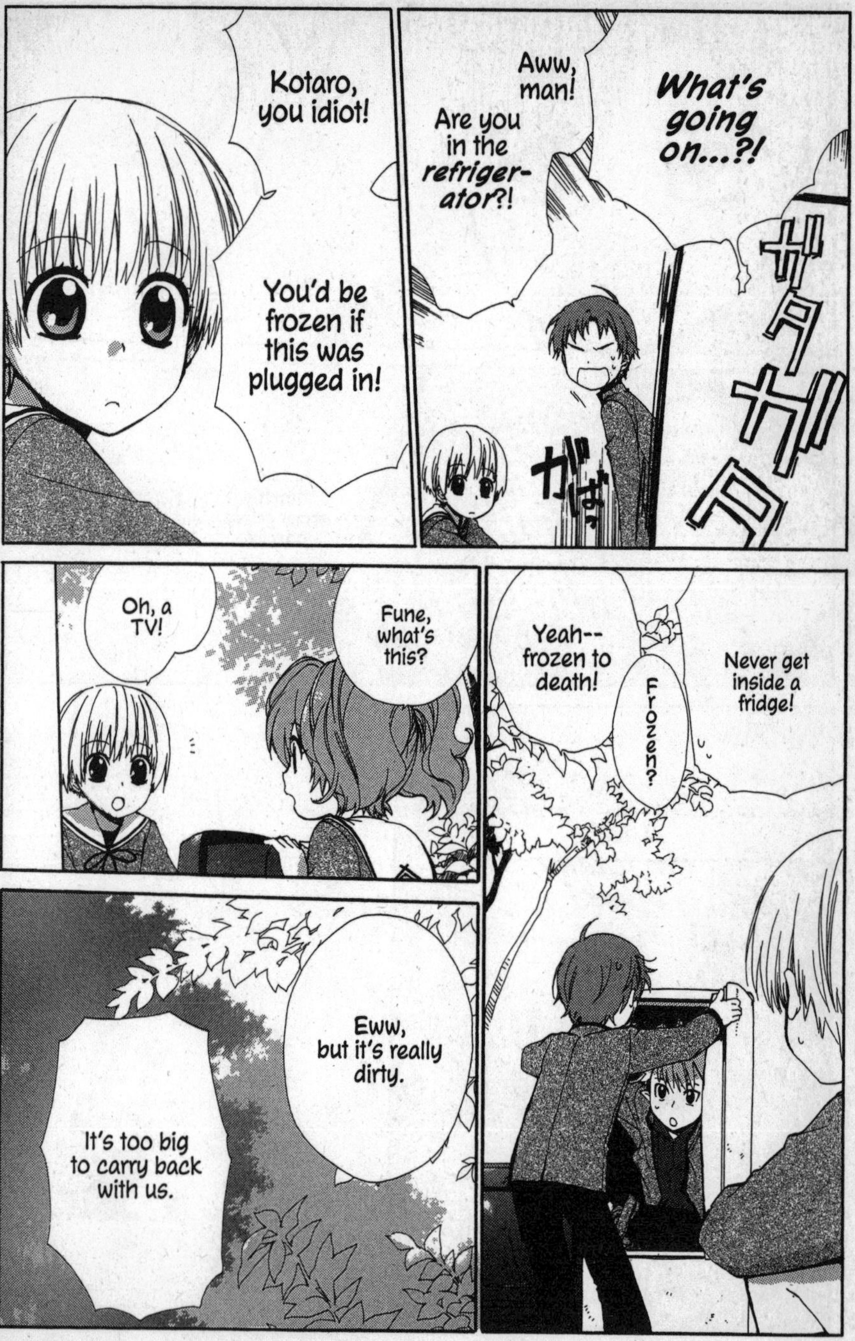
What's going on...?!
Aww, man!
Are you in the refrigerator?!
ガタガタ
がばっ
Kotaro, you idiot!
You'd be frozen if this was plugged in!
Never get inside a fridge!
Frozen?
Yeah-- frozen to death!
Fune, what's this?
Oh, a TV!
Eww, but it's really dirty.
It's too big to carry back with us.

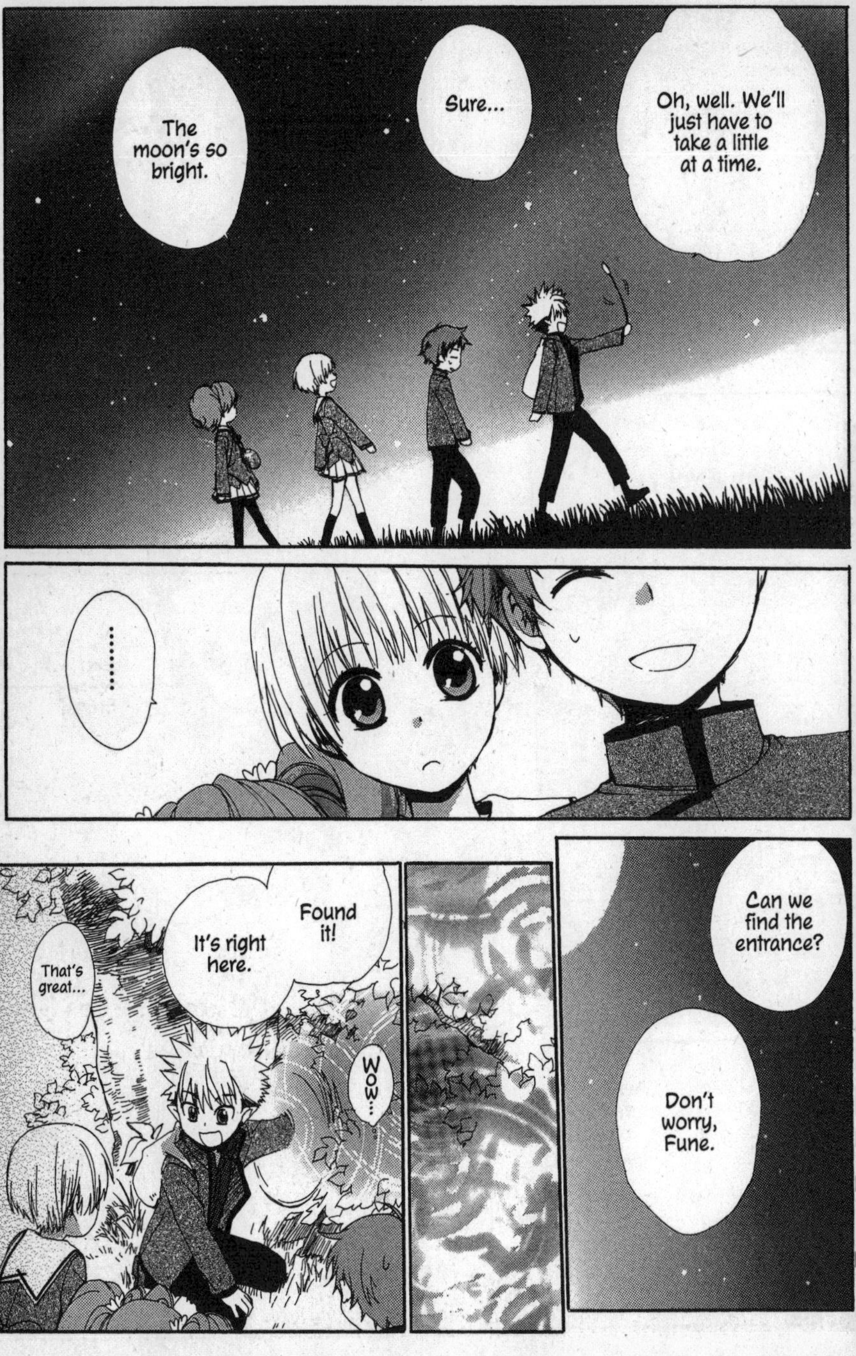

Oh, well. We'll just have to take a little at a time.
Sure...
The moon's so bright.
......
Can we find the entrance?
Don't worry, Fune.
Found it!
It's right here.
That's great...
Wow...

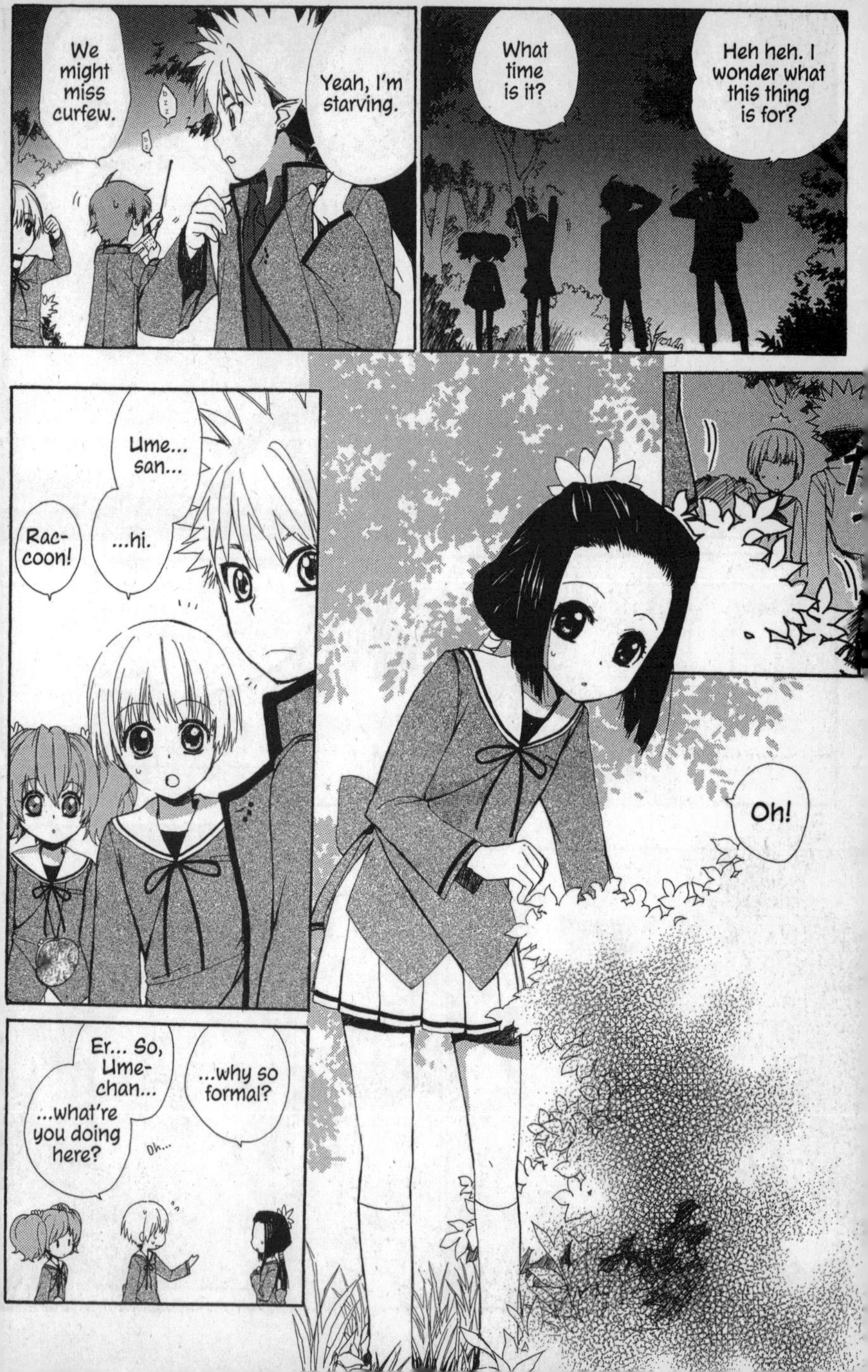
Heh heh. I wonder what this thing is for?
What time is it?
Yeah, I'm starving.
We might miss curfew.
Oh!
Ume... san...
...hi.
Rac-coon!
...why so formal?
Er... So, Ume-chan... ...what're you doing here?
Oh...

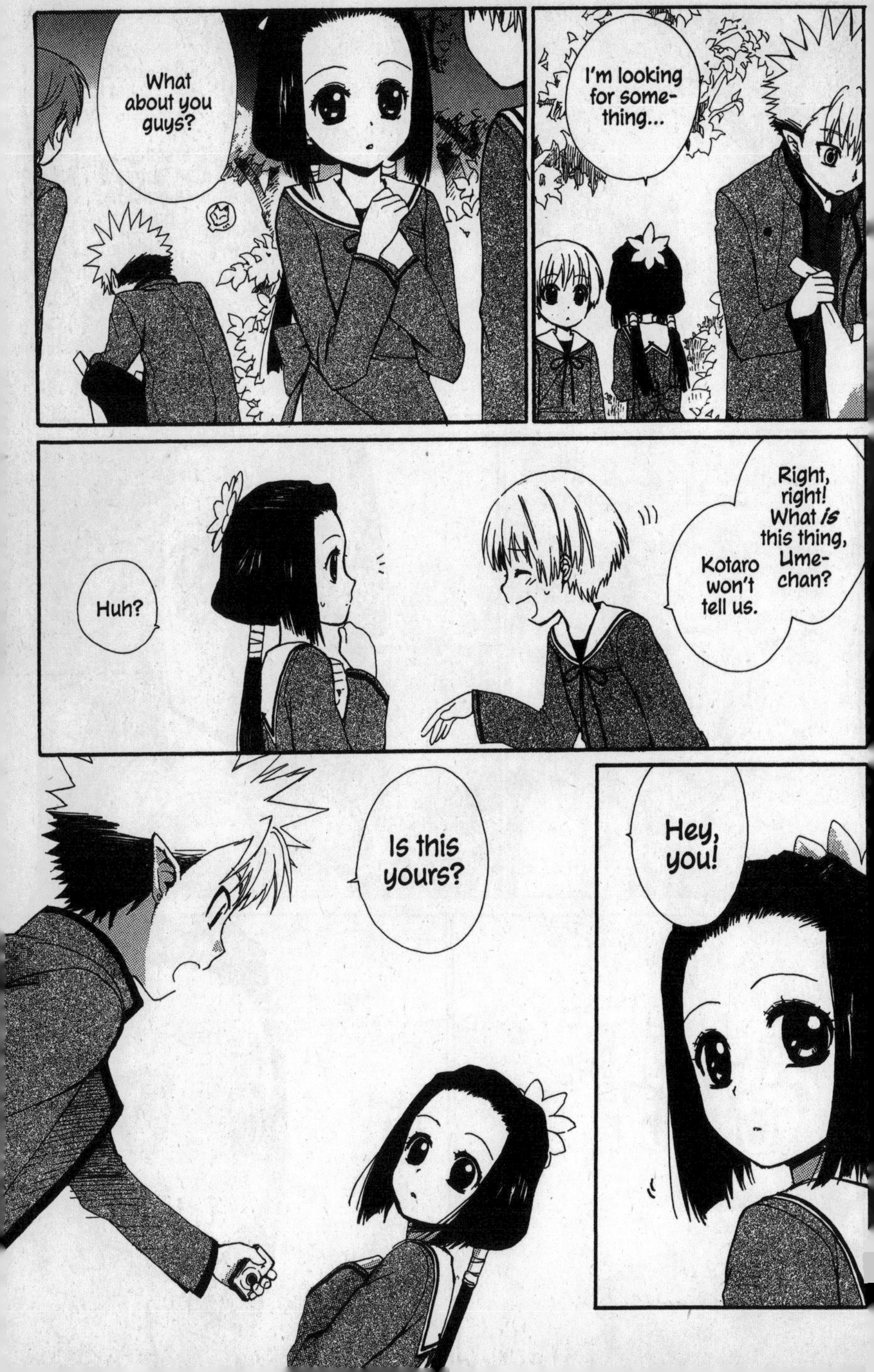
I'm looking for some-thing...
What about you guys?
Right, right! What *is* this thing, Ume-chan?
Kotaro won't tell us.
Huh?
Hey, you!
Is this yours?

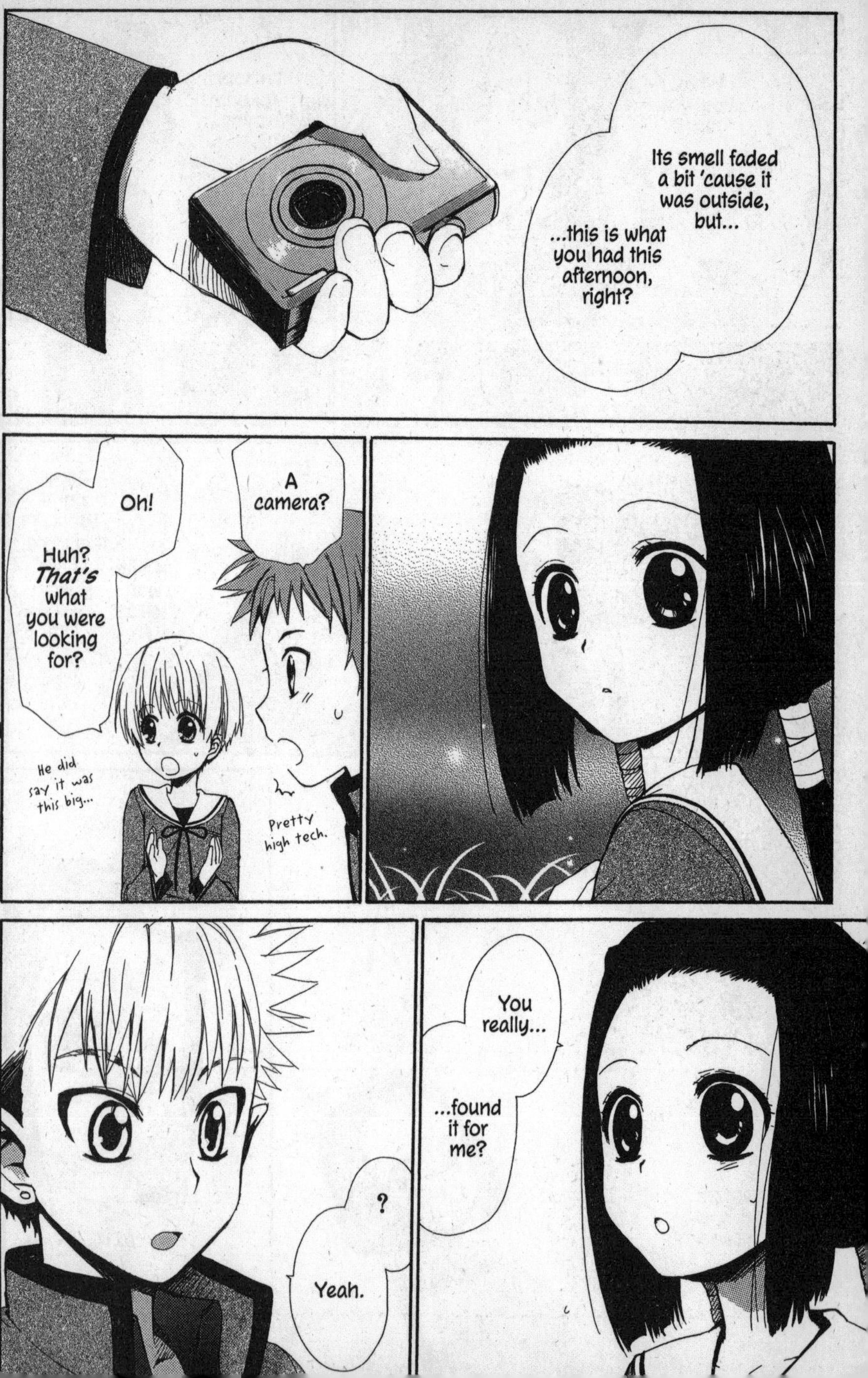
Its smell faded a bit 'cause it was outside, but...
...this is what you had this afternoon, right?
A camera?
Oh!
Huh? *That's* what you were looking for?
Pretty high tech.
He did say it was this big...
You really...
...found it for me?
?
Yeah.

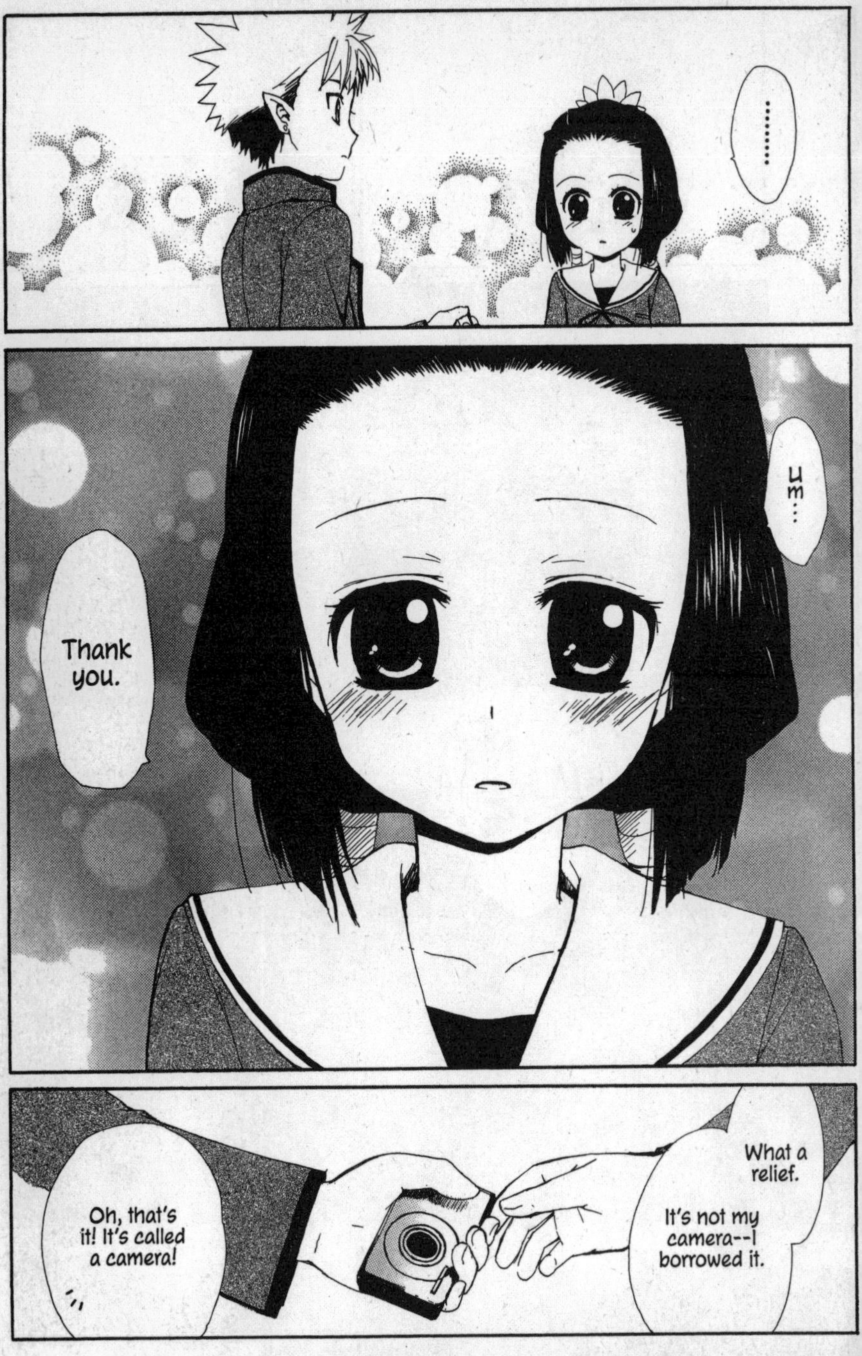
......
Um...
Thank you.
What a relief.
It's not my camera--I borrowed it.
Oh, that's it! It's called a camera!

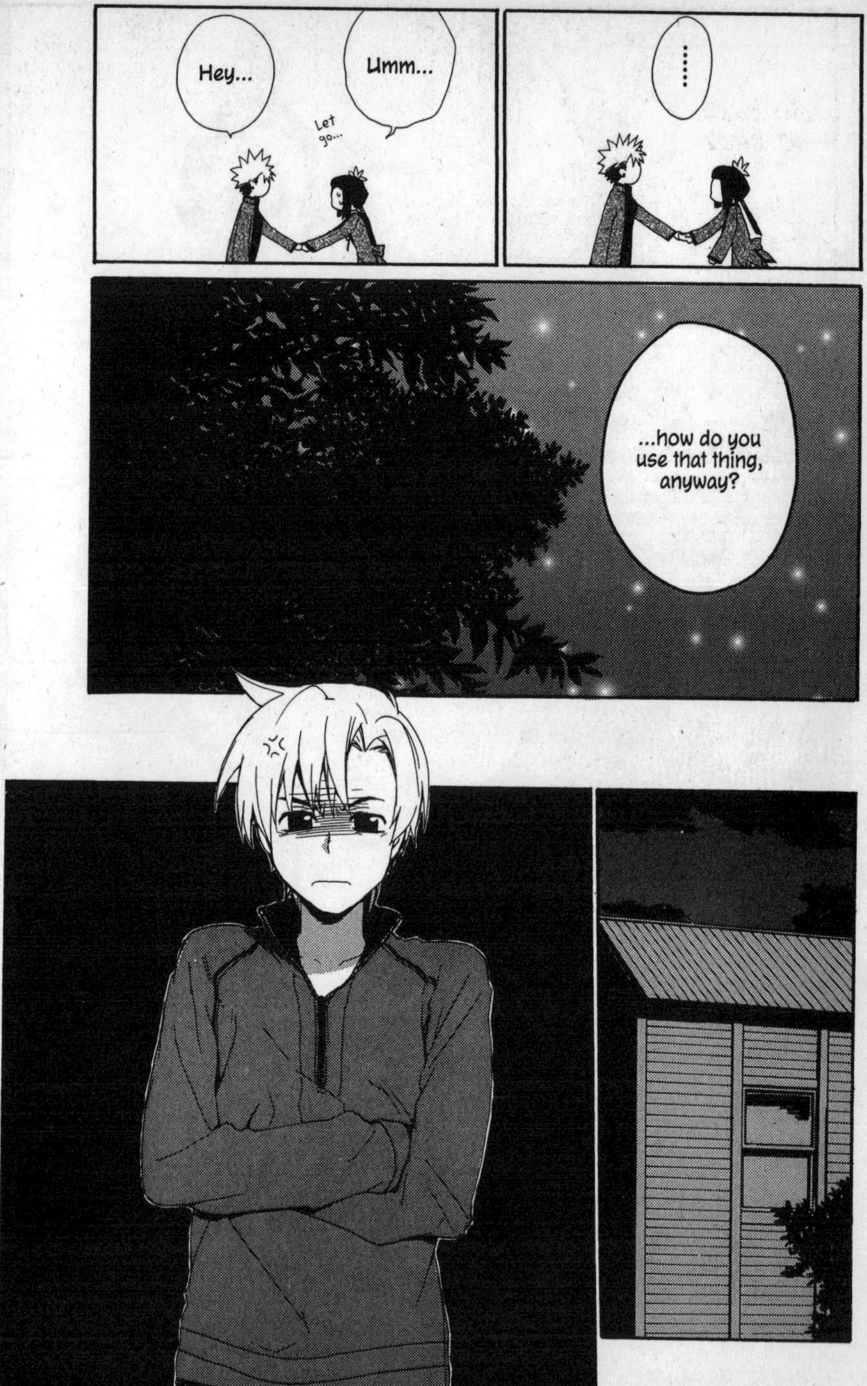
......
Umm...
Let go...
Hey...
...how do you use that thing, anyway?

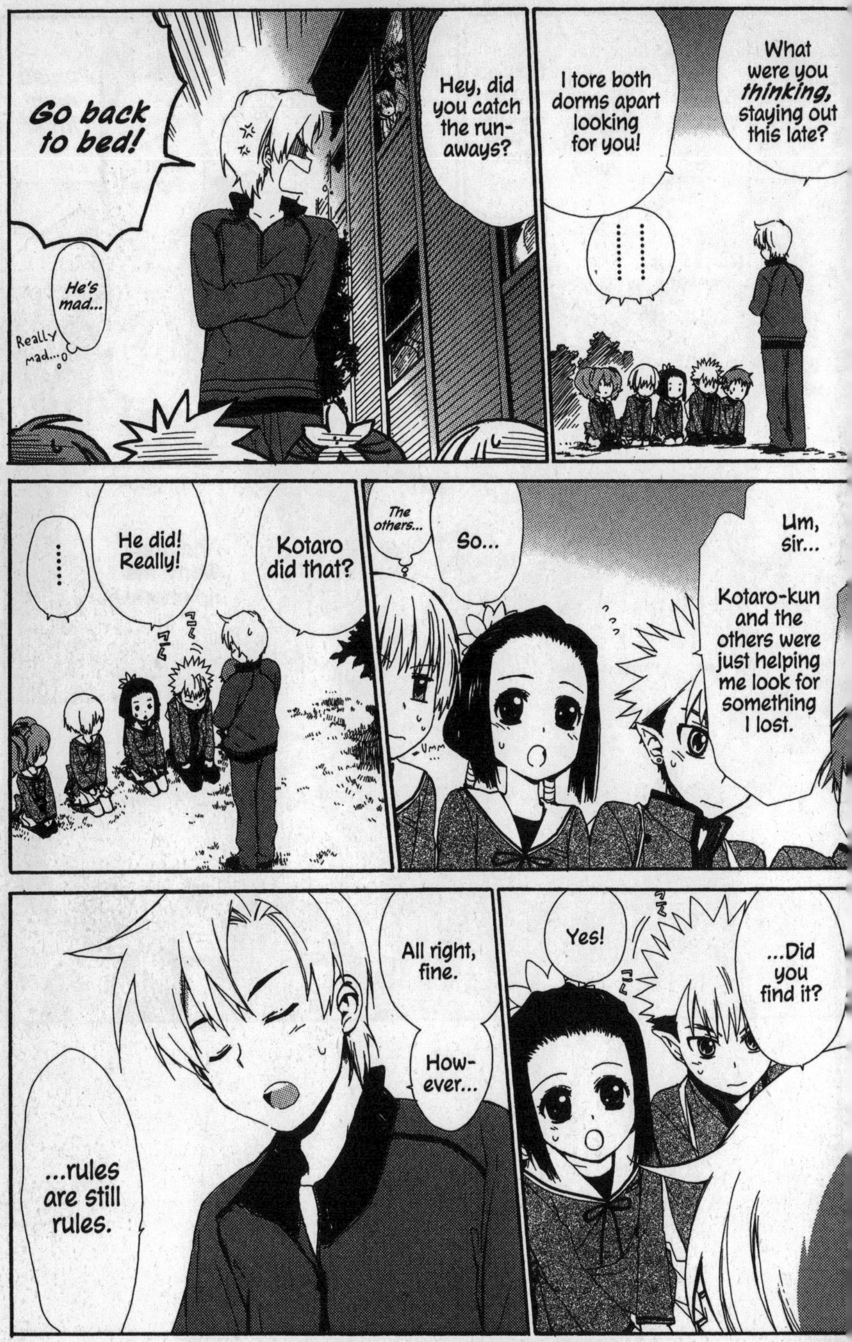
What were you *thinking,* staying out this late?
I tore both dorms apart looking for you!
......
Hey, did you catch the run-aways?
Go back to bed!
He's mad...
Really mad...
Um, sir...
Kotaro-kun and the others were just helping me look for something I lost.
So...
The others...
Umm...
Kotaro did that?
He did! Really!
......
...Did you find it?
Yes!
All right, fine.
How-ever...
...rules are still rules.

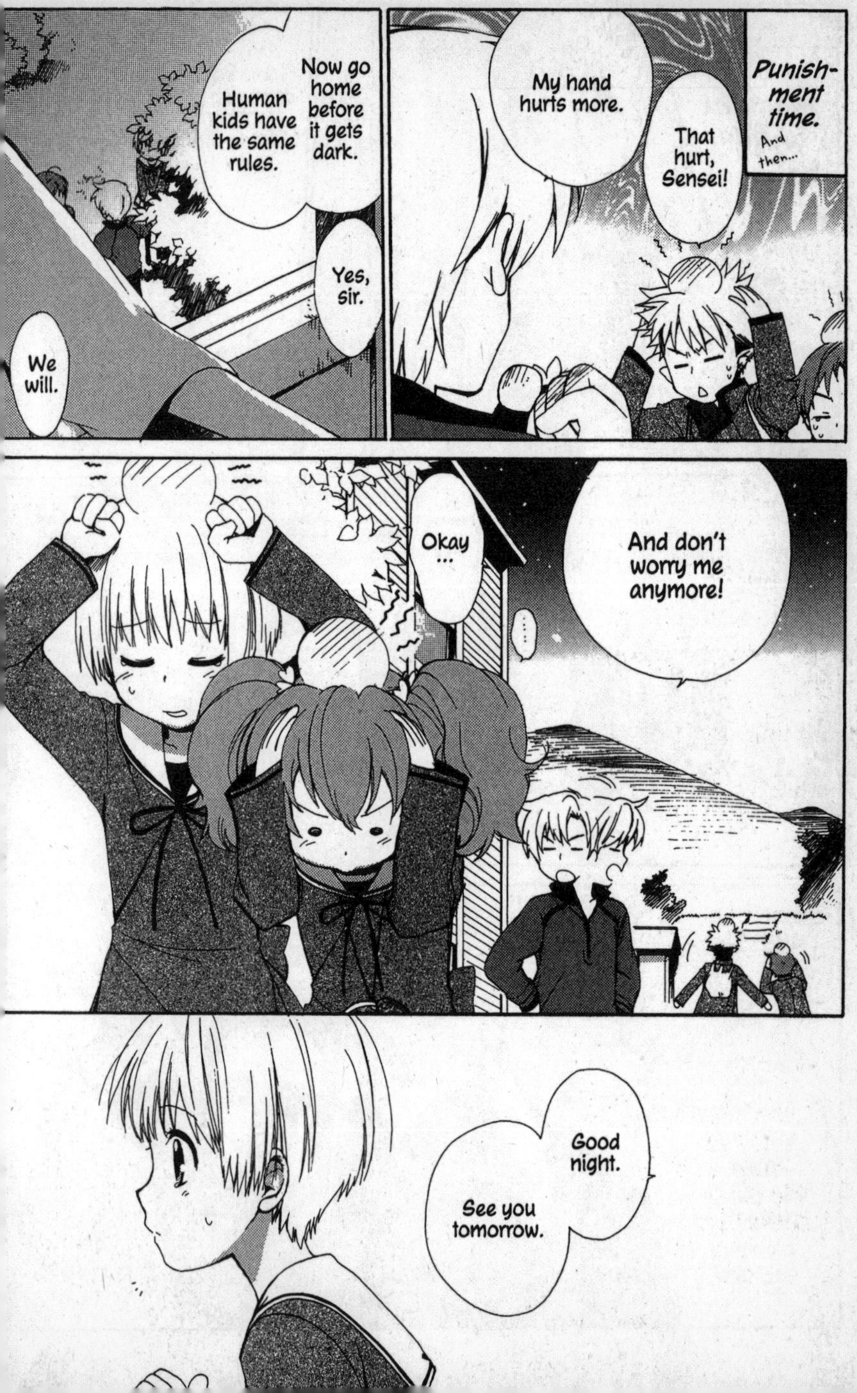
Punishment time.
And then...
That hurt, Sensei!
My hand hurts more.
Now go home before it gets dark.
Human kids have the same rules.
Yes, sir.
We will.
And don't worry me anymore!
...
Okay ...
Good night.
See you tomorrow.

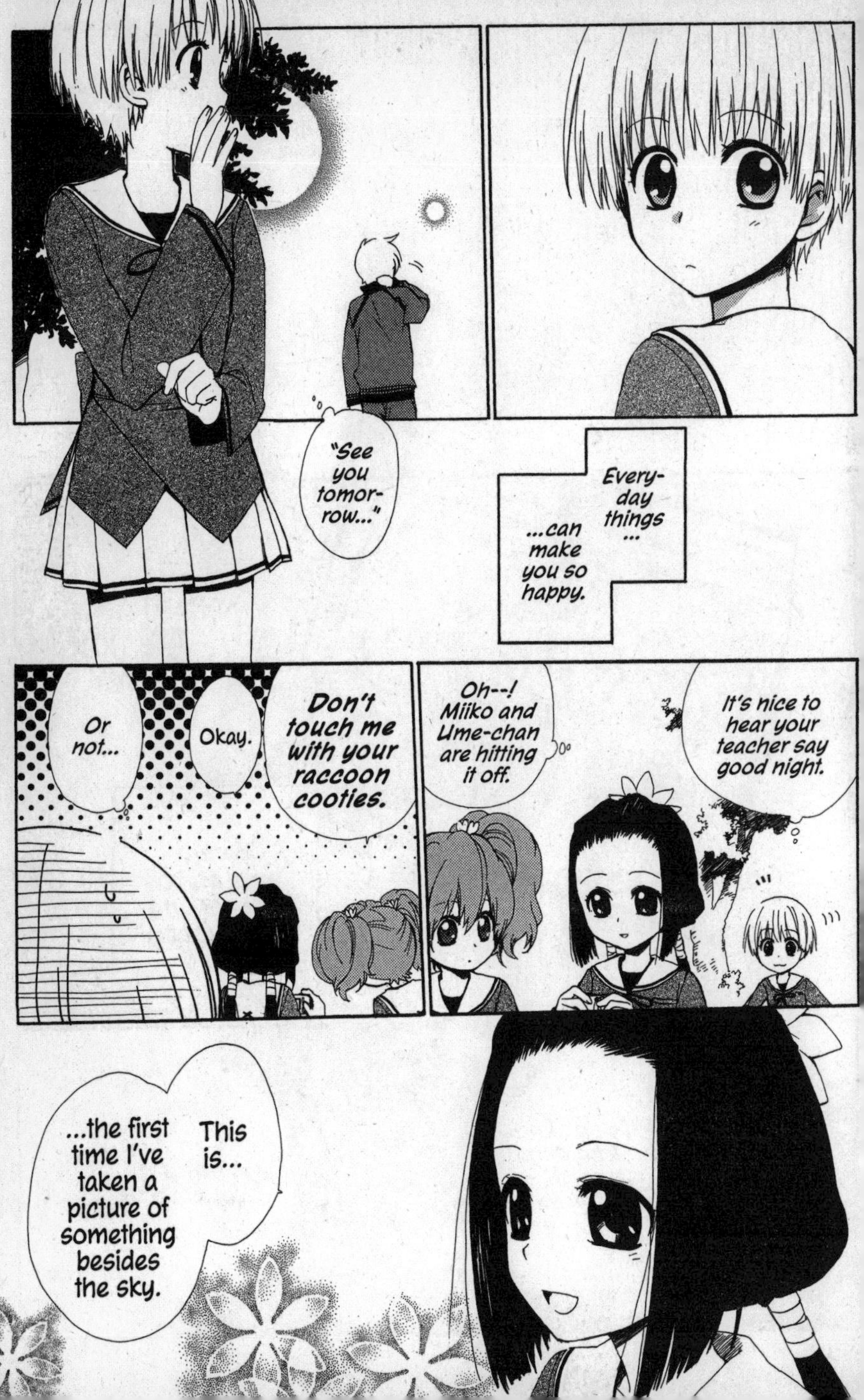
"See you tomorrow..."
Everyday things...
...can make you so happy.
It's nice to hear your teacher say good night.
Oh--! Miiko and Ume-chan are hitting it off.
Don't touch me with your raccoon cooties.
Okay.
Or not...
This is...
...the first time I've taken a picture of something besides the sky.

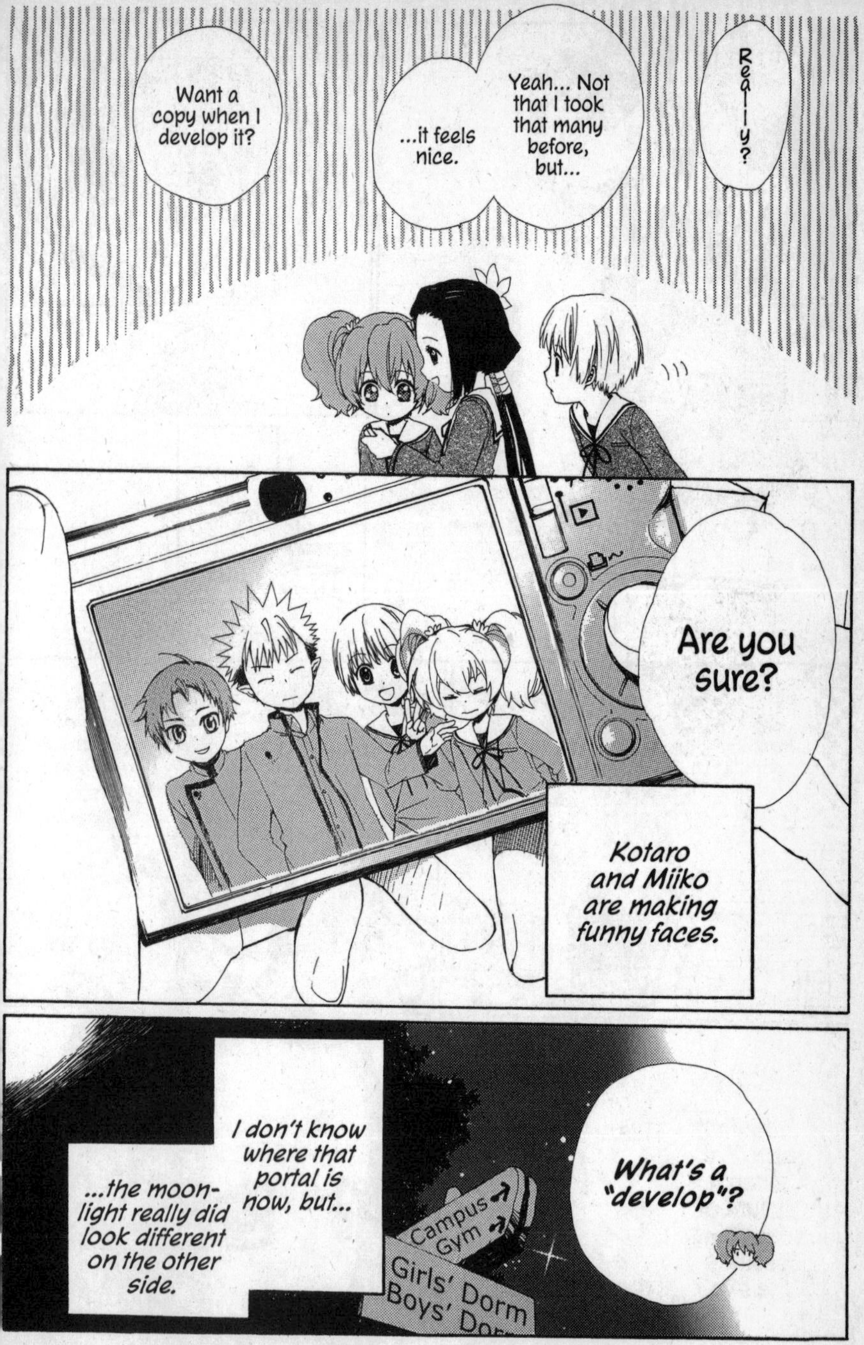
Really?
Yeah... Not that I took that many before, but...
...it feels nice.
Want a copy when I develop it?
Are you sure?
Kotaro and Miiko are making funny faces.
What's a "develop"?
I don't know where that portal is now, but...
...the moon-light really did look different on the other side.
Campus
Gym
Girls' Dorm
Boys' Dor

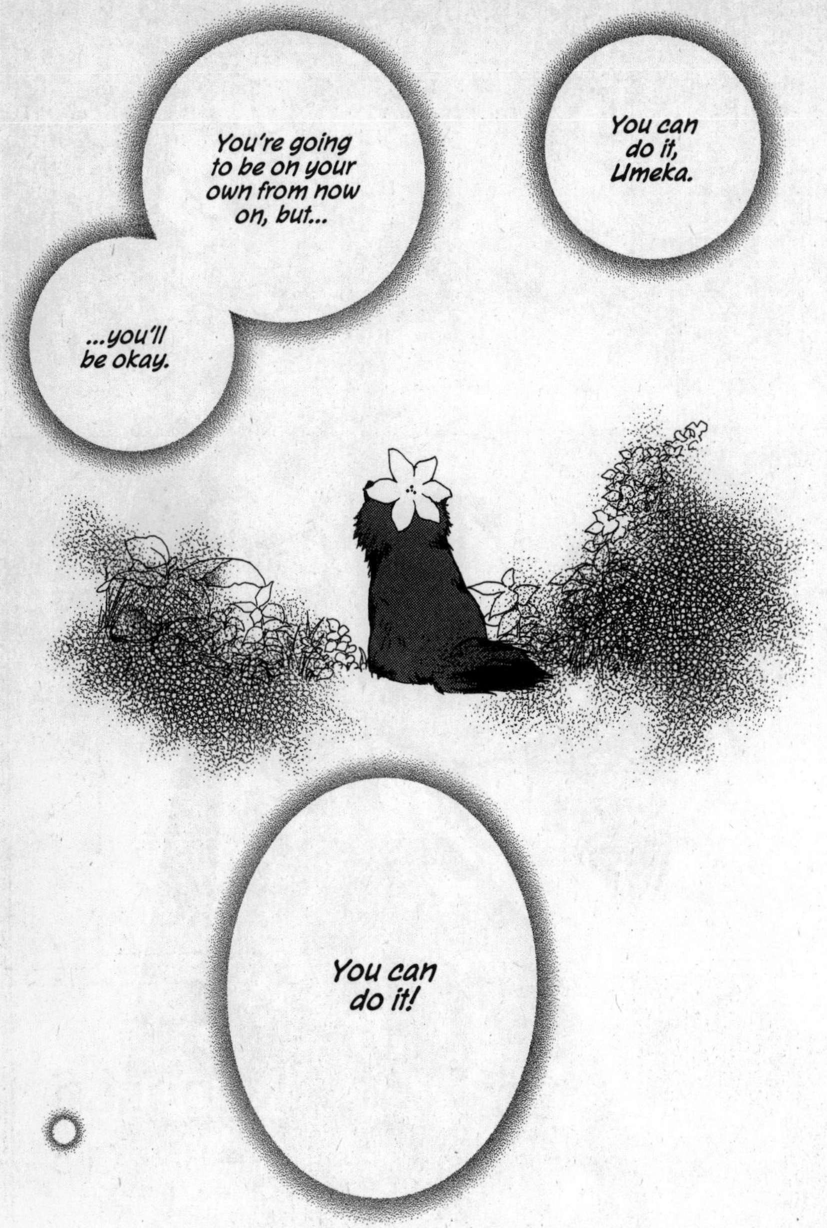
You can do it, Umeka.
You're going to be on your own from now on, but...
...you'll be okay.
You can do it!

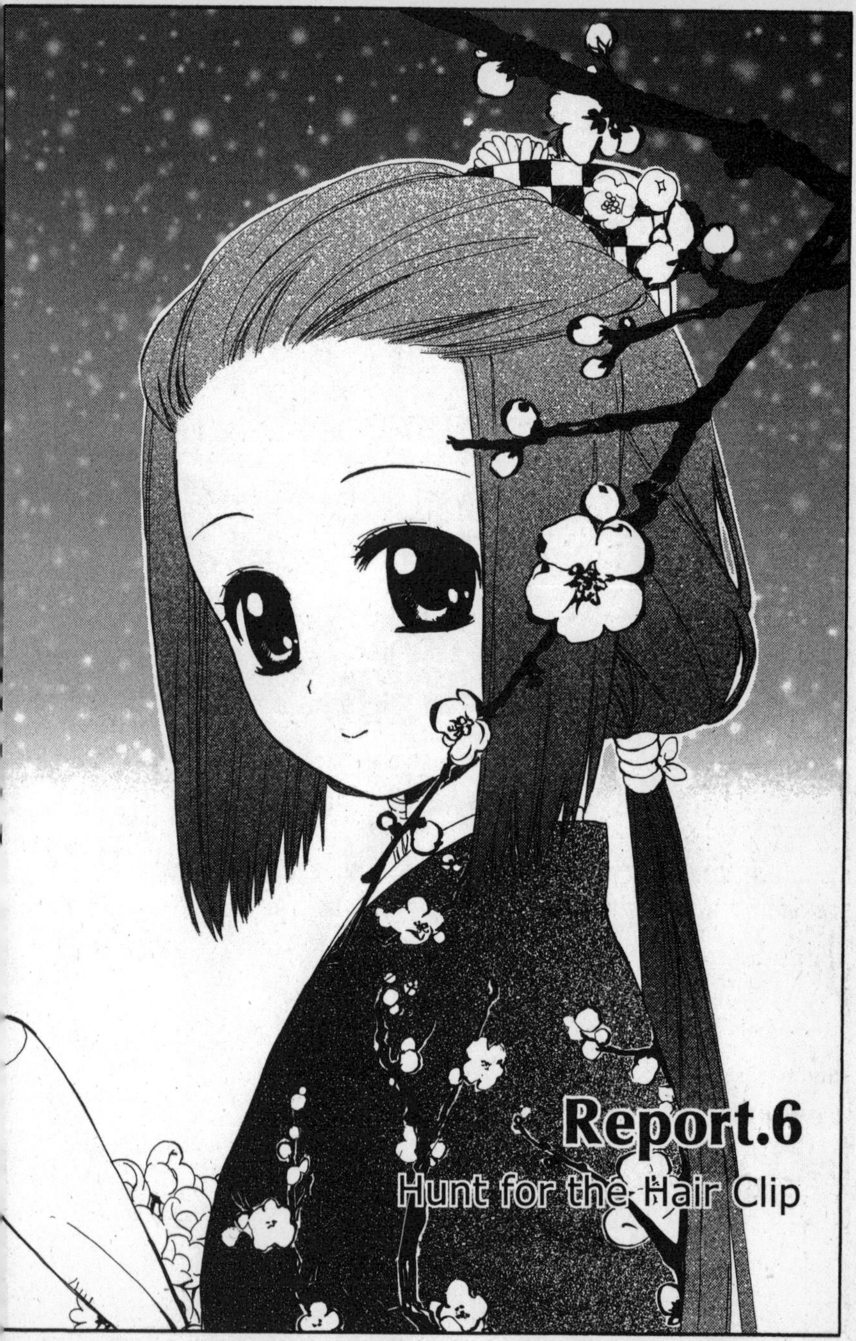
Report.6
Hunt for the Hair Clip

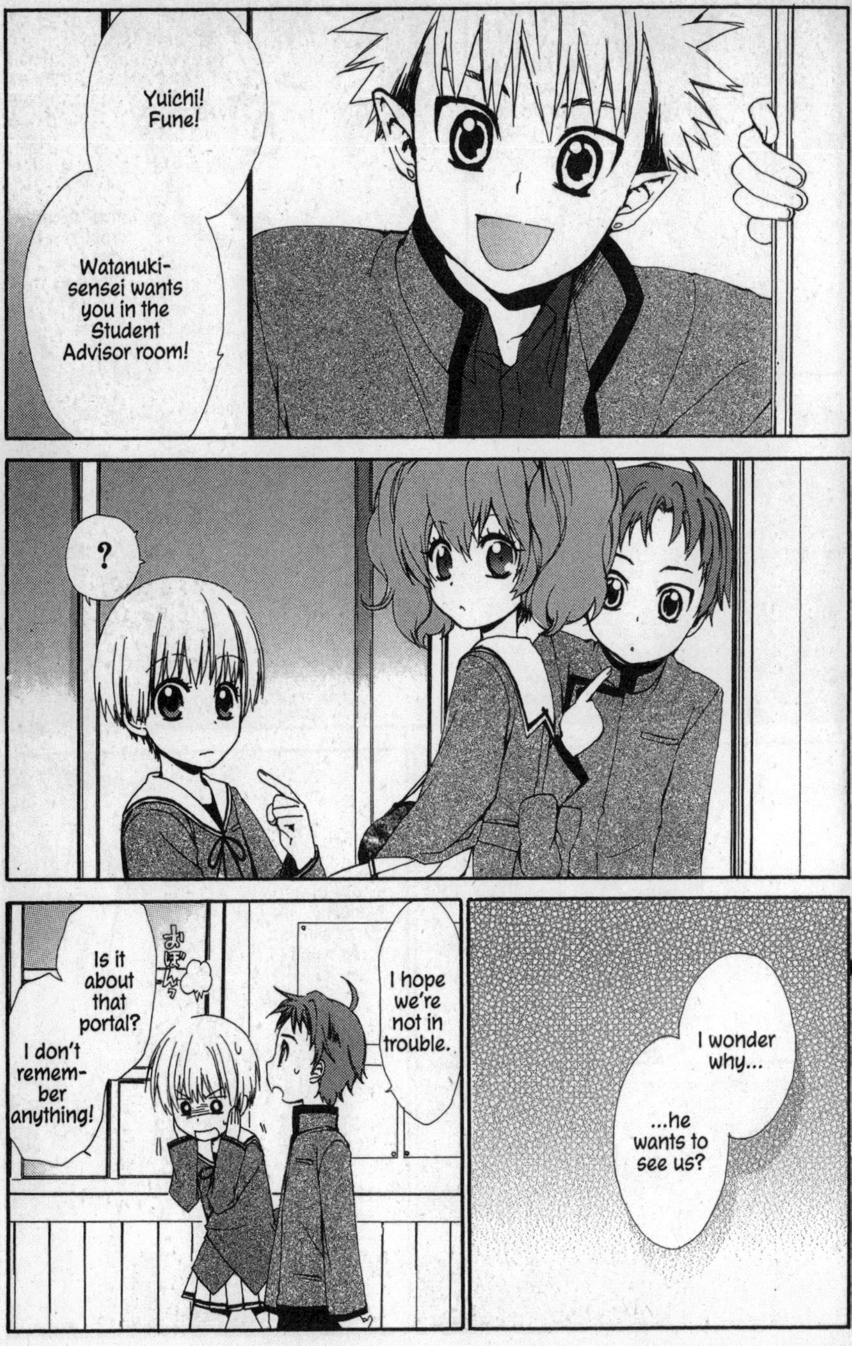
Yuichi! Fune!
Watanuki-sensei wants you in the Student Advisor room!
?
I wonder why...
...he wants to see us?
I hope we're not in trouble.
おぼんっ
Is it about that portal?
I don't remember anything!

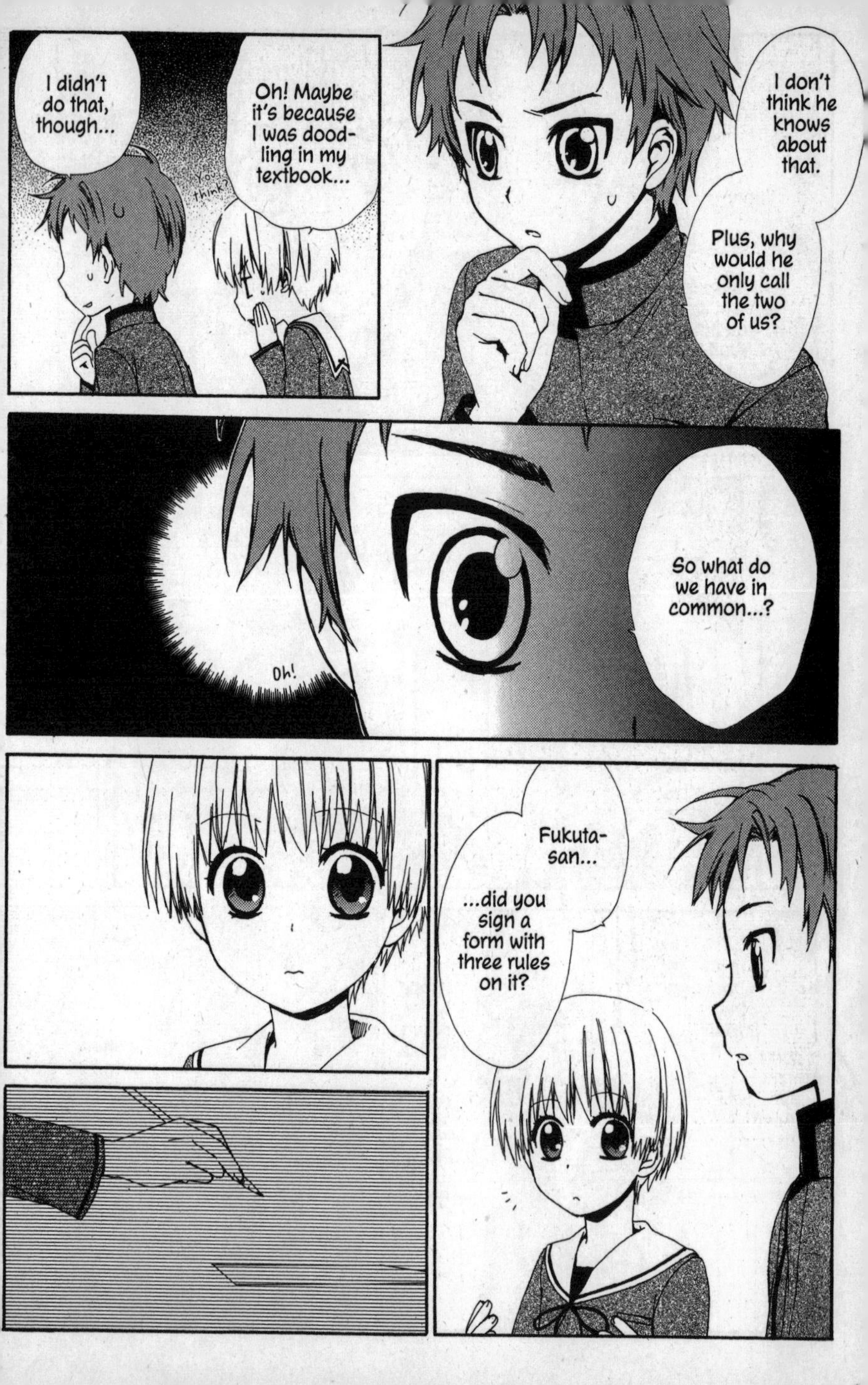
I don't think he knows about that.
Plus, why would he only call the two of us?
Oh! Maybe it's because I was dood-ling in my textbook...
You think?
I didn't do that, though...
So what do we have in common...?
Oh!
Fukuta-san...
...did you sign a form with three rules on it?

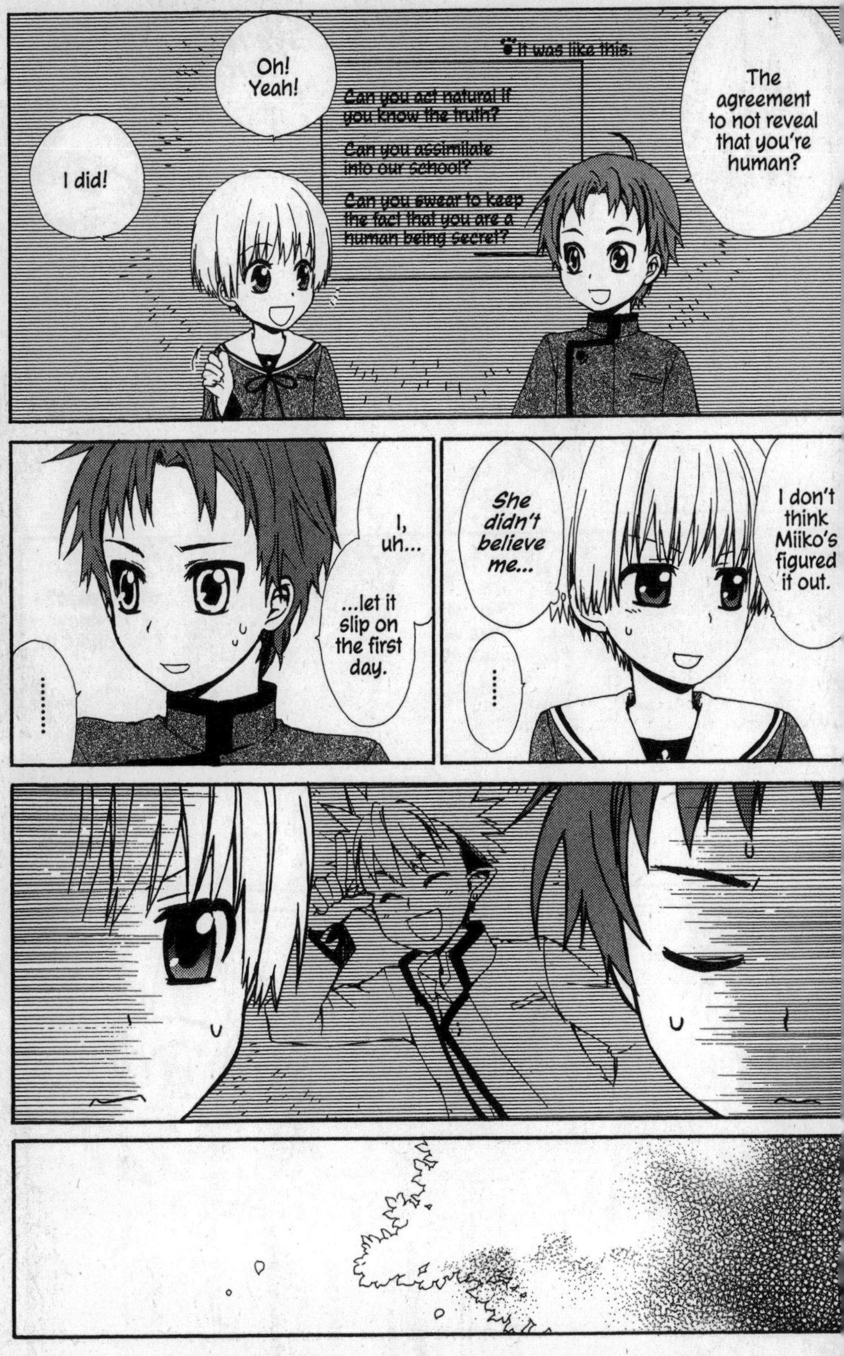
The agreement to not reveal that you're human?
It was like this:
Can you act natural if you know the truth?
Can you assimilate into our school?
Can you swear to keep the fact that you are a human being secret?
Oh! Yeah!
I did!
I don't think Miiko's figured it out.
She didn't believe me...
......
I, uh...
...let it slip on the first day.
....

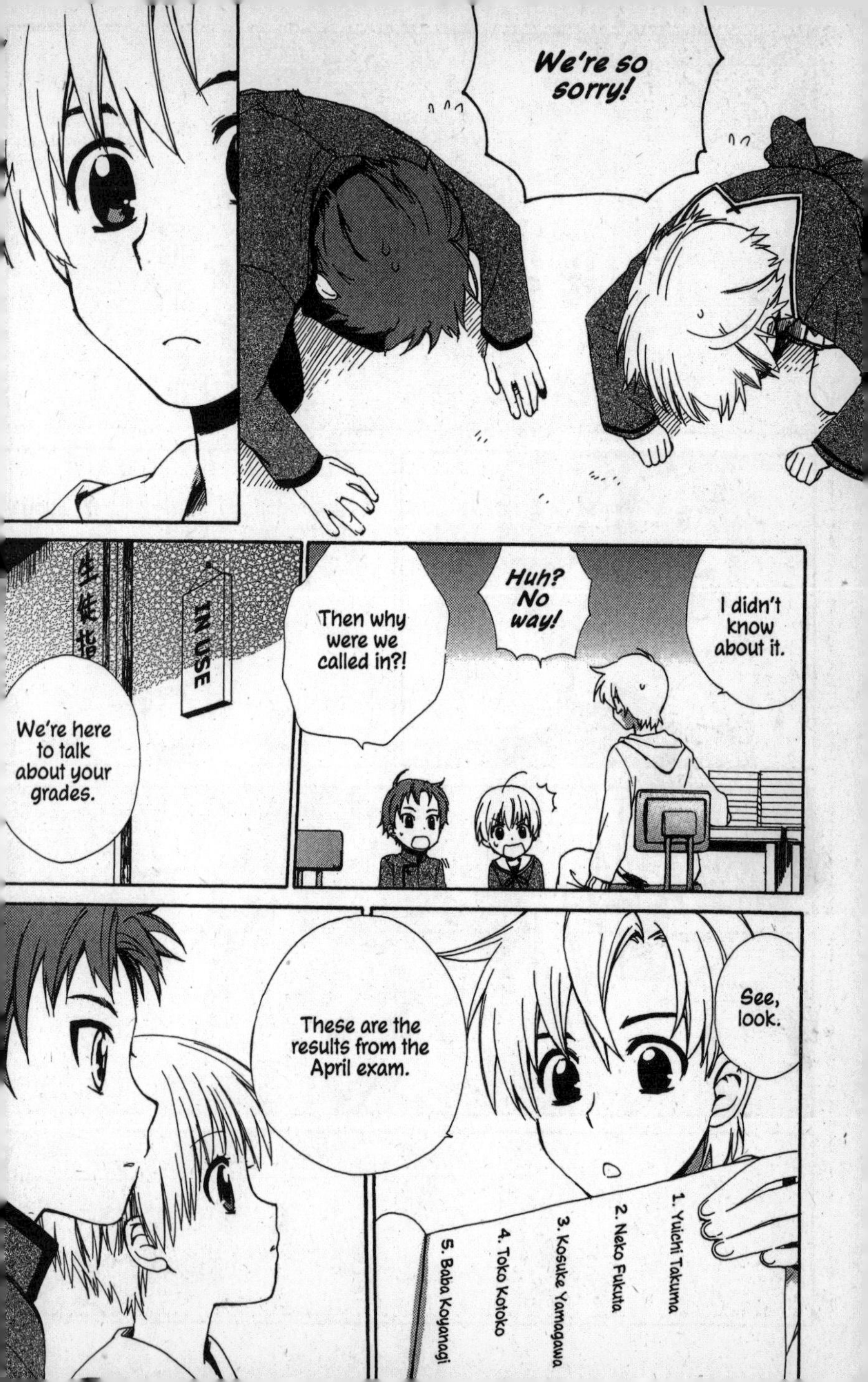
We're so sorry!
I didn't know about it.
Huh? No way!
Then why were we called in?!
生徒指
IN USE
We're here to talk about your grades.
See, look.
These are the results from the April exam.
1. Yuichi Takuma
2. Neko Fukuta
3. Kosuke Yamagawa
4. Toko Kotoko
5. Baba Koyanagi

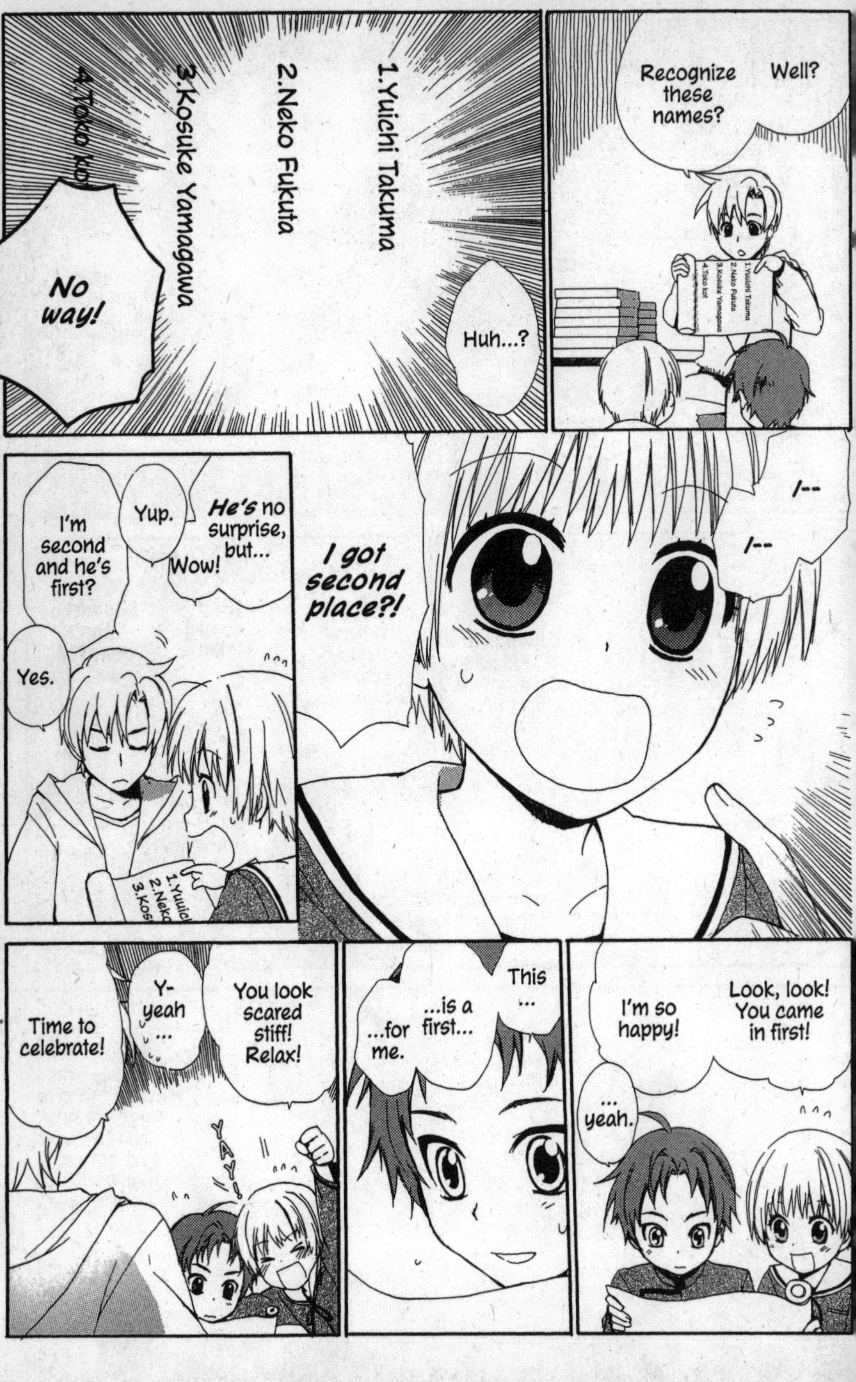
Well?
Recognize these names?
1. Yuichi Takuma
2. Neko Fukuta
3. Kosuke Yamagawa
4. Toko koi
Huh...?
1.Yuichi Takuma
2.Neko Fukuta
3.Kosuke Yamagawa
4.Toko ko
No way!
/--
/--
I got second place?!
He's no surprise, but...
Wow!
Yup.
I'm second and he's first?
Yes.
Look, look! You came in first!
I'm so happy!
... yeah.
This ...
...is a first...
...for me.
You look scared stiff! Relax!
Y-yeah ...
Time to celebrate!
YAY!

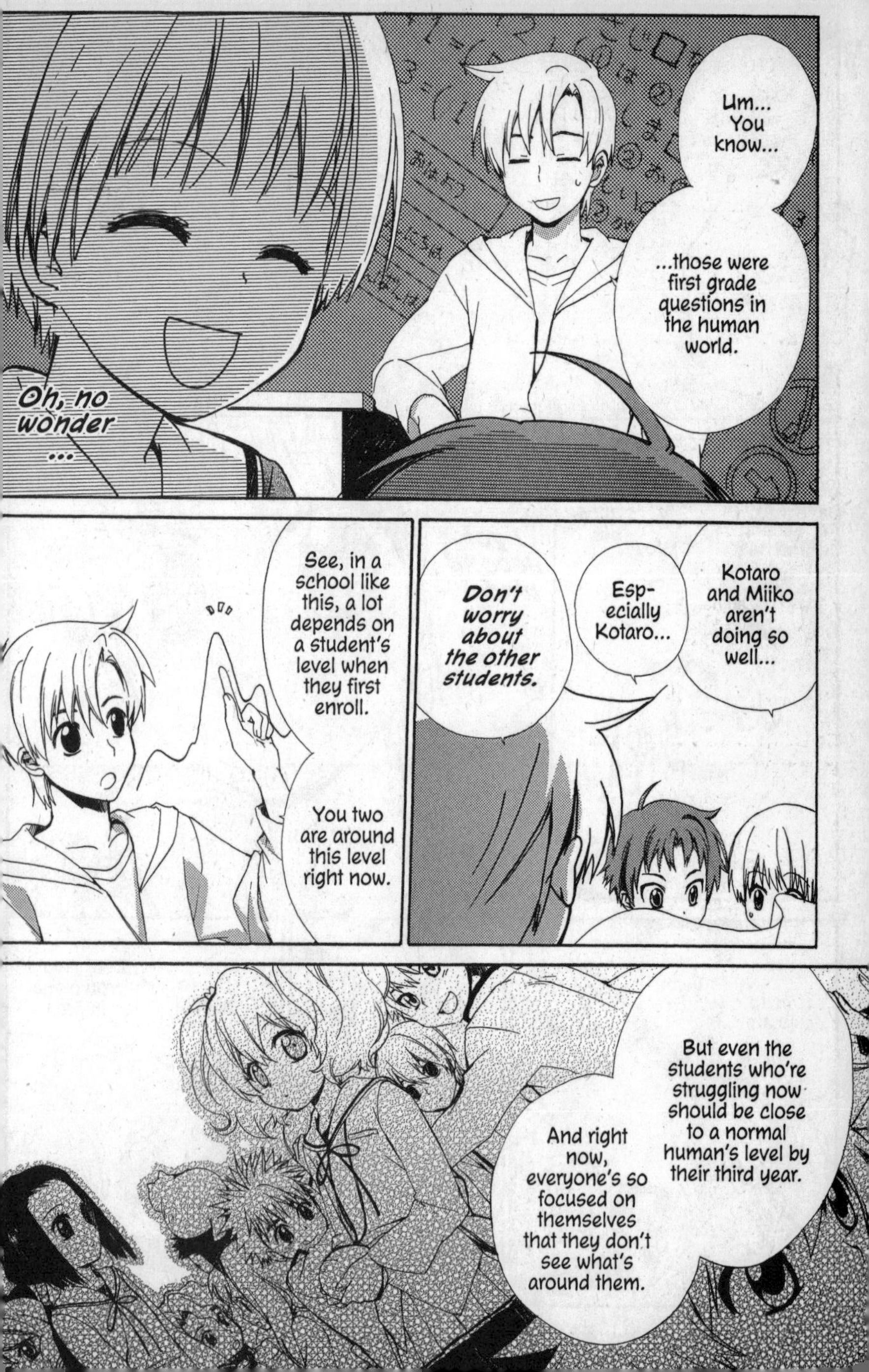
Um... You know...
...those were first grade questions in the human world.
Oh, no wonder ...
Kotaro and Miiko aren't doing so well...
Esp-ecially Kotaro...
Don't worry about the other students.
See, in a school like this, a lot depends on a student's level when they first enroll.
You two are around this level right now.
But even the students who're struggling now should be close to a normal human's level by their third year.
And right now, everyone's so focused on themselves that they don't see what's around them.

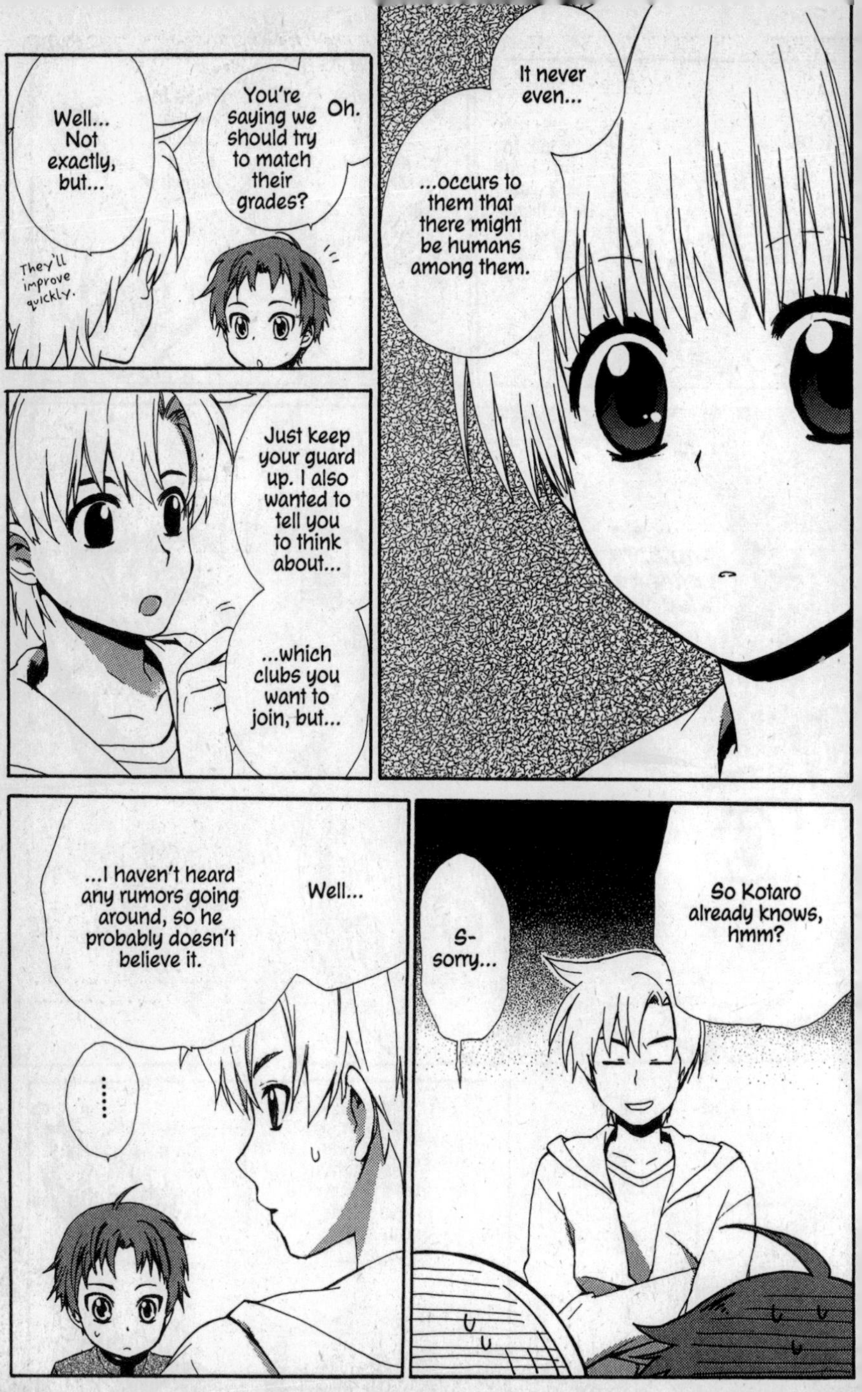
It never even...
...occurs to them that there might be humans among them.
Oh.
You're saying we should try to match their grades?
Well... Not exactly, but...
They'll improve quickly.
Just keep your guard up. I also wanted to tell you to think about...
...which clubs you want to join, but...
So Kotaro already knows, hmm?
S-sorry...
Well...
...I haven't heard any rumors going around, so he probably doesn't believe it.
......

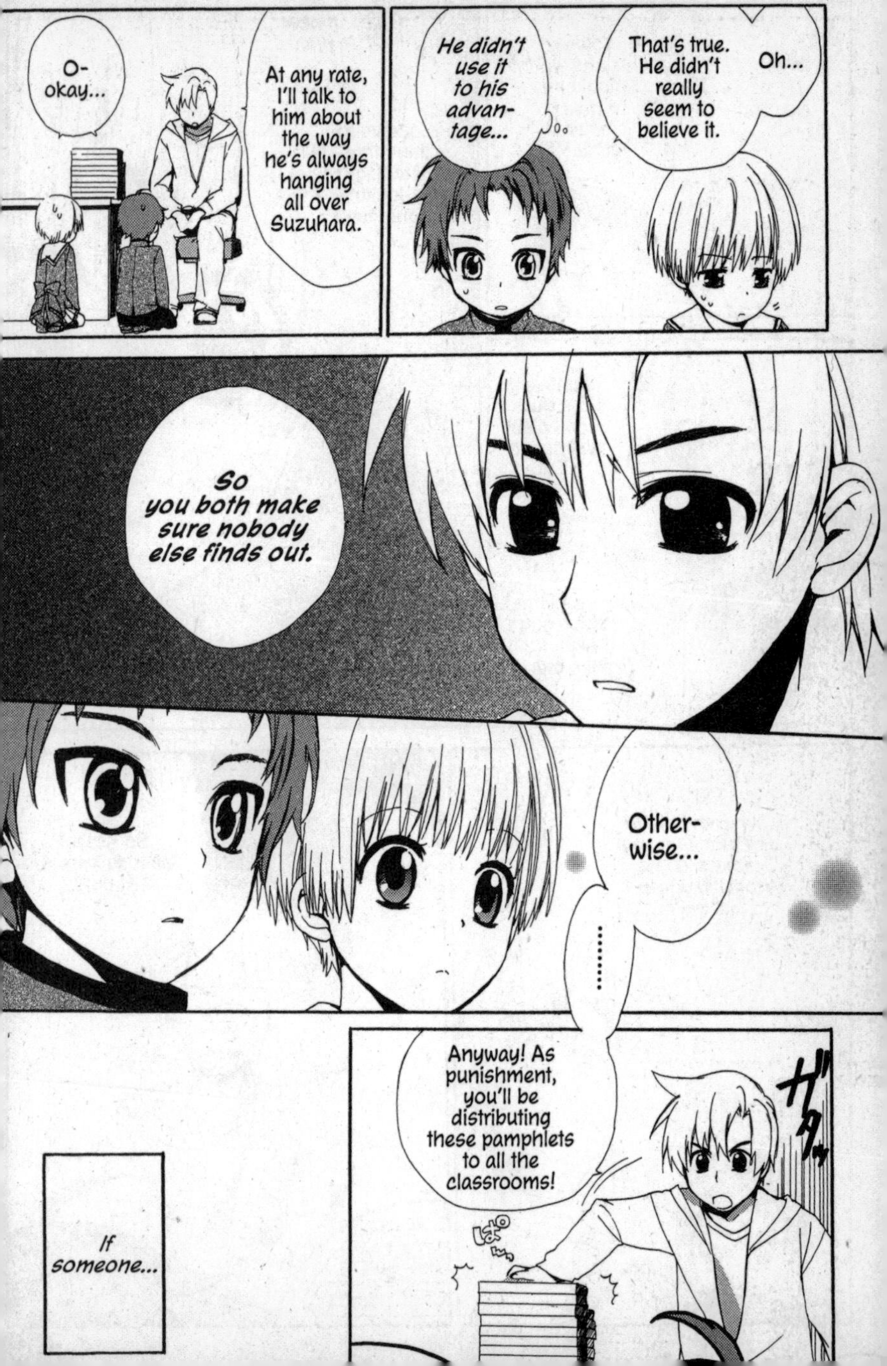
Oh...
That's true. He didn't really seem to believe it.
He didn't use it to his advantage...
At any rate, I'll talk to him about the way he's always hanging all over Suzuhara.
O-okay...
So you both make sure nobody else finds out.
Other-wise...
......
ガタッ
Anyway! As punishment, you'll be distributing these pamphlets to all the classrooms!
If someone...

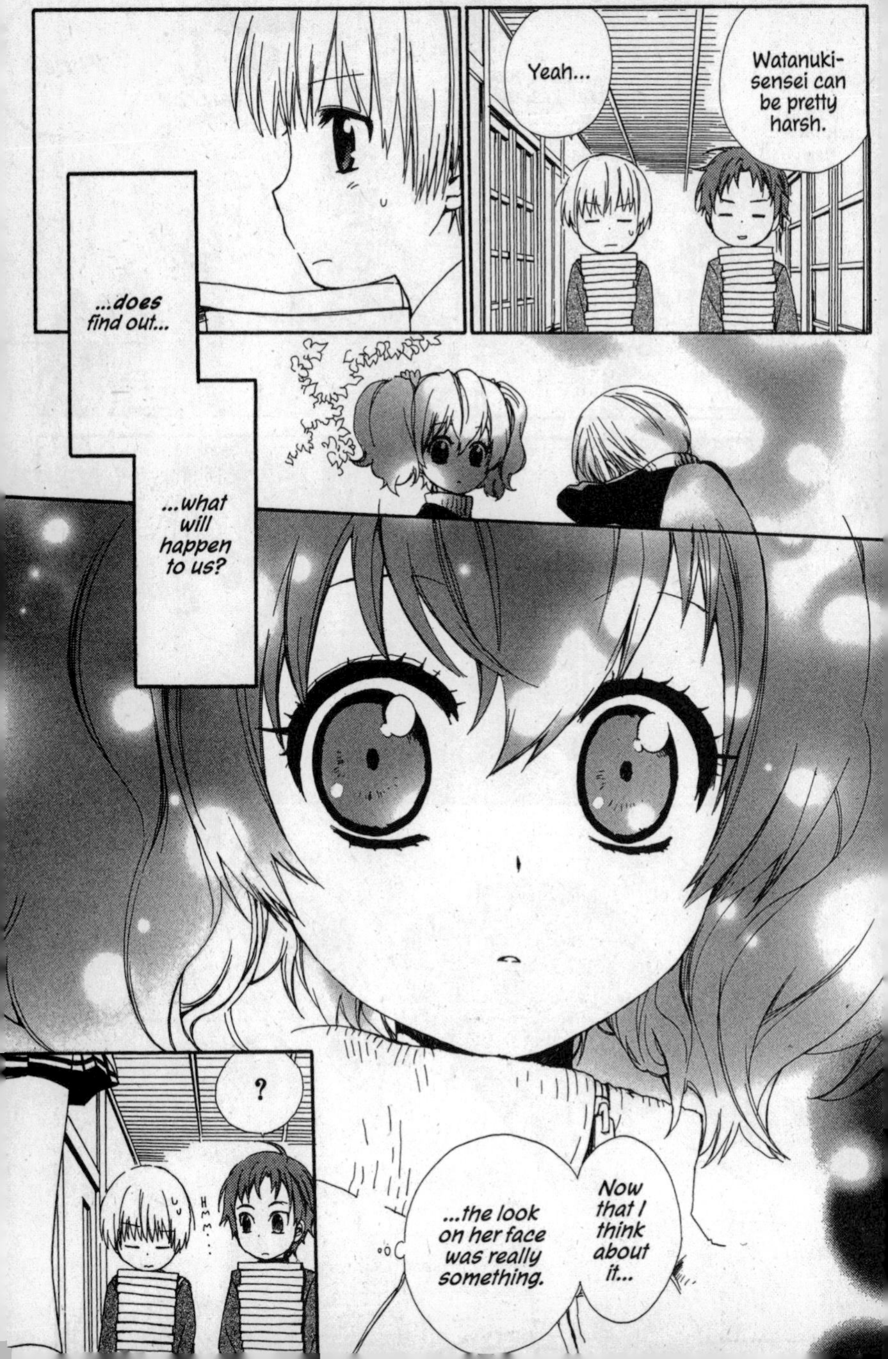
Watanuki-sensei can be pretty harsh.
Yeah...
...does find out...
...what will happen to us?
Now that I think about it...
...the look on her face was really something.
?
HMM...

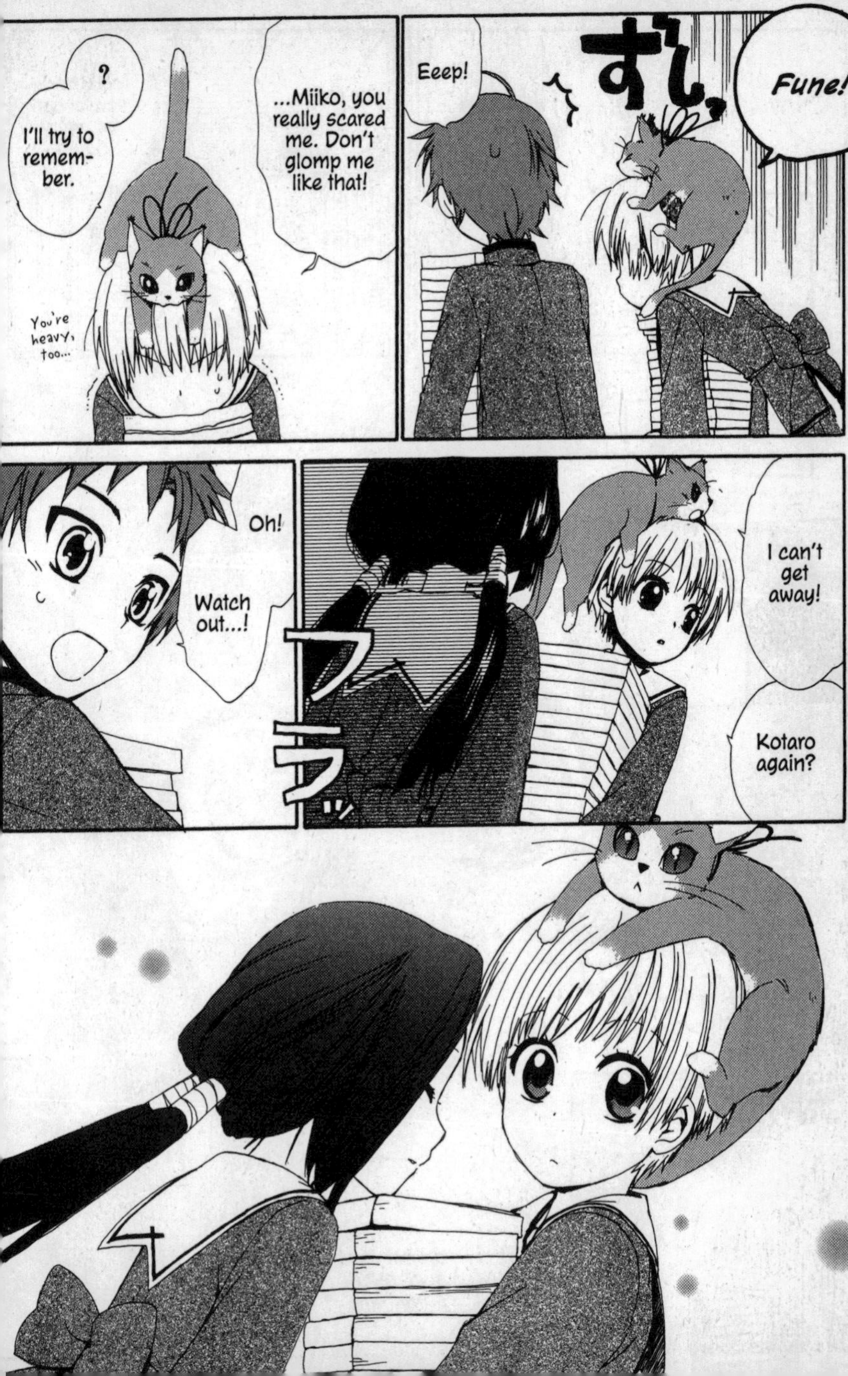
Fune!
ずし
Eeep!
...Miiko, you really scared me. Don't glomp me like that!
?
I'll try to remem-ber.
You're heavy, too...
I can't get away!
Kotaro again?
フラッ
Oh!
Watch out...!

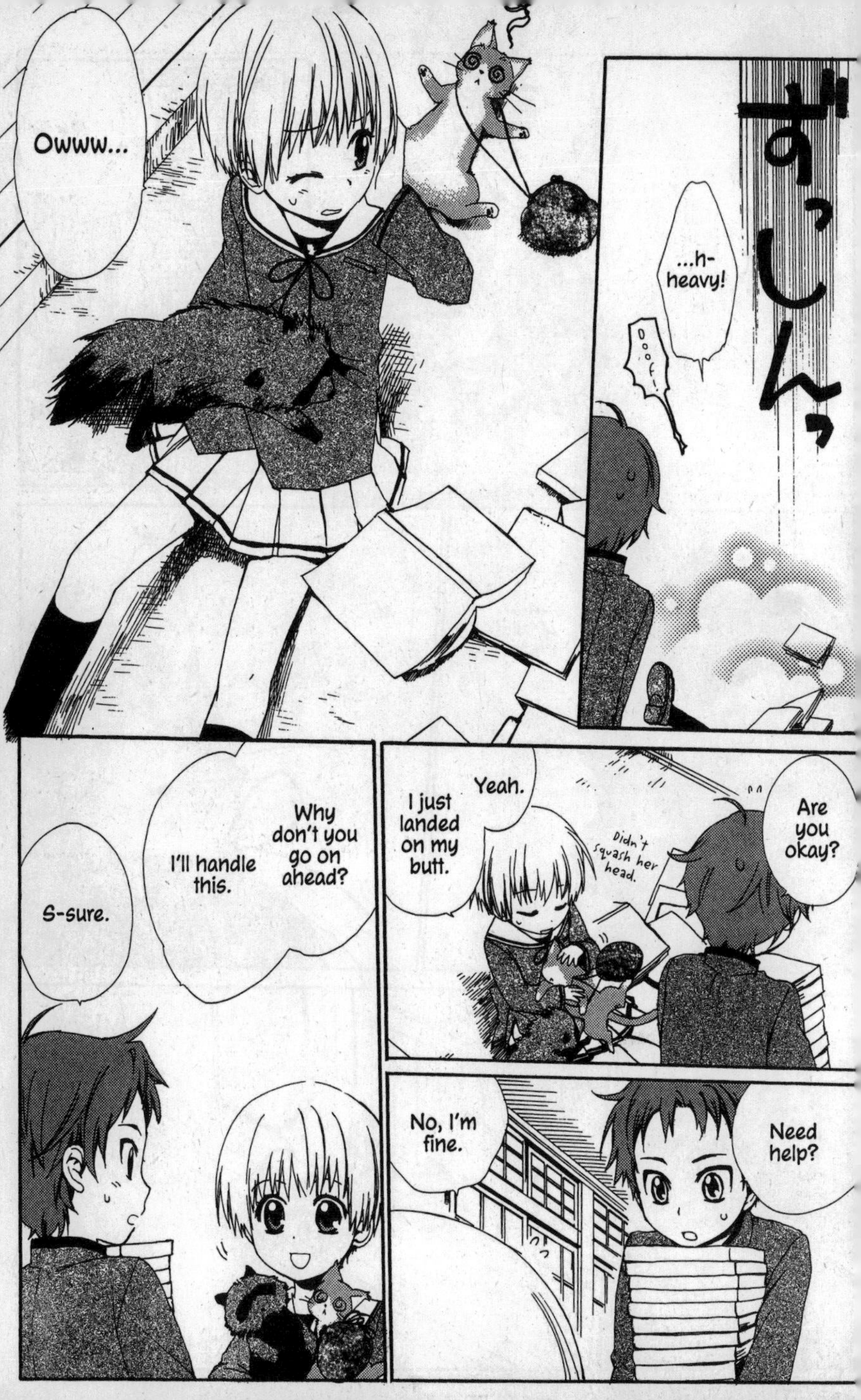
ずっしんっ
...h- heavy!
Dooof!
Owww...
Are you okay?
Didn't squash her head.
Yeah.
I just landed on my butt.
Need help?
No, I'm fine.
Why don't you go on ahead?
I'll handle this.
S-sure.

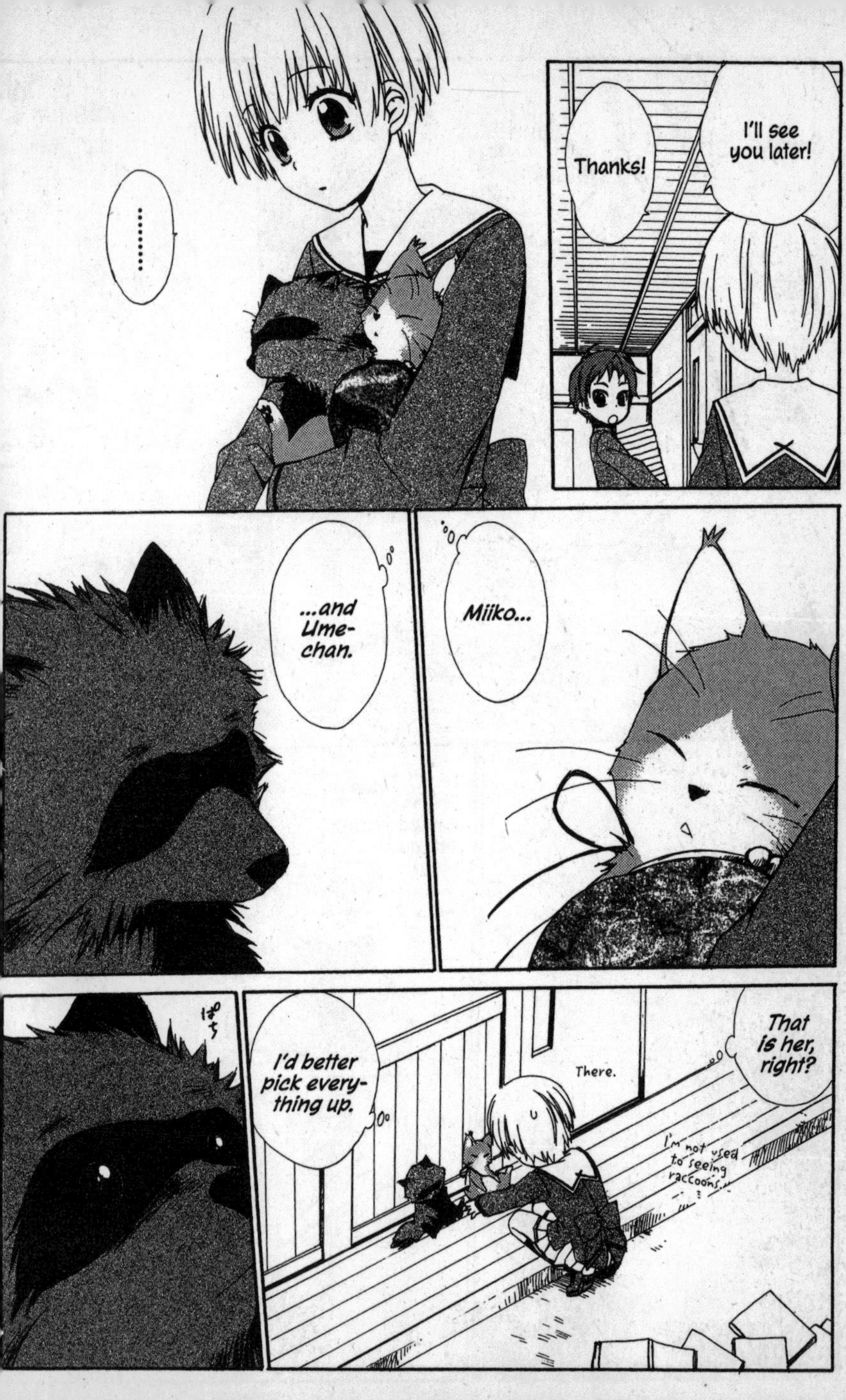
I'll see you later!
Thanks!
......
Miiko...
...and Ume-chan.
That is her, right?
There.
I'm not used to seeing raccoons...
I'd better pick every-thing up.
ぱち

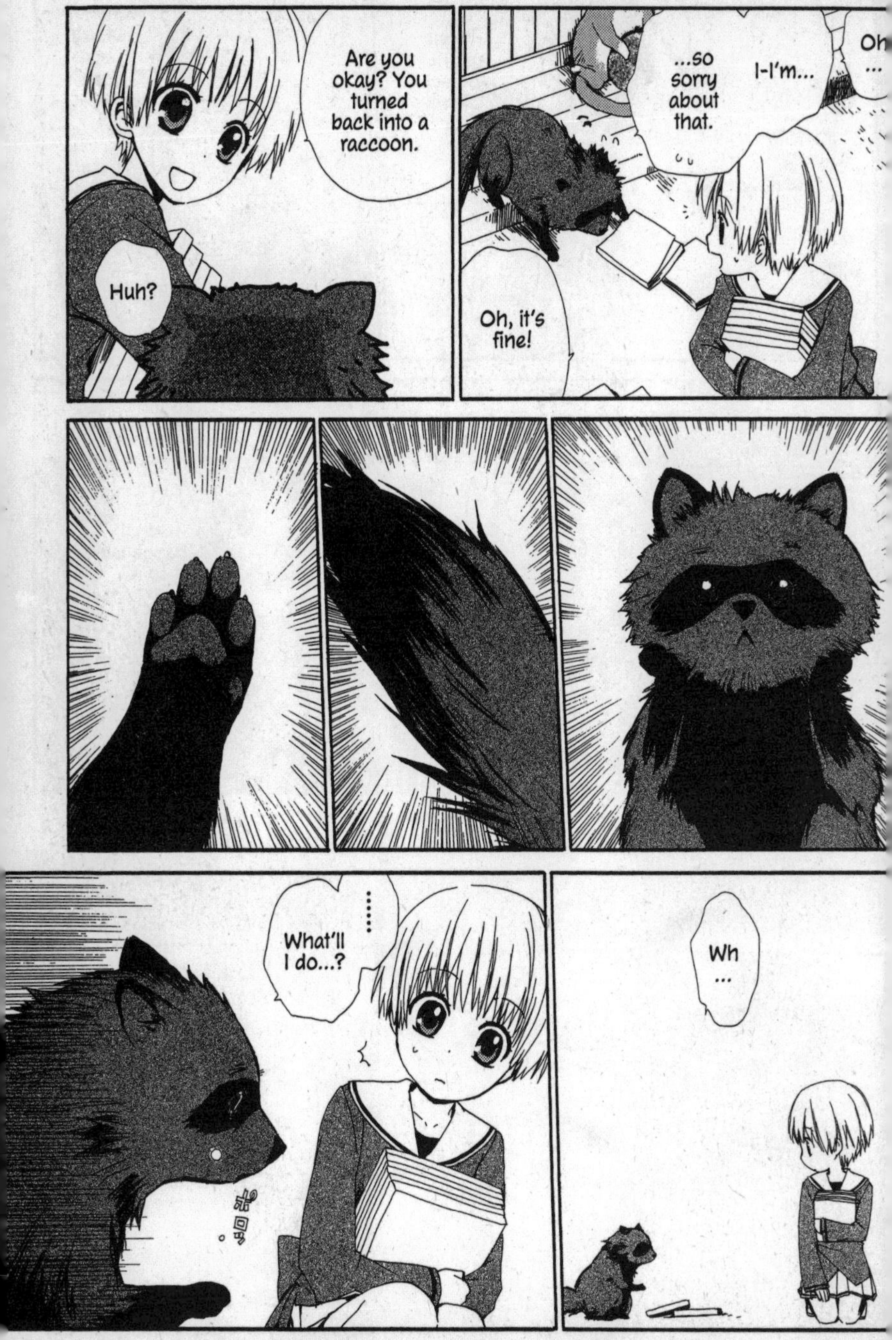
Oh ...
I-I'm...
...so sorry about that.
Oh, it's fine!
Are you okay? You turned back into a raccoon.
Huh?
Wh ...
......
What'll I do...?

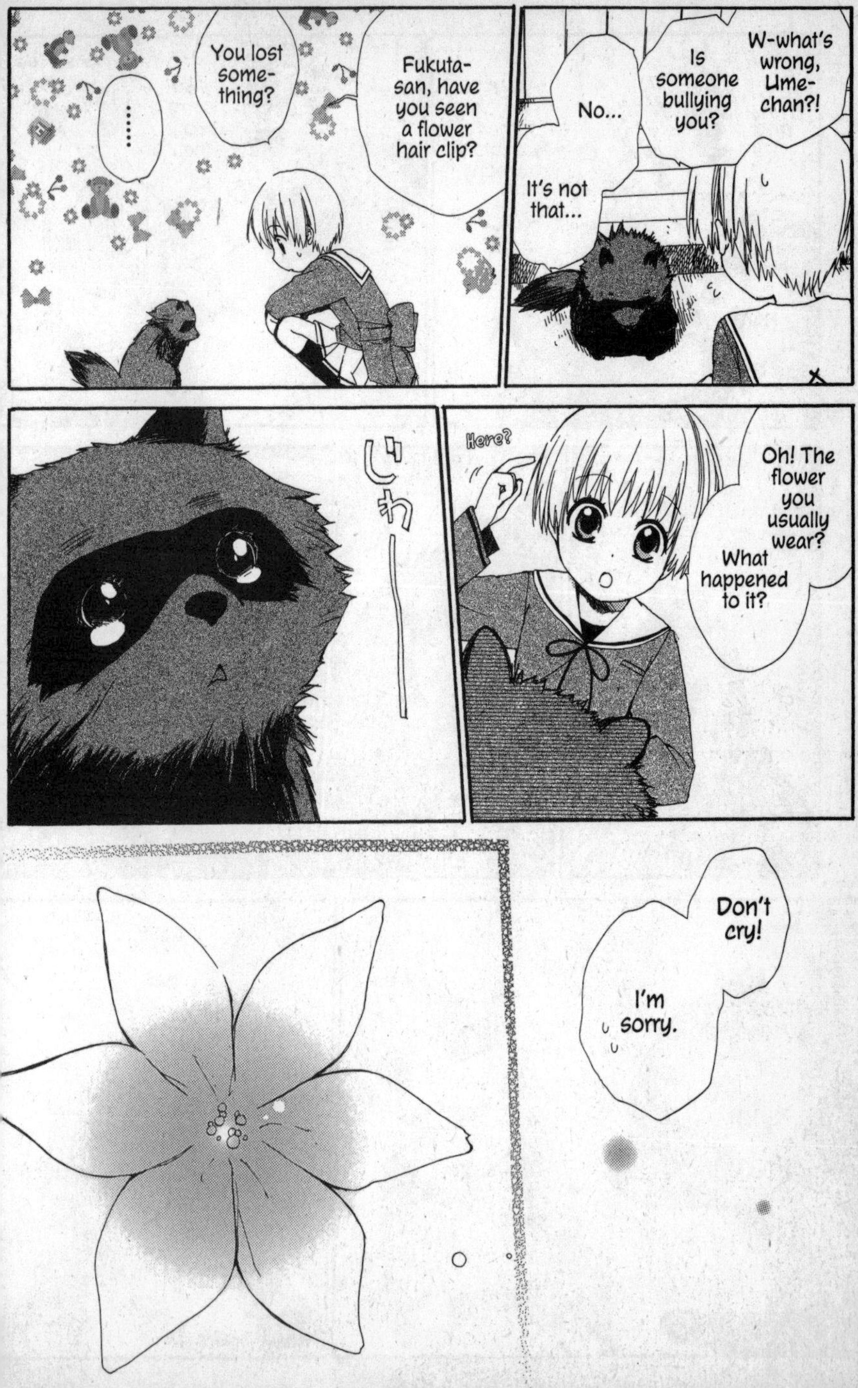

W-what's wrong, Ume-chan?!
Is someone bullying you?
No...
It's not that...
Fukuta-san, have you seen a flower hair clip?
You lost something?
......
Oh! The flower you usually wear?
What happened to it?
Here?
じわー
Don't cry!
I'm sorry.

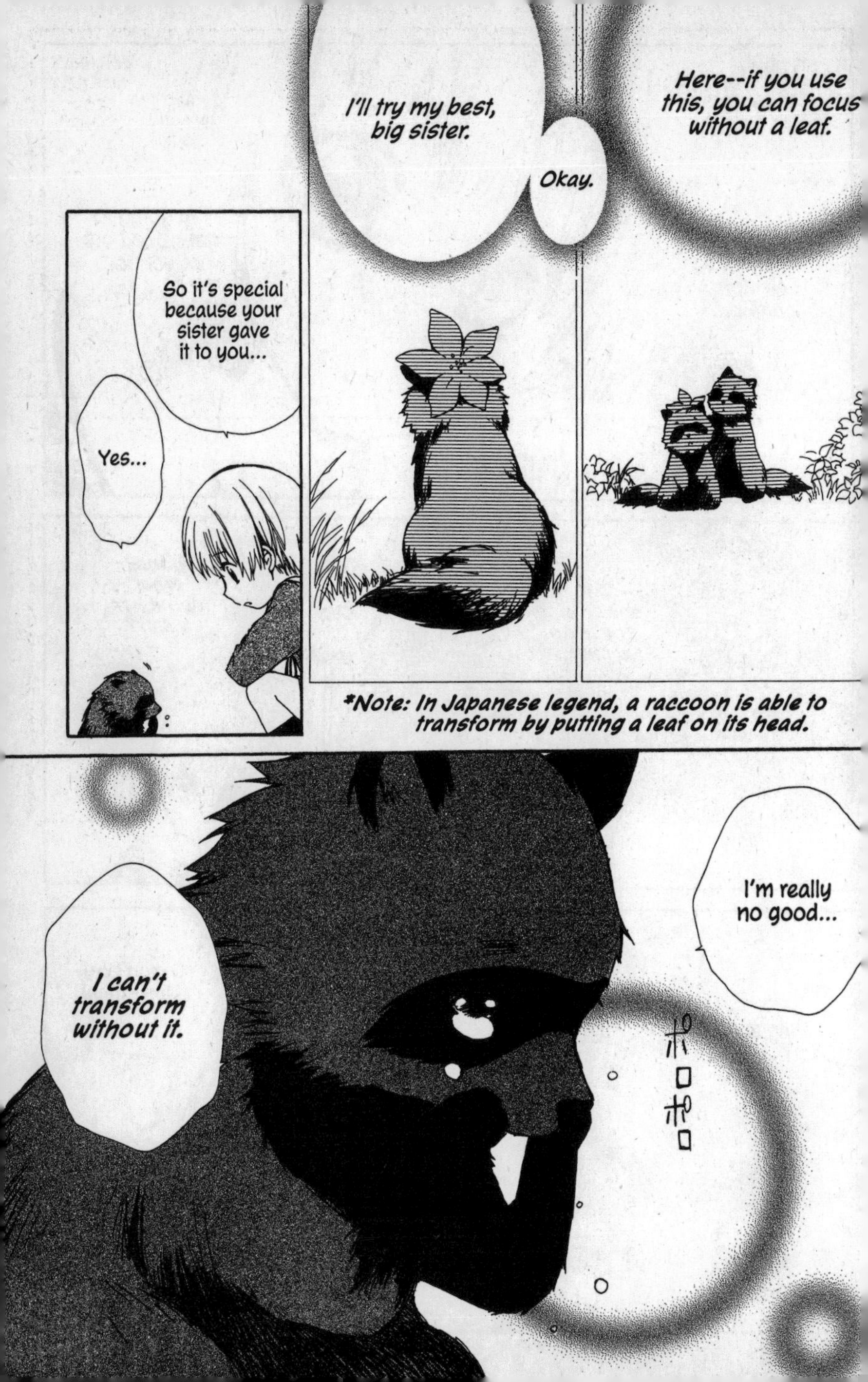
Here--if you use this, you can focus without a leaf.
Okay.
I'll try my best, big sister.
So it's special because your sister gave it to you...
Yes...
*Note: In Japanese legend, a raccoon is able to transform by putting a leaf on its head.
I'm really no good...
ポロポロ
I can't transform without it.

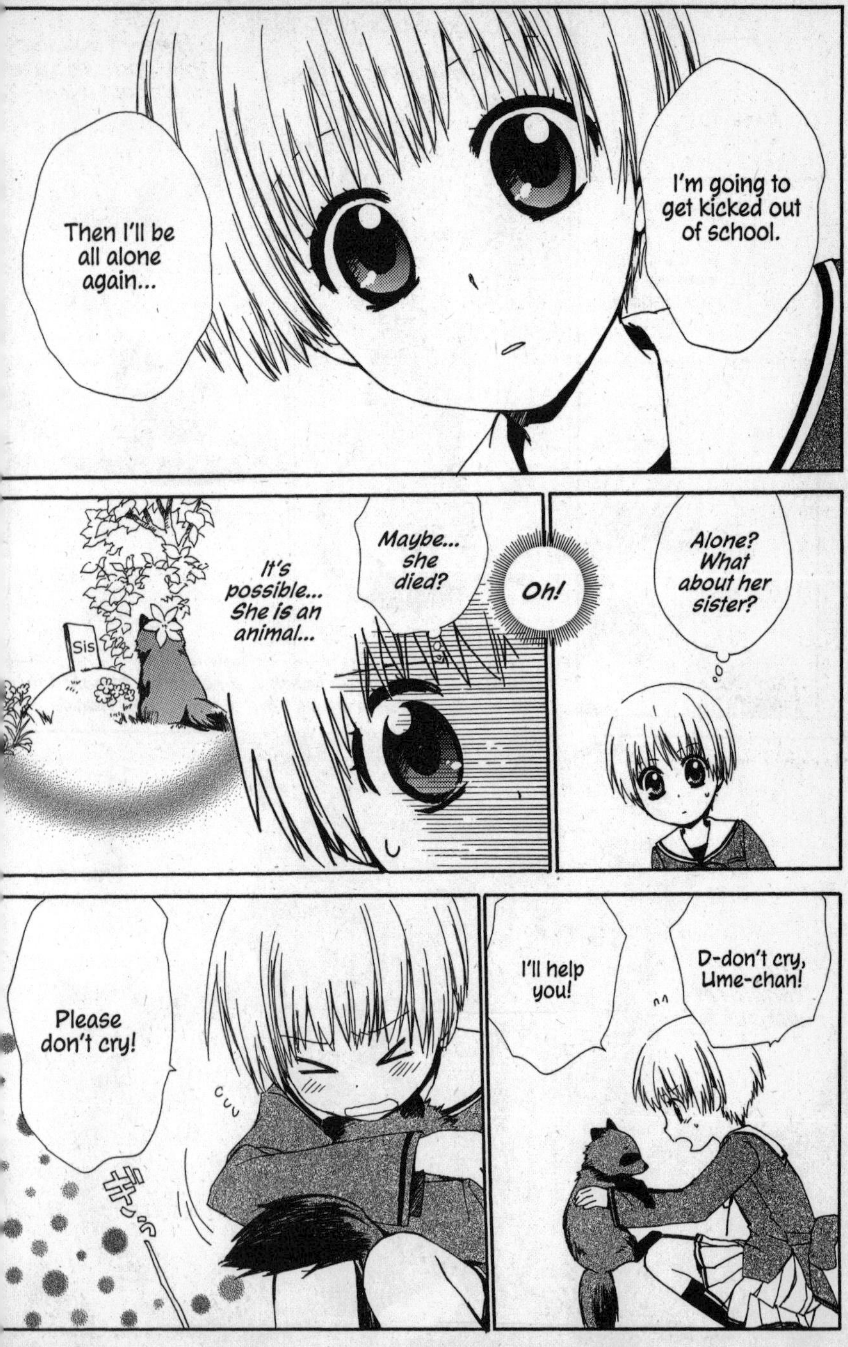

I'm going to get kicked out of school.
Then I'll be all alone again...
Alone? What about her sister?
Oh!
Maybe... she died?
It's possible... She is an animal...
Sis
D-don't cry, Ume-chan!
I'll help you!
Please don't cry!

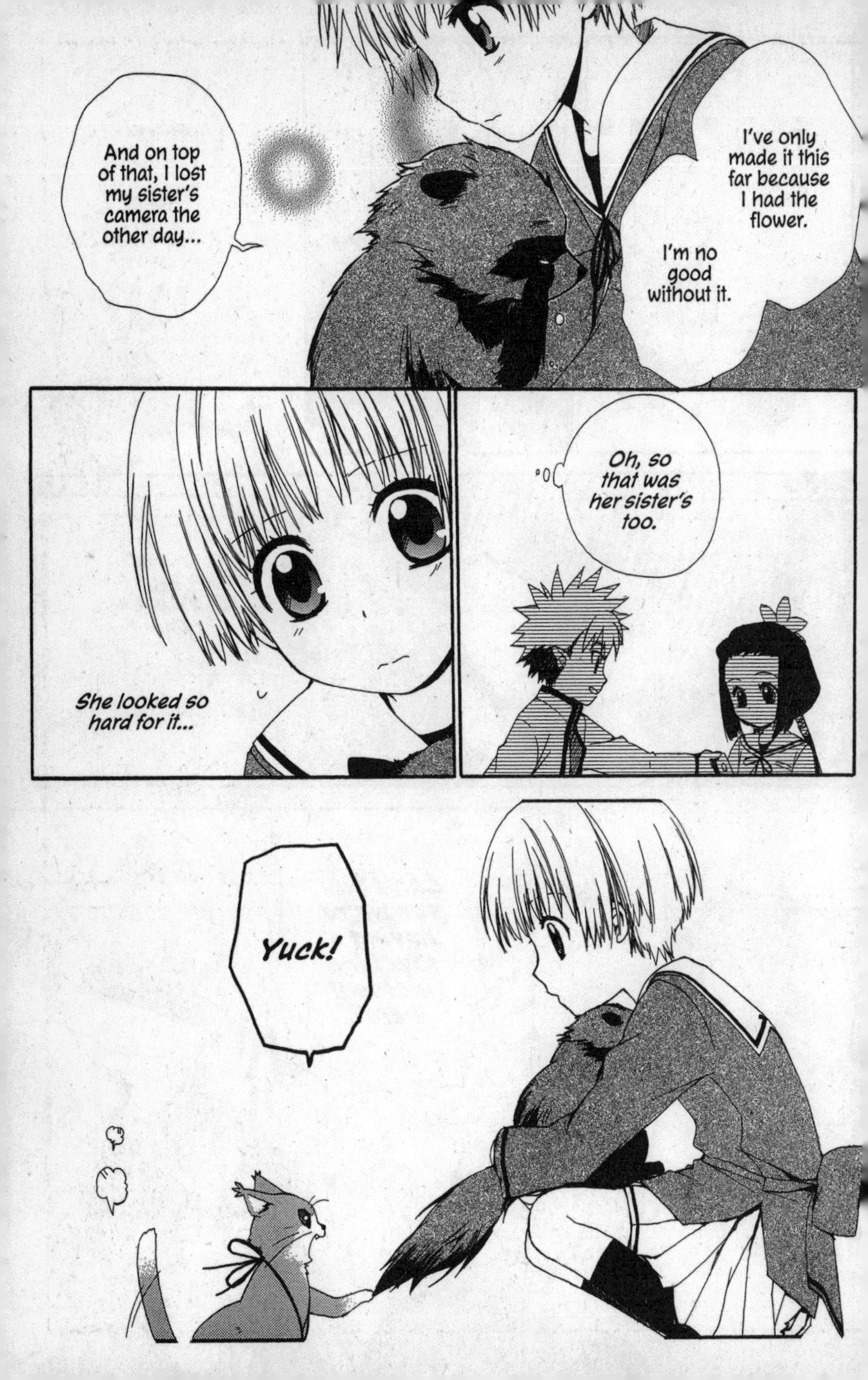
I've only made it this far because I had the flower.
I'm no good without it.
And on top of that, I lost my sister's camera the other day...
Oh, so that was her sister's too.
She looked so hard for it...
Yuck!

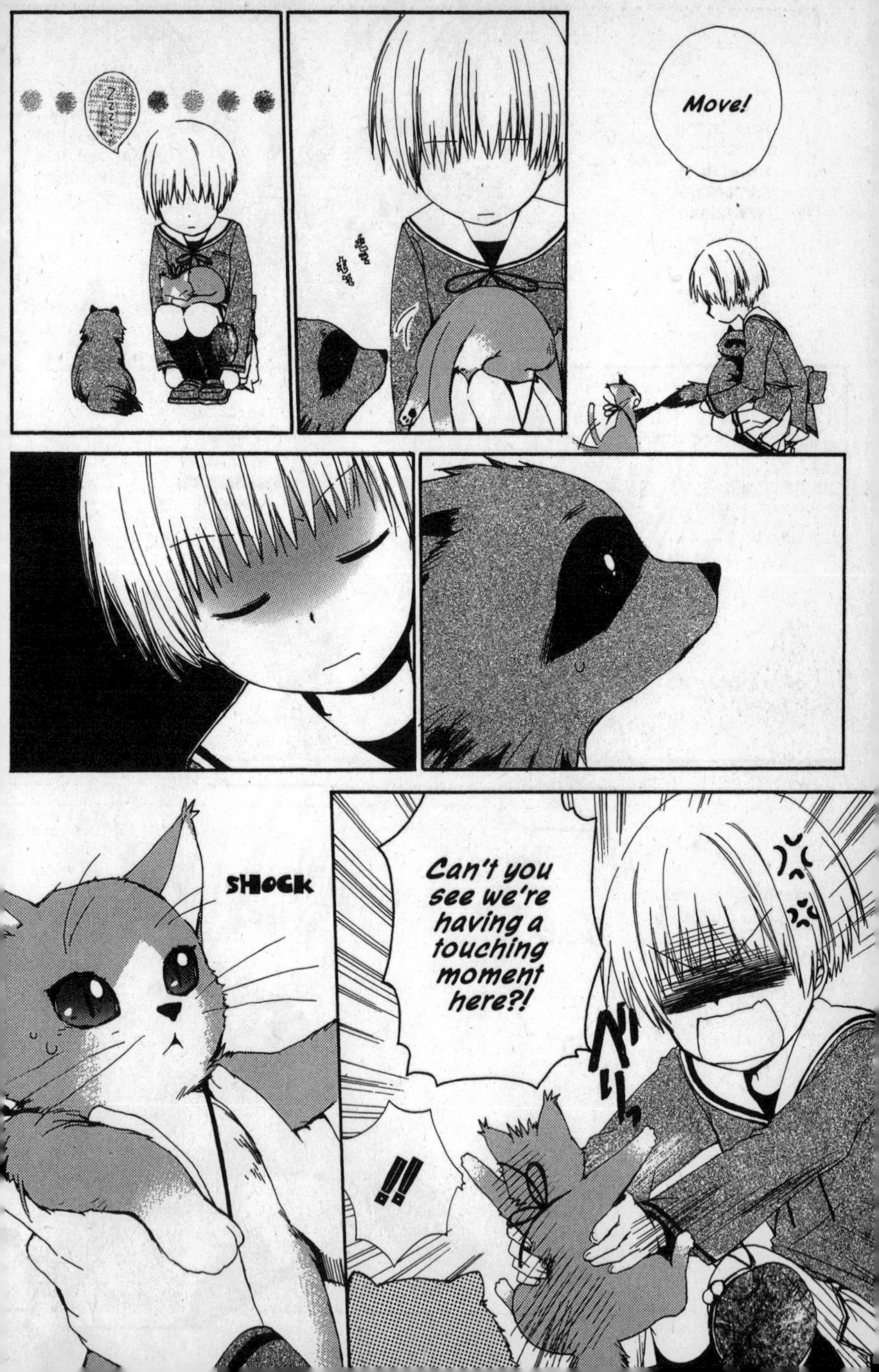
Move!
ZZZ
Can't you see we're having a touching moment here?!
!!
SHOCK

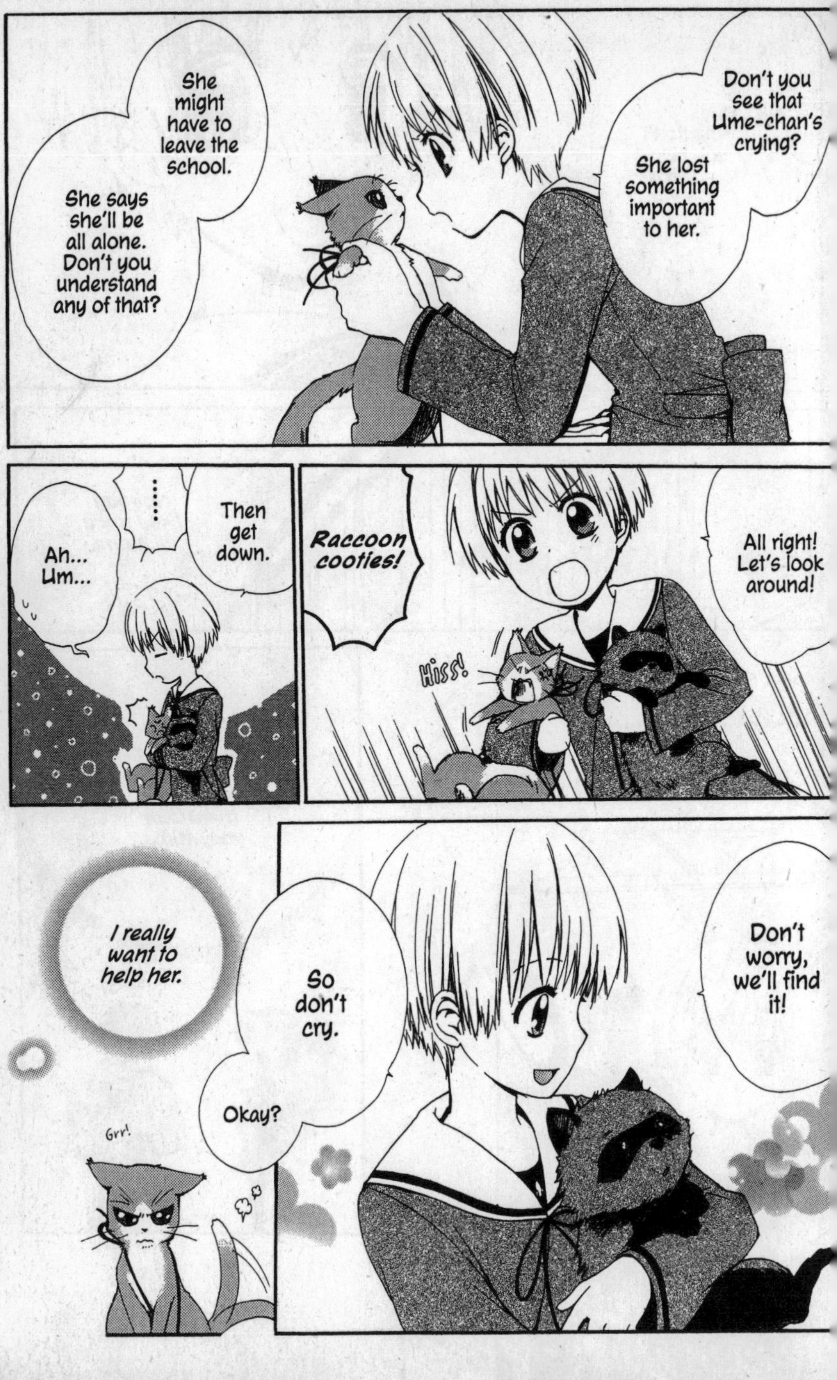
Don't you see that Ume-chan's crying?
She lost something important to her.
She might have to leave the school.
She says she'll be all alone. Don't you understand any of that?
All right! Let's look around!
Raccoon cooties!
HISS!
Then get down.
......
Ah... Um...
Don't worry, we'll find it!
So don't cry.
Okay?
I really want to help her.
Grr!

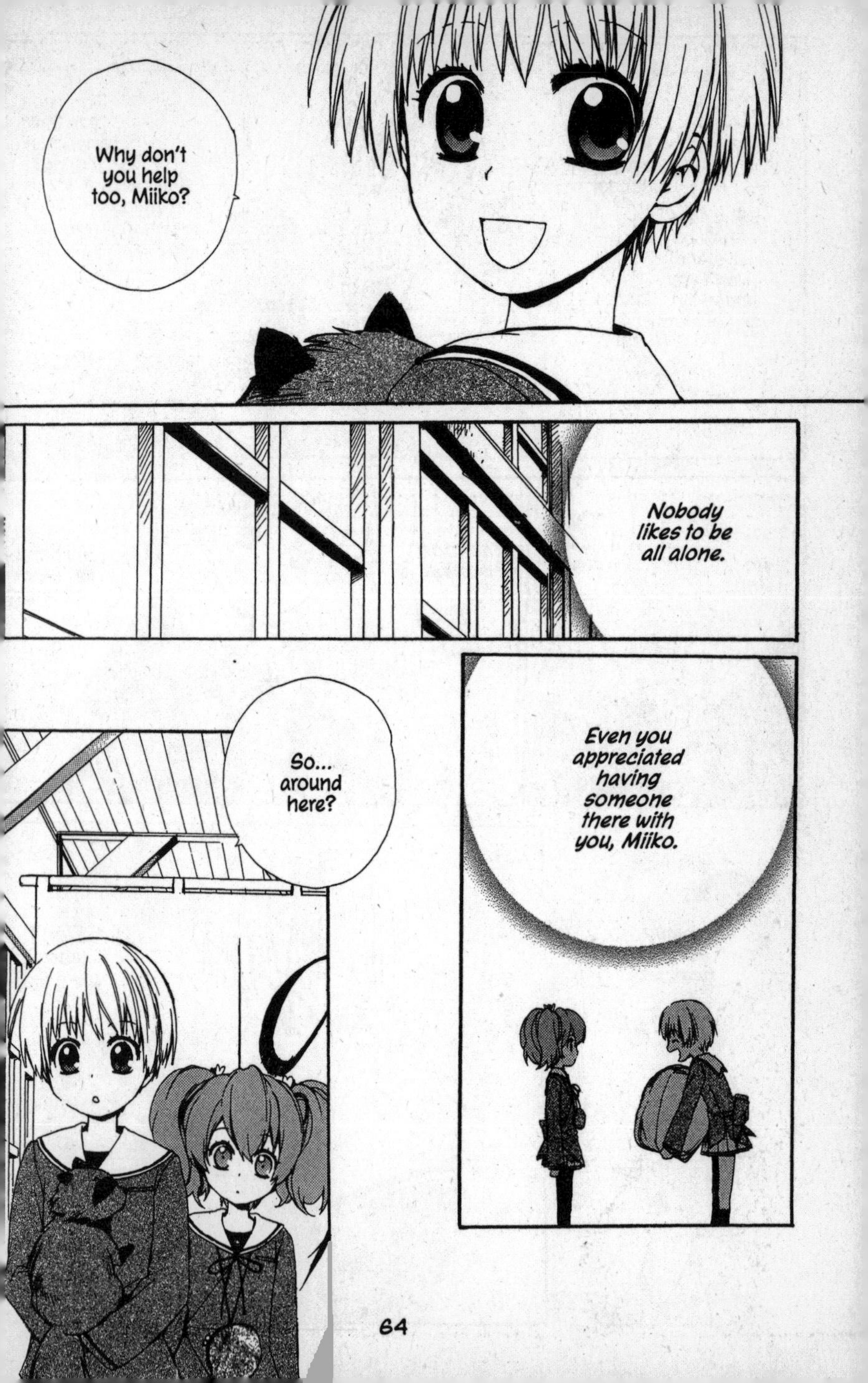
Why don't you help too, Miiko?
Nobody likes to be all alone.
Even you appreciated having someone there with you, Miiko.
So... around here?

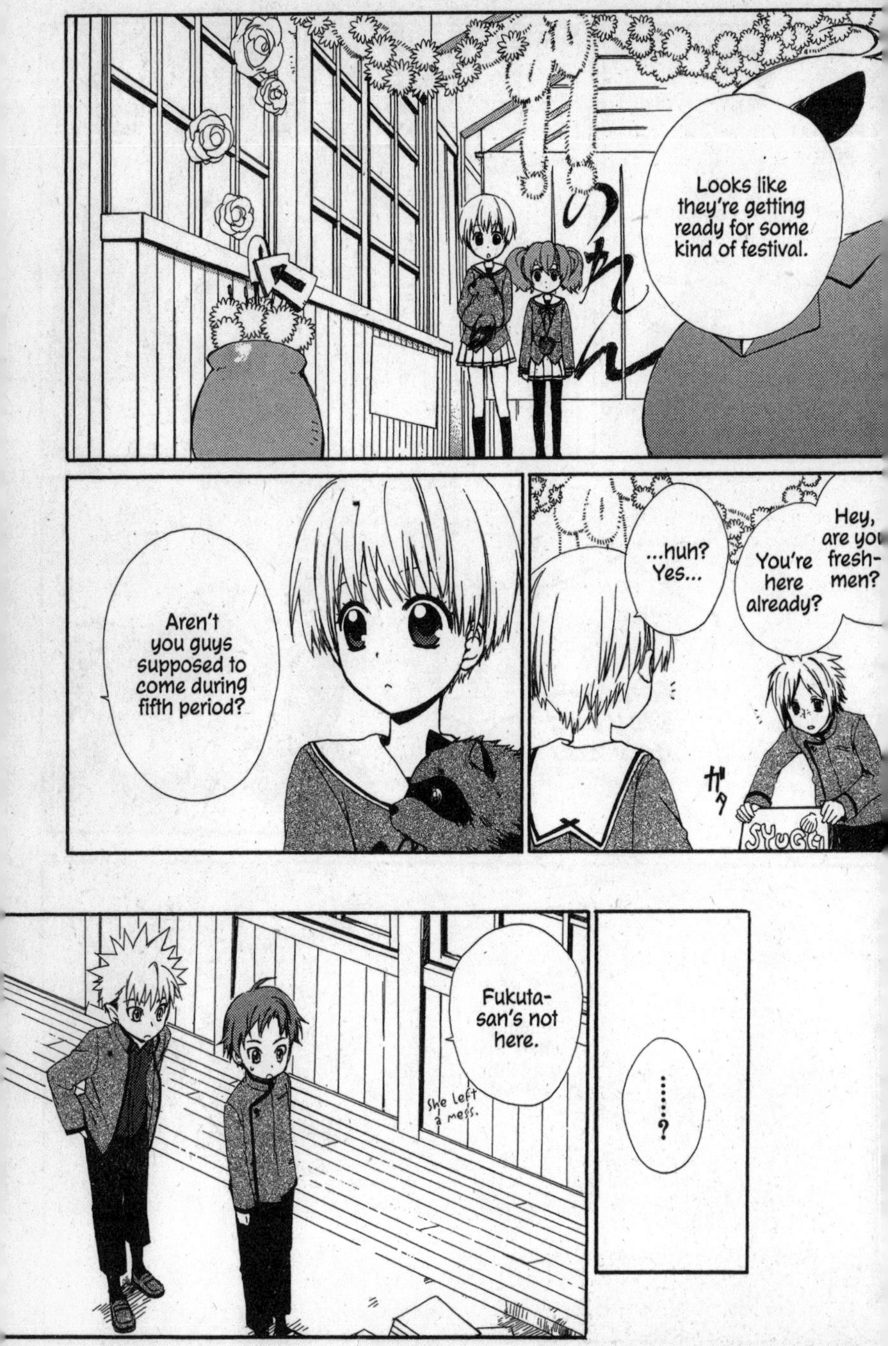
Looks like they're getting ready for some kind of festival.
Hey, are yo fresh-men?
You're here already?
...huh? Yes...
ガタ
Aren't you guys supposed to come during fifth period?
......?
Fukuta-san's not here.
She left a mess.

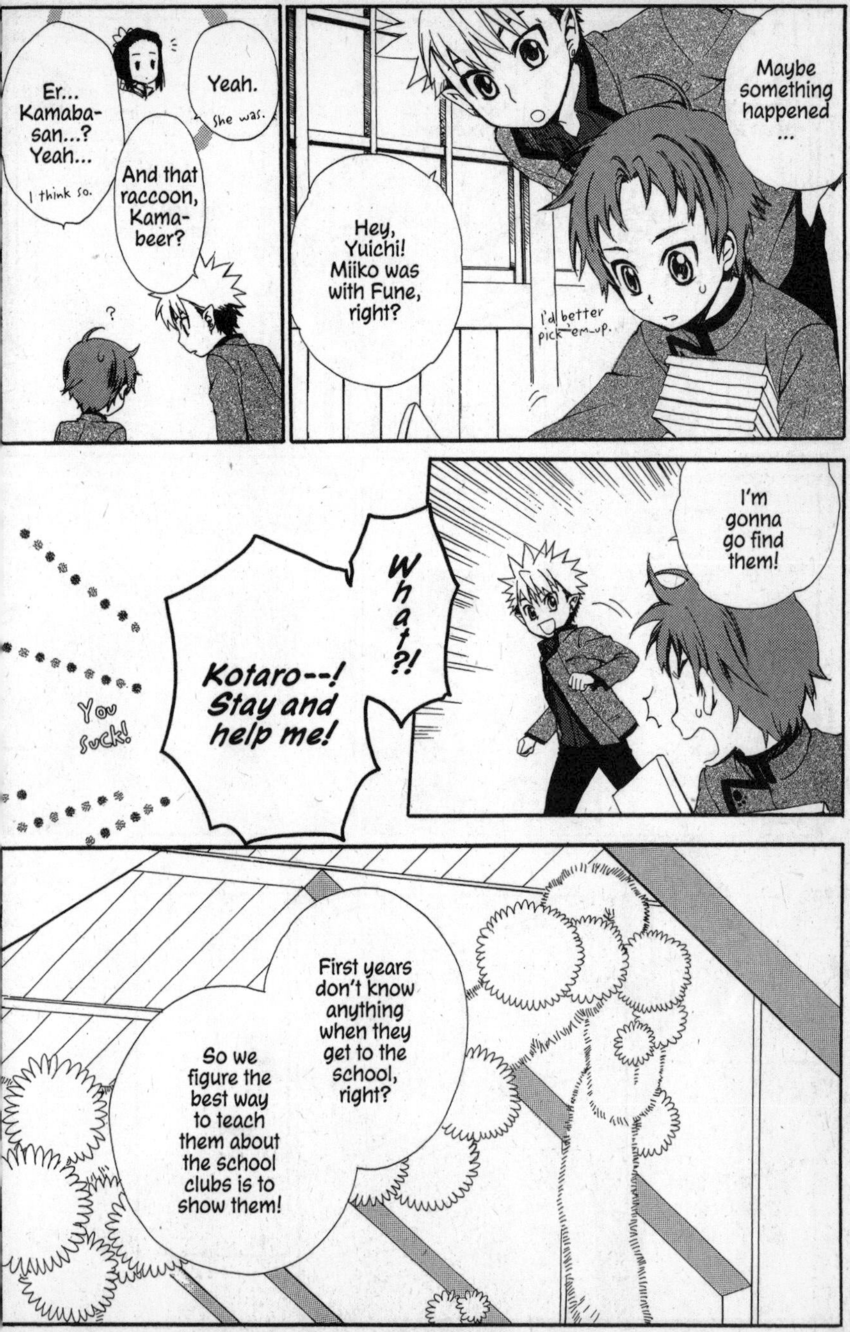

Maybe something happened ...
Hey, Yuichi! Miiko was with Fune, right?
I'd better pick 'em up.
Yeah. She was.
Er... Kamaba-san...? Yeah... I think so.
And that raccoon, Kama-beer?
?
I'm gonna go find them!
What?!
Kotaro--! Stay and help me!
You suck!
First years don't know anything when they get to the school, right?
So we figure the best way to teach them about the school clubs is to show them!

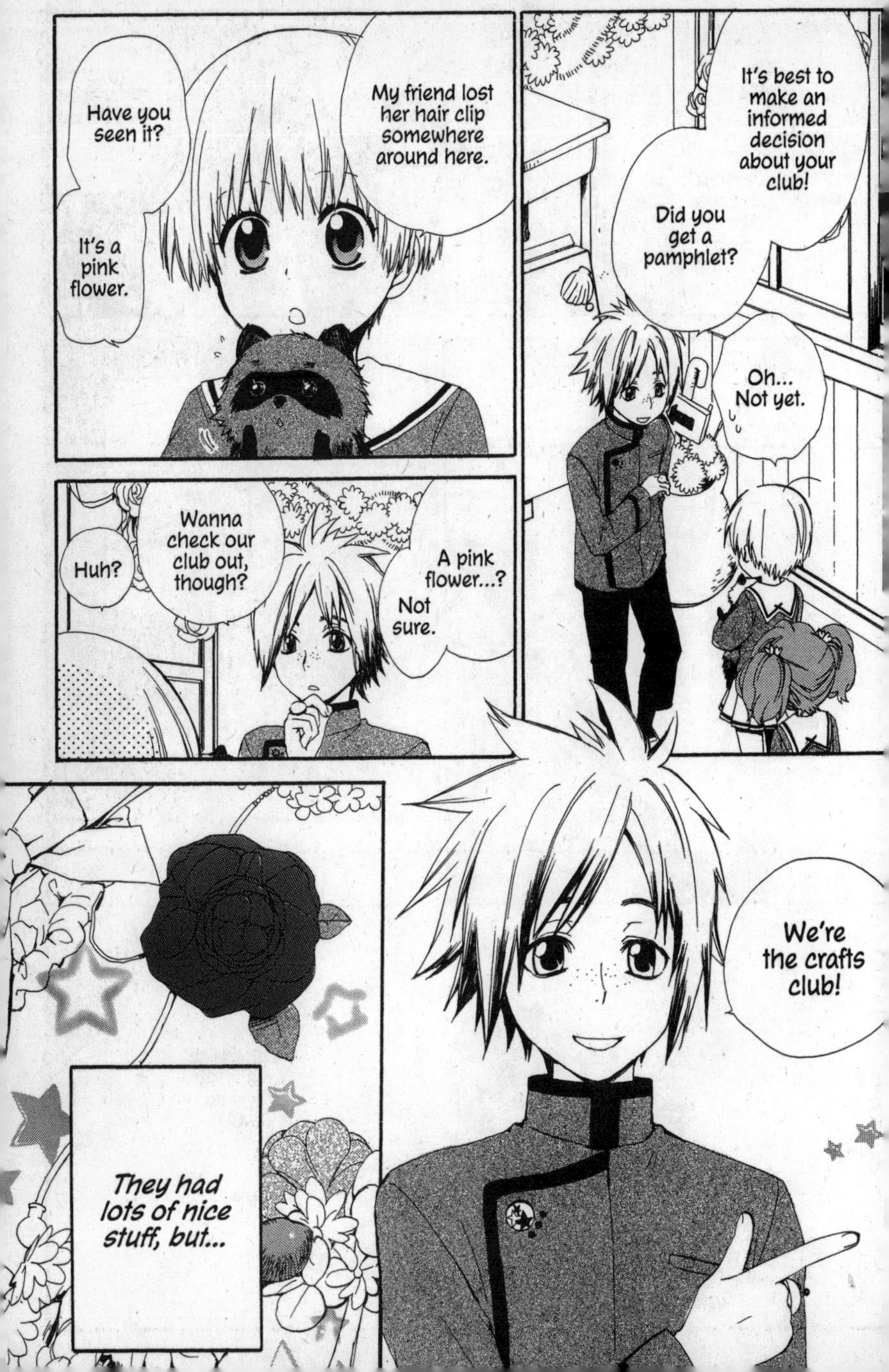
It's best to make an informed decision about your club!
Did you get a pamphlet?
Oh... Not yet.
My friend lost her hair clip somewhere around here.
Have you seen it?
It's a pink flower.
A pink flower...?
Not sure.
Wanna check our club out, though?
Huh?
We're the crafts club!
They had lots of nice stuff, but...

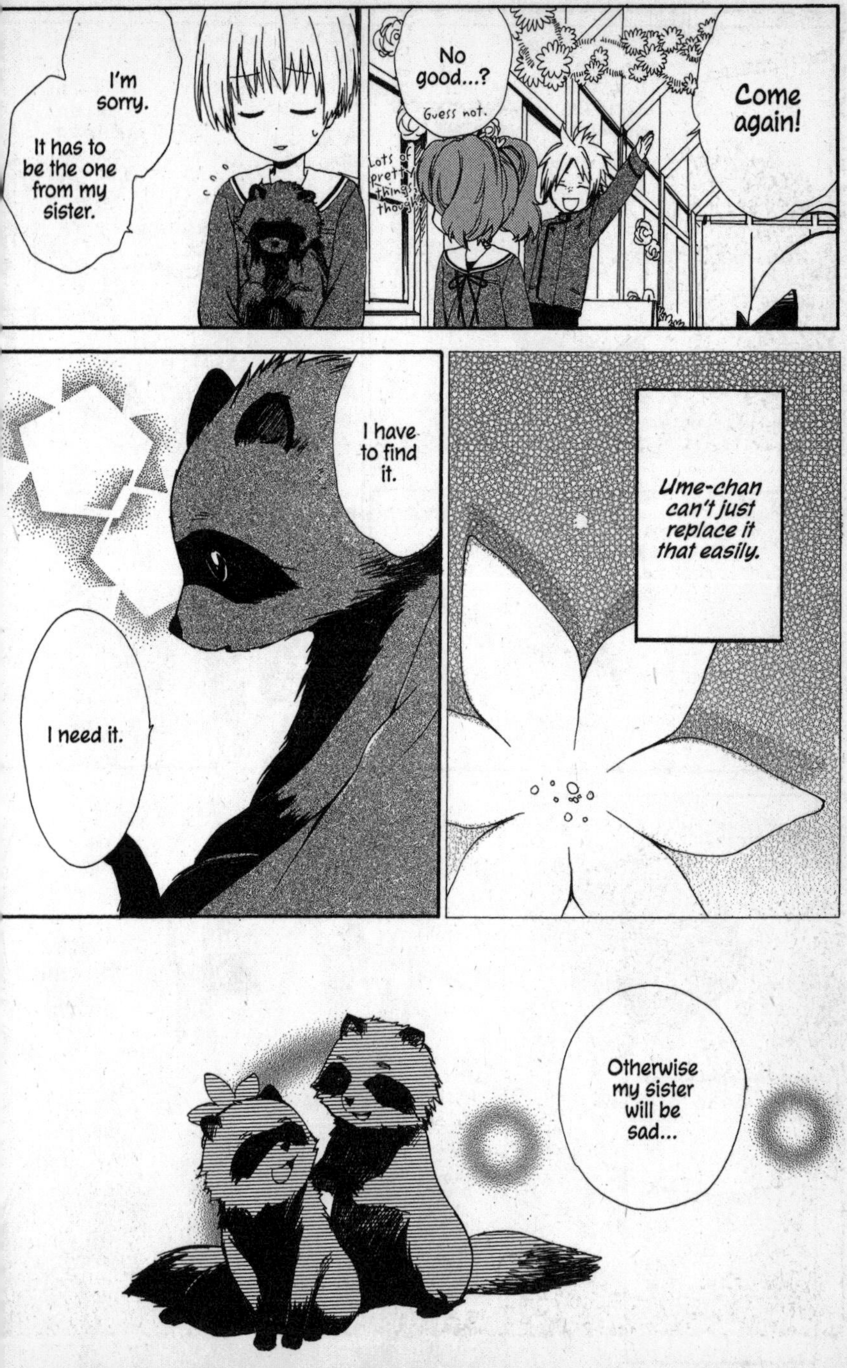
Come again!
No good...?
Guess not.
Lots of pretty things, though!
I'm sorry.
It has to be the one from my sister.
Ume-chan can't just replace it that easily.
I have to find it.
I need it.
Otherwise my sister will be sad...

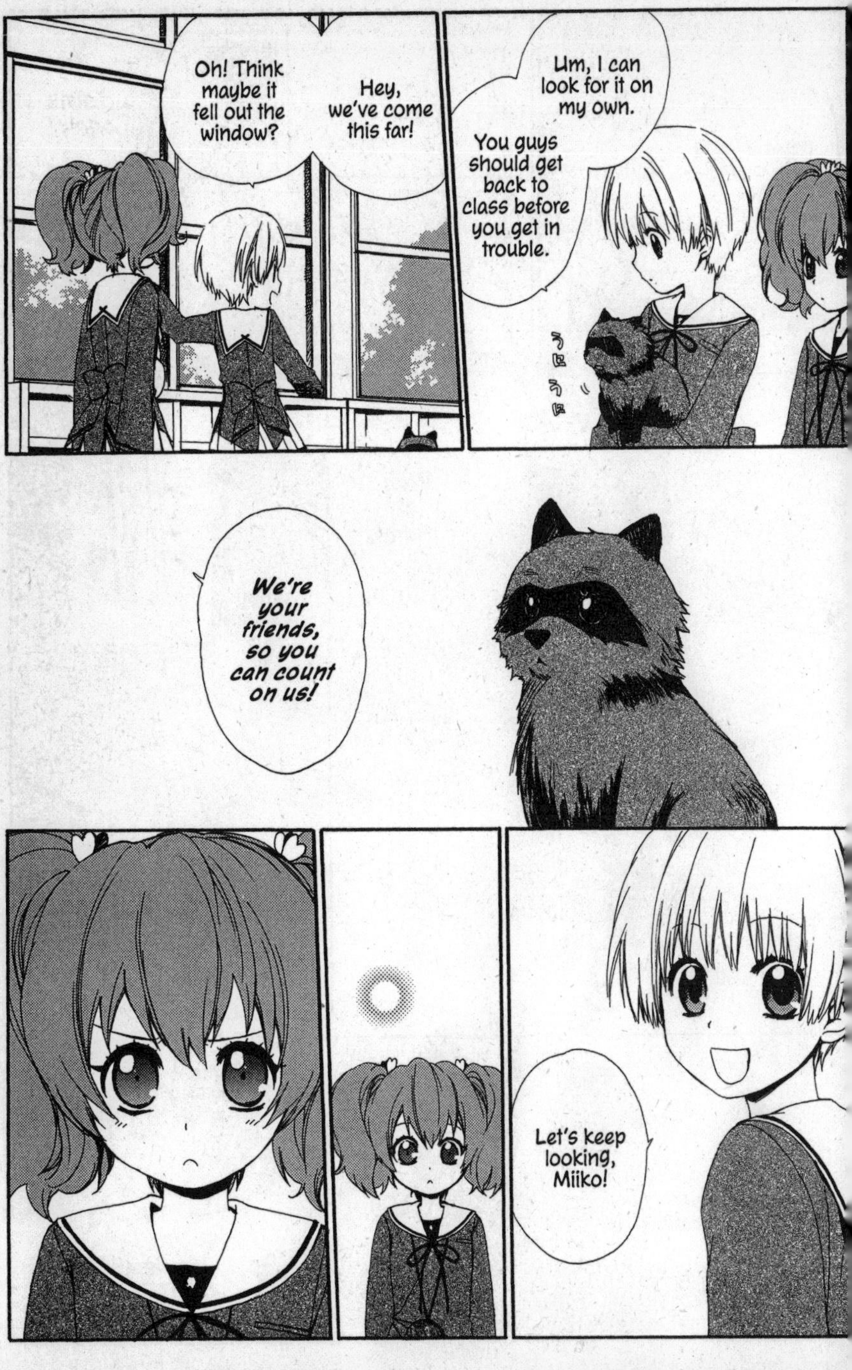
Um, I can look for it on my own.
You guys should get back to class before you get in trouble.
Hey, we've come this far!
Oh! Think maybe it fell out the window?
We're your friends, so you can count on us!
Let's keep looking, Miiko!

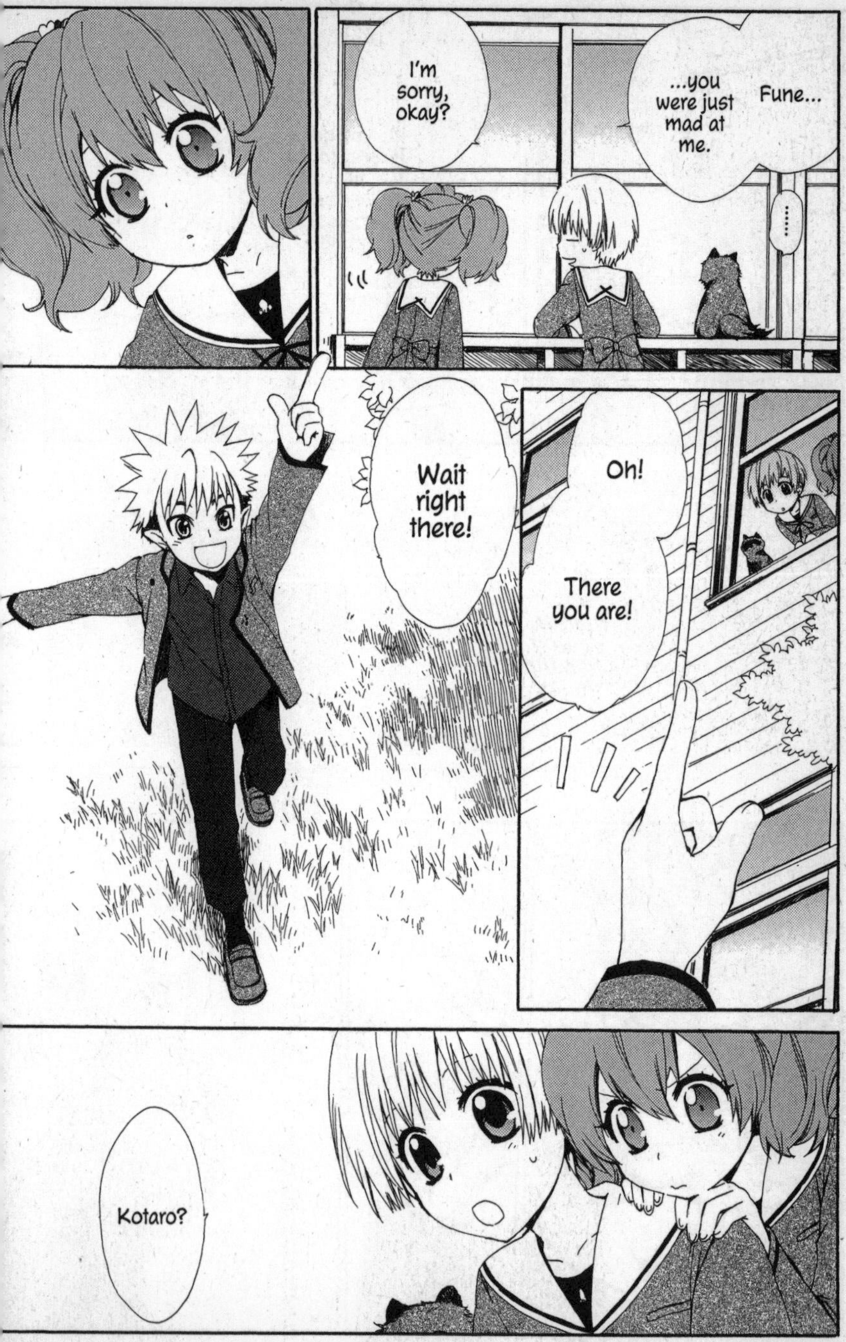
Fune...
...you were just mad at me.
......
I'm sorry, okay?
Oh!
There you are!
Wait right there!
Kotaro?

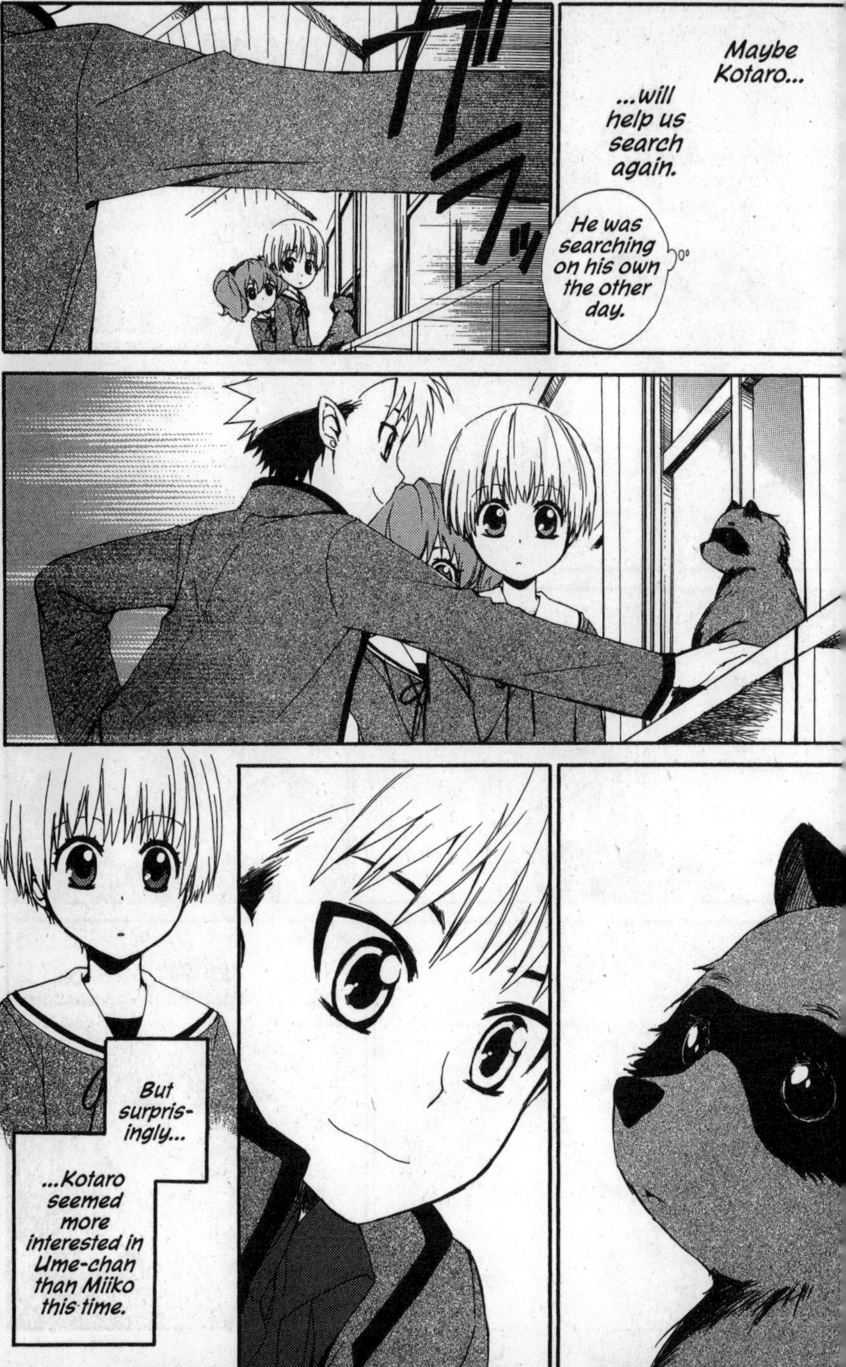
Maybe Kotaro...
...will help us search again.
He was searching on his own the other day.
But surpris-ingly...
...Kotaro seemed more interested in Ume-chan than Miiko this time.

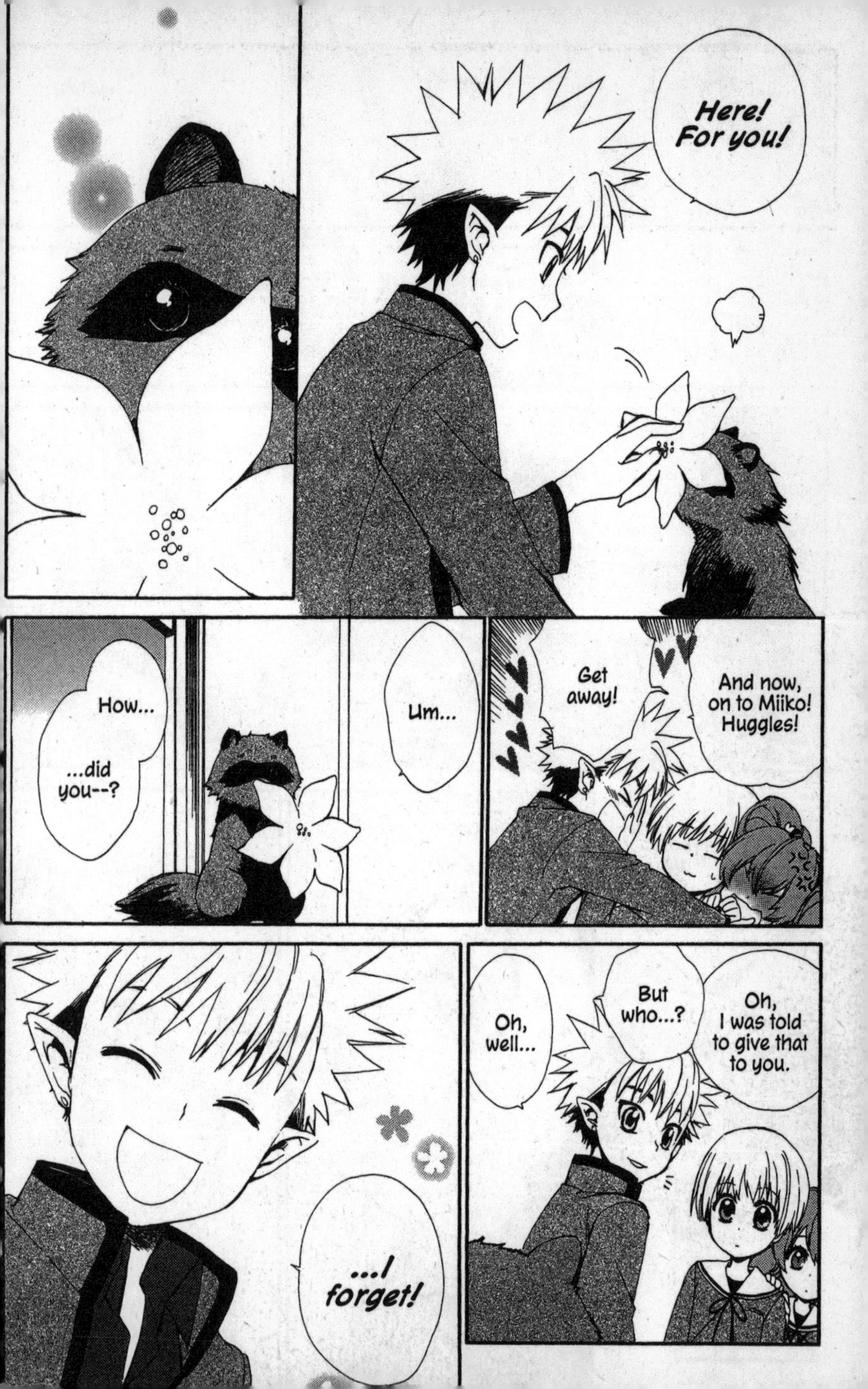
Here! For you!
And now, on to Miiko! Huggles!
Get away!
Um...
How...
...did you--?
Oh, I was told to give that to you.
But who...?
Oh, well...
...I forget!

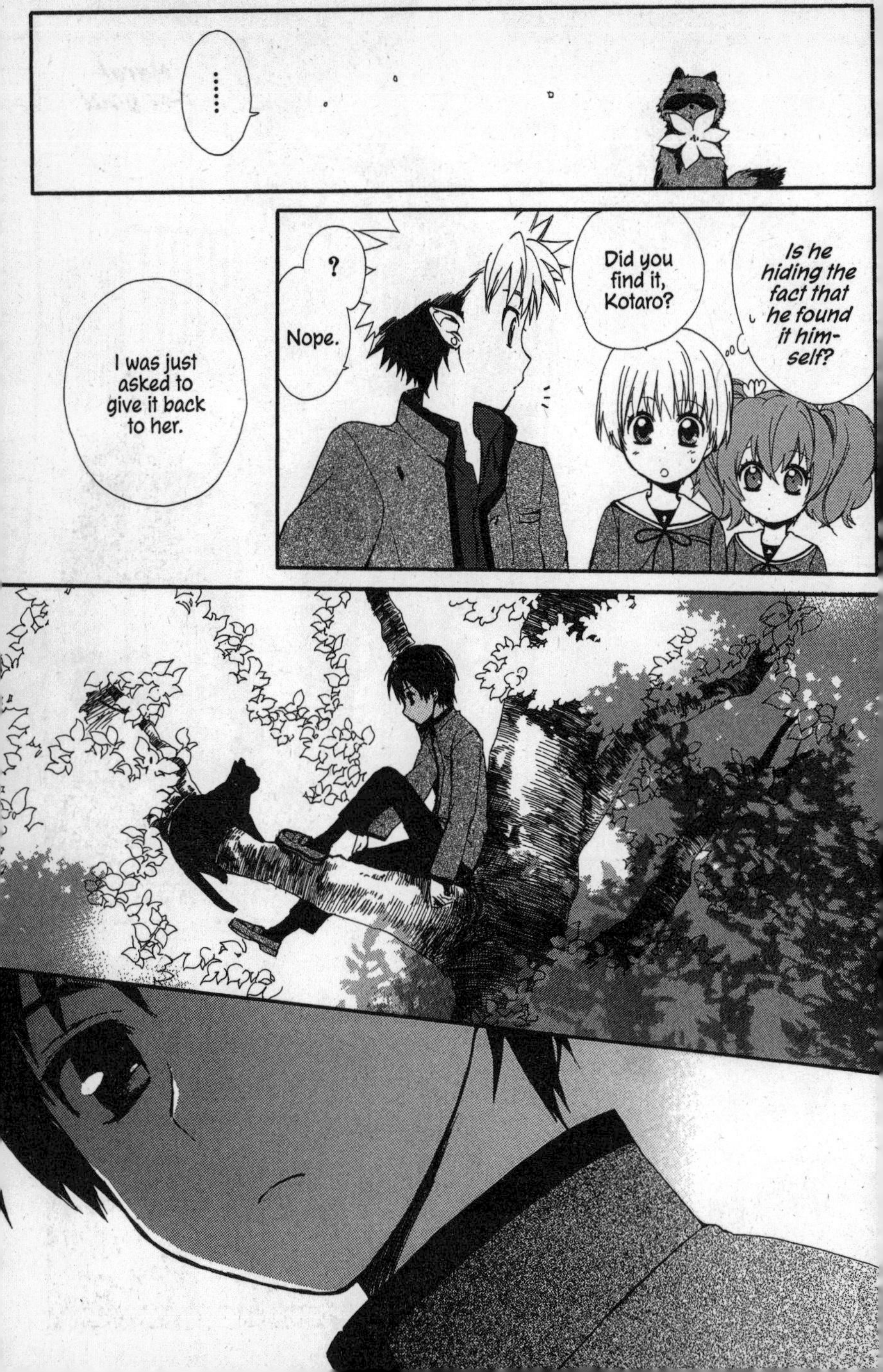
……
Is he hiding the fact that he found it himself?
Did you find it, Kotaro?
?
Nope.
I was just asked to give it back to her.

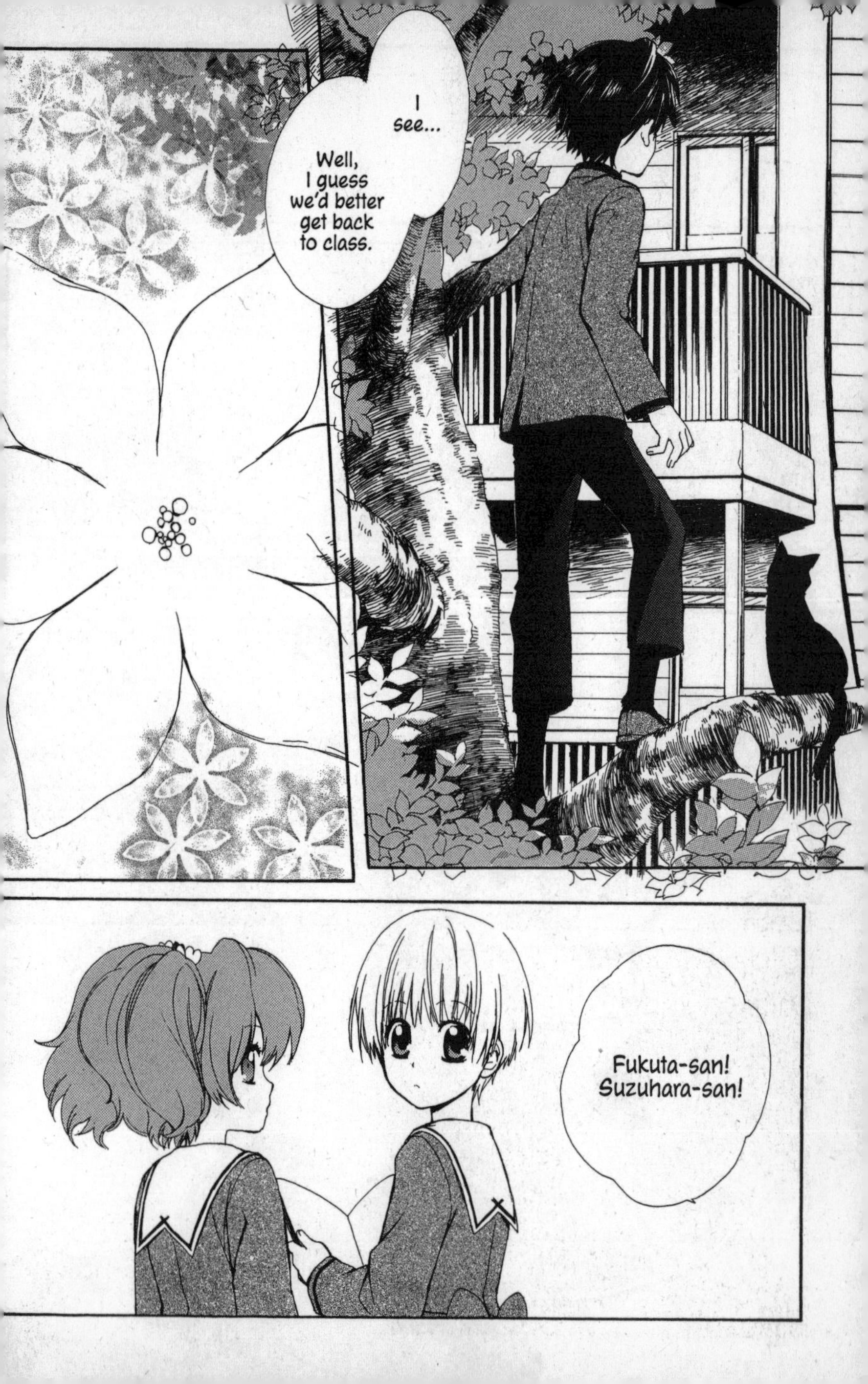
I see...
Well, I guess we'd better get back to class.
Fukuta-san! Suzuhara-san!

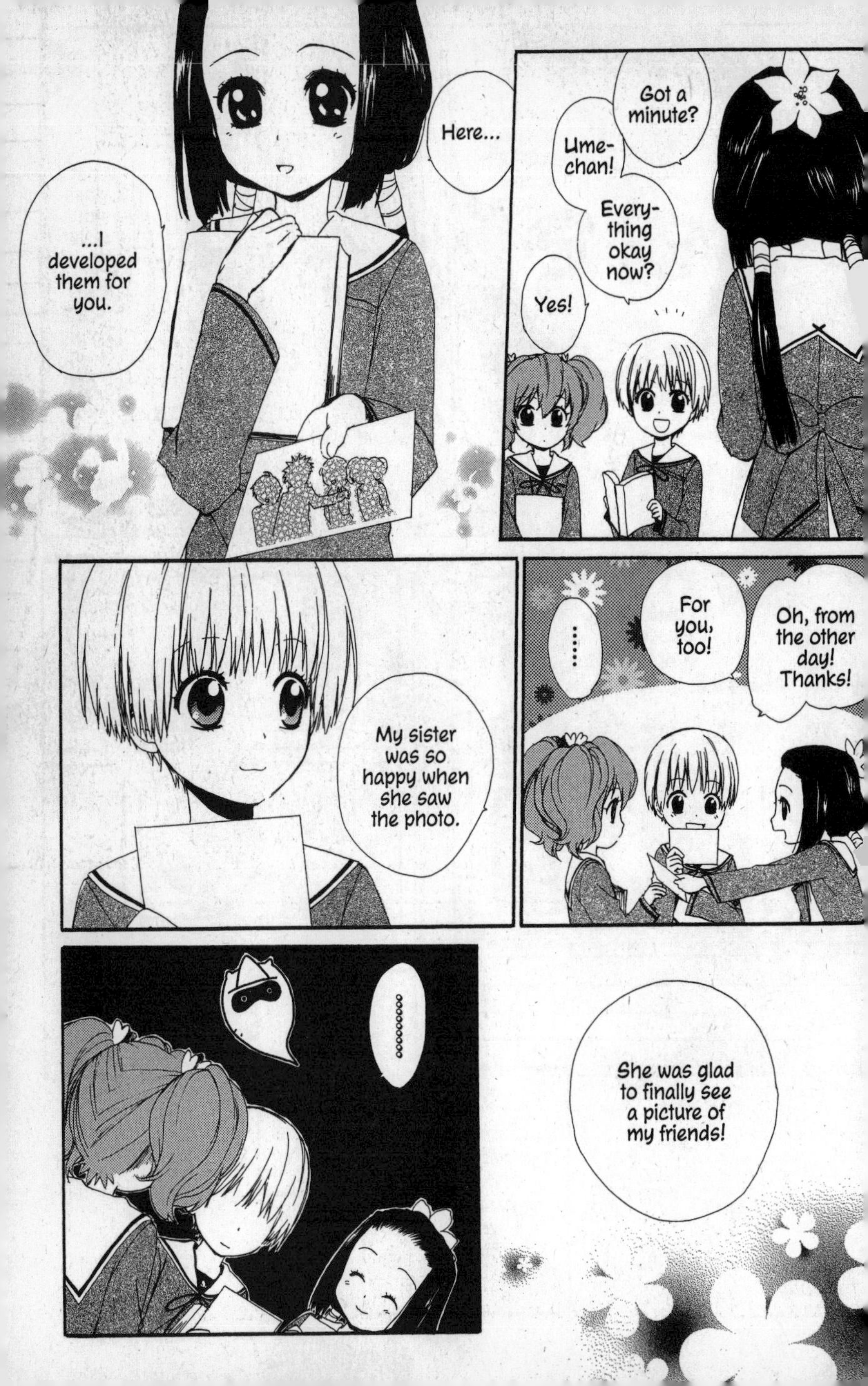
Got a minute?
Ume-chan!
Everything okay now?
Yes!
Here...
...I developed them for you.
Oh, from the other day! Thanks!
For you, too!
......
My sister was so happy when she saw the photo.
She was glad to finally see a picture of my friends!
....

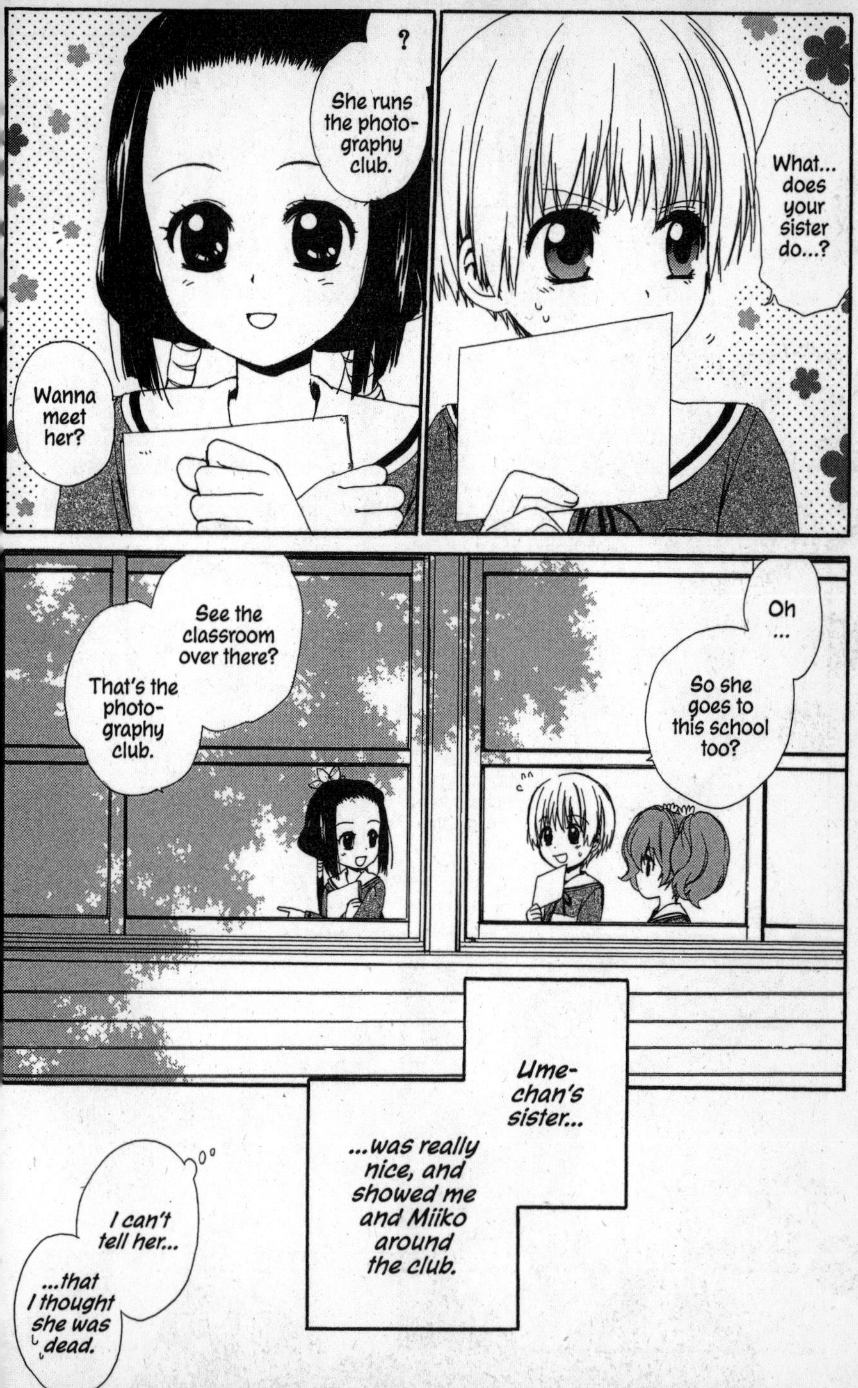
What... does your sister do...?
?
She runs the photography club.
Wanna meet her?
Oh ...
So she goes to this school too?
See the classroom over there?
That's the photography club.
Ume-chan's sister...
...was really nice, and showed me and Miiko around the club.
I can't tell her...
...that I thought she was dead.

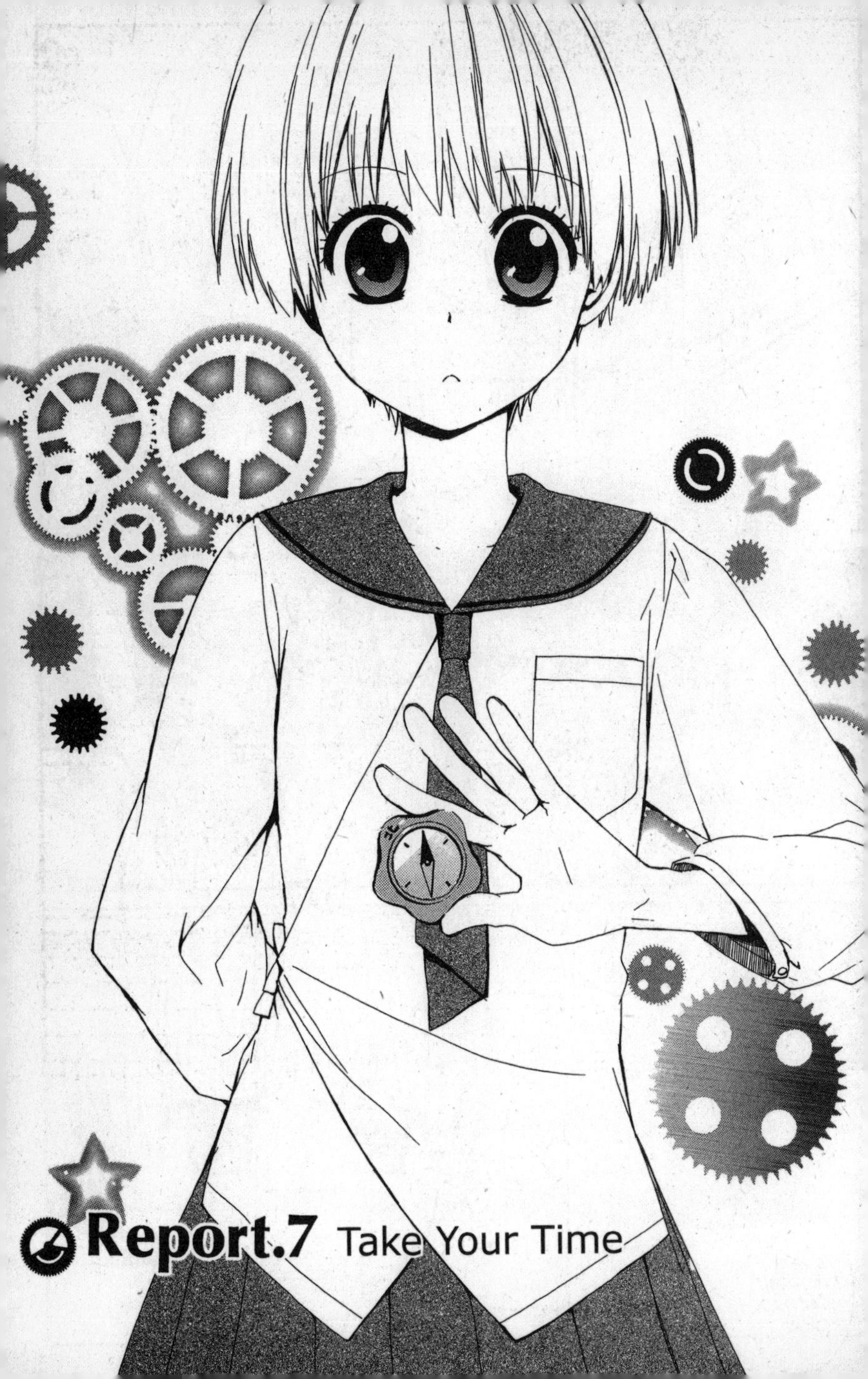
Report.7 Take Your Time

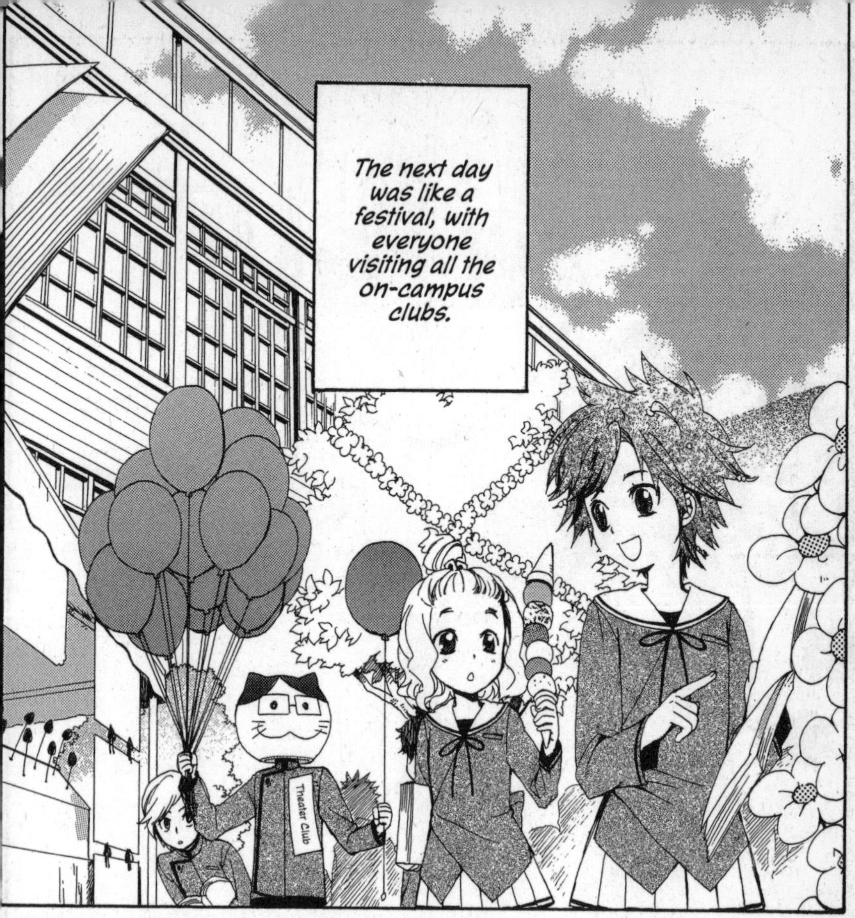
The next day was like a festival, with everyone visiting all the on-campus clubs.
Theater Club
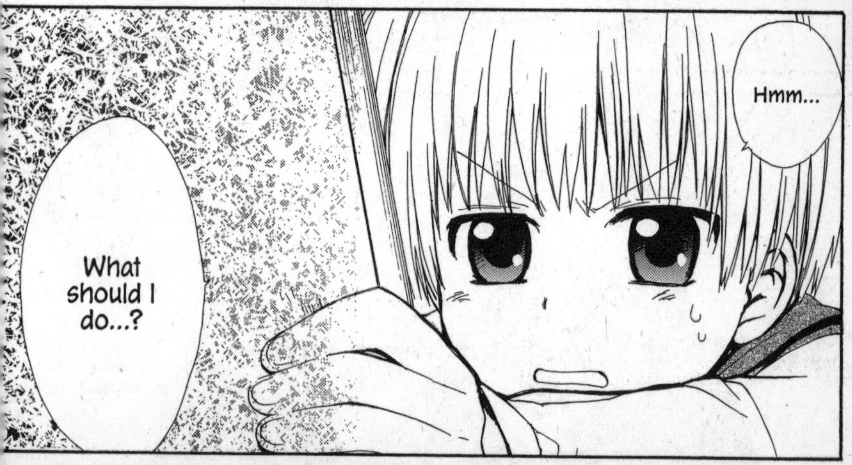
Hmm...
What should I do...?

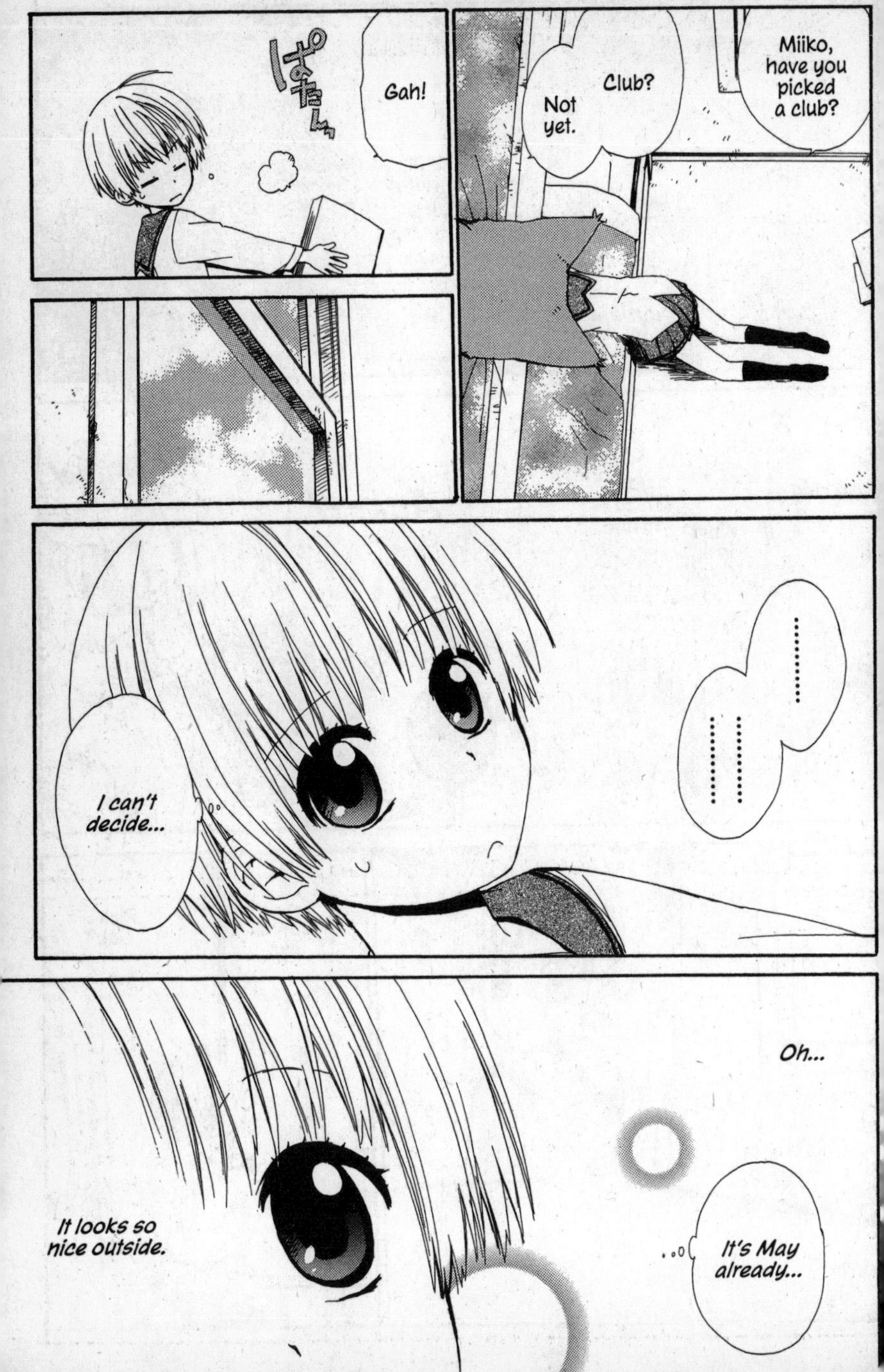
Miiko, have you picked a club?
Club?
Not yet.
ぱたん
Gah!
......
I can't decide...
Oh...
It's May already...
It looks so nice outside.

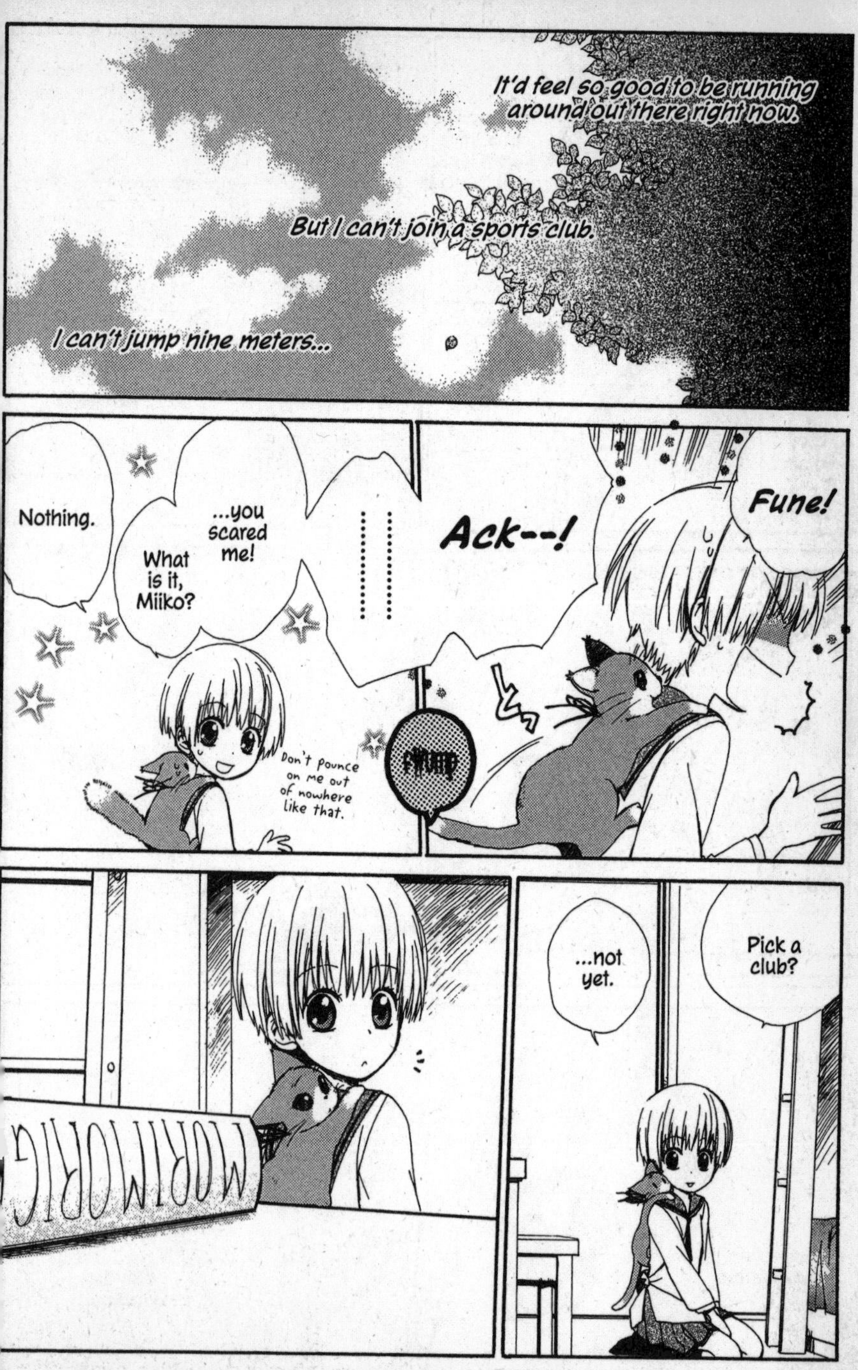
It'd feel so good to be running around out there right now.
But I can't join a sports club.
I can't jump nine meters...
Fune!
Ack--!
......
...you scared me!
What is it, Miiko?
Nothing.
Don't pounce on me out of nowhere like that.
Pick a club?
...not yet.

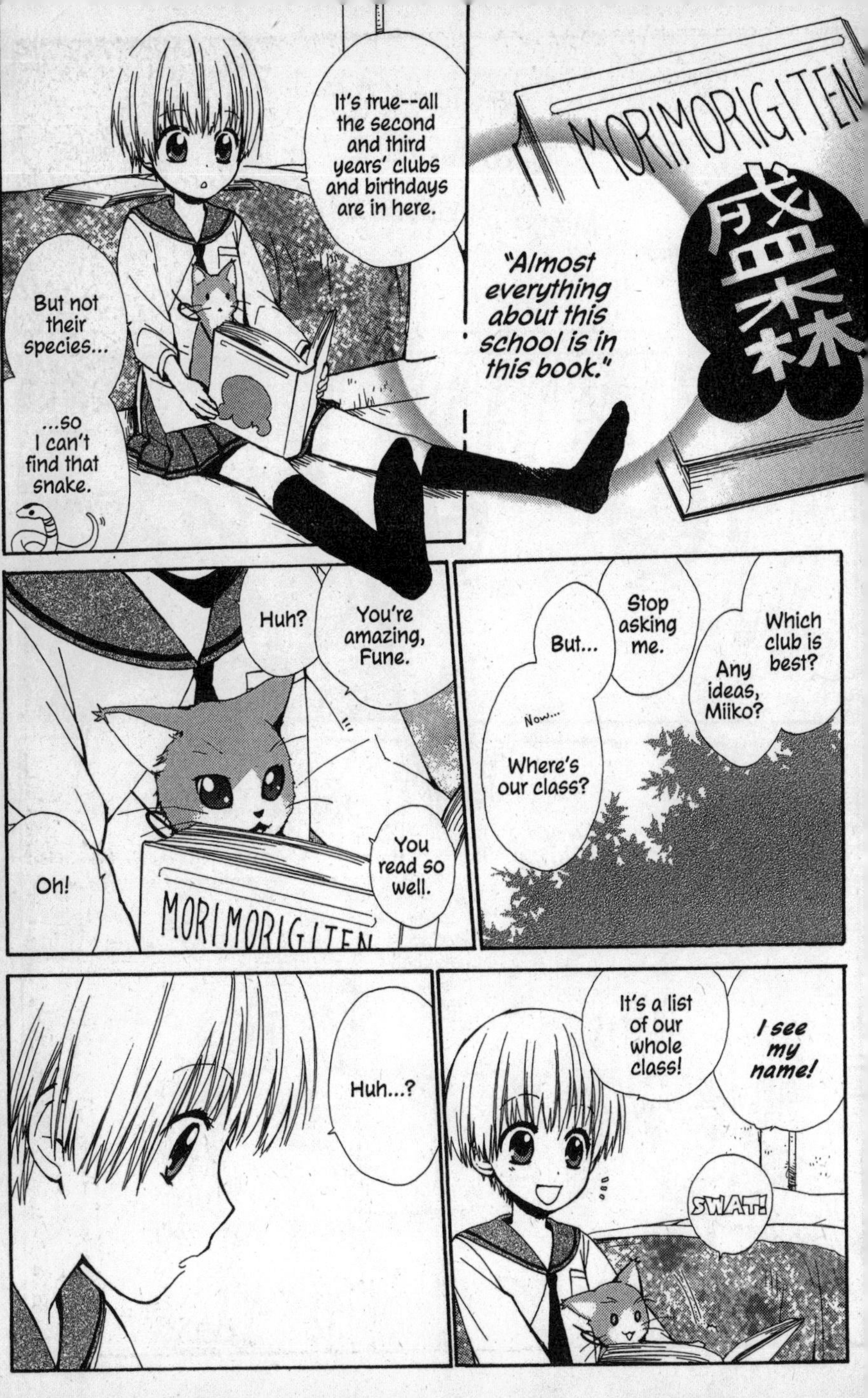
MORIMORIGITEN
盛森
"Almost everything about this school is in this book."
It's true--all the second and third years' clubs and birthdays are in here.
But not their species...
...so I can't find that snake.
Which club is best?
Any ideas, Miiko?
Stop asking me.
But...
Now...
Where's our class?
You're amazing, Fune.
Huh?
You read so well.
Oh!
MORIMORIGITEN
I see my name!
It's a list of our whole class!
SWAT!
Huh...?

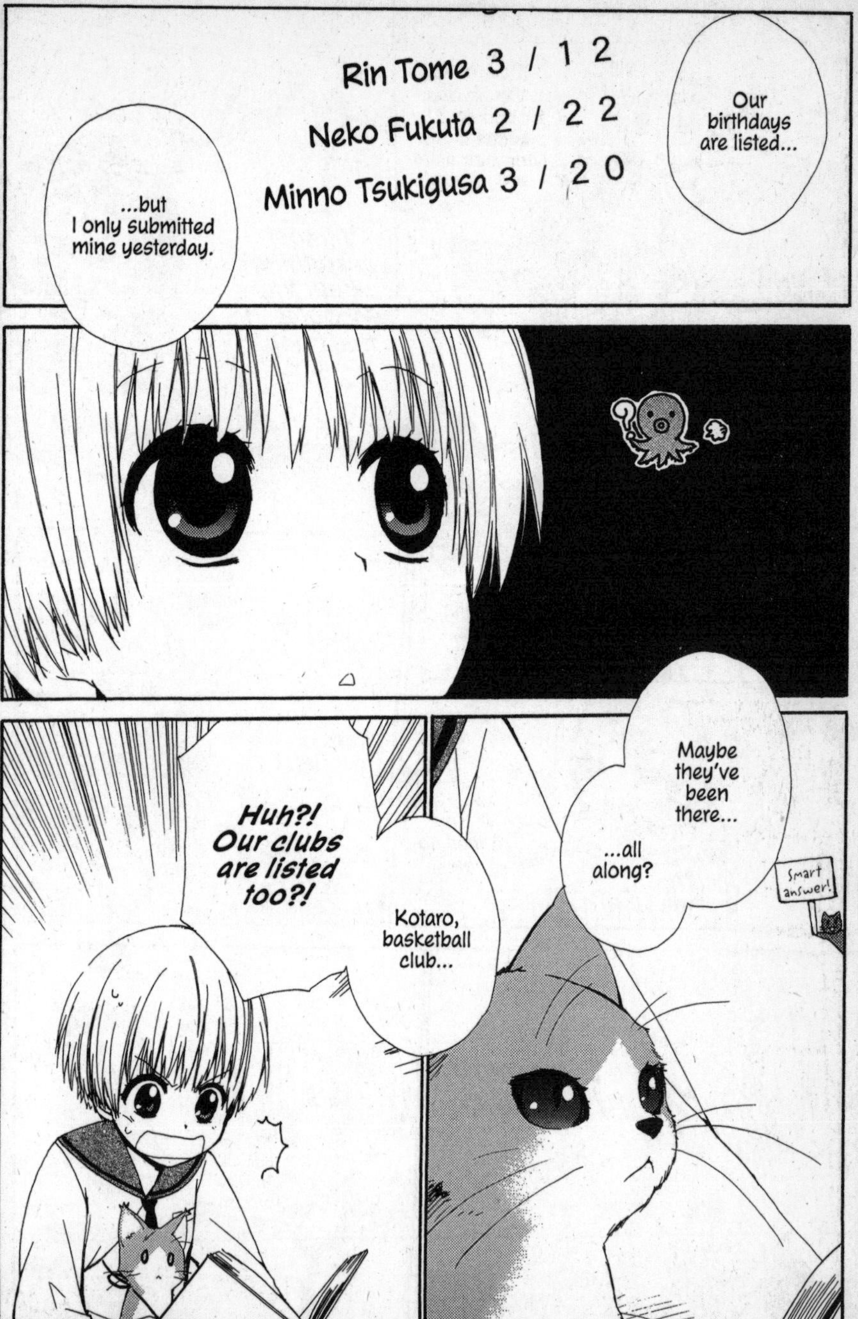
Our birthdays are listed...
Rin Tome 3 / 12
Neko Fukuta 2 / 22
Minno Tsukigusa 3 / 20
...but I only submitted mine yesterday.
Maybe they've been there...
...all along?
Smart answer!
Kotaro, basketball club...
Huh?! Our clubs are listed too?!

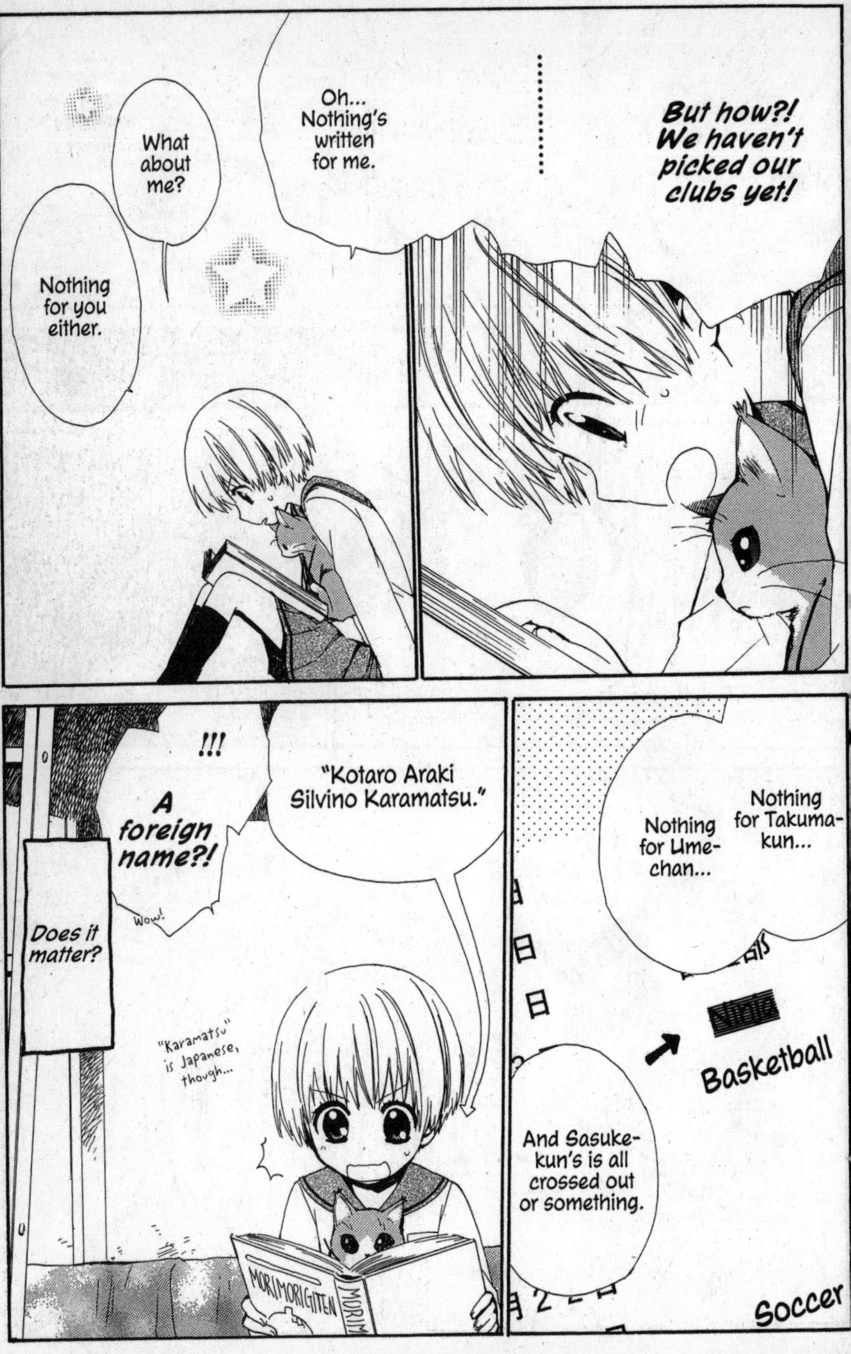
But how?! We haven't picked our clubs yet!
......
Oh... Nothing's written for me.
What about me?
Nothing for you either.
Nothing for Takuma-kun...
Nothing for Ume-chan...
Basketball
Soccer
And Sasuke-kun's is all crossed out or something.
"Kotaro Araki Silvino Karamatsu."
!!!
A foreign name?!
Wow!
Does it matter?
"Karamatsu" is Japanese, though...
MORIMORIGITEN

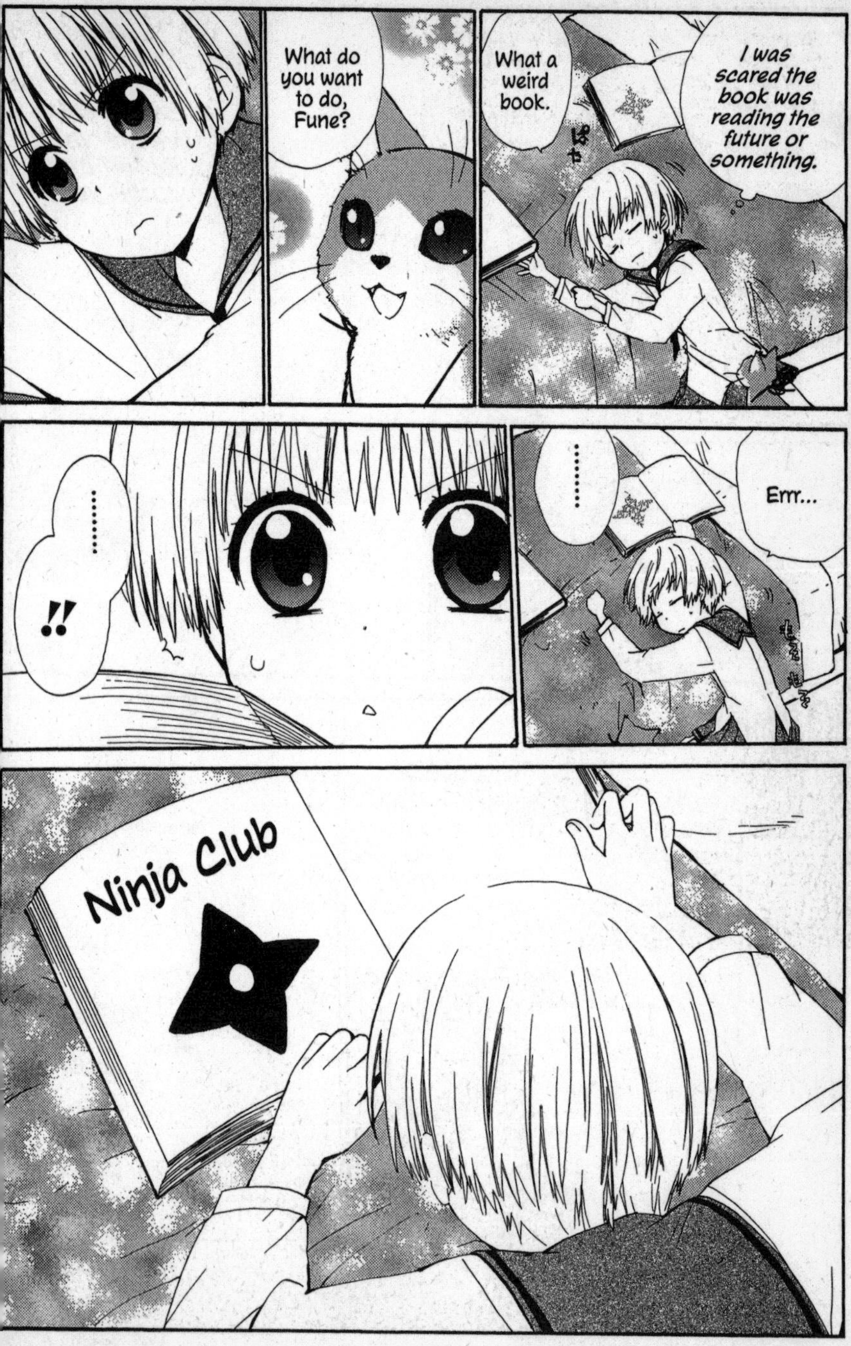
I was scared the book was reading the future or something.
What a weird book.
What do you want to do, Fune?
Err...
......
......
!!
Ninja Club

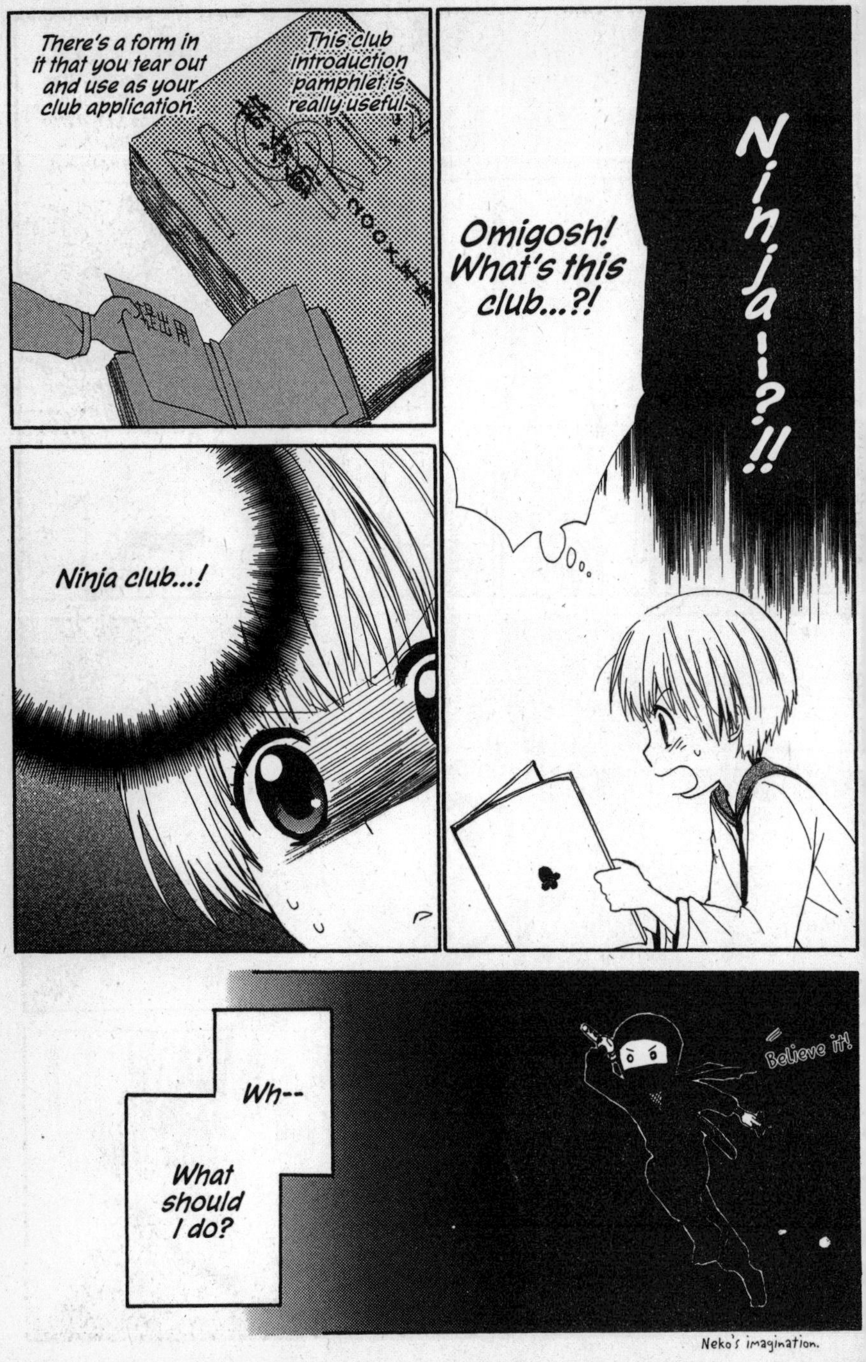
Ninja!!?!!
Omigosh! What's this club...?!
This club introduction pamphlet is really useful.
There's a form in it that you tear out and use as your club application.
Ninja club...!
Believe it!
Wh--
What should I do?

Neko's imagination.

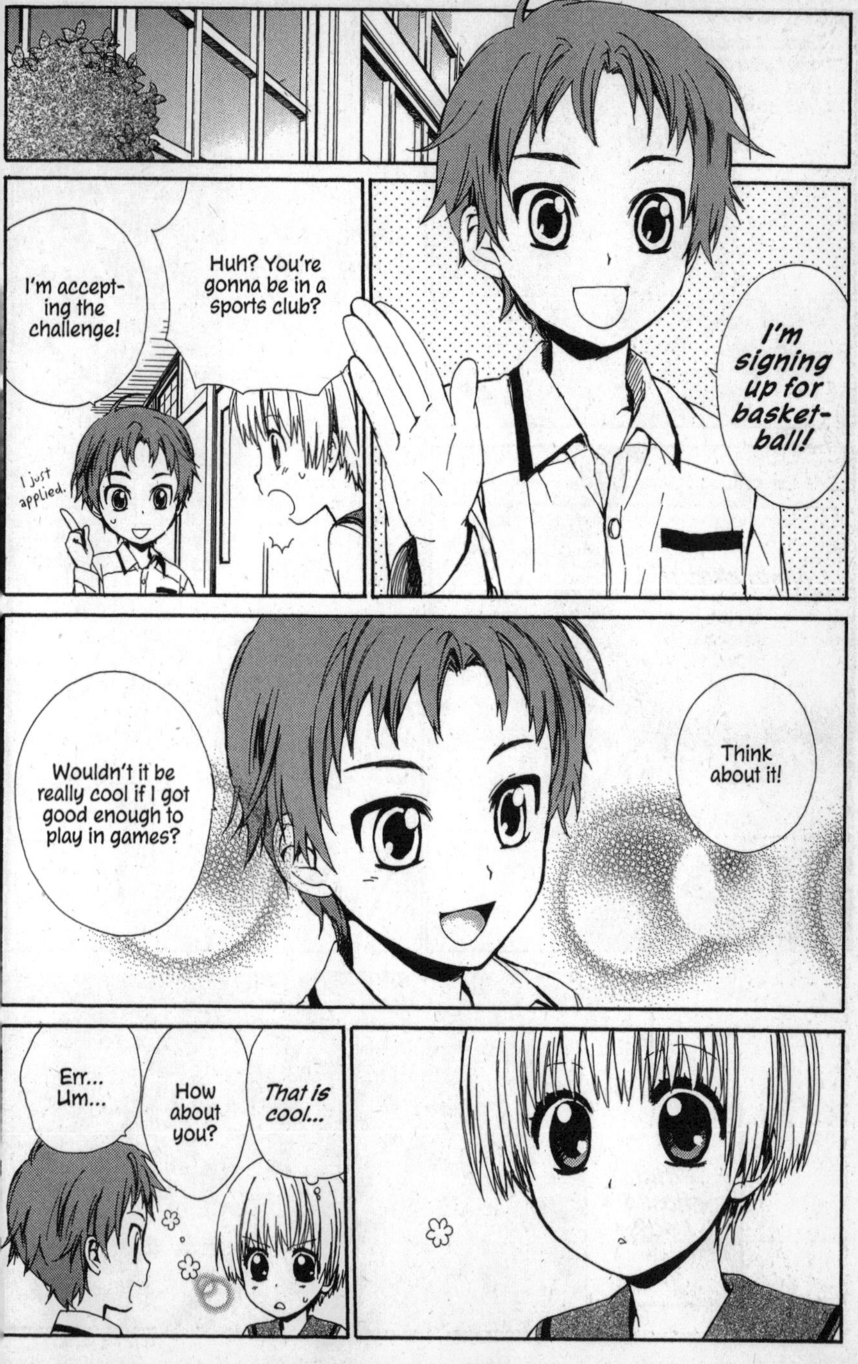
I'm signing up for basketball!
Huh? You're gonna be in a sports club?
I'm accepting the challenge!
I just applied.
Think about it!
Wouldn't it be really cool if I got good enough to play in games?
That is cool...
How about you?
Err... Um...

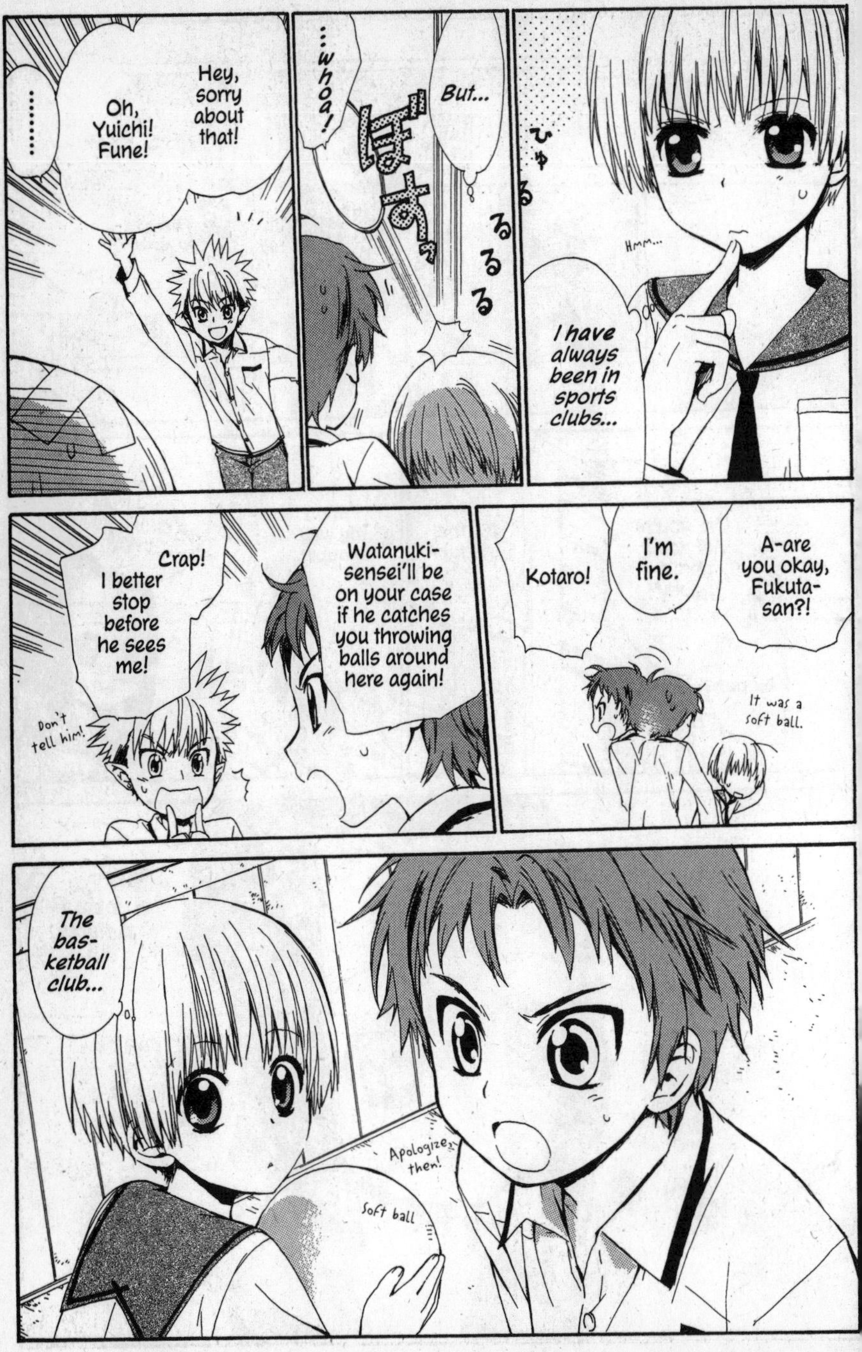
ひゅるるるる
Hmm...
I have always been in sports clubs...
But...
...whoa!
ぽすっ
Hey, sorry about that!
Oh, Yuichi! Fune!
....
A-are you okay, Fukuta-san?!
I'm fine.
Kotaro!
It was a soft ball.
Watanuki-sensei'll be on your case if he catches you throwing balls around here again!
Crap! I better stop before he sees me!
Don't tell him!
The bas-ketball club...
Apologize then!
Soft ball

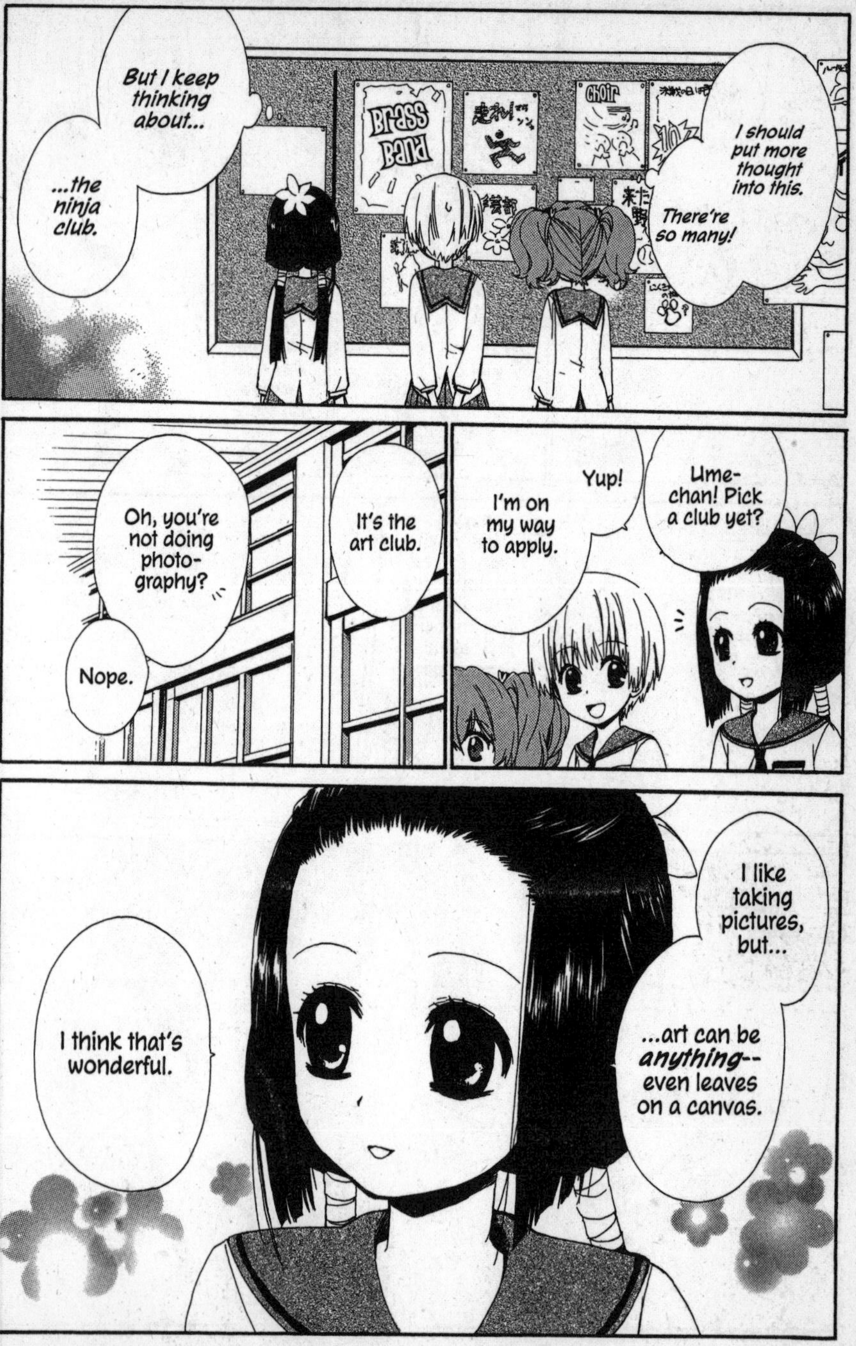
I should put more thought into this.
There're so many!
Choir
Brass Band
But I keep thinking about...
...the ninja club.
Ume-chan! Pick a club yet?
Yup!
I'm on my way to apply.
It's the art club.
Oh, you're not doing photo-graphy?
Nope.
I like taking pictures, but...
...art can be *anything*--even leaves on a canvas.
I think that's wonderful.

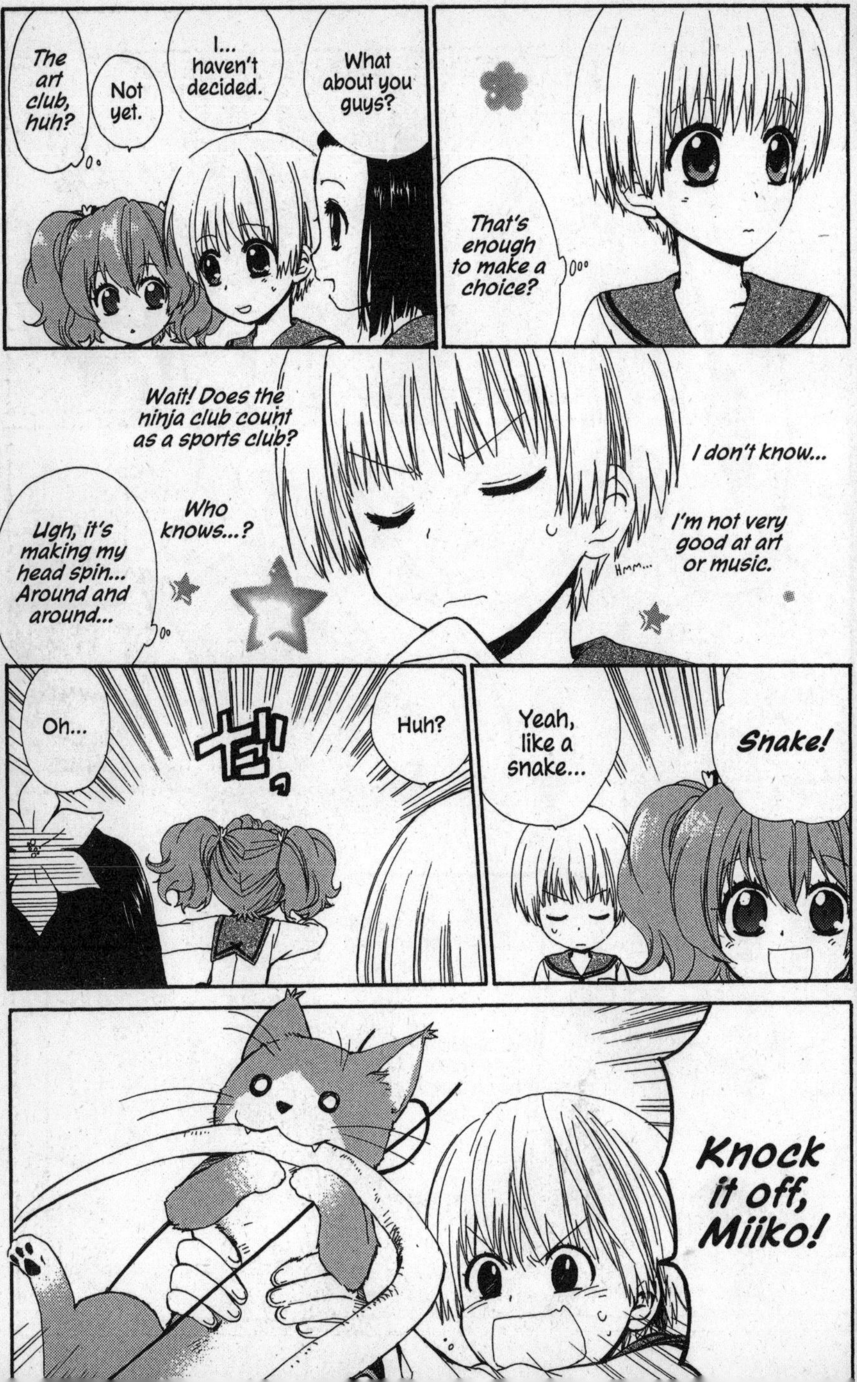
That's enough to make a choice?
What about you guys?
I... haven't decided.
Not yet.
The art club, huh?
I don't know...
I'm not very good at art or music.
Hmm...
Wait! Does the ninja club count as a sports club?
Who knows...?
Ugh, it's making my head spin... Around and around...
Snake!
Yeah, like a snake...
Huh?
Oh...
Knock it off, Miiko!

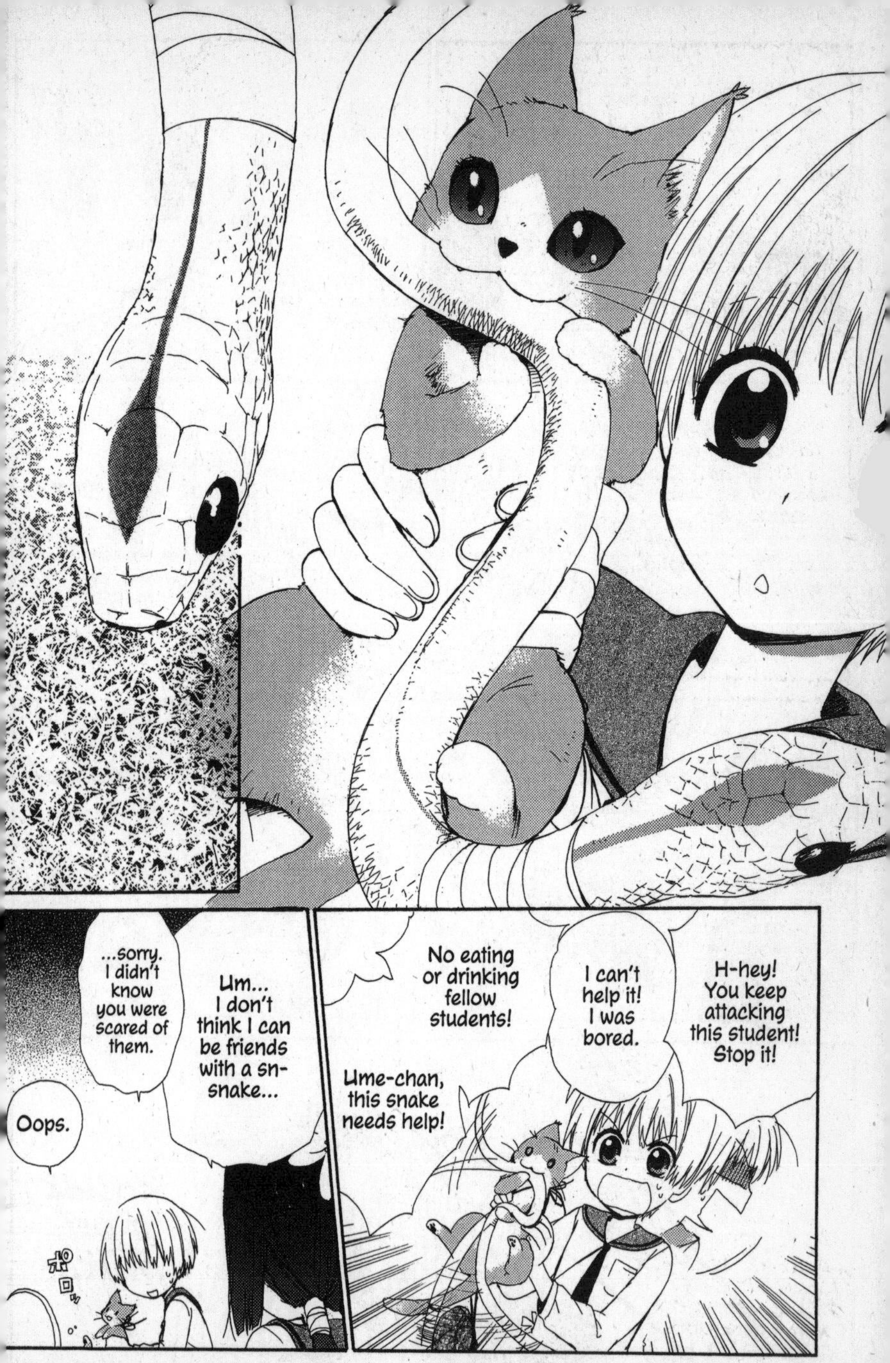
H-hey! You keep attacking this student! Stop it!
I can't help it! I was bored.
No eating or drinking fellow students!
Ume-chan, this snake needs help!
Um... I don't think I can be friends with a sn-snake...
...sorry. I didn't know you were scared of them.
Oops.
ポロッ

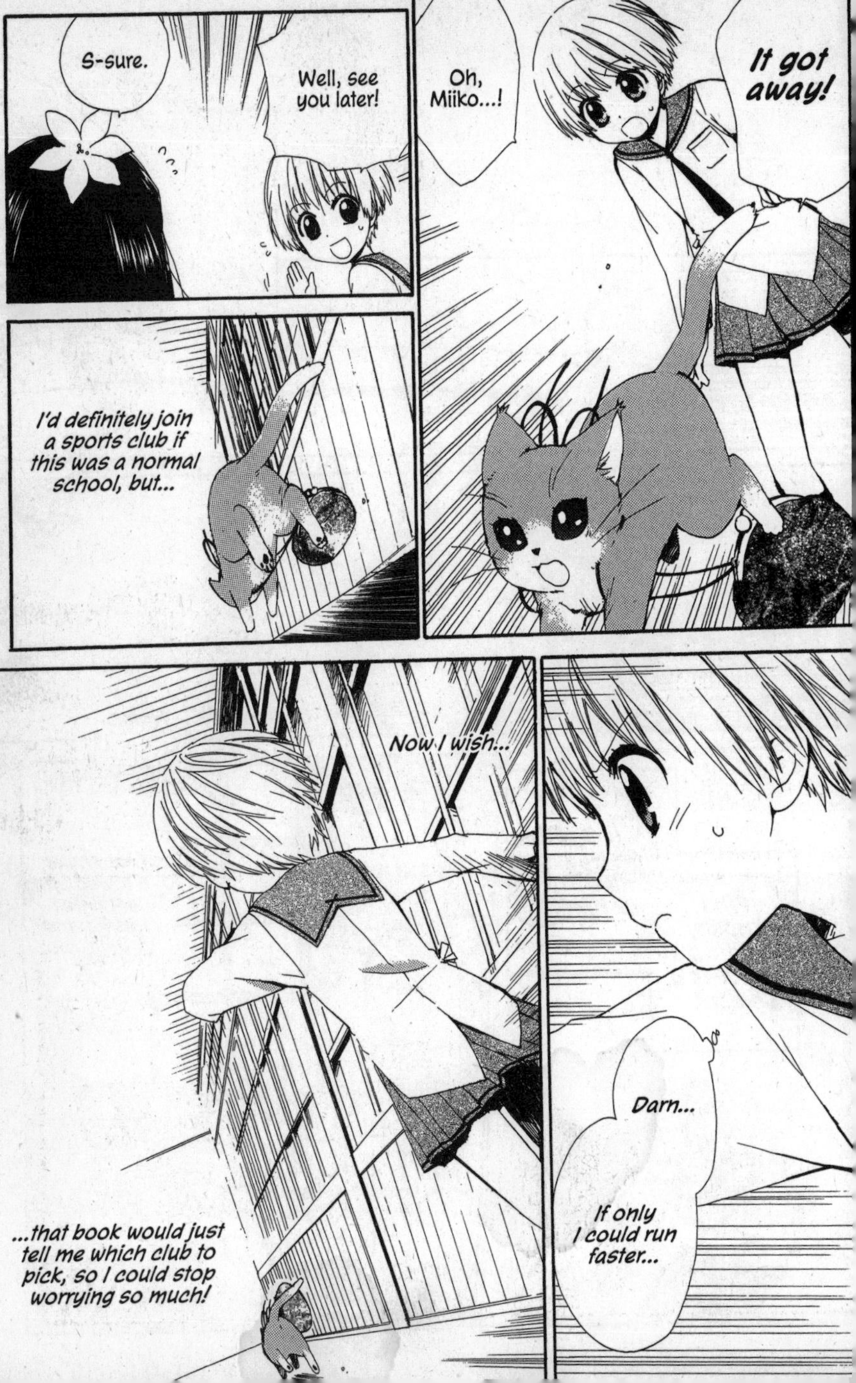
It got away!
Oh, Miiko...!
Well, see you later!
S-sure.
I'd definitely join a sports club if this was a normal school, but...
Darn...
If only I could run faster...
Now I wish...
...that book would just tell me which club to pick, so I could stop worrying so much!

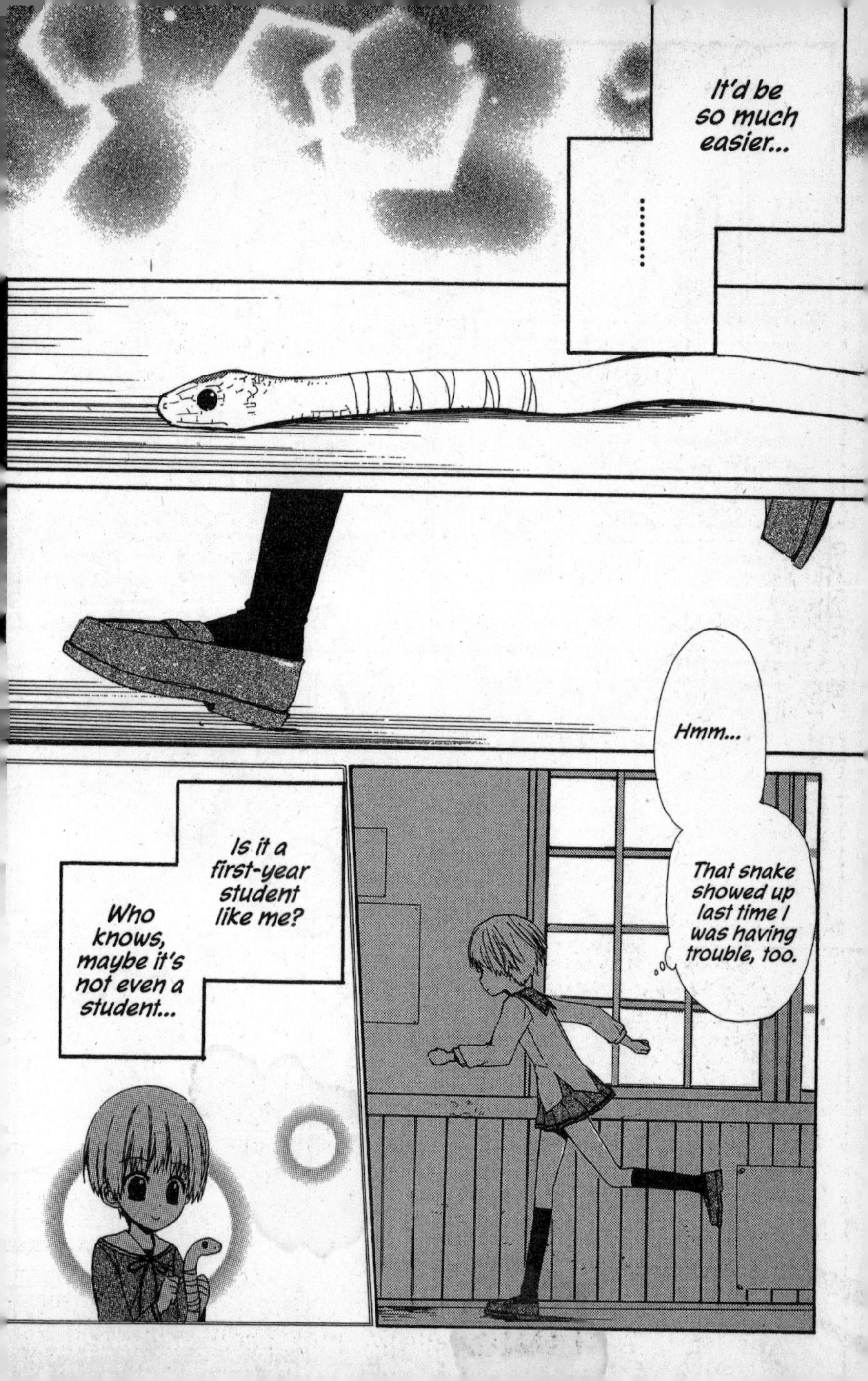
It'd be so much easier...
....
Hmm...
That snake showed up last time I was having trouble, too.
Is it a first-year student like me?
Who knows, maybe it's not even a student...

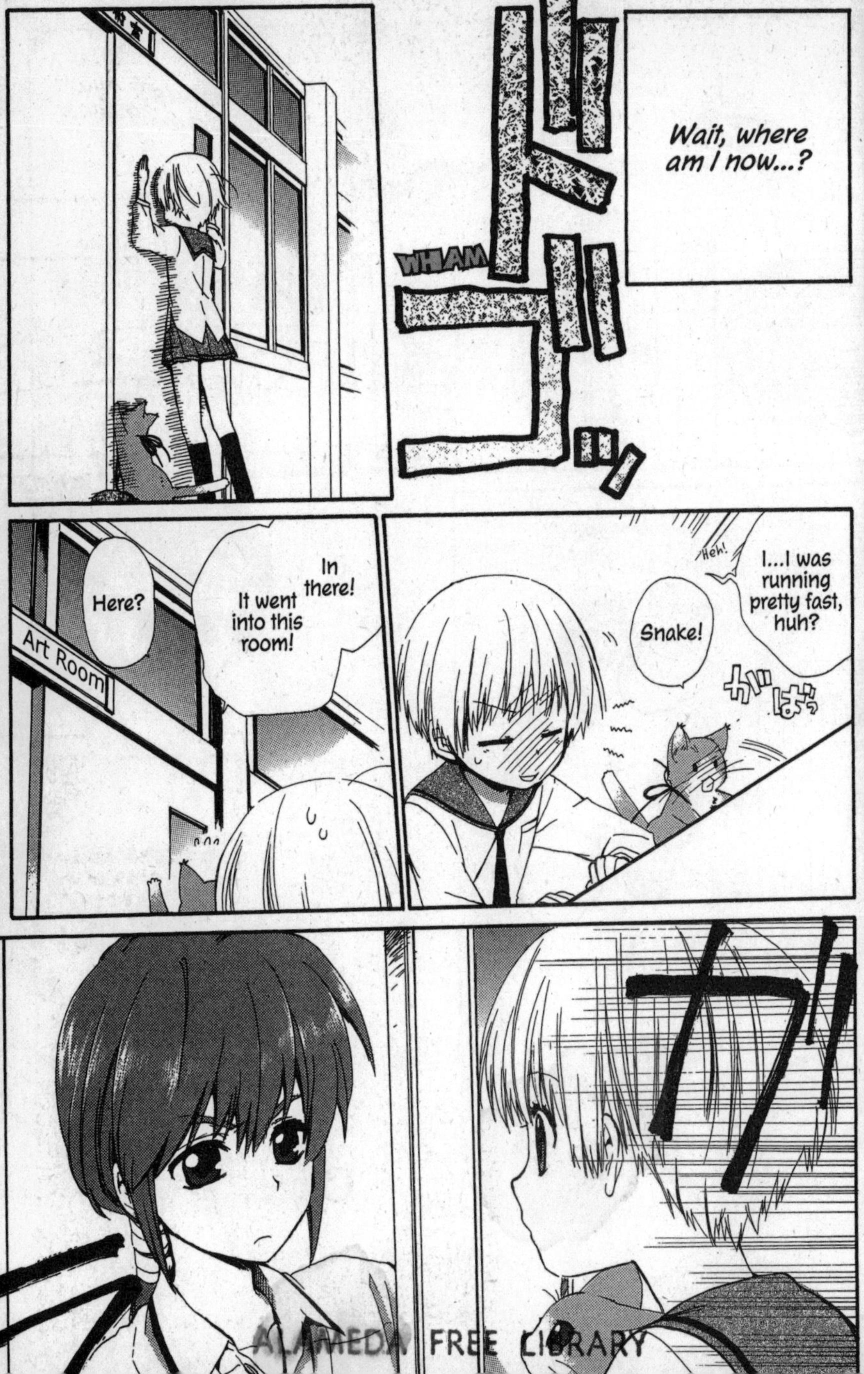

Wait, where am I now...?
WHAM
Heh!
I...I was running pretty fast, huh?
Snake!
In there!
It went into this room!
Here?
Art Room

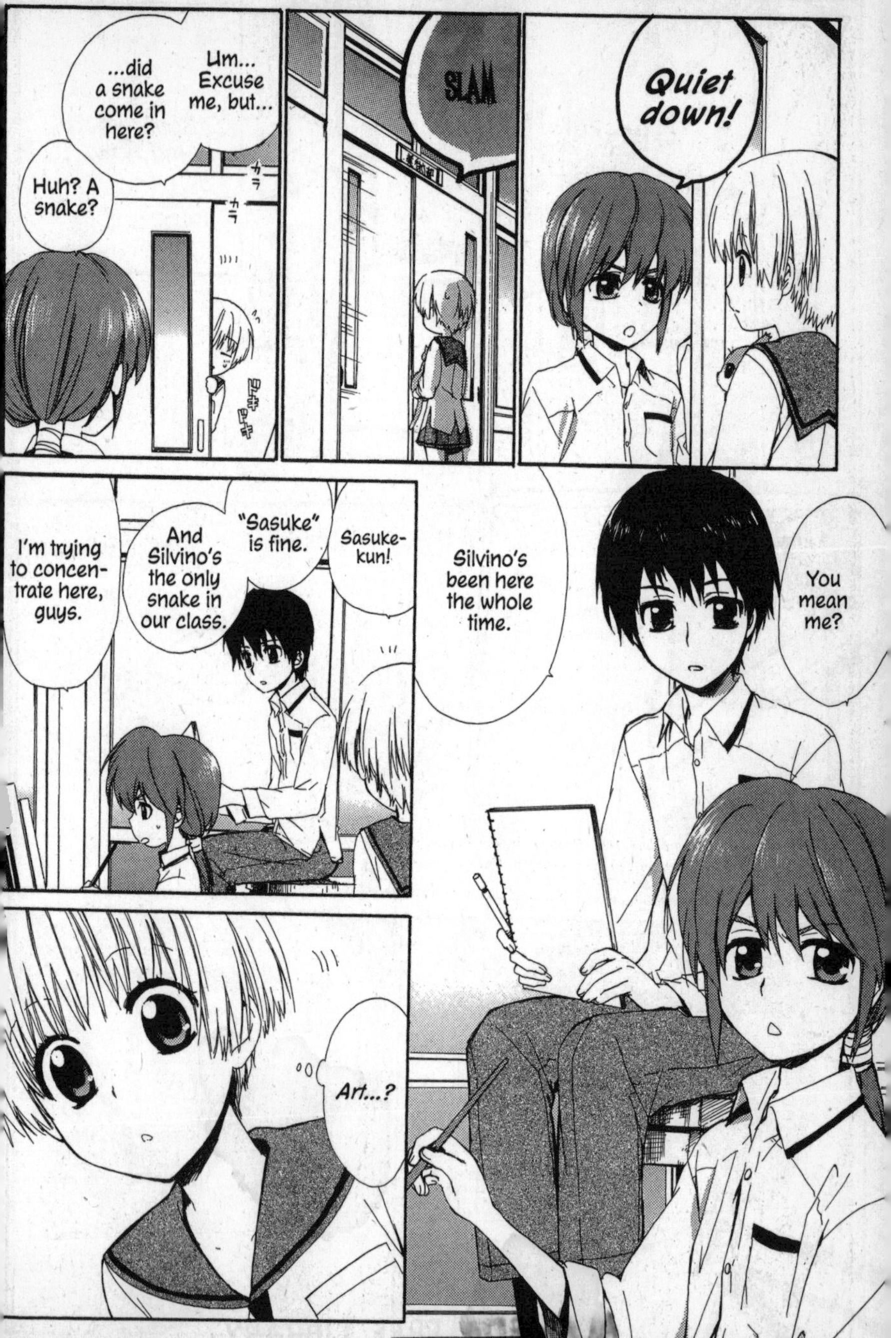
Quiet down!
SLAM
Um... Excuse me, but...
...did a snake come in here?
Huh? A snake?
You mean me?
Silvino's been here the whole time.
Sasuke-kun!
"Sasuke" is fine.
And Silvino's the only snake in our class.
I'm trying to concentrate here, guys.
Art...?

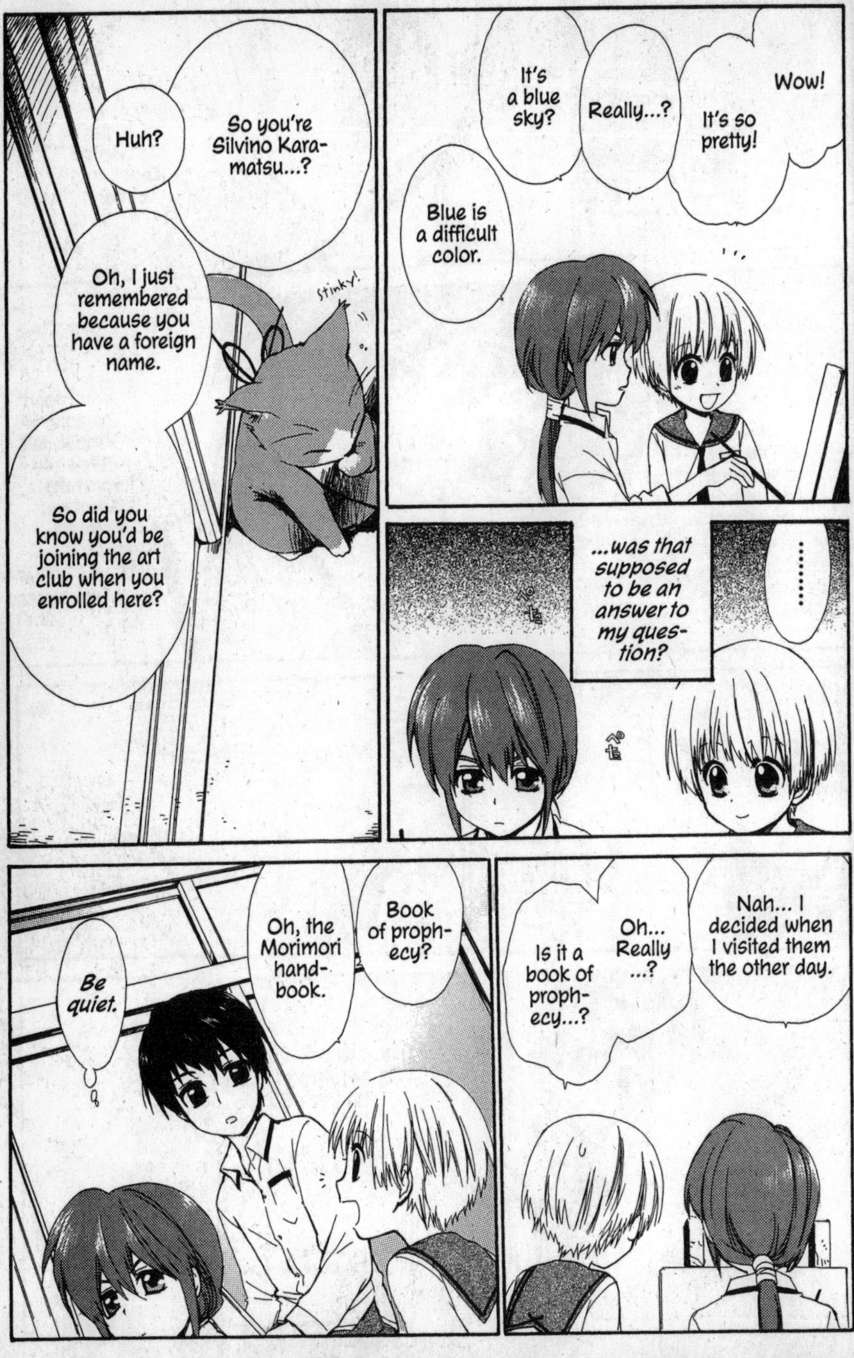
Wow!
It's so pretty!
Really...?
It's a blue sky?
Blue is a difficult color.
......
...was that supposed to be an answer to my question?
ぺた
ぺた
So you're Silvino Karamatsu...?
Huh?
Oh, I just remembered because you have a foreign name.
Stinky!
So did you know you'd be joining the art club when you enrolled here?
Nah... I decided when I visited them the other day.
Oh... Really ...?
Is it a book of prophecy...?
Book of prophecy?
Oh, the Morimori handbook.
Be quiet.

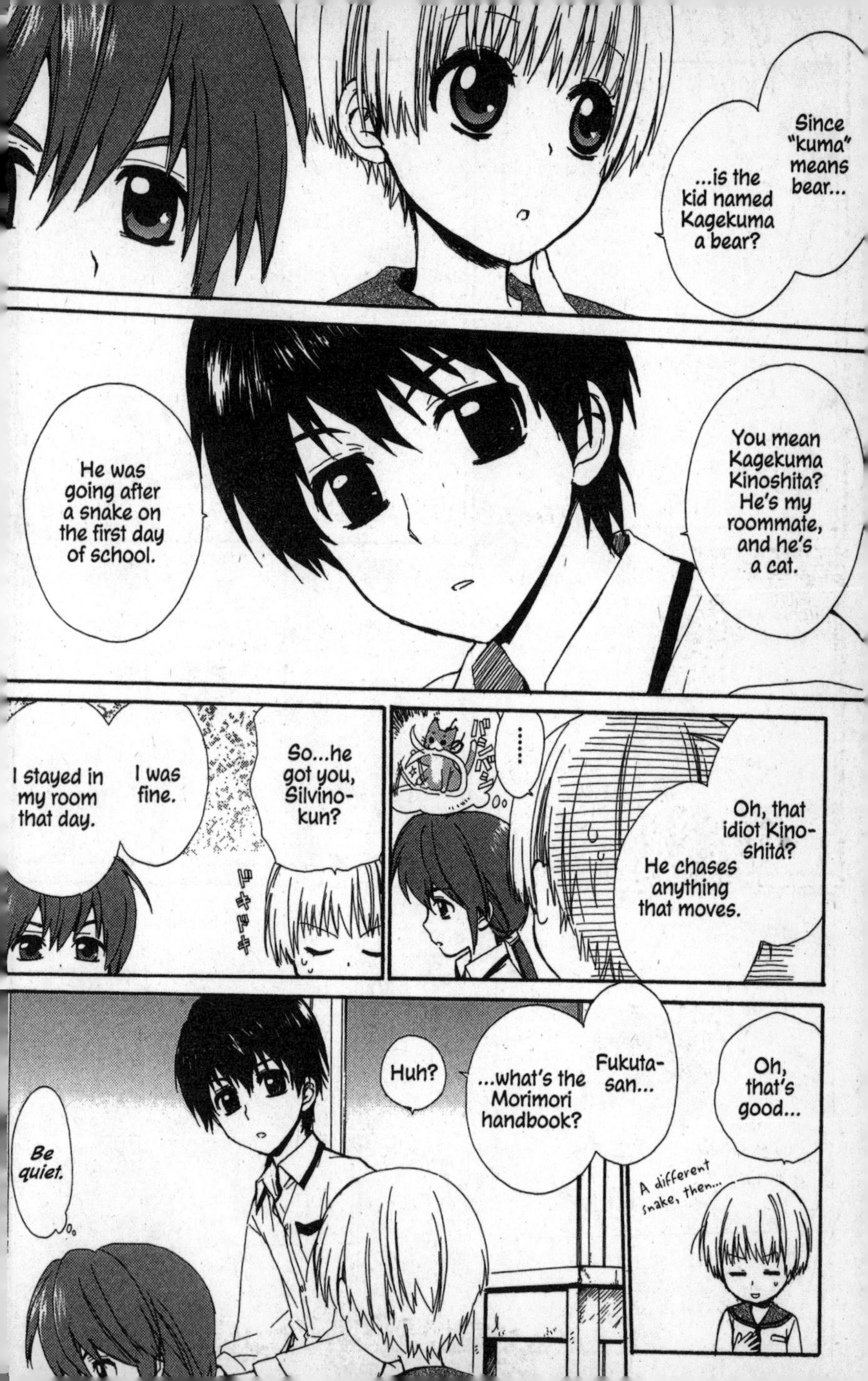
Since "kuma" means bear...
...is the kid named Kagekuma a bear?
You mean Kagekuma Kinoshita? He's my roommate, and he's a cat.
He was going after a snake on the first day of school.
......
Oh, that idiot Kinoshita?
He chases anything that moves.
So...he got you, Silvino-kun?
I was fine.
I stayed in my room that day.
Oh, that's good...
A different snake, then...
Fukuta-san...
...what's the Morimori handbook?
Huh?
Be quiet.

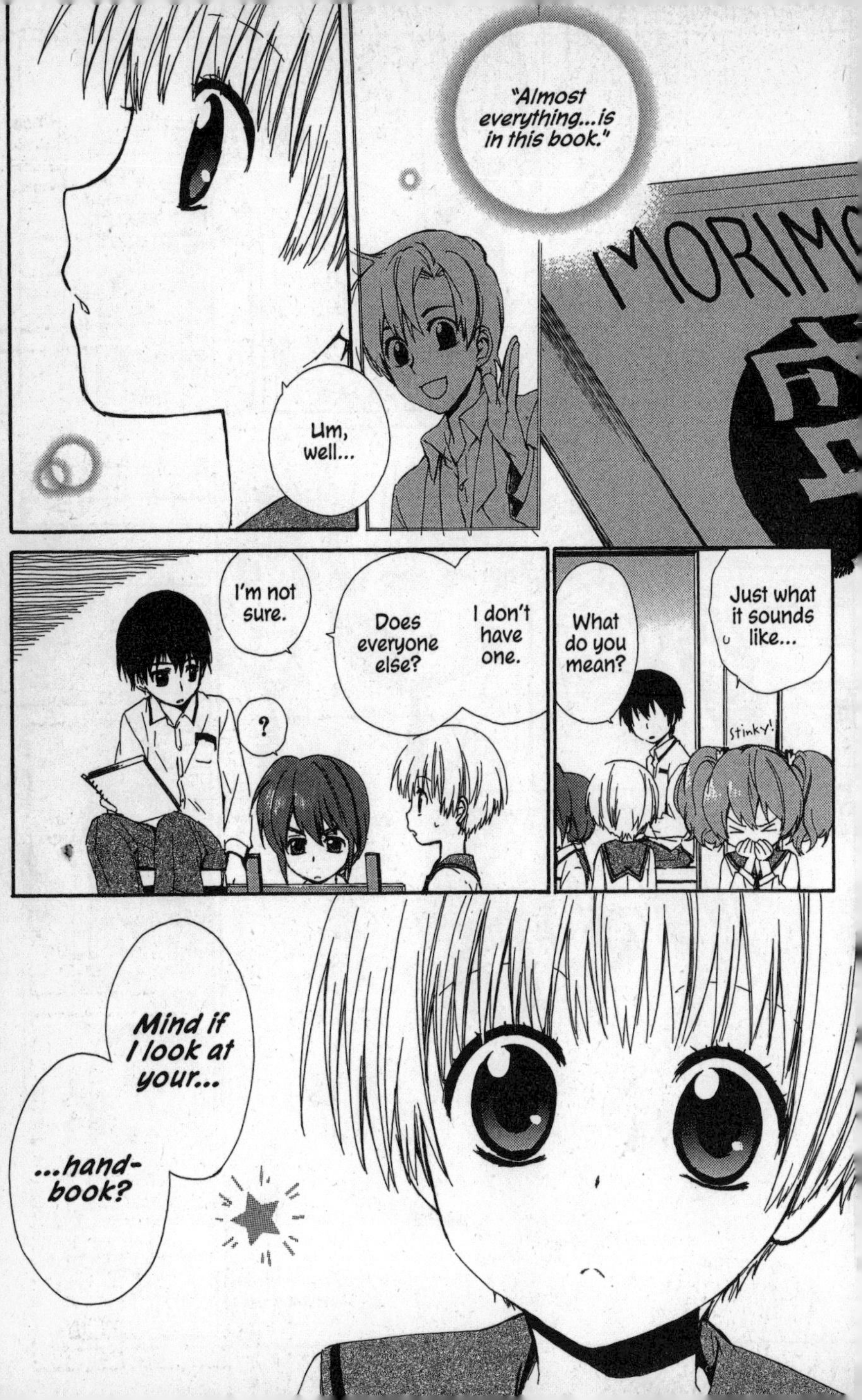
"Almost everything...is in this book."
Um, well...
Just what it sounds like...
What do you mean?
Stinky!
I don't have one.
Does everyone else?
I'm not sure.
?
Mind if I look at your...
...hand-book?

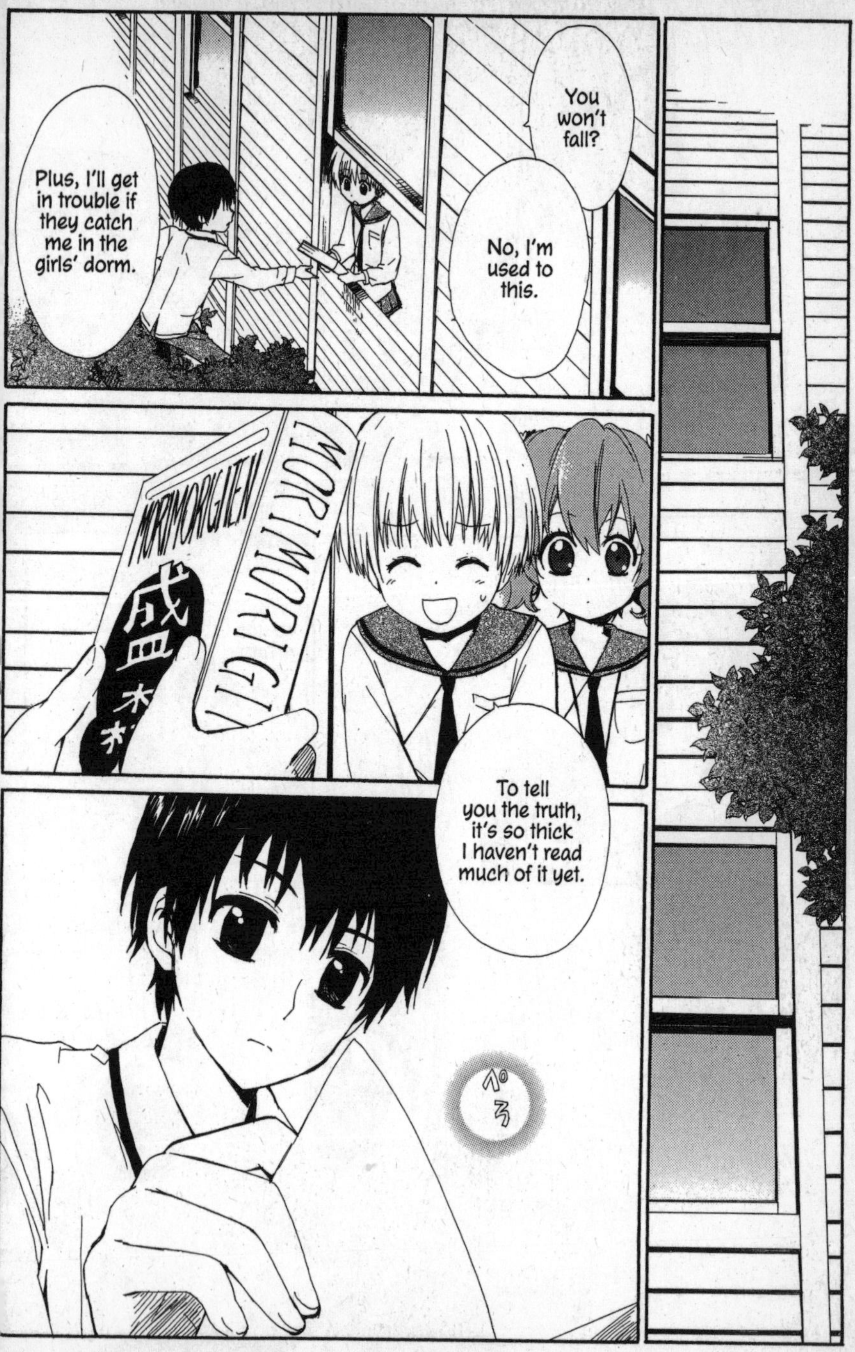
You won't fall?
No, I'm used to this.
Plus, I'll get in trouble if they catch me in the girls' dorm.
MORIMORIGIEN
盛
To tell you the truth, it's so thick I haven't read much of it yet.
ぺろ

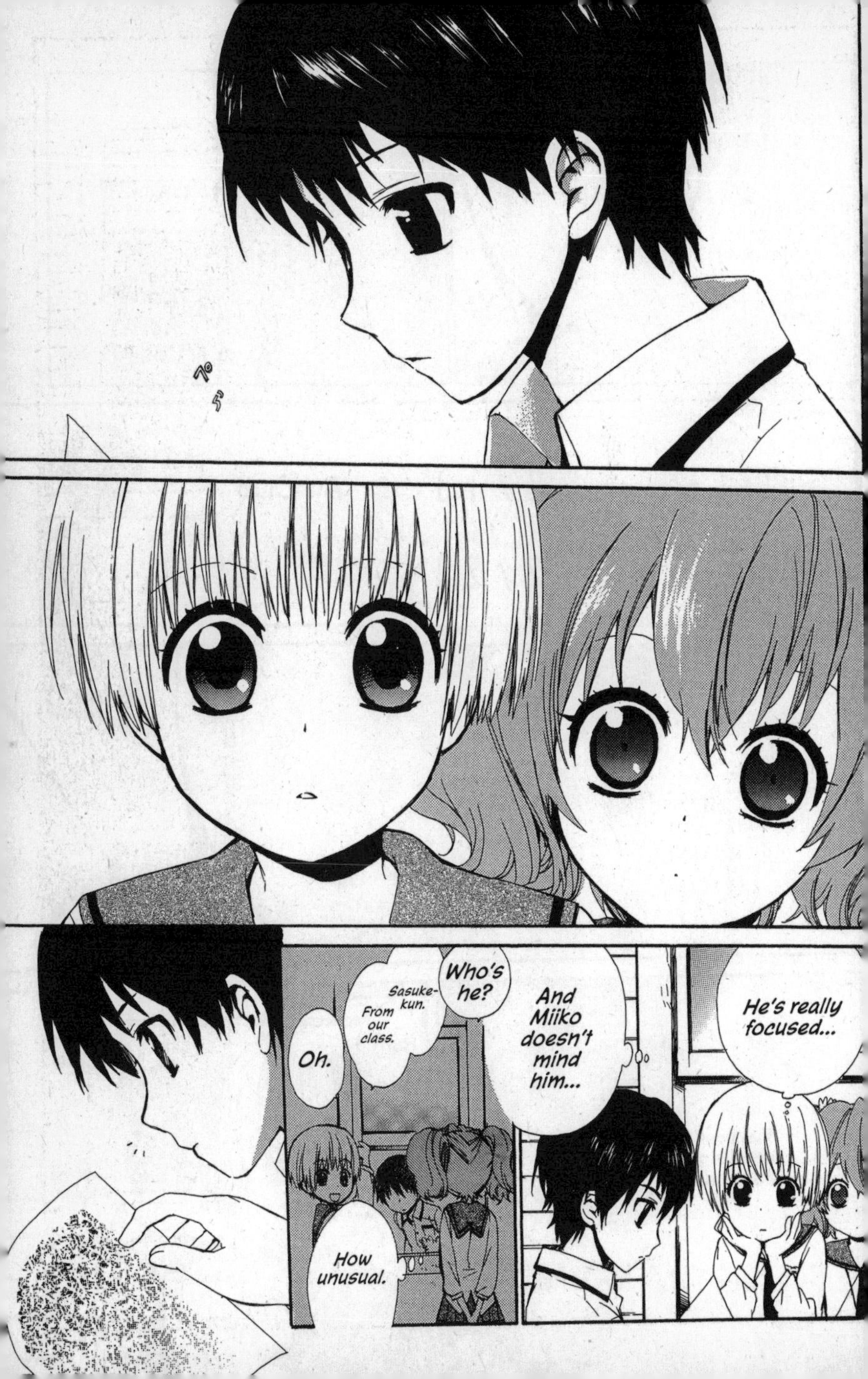
He's really focused...
And Miiko doesn't mind him...
Who's he?
Sasuke-kun. From our class.
Oh.
How unusual.

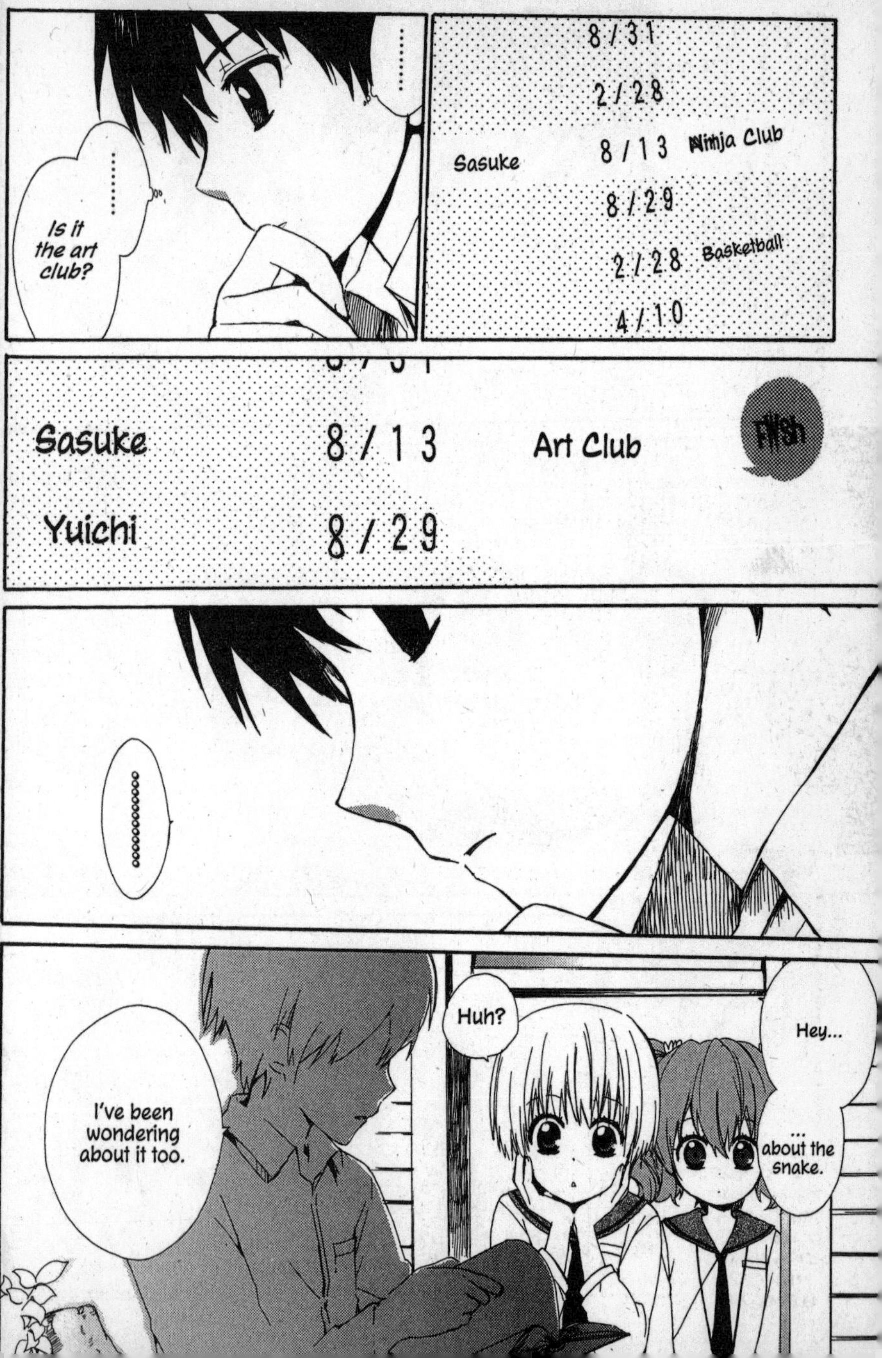
8/31
2/28
Sasuke 8/13 Ninja Club
8/29
2/28 Basketball
4/10
......
......
Is it the art club?
Sasuke 8/13 Art Club
Yuichi 8/29
FWSH
....
Hey...
...about the snake.
Huh?
I've been wondering about it too.

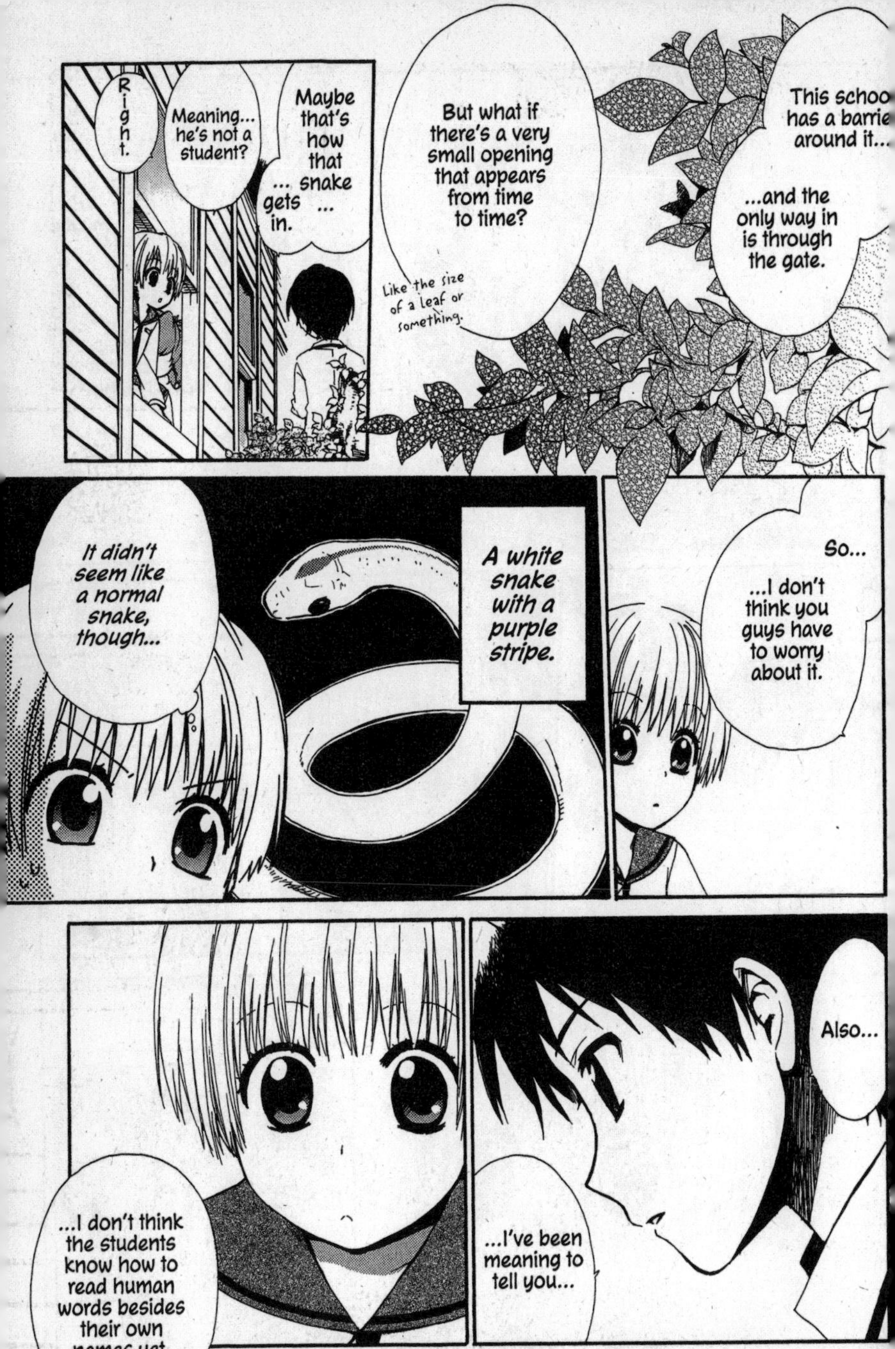
This schoo has a barrie around it...
...and the only way in is through the gate.
But what if there's a very small opening that appears from time to time?
Like the size of a leaf or something.
Maybe that's how that snake ...
... gets in.
Meaning... he's not a student?
Right.
So...
...I don't think you guys have to worry about it.
A white snake with a purple stripe.
It didn't seem like a normal snake, though...
Also...
...I've been meaning to tell you...
...I don't think the students know how to read human words besides their own names yet.

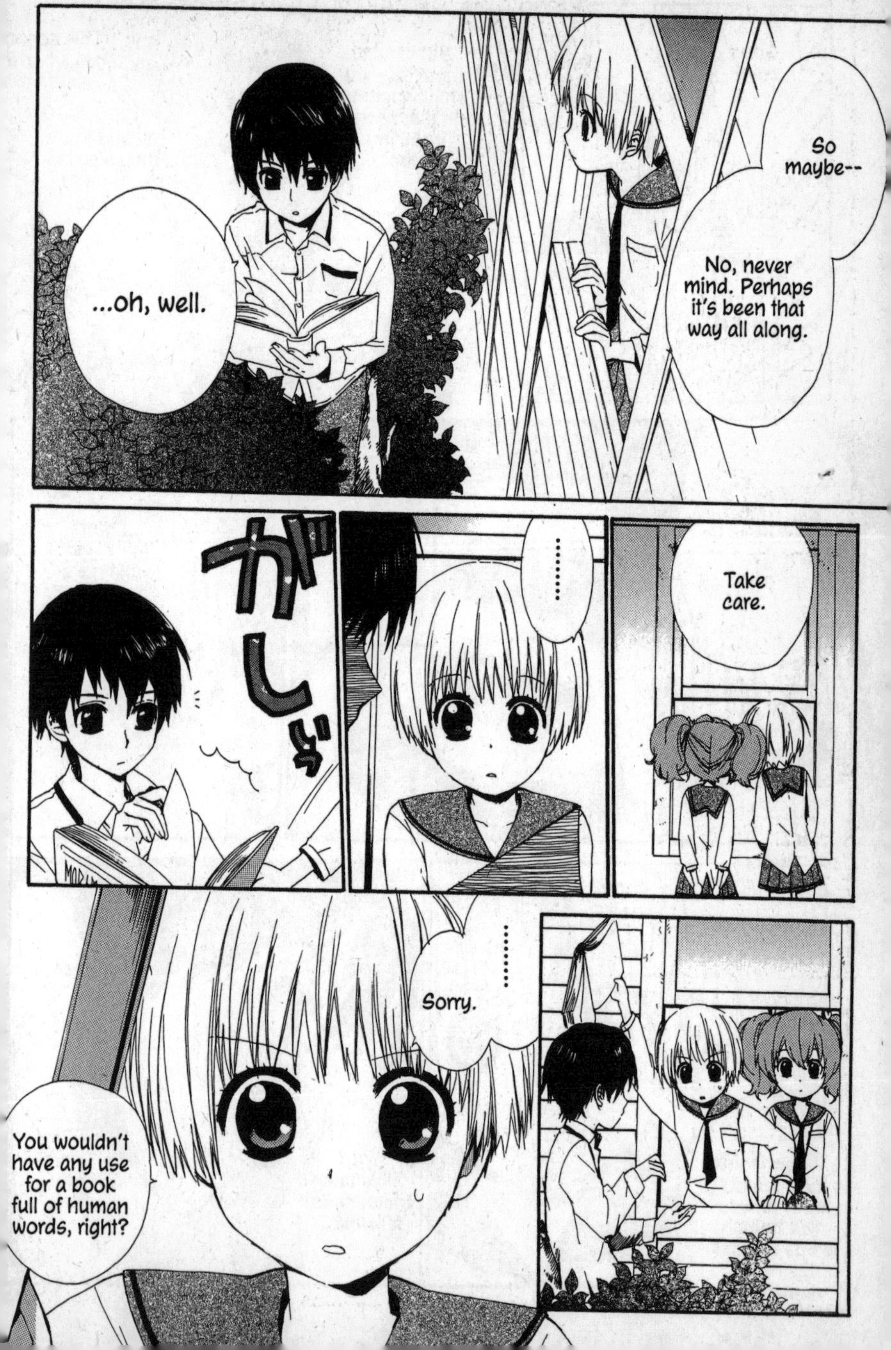
So maybe--
No, never mind. Perhaps it's been that way all along.
...oh, well.
Take care.
......
がしっ
......
Sorry.
You wouldn't have any use for a book full of human words, right?

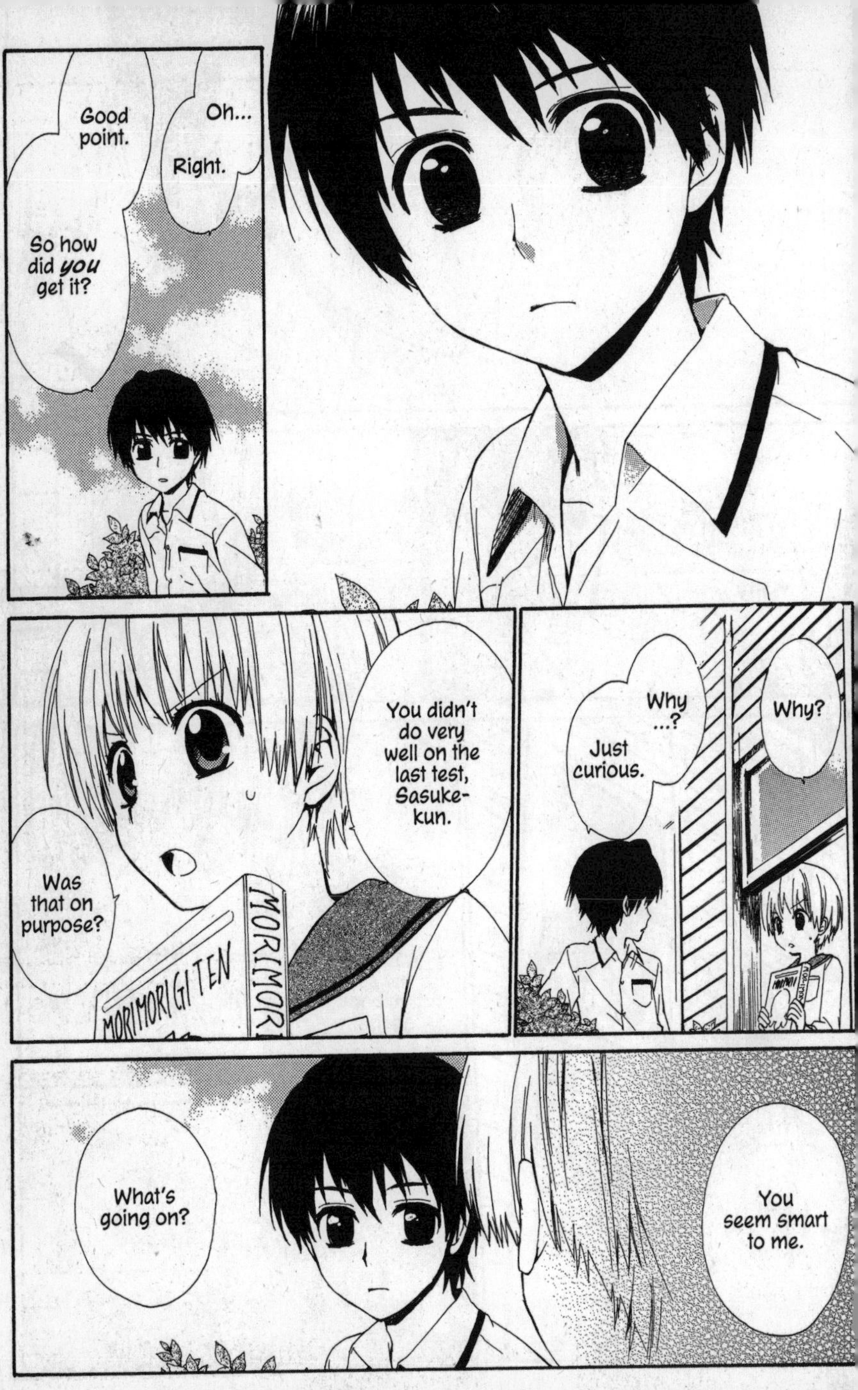
Oh...
Right.
Good point.
So how did *you* get it?
Why?
Why...?
Just curious.
You didn't do very well on the last test, Sasuke-kun.
Was that on purpose?
MORIMORI GI TEN
You seem smart to me.
What's going on?

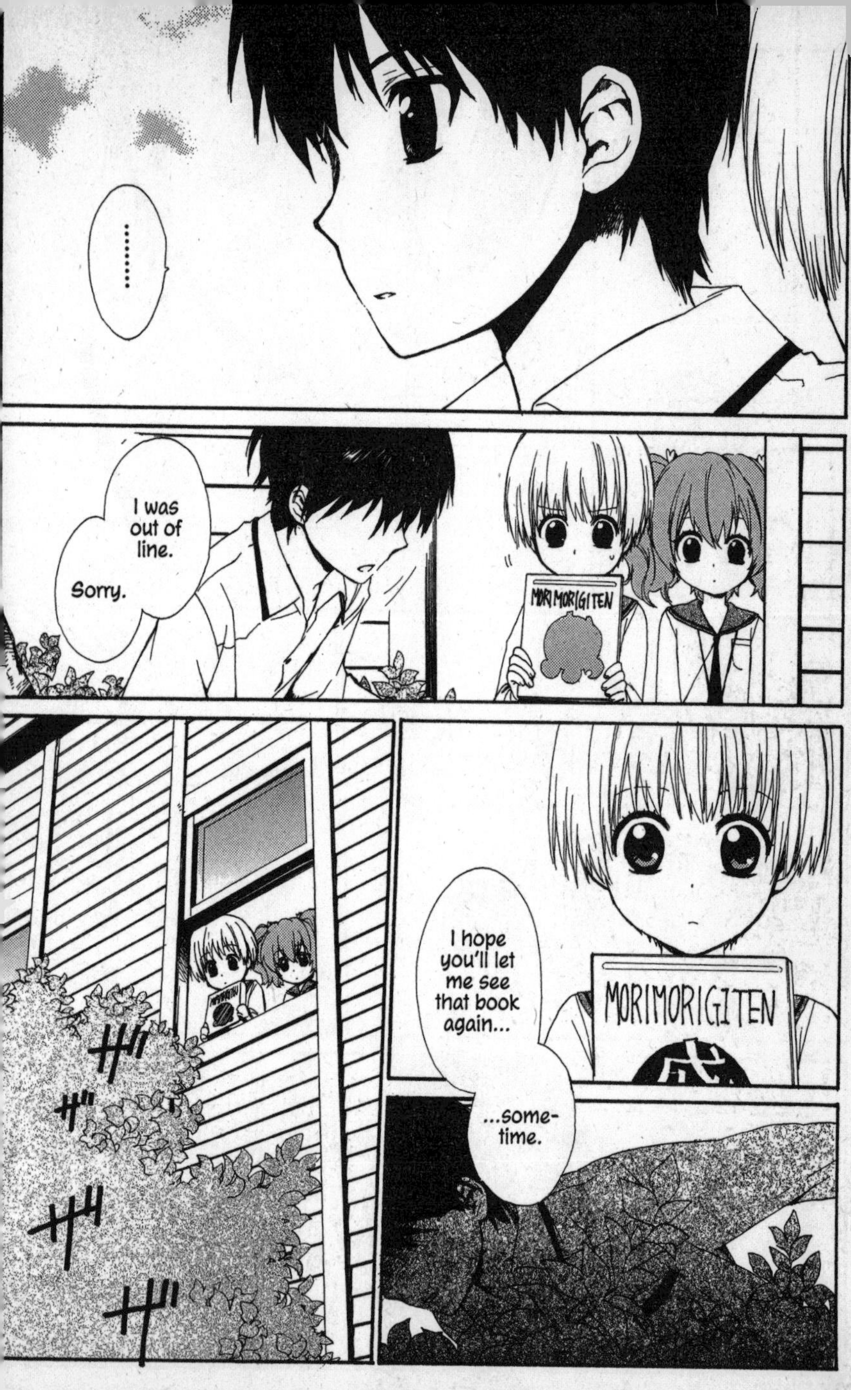
……
MORIMORIGITEN
I was out of line. Sorry.
MORIMORIGITEN
I hope you'll let me see that book again...
...some-time.
ザ
ザ
ザ
ザ

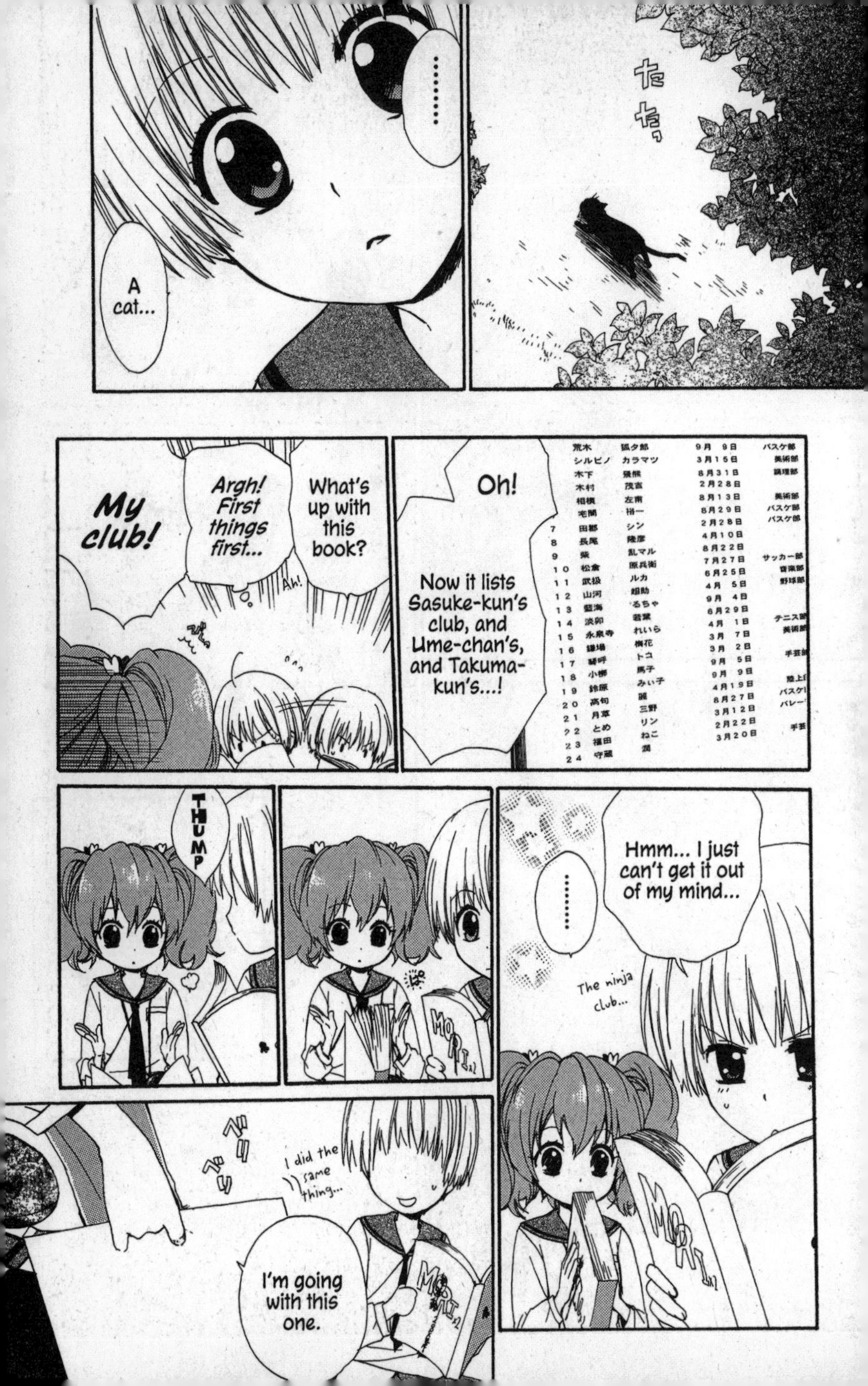

たたっ
......
A cat...
Oh!
Now it lists Sasuke-kun's club, and Ume-chan's, and Takuma-kun's...!
What's up with this book?
Argh! First things first...
Ah!
My club!
Hmm... I just can't get it out of my mind...
......
The ninja club...
THUMP
べりべり
I did the same thing...
I'm going with this one.

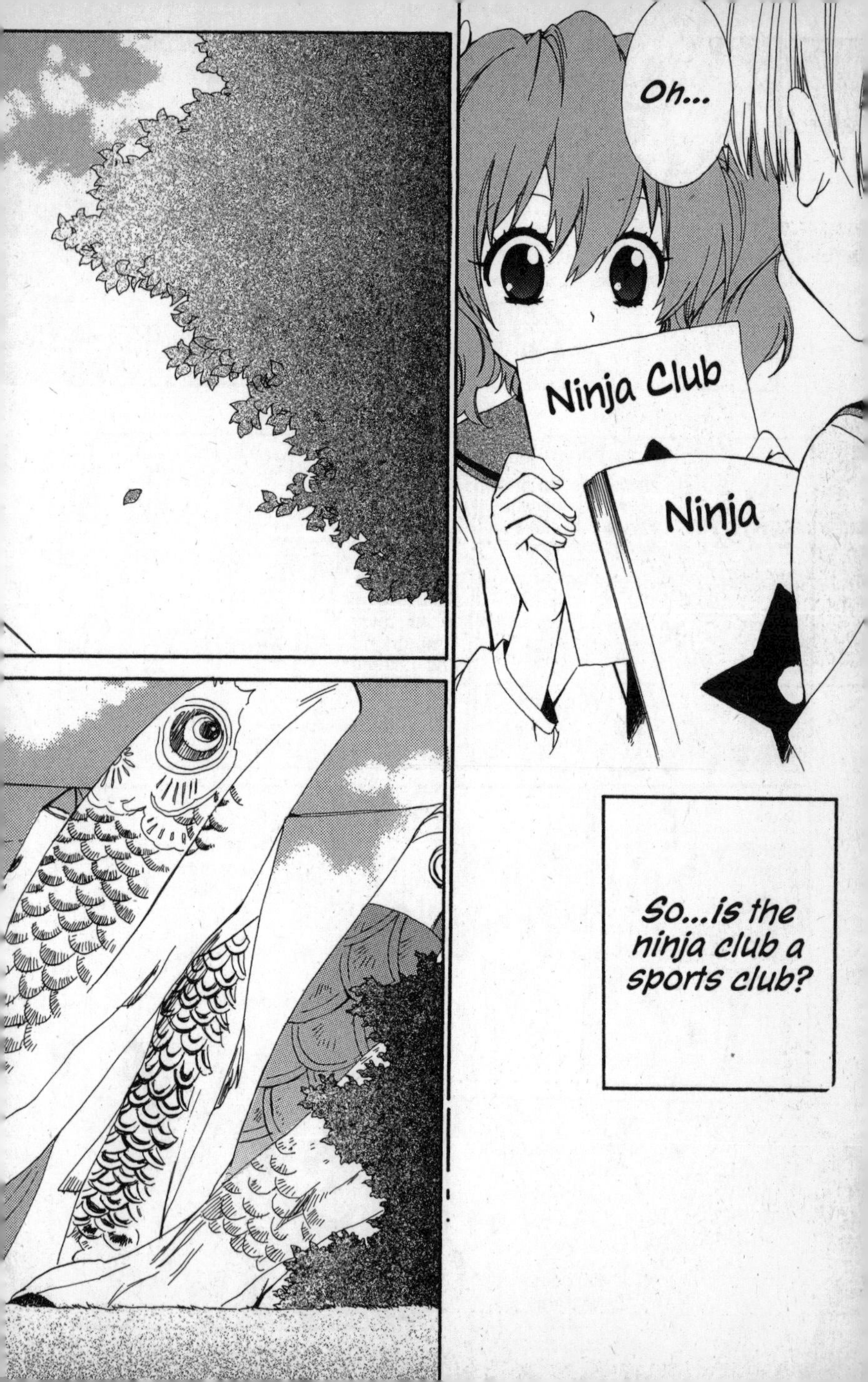
Oh...
Ninja Club
Ninja
So...is the ninja club a sports club?

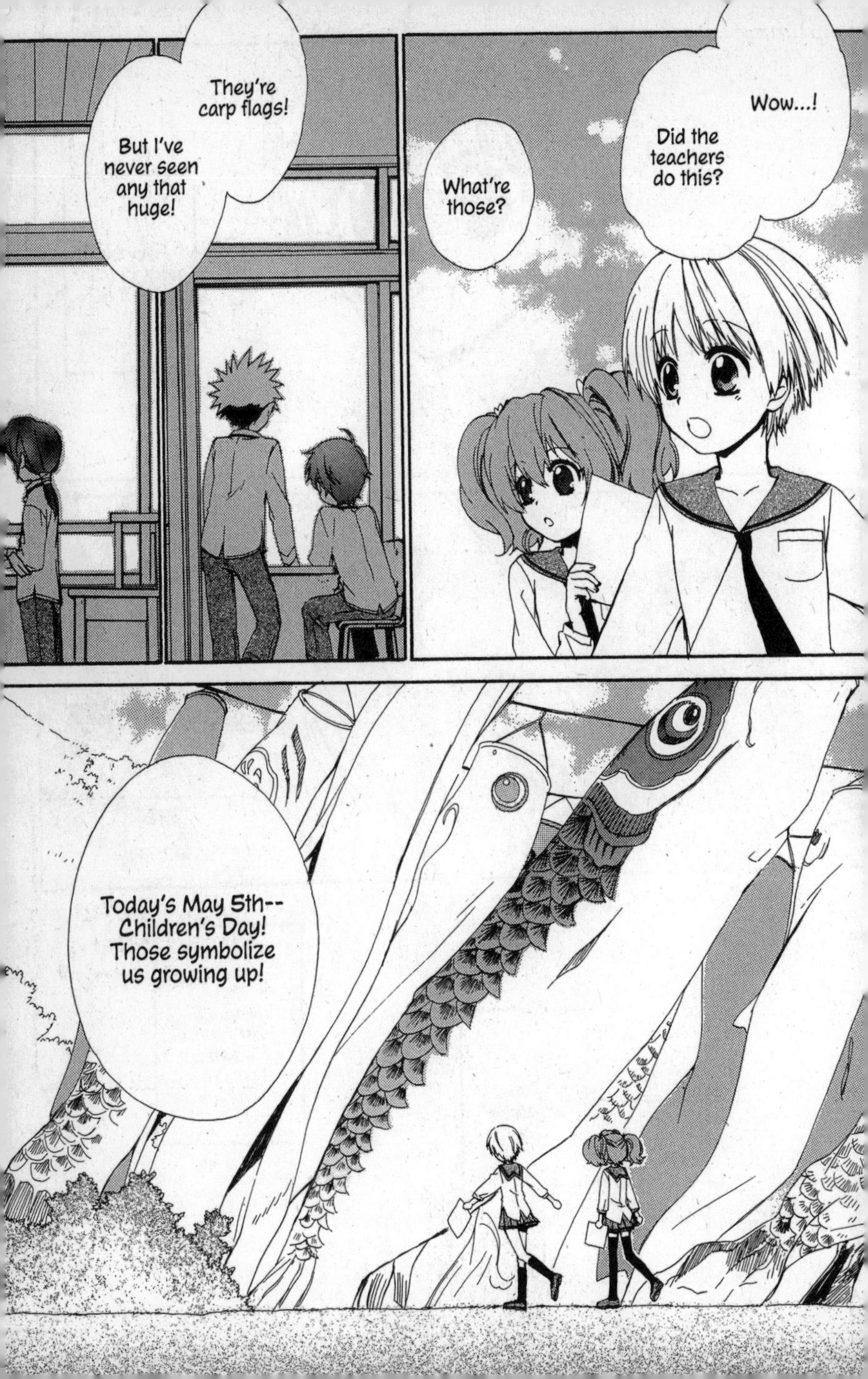
Wow...!
Did the teachers do this?
What're those?
They're carp flags!
But I've never seen any that huge!
Today's May 5th-- Children's Day! Those symbolize us growing up!

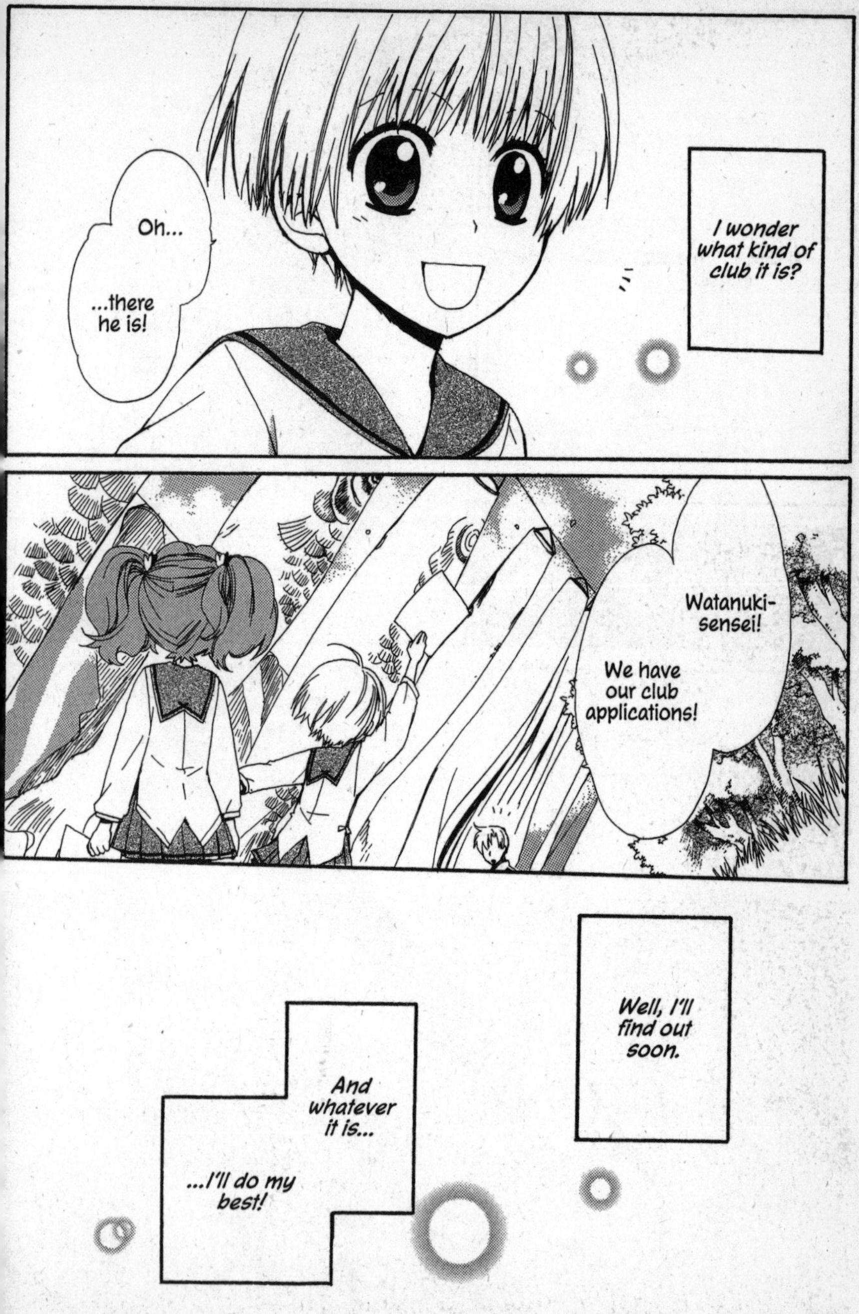
I wonder what kind of club it is?
Oh...
...there he is!
Watanuki-sensei!
We have our club applications!
Well, I'll find out soon.
And whatever it is...
...I'll do my best!

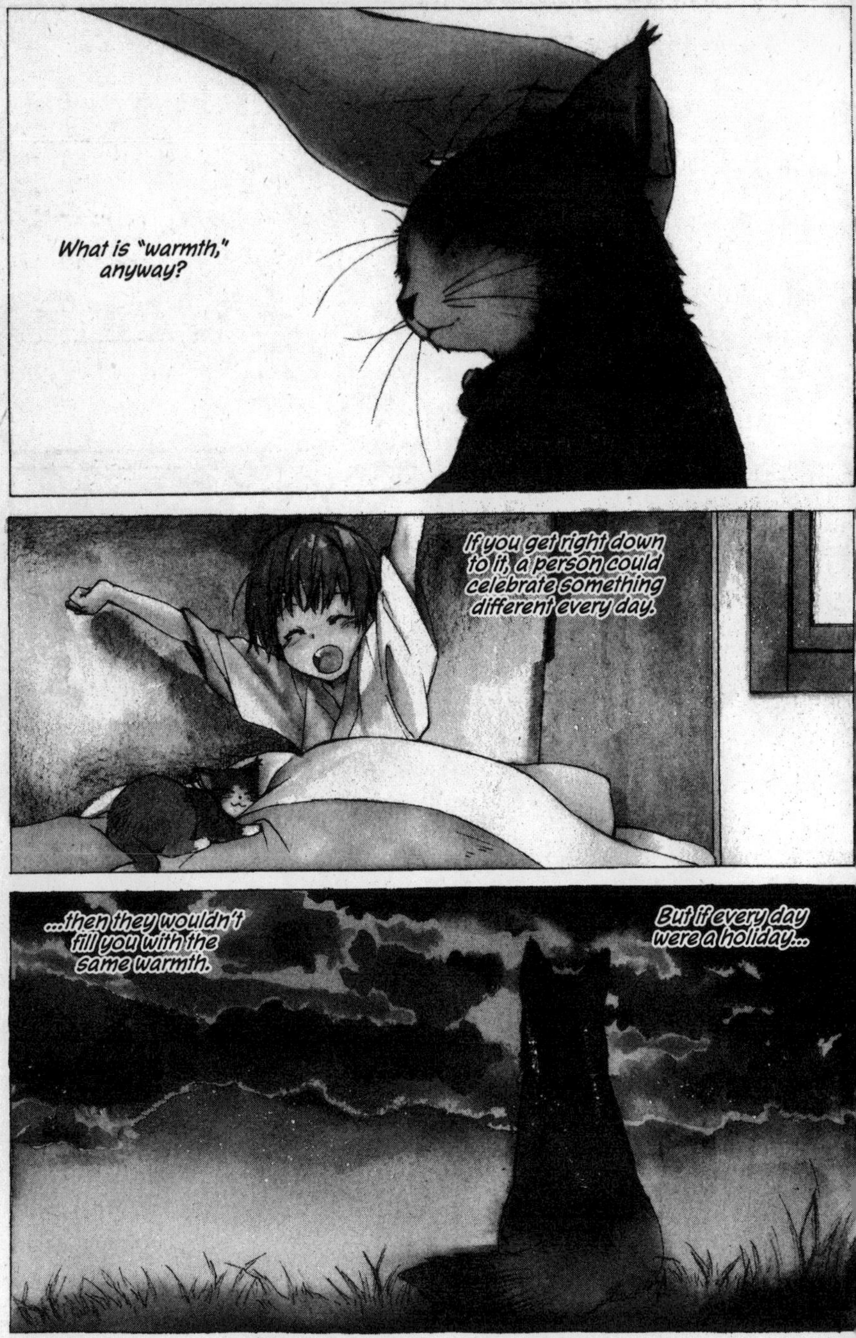
What is "warmth," anyway?
If you get right down to it, a person could celebrate something different every day.
But if every day were a holiday...
...then they wouldn't fill you with the same warmth.

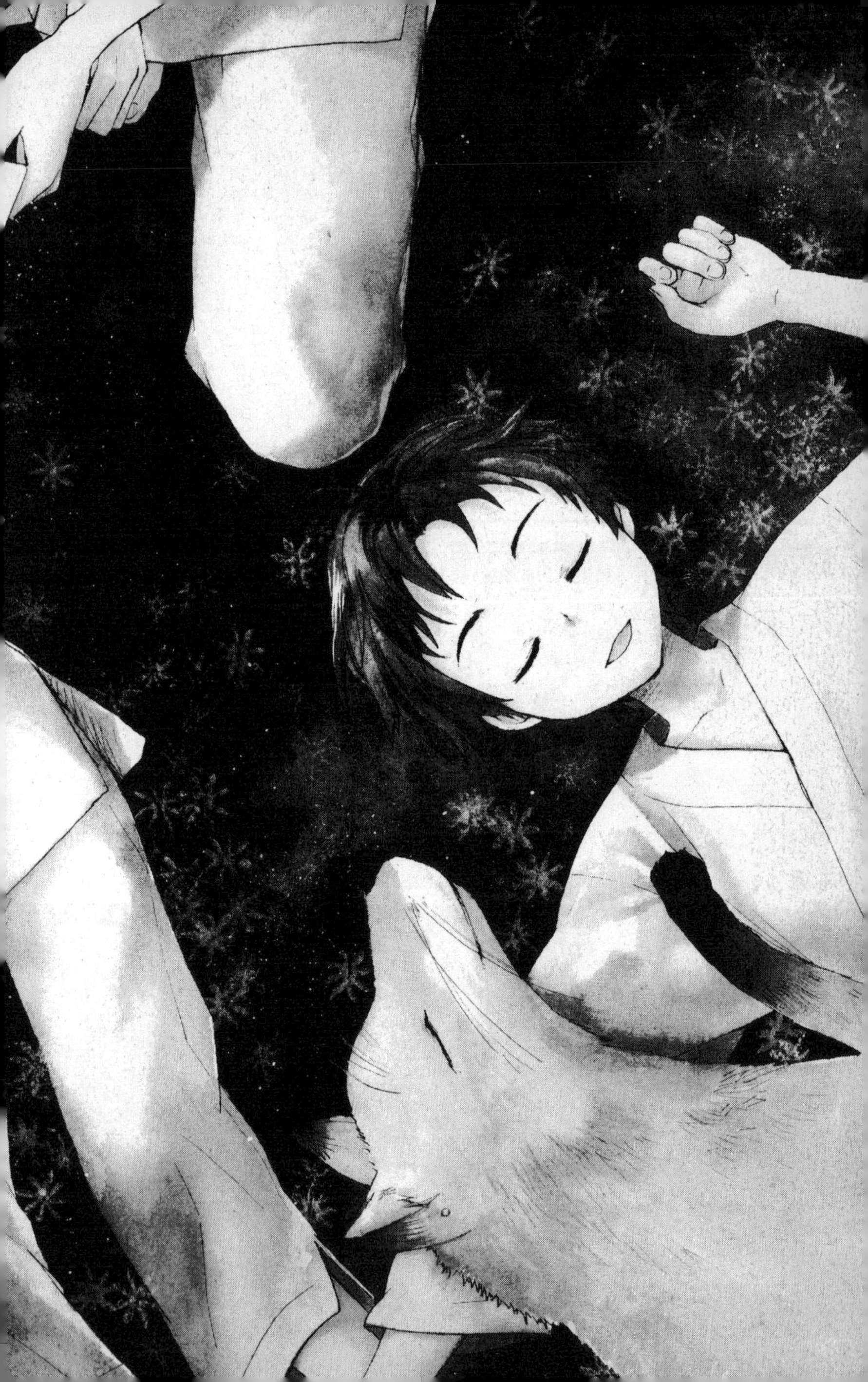

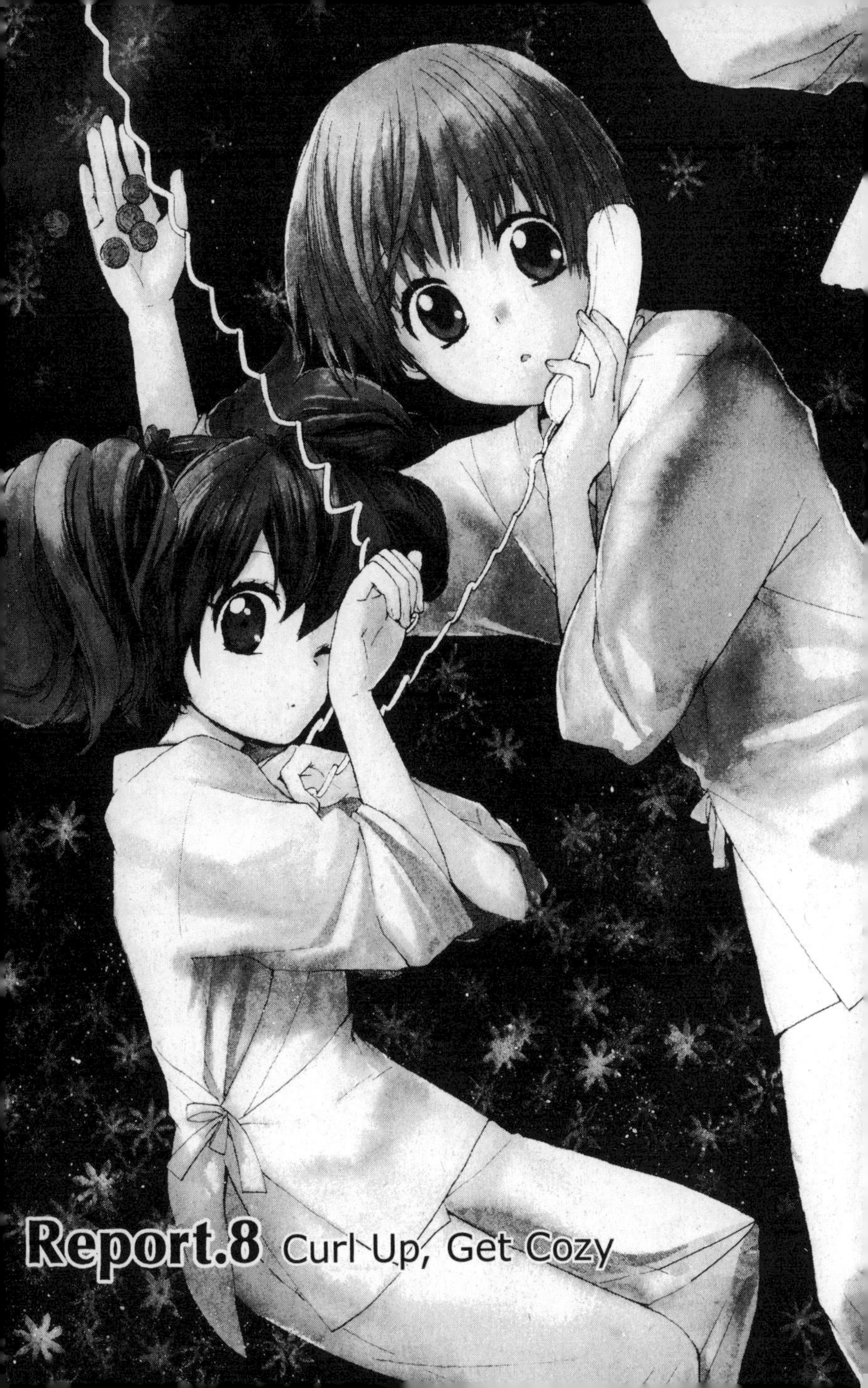
Report.8 Curl Up, Get Cozy

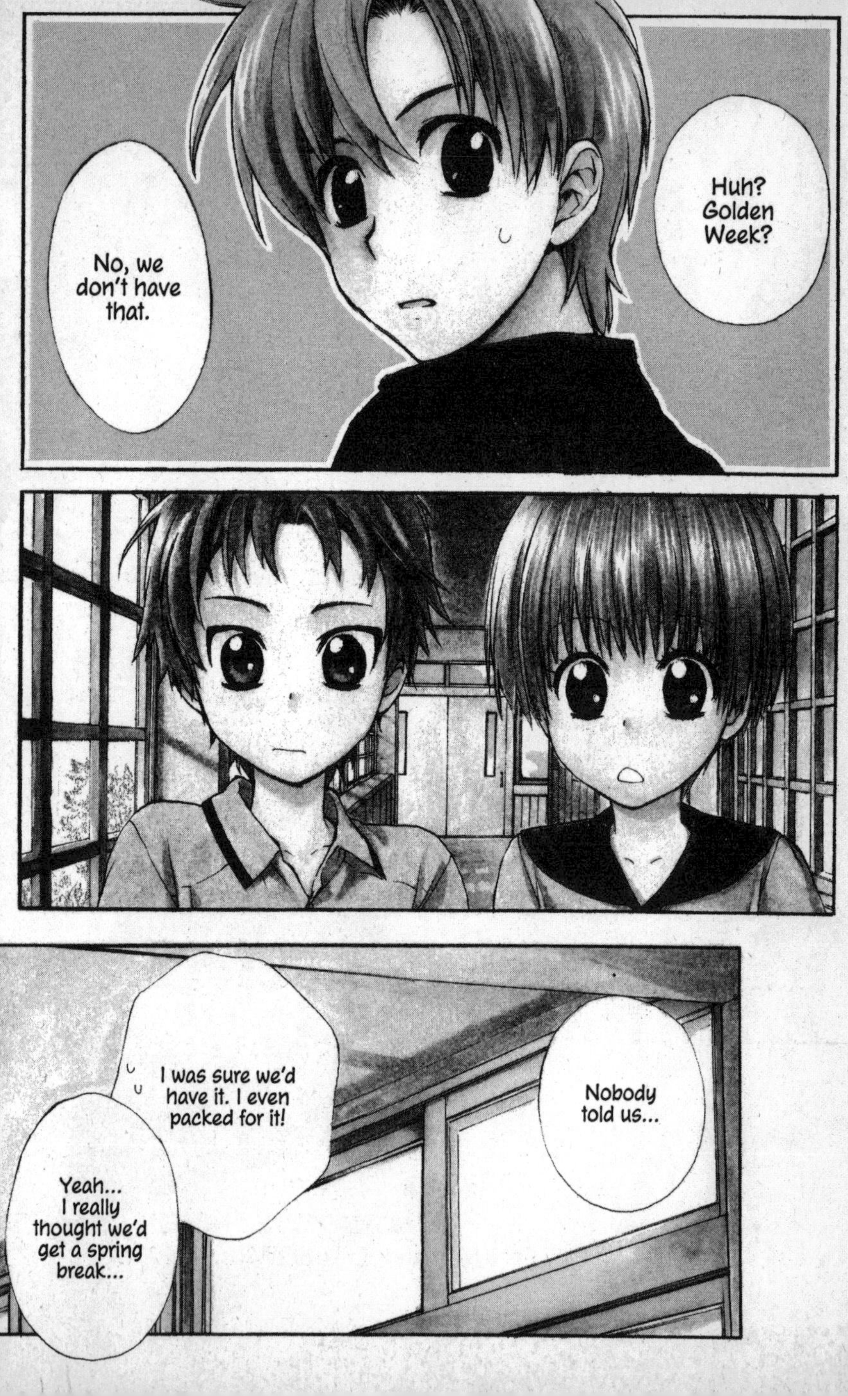

Huh? Golden Week?
No, we don't have that.
Nobody told us...
I was sure we'd have it. I even packed for it!
Yeah... I really thought we'd get a spring break...

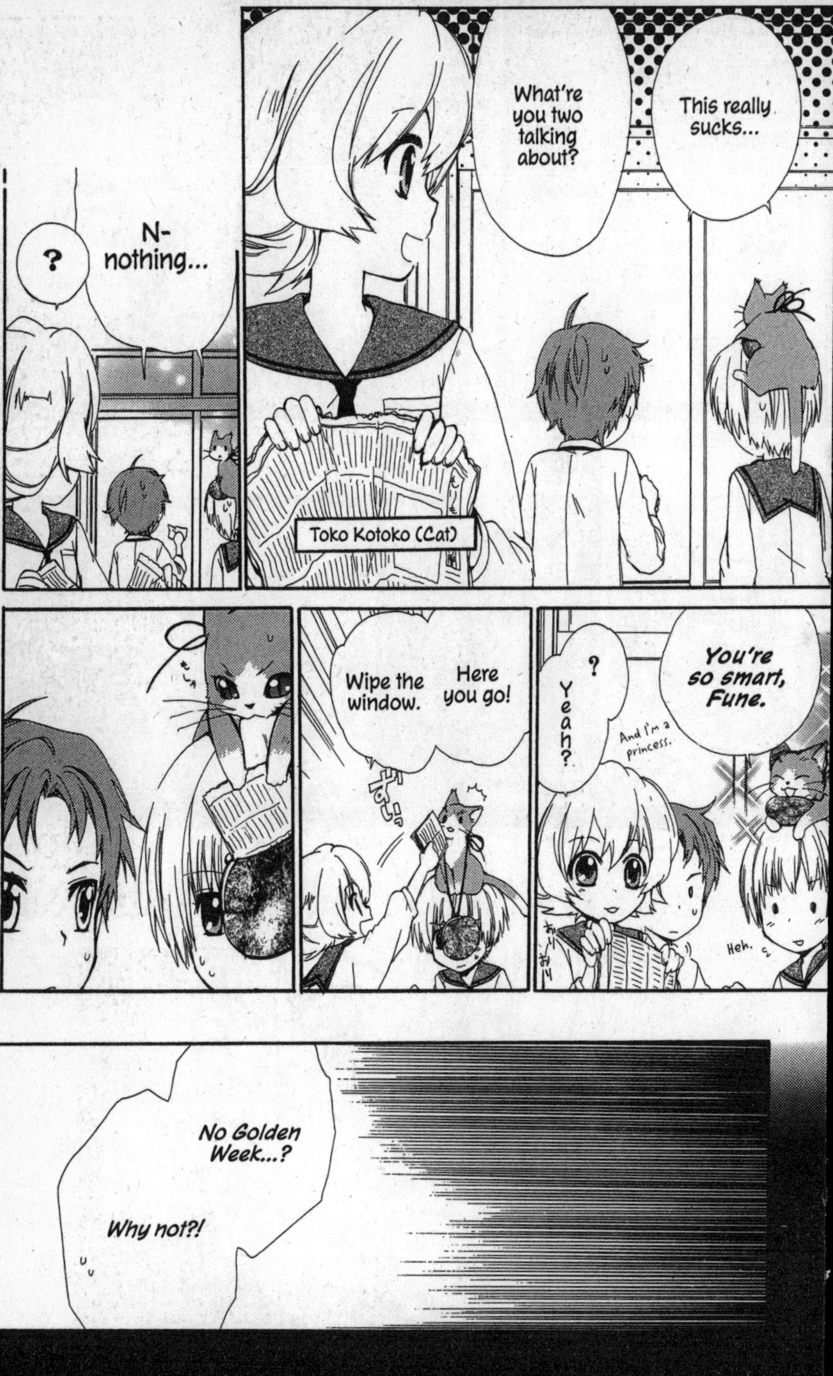
This really sucks...
What're you two talking about?
Toko Kotoko (Cat)
N- nothing...
?
You're so smart, Fune.
?
Yeah?
And I'm a princess.
Heh.
Here you go!
Wipe the window.
No Golden Week...?
Why not?!

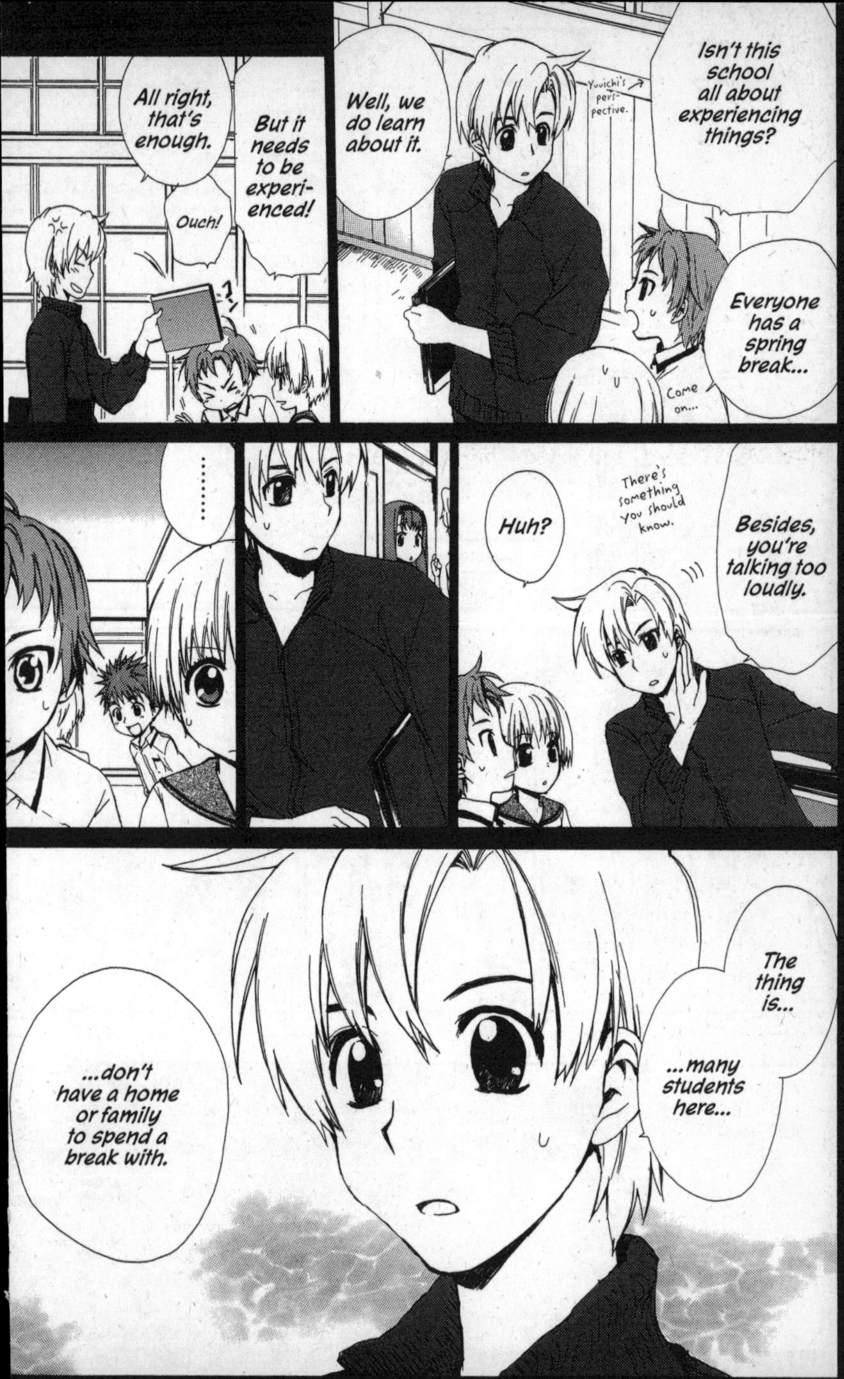
Isn't this school all about experiencing things?
Yuuichi's perspective.
Well, we do learn about it.
Everyone has a spring break...
Come on...
But it needs to be experienced!
All right, that's enough.
Ouch!
Besides, you're talking too loudly.
There's something you should know.
Huh?
......
The thing is...
...many students here...
...don't have a home or family to spend a break with.

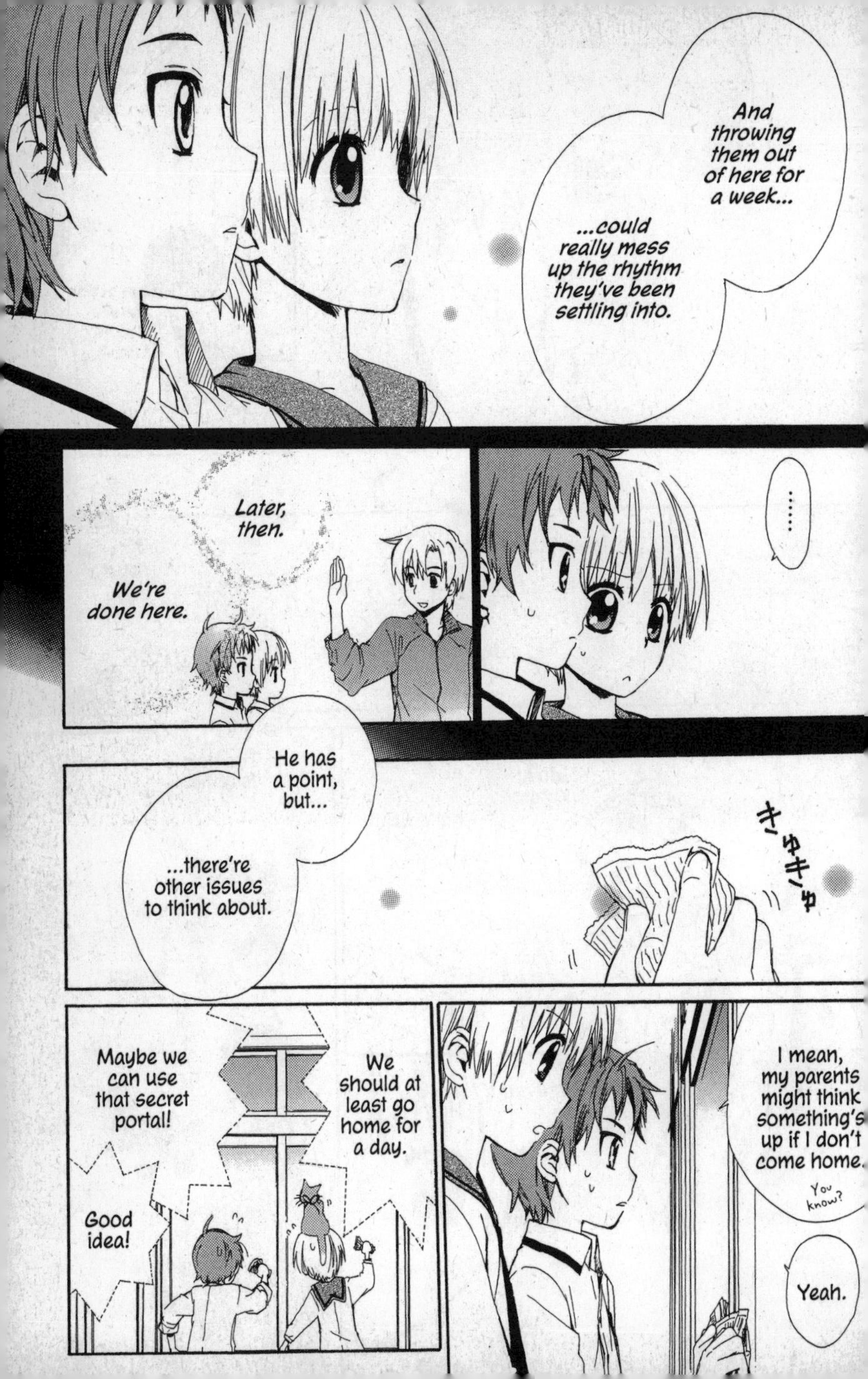
And throwing them out of here for a week...
...could really mess up the rhythm they've been settling into.
......
Later, then.
We're done here.
He has a point, but...
...there're other issues to think about.
キュキュ
I mean, my parents might think something's up if I don't come home.
You know?
Yeah.
We should at least go home for a day.
Maybe we can use that secret portal!
Good idea!

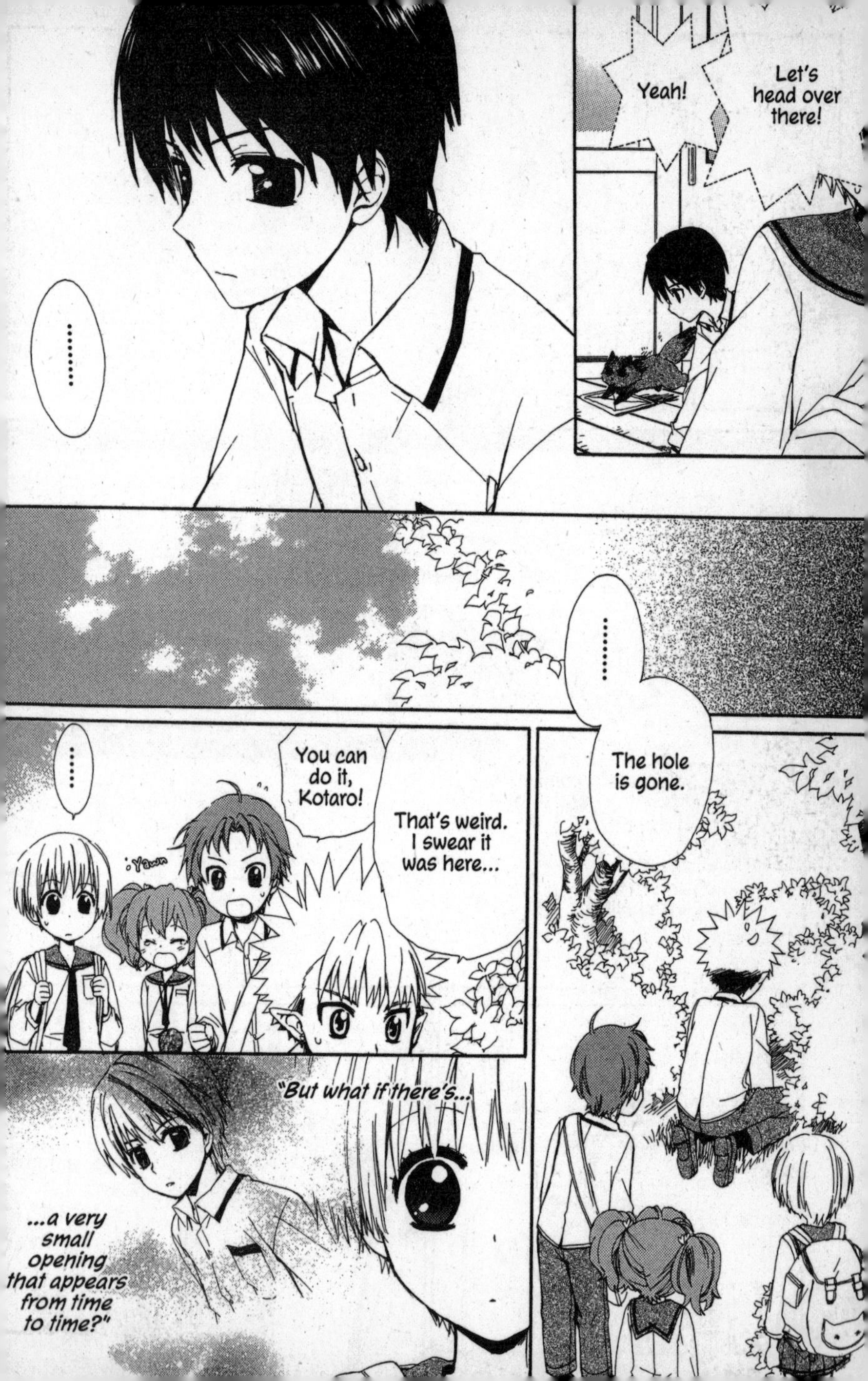
Let's head over there!
Yeah!
......
......
The hole is gone.
That's weird. I swear it was here...
You can do it, Kotaro!
Yawn
......
"But what if there's...
...a very small opening that appears from time to time?"

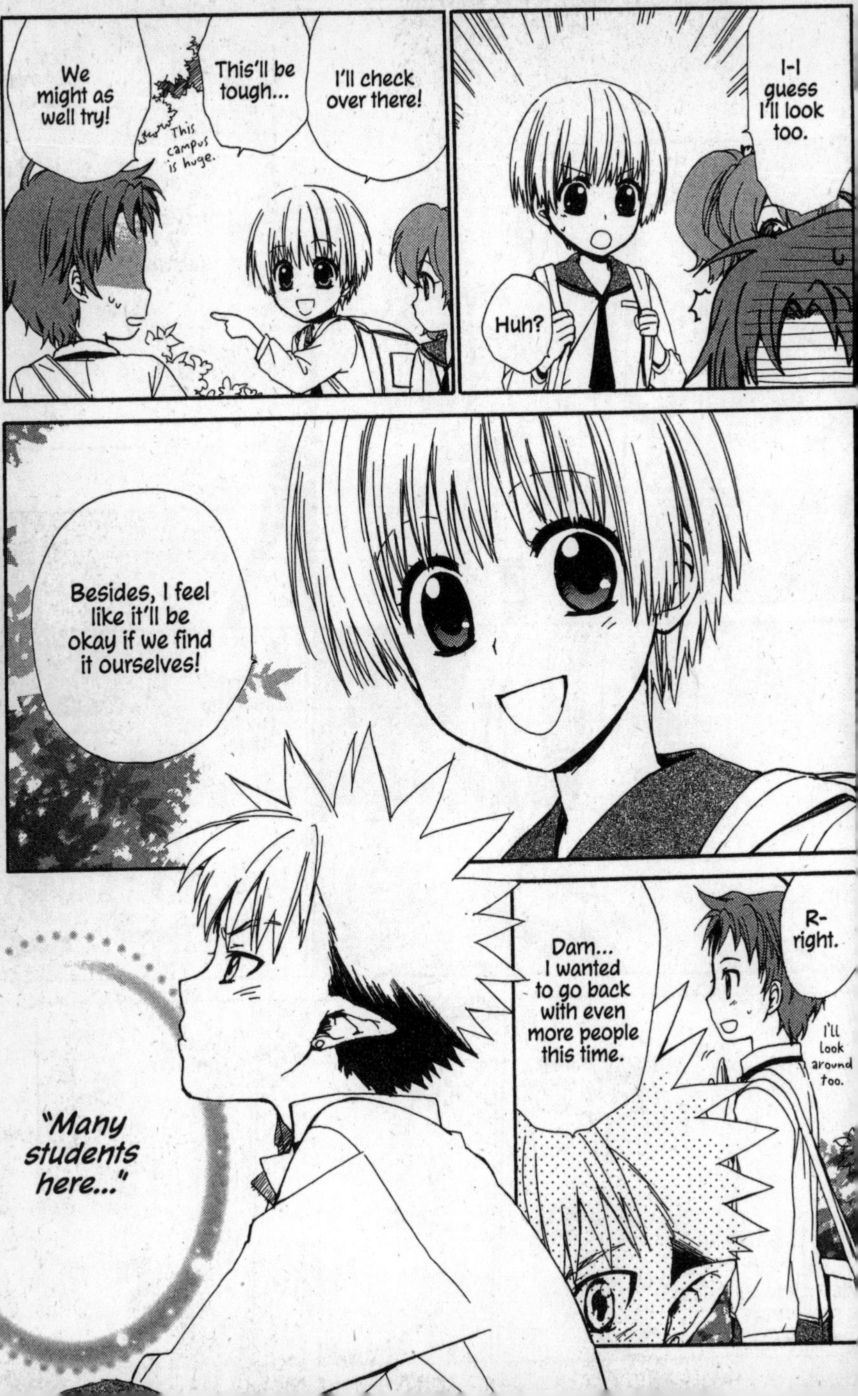
I-I guess I'll look too.
Huh?
I'll check over there!
This'll be tough...
This campus is huge.
We might as well try!
Besides, I feel like it'll be okay if we find it ourselves!
R-right.
I'll look around too.
Darn... I wanted to go back with even more people this time.
"Many students here..."

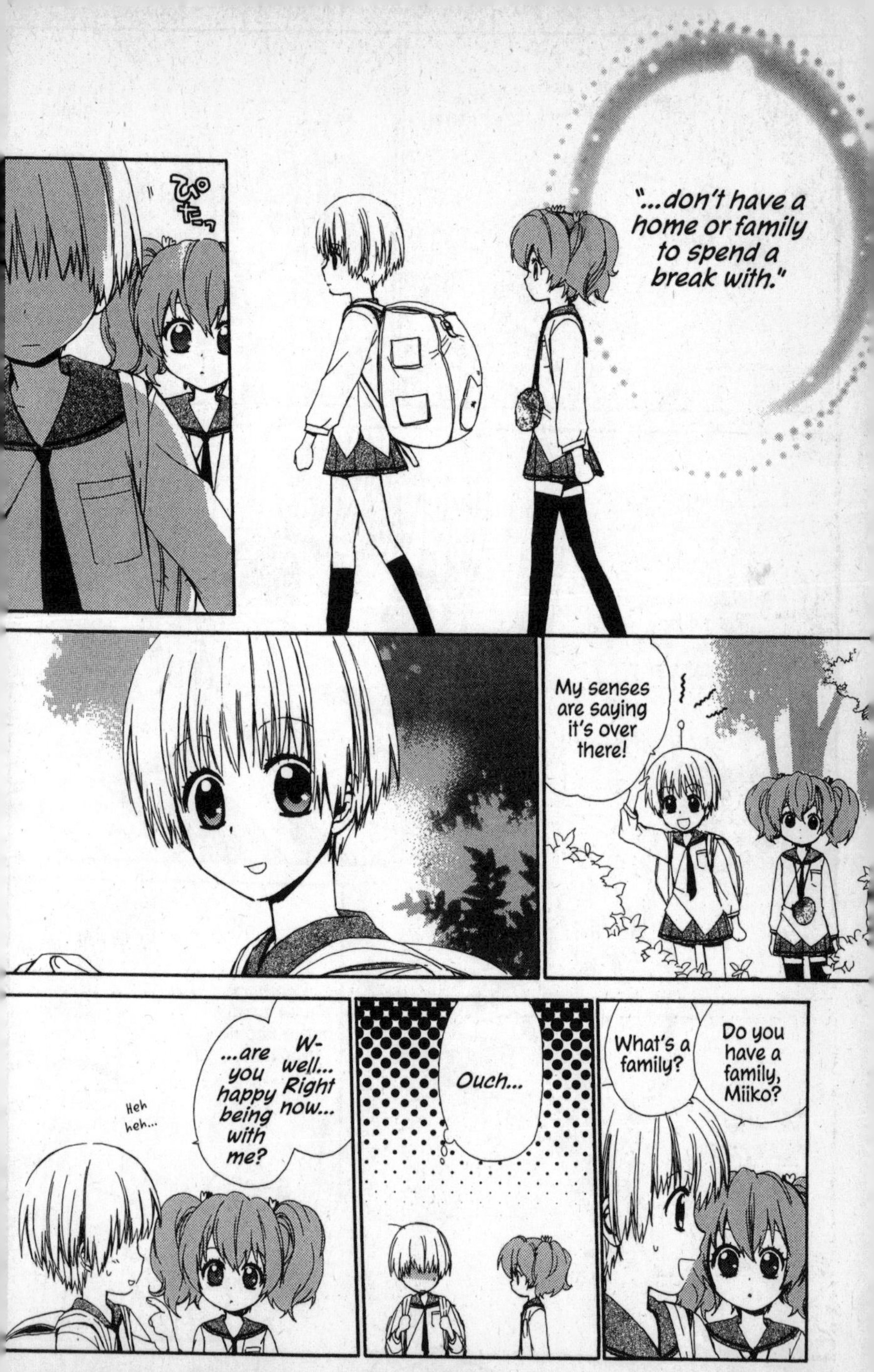
"...don't have a home or family to spend a break with."
ぴたっ
My senses are saying it's over there!
Do you have a family, Miiko?
What's a family?
Ouch...
W- well... Right now...
...are you happy being with me?
Heh heh...

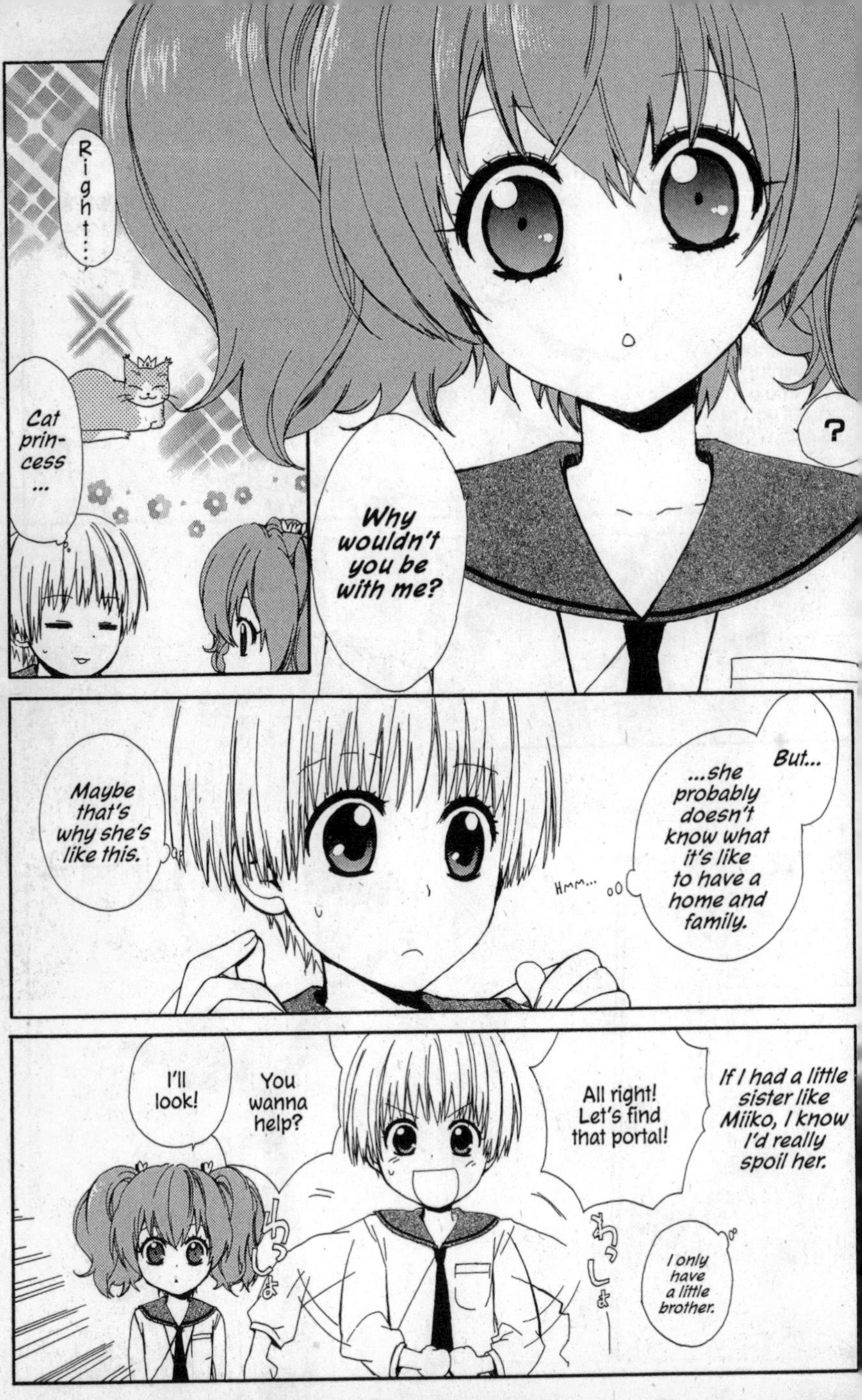
?
Why wouldn't you be with me?
Right...
Cat princess...
But...
...she probably doesn't know what it's like to have a home and family.
HMM...
Maybe that's why she's like this.
If I had a little sister like Miiko, I know I'd really spoil her.
I only have a little brother.
わっしょ
All right! Let's find that portal!
You wanna help?
わっしょ
I'll look!

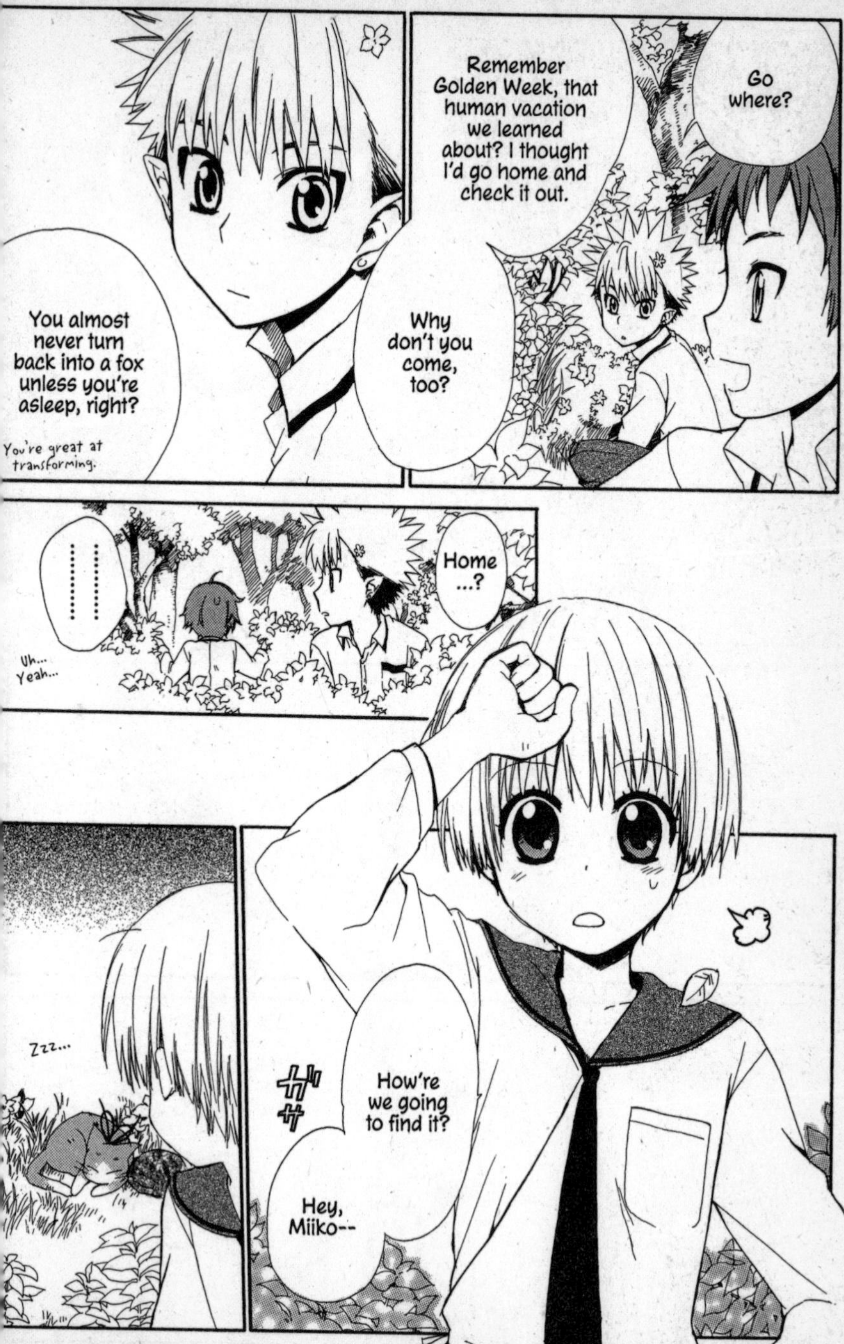
Go where?
Remember Golden Week, that human vacation we learned about? I thought I'd go home and check it out.
Why don't you come, too?
You almost never turn back into a fox unless you're asleep, right?
You're great at transforming.
Home ...?
......
Uh... Yeah...
How're we going to find it?
Hey, Miiko--
Zzz...

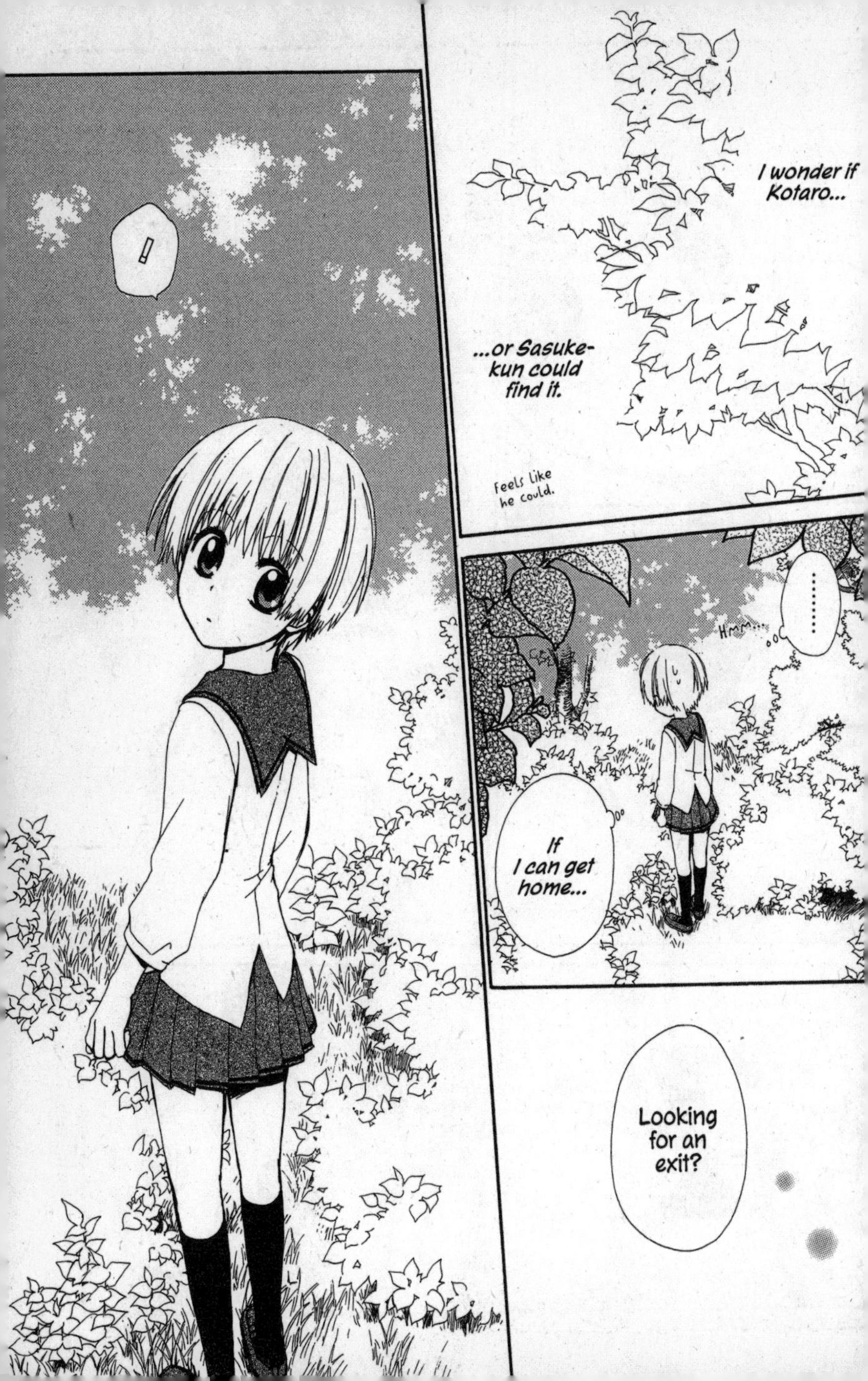
I wonder if Kotaro...
...or Sasuke-kun could find it.
Feels like he could.
......
Hmm...
If I can get home...
Looking for an exit?
!

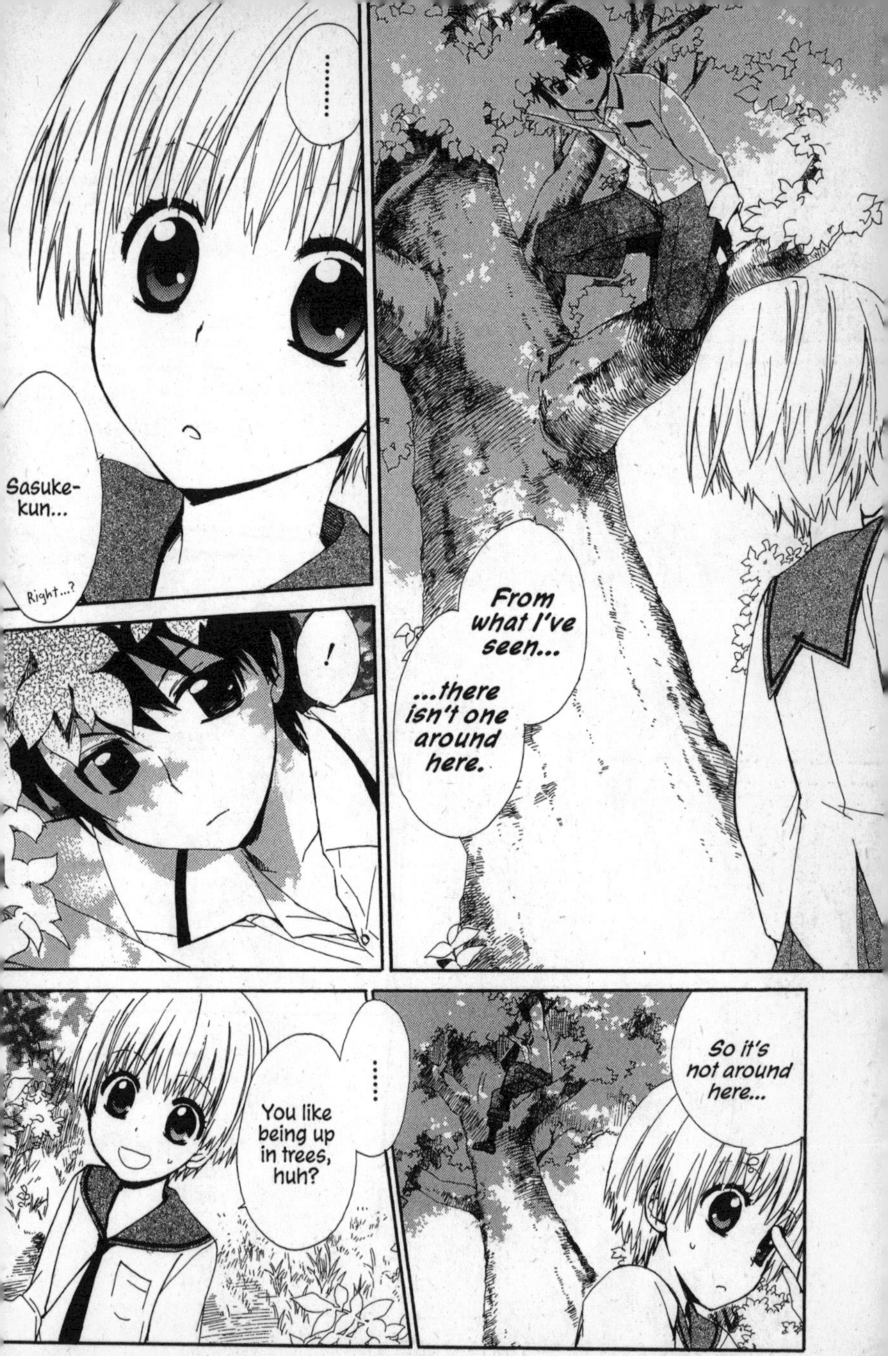
From what I've seen...
...there isn't one around here.
......
Sasuke-kun...
Right...?
!
So it's not around here...
......
You like being up in trees, huh?

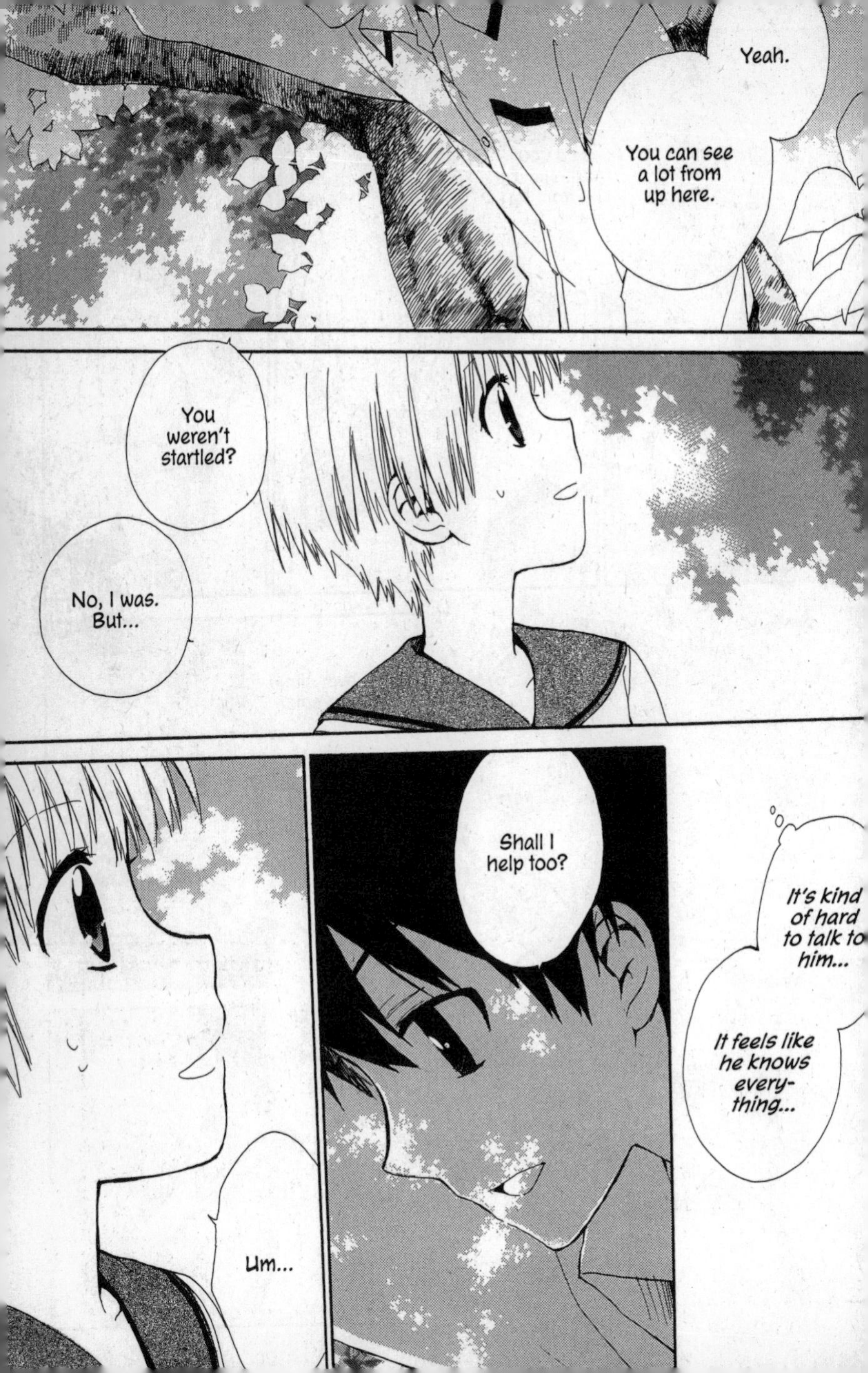
Yeah.
You can see a lot from up here.
You weren't startled?
No, I was. But...
Shall I help too?
It's kind of hard to talk to him...
It feels like he knows every-thing...
Um...

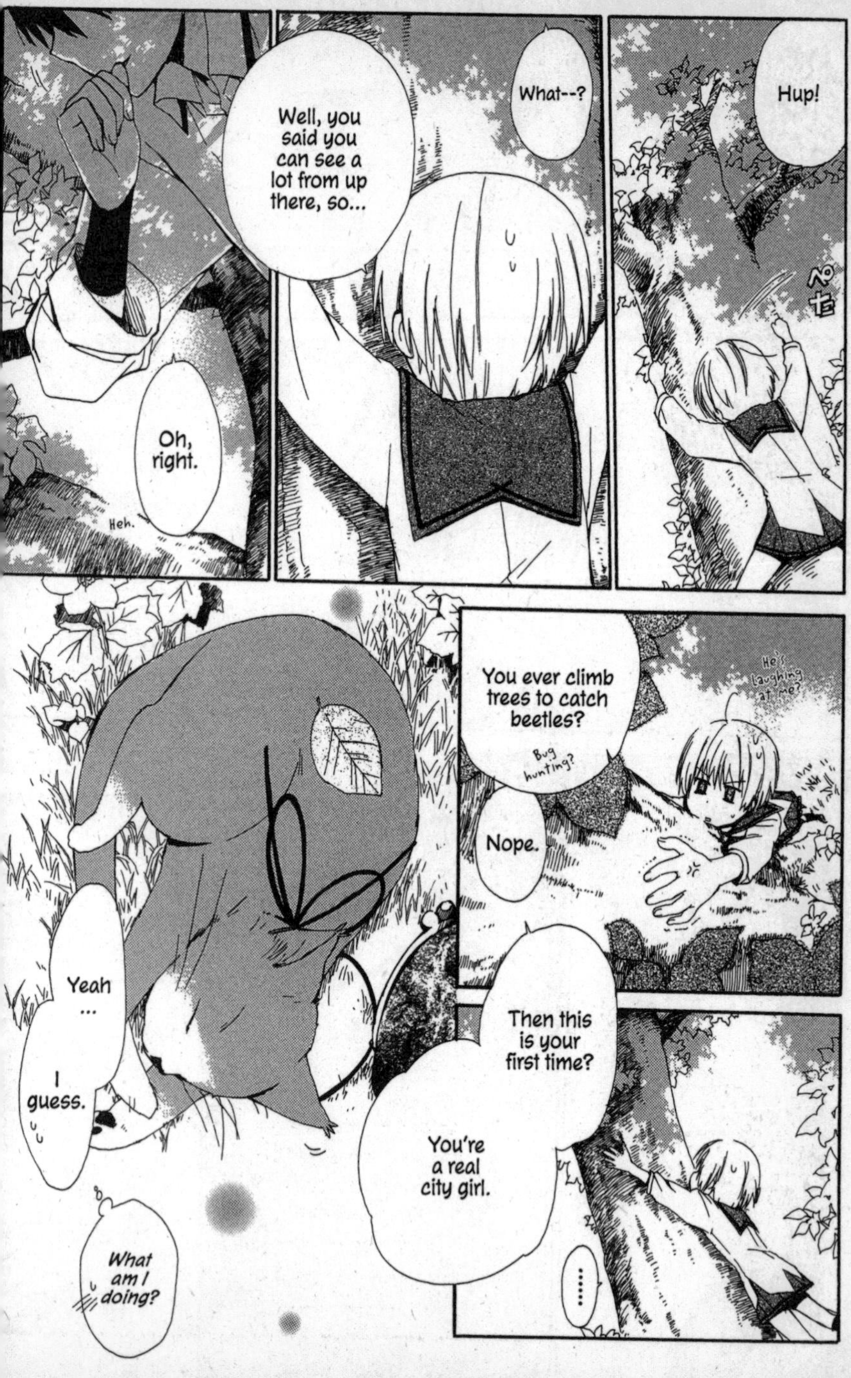
Hup!
へた
What--?
Well, you said you can see a lot from up there, so...
Oh, right.
Heh.
You ever climb trees to catch beetles?
He's laughing at me?
Bug hunting?
Nope.
Then this is your first time?
You're a real city girl.
......
Yeah ... I guess.
What am I doing?

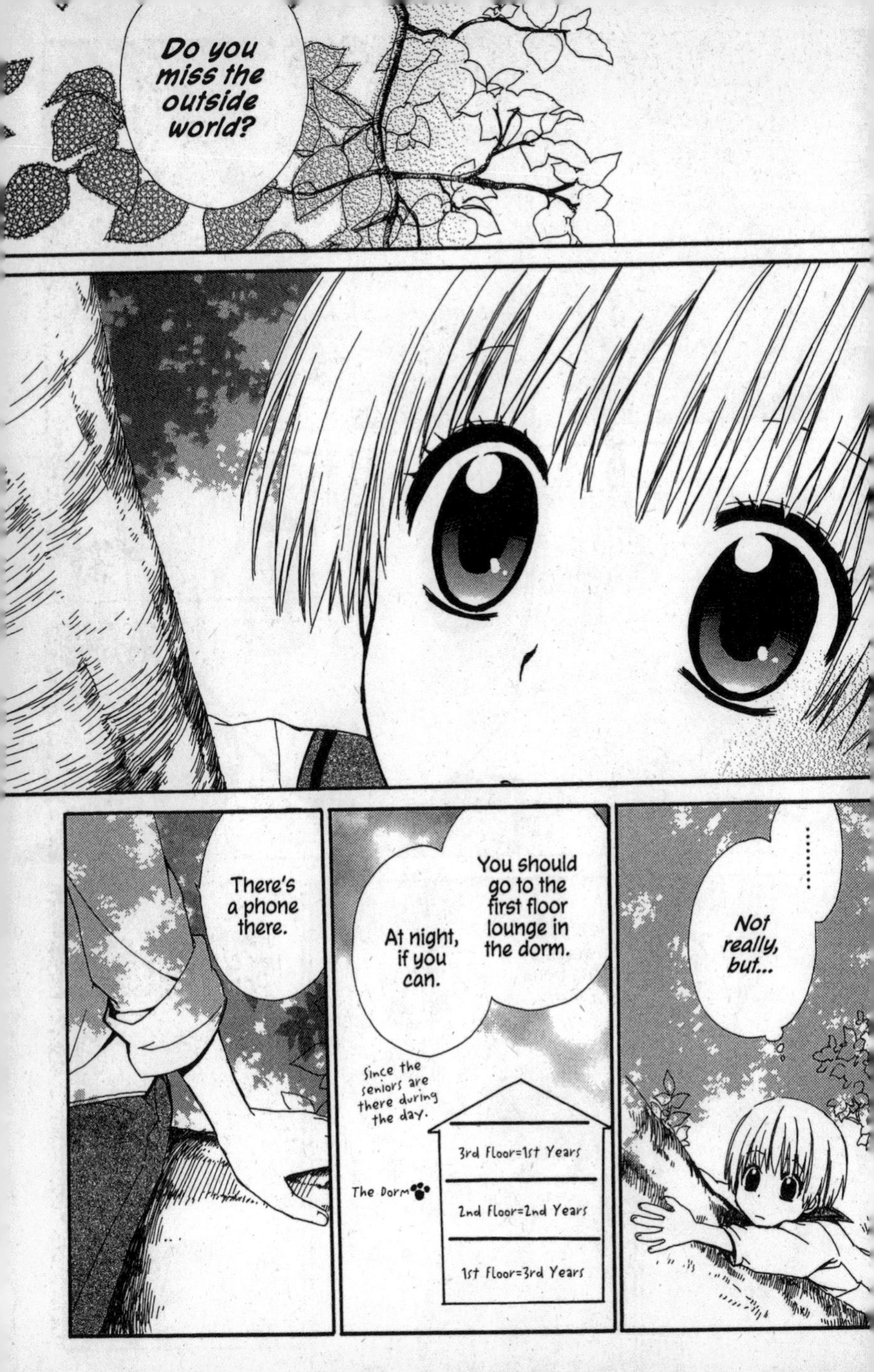
Do you miss the outside world?
......
Not really, but...
You should go to the first floor lounge in the dorm.
At night, if you can.
Since the seniors are there during the day.
The Dorm
3rd Floor=1st Years
2nd Floor=2nd Years
1st Floor=3rd Years
There's a phone there.
...

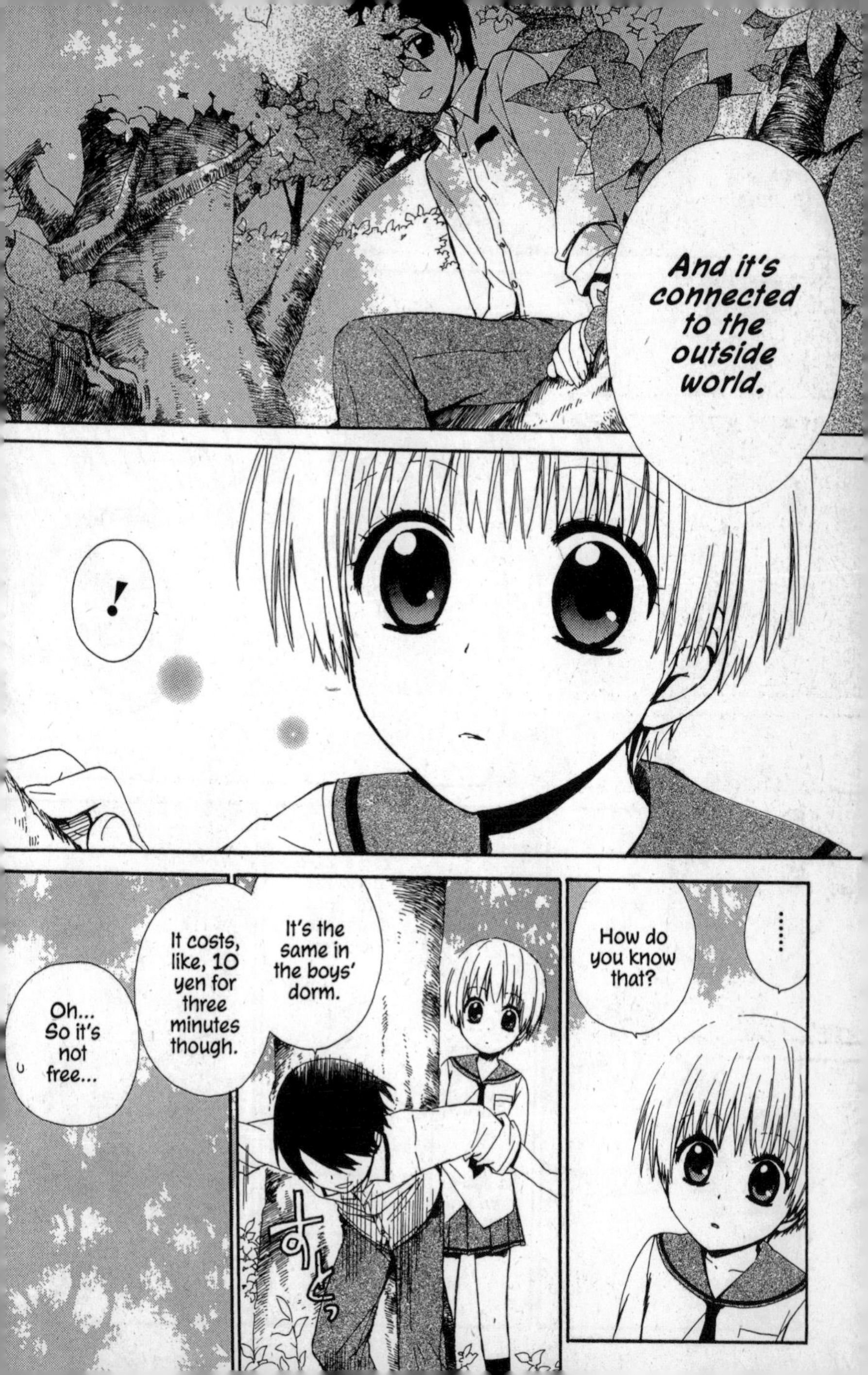
And it's connected to the outside world.
!
......
How do you know that?
It's the same in the boys' dorm.
It costs, like, 10 yen for three minutes though.
Oh... So it's not free...
すとっ

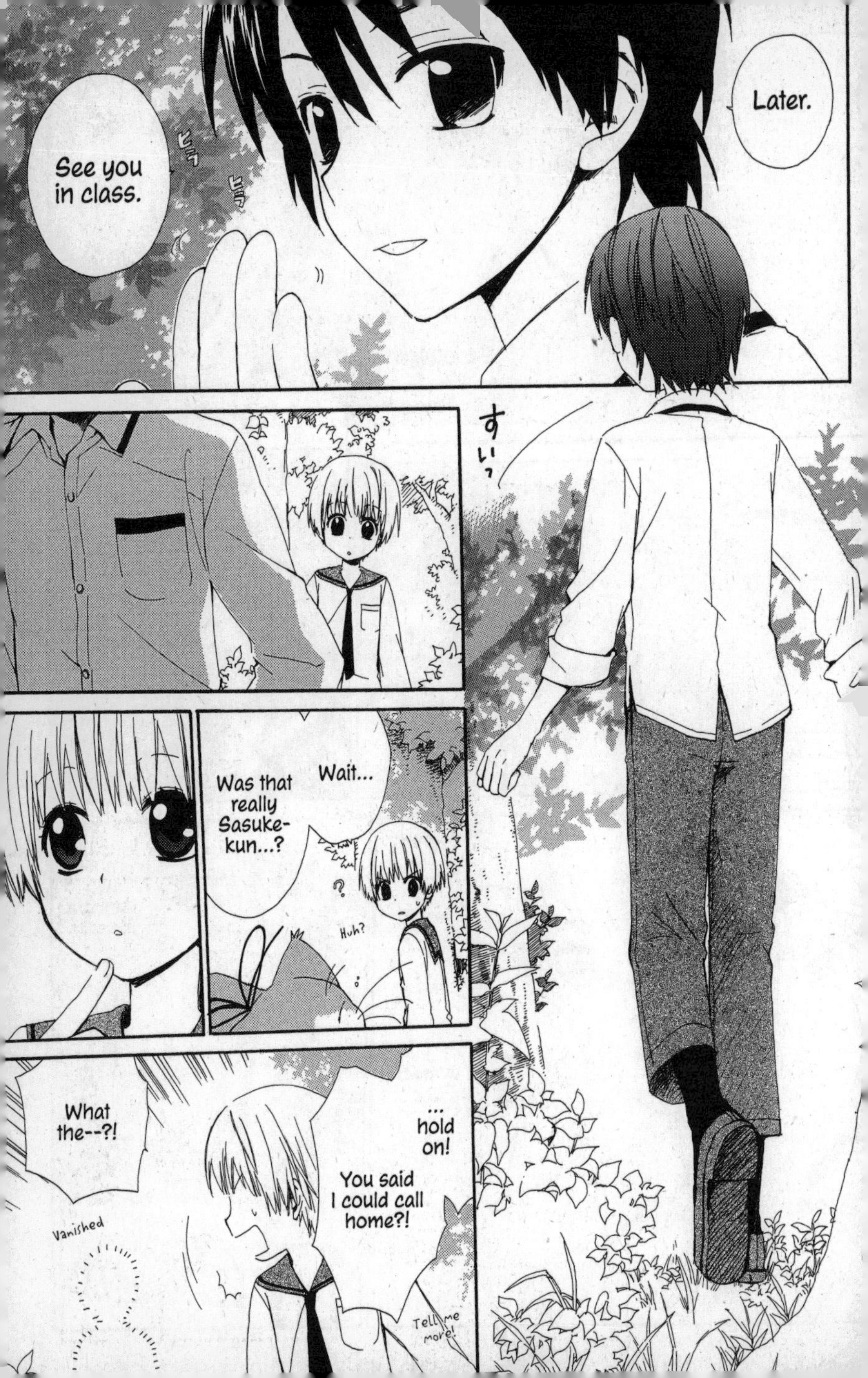
Later.
ヒラ ヒラ
See you in class.
すいっ
Wait...
Was that really Sasuke-kun...?
Huh?
... hold on!
You said I could call home?!
What the--?!
Tell me more!
Vanished

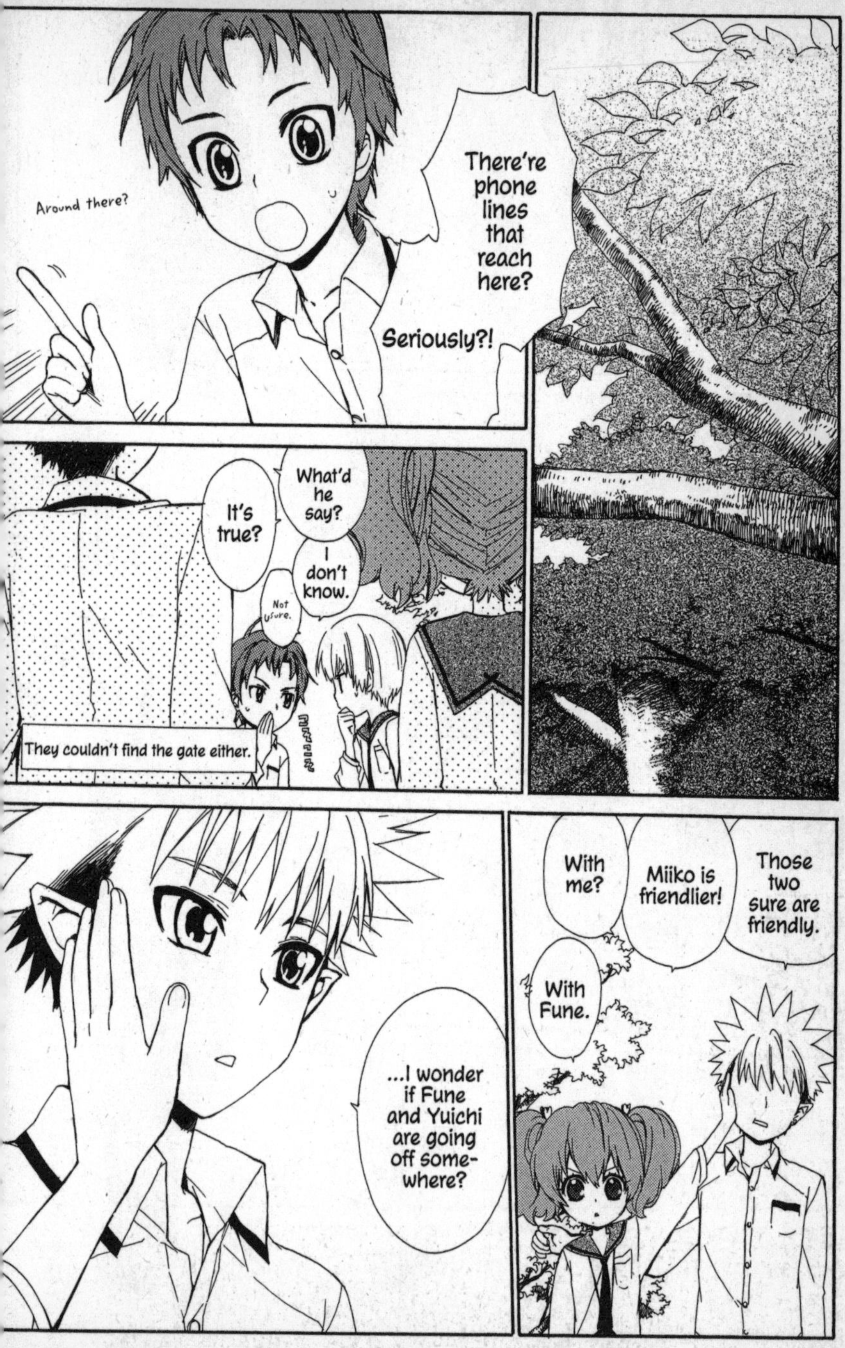
There're phone lines that reach here?
Seriously?!
Around there?
What'd he say?
It's true?
I don't know.
Not sure.
They couldn't find the gate either.
Those two sure are friendly.
Miiko is friendlier!
With me?
With Fune.
...I wonder if Fune and Yuichi are going off some-where?

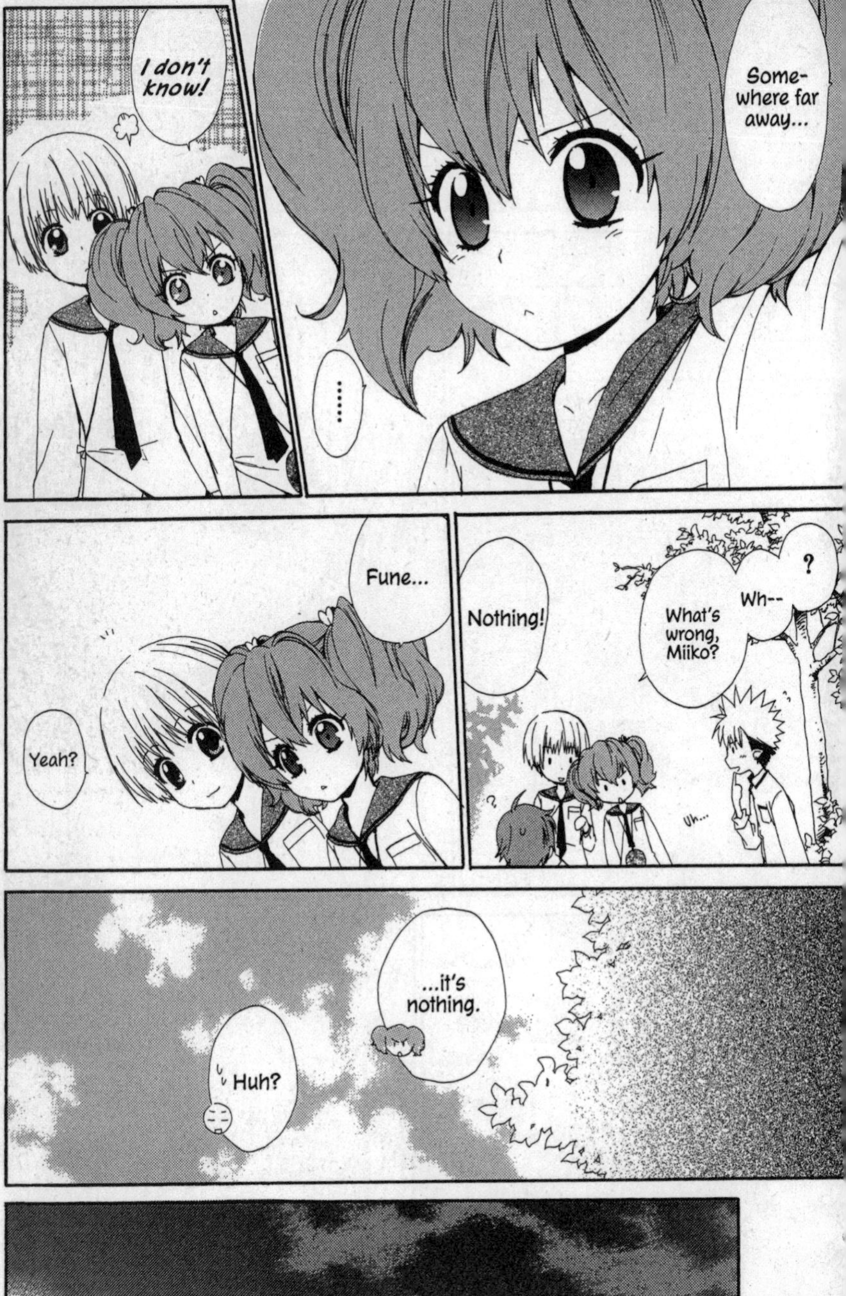
Some-
where far
away...
......
I don't
know!
?
Wh--
What's
wrong,
Miiko?
Nothing!
Uh...
Fune...
Yeah?
...it's
nothing.
Huh?

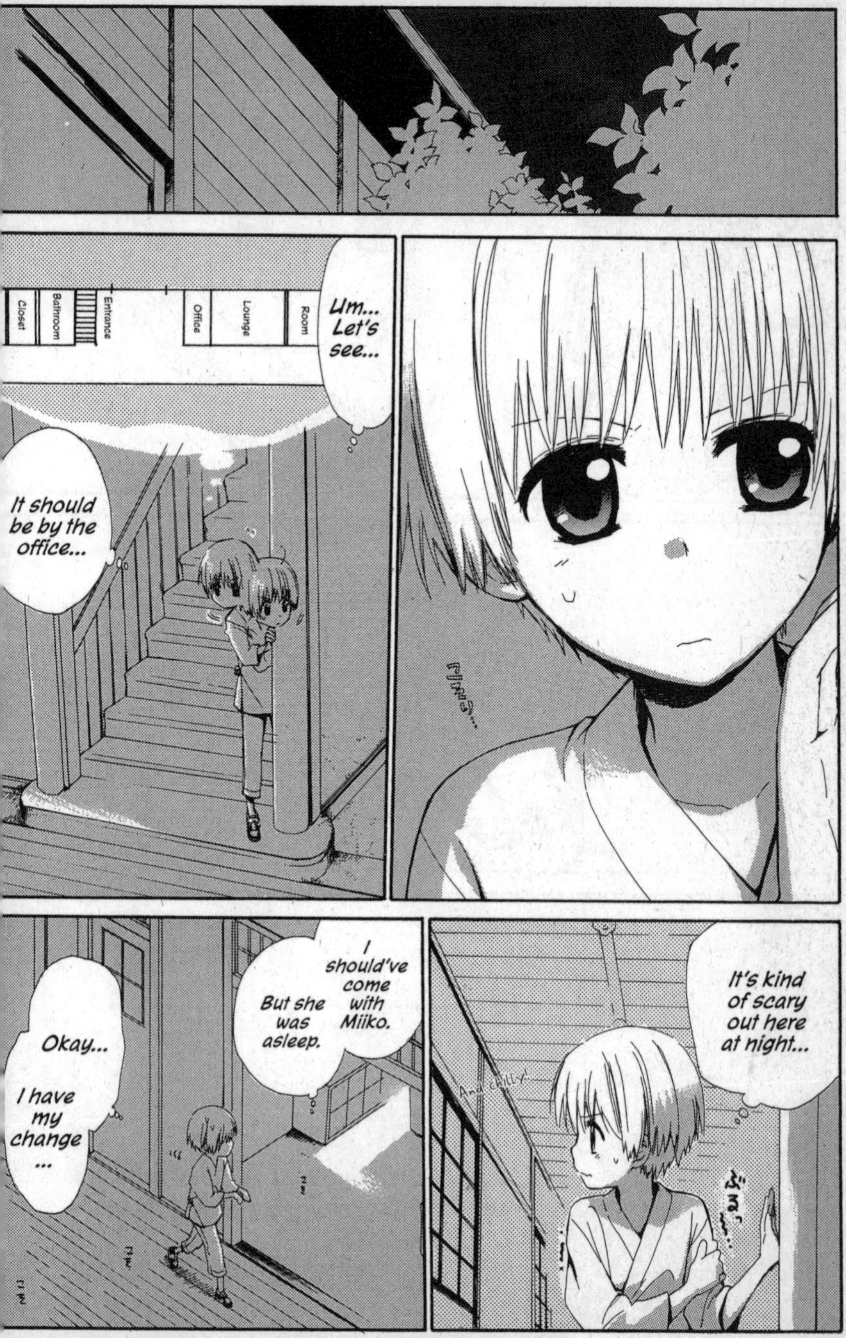
Um... Let's see...
Room
Lounge
Office
Entrance
Bathroom
Closet
It should be by the office...
It's kind of scary out here at night...
And chilly!
I should've come with Miiko.
But she was asleep.
Okay...
I have my change ...

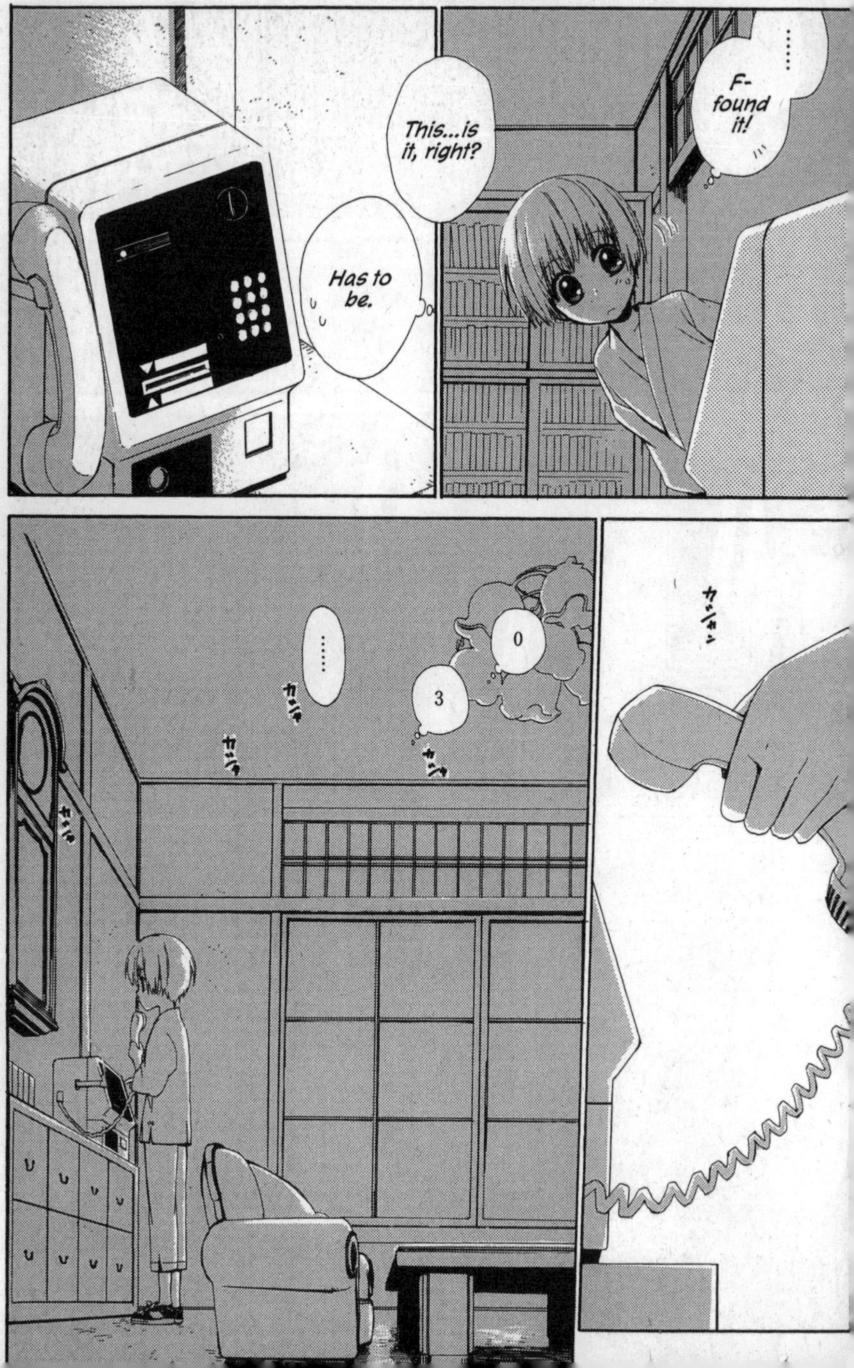
......
F-found it!
This...is it, right?
Has to be.
......
0
3

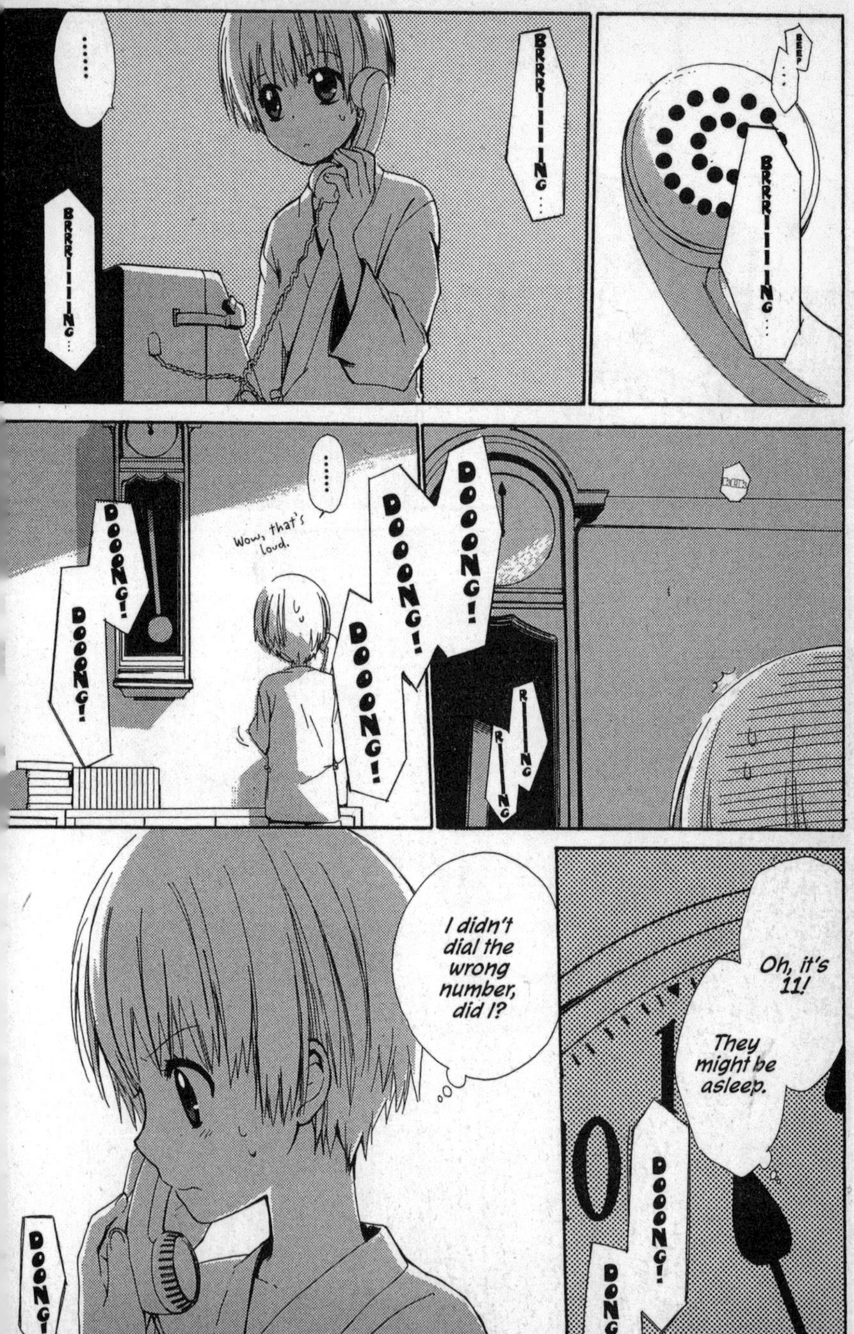
BEEP...
BRRRIIIING...
BRRRIIIING...
......
BRRRIIIING...
KLIK
RIIING
RIIING
DOOONG!
DOOONG!
DOOONG!
......
Wow, that's loud.
DOOONG!
DOOONG!
Oh, it's 11!
They might be asleep.
DOOONG!
DONG!
I didn't dial the wrong number, did I?
DOOONG!

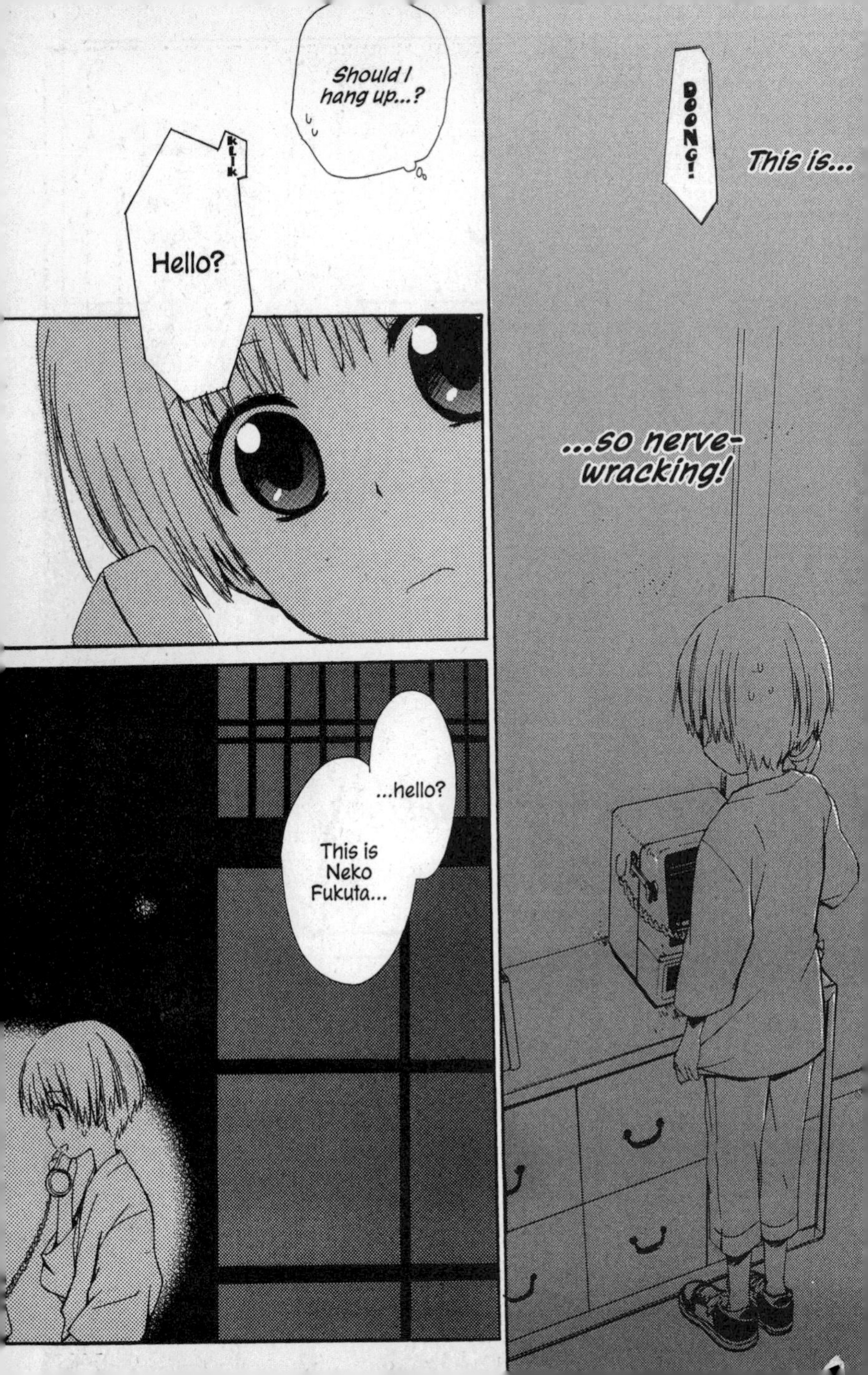
DOONG!
This is...
...so nerve-wracking!
Should I hang up...?
KLIK
Hello?
...hello?
This is Neko Fukuta...

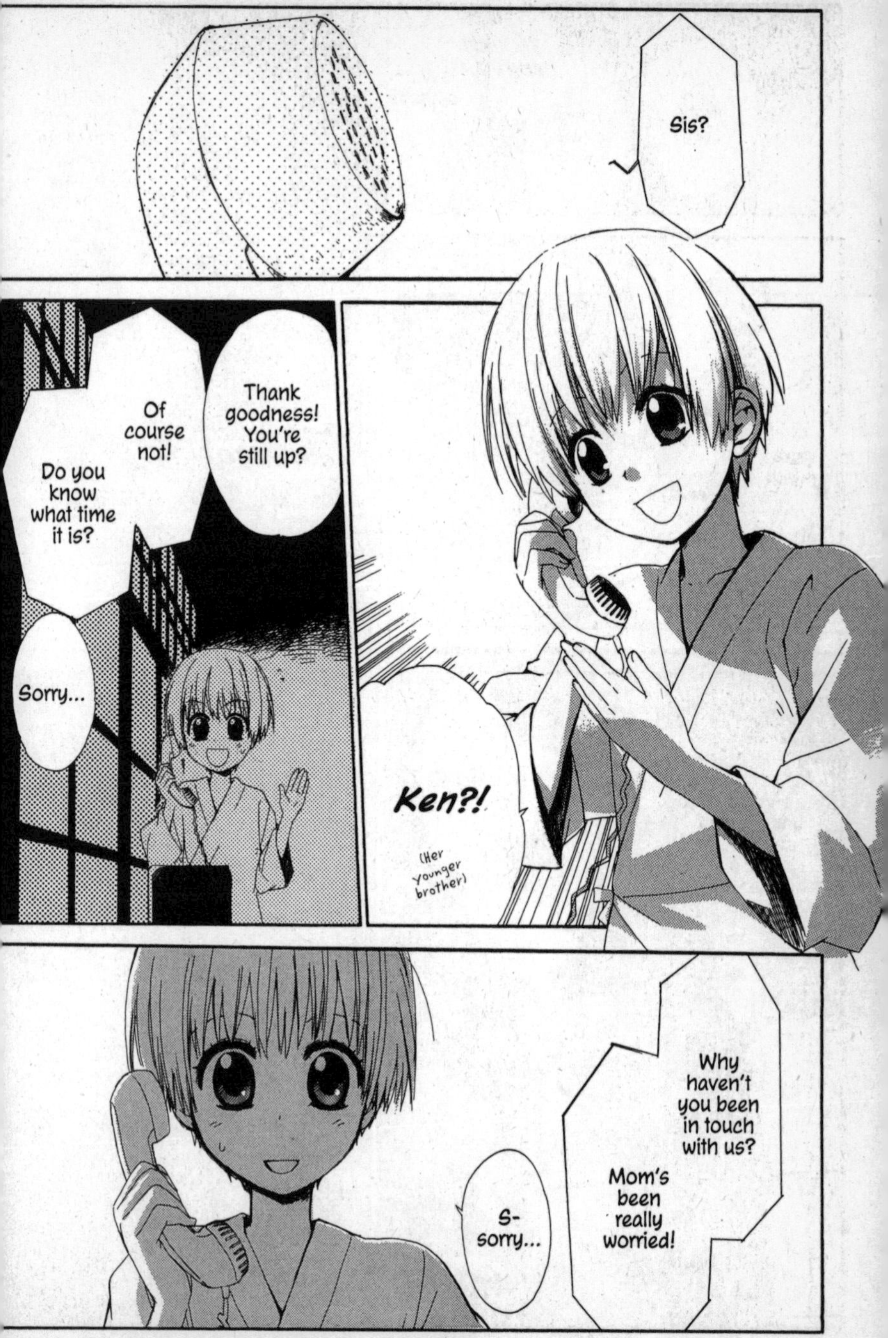
Sis?
Ken?!
(Her younger brother)
Thank goodness! You're still up?
Of course not!
Do you know what time it is?
Sorry...
Why haven't you been in touch with us?
Mom's been really worried!
S-sorry...

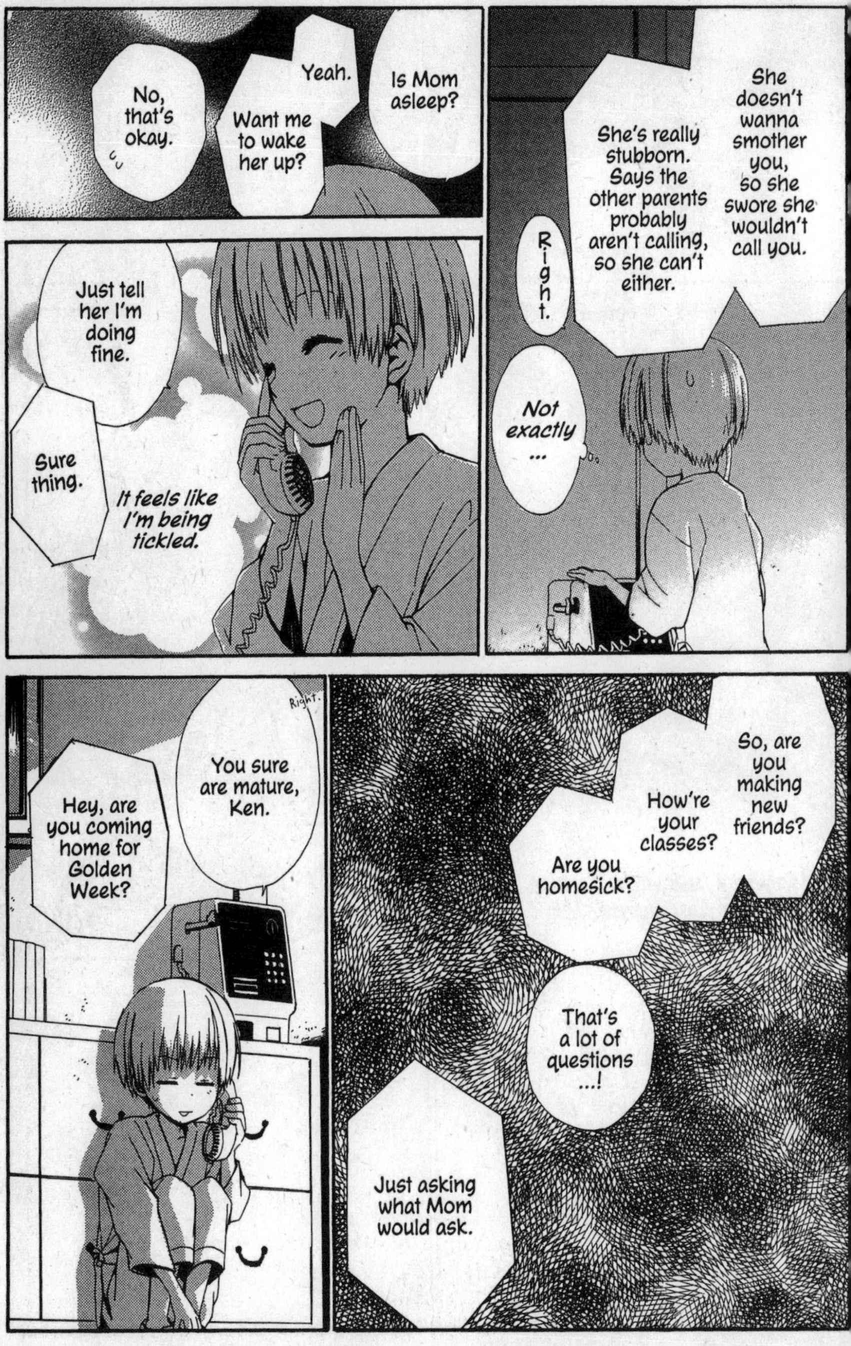
She doesn't wanna smother you, so she swore she wouldn't call you.
She's really stubborn. Says the other parents probably aren't calling, so she can't either.
Right.
Not exactly ...
Is Mom asleep?
Yeah.
Want me to wake her up?
No, that's okay.
Just tell her I'm doing fine.
Sure thing.
It feels like I'm being tickled.
So, are you making new friends?
How're your classes?
Are you homesick?
That's a lot of questions ...!
Just asking what Mom would ask.
Right.
You sure are mature, Ken.
Hey, are you coming home for Golden Week?

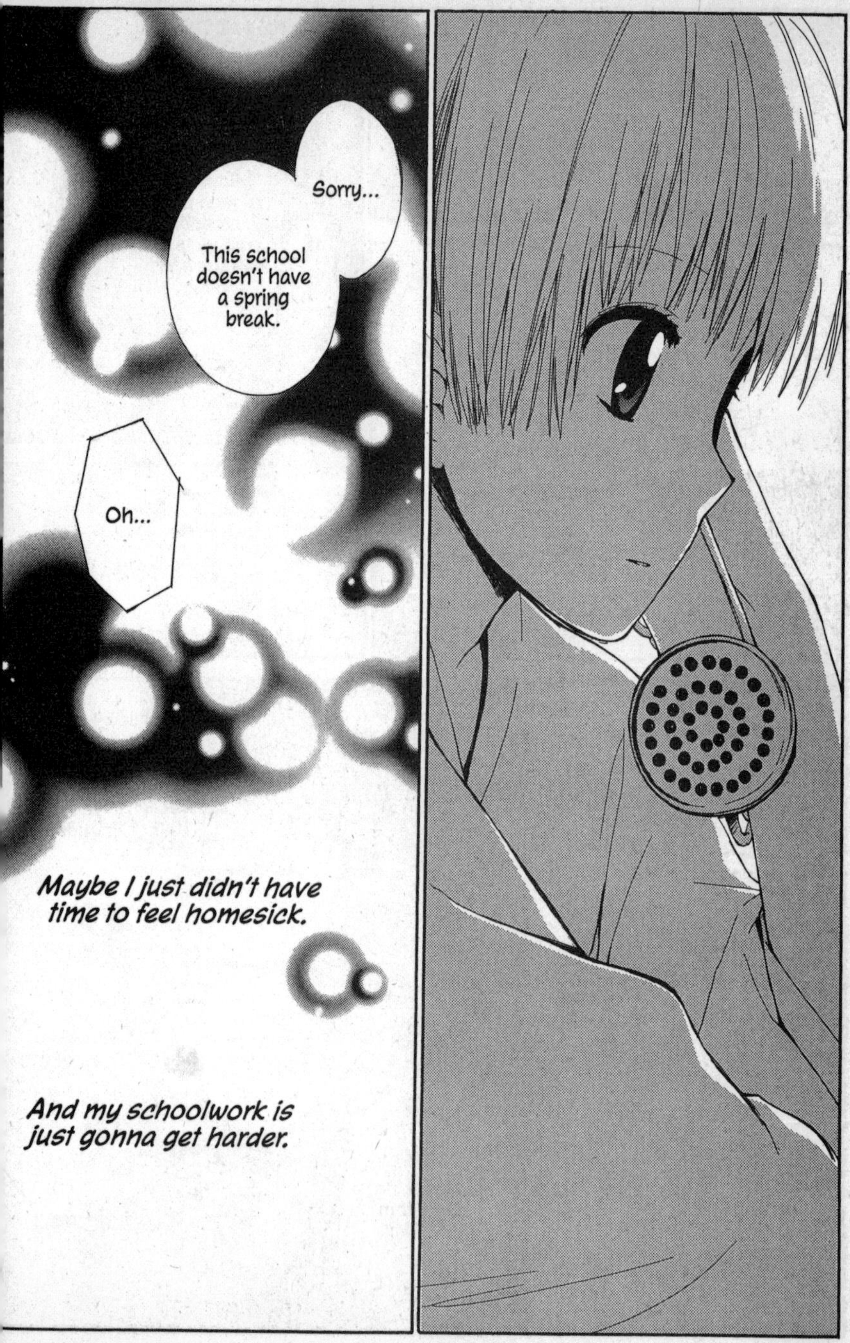
Sorry...
This school doesn't have a spring break.
Oh...
Maybe I just didn't have time to feel homesick.
And my schoolwork is just gonna get harder.

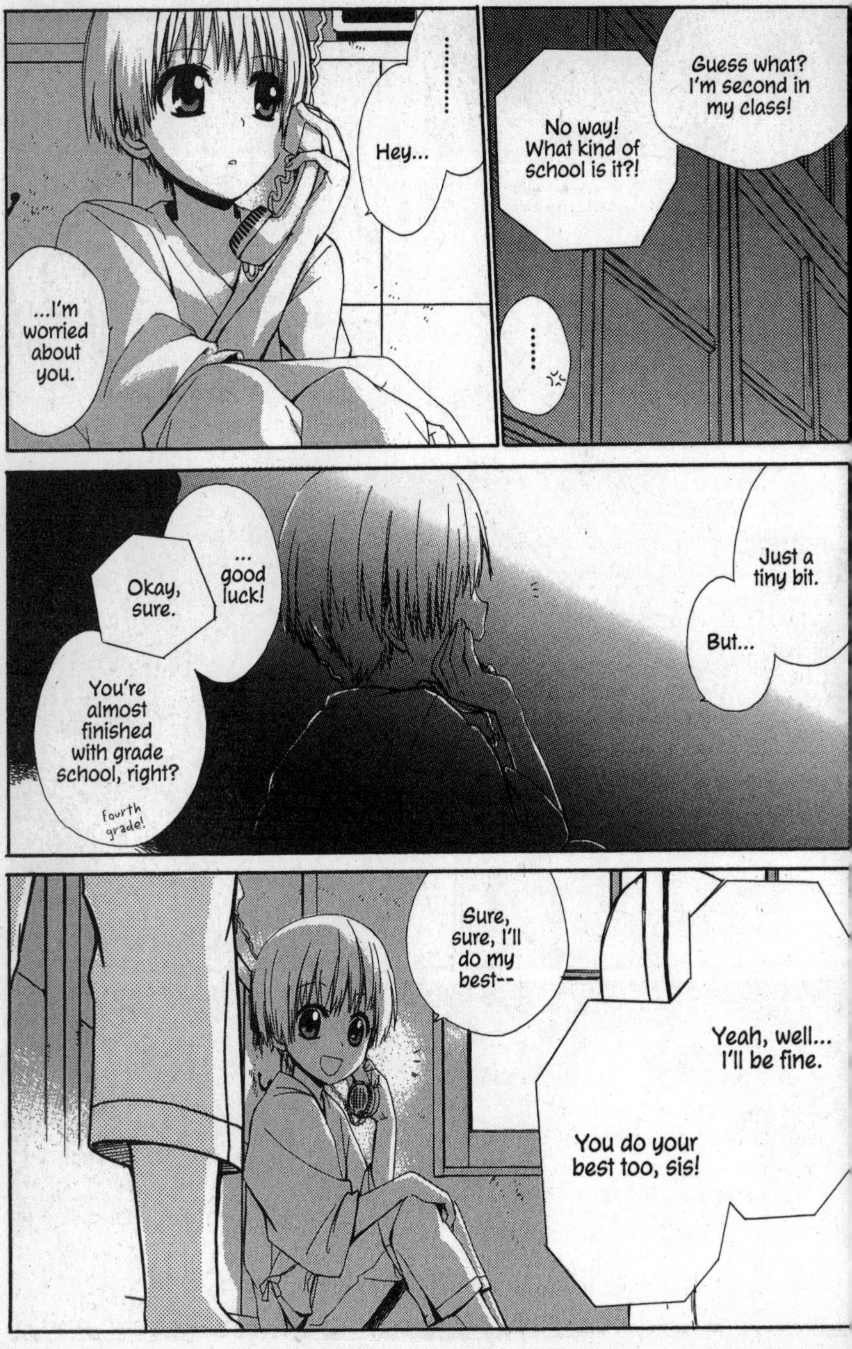
Guess what? I'm second in my class!
No way! What kind of school is it?!
......
......
Hey...
...I'm worried about you.
Just a tiny bit.
But...
... good luck!
Okay, sure.
You're almost finished with grade school, right?
fourth grade!
Yeah, well... I'll be fine.
You do your best too, sis!
Sure, sure, I'll do my best--

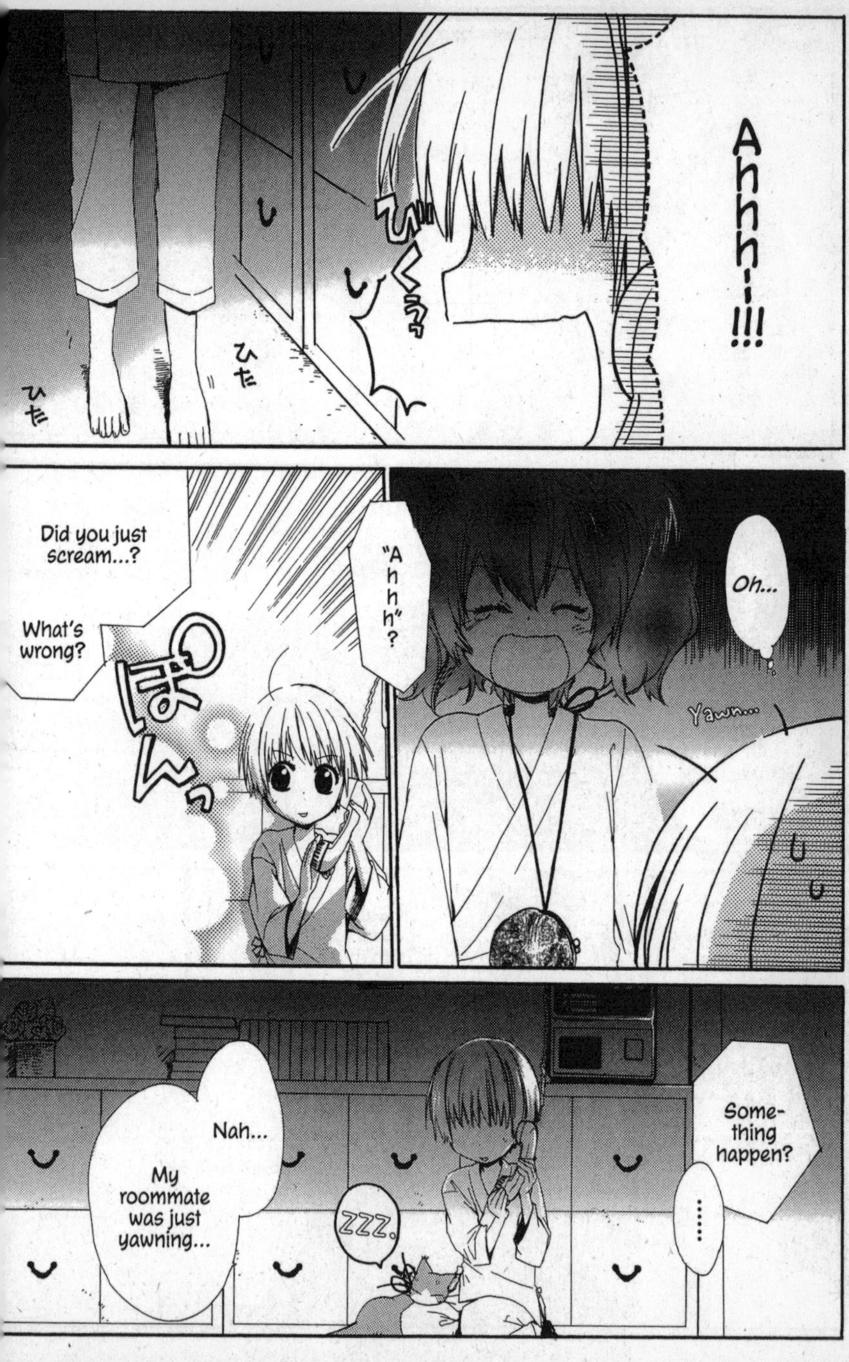
Ahhh--!!!
ひた
ひた
Oh...
Yawn...
"A h h h"?
Did you just scream...?
What's wrong?
ぽんっ
Some-thing happen?
......
Nah...
My roommate was just yawning...
ZZZ.

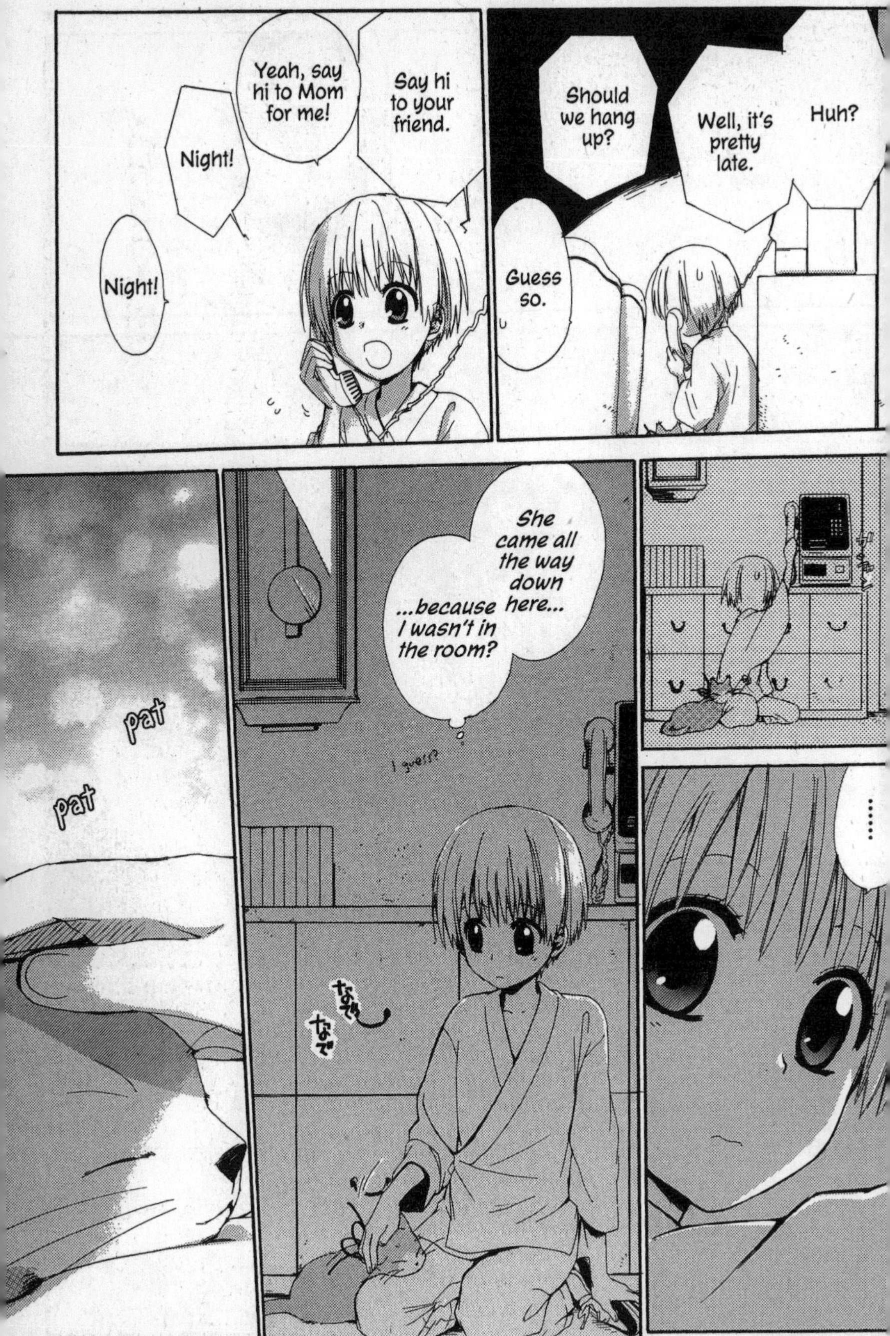
Huh?
Well, it's pretty late.
Should we hang up?
Guess so.
Say hi to your friend.
Yeah, say hi to Mom for me!
Night!
Night!
......
She came all the way down here...
...because I wasn't in the room?
I guess?
なで なで
pat
pat

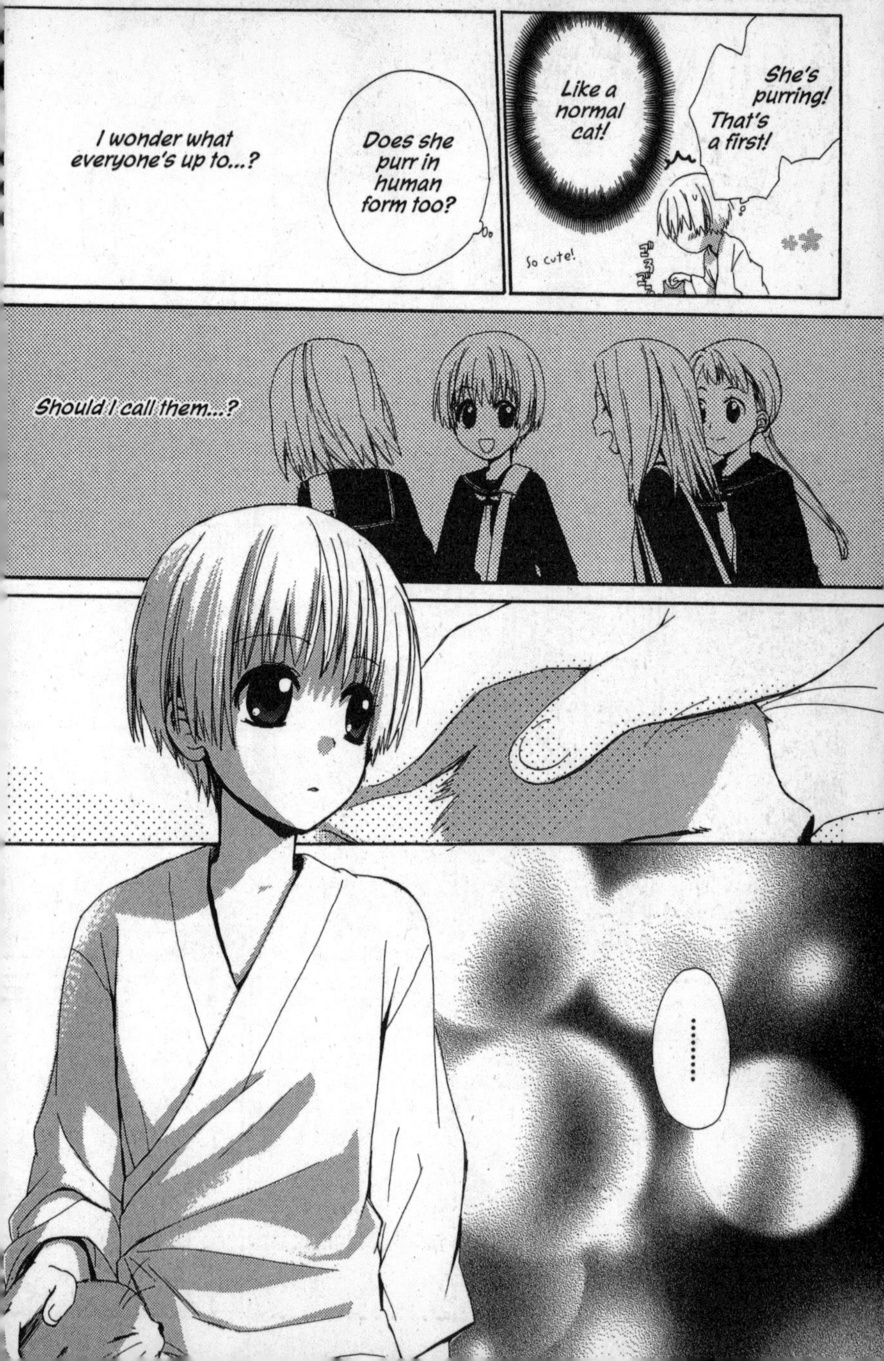
She's purring!
That's a first!
Like a normal cat!
So cute!
Does she purr in human form too?
I wonder what everyone's up to...?
Should I call them...?
....

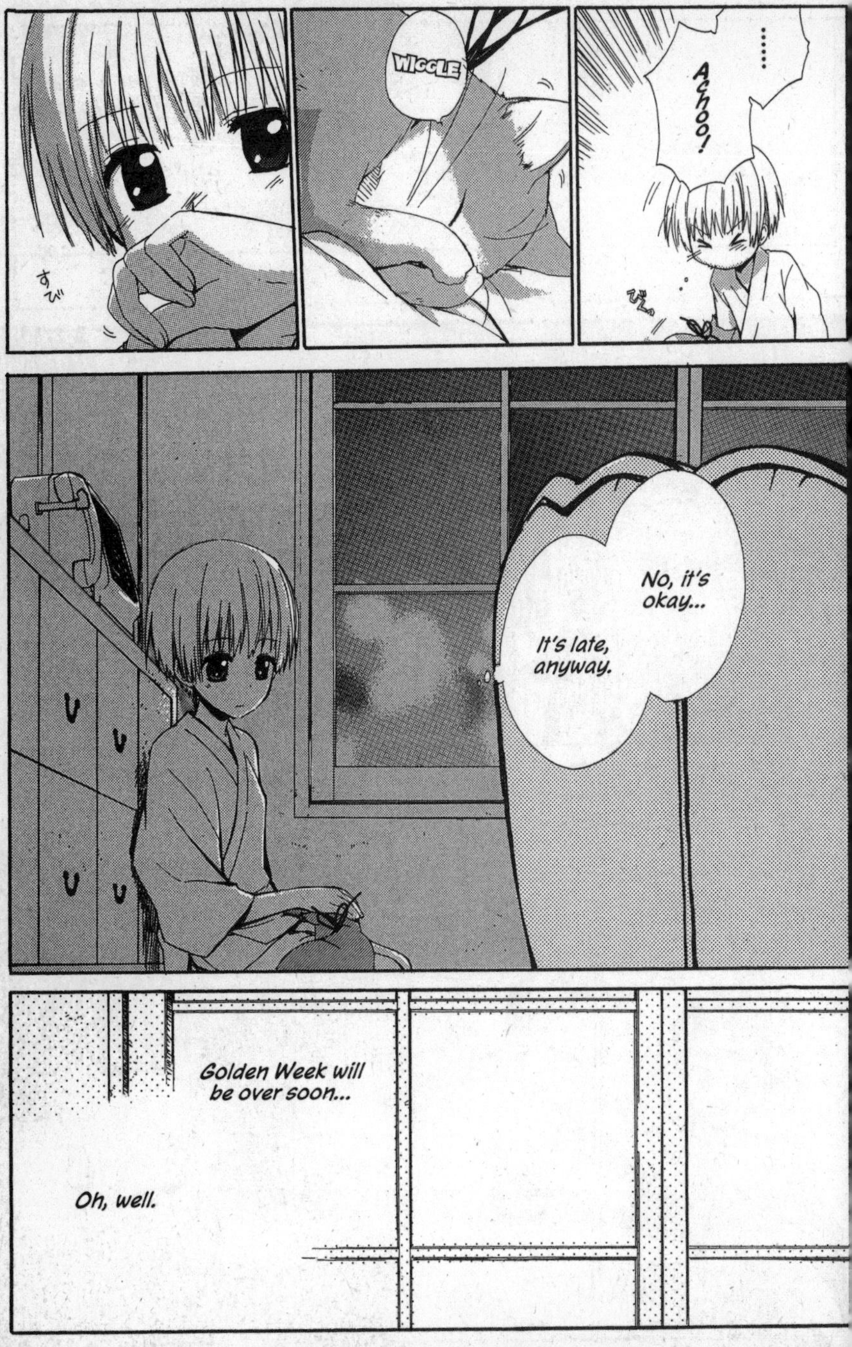
......
Achoo!
WIGGLE
No, it's okay...
It's late, anyway.
Golden Week will be over soon...
Oh, well.

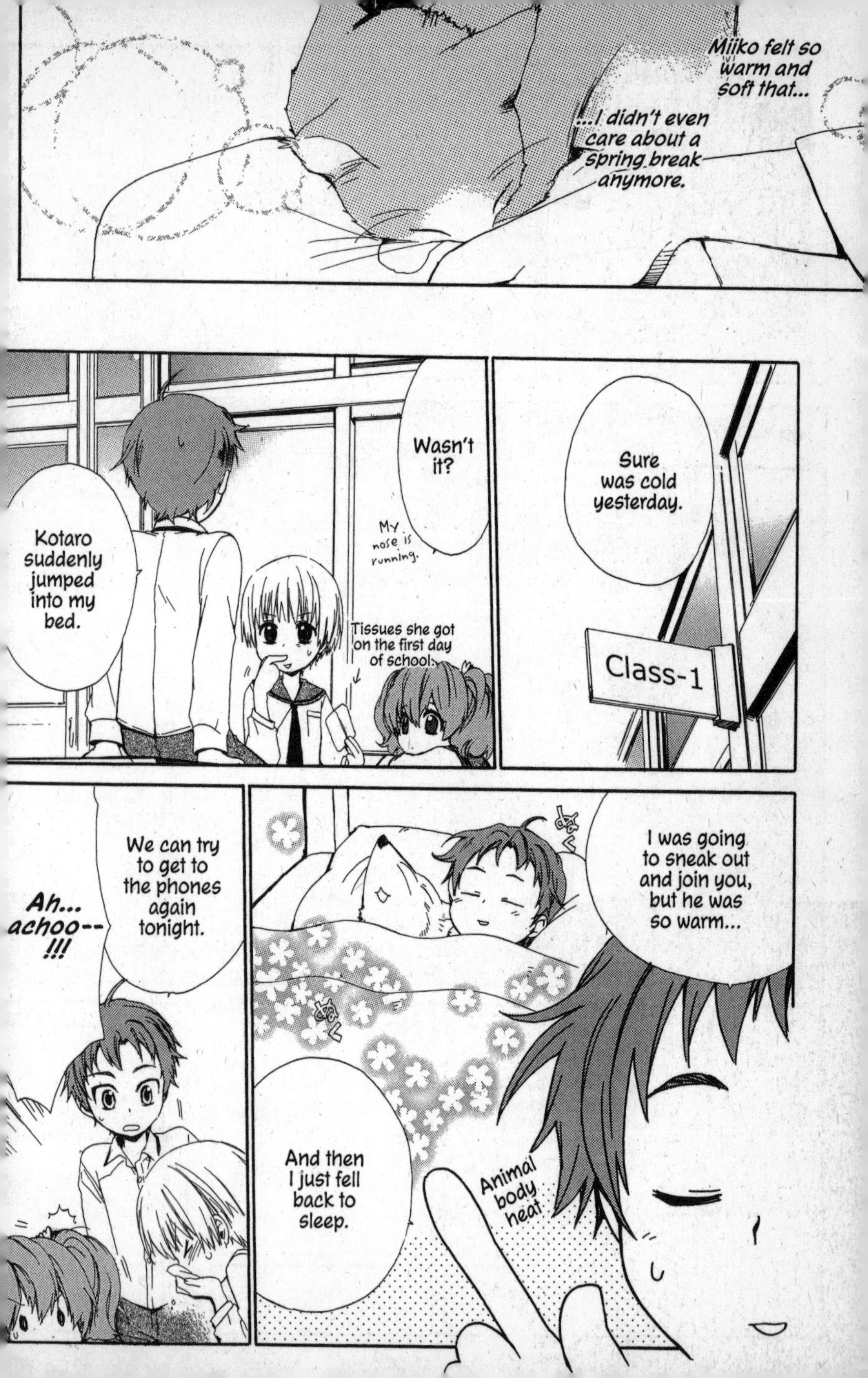
Miiko felt so warm and soft that...
...I didn't even care about a spring break anymore.
Sure was cold yesterday.
Class-1
Wasn't it?
My nose is running.
Tissues she got on the first day of school.
Kotaro suddenly jumped into my bed.
I was going to sneak out and join you, but he was so warm...
And then I just fell back to sleep.
Animal body heat
We can try to get to the phones again tonight.
Ah... achoo--!!!

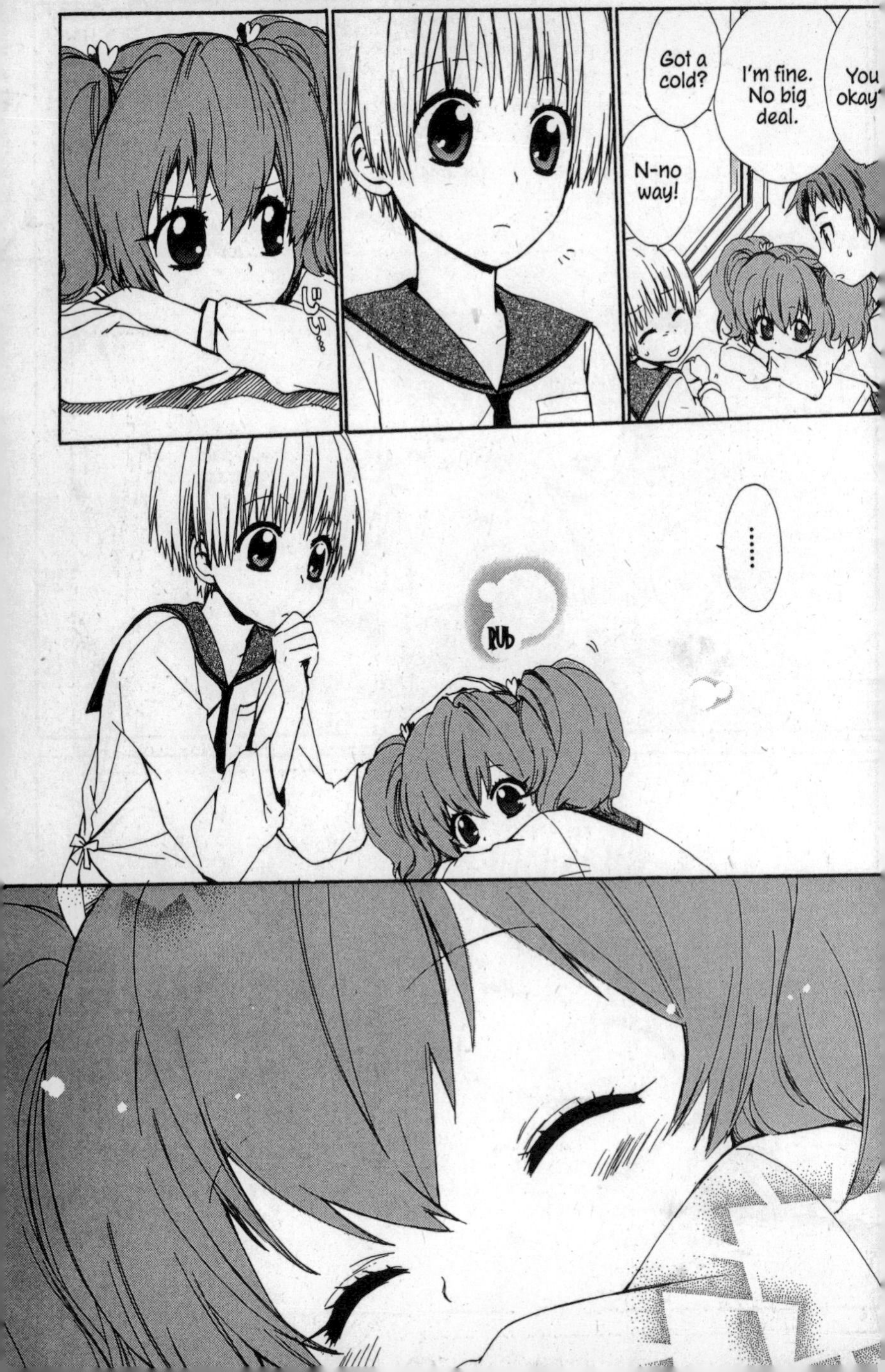
You okay
I'm fine. No big deal.
Got a cold?
N-no way!
......
RUB

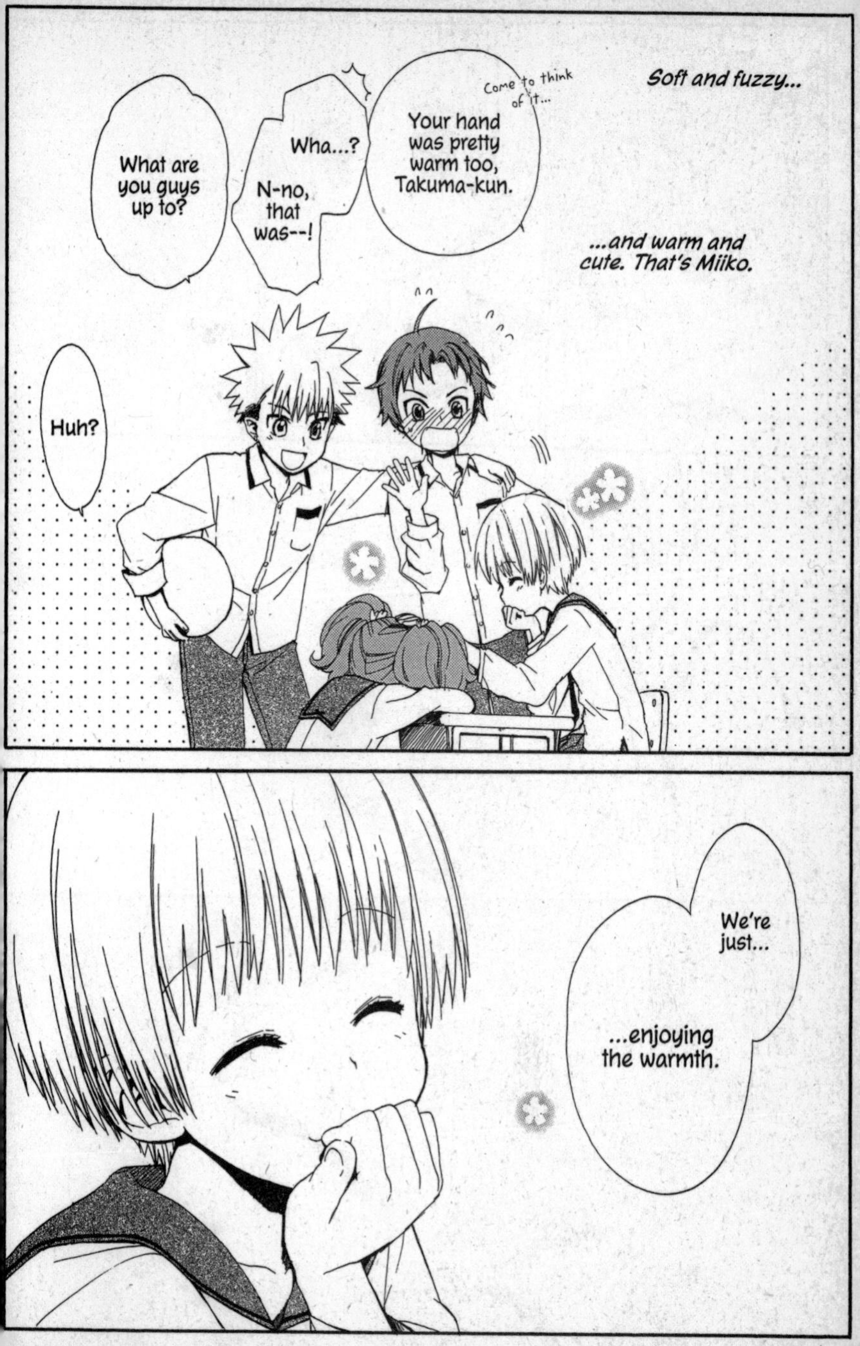
Soft and fuzzy...
...and warm and cute. That's Miiko.
Come to think of it...
Your hand was pretty warm too, Takuma-kun.
Wha...? N-no, that was--!
What are you guys up to?
Huh?
We're just... ...enjoying the warmth.

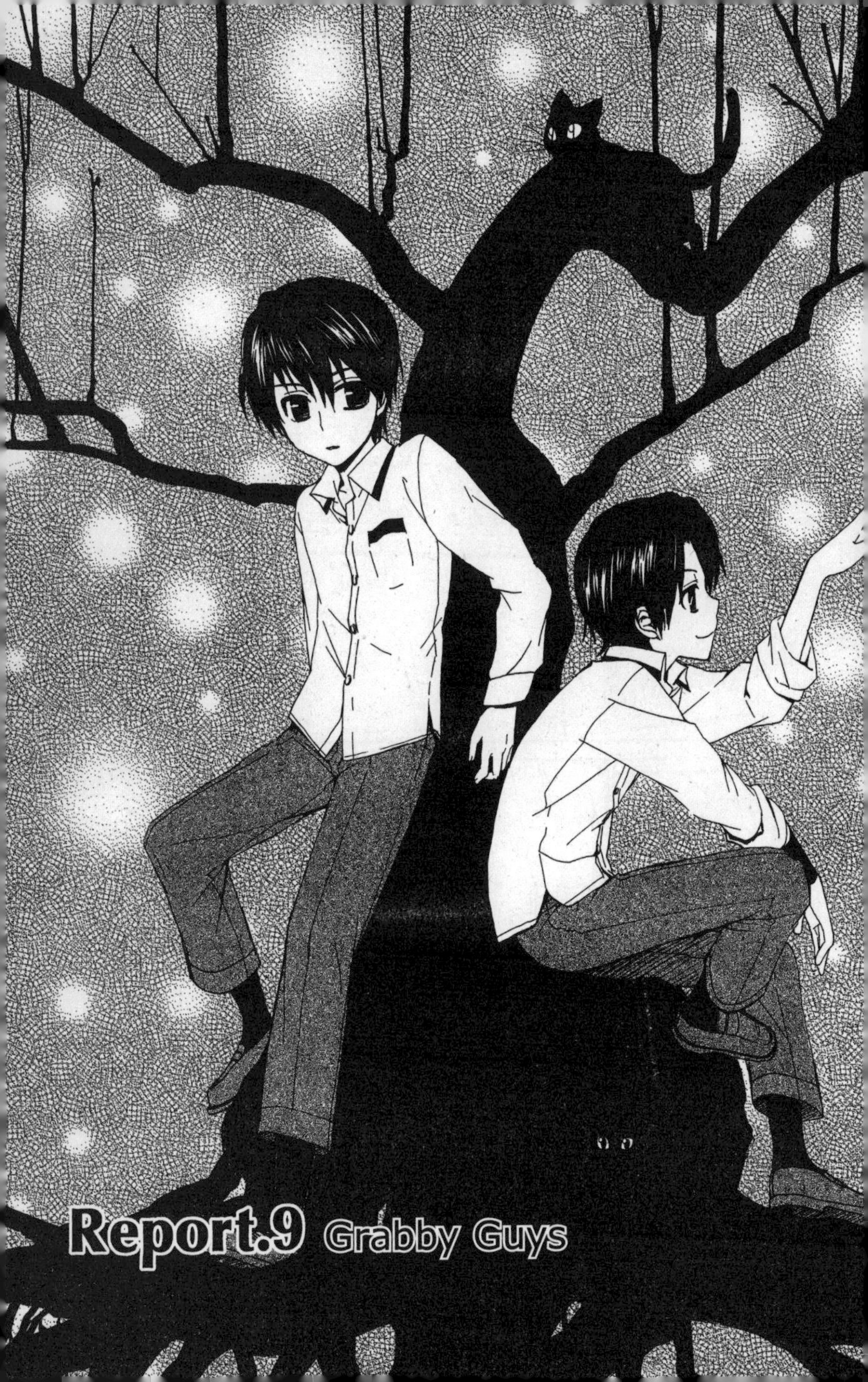
Report.9 Grabby Guys

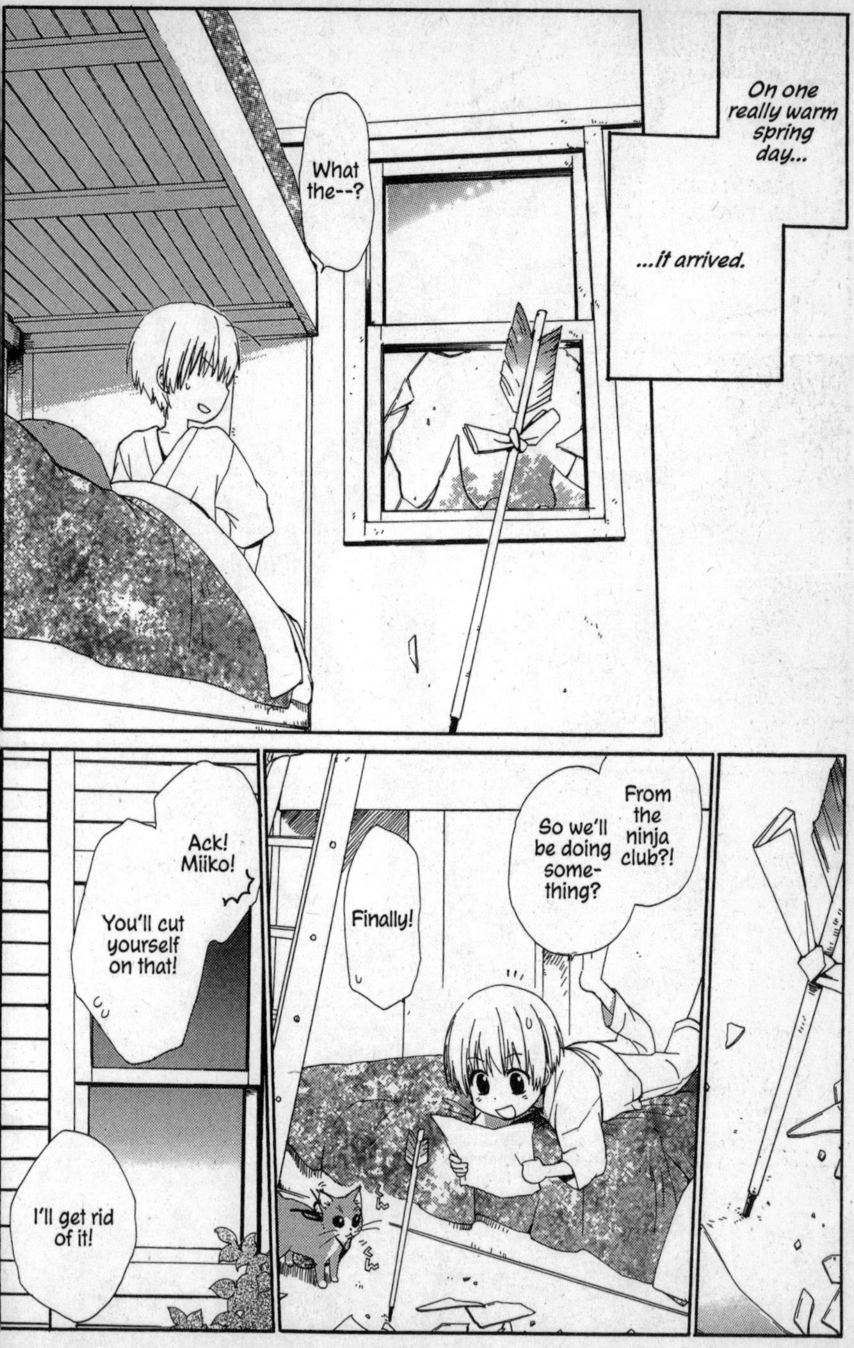
On one really warm spring day...
...it arrived.
What the--?
From the ninja club?!
So we'll be doing some-thing?
Finally!
Ack! Miiko!
You'll cut yourself on that!
I'll get rid of it!

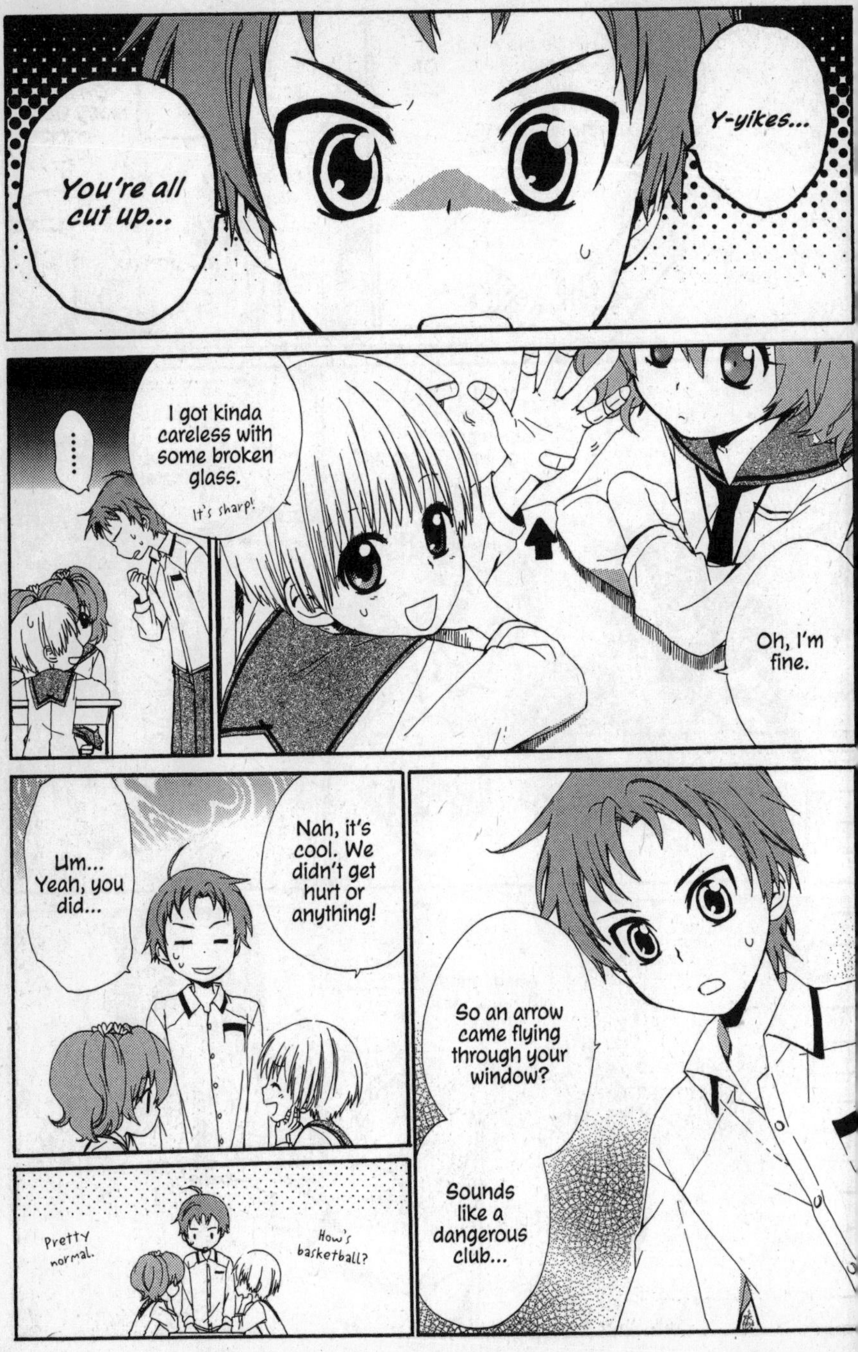
Y-yikes...
You're all cut up...
Oh, I'm fine.
I got kinda careless with some broken glass.
It's sharp!
......
So an arrow came flying through your window?
Sounds like a dangerous club...
Nah, it's cool. We didn't get hurt or anything!
Um... Yeah, you did...
How's basketball?
Pretty normal.

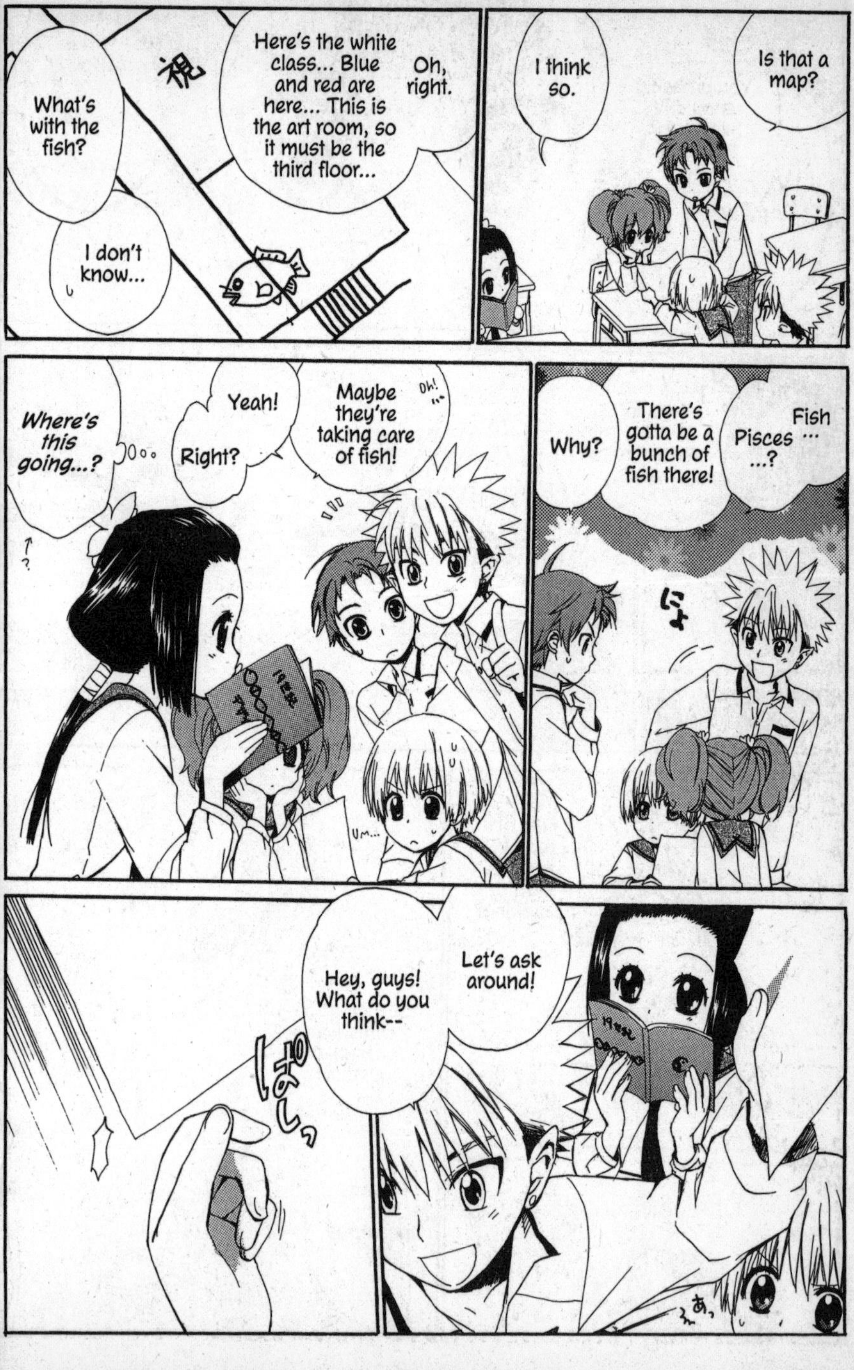
Is that a map?
I think so.
Oh, right.
Here's the white class... Blue and red are here... This is the art room, so it must be the third floor...
視
What's with the fish?
I don't know...
Fish...
Pisces...?
There's gotta be a bunch of fish there!
Why?
にょ
Oh!
Maybe they're taking care of fish!
Yeah!
Right?
Where's this going...?
Um...
Let's ask around!
Hey, guys! What do you think--
ぱしっ
あっ

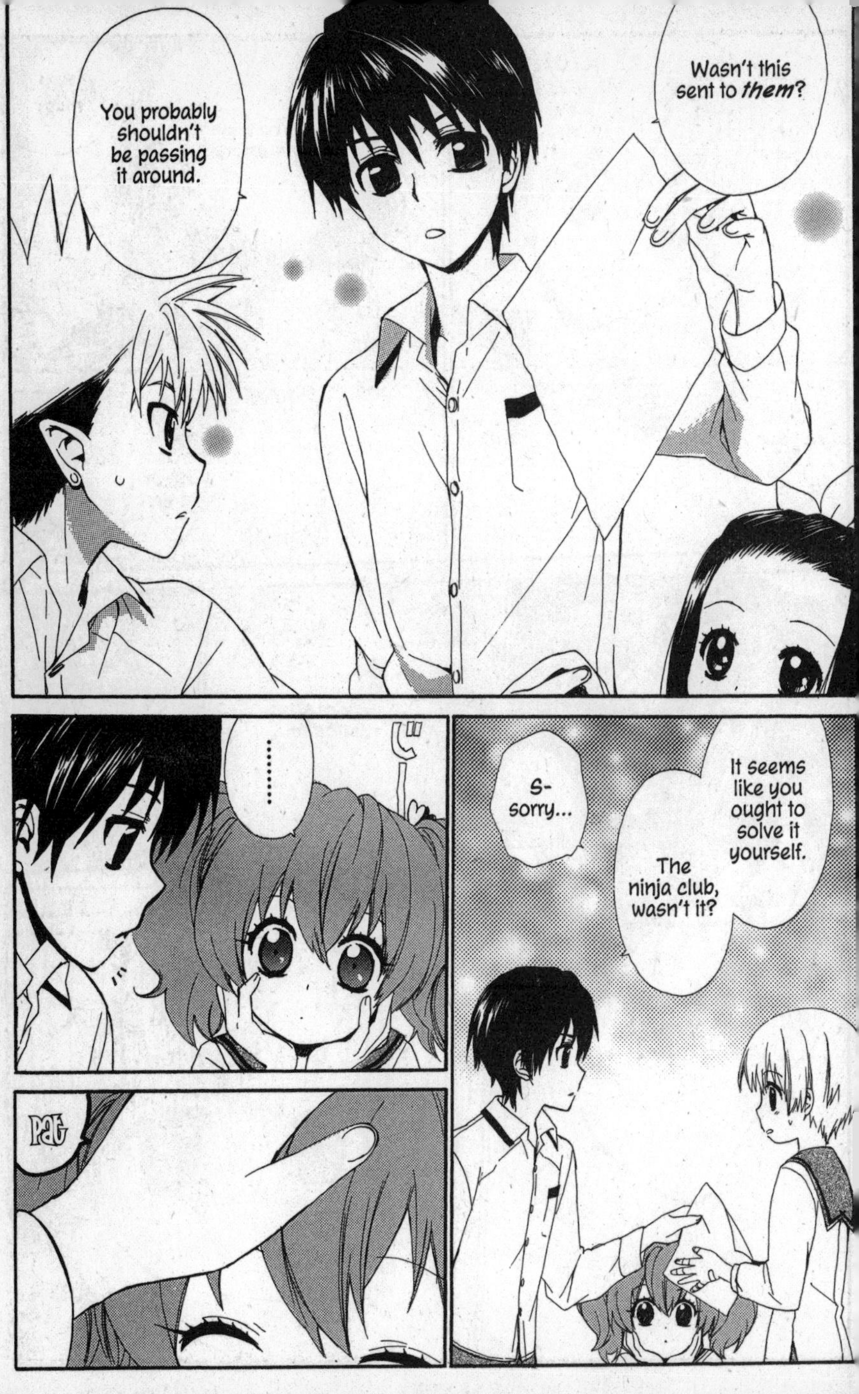
Wasn't this sent to *them*?
You probably shouldn't be passing it around.
It seems like you ought to solve it yourself.
The ninja club, wasn't it?
S-sorry...
......
じ
PAT

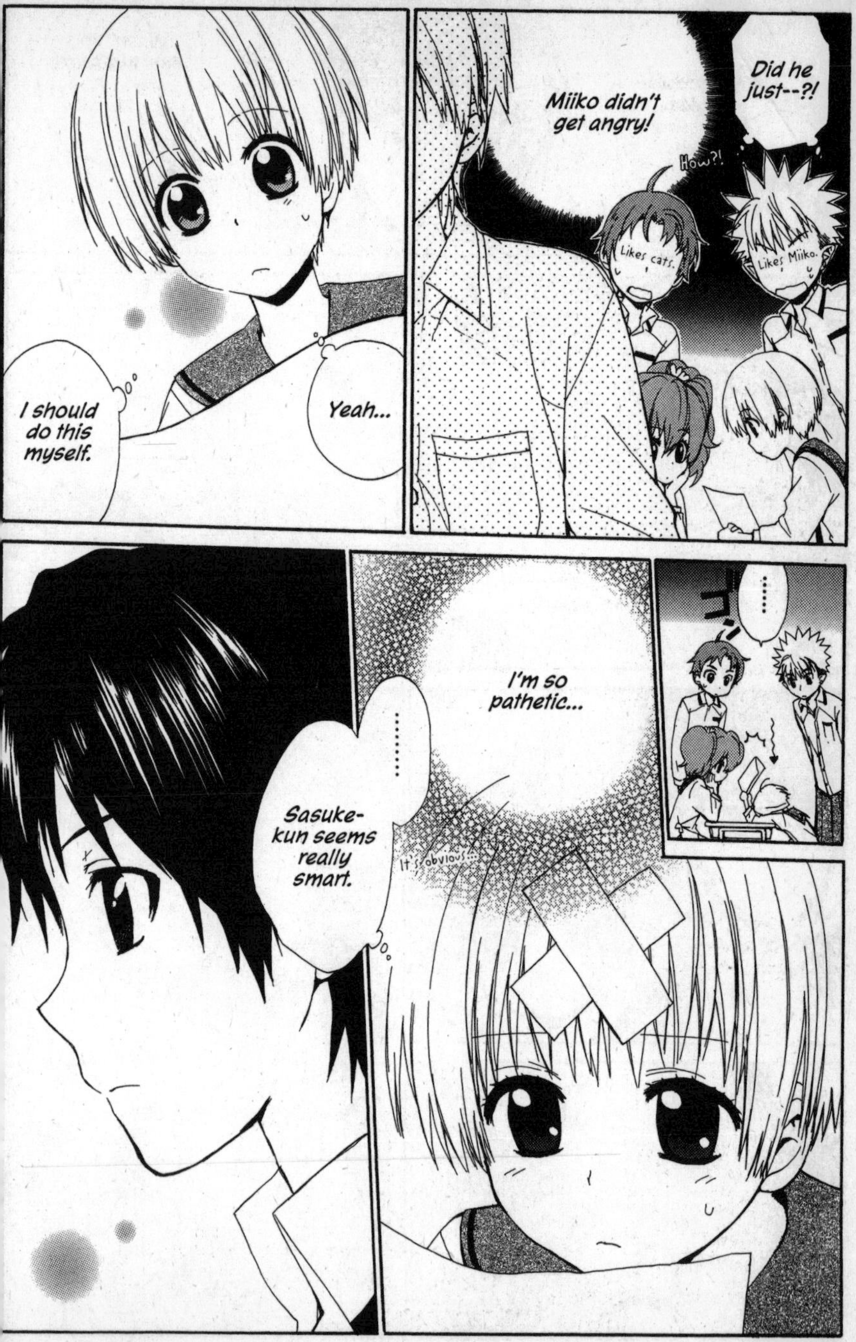
Did he just--?!
Miiko didn't get angry!
How?!
Likes Miiko.
Likes cats.
Yeah...
I should do this myself.
......
I'm so pathetic...
It's obvious...
......
Sasuke-kun seems really smart.

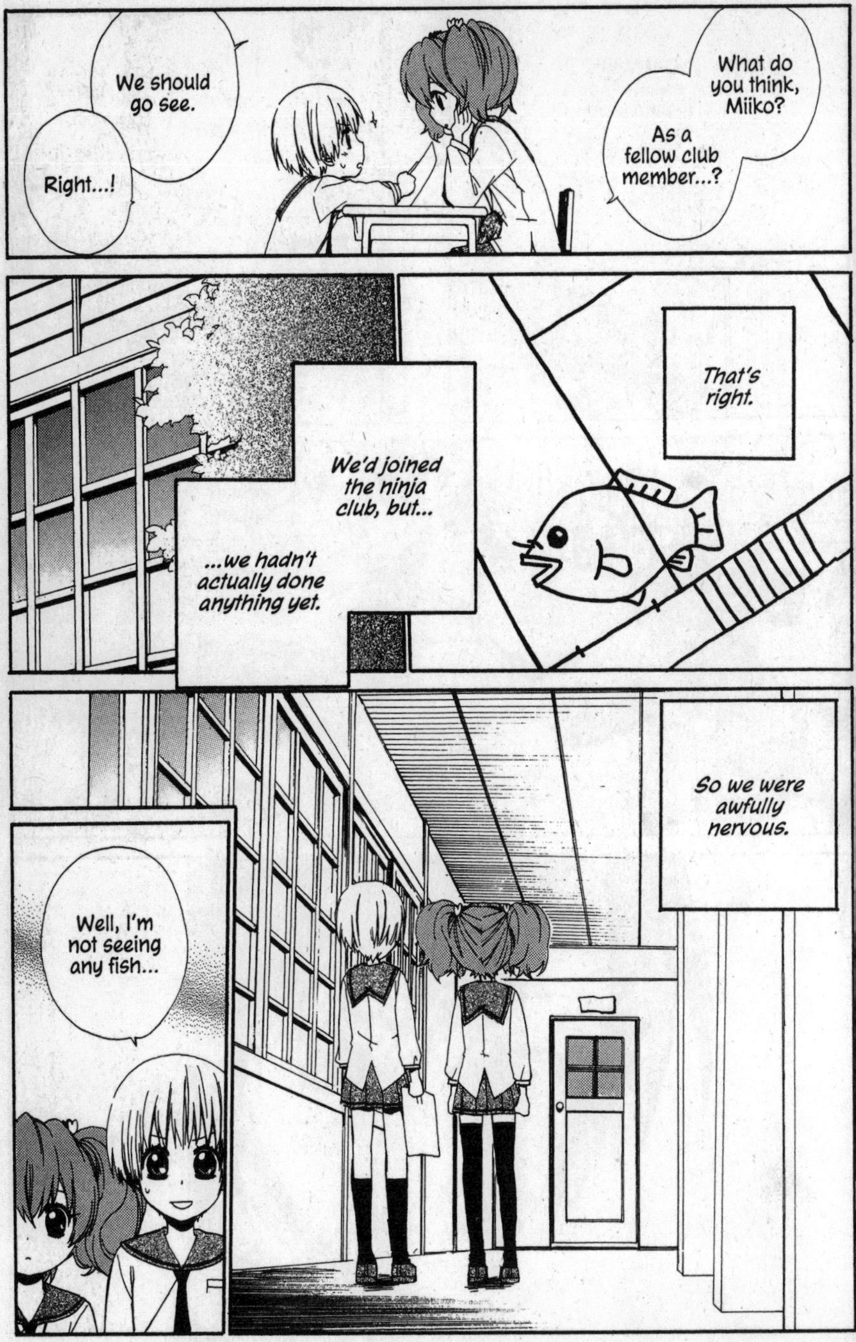
What do you think, Miiko? As a fellow club member...?
We should go see.
Right...!
That's right.
We'd joined the ninja club, but...
...we hadn't actually done anything yet.
So we were awfully nervous.
Well, I'm not seeing any fish...

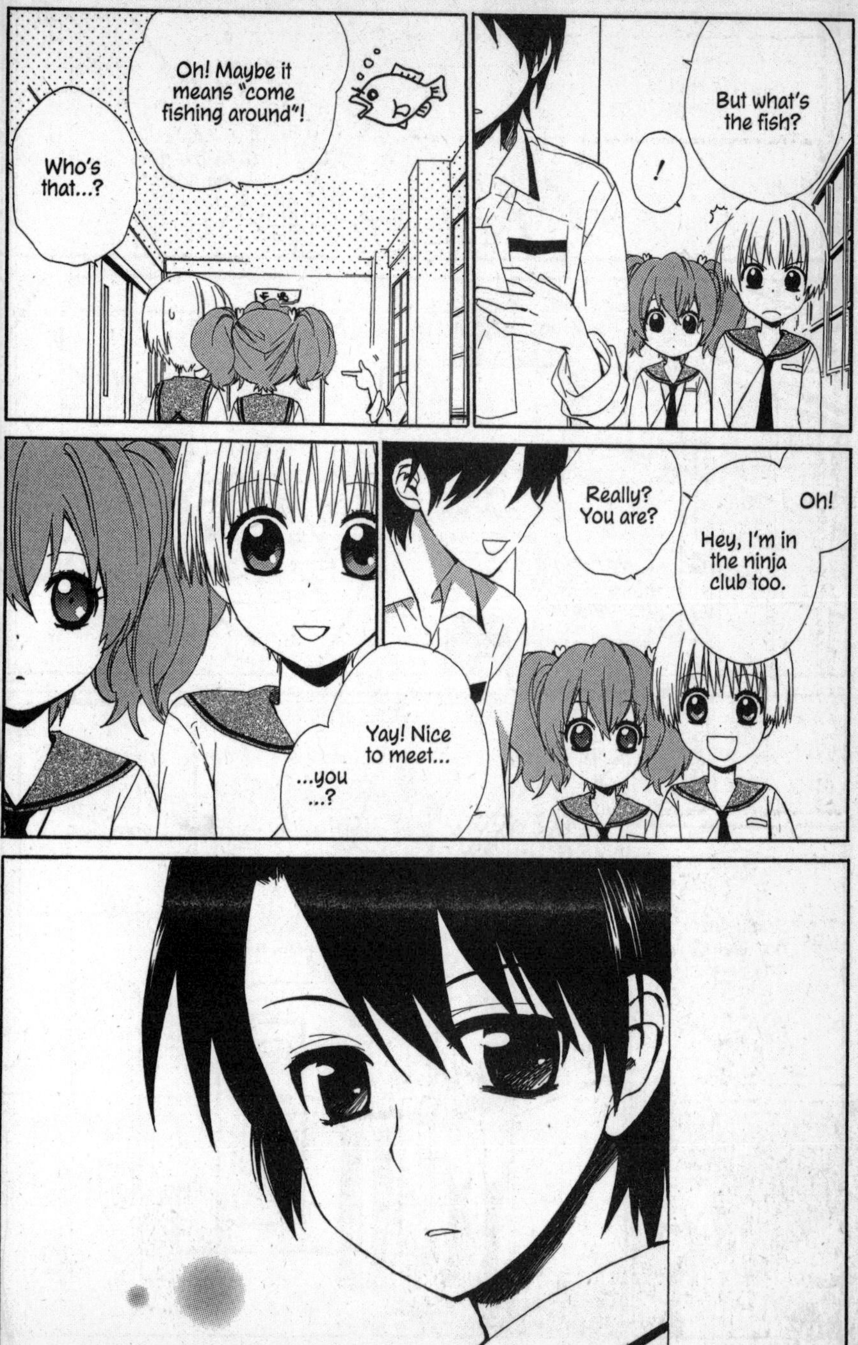
But what's the fish?
!
Oh! Maybe it means "come fishing around"!
Who's that...?
Oh! Hey, I'm in the ninja club too.
Really? You are?
Yay! Nice to meet...
...you ...?

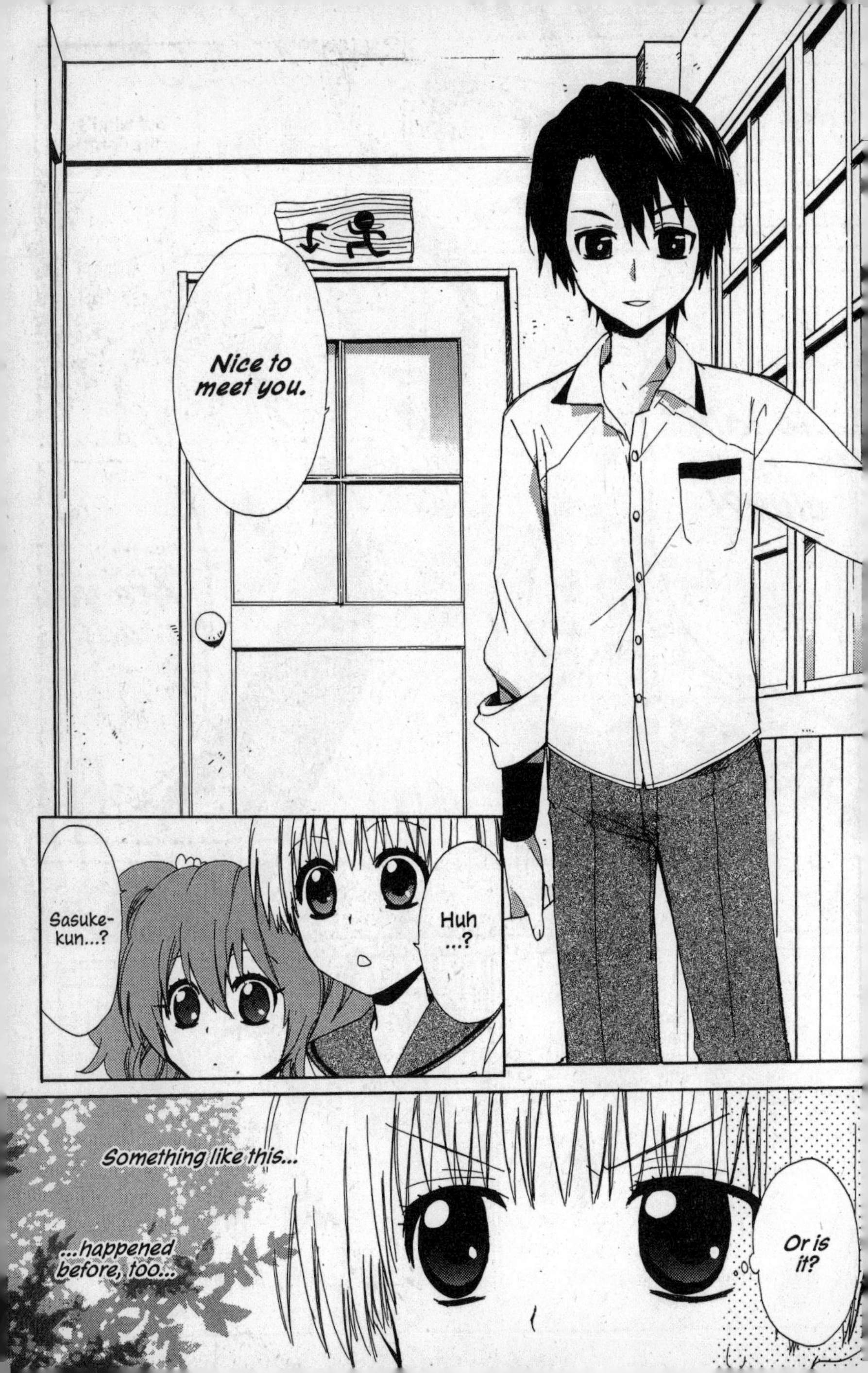
Nice to meet you.
Huh ...?
Sasuke-kun...?
Something like this...
...happened before, too...
Or is it?

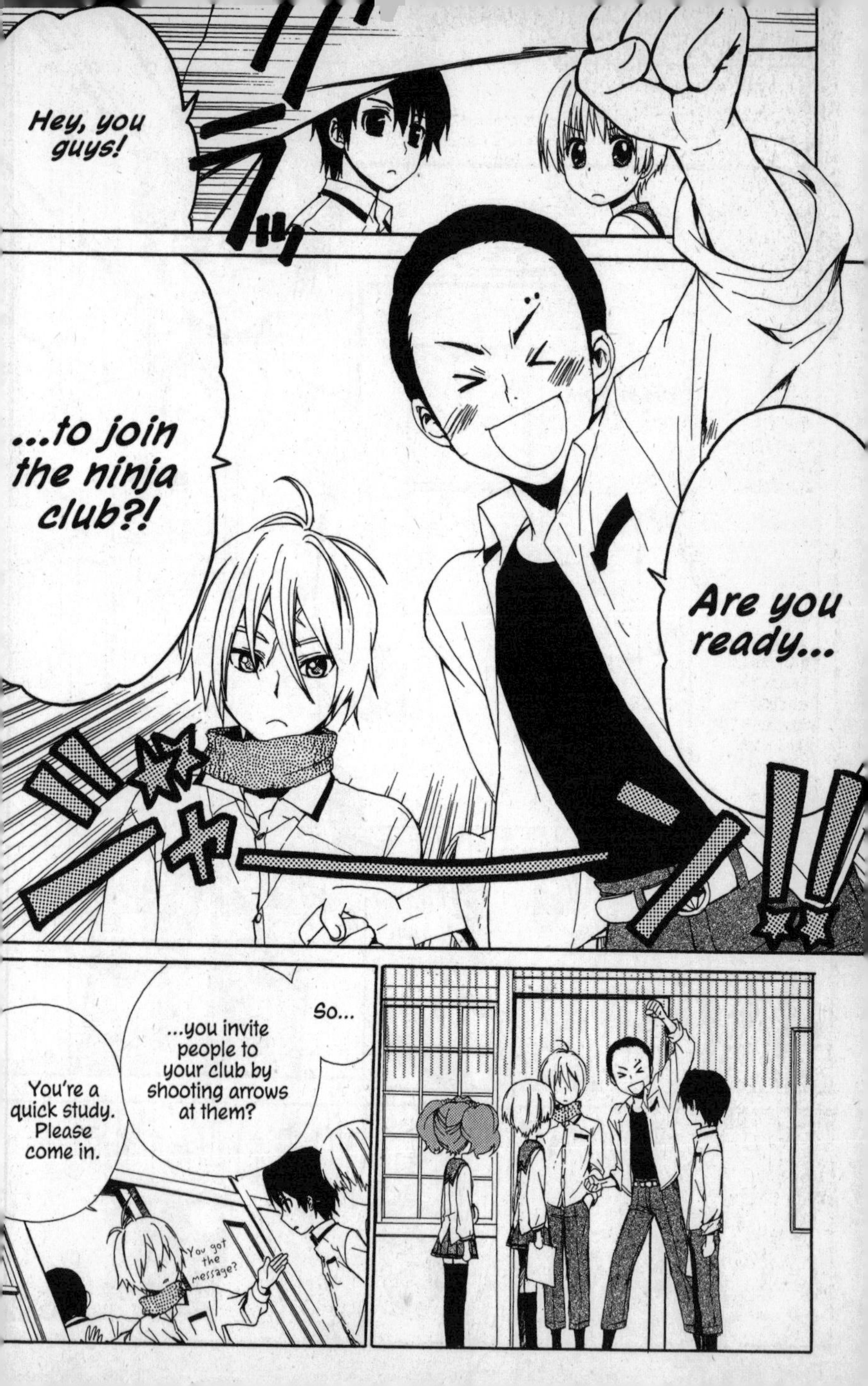
Hey, you guys!
Are you ready...
...to join the ninja club?!
So...
...you invite people to your club by shooting arrows at them?
You're a quick study. Please come in.
You got the message?

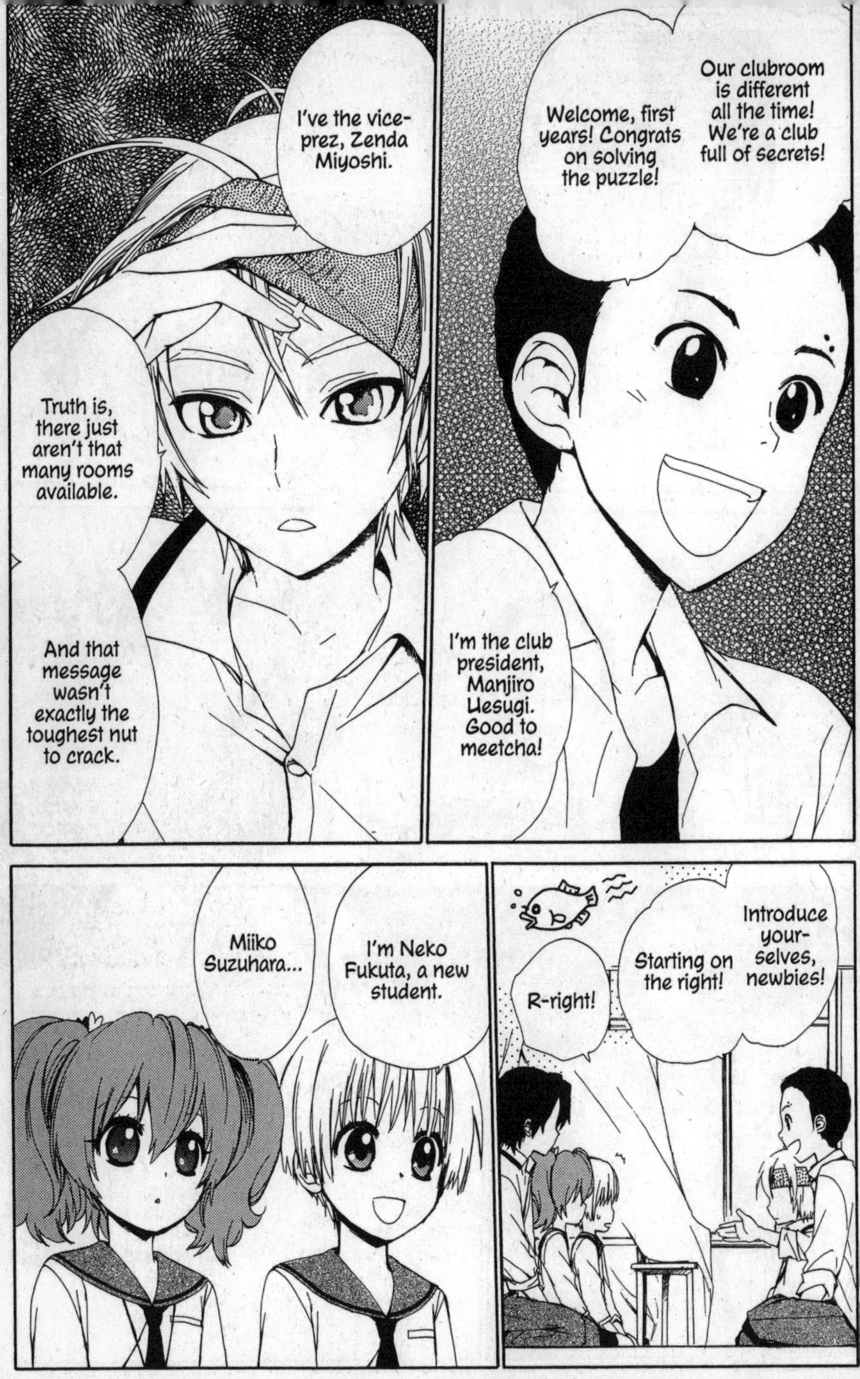
Our clubroom is different all the time! We're a club full of secrets!
Welcome, first years! Congrats on solving the puzzle!
I'm the club president, Manjiro Uesugi. Good to meetcha!
I've the vice-prez, Zenda Miyoshi.
Truth is, there just aren't that many rooms available.
And that message wasn't exactly the toughest nut to crack.
Introduce your-selves, newbies!
Starting on the right!
R-right!
I'm Neko Fukuta, a new student.
Miiko Suzuhara...

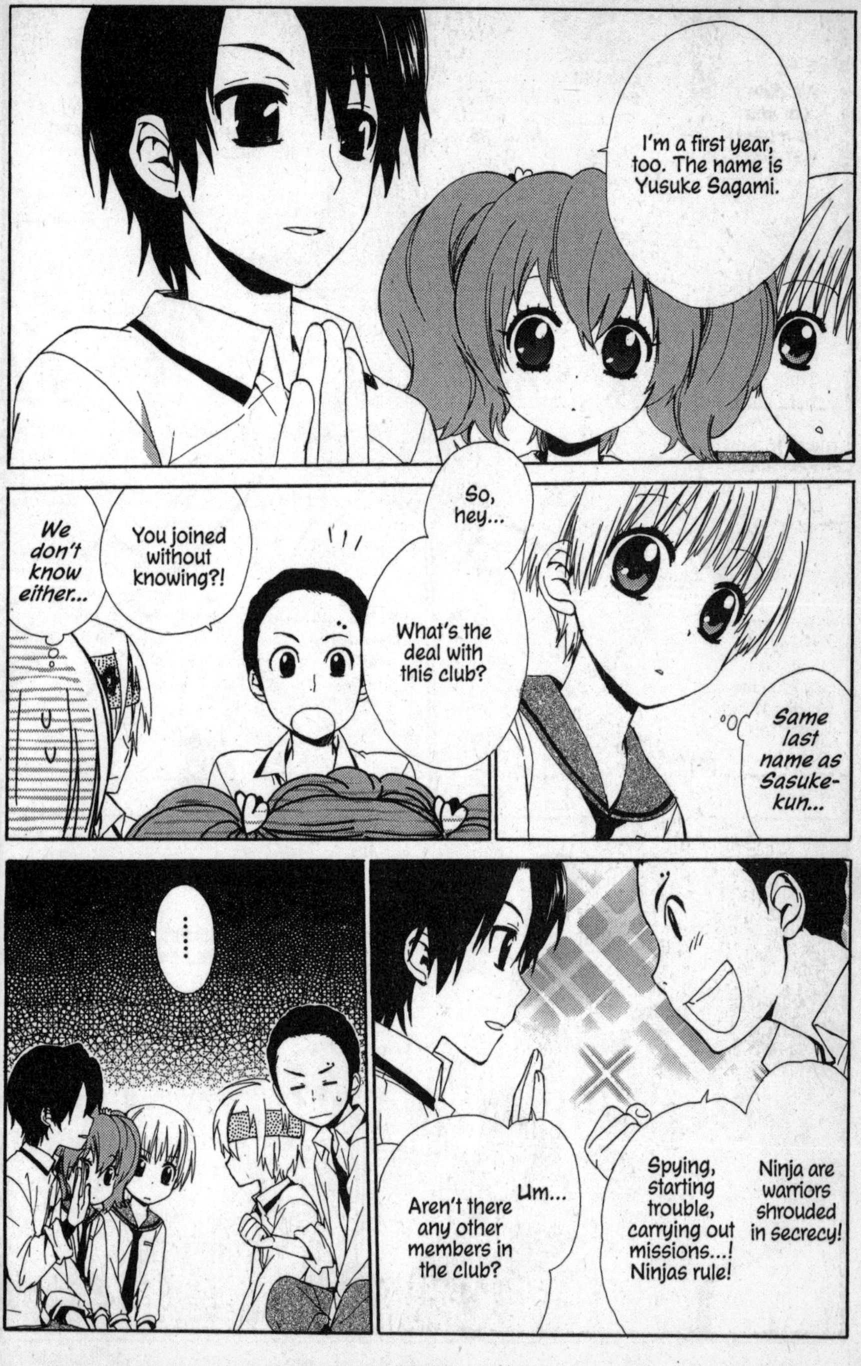
I'm a first year, too. The name is Yusuke Sagami.
Same last name as Sasuke-kun...
So, hey...
What's the deal with this club?
You joined without knowing?!
We don't know either...
Ninja are warriors shrouded in secrecy!
Spying, starting trouble, carrying out missions...! Ninjas rule!
Um...
Aren't there any other members in the club?
......

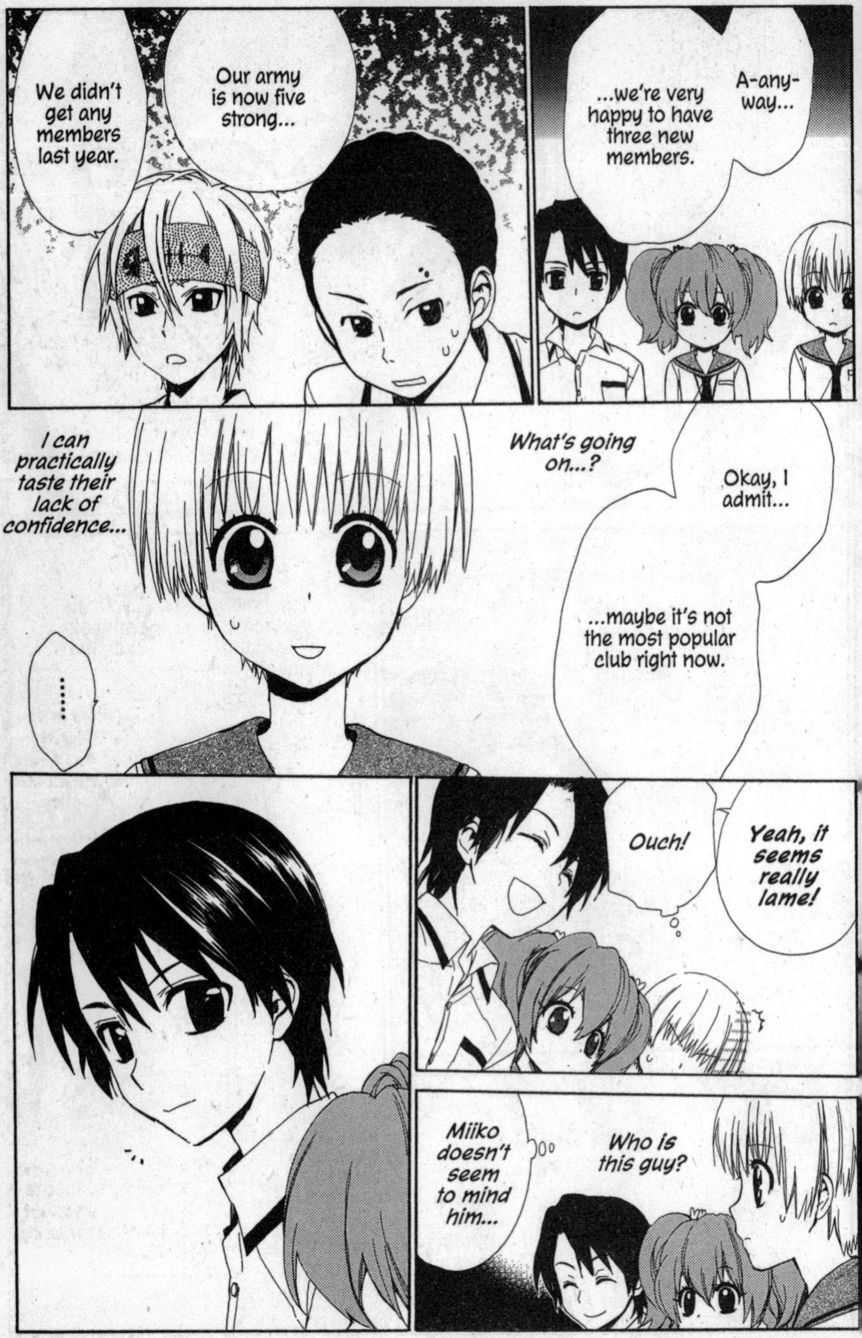
A-any-way...
...we're very happy to have three new members.
Our army is now five strong...
We didn't get any members last year.
Okay, I admit...
...maybe it's not the most popular club right now.
What's going on...?
I can practically taste their lack of confidence...
......
Yeah, it seems really lame!
Ouch!
Who is this guy?
Miiko doesn't seem to mind him...

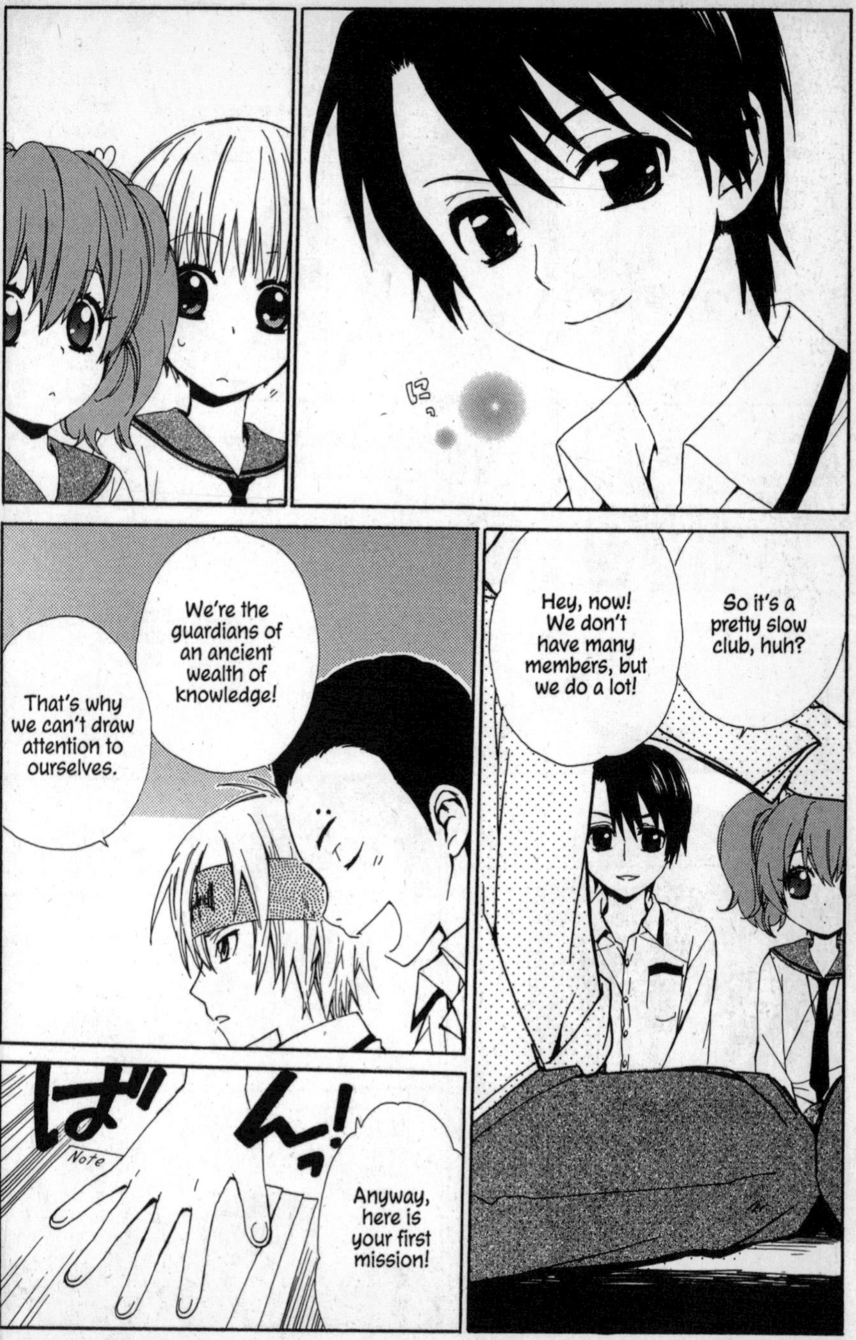
にっ
So it's a pretty slow club, huh?
Hey, now! We don't have many members, but we do a lot!
We're the guardians of an ancient wealth of knowledge!
That's why we can't draw attention to ourselves.
ばんっ!
Note
Anyway, here is your first mission!

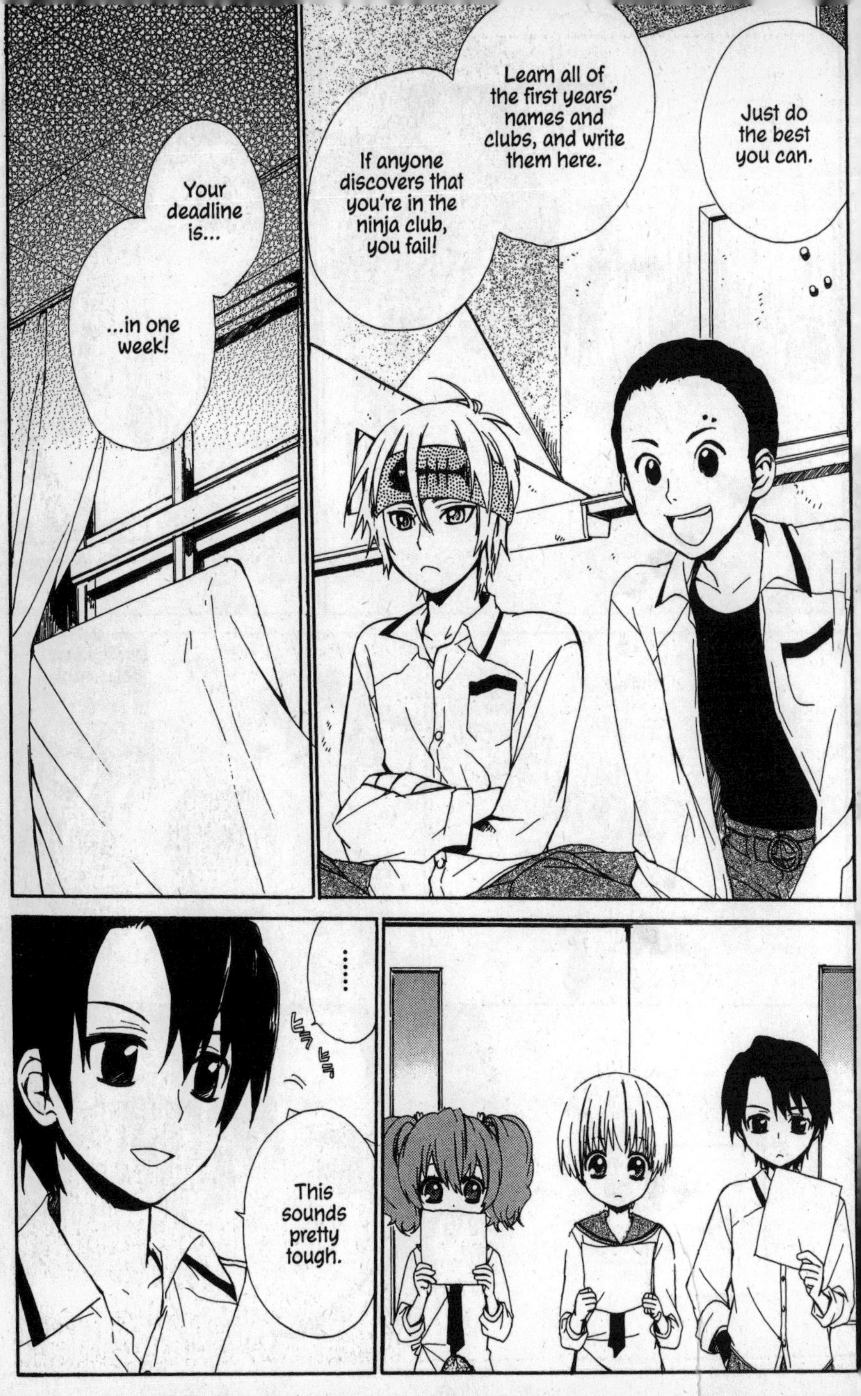

Just do the best you can.
Learn all of the first years' names and clubs, and write them here.
If anyone discovers that you're in the ninja club, you fail!
Your deadline is...
...in one week!
......
ヒラ ヒラ
This sounds pretty tough.

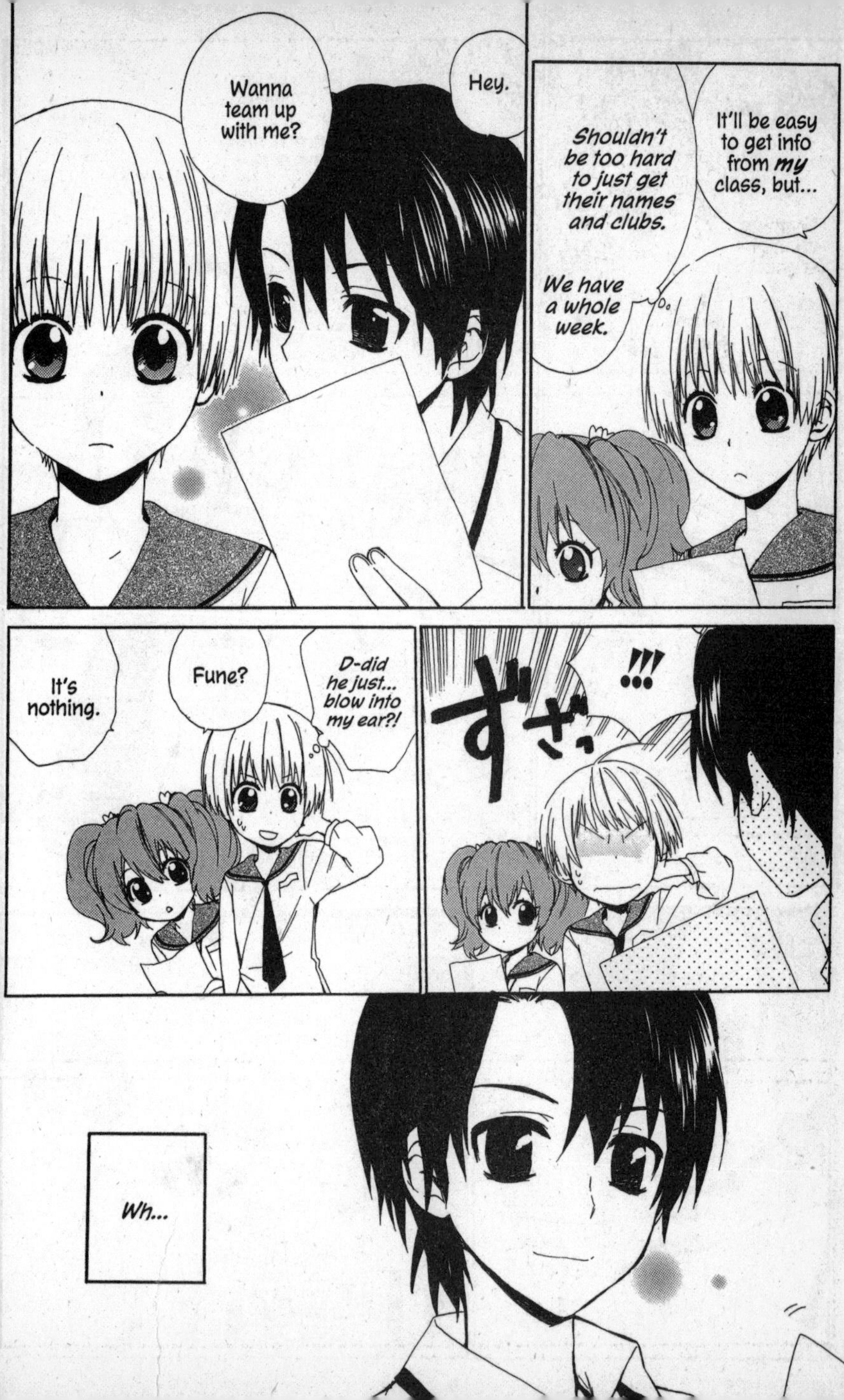
It'll be easy to get info from *my* class, but...
Shouldn't be too hard to just get their names and clubs.
We have a whole week.
Hey.
Wanna team up with me?
ずざっ
!!!
D-did he just... blow into my ear?!
Fune?
It's nothing.
Wh...

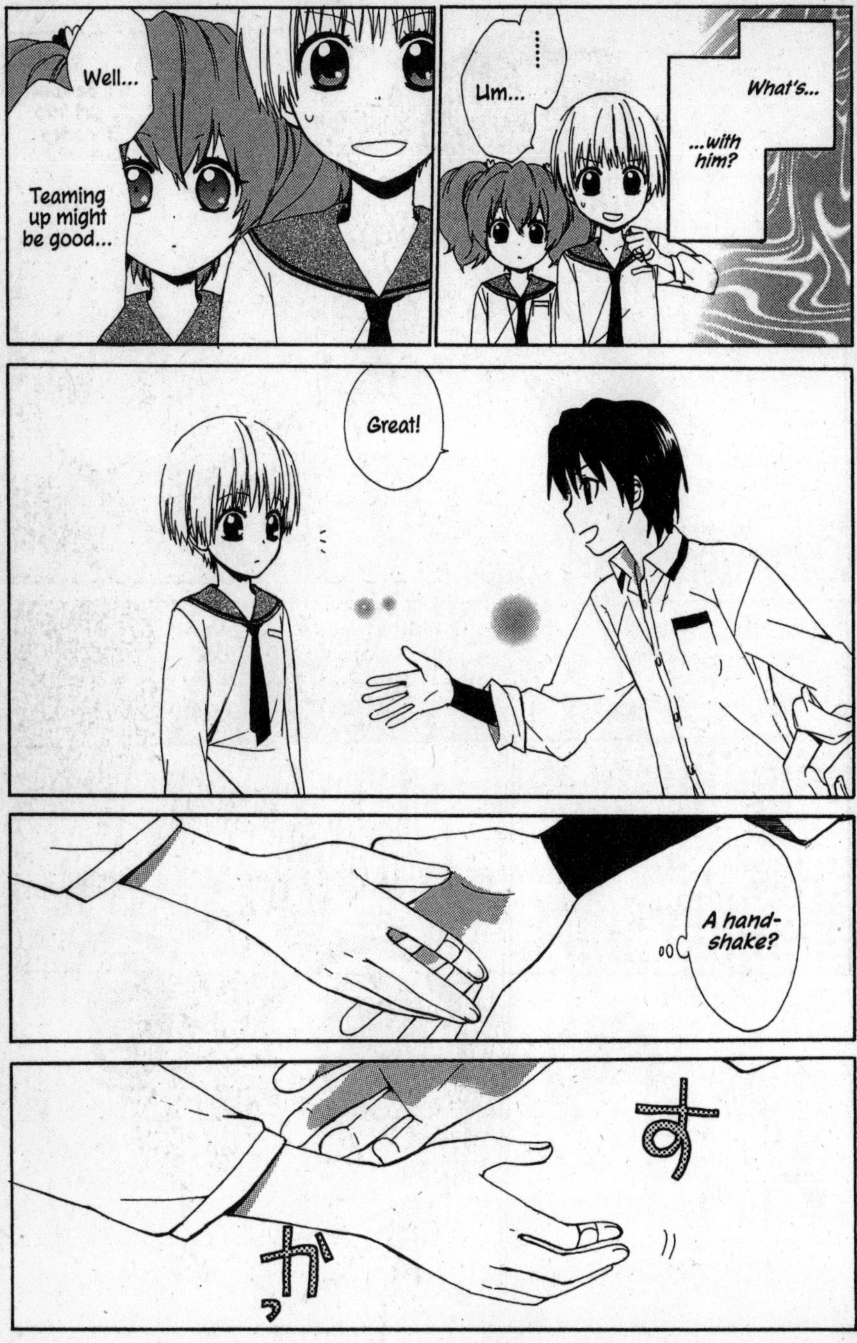
What's...
...with him?
......
Um...
Well...
Teaming up might be good...
Great!
A hand-shake?
すかっ

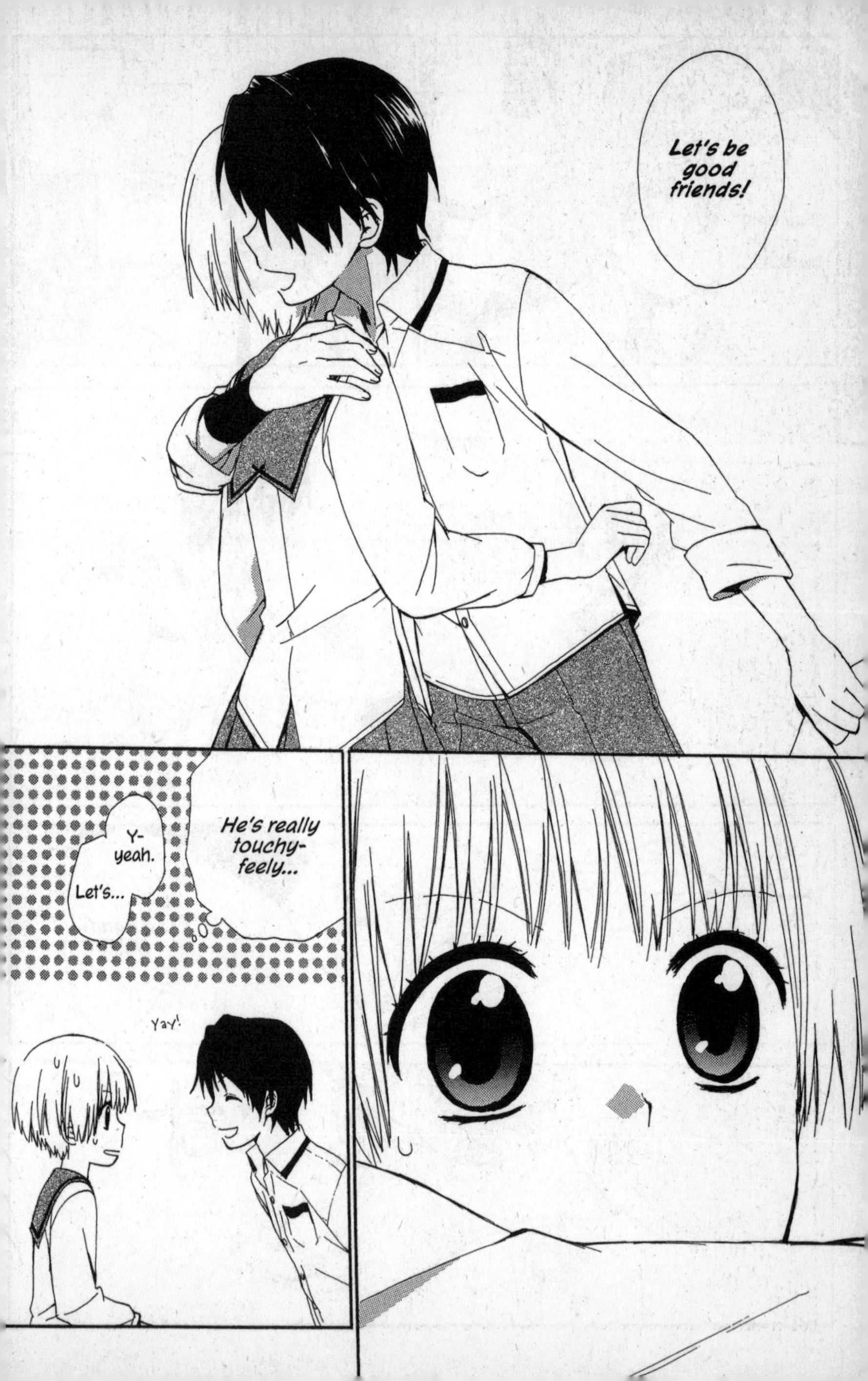
Let's be good friends!
He's really touchy-feely...
Y-yeah. Let's...
Yay!

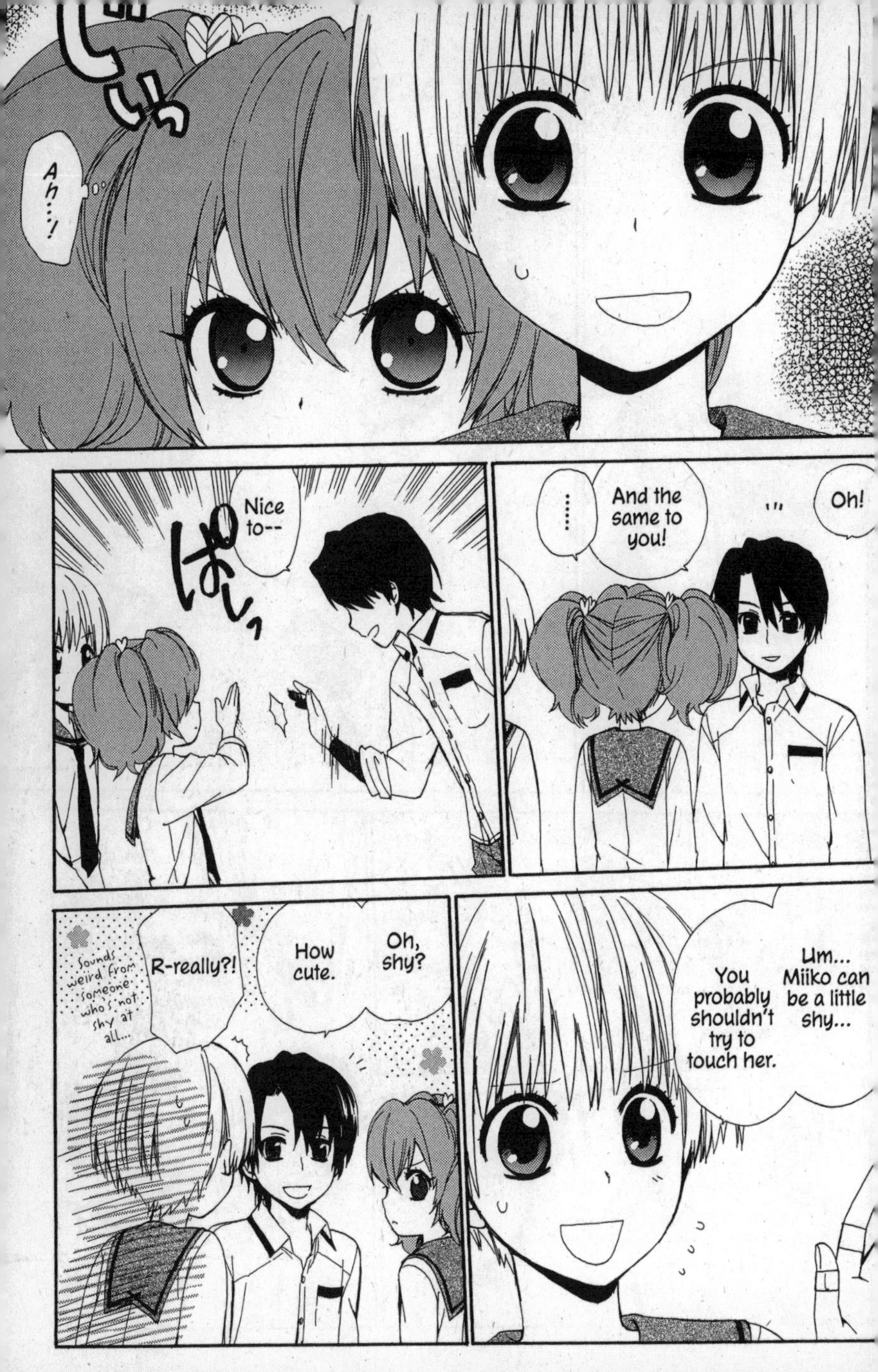
Ah...!
Oh!
And the same to you!
......
Nice to--
ぱしっ
Um... Miiko can be a little shy...
You probably shouldn't try to touch her.
Oh, shy?
How cute.
R-really?!
Sounds weird from someone who's not shy at all...

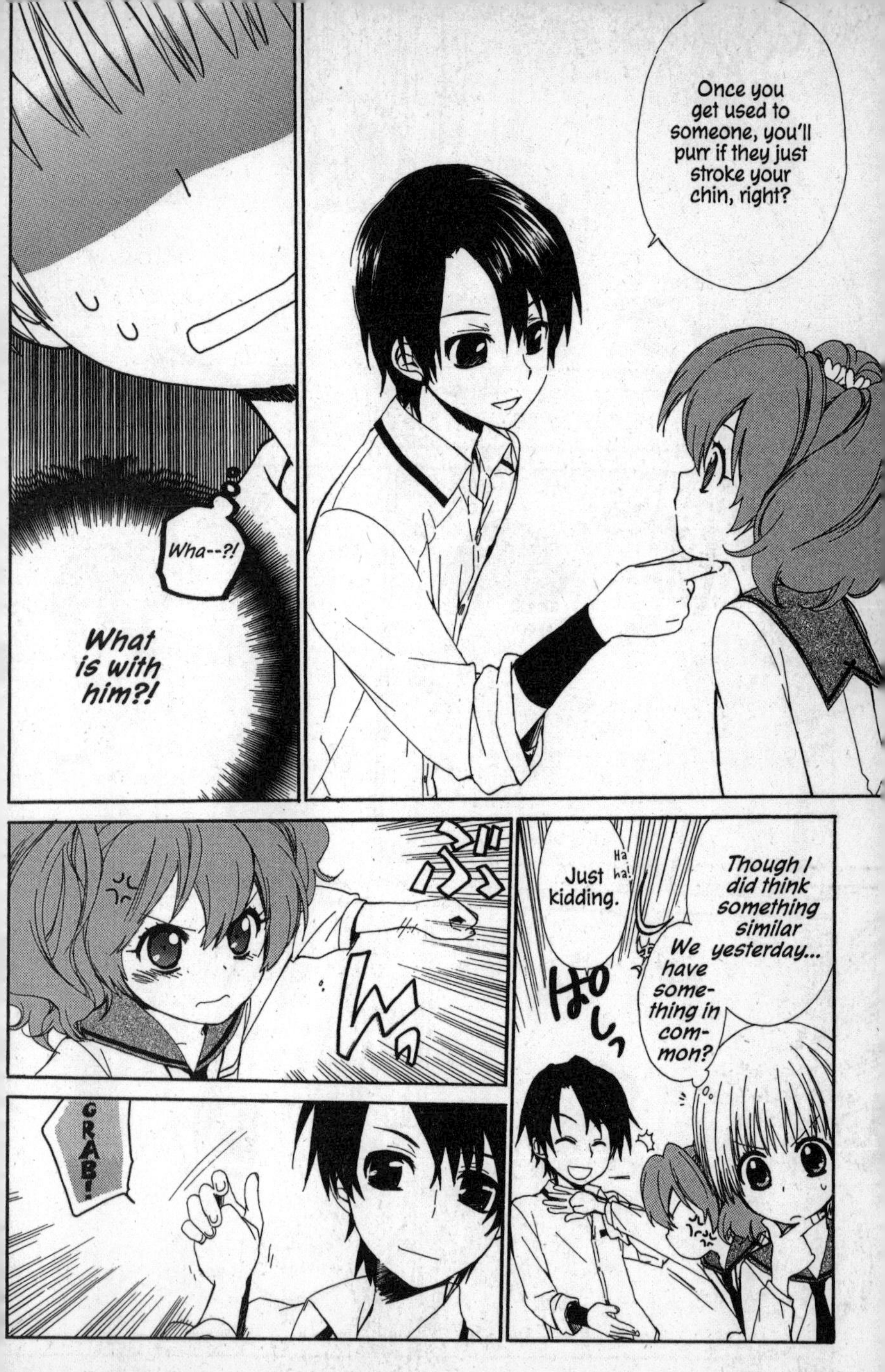
Once you get used to someone, you'll purr if they just stroke your chin, right?
Wha--?!
What is with him?!
Though I did think something similar yesterday...
Ha ha!
Just kidding.
We have something in common?
ぱしっ
GRAB!

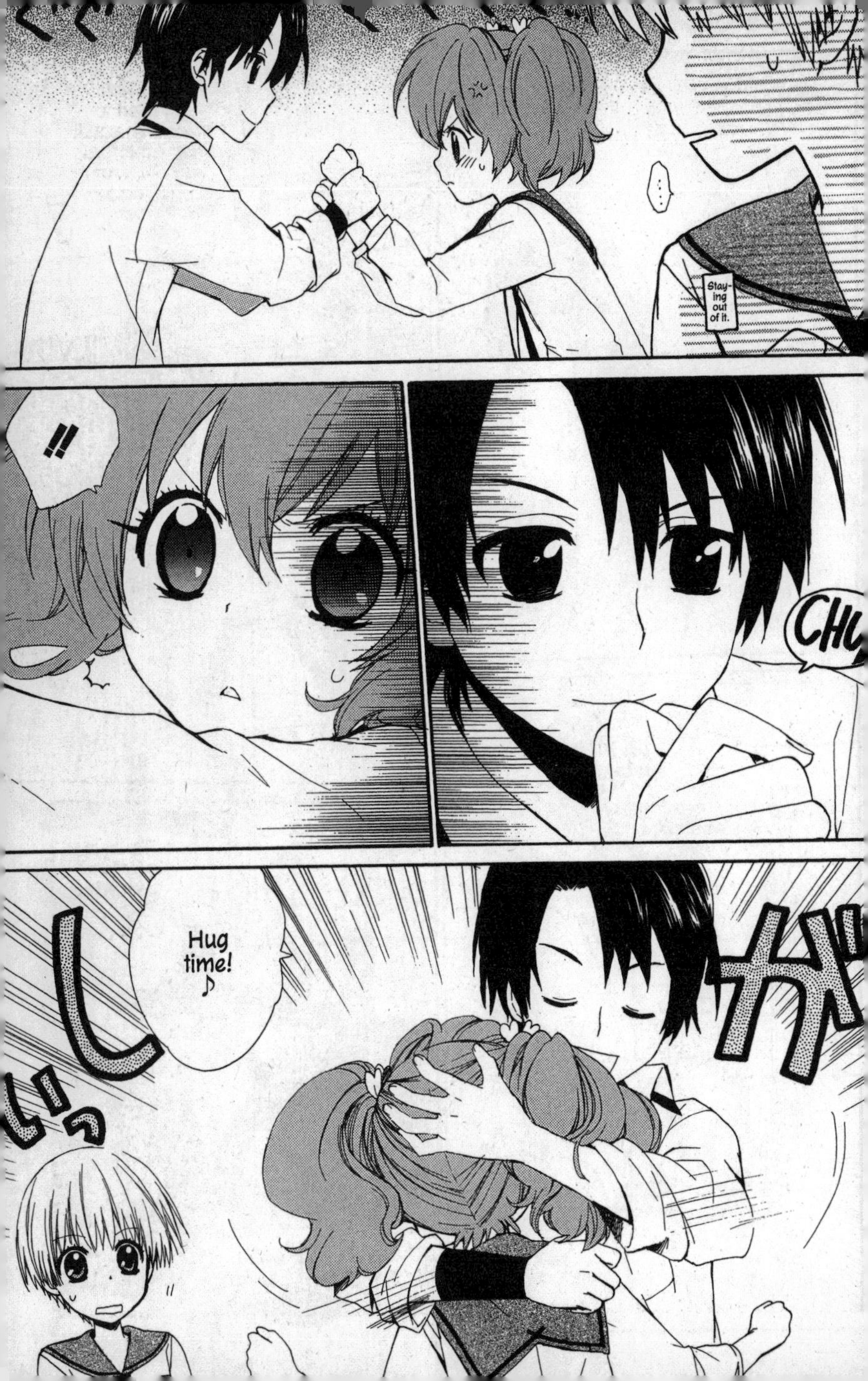
...
Stay-ing out of it.
CHU
!!
Hug time! ♪

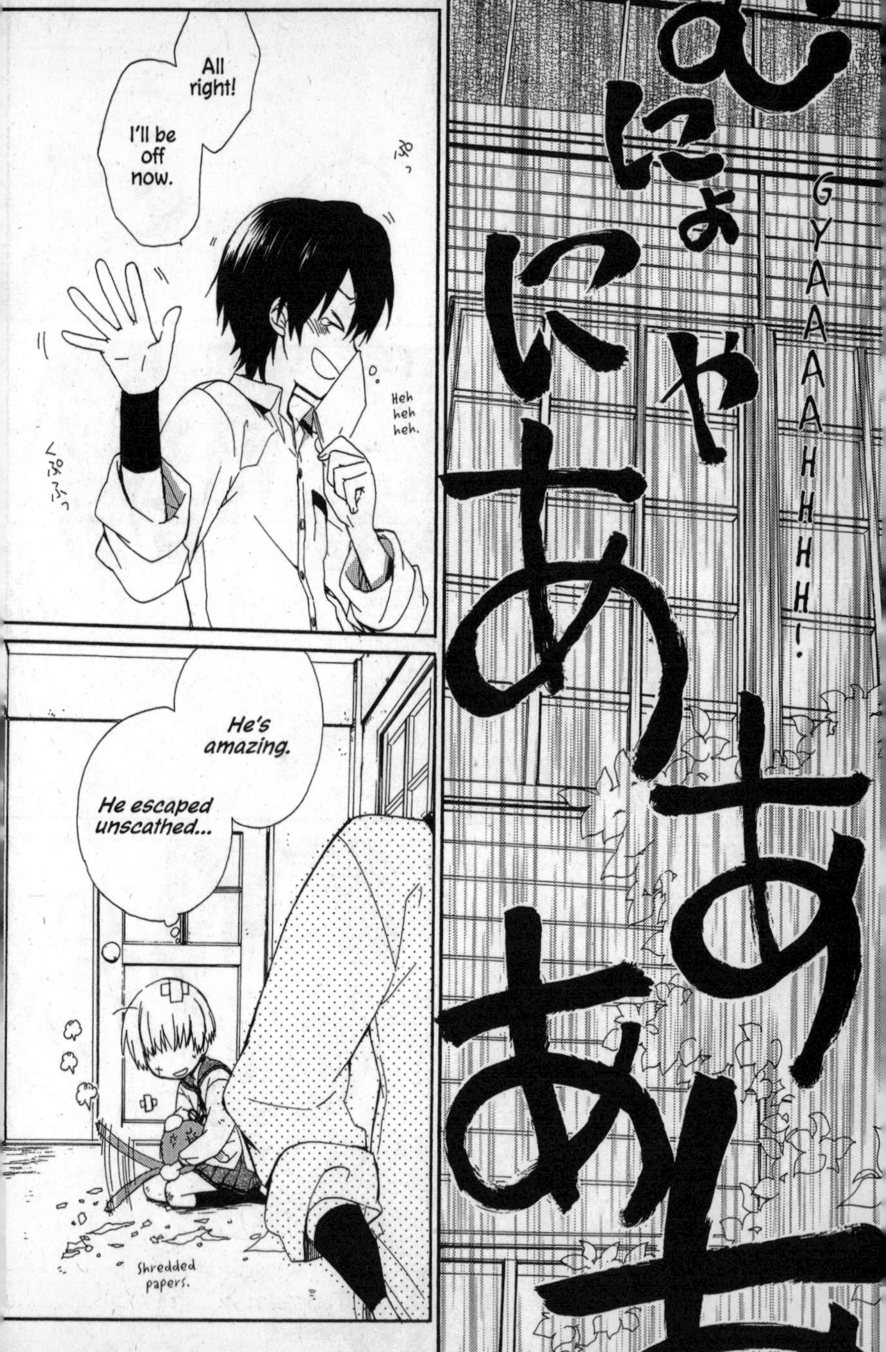
GYAAAAHHHHH!
All right!
I'll be off now.
Heh heh heh.
He's amazing.
He escaped unscathed...
Shredded papers.

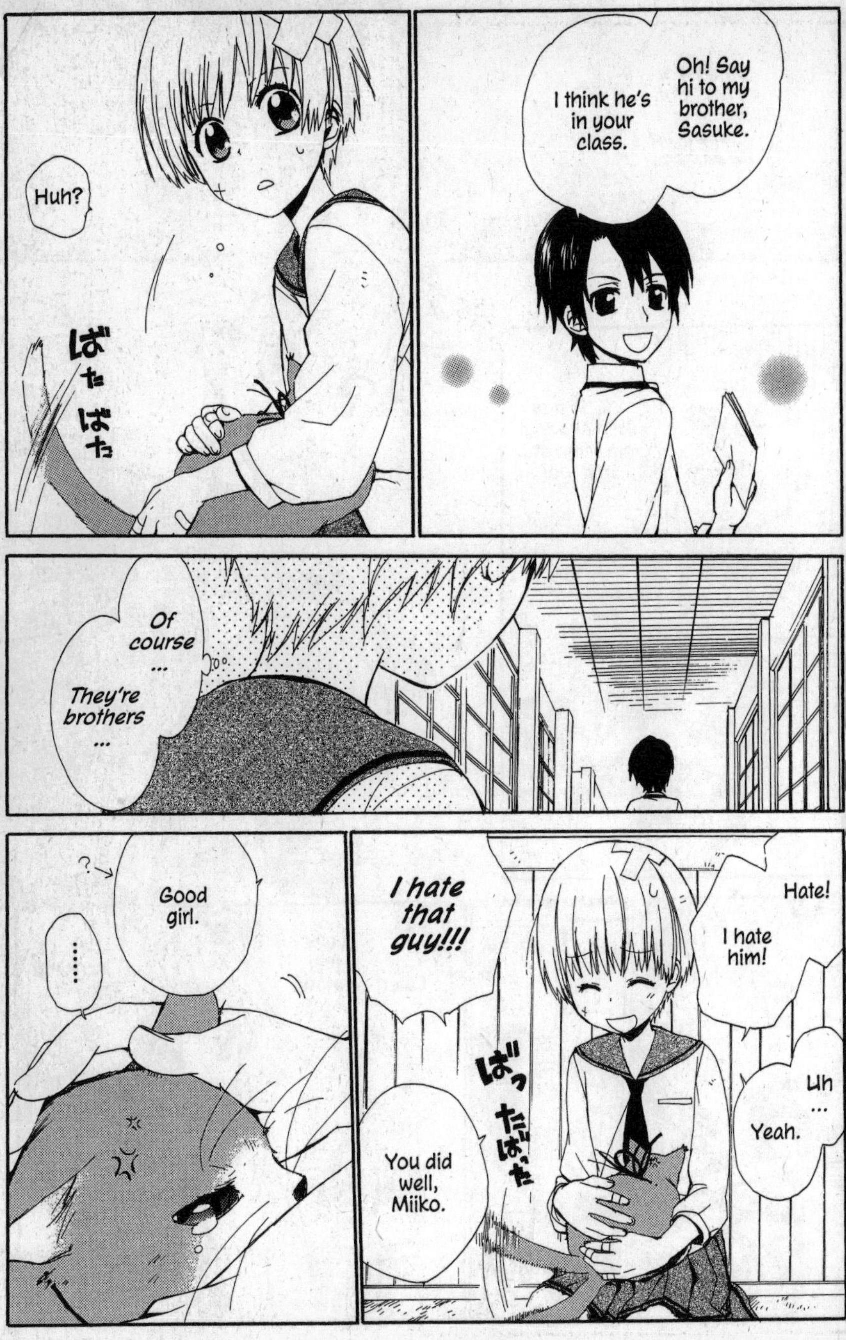
Oh! Say hi to my brother, Sasuke.
I think he's in your class.
Huh?
ばた ばた
Of course ... They're brothers ...
Hate!
I hate him!
Uh ... Yeah.
I hate that guy!!!
ばっ たばった
You did well, Miiko.
?
Good girl.
......

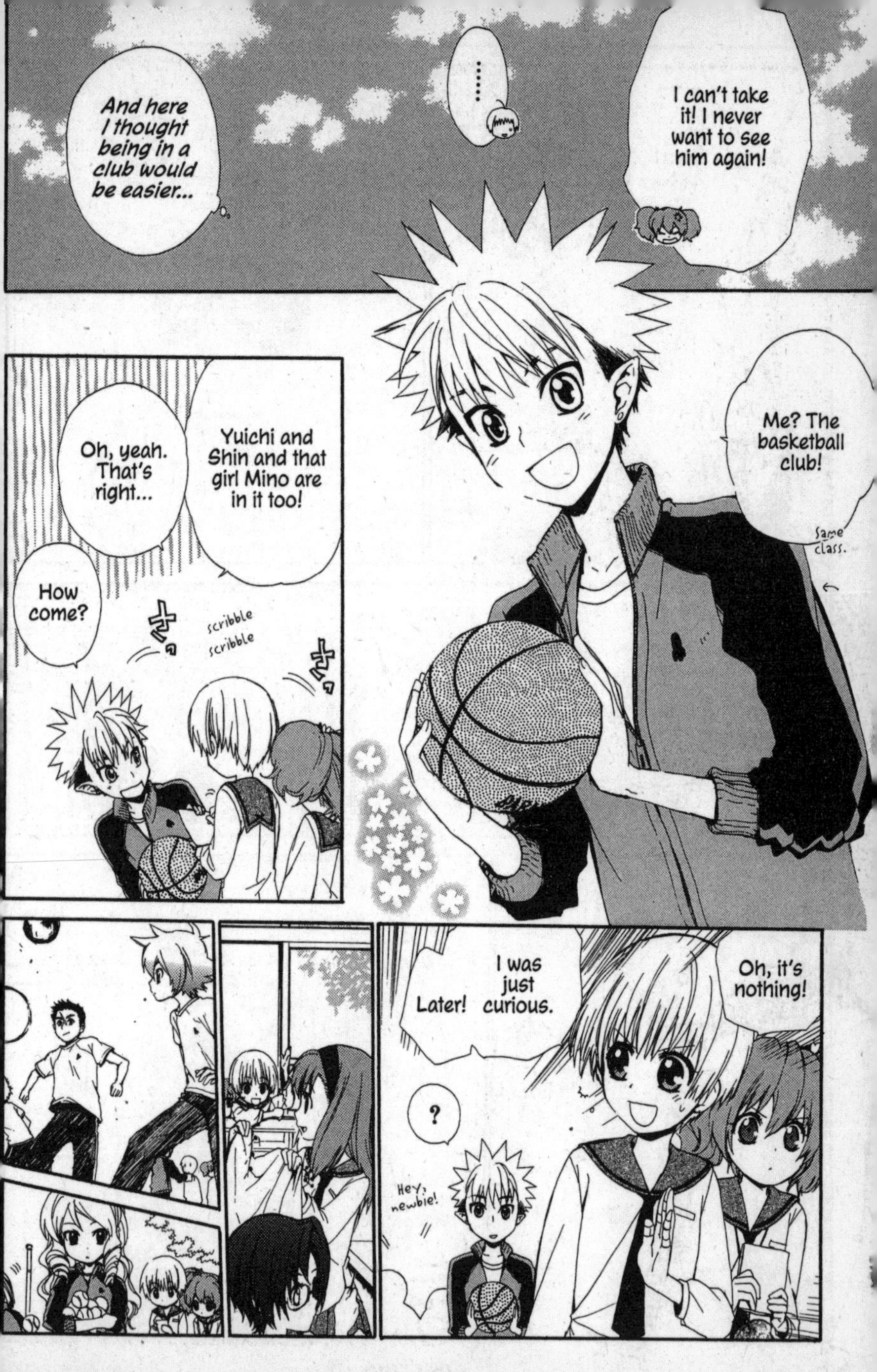
I can't take it! I never want to see him again!
......
And here I thought being in a club would be easier...
Me? The basketball club!
Same class.
Yuichi and Shin and that girl Mino are in it too!
Oh, yeah. That's right...
How come?
scribble scribble
Oh, it's nothing!
I was just curious.
Later!
?
Hey, newbie!

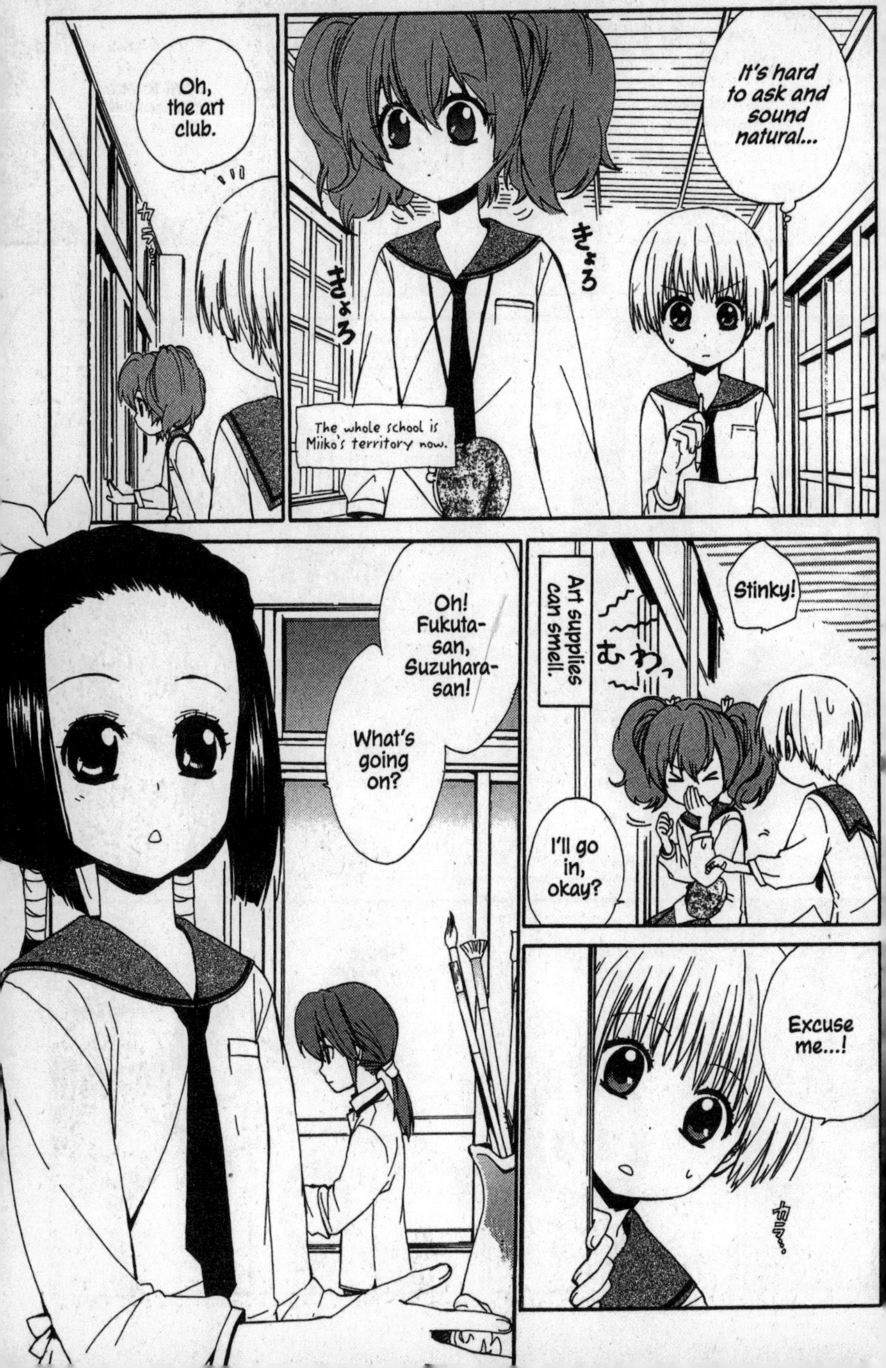
It's hard to ask and sound natural...
きょろ
きょろ
The whole school is Miiko's territory now.
Oh, the art club.
Stinky!
Art supplies can smell.
むわっ
I'll go in, okay?
Excuse me...!
Oh! Fukuta-san, Suzuhara-san!
What's going on?

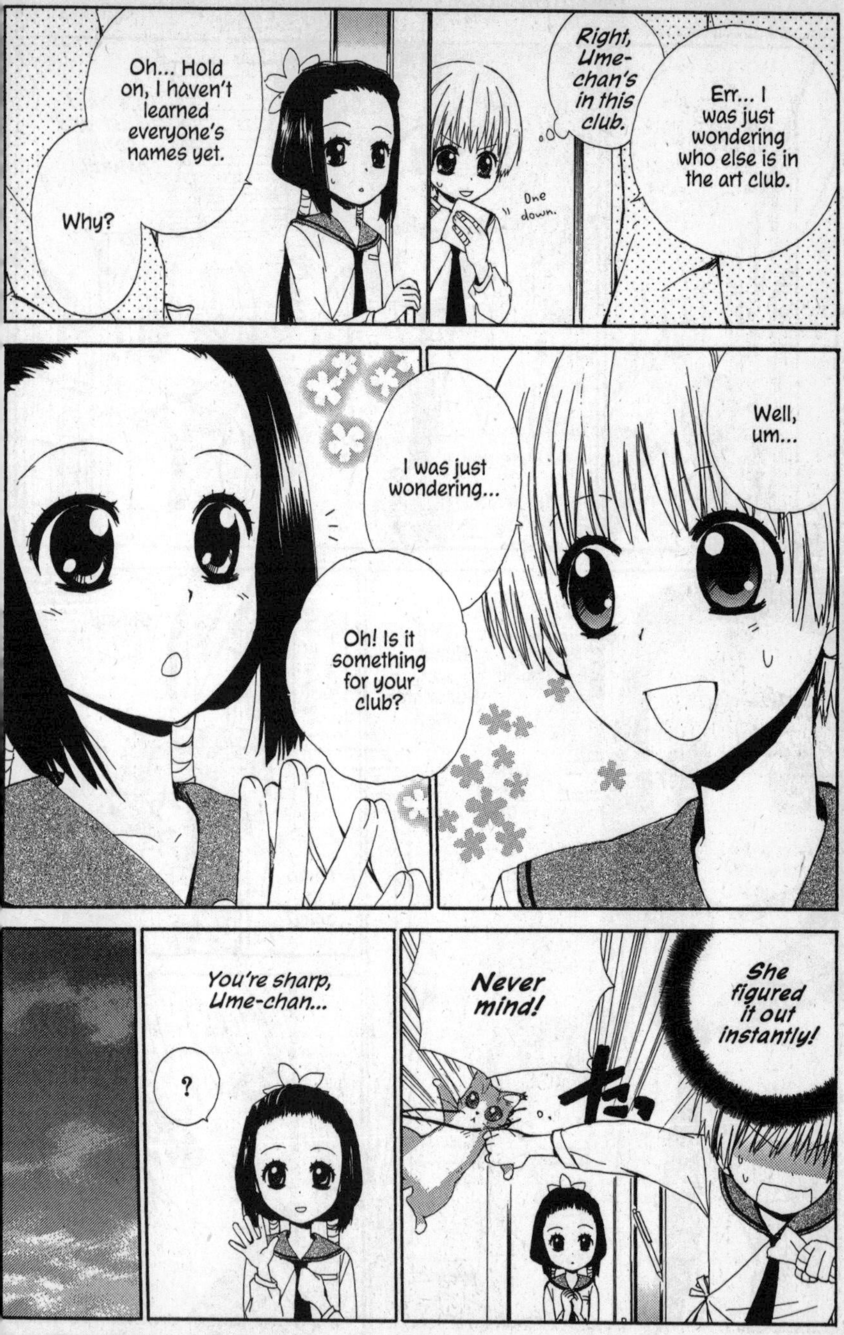
Err... I was just wondering who else is in the art club.
Right, Ume-chan's in this club.
One down.
Oh... Hold on, I haven't learned everyone's names yet.
Why?
Well, um...
I was just wondering...
Oh! Is it something for your club?
She figured it out instantly!
Never mind!
You're sharp, Ume-chan...
?

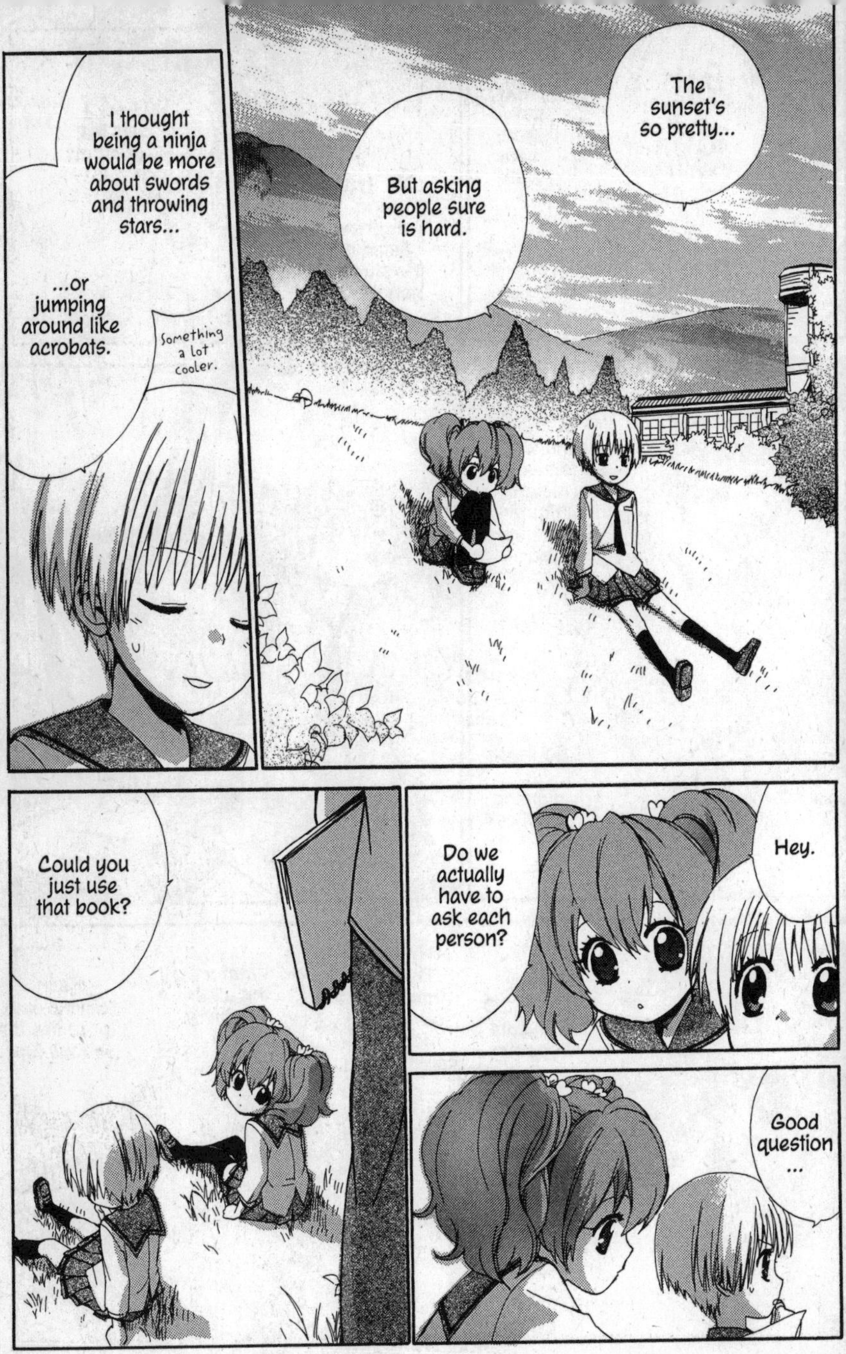
The sunset's so pretty...
But asking people sure is hard.
I thought being a ninja would be more about swords and throwing stars...
...or jumping around like acrobats.
Something a lot cooler.
Hey.
Do we actually have to ask each person?
Good question ...
Could you just use that book?

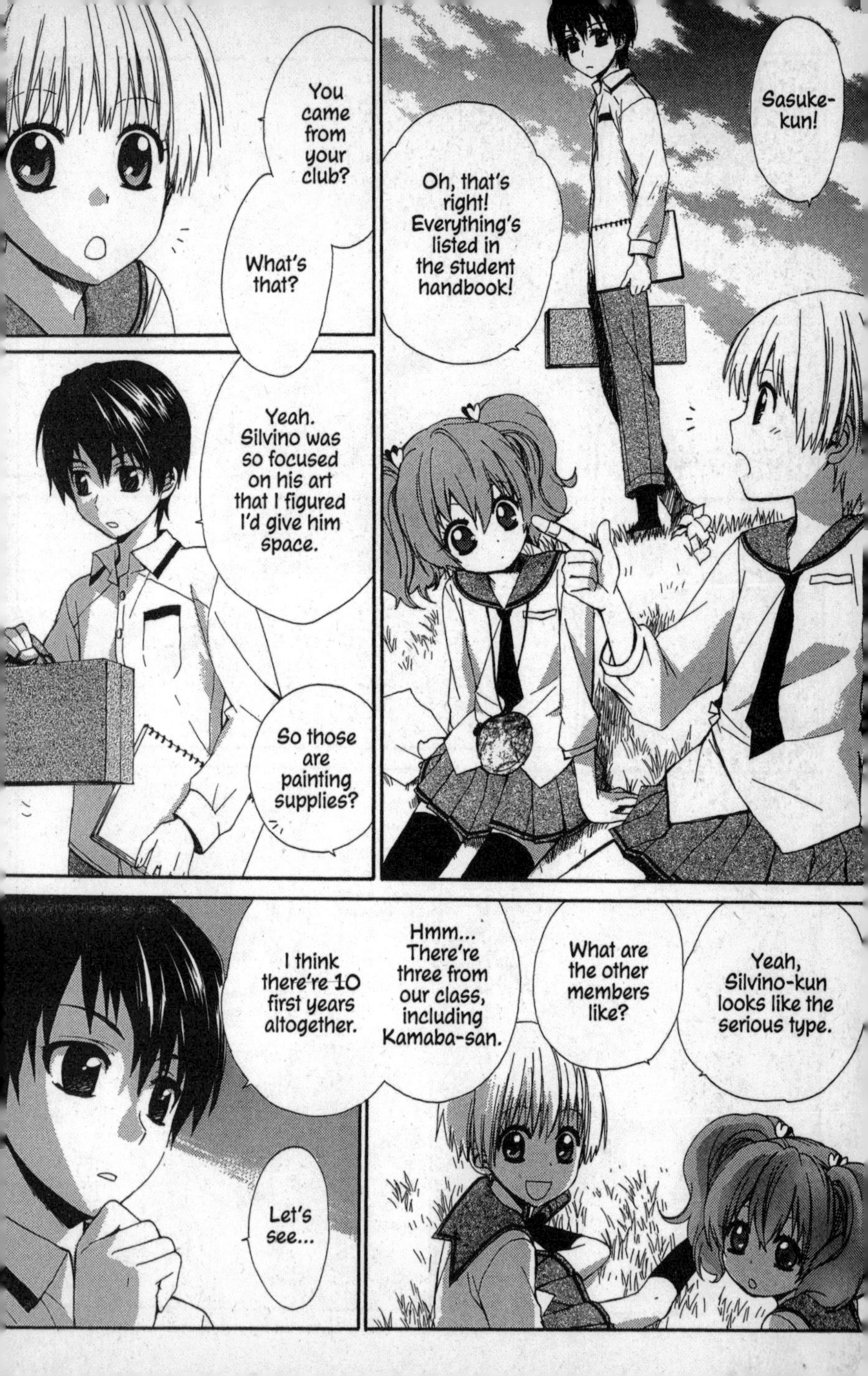
Sasuke-kun!
Oh, that's right! Everything's listed in the student handbook!
You came from your club?
What's that?
Yeah. Silvino was so focused on his art that I figured I'd give him space.
So those are painting supplies?
Yeah, Silvino-kun looks like the serious type.
What are the other members like?
Hmm... There're three from our class, including Kamaba-san.
I think there're 10 first years altogether.
Let's see...

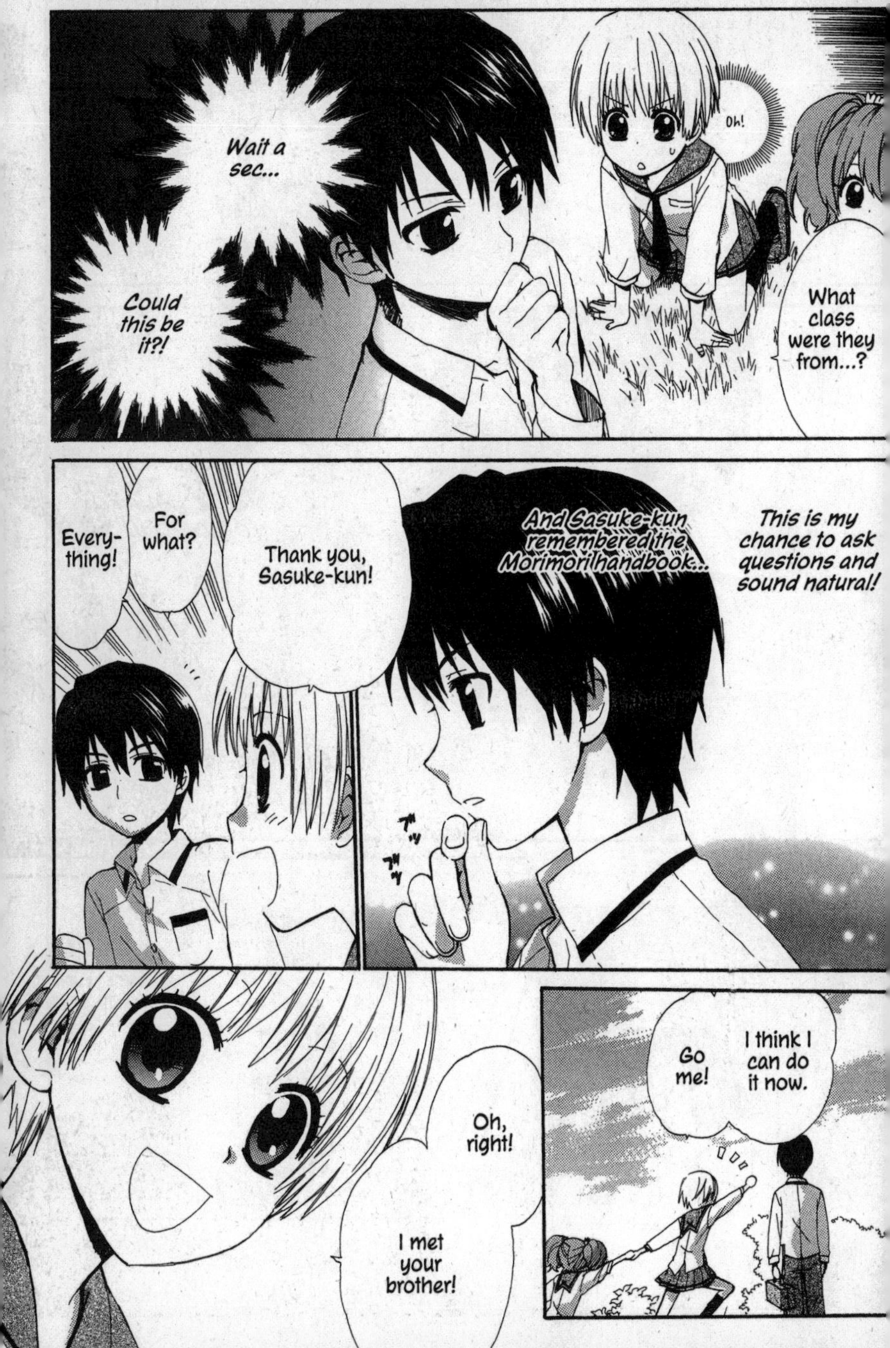
What class were they from...?
Oh!
Wait a sec...
Could this be it?!
This is my chance to ask questions and sound natural!
And Sasuke-kun remembered the Morimori handbook...
Thank you, Sasuke-kun!
For what?
Every-thing!
I think I can do it now.
Go me!
Oh, right!
I met your brother!

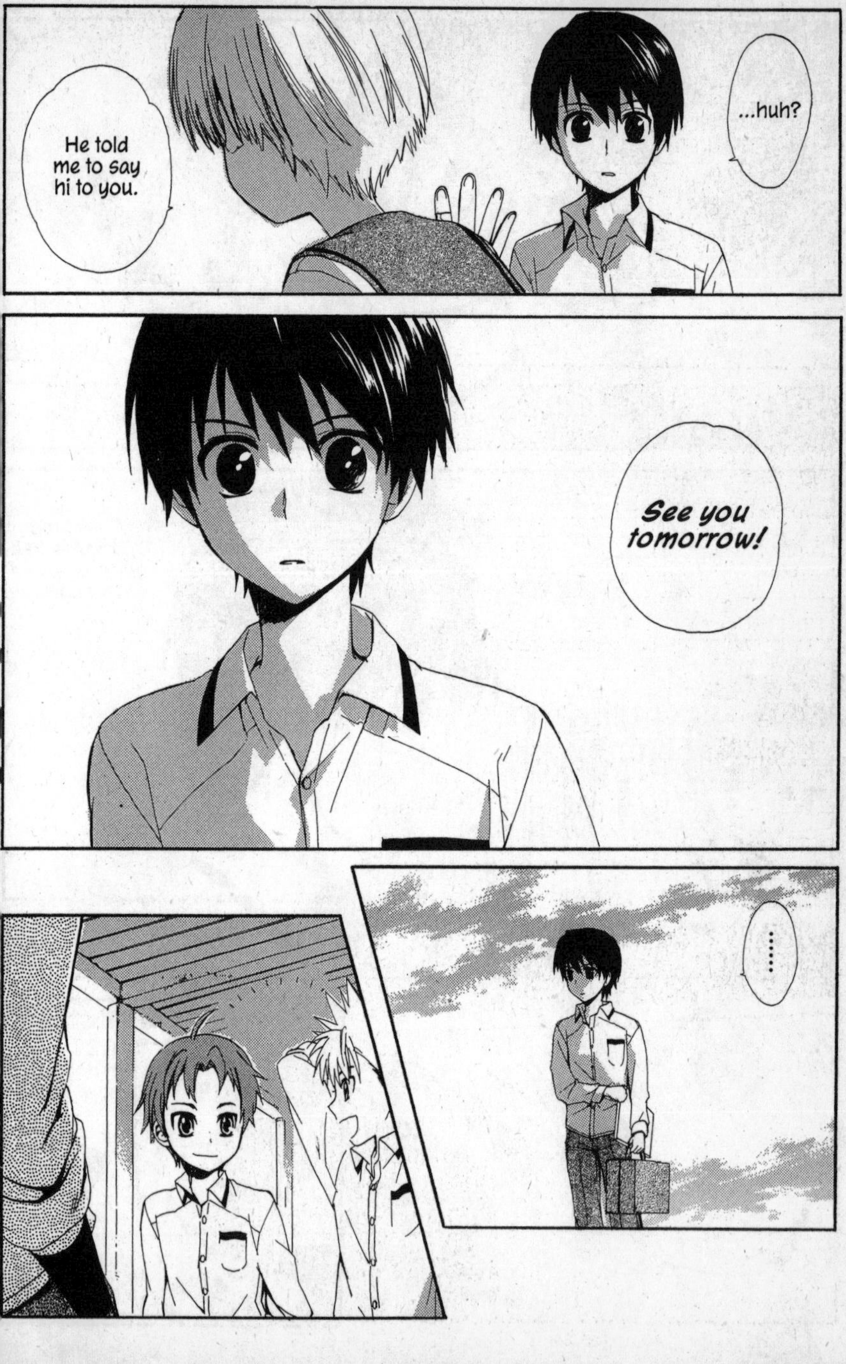
...huh?
He told me to say hi to you.
See you tomorrow!
......

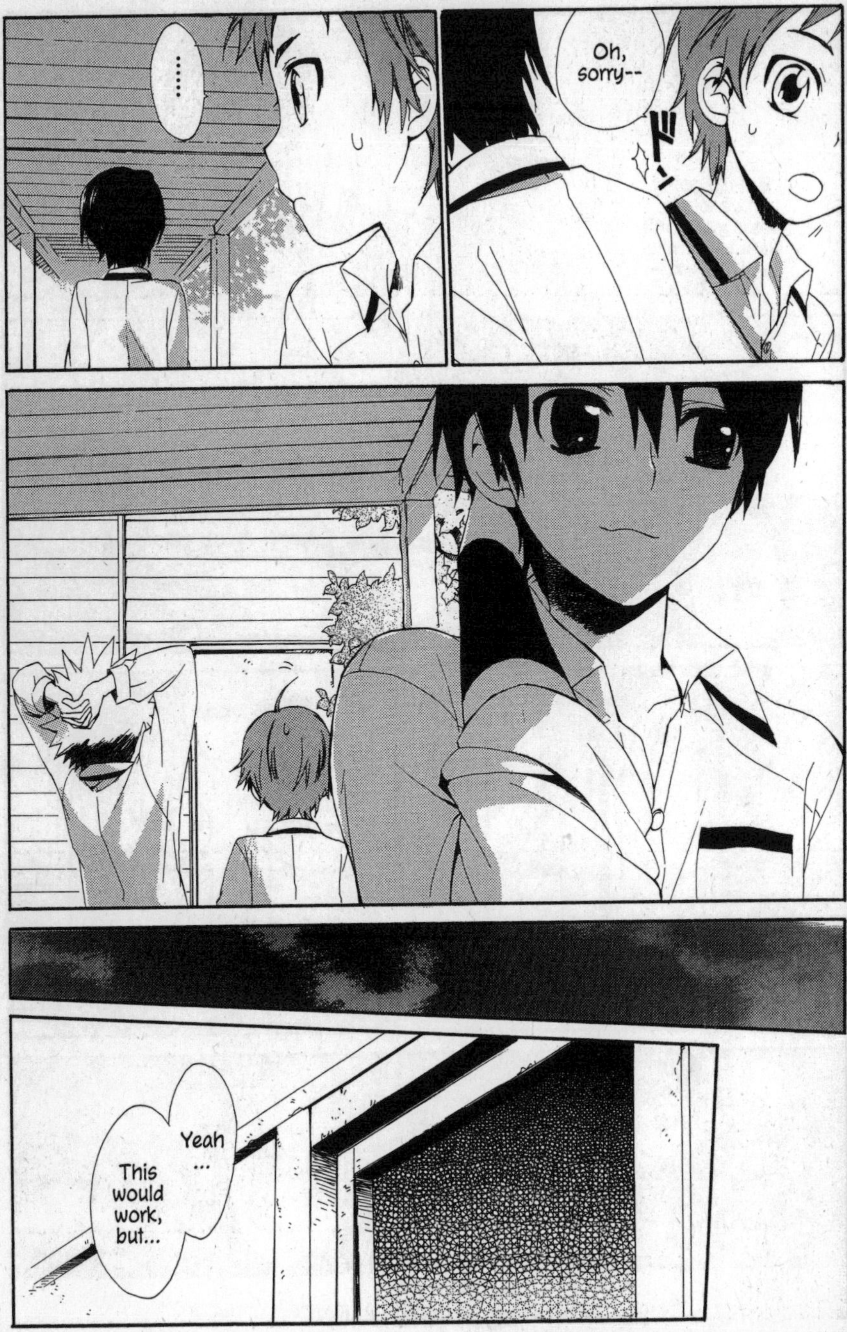
Oh, sorry--
ドッ
......
Yeah ...
This would work, but...

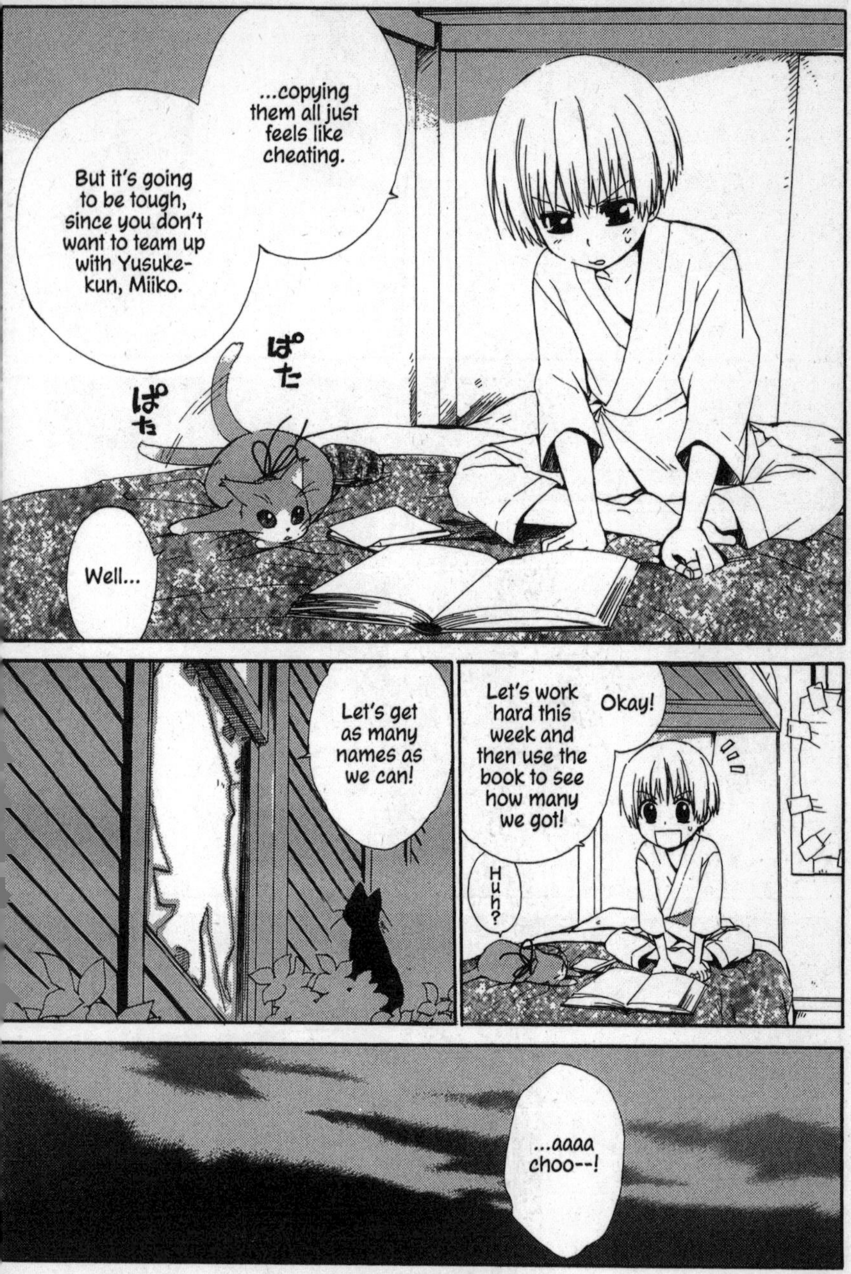
...copying them all just feels like cheating.
But it's going to be tough, since you don't want to team up with Yusuke-kun, Miiko.
ぱた
ぱた
Well...
Okay!
Let's work hard this week and then use the book to see how many we got!
Huh?
Let's get as many names as we can!
...aaaa choo--!

Animal Academy 2/END

Morimori
athletic
uniform

Postscript [2]

~Hamster~

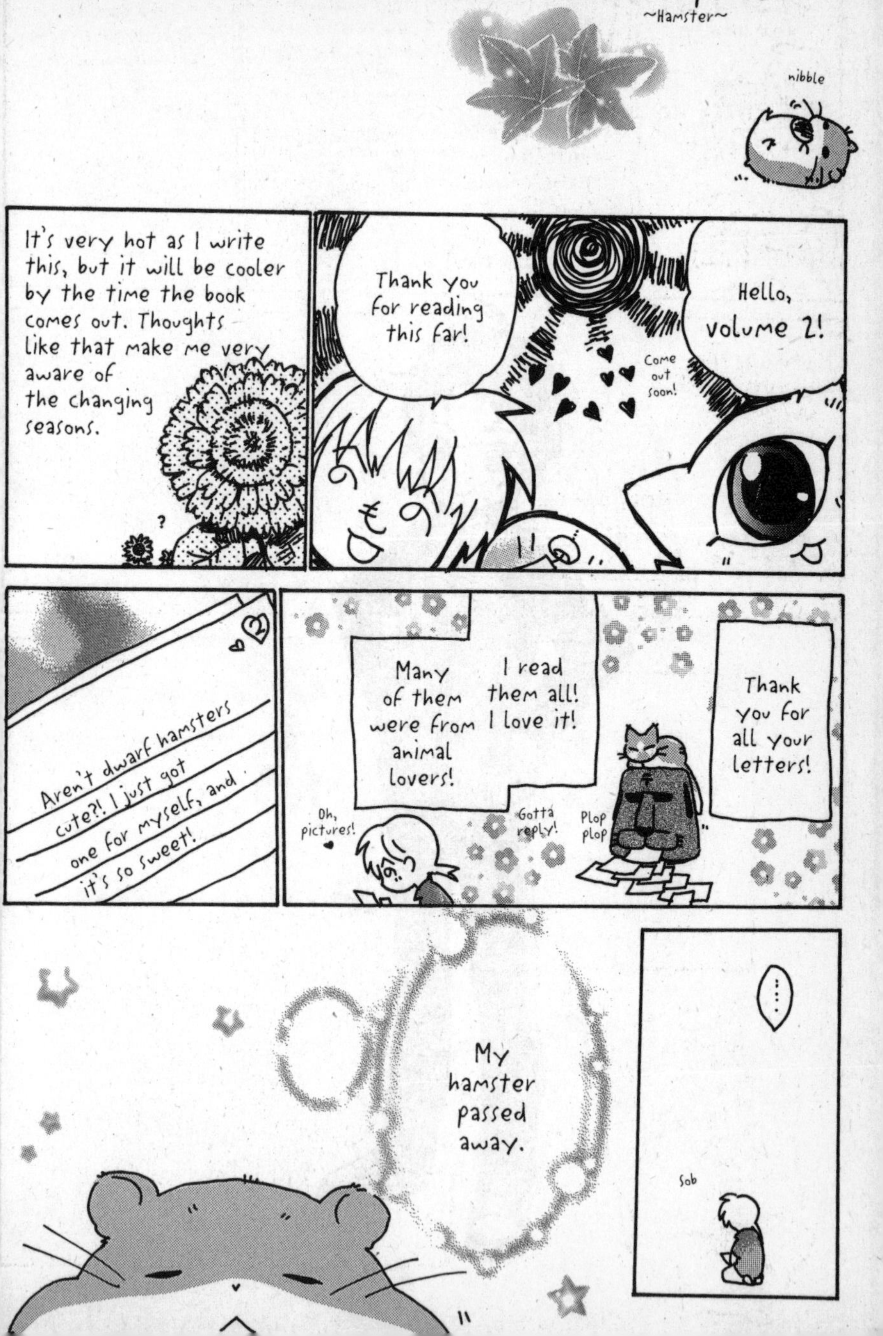
nibble
Hello, volume 2!
Come out soon!
Thank you for reading this far!
It's very hot as I write this, but it will be cooler by the time the book comes out. Thoughts like that make me very aware of the changing seasons.
?
Thank you for all your letters!
I read them all! I love it!
Many of them were from animal lovers!
Plop plop
Gotta reply!
Oh, pictures!
Aren't dwarf hamsters cute?! I just got one for myself, and it's so sweet!
......
Sob
My hamster passed away.

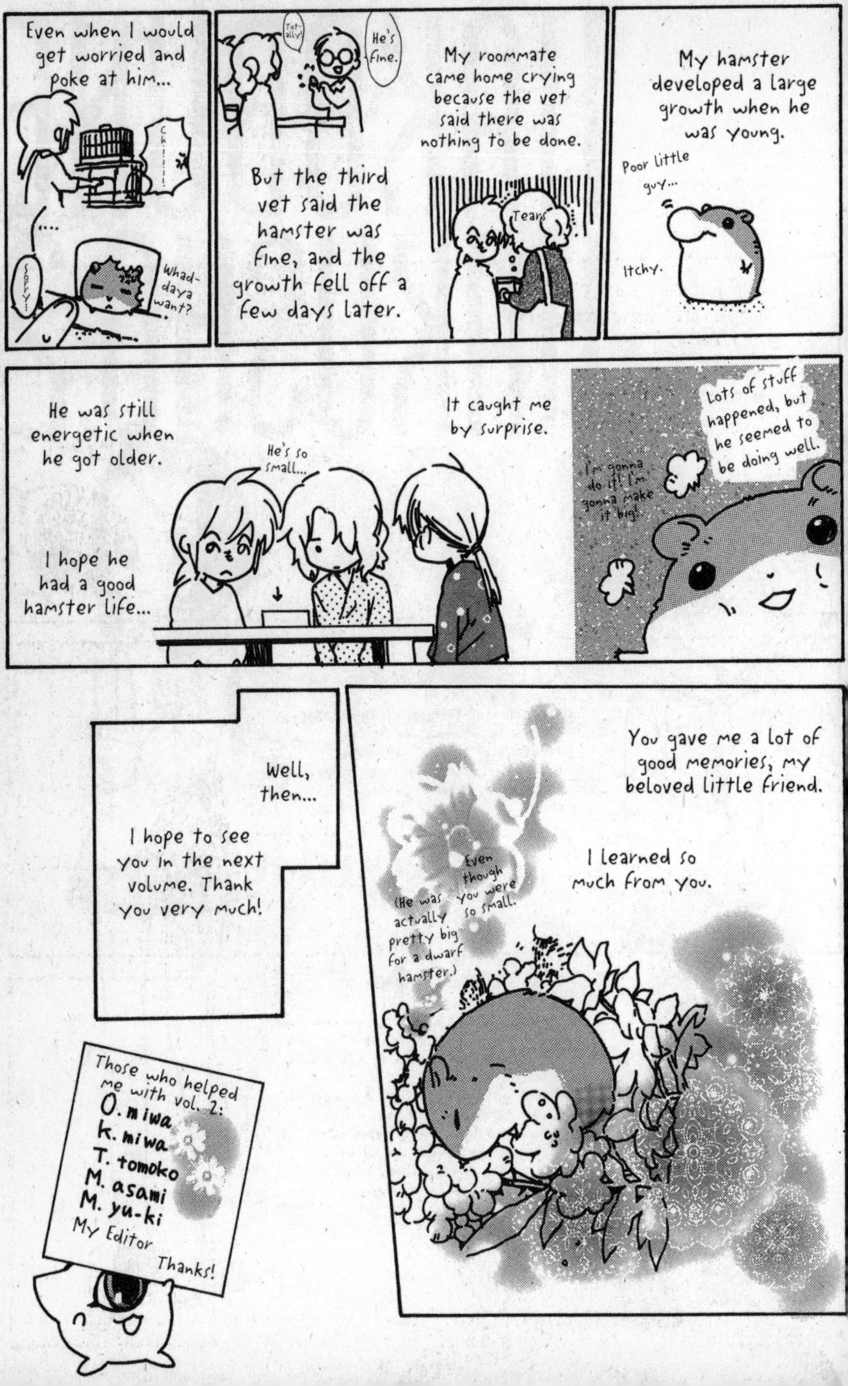

My hamster developed a large growth when he was young.
Poor little guy...
Itchy.
My roommate came home crying because the vet said there was nothing to be done.
Tears
He's fine.
Tot-ally!
But the third vet said the hamster was fine, and the growth fell off a few days later.
Even when I would get worried and poke at him...
Chi!!!
....
Whad-daya want?
Sorry...
Lots of stuff happened, but he seemed to be doing well.
I'm gonna do it! I'm gonna make it big!
It caught me by surprise.
He's so small...
He was still energetic when he got older.
I hope he had a good hamster life...
You gave me a lot of good memories, my beloved little friend.
I learned so much from you.
Even though you were so small.
(He was actually pretty big for a dwarf hamster.)
Well, then...
I hope to see you in the next volume. Thank you very much!
Those who helped me with vol. 2:
O. miwa
K. miwa
T. tomoko
M. asami
M. yu-ki
My Editor
Thanks!

HAKOBUNE HAKUSHO.2

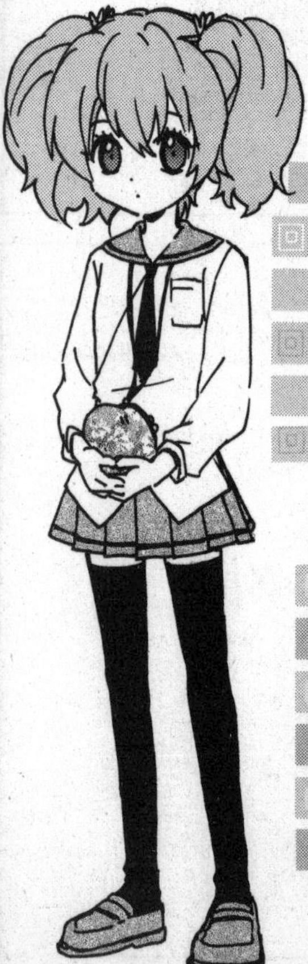

← Miiko Suzuhara

- Cat •Morimori High school 1st year student, White Class
- Seat Number 19 •Species: Felix catus
- She's a little immature for her age. Has high athletic capabilities, and a self-centered, princess-type personality. Watanuki-sensei just picked a random day as her birthday while filling in her application forms.

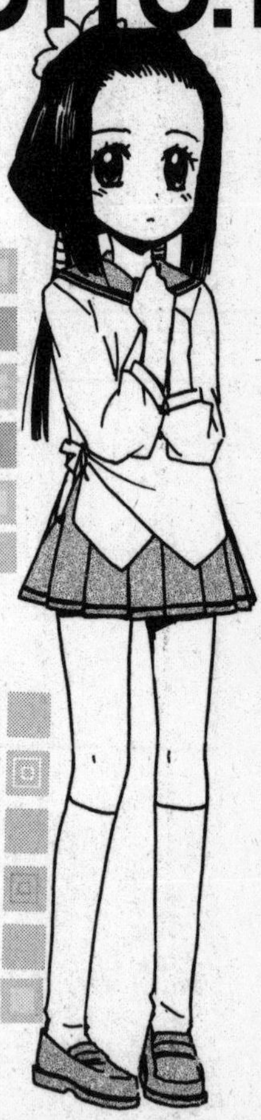

Umeha Kamaba →

- Raccoon Dog (tanuki) •Morimori High School 1st year student, White Class.
- Seat Number 16 •Species: Nyctereutes procyonides
- She got to see a lot of human magazines even before she came to school, so she's a little better at reading than the average student. Omnivorous, so there are few foods she particularly likes or dislikes. Faints easily.

A Kitty Gourmand

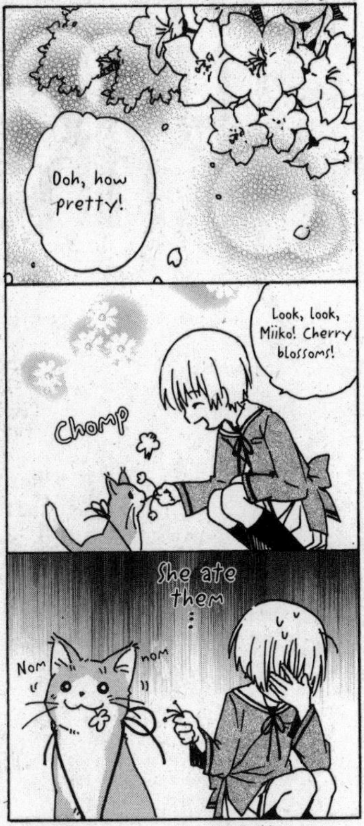
Ooh, how pretty!
Look, look, Miiko! Cherry blossoms!
Chomp
She ate them...
Nom nom

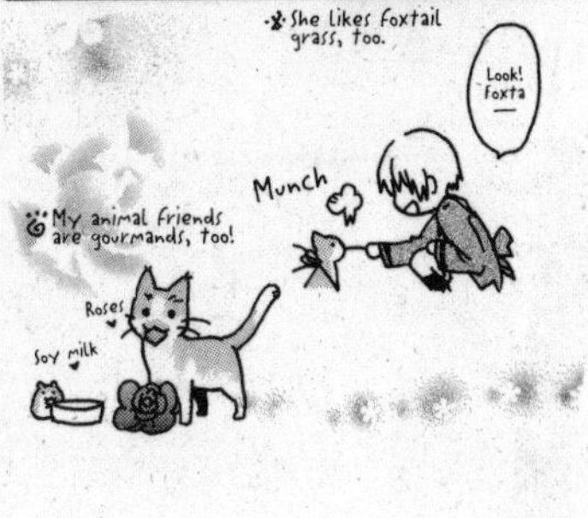
She likes foxtail grass, too.
Look! Foxta—
Munch
My animal friends are gourmands, too!
Roses
Soy milk

HAKOBUNE HAKUSHO

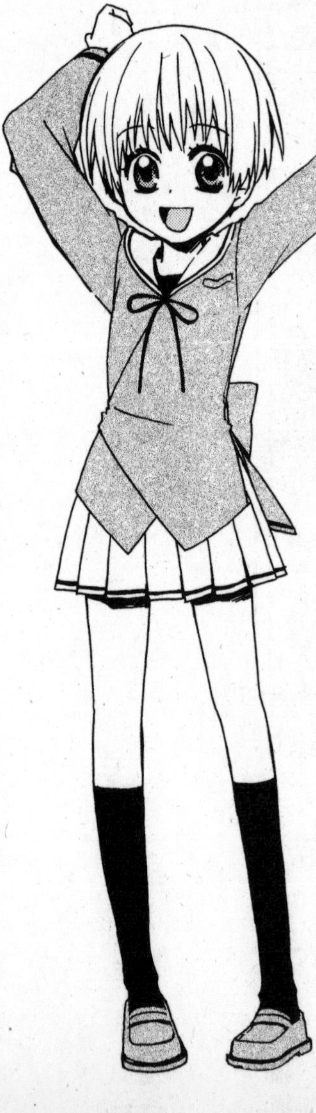

Question.1
Can you be your natural self, if you know the truth?

Question.2
Can you assimelate into our school?

Question.3
Can you pledge secrecy that you are a human being?

[1]

Neko Fukuta

•Human •Morimori High School 1st year student, White Class
•Seat Number 23 ~Is believed to be a cat
•15 years old and a bad student. Her family includes her mother, father and little brother. Her athletic ability is (just barely) decent.

Meaningless Manga

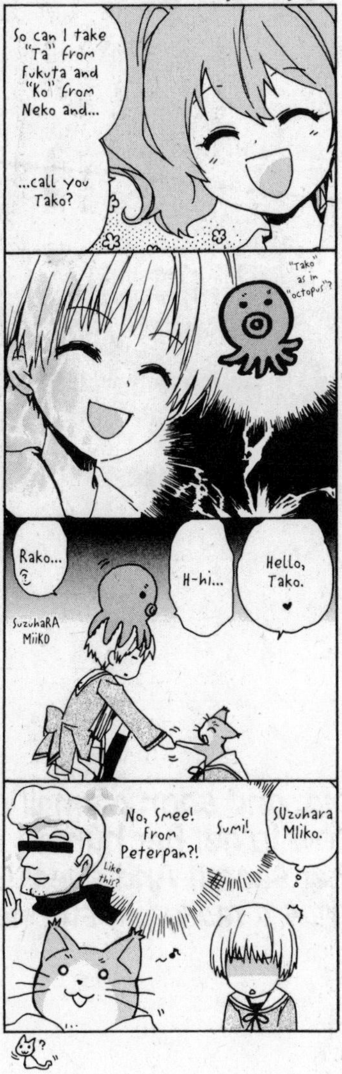
So can I take "Ta" from Fukuta and "Ko" from Neko and...
...call you Tako?
"Tako" as in "octopus"?
Hello, Tako.
H-hi...
Rako...?
SuzuhaRA MiiKO
SUzuhara Miiko.
Sumi!
No, Smee! From Peterpan?!
Like this?

*Idea from my friend S.

In the next volume of...

Animal ACADEMY
HAKOBUNE HAKUSHO
はこぶね白書

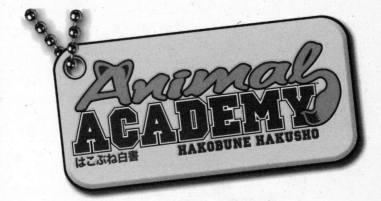

Neko's got a cold, and soon a small conspiracy begins regarding how to get her human cold medicine without revealing her secret! And speaking of secrets, Yuichi Takuma has a really big surprise in store!

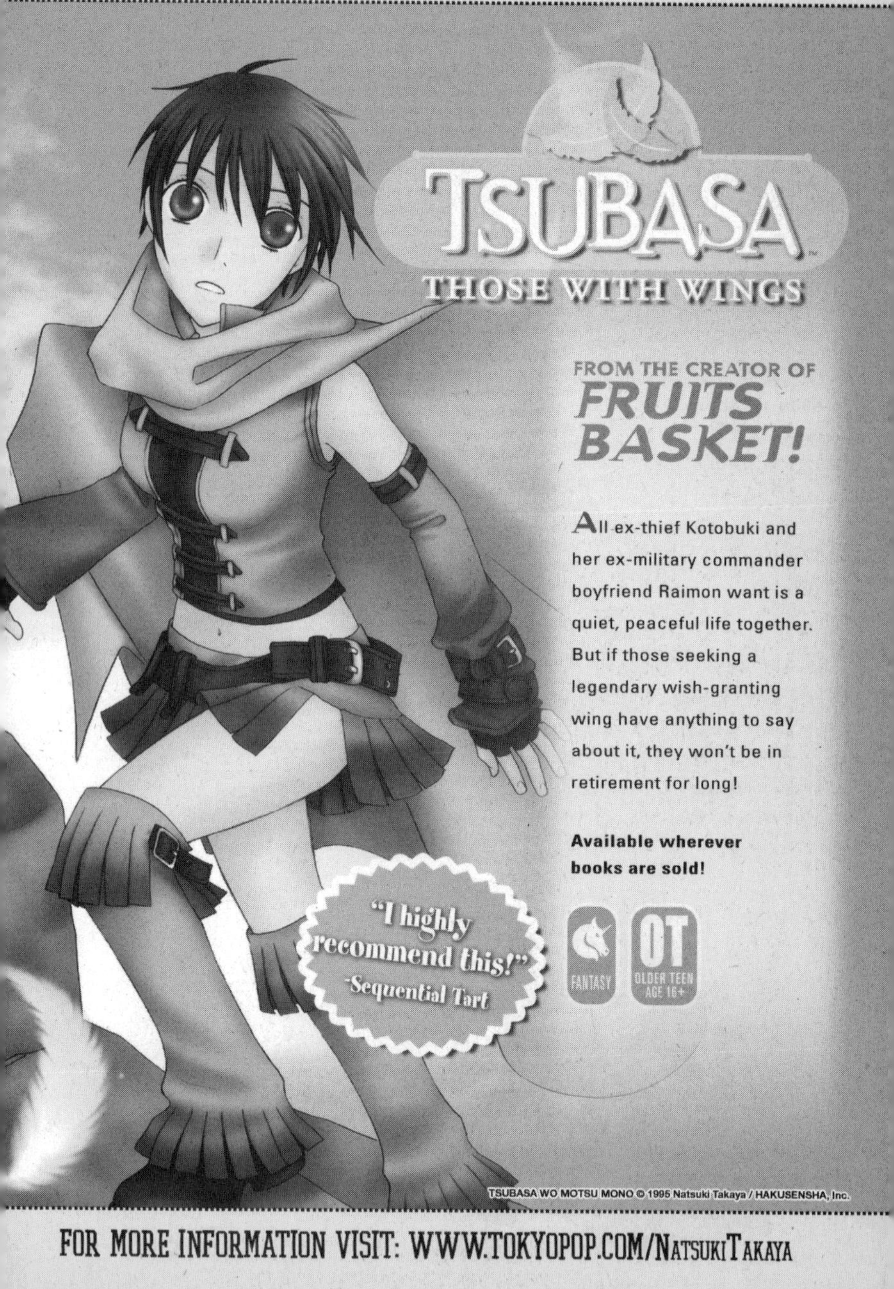
TSUBASA
THOSE WITH WINGS
FROM THE CREATOR OF
FRUITS BASKET!
All ex-thief Kotobuki and her ex-military commander boyfriend Raimon want is a quiet, peaceful life together. But if those seeking a legendary wish-granting wing have anything to say about it, they won't be in retirement for long!
Available wherever books are sold!
"I highly recommend this!" -Sequential Tart
FANTASY
OT
OLDER TEEN AGE 16+
TSUBASA WO MOTSU MONO © 1995 Natsuki Takaya / HAKUSENSHA, Inc.

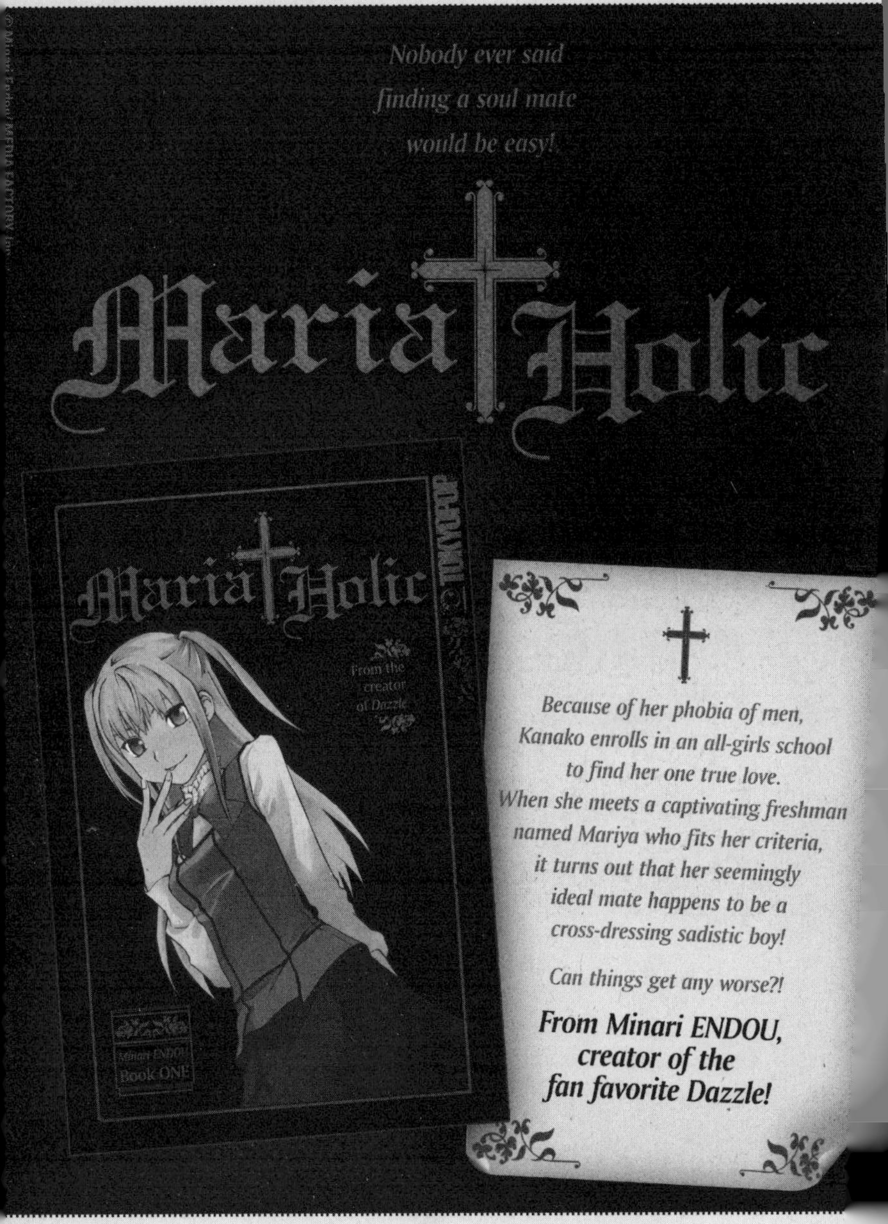
Nobody ever said
finding a soul mate
would be easy!
Maria Holic
Maria Holic
From the creator of Dazzle
Minari ENDOU
Book ONE
TOKYOPOP
Because of her phobia of men,
Kanako enrolls in an all-girls school
to find her one true love.
When she meets a captivating freshman
named Mariya who fits her criteria,
it turns out that her seemingly
ideal mate happens to be a
cross-dressing sadistic boy!
Can things get any worse?!
From Minari ENDOU,
creator of the
fan favorite Dazzle!

STOP!

This is the back of the book. You wouldn't want to spoil a great ending!

This book is printed "manga-style," in the authentic Japanese right-to-left format. Since none of the artwork has been flipped or altered, readers get to experience the story just as teh creater intended. You've been asking for it, so TOKYOPOP® delivered: authentic, hot-off-the-press, and far more fun!

1
2
3
4
5
6
7
8
9
10

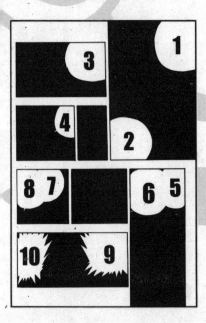

DIRECTIONS

If this is your first time reading manga-style, here's a quick guide to help you understand how it works.

It's easy... just start in the top right panel and follow the numbers. Have fun, and look for more 100% authentic manga from TOKYOPOP®!

THE MANGA REVOLUTION • LEADING
漫画革命
THE MANGA REVOLUTION • LEADING

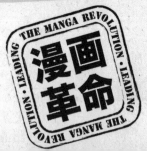